Paperback Edition

I0635122

* * * * *

PUBLISHED BY:
Exaggerist Edutainment, USA
Copyright © 2013 by Jaya Drats
JayaDrats@Hotmail.com

Forward by Konrad Lorenz and E.O. Wilson*

Thank you purchasing this book.
The author appreciates your support and respect for this property
(over 10 years in the making).

= Dedication = To the humans I know, and the ones I've never met,
for forcing me to write this book; and to Earth's unbelievable
Wildlife, for forcing me to protect it.

HN3H It's Spreading!

*It would have been great to have Lorenz write the forward before he died. He would have had something interesting to say regarding innate Human behavior no doubt. Another wish gone forever. We can only hope Wilson will add his inimitable pith before another great scientific mind passes. Alas.

This best-selling literary novel has readers inspired, and looking at the world through a new lens. Thousands of readers have commented that they have found the wildlife fascinating, the poignant relationship issues resonant, and the action compelling; a unique voice in literature. Don't be afraid to laugh, or cry, . . . or lend a hand. Join the HN3H movement, and become part of the solution. It's spreading!

"A self-help book for the other 20 million species on The Planet!"
-- Marlyn M., MA, Family Resource Advocate

Table of Contents

What is the appropriate behavior for a man or a woman in the midst of this world, where each person is clinging to his piece of debris? What's the proper salutation between people as they pass each other in this flood? --- Leonard Cohen

December 1997 to early 2000 A.D. The turn of The Millennium. Y2K

Chapter 1: The Ocean is Big

Here I swim.

In the middle of the biggest ocean of the only planet we know.

What Happened?

Even in my last thoughts, my attention span spills off randomly all over the place.

How did I get here?

Speedboats bounce on the waves, frenetically.

For all of the hard work and crazy energy, did it matter? Did my love for nature and my passion to protect the other two million species on The Planet work? Who did I influence or "help"? Did I just piss people off, . . . harden my enemies? Did it backfire, ... blow up in my face? I can't imagine how I would have done any of it differently. It wasn't possible for me to be anymore honest, or earnest.

Yet, here I swim. Slowly, . . . methodically, waiting. I remember everything. I can see myself, innocently traveling out here, on that first day . . . not knowing I would become a self-encapsulated metaphor of a chronicling of the survival of humanity; the solo nucleus of a homocentrically driven story. The type of story faunacentric people like me typically shun.

I remember being in one of the big stopover hubs. Was it JFK? I watched a rich, gray-haired doctor trying his darnedest to read his golf magazine, as his much younger Asian wife returned with a vest she had just shopped for at Exofficio, or LaCoste, or LaVie Expensivo, or someplace. Does she think she is getting a "Duty

Free Deal"? That's rich. She models the vest for the husband, as Cyndi Lauper blares over the scratchy speakers in the background. No one in this crowded airport terminal seems to know or care that a song about masturbation (*She Bop*) plays. Interrupted by imperceptible gate announcements, she begs with an accent, "How's it look? You like?" The doctor wrenches his eyes up from his all-important magazine for all of a millisecond. "Mm. Mm." he grunts like Australopithecus. He could give a shit. He wishes she would just shut up and buy shit with his money. He needs to read his golf magazine. He needs to!

Next, I remember being on a little 19-seater, staring down at the ocean wondering what lies ahead. I've been on this twin-propped Gulf Stream turbo for a few hours now, and still have a couple of hours to go. Waiting. Just waiting; and staring down at nothing but big blue Pacific. I will learn the fine art of waiting when I arrive at my destination and live out there for just over 2 years, 17 days, and 43 hours. Waiting waiting waiting. Waiting to die. Cause, as it turns out, I die out there, . . . but back to the big blue ocean. I knew it was big. I've studied globes and *National Geographic* since I was four, with dreams of becoming an archeologist, or animal behaviorist, or, a rock singer or Hollywood stuntman. Why not? Why couldn't a lower-middle class bricklayer's son from a little burb in Boston be a scientist or a rock star? I'm hyper; always have been. That's a good start, but not good at waiting am I. I love animals, and I love singing. Ah, the dichotomy. Can I be the singing paleontologist, presenting my finds in true Broadway musical fashion? Scratch that. I actually loathe cheesy Broadway. It would have to be in true Off Off Broadway fashion.

In my vivid imagination, as I look at the clouds, I'm suddenly on stage with lights flashing and media clambering to get the scoop. A deep voice rasps, "Is it true you found living dinosaurs in the tepuis in Venezuela?"

A harsh voice squeals, "Which species did you discover?"

A Latvian-sounding professor belches, "Do you have proof? We must demand proof?"

As I surreally take my time scanning the horde of leeches, moving my head slowly like a reeling Rastifari in a Noh play, the music swells, the audience hushes, the lights dim and the spotlight intensifies. I sing with my extremely heavy Boston accent as improvised lyrics pop into my head:

You may think that I'm a childish fool. A boy too young and should be in school.

But if you saw just what I saw, you'd swear it was a dinosaur!
The audience screams as the curtain behind me drops to the floor like a sheet of lead chain mail, with blaring electric guitar and massive taiko drums pounding. Flashbulbs strobe against an Allosaurus held in shackles. I sing and dance, kicking across the stage, a cross between some kind of twisted Stravinsky ballet and Mick Jagger strut.

I snap back to the present.

"Are you feeling okay?" Jewel, the southern-bell flight attendant says with a Georgian drawl. "You're not feeling sick now are you honey?"

"No, not at all. I never get seasick, ah motion sick." I fumble, trying to keep my eyes on hers while I can't help but notice everything else. Ay Carumba! She looks to be in her 30s, definitely makes a good, warm first impression, and has a pretty face and a nice body to boot.

Her drawl is long and languid, and soft. Not ignorant sounding, but soothing and nice. "First time out to Halfway honey?" she asks.

"Yeah, I'm the first ranger," I respond proudly.

"Well good for you. Would you like a cool refreshment?" she asks.

"Sure," I say.

"We have fruit juices from Kauai. Mango, papaya, *passion fruit,*" she emphasizes with a hint of a smile.

Passion fruit! Now she's fuckin with me. Man, already? What the hell is wrong with me. This is my first opportunity at a serious career move in a field I've been dying to get into. I just finished my Master's and left that horrible, miserable university behind with all its evil staff in the Dean's Office and Student Union. I have a chance to really make a name for myself out here, and to make a major positive impact for the environment; the first ranger for the U.S. Animal Protection Service (APS) on Halfway Atoll Wildlife Sanctuary (HAWS), and all I can crassly think about is squeezing her passion fruits? Fuck, I'm such an idiot. What was that quote I always loved? Oh yeah, . . .

Act the way you'd like to be and soon you'll be the way you act.

6

- George W. Crane

"Huh huh, passion fruit, really?" I stumble.

"Yep, we sure do. Here you go honey", she says under her breath as she slowly wipes the top of the can with a napkin and passes it to me.

'Honey?' Oh man. That accent is hotter than Georgia asphalt in Juuuuuuly!

I ask, "You been out to Halfway before?" trying to keep the conversation going.

"A couple of times," she responds as she sits in the seat next to me.

"DD-Don't you get in trouble for sitting down on your shift?" I quip nervously.

"Not on a five-and-a-half-hour flight with 19 seats and only half of em full o bodies. Everybody looks asleep anyway," she says, flipping her hand forward and down.

Okay, I've been lucky before. Way too lucky. It's amazing that I've made it to 32 years-old without getting AIDS, killed, or slammed in jail, but this smacks of set-up to me. Too Hollywood, too mile-high pie in the sky. I have to admit to myself, I'm interested.

"Now that the Pill-a-pinos are on island, the Navy doesn't have to do the services anymore, which is good, cause I like the Pill-a-pino masses better, even though some of it is in their language" she explains with a sweet smile.

D'oh! I knew there was a catch. She's trying to convert me. Fuck! Whenever a hot girl is that nice to ya, there's a reason, like in Vegas, or like those gorgeous Moonies I met on the quad in front of the Women's Gym on the UCLA campus. I quickly flash back to that day. A little late for class and moving at a fast clip, a blond sitting on a large blanket says 'hi' to me, like a siren. I stop in my tracks, and say hello back, and then she asks where I am going and if I could sit down with her for a while. I kneel on the blanket as a second, just as beautiful girl, arrives and sits down all chummy with her. I was so psyched, only to have them ask me if I know of the Reverend Sun Myung Moon. I bailed to class and never saw them again.

Coming back to the present, I look at Jewel and say, "You mean Tagalog, right?" knowing she must mean 'Filipinos'.

She looks into my eyes with a gentle smile. "Is that what it is? Kinda sounds Mexican."

"Well, that's interesting because there is a lot of Spanish influence, and English too, since they were occupied so much." I cut myself short. She's gonna think I'm an arrogant, stuck-up know-it-all, trying to hit on her. I've dealt with that for a long time in my life with my family, girlfriends, friends. I gotta stop right here and pull my shit together. I awkwardly pause and look out the window. Okay: First thing, she works for Halfway Icarus Corp. (HIC), the cooperator with APS and the Navy out on Halfway. Secondly, she's a Christian. I do not need to get into any shit my first day out here. My philosophy with relationships has always been to jump right in with both feet and swim or drown. Sometimes I swim, most of the time I drown, but at least I'm in the water. How else do you find the love of your life? Trial and error. Crash and burn, that's the only way to learn.

Wow, funny how I think, ha? I see myself as a hetero boy who loves women, not a masher or a cad. Is that how people see me? Even if I were to start writing a diary to explain myself to myself, I don't think I would *really* be expressing what I think or how I feel. Salvador Dali could put anything he could imagine on a canvas. When I look at his work, I think it is the greatest art ever. The depth and surreal quality, and the masterful ability blew me away long before I knew he was a fascist or misogynist. For me, there are two Worlds: The world that's in my head, and then there is the rest of the World. I know, that sounds obvious right? Do you ever think about that though, and what makes us different? The world that's in my head is so intricate and complex, and has so many ideas, and is so positive with so much energy, and that World is a big, beautiful happy place. The thing is, I thought for many years, people were just like me and understood my thoughts innately, and that many things just simply go without saying. But no one knows what I'm really thinking. No one knows my thoughts, and my world. Even if I were to try to articulate it in a novel, there's no way anyone could ever really understand my mind. Just like no one can ever really study animals without them knowing that humans are there, or in the same way that no one really knows what Shakespeare was saying, or how he felt, or who exactly he even was. Or like trying to understand my friend Drats' poems, artwork, performance, or his novel! A hundred times, I must have said to him, "What Do You Mean By That?"

If I were to write, it couldn't be about me and my mind, just like Drats' novel isn't about him. It's about audiences understanding and perceiving it. It's about how it hits someone else viscerally or stimulates someone cerebrally. What do you feel or think? We really are alone.

Flying straight into the flaming sunset; our wings whip the clouds.

"See anythang?" she interrupts again.

Can't she see my mind is racing and she should cut me some slack to compose myself? I scan for a moment. What a dumb question; 'See anything?' Pufh. Water, waves, white puffy clouds. I'm straining to look for whales but at 30,000-feet, I doubt even I, with my 'ultra-super vision', would be able to pick one out. Though my hearing may be going from singing in bands and going dancing, people are always impressed with my animal identification skills from way off.

Suddenly, "Yes, . . . I do see something. What is that?"

Jewel leans over, pressing her right shoulder into my left clavicle for a sincere look.

"I don't know. I never know what those little islands are" as she slumps back to her seat, brushing her soft hand along my hairy arm. I can't believe a girl could be so unconscious as to do that by accident. I like it, so I keep my mouth shut.

Little islands eh? I studied the map before I came out here from my work on the turtle project on the Big Island, as I always do. Why? Why do I always have to study everything, and know where I'm going, and know which bird species might be there, and read *Lonely Planet* to make sure not to miss anything cool and avoid the tourist traps and malls? Why?

Why again? Why does someone write a novel? Why do we read them? Why? Why on Earth would anyone want to read a novel? This novel? A novel Drats wrote? Typically, authors use big pompous words to browbeat the reader down into thinking the author is god, or at least way better or way smarter than the reader, and therefore worth reading. I think Drats would agree that those stuck-up, Hawthorne-quoting elitists can go squat on an albatross egg! Should only really smart or really funny or really stupid or really tragic people write? Why shouldn't a "normal" person write about normal things that happen, that document an existence, a slice of life, a time capsule? Would other people reading it relate, feel less isolated, feel more of a connection, more warmth, more love? Fuck! I don't know. I don't know why. It's happening! It's happening right now. Their fingers are moving. Crazy authors like Drats click and clack at their keyboards. Why?

Why? I'll tell you why. Because one of those snobby spoiled little rich boys at BU told me off on my last day supervising him, saying "You are a crazy psycho, Falco."

I looked at this wussy work-study pupil with a laugh. "I might be crazier than anyone you know, but how do you know *you're not* crazier than me?"

He froze. He possessed no evidence from any reputable source to gauge our relative craziness levels. What, he thinks he's not crazy at all? Like, I'm the only crazy one? Don't make me laugh. Don't make me laugh. At least I embrace my crazy, just like Drats apparently embraces his. Is this what drives anyone from normal to crazy: To write a book, to climb Everest, to compose a love song? Why shouldn't we? Subjective sanity?

Straining to see, with my forehead and eye shmushed against the window at an oblique angle, I can see now that it is an island, and I deduce from my cognitive map and the number of flight-hours behind us that it must be either Laysan or Lisianski.

"Excuse me." I climb over Jewel with my 35-inch hurdler's legs and pull my camera from the baggage compartment. I always keep my long lens on the camera, cause I had already learned from years of wildlife photography that anything you are gonna need to shoot quickly needs a 300 zoom, whereas landscapes and people generally patiently cooperate while I switch to my 28-75mm. Unlike me, mountains and streams will wait.

Getting back in my seat and wiping the fog off of the window from my panting breath, I angle the camera to zoom in on it. Yup, it's Laysan, for I can actually make out the large lake in the middle; a feature I had studied while reading about the critically endangered Laysan Duck, that snap their bills after flies by the briny lake. Cheerwerr cheerwerr. I snap off two shots.

"Dya get it?" Jewel politely inquires.

"Yeah, I think so. That's Laysan."

"Isn't that the same name of the goonies?" She replies, expecting another intelligent answer.

"You mean the albatross, right?"

"Yeah, but everybody calls them gooon-nneeees" she states, correcting me to the reality of the situation out there. These are not scientists, but Navy personnel and their contractors.

A massive Black-footed Albatross lifts off a safe distance away from the Halfway tarmac.

"Yes. There are Black-footed and Laysan Albatross on Halfway, but I don't know why they are called Laysan." Shit, I don't why? I am good about being humble and acknowledging when I don't know something. I really am. But, shouldn't I know that one? I mean the albatross are the centerpiece of the whole enchilada out there. Rrrmmmmm. The props continue to hum. Pregnant pause, and Jewel rests her eyes peacefully.

Halfway, ready or not, here I come.

Chapter 2: First Impacts

Since the plane is so small and empty, the pilots invite us to break up their boredom gladly. The co-pilot, a weird Texan with short, portly chubby cheeks, waves me up to the cockpit. I can't remember his name. Tex? Tex would fit. Tex doesn't have cute chubby cheeks, but more like cheesy-pizza lookin moon-face cheeks; kind of like a guy with a disease, or who had eaten unhealthy shit all his life, but isn't obscenely obese. He could stand to drop a good 30-pounds off the stomach though. The other, a totally standard captain guy, invites me to look through the windshield. Compared to Tex, he's kind of like Captain America: Good looking, well spoken, neatly appointed; obviously the captain Tex wants to be.

As the sun seemingly hangs in the air, dead in front of us, above a landscape of white puffy cumulous, the clouds separate and remerge, giving us our first glimpse of the atoll. I look over the pilots' shoulders as the humming engines, ever so slightly, become lower, softer, and deeper.

"There she is," Tex exclaims proudly, "Halfway Island," taking credit as if he just produced the freakin atoll.

He's right, there are three islands visible, but that name is a throw back to the Navy days when no one bothered to learn anything about where they were, or cared. It was a duty station. A place you went to so you could get off of it as much as possible as soon as possible. A place you got shipped to; where you went to work, like 'The Artic' or 'The Russian Front' or 'The French Foreign Legion'. Ya know, a place like that. A place where you went to take orders, were punished by scrubbing toilets with toothbrushes, and where you went to the brig for fighting with The Marines. A kind of place where you have to wait. Waiting. Waiting. Wait. Halfway was a Naval Air Station. At the peak of the Navy's occupation, they had crowded the goonies off and squeezed over 3000 servicemen onto Sand Island. Not just men though. Officers were allowed to have their families out here, and yes actually, humans were born here. How's that for an aberration of geographical evolution? *Homo sapiens*, as with any other type of terrestrial mammal, should not be able to breed on a remote atoll, for the single basic fact that they simply couldn't get there. Don't get me wrong; . . . Halfway *was* an island once. About 29 million years ago, Halfway once sat over what we think of as the Hawaiian hot spot now; the same hot spot which now creates a new island some 41 miles southeast of the currently irrupting Kilauea Volcano on Hawaii, the most active volcano in the World, by-the-way. Did you know that? Did you know that the most active volcano in the World is in the U.S.? I thought volcanoes were for third world countries where all the worst disasters happen. I'm shocked by what I don't know, especially something of this magnitude. I can't imagine what it must have been like with 3,000 service men on one square mile of runway atoll. Tex's slimy cheeks glisten in the sunlight. I suddenly recollect that manic song by Drats:

Speedy Little Pizza Man
by Drats

Speedy Little Pizza Man, racing toward me now
Melted cheese and steaming grease, staining grey cardboard and asphalt
Super-size my combo-gulp, consume I must now
I can't hear your rumble yet. Is that you, are you close?
Hurry, hurry Mr. Pizza Guy, I'm all alone and I don't have much time
I'm only here for the blink of an eye, a wink and a new baby arrives,
I choke down a slice and I'm gone.
Speedy Little Pizza Man, the sauce shifts and slides
Patter to me before I pitter away, for if I die, who will pay?
Rush rush rush --- Race toward me now
Hurry, hurry Mr. Pizza Guy, I'm all alone and I don't have much time
I'm only here for the blink of an eye, a wink and a new baby arrives,
I choke down a slice and I'm gone.
It's all about me. It's all about me.

Actually a rocky basalt island once, Halfway crawls three inches a year to the northwest, as the Pacific plate moves under the Eurasian plate. Halfway sinks, erodes, and eventually now sits over twelve-hundred miles from Honolulu. Why do I know this? A ranger who don't know shit ain't worth shit. There's nothing worse than a ranger who keeps saying 'I don't know', except a ranger who bullshits you. That's why I promised myself when I took this job, that I would never be like one of those hokey rangers that bore you with lame jokes. I promised that I would never lie or exaggerate, finding truths that are way more mind-blowing than any fiction, and I definitely won't pull weak stunts, like pretending a Baby Ruth was Monk Seal scat and then eating it in front of the crowd. Unfortunately, a lot of people don't know when a ranger is bullshitting them. Perception is more important than reality. Halfway is not an island or islands! It's an Atoll. I'm not splitting hairs here. There is a big difference. An island is alive. It has a lifespan that seems to go on beyond time. Sand, Eastern, and Spit especially, are ephemeral. The island itself sank long long ago. Only a coral ring, of living organisms dying, and living, and dying on top of each other, and growing to reach the sun, make an atoll. The actual island itself, the basalt rock, is long gone and hundreds of feet below. Dead. Atolls, like island skeletons in a ring, and the coral, like parasites coming to feed on the calcium and marrow carcass, are akin to zombies: The living dead. Halfway continues to creep towards the Darwin Line at 29-degrees north, on the Pacific Plate, where all Hawaiian atolls go to die. All atolls have finite and pressing deadlines; final gasps in muted sunlight, warped by waves. All of these thoughts flash through my mind in the blink of an eye, as they always do.

Sand, Spit, and Eastern, the little "islands" that make up Halfway Atoll.

Still standing over Tex's shoulder, I think to myself, 'Dumb ass, doesn't he know anything about where he's flying to? Halfway Islands? No. But wait, I'm the dumb ass for thinking he should know or bother to know. He can fly a plane, sort of, and I can't, so he may not be the dumb ass.

Whenever my Dad called me a smart ass, I'd quickly counter, 'Better than being a dumb ass'. He didn't like that. Too sharp? Acerbic? We all disrespected our Dads. Maybe that's one of the reasons mine checked-out at only 65; a long, slow, boozey suicide.

"Where you from?" Tex quips.

"Boston, originally," I reply gleefully.

"Oh my god, Ted Kennedy and everyone from that state should be nuked, seriously," Tex replies brainlessly. At least he has heard of The Kennedys. Little does he know that a lot of my ignorant relatives who still live in Mass. vote Republican, even though it continues to hurt US. Like Tex, they are easily duped fools who have really spent no time studying politics and, like most Americans, fall for the easy, lazy answer issues fed to them by Fox News, CNN, and the like.

The captain interrupts my thoughts, giving coordinate orders and training Tex on how to call the tower, to land the plane.

"You gonna let me do it?" Tex says like a kid.

Holy shit! Is he? This is gonna be a really short book if he lets Tex land the plane.

"No, I'll be landing her this time."

"Oowww," Tex sulks bitterly.

"You stay focused on bird strike hazards," the captain commands.

Bird strike hazards? What the hell is that? Suddenly I see a pterodactyl-sized seabird heading straight toward the cockpit and then swoop-dive below the nose.

"Wow, that one was up at 1400 feet!" Tex quips.

"You have to buckle up now," the captain orders professionally.

"Yeah," Tex concurs, a little late on the draw.

At that exact moment I feel the gentle touch of an angel on my shoulder. Am I really going to die right now, so soon?

Oh; it's just Jewel invading my personal space again. "Everyone has to be seated for landin shhhugar." Her hand is soft, and smells kinda minty-creamy good.

"No prob," I return back to my window and start snapping off killer aerials.

I hope the generous publisher of Drats' book has the brilliance to print these photos.

Landing at Halfway with gooney and frigate squadrons about.

The atoll waters glow in the most surreal way. No one, including the most incredulous of my kin, is going to believe this. They are going to assume I used a tricky polarizing filter. With a bit of turbulence and what kind of feels/sounds like 2 bird strikes, we begin to glide down to the runway. In the dark green, almost black looking Bermuda Grass fields below, I see what looks like a few, and then suddenly hundreds and thousands of black and white soccer balls scattered about. As we descend I see that each is an albatross, most sitting on nests. It is December after all.

After a smooth as silk landing, I meet Ben at the airport. This big, introverted wookie of a man from Missouri (or is it Misery) has very limited ways of expressing how overjoyed he is that I have arrived. A whiff of guano wafts through the air.

"You Kestrel?" Ben asks.

"Yeh, Hi, Kestrel Falco, and you?"

"I'm Ben Messihammer, temp sanct manager. How'd ya like the flight?" he says dryly.

"Great! Loved it. Very interesting," I say as I catch a glimpse of Jewel standing at the foot of the stairs, on the tarmac, trying to act all diplomatic and professional, flashing me a beautiful smile; pulling off her best Vana White.

Ben doesn't appear to notice as he states, "Well, here's your bike. You will be bathroom buddies with Zart. You're gonna like him. He's a great guy and he really likes beer. You like beer right?"

"Ya, sure. What about my bags?" I don't really care about alcohol, including beer, but I feel pressured to sound like one of the boys.

"The Foreign Nationals will bring them by your room in the Dolphin Van. Don't worry about crime around here. No one has anywhere to go. Hm. We're all stuck out here and it would even take a Coast Guard C-130 four hours to get here."

"Whoaw. We are out here," I say with elated gutsy bravado. After all, I'm an adventure guy. "I've already hit the cactus forest hell of Mona Island in Puerto Rico, and the awesome jungles around the Amazonian waterfalls in my short, economically challenged life, so why not Halfway ey?" I try to strike up a conversation, but Ben just doesn't believe in goin on jawin much.

Ben and I leave the Hangar area, then cruise through the parade grounds, through a sea of what has to be 100,000 goonies, many 'squawnking' as I call it.

"Try not to hit any albatross on the road", he says factually, though I assume it to be some kind of rye atoll humor. It isn't. I find myself regularly swerving to give the goonies a wide berth. If you bike by too close, it's kind of like a magnetic mine. The birds pop their long, tube-nosed bills from between their wings and up off their backs, then they start whipping their heads around frantically, then, they flip out their wings under your tires and jump up and stick their necks through your spokes. With the precision of a Musketeer, albatross can lunge their bills quickly between the spokes, but if the knot of the skull slips through, it can be hard for them to back out.

We turn through some dark trees, pass some kind of seaman's shrine to The Blessed Virgin, and some small cottage-like houses with dim golden-mustard lights glowing under their little porches and from inside. The air feels cooler than Hawaii, except up at Volcanoes.

Ben continues as we peddle, "That's The Galley, where you should report for breakfast at O-six-forty tomorrow. We will have a morning meeting at O-seven-hundred, and then you have to attend Orientation at eight."

As we turn toward a group of larger structures, I notice a large satellite dish in the distance.

"What's that for?"

"You didn't know? The Navy put a dish out here for TV. We get HBO," Ben announces.

"For how much?" I ask.

"Free," he replies.

"I mean, how much will it be for me?" I look for clarification.

"Free. We get all our TV, like about 20 or 30 stations, for free. And HBO."

Wow. Peace dividend! I'm on one of the most remote places on Earth and for the first time in my life I get HBO, and, for free! Wow! Weird. Couldn't have called that one. I wonder if there will ever be anything on HBO I'd ever actually want to watch? I guess it's not really free, cause it's paid for with our taxes, and I pay taxes, so I am paying for it, just like you. Yippie!

I look at the satellite dish as we peddle by. It is huge, and there is a second array over to the left on the hillside by some Ironwood Trees. I'm sure these massive dishes handle a lot more than HBO, like spy transmissions and the like.

At that moment a dark "bat" darts down in a swoop and nails me right in the back of the head.

"Ooaw!" involuntarily spurts from my throat.

I look back to see it flutter up off the road and into the black sky with an 'ettehh' call, sounding like a nasal, grinding rusty hinge on a moldy shutter.

"What the hell was that?" I stammer.

"You were christened. That's good luck. You're gonna have good luck out here?" Ben says with a little chuckle.

"Well, I hope I don't get christened in the face. That hurt. What was that?" I say.

Ben says, as we continue biking without missing a beat, "Bonin Petrel. Banette is writin a paper up on em right soon. We have about 45,000 of them nestin out here, that's why ya can't walk off the pavement." He gestures at an empty field with a slow, heavy arm.

My mind snaps back to studies. These nocturnal seabirds have counter-shading patterns, (like a World War II Avenger torpedo plane), and they dig burrows, lay eggs underground, and can smell their chicks. They bite the hell out of your cuticles when held in hand for banding. They rock! It's funny how Bonin Petrels will end up being my favorite bird on the atoll. If I hadn't died before I left Halfway, I would be telling everyone how cool they are and why we should protect them.

I would also learn that the prettiest bird on the atoll would be the Pacific Golden-Plover, especially in breeding plumage. It looks like a golden statue. The toughest bird would be a toss-up between the nasty-tempered Black-footed Albatross, and the aerial pirate, the Great Frigate Bird. The award for loudest ear-splitter on the atoll would go to the Red-tailed Tropicbird. I would learn of all these critters in short course on Halfway, but for now, Ben brings me to the Bachelor Officer's Quarters (BOQ), a 3-story, quickly built, cinderblock rectangle reminiscent of third world jail construction. I don't care. I am psyched to be here and to have already been smacked by a petrel. I leave my bike in the rack and climb the concrete stairs to the 3rd floor. Fine with me again. I'm in great fucking shape and want to take on the World; with a view preferably.

Ben says as he turns down the hall, "We'll get ya a surplus TV tomorrow. Have a good night, and see ya at breakfast."

I say, "Okay, ah, bye," and boom, he is gone.

Wow, does he hate me, or is that just him? I wouldn't have minded a little more chatter and a game of twenty questions. I am so wound-up. I guess there will be time for that. There is always plenty of time on Halfway. Too much time, it will turn out. Waiting waiting waiting. Always waiting for something on Halfway. Waiting for the goonies to return. Waiting for the HIC flight to bring us bananas so our potassium levels don't shrink. Waiting for oranges so we don't get scurvy. Waiting, waiting, waiting. Animals do a lot of waiting, like the albatross chicks, waiting for a regurgitated meal from far off seamounts. Waiting for a new video to arrive to show at The Station Theater. Ya know, waiting!

Kestrel and an APS biologist test Halfway chicks for lead in their blood; from eating chipping paint left behind on the Navy buildings.

I stand at the window and stare down at the quad below the streetlights. Some of the albatross dance. Some of them don't move at all. I swear some of them look dead. Some of them look like they are walking around looking for something or someone. Every 2 minutes or so, one streaks by or comes in for a landing, even though, supposedly, they tend to stay pretty grounded after dark. It's the Black-footed Albatross, "the evil ones" as they were known by the Navy and their brats, which hunt for squid glowing at night, and shiny flying-fish eggs floating on the surface like a humongous sushi barge had flipped at sea, leaving glistening orangey roe dancing in the moonlight. Wow, what it must be to be an albatross; flying over the ocean day after night after night after day, with the moon, sun, and wind on your back, looking down at the endless swells. So stealthy, you'd never see a black-foot coming down on you at night until you were in its mouth. But, still, this is a bird colony; a bird colony of over a million, with another species, overlapping the first bird colony of 50 thousand, and another colony of 35,000, and two subterranean species colonies of about 48,000, and an Eastern Island colony and Spit Island colony of 55,000 and 4,000 respectively. On and on the birds go, with maybe as much individual variation in each as in people in Upper Manhattan or in Shinjuku San Chome. 11 species in all breed on the atoll, and that's why it became an animal sanctuary, eventually. What the hell am I doing out here? It's one of those moments again, isn't it? The hollow lonely lost pit in my stomach again. I

21

want a hug. Boo hoo hoo. Did I fuck up? What am I doing out here? Breathe. Breathe. It's cool. Just keep telling myself. It's cool. This place is cool. Rad. Cool. Okay.

I feel out-of-place. Ya know that feeling when you feel like you are in the wrong place and you really really don't belong? I love Boston, but I could never be me in the hood I grew up in? I think of my long-term girlfriend, now my ex. Back in the 80s and 90s, she lived with me in Boston for four-and-a-half-years. When she was moving back to LA, of all the rat holes to return to, she said, "Boston is such a beautiful town. It's too bad the people are so ugly." I'm sure a dapper looking bunch of Bostonians would take exception to that remark. Of course, she referred to personality, and was mainly referring to E.B. and Revere, not The Back Bay and Beacon Hill so much. If you've been in a parking dispute in Chelsea, you know exactly what she meant. She did not feel that such a delicate flower should live in such an abusively hostile environment. I met her at Chrysalis Music in LA, while I worked an internship as I finished up at UCLA. I liked it there, but talk about a fish out of water. I could not deal with the "music biz". For example, at one 'function' held by the A & R department to shmooze-up clients, I had this guy walk up to me, tell me he was Billy Idol's cousin, ask me what I do, then, once he realized I was a nobody intern, tell me to never namedrop, cause it 'makes ya look needy'. What? I don't belong in that world of irony anymore than I belong down in Needles with the meth addicts and desert loners. I guess the smart enough players know it's bullshit and just roll with it, but I like to be real. Nature is real, very real, and natural. That's why I like to be in nature. I've never had a Bufflehead or Bobolink bullshit me, although Killdeer make a compelling argument with their feigned complaints.

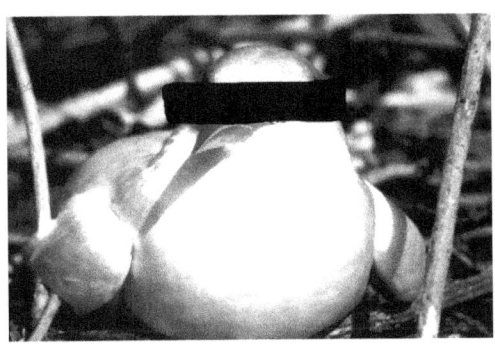

Not only albatross, but a number of other seabirds, like the robust Red-tailed Tropicbird, colonize the atoll.

Snapping out of my glaring gaze, I lay down on my firm, hard dusty bed. That's fine with me, I like it, but, there is no way I am going to pull my usual narcoleptic pass-out-crash maneuver. I don't have any way to play music right now. When I was in college, I had one of those Brady Bunch style cassette tape player recorder things with the top that opens like a hatchback and those noisy square buttons. I would put a tape in right by my head, then hit play, usually falling asleep before the first song finished. Sometimes, when the tape would end, the click of the cassette player stopping would wake me momentarily, but most of the time I slept through it. When I was at UCLA, one of my favorite tapes was Kate Bush, *The Dreaming*. My sissy friends in the Theatre Department thought it would give me nightmares. I loved it, but remember, I only got to hear the first few songs on each side of the tape. Many of the songs, later on the tape, were a mystery to me for a long time. Hearing her sing her bizarre lyrics in my sleep had such a weird effect on me, and I almost thought she was right there, and could feel her whispering to me in my ear. Tonight, the clatter of the albatross will be my lullaby.

So, instead I start reading a book on the history of The Battle of Halfway. Wow, ocean warfare. When you die an infantry soldier, you lay in a field in your blood, and you wait for a Medic or die. "Infantry". Huh. That's funny. "Infant tree." What are they trying to say, that you are like a stupid little infant, a sapling, no more important than any other infantryman, expendable? Why don't they just call them 'pawns' or 'peasants' or 'minorities' or 'white trash' instead? How many of the Richie Riches end up in the infantry? My "little" brother Manat falls for the military crap, but luckily, he never got sucked-in to the god stuff like two of my other brothers. Manat thinks everyone is full of shit. That's his defense mechanism because he knows he isn't very smart, and that he is full of shit, and all the firemen he hangs around with are full of shit, and therefore (to use transitive property), the liberal media, the plumber next-door, the barber down the Centre; they're all full of shit. Unless. . . , ah ha, unless it's something he happens to agree with, like say, Fox News, or the NRA. Then, Manat can switch off his wall of cognitive dissonance, and they ain't full of shit. They're gospel.

Manat was programmed by the recruiters to believe that, and I quote, "The Air Force is the best branch, cause day treat ya like a U-man bean."

"Who told you that?" I replied.

"The recruiter. They're bonded. They can't lie or day can be couwrt mahshaled," Manat replied with an exterior confidence, but revealing a shallow insecurity beneath his 'tough-guy' Boston accent.

They also told him a lot, a lot more "shtuff" we shall call it. Shtuff like, "You can fly helicopters" turned into, "You're too big", and "You can work with K-9s", turned into "Sorry", without so much as an explanation. Instead, he was stuck in Lakenheath guarding our nukes on a RAF base. Day and night, especially night, in a place so unlike Halfway, with a bone-chilling raw fog, and mind atrophying duty, he marched about the aircraft inside the razor-wire fence. After the U.K., a DUI at his next station in Utah led to a quick escape from Mormonland to get out clean. He was quick to say, "No regrets!" He could never admit to being a loser, though he can't hide the feeling in his eyes. For some reason he feels like a loser around me. I know, I can hear and see what I am thinking here, and how can I say such a thing about my "little" brother. It's not that I don't love him. I think once I left for college, and with all the fights and shit that went down as kids, he never felt he could trust being tight with me. I can see that. I gave him plenty of reasons *not* to trust me as a kid. I think what he really needs is a really good friend. I can't be that friend. Too much water under the bridge and he will never trust me or anybody, no matter how sincere I am with him now. The fucked-up thing is, that you would think that if he didn't think he was a loser, he wouldn't be, but thinking he is makes him one. Self-fulfilling prophecy. Yiyyi! So, he lives by the "Ya right" attitude. It's the tough guys "whatever". "Puhf, ya, . . right". Kinda like "NOT" at the end of a statement. By revealing all of this to my friends, as I do openly but not overly, I think they think I really do hate him. I don't. You can be mad, and bummed, and frustrated, and disappointed til the cows come home, but ya can't hate him anymore than you could hate a mongoloid or a mongoose. They're just what they are. Over the years I asked him to star in some of my videos, and he has given me spare camo gear. He brought me to and from Logan Airport; so though you can tell he hates me, he doesn't really hate me anymore than other emotionally fucked-up siblings might. It's average hate, but still too much for me to take. I wish I could somehow reach him positively, but I think anything I say or do he would react against, so it's better to bless and release, and let him realize that anything that happens in his life, good or bad, has nothing to do with me, the ultimate scapegoat.

Realizing that I have been staring at the page, thinking about my brother, I force myself to concentrate on the text again. I read on about World War II history. On a ship, man, on a ship, you end up in the fuckin water. Not good. Not a good option, ever. Why the hell would I join the Navy over the Marines, Army, or Air Force? Did one of the guys that slept in this room get killed during the war? Wow, I just learned they didn't have an air force back then, so the Army flew the bombers, and the Navy off the aircraft carriers. Wow. Crazy shit. People are crazy: Knights in armor with maces, smashing the shit out of their enemy's skull; Assyrians disemboweling people; rapes of Nan King and Nam and grand mom. How the fuck do these stupid things happen, and why? I think about Ben Hur, and the oarsmen shackled in place. I think about the aqua naumachia, or whatever the Romans called it when they would flood the Coliseum to have the gladiators fight mock sea battles for the spectators, to the death. It's amazing how crafty we are about being evil to each other.

The shabby BOQ; my first HAWS abode, with its neutering palette.

I fall asleep with the light on and the book on my chest, dreaming of war and humans and birds fighting in colonies. My brain darts and fragments, stream-of-consciousness alpha-state muddles: First night in barracks. Adventure awaits. Lying in bed. Staring at the ceiling. Waiting. Get use to it. Always feel like waiting on Halfway. Always waiting for something. Singing career lost? On hold? Never to return again? Did I lose my friends? What about that sweet little masochist Messycka? Mmmmm, mmm mmm. Messycka; I love that name, and that girl, but I just can't trust her. Note all the m's I used to describe her. Eleven. Will I ever be in a rock opera again? Scared, alone. Plunge myself into my studies, and work. No control over my destiny. Nothing. How did my path go to UCLA, BU, Halfway? I was Danny Zuko in Grease in high school. I was the captain of my spring track team and still hold unbroken records. I put myself through UCLA and BU with absolutely no help from family, working full-time. How can someone who has accomplished so much have such a blabby, unfocussed brain? I am an award-winning video producer, and now, the first ranger on Halfway Atoll. Alpha-state stream. Reaffirmation. Relax. Rewind. Recoup. Recharge.

Blackness.

Waves roll on day after day, hour after hour, over the massive Pacific. Ceaselessly, the cycle's unyielding: Corals and crustaceans, seabirds and seals, phytoplankton and fishes. From the minute rhythms of microscopic whip-cracking flagella to the generally gargantuan marine oscillations that pulse throughout the Pacific, the ocean thrives like a massive chorus of one.

Drizzle hits my windows as I sleep deeply. The petrels don't care. They keep blasting around all night, looking for some other new arrival to the atoll to crash into. Outside my window, the light-tower beam shines in circles against the clouds. Red lights blink on top of eight-story fuel tanks. I can see them from my stale pillow when I peak my eyes open. In the glimmering shallows beyond, Sea Cucumbers filter each piece of coral sand through their digestive systems and squeeze them back out through their tiny sphincters.

Are writers psychotic insomniacs? Why does Drats start writing at 1:11am; only when he's disturbed,. . . pissed-off? It would be funny to call him an 'angry young man'. He is not really that angry and doesn't really have the right to be that angry about anything, other than the complete annihilation of The Planet by one species, *Homo sapiens*. A lot of people would certainly argue that he's not young, albeit immature. Well, 80-year-olds would call him young. I wonder if an 80 year-old will read this. I wonder if they would like it. Would Drats' themes and style be universal enough? William S. Burroughs might have liked it. It's all relative. When I was little I use to think teenagers were old.

"Oh no, what happened?" the sympathetic adult would whine. "Those teenagers were mean to me," I would reply with a sob. Teenagers were the meanest. They were the meanest people in the World. Somehow, they were worse than the Nazi Germans. Why did we always fight the Germans as kids when we were playing Army? And why did we always play Army? We never played Air Force, Navy, or Marines. WWII movies? There were Japanese movies out there too, but, I don't know. Jungle warfare? Sea battles? Just didn't do it for us. We wanted tanks in the European theater. Theater? Hmmm. Like it's a play? Like no one really gets killed. They just try to hold their breath and keep their stomach from heaving so the audience won't see. Have you tried that? It sucks. One of the worst parts you can have in a play is having to die on stage with minutes left in the scene; minutes that feel like a lot of minutes. Corpses don't sweat either. Waiting. Waiting for the scene to end. Waiting for the curtain to fall. Just waiting to fade to black.

Octogenarians would say I died young, but teenagers already think I'm old.

With a scratchy, hoarse voice, they would proclaim, 'He died in the prime of his life. Oh to be that young again. If I knew then what I know now, I would have ruled the world.' The clichés fall away.

'*With alcohol I rule the world with a little word*,' Stump once blathered poetically.

'*I shake with emotion, by swallowing the ocean.*' Ah Stump; so, so woefully under-rated and underappreciated as a kooky UK art band. But angry? I can play angry on TV. I don't think people really get angry. They just play angry. It's a choice.

Yeh, we *choose* to get angry. It makes US look tough. It makes US look mean. Clint's *Dirty Harry* always looked mean, but he never looked angry.

Ya, we never fought the Japs for some reason as kids, and fighting the Italians was certainly out of the question. Most of the time we didn't even bother with toy guns. We mimed our sub-machineguns and *hang grenades* (as we erroneously called them), and bazookas. I didn't even know the Italians were in the war until I developed into one of those mean teenagers myself, but actually, once I became a teenager, they weren't quite so mean anymore. I certainly wasn't mean. Well, not as mean as the teens in the early 70's. They were wicked mean, and dangerous. They thought they were gonna get drafted to go to Nam, so they didn't give a shit about anything. They knew Nixon was a creep, like all the stodgy good 'ol boys types. Pipe bombs in school toilets, mescaline in homeroom at 8:17am, bomb scares monthly, and rashes of stabbings in Dorchester and Roslindale. They used to walk down the street with their hands in their denim jackets, spitting, and flipping their long hair out of their face. Mean. White punks on dope. Mean mean mean.

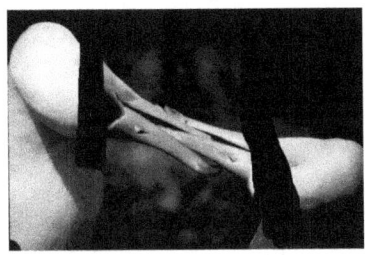

Humans, like Albatross, battle for superiority.

I was wicked confused when I watched McHale's Navy and they were in Italy, and Ernest Borgnine, obviously a big chunky Italiano guy, was named McHale. What was up with that? Oh yeah, and what was up with Ginger and Mary Ann? I thought I was a 'fem' (as the mean teenagers would call me), or something was wrong with me. I knew I was supposed to like Ginger, based on how adult men (like the Professor and the Skipper) would react to her every little adjustment, but I was blown away by Mary Ann. Did real men like Ginger Grant? Real angry young teenage men? Did the octogenarians like Ginger too, or were they digging Lovie? Yea, she was a sugar momma, but no, No. That's like digging Mrs. Cunningham. I heard Fonzi had a thing with her during the show, and Mrs. Brady did Greg, and Shirley Jones seduced David Cassidy. Was nothing incestually sacred back then? Rumors abounded among the teenagers. They thought they knew everything and that grown-ups were idiots. Hey, the grown-ups created Nam. What would growing-up life have been like without black and white reruns of McHale's and Gilligan's? I don't know, but even now, as an adult who almost has most of my shit together, I still think I'd take Mary Ann, for a roll in the hay or to be my life-long loving soul mate, over Ginger, either way. I'm sorry, I would. Would you?

I made a Savoia-Marchetti SM79 once. You know, the Italian torpedo plane. I glued it together with that lethal air-plane glue. I finished the WWII craft with my toxic paints and did a killer camo pattern on it. When it was done, I 'flew' it, by hand, down the stairs, which were giant waterfalls pouring down from the Swiss Alps. Then, I turned past the banister, which was actually a monolithic pinnacle in my mind. Then, through the kitchen canyon and out to sea to sink some unsuspecting target in the sunroom. My Dad looked at the plane and took it from me.

"Wow, great job. Hey Saintia, look at the job he did on this plane. That's a heck of a paint job," he yelled at my Mom, over by the sink in her apron.

He was totally sincere. Totally. There is no way my Dad would ever say anything nice, even if you deserved it, unless he really meant it. That was being tough. Not mean, not angry, just tough. That way, you can survive in life. Being the youngest of a family of 9, my Dad knew all about tough love. I picked-up some of that; some of it in a good way, and some of it in a bad way.

He examined the plane. "What is this?" he asked.

"It's a Savoia-Marchetti," I explained proudly, butchering the Italian.

"Oh, that's an Italian plane," he said.

I thought for a minute. 'It is? What the fuck am I doing with an Italian plane? Were the Italians in WWII? They must of fought with US, right?'

"Ya know what kind of plane this is?" he queried.

"Yeah, it's a tor—pee-dddooo" and as the words 'torpedo plane' slowly dripped from my mouth, I realized that I had spent hours on an awesome jungle camouflage paint job on a plane that would be spending 80% of its time over the water. FUCK! I was always clueless. Always oblivious. Always fucked! Well, maybe enemy planes from above would think it was a tiny island shaped like a plane, and moving wicked fast? At least when parked in the jungle no one could see it. Fuck, are there any jungles in Italy?!

Funny thing though, my Dad didn't react. He didn't do anything negative or positive. Nothing. He just looked at the workmanship and didn't appear to care that I didn't know shit. I think he kind of wished he had painted that plane. It looked good. He had dabbled in some paint-by-numbers type art before; just another way he and I seemed so different from all of my siblings who never showed any interest in anything other than destructive behavior as teenagers and as adults.

"Hey Saintia, did you take a look at this?"

He handed it back to me and went back to the paper. I flew back through the fjord, glancing past the cabinet door precipices, and off onto the attack, wondering, what gave me the idea to paint a camo seaplane, and what the hell were the Italians doing in WWII? I never heard about Mussolini until I made it to 8th grade. That's why we couldn't speak Italian in the house?

That is still one of the few times I ever remember my Dad giving me positive reinforcement. It had to be tough love or you'd turn into a pussy. When I broke the high school record in track, he said, "Well, what do you expect? He's a natural runner. A lot of the Falco's are natural runners."

NOT. I'm the only one I ever knew of who ever ran. This is how these family myths get started, like my older brother Sproc is the motorcycle guy in the family. What a myth. I have more time on bikes than Doger, Sproc and Rosmarus combined, and I've owned more bikes than them too. When I worked hard on my paper route, and had saved almost a thousand dollars (more than I have saved right now), my brother Rosmarus, 5 years my senior, was pissed.

Bloodied albatross, after it got its cloaca kicked.

Rosmarus would demand in a deep voice, masculine beyond his age, 'Ma, I need five bucks, I'm going out.' You know, pubescent boys trying so hard to sound like men, but still in the mean teenager phase.

I've never been in a rush to manhood. Even now, most people still see me as a kid. Man-child. Like Jim Carey or something.

"Five bucks?!" Our Dad would pipe in with his heavy North End accent. "Why don't yah get ah job like Kestrel?"

Then he'd make one of our famous family myth statements like, "Of course he's makin good money. It runs in dah family. My brothas ahre all hahd workahs."

Now that was true. The entire family always had a really strong work ethic, proud of their jobs. I'm so glad I had that going for me. Thanks Mom and Dad. I guess I should have told them that while I was alive. Anyway, like many families across the World, myths develop and are perpetuated. 'Kestrel Falco can't tie his shoes or cross the street safely, cause he went to college' for example. This is the old "Absent-minded Professor" cliché. If tough mean guys can't find a way to make smart guys look wussy, then they feel inferior. I think that's another one I had figured-out by third of fourth grade, but was still way to small and dumb to do anything about. Like adults today; we know what the problems are and what the answers are, but we don't know how to get to the solutions. Every time ya try to end war, someone drops a bomb.

I heard one of my brothers telling my other brothers once, "I may not have an education, cause I didn't want ta do homework, but at least I can walk across the street without gettin killed.' Ya know, that kind of myth; totally unfounded in anything rational. If they don't call you a clutz or dweeb or wuss or 4-eyes, than what do they got on ya? What if a guy who feels lame about himself meets a guy like me? They hate me. Insecure bully-type guys hate me right away. My problem is I care, and I don't want them to hate me, but I can't suddenly get dumb, fat, and weak, though I try to lower myself to being that way when I meet these types. If I dumb-it-down for them they don't feel as insecure, and sometimes I even act obsequious around them just so they won't feel threatened by me. Then we can be friends. That sucks, but I still can't find a better way to handle it. And look at how *Homo* all of these cultural traps are now. All *Homo*. Absolutely nothing to do with the rest of the world, yet critically important to US somehow.

When I took a date to the movies, at 17, still a virgin who knew nothing, I mean nothing, my Dad whispered under his breath, "Ya know how to protect ya self, don't ya."

"Daaaaaaaaaad." I responded with shear embarrassment even though no one else heard. I really had no idea what he was talking about, but, he loved that Savoia-Marchetti. If we had established a more open, communicative relationship from the get-go, we could have had a better chance at connecting on these crucial father-son moments; but we didn't. We are Italian/Swede/Irish Boston Catholics. We are way too religioned-out to discuss sex. If you didn't grow up in this type of family in the early 70's, it would take a whole book for me to describe what it was like.

I should write a play while I'm on Halfway. Hmmm, what could I write? It should be cool of course. I have to make sure my cool side shows. It can't be weak, and play-like; like all those plays I hate and that always drove me away from the theatre. People should definitely get killed in it, especially people who suck of course, but some non-suckers should die too, so the audience can feel pain, and unsettled. *The Theatre of Cruelty!* Ha ha ha. Artaud. What a bastard. I could snag some of his methods, but if anyone dies, including me, I can't leave them on stage too long, waiting, trying to hold their breath. That sucks. I should have them drop off into the wings or orchestra pit.

Suddenly I realize I'm coming out of alpha state, and the random tangents above were my synapses firing off like crazy again. The sun is shining, glowing in my bright, pale, practically colorless room: A room that may have been kind of white once, but now has a tinge of yellow. The goonies out on the parade ground have never stopped. They clack and purr away, dancing and strutting. To see it once on TV is funny, entertaining. To stare down on it, . . . mind-blowing! I will learn to live with it, for days, weeks, and months: Nothing less than brain eroding. Some people who think I'm an exaggerist (euphemism for 'full of shit') could never in a million years understand what it is like to live with 2 million goonies. Ask someone who was there. Pry. Ask them what it was really like on HAWS (Halfway Atoll Wildlife Sanctuary).

I break from the cacophonous mayhem at the window to enter my bathroom for the first time. Straight ahead of me, the first thing I notice is a door, just like mine. Oh yeah, that guy Zart is my bathroom buddy. I notice a deadbolt on the door, and I turn to look at mine too. Ahhh, so I can lock him out and he can lock me out.

33

Note to self: Don't lock him out if I don't want to be locked out. To my right, in this narrow corridor, a toilet, then a shower. Just outside, on the windowsill, two White Terns look up at me, delicate and fearless. I lean forward and look back over to my sink, which protrudes from the cinderblock wall back in my room, under a smudgy half-sized mirror, bolted hastily. Innnterrresssssting. They put sinks in our rooms but we have to share the toilet and shower. Why not share a sink too? I never figured that one out. I keep saying I'm not a know-it-all, whether I strive to know why why why, or not. I'm guessing it must have had something to do with shaving, cause 8 men sharing a shower and toilet could work, I guess, but shaving, especially in the Navy where they were forced to shave daily, must have been a log jam.

I put on my APS (Animal Protection Service) uniform and head down the stairs to my bike. On the stairs I run into a construction worker on his way out. He looks at me with a stabby glare.
"Hi," I say jovially.
He gives me the cool-guy nod without an oral utterance, like a Fence Lizard on some sunny shale. Hate fills his eyes and soul, as he looks at me the same way my "little" brother Manat does. Hmm, hostility? Not out here in paradise.

I get on my beach cruiser, and pedal toward The Galley, albatrosses everywhere! In the air, on the ground, in the streets, on the porches, . . . everywhere! One sits on the floor of a charging golf cart, parked by the ASS house. One dabbles in a puddle by a fire hydrant. They still sing of course, if you could call it that. Occasionally, a pair of White Terns float by effortlessly, like angels. I pass a few people who had been on the plane with me. They meander around, possessed by the gooney dance and taking photos. I see loose strings of other people up ahead. They all appear to be heading in the same direction. That must be the place. I pull my bike into the rack, dismount, and look to see that most, . . . no, . . . all of the people are not only guys, but not a one is white. They all sport dark skin with indiscernible ethnicity. Wow, no one told me anything about that. I'm suddenly starting to realize I am way less prepared than I thought I was for this place, even after all of my studying. Some things just don't make it into print, do they?

I know there was no indigenous population on the atoll, and that it had been a U.S. possession since 1858 or something like that, so what are these guys doing here?

As I enter The Galley, one of the men holds the screen door open for me and says "Good morning Mr. Kestrel" with a strong accent. Hmm. He knows my name. There is a line. This large cafeteria with 20 or so long tables, looks shiny and clean, with the typical low mumble of voices and shuffling hums. As I approach the cashier, another tells me to move along. I don't have to pay, yet. Just like any other cafeteria, we slide our trays along the metal rack and watch in horror as greasy, buttery, meat-laden chow shlopps onto our plates.

I notice a semi-white toddler running around one of the crowded, long tables, then, he runs toward the counter, playing with his reflection in the shiny stainless steel. Unfortunately, what he doesn't realize is that the tray rack protrudes about a foot and a half out, and happens to be exactly at his forehead level. As he stomps forward quickly and reaches out to tag his metallic reflection, BOOOONG!, his forehead bangs into the tray rack like a gong and he drops backwards to his padded diaper butt with a squishy thunk. He starts crying, but it comes as one of those silent cries, where the kid's mouth opens, and the tears trickle, and everybody looks in shock, and that pregnant pause hangs like fog, and then, WWWhhhhhhaaaaaaaaaaaaaaaaa! It hits. At least he wasn't knocked cold. The foreign men all rush to his aid. The mother, who looks Filipina, rolls her eyes and downs some scrambled eggs. I later learn that she happens to be the doctor's wife, and that is just one of three kids they have on atoll.

I scan my surroundings. Where to sit? Does this happen to you? I'm the first ranger on Halfway. I see people in APS uniforms at one table, and all these friendly brown-skinned guys at another. I gotta guess Southeast Asian by now. I see the construction workers, and I see Jewel and the flight crew. Man, I really want to sit with Jewel, but how would that look? So, I amble over to the APS table where Ben and several others sit.

"Good morning," I announce, trying to start things off on a bright and positive note.

"Mornin'," Ben replies, just like he is from the boonies. "This is our first-ever ranger, Kestrel."

A bunch of simultaneous hellos erupt.

"How'd ya sleep?" Ben asks.

"Well," I say, "I love all the birds, don't get me wrong, but it looks like it's going to take some getting used to."

Everyone chuckles politely, like when a celebrity or foreign dignitary makes some kind of indiscernible joke.

"Everyone seems to have that problem," Ben replies. "I can get ya some earplugs."

"Or run the AC," says a plain, fake-blond, sitting next to Ben. "That will mumble right ovah dah sound, you bet cha."

AC? I friggin hate AC. I've hated it my whole life. It makes my nose stuffy. It makes it hard for me to acclimate to the heat outside the AC. It dries my eyes out. It makes my head feel all funny inside and the dust triggers my allergies. It wastes way more energy than a ceiling fan. I hate AC. Who would propose such a thing to ME?

"This is Myhel. She's our seal monitor for The All-world and Sea Society, better known around here as A-S-S," Ben spells out. "And this is Han. He works with us too from Sri Lanka. If you need anything, Han's the man," Ben continues, obviously more animated with girls like Myhel around.

"Hello Mr. Kestrel. Are you coming to our Merry New Year Party?" Han says, sounding Indian, and very polite.

"Oh, great! There's going to be a party? I love to party," I reply enthusiastically. "Sure, but please, don't call me Mr. Kestrel. Kestrel is fine."

Han's smile fades as Ben nods his head in a 'no' to me. Utt ohh, faux pas already?

Myhel bats her eyes at me while Ben continues on with a number of other introductions.

"This is Banette. She's our biologist, and this is Kilgro, she's the dolphin project leader for A-S-S too. She works with Myhel."

Banette says 'hi' in a kind of nasal Fran Drescher way. She is small, petite. A wee person one might say, but not a midget; maybe

Japanese, or Malaysian, and looks like a serious professional biologist. Though cuter than anyone on the atoll with the exception of Jewel, Banette right away appears way too little-boy-like for me. Like men tested worldwide, I like curves. Of course there is a lot more to someone than their physique. I'm just talking pure, raw first impressions here.

Before Banette gets another word in, Kilgro chimes-in with a voice that would make Patty and Selma, and Rosanne, sound like the sweetest love sirens from Venus. She burps, "Nice to meet you. When I was in Belize . . . "

I don't even hear the rest of the sentence. All I can do is be completed distracted by how repulsed I feel. She starts to rant like a banshee, with a sentence structure straight from Prime Time news shows. Everything she says is boring and bland, and sounds like she has said it before. She is probably 5'1", as heavy as me, with breasts the size of honeydews, and black, lifeless eyes, barely visible through her glasses. I'm having trouble swallowing my food, and I wish she would turn the bull-horn down, but I can't be so rude as to ask her to squeeze the volume down a notch on my first day on the atoll, at my first meal in The Galley.

She continues un-phased by my expression, "I love to study dolphins cause they're the only animals in the animal kingdom known to enjoy sex. They're doin it all the time," Kilgro grinds.

I think to myself for an instant. I am a human animal in the animal kingdom and I like sex. Maybe she is a biologist who counts US separate from The Animal World. Also, from my studies, I thought it had to do with social behavior and pecking order, not necessarily pleasure. How can a scientist gauge pleasure? And isn't there also evidence that some great apes, and even the most primitive ones, the baboons, appear to produce increased endorphin levels during coitus? Hmmm, what would Lorenz say? He studied geese, not dolphins. Maybe everything likes sex and gets off on the dopamine shit. US homocentric arrogant bastards think we enjoy exclusively?! How can that be when we've all come up from fish and lizards?

I jump into the gap before she can finish her next breath, "You mean to say it's documented that some cetaceans engage in recreational sexual activity for pleasure?" as Mr. Know-It-All makes an appearance.

"Well," she says with a shock, "today many . . . blah blah blah" she tries to respond, but my ears stay clogged by the grating sound of her voice, and my eyes can't possibly disguise my struggle in the ability to get beyond what I am experiencing. It's my first day. I have jetlag. I didn't sleep very well. There are 200 people walking and clanking and chewing and laughing, and this is the last thing I want to be talking to. I know I'm judging books by covers here, but her personality is so extremely obnoxious.

". . .and I'm glad you used the proper scientific term for 'cetaceans'," Kilgro ends.

"Oh, thanks," I say, trying to avoid sarcasm while swallowing her condescension politely.

"Better chow down," Ben says. "Orientation will be in 10 minutes. As soon as you are up for it, let me know, cause I need you to take over."

"Great!" I say like an enthusiastic Tony the Tiger.

After following everyone to the tray bus window, I hop on my bike and follow Ben to the office, where he picks up the flight manifest with a list of the passengers and a few other items. Then we ride to the large, rectangular, 3-story Hangar. There, we park our bikes again, climb the navy blue concrete stairs, and enter a windowless conference room with a long table and a slide projector.

Nothing is ready. Ben has been doing the orientations for the new visitors, primarily pallid wildlife tourists, and an assorted lot of contractors and others who make their way out here one way or another. He's an okay guy, don't get me wrong, but definitely not a people person. He awkwardly stands up in front of the new visitors in this creepy room by the runway, with bluish Navy paint peeling off the walls. His face looks red. His forehead sweats profusely, continuously. Oh, it's painful.

He says "Hi. Welcome to Halfway. This is a sanctuary. Blah blah blah." Poor biologist. Poor, poor biologist. Ahh, to be a scientist. Fuck. I have to do that, in front of this unwilling audience of atoll visitors and new employees, who want to be anywhere but here. Doesn't he know how to use action verbs? Keep it exciting, god. This job is gonna suck. Wait a minute. I don't have to do it *that* way, right? I wonder if he'll give me any play with this whole thing. I wonder if I should do a musical version? People will be singing the orientation jingles while they violate the atoll.

'And don't forget-het, everyday-yay, from the monk seals stay 100 feet away-yay.'

I wonder if I were to write a play, if Ben won't be hurt if I don't cast him? Probably not. He goes on to say that currently on Halfway there are '200 men and 11 women, and that most of them are foreign nationals, contracted by the Navy, from Sri Lanka, Thailand, and The Philippines.' That explains why I couldn't figure out where they were from. First off, they are from three different countries/cultures. Secondly, have you ever seen a bunch of guys together from those 3 countries? They all kinda look like they could be from the same place; like Canadians, Australians, and Russians; but eventually it becomes obvious that they are very, very different, and they will let you know. I gotta watch myself out here and really get started on the right foot.

I take notes on the orientation and the tour. After returning from the Historical Tour, I start my obligatory first-day-on-the-job behavior. I follow Ben around, pretend I'm not bored, try to limit my yawns to when his back is turned, and try to stay focused and remember everything he shows me. Why is the first day always like this? A combination of nerves, trying really hard, but having no autonomy; must be how a horse feels with a rider. Ben shows me which keys to use, and the location of my desk in the corner, with its back to the window. I will change that immediately. I learned in 8th grade that it's key to be near a window; wishing you could be running in the shining sunlight, filling your lungs with the crisp air. Then, the bureaucracy! I'm handed a pile of government paper work and forms. Waiting waiting waiting for the forms to be given to me, then to fill and complete, then to send in and confirm. Did I do it right?

"Here ya go," as Ben gives me my first government cell phone; a big, clunky, old, full-sized cell phone with one of those plastic-leather protective cases so I can clip it onto my belt.

So the task before me? Write tours. Can't write if I don't know anything. I start looking around the office, and I see three books and 4 videos on Ben's little makeshift library (three shelves in the office), and stuff them into my trusty, albeit beaten, backpack, with its broken zippers and ripped stitching. The safety pins make it look like Johnny Rotten's, but this is by true poverty, not fashion-poser design.

I hear a squealing Purreewwww! I have to stop for a moment and behold the scene in front of my office. Albatross; glorious, black and white albatross all over the place; on the lawns, and around the monument. The monument happens to be a giant gooney that looks more like a bowling pin than a seabird. On the sidewalk in front of the bowling alley, scratching their nails against the concrete ramp; on the street; everywhere I look, everywhere I listen, everywhere I see something move or flutter. Goonies goonies goonies everywhere!

Suddenly, I hear someone whistle in fast succession. Deee-ooo-wiiiiii. Deee-ooo-wiiiiii. Deee-ooo-wiiiiii. I flick my head about but see no one. I hear it again, then, about 60 meters out at almost 1 O'clock low, I catch a roundish brown football apparently running under its own power. My eyes refocus, and there, making its way through the goonies and under the shade, darts something out of a Warner Bros. classic Bugs Bunny alien episode. It is (get ready to laugh your ass off at this one) a Bristle-thighed Curlew!

First of all, who gets to name this shit! I am so pissed that the AOU let this slip through, so pissed. Can you see the bristles, ever, really? Can you even find the friggen thighs on these chunky little bastards? No. No. And, no. I must immediately learn how to separate Bristle-thighs from other curlews and Whimbrel. The whistle almost has a flute quality to it, and the notes resemble some of the flute parts I play in a song that I'm not sure would actually be in the rock musical by Drats called **Rudy the Red Bat,** should it ever be produced.

That Anasazi Song
by Drats

Just like the Anasazi, we had it all
Walls to never crumble, nor civilizations fall.

Overpopulation, depleted the land
Overpopulation, water usage banned
Murals in kivas, ritualistic sites
Organized societies, flutter like kites

Just like the Anasazi, we had it all
Walls to never crumble, nor civilizations fall.

It's a parallel culture, history will repeat
The cycle's unyielding, history will repeat
They're all parallel cultures, history will repeat
history will repeat
history will repeat
history will repeat
history will repeat
history will repeat

Now we have no water and we have no land
Overpopulation, we slip from god's hand
Now we vanish, but we had it all
Just like the Anasazi, ancient ones we're called.

My attention suddenly breaks when I notice the curlew running something down. I reach into my backpack for my camera and start twisting my lens-covers off by feel, without taking my eye of this shifty "atoll road runner" of Halfway, when suddenly, it catches something and holds it up in its bill. The flute melody still plays in my head. Then I see, it holds a *Mus musculus*. That's right Latin nerds, the House Mouse, by way of Europa. I focus my lens and

41

start reeling off shots. A quick aperture adjustment, then 3 more shots. Maybe if Drats' publisher isn't lame, they will put these photos in. They are dark, but diagnostic. The curlew takes a few steps, pauses, moves its head slightly to scope the scene, and then moves the live mouse down its long, curved bill. At the mouth, which surprisingly becomes big and round quickly, down goes the live but shaken mouse, headfirst.

I hear another whistle, so I copy it. One curlew comes within my focal range, and then, too close to shoot. Click. I get a couple of great shots as it moves off. These would end up being the first slides I would add to Ben's slideshow. I whistle more to play with them, then hear another whistle, and look up to see Tex on his bike mimicking me. I get up off of my belly to go talk with him. Tex tells me, as if to proclaim upon me some universal truth all good people should know, "What the hell are you doing weirdo? You don't belong down there with the animals n shit."

At that same moment, a slim figure with a buzz-cut halts his bike on the road. It's Loon.
"Hey, leave the birds alone!" he barks.
"Oh, great, . . . you bird protector?" Tex replies with a drawl. "We got enough of those in this country."
I try to jump in, "Hi, I'm just taking pictures. I'm . . .". The explanation means nothing to either of them. They're already embroiled.
"Where the hell did you come from?" Loon interjects.
"I'm the pilot, dumb-ass. You better watch how you talkin boy, if you ever wanna get off this rock again," Tex fires back, like he has power to keep us stranded here or something.
Isn't that funny? Daniel the real pilot would be too modest to say that, and Tex, the wanna-be pilot, is all proud bravado. Ha.
Loon immediately realizes the intellectual level he deals with here, like I did in the door of the cockpit of the Gulfstream turbo. He tempers toward the rational, and stows the radical, "Hey, I actually worked in Texas on armadillo surveys. I know the area, and they have some good people working down there." Loon challenges, "I did meet good folks down there too. You don't *have* to be that way."

"What way?" Tex pulls air into his chest and flexes his pecks like a silverback. Strike that: Silverbacks do it with a lot more style and charisma.

Loon answers, "Texan. Like a Texan. You don't have to act like a Texan. You are not forced to act like a Texan. Sometimes, it's refreshing when someone from New York City is polite and kind, and someone from Texas is smart and non-aggressive."

Tex looks at Loon, puzzled for a minute. He thought he was in a fight, but now he can't tell if Loon attacks with backhanded insults, or empathizes with deep sincere understanding.

Having been on the atoll for less than 24-hours, I have to say, my mind has already been blown. What have I gotten myself into out here? I look at both of them for a second. They stare at each other in silence. I slip onto my saddle and quietly push off to a glide, giving a little whimper of a goodbye. Entering The Galley, I look back to see if it has come to blows. They both bike off on their ways. After eating my lunch, I ride up the smooth concrete ramp and into the breeze-way between my office and the little store. I walk in to find a skinny Filipino behind the counter.

"Hello Mr. Kestrel," he says. "Welcome, please buy everyathing."
"Thank you," I say, trying to look unsurprised.

How does everyone already know my name out here? I'm used to living in Boston, LA, Tokyo, and San Francisco. I'm used to anonymity, and seeing thousands of new faces every single day.

I walk up and down a few isles in a room that probably once functioned as some kind of office. The long, fluorescent, rusting bulbs hang down below the dilapidated hanging ceiling, and most of the shelves look dusty and bare. I grab a stale box of raisins and some emergency candy bars for my room, and then spin out of there quickly. As I glance up, across the way, I notice a tiny room with a window. A donation library with books and videos sits locked and dark across the breezeway. Mental note: Get a bunch of free reading and vid-watching done while on the atoll. See, you don't have to have money to have fun. I've been having fun with no money my whole life. Fuck money. I don't pay to workout; I climb trees and do pull-ups on poles. Libraries, forests, parks, downtowns; they're all free, man. Free free free. Like me.

As I ride along with my backpack in my little basket, I think back about meeting all of these tripped-out characters so far on this sanctuary, and that's what makes the next meeting so shocking. I actually am about to come upon a nice, normal person. Not a guy in the 'guy' sense, but a true buddy. Like I said, I'm not a 'guy'. At first, I see her apparently taking some kind of measurement on one of the lawns. Then I see her raise her clipboard up and slip it tightly under her armpit, then she flicks open a knife and whittles her short pencil sharp.

"Survey?" I guess.
"Yup. Hey you must be the new ranger they were sending out. I'm Dietera," she says with a calm, mellow voice, as she folds the knife closed, puts the pencil in her lips and reaches to shake my hand. "I set up the albatross success plots here."
Dietera's calm seems to be the antithesis of Kilgro's vomitive expulsion of exposition.
"Wait, for US?" I thought Banette was the biologist.
"Yeh, well I am the biologist for ASS, under contract with the APS."
"Oh, so what do you do?" I continue, always having to know everything about anything.
"Well," she continues very humble and matter-of-fact, "Right now I am just designating a plot so the volunteers know which nests are in. Then they will collect data on a sheet like this. We are mainly looking at breeding success. How many parents in a plot have eggs hatch? How many fledge? And this year we will also be banding fledglings to try to determine how many make it off the atoll."
I say, "Wow that's a lot of work."
"I know, that's why we were glad to hear you ran track and play ultimate," she says sincerely. "You can help us chase down the albatross fledglings for banding before they leave the atoll."
"I would love to." I say, "How do you and everybody else already know stuff about me?" I wonder.
"Well, I don't know about everyone else, but I just spoke with Gerry the other day in Hono and he was excited to have you

coming out. Then Tirgut I guess also got your profile from APS. It's a small atoll."

"I'm learning that quickly," I respond. "1200 acres? I grew up on kind of a small island east of Boston. . . 1-square-mile, 23,000 people. Everybody knew everybody there too. The cops treated me like they were my uncles," I tell her.

She grins, displaying bright white teeth beneath her dark tan. She is attractive, maybe has seven to ten years on me or so, and looks to be pretty down-to-Earth.

I go on, "It's true. When the cops caught me drinking with four of my friends in my Dad's Chevy Citation, up at the public landing, they came up and said, "Okay lil'Falco, step out of dah cah with all yah friends and pouh all da beah down the sewah.""

Dietera laughs at my impression of Boston cops and says sympathetically, "That really hurt, cause buying beer was not only a major expense at that age, but pretty hard to do too."

"Ya." I say. "The drinking age was only 18 when I first started trying to get beer, but then it went up to 20, and then eventually, 21, staying ahead of me year by year. That's okay. I don't really like drinking that much."

"Did you meet Zart yet?" Dietera asks.

"No."

"Oh, yah, he's off atoll right now," Dietera answers herself. "He's a great guy. You guys are gonna get along great."

Funny, that's almost the same thing Ben said.

She ends, "He went back to visit his family for the holidays. He should be bringing some special micro brews," swinging her long, flat, straight black hair out of her eyes.

"Well nice meeting you and keep up the good work," I say as one of my usual salutations, and glide off on my cruiser to my barracks.

I push my front tire into the bike rack as I dismount, causing a gooney on the other side to startle up onto its feet and bray at me in defiance.

"Sorry little buddy," I say in a high, soft falsetto.

The gooney falls forward clumsily and gets its head caught in my spokes.

Ya ever do that? At Baggiano's, the funeral home I played at when I was 6 to 12, I flung a broken hockey stick at Markysarkywarky's spokes; the youngest of the Baggiano's family and a huge crybaby. The stick slid through the spokes, then hit the front forks, flipping the crybaby over the handle bars and onto the asphalt. Funny as hell, especially to us pre-teens, on the first steps to becoming those mean teenagers.

I never thought of jail as an option, like some kids do, and I never thought anyone would seriously consider putting a kid like me in juvie, even though I might have deserved it at times, at least, a little bit. The Baggiano's funeral home was an easy place to get into trouble, especially looking through the windows to watch the embalming procedures. I got busted by the police there too, with my "little" brother Manat, but watching old ladies' feet shrivel up on the table must be part of what we are now. That song Drats wrote, *All In Jail*, for the **Rudy the Red Bat** rock opera, pops into my head:

All In Jail
by Drats

Jury found me guilty, I am lost to jail
No way around it, no plea-bargain bail
You're right, I was wrong
But one thing that makes me strong
My unstoppable love for wild, random mutants belong
In jail I'll do my time but I'll never promise to be blind
to the wrongs that we have done, breakout from stagnant mind
And I'll fight for rights when I get out
Sure I'll follow the law, hell that's true
But I can't settle for what's wrong with you
If one of US is in jail we're all in jail
Every creature on Earth in a human cage
Every single thing trapped in a mental jail
Refuges tiny, zoos isolated
6 billion deviant G.E. forms, castrated
Elk locked, to our walls
Redwoods for rich dining halls
Our potential in the extreme, South Bronx uranium balls

In jail I'll do my time but I'll never promise to be blind
To the wrongs that we have done, breakout from passive mind
And we know we can't keep living this lie
Sure borrow time at what consequence?
Unlimited profit at the soul's expense
If one of US is in jail we're all in jail
Every creature on Earth in a human cage
Every single thing trapped in a mental jail

I agree with a lot of the sentiments in that song. In a sense, we are all in a mental jail; a construct created by US; by gods and guns and credit, and precious objects and minerals.

I think all these thoughts as I climb the stairs of the Bachelor Officer's Quarters, or the BOQ, (you know the government loves their acronyms), fumble with my key, nudge the door ajar to slip through, and dump a number of work materials and other items onto my bed, lacking any other piece of furniture. I stand there for a moment, like a zombie, looking out and down at the goonies below again, and listening to the silence in the long hall behind me. My god. My god. What the fuck. What a trippy fuckin place. My god. That's all I can think.

Well, I don't really have anything else to do right now, and though I feel I could pull-off a nap, I feel kind of antsy, so I put my Desert Storm-type camo hat back on, and my shades, and head back down the long, dark, cinderblock hallway, with 2 inches of cream paint over the walls. When I get down to my bike, the same gooney still sits in the same spot. This time, I gently try to pull my bike out slowly, but it still jumps up and flicks its wings like the last time, attacking my spokes in the process with a quick jab of its sharply hooked bill. I decide to head back to my office to start working on maps right away. I have just taken Computers in Communication at BU last summer, so I think I will be a stud on the Mac map programs. Little did I know, the government uses PC exclusively. "Watch-it! They'll getcha!" I hear a creaky, wretched sounding voice. I look up to see two female humans creeping up on me, their eyes transfixed with hunger.

"HI, I'm Kilgro, and this is my assistant Myhel," she says, in a voice that is much harsher and creepier than Myhel's.

47

"Hi, I'm Kestrel. Nice to meet you," I say with slow confusion, unsure of whether or not this is a joke or a game. With my hands firmly grasping the grips as I continue to pull my bike backward slowly, I am able to avoid having to shake hands with this potentially syphilitic beast Kilgro, and her cohort Myhel.

"Oh, *we know who **you** are*," Myhel says with a seductive smile and a grin.

"Yeh, we've been looking forward to having you out here," joins Kilgro, twisting her fingers behind her back.

Wow, I have never felt so creeped-out in my life. Yikes.

"Yah, we are tired of the stale Navy fish around here, and I won't miss being called 'squid' when they leave," Kilgro continues, as her giant, cantaloupe-sized mammaries bubble beneath the top of her over-stretched, one-piece spaghetti-strapped bustier type thang.

I don't understand why the Navy gents would demean women with a name like 'squid'. I imagine it must be some kind of sophomoric male-bonding crap.

"They, they call you squid?" I say as they follow me down the cracked concrete path among the throng of goonies, between the triangular quads of grass.

"They call every girl 'squid'. It's a big put-down. Like every chick is a squid," Myhel says with a bit of a Canadian-sounding accent.

"Being called a squid is definitely off the list."

Interesting. "Well, gotta go, but I'm sure I'll be seeing you around," I say as a dismissive goodbye.

They wave and say goodbye. I don't look back.

Wait a minute. These were the same women I met at The Galley. We had even talked a bit at the table. Yet, they introduce themselves to me again. There's no way they had already forgotten meeting me. Hmmm. They just couldn't think of an excuse to talk with me, . . . is that what it is; or, is everyone a little mad on this atoll?

At the office, I try to get on the computer, but it's fucked up. Ben apologizes, "Sorry Kestrel. A lot of the stuff just don't work around here. Ya know, government stuff. You have to be pretty self-reliant. Good thing that the Foreign Nationals are here.

48

Usually at least one of them knows something about everything on heaven and Earth."

I get down on the floor and start working on pulling plugs and cables in and out. After about an hour of frustration, I get the computer going, then go into CorelDraw, with full intentions of working late; my nose now filled with fine dry dust and gooney dander.

Ben says, "Hey, you coming to dinner?"

"Nah; I want to finish this," I respond half-consciously.

"No you can't," Ben states. "The Galley will close. I want to shut the lights and lock up."

So with that, Ben makes me leave on my first full day/night of work. He is right. I shouldn't start out like an over-achieving psycho. After all, I'm not even on the payroll yet, technically. They are paying me a stipend as an intern until the paperwork comes in though Hono from DC, making me an official ranger.

I go to dinner. It looks like my only option is the hot curry. As I hold my plate up to the Filipino server, I ask him carefully, "Is it hot? You know, spicy?"

"No, no Mr. Kestrel. Not so spicy for you," he assures me sincerely.

After a few mouthfuls at the long cafeteria table, my face profusely sweats, as does Ben's, like a mirror to mine, which has also turned fire red. Ben puts his spork down for a second to bring a napkin stained with orangey sauce to his mouth, and then across his percolating forehead.

"Kestrel, meet Han," Ben blurts out with a burnt voice.

Han puts his hand out to shake mine, laughing, since he and I know that Ben has already introduced us at breakfast. "Great to meet you Mr. Kestrel. You come from cold place," he states.

"Yes, that's correct, I am from Boston," I respond slowly and clearly.

"So you not like dee curry?" he asks with a smile.

"No, I like it a lot. It's great. It's just hot," I admit.

Han reaches to the center of the table to grab a foot-tall, white, heavily shellacked, vase; ya know, the kind you get for 99-cents at a church bizarre. He pulls the plastic flowers out and then dumps some tiny hot chili peppers into his hand.

"You want try one these Mr. Kestrel?" as he laughs.

49

Ben's eyes glance at me below his sweaty brow, "I wouldn't if I were you."

"No thanks, my curry is plenty hot already," I say quickly, trying not to offend.

"Okaaaay," Han says, a little bit disappointed, as he breaks the peppers into tiny bits with the tips of his slender, boney, dark fingers, and drops it into his curry. With relish, he heaps spoonfuls of 5-Alarm curry down his gullet. At that moment Kilgro and Myhel slide their trays onto the shiny table, next to Ben and I.

At the asbestos party, Kilgro stuffs chicken in her face as fast as possible.

"You likin the curry?" Kilgro announces with a loud screech to obliterate anything Myhel might try to say first.

"He's doin fine," Ben defends.

"The first time I had it I was shocked," Myhel empathizes. "Being from the U P and all. I never had spicy food growin up."

"U P?" I ask.

"Yup, you betcha. You never heard of the U P? It is the Upper Peninsula of Michigan," she gleams.

Kilgro bursts in, "When I was in Belize, I worked with cetacean mating behavior. I like to study dolphins. They are the only animal that likes copulating, other than *US*," she says 'US' with a glimmer in her eye, like she means 'her and I' US.

That, in combination with the burning hot curry, and the disgusting glimpses of Ben's lonely eyes toward Myhel's chest; mainly her chest, make me feel close to yakking. All of these people have already met me today and why do they keep repeating themselves?

50

Ben, the entire time he is eating, keeps looking over at Myhel, and talking with her, and really engaging her like nobody else sits at the table. It becomes immediately very obvious to me that he sees her as some kind of goddess that he can never attain because he's so kind-of back-woodsy shy-hick from the boonies, with no confidence, and therefore feels she's way out of his league; a trophy-wife fantasy to him.

For me, like I said, I feel the bile start to bubble up in the bottom of my gizzard. I have hopes of running into renowned scientist types, like Dietera, and not insipid, pain-in-the-ass annoyers.

I glance up at Ben discreetly. Wow, he looks like he is beating-off over her right now, right in front of me, . . . in front of all of us. Myhel dressed up for dinner, in a little casual dress with strappy sandal shoes. I think she isn't really as bad looking as I had previously thought. Kilgro really drags her down. Guilt by association maybe. Shit! I've only been here a day and one of the girls who originally repelled me is starting to look good already? Yikes!

He who sees the truth, let him proclaim it, without asking who is for it or who is against it. --- Henry George

As these thoughts occur to me, I begin looking around the crowded galley at dusty construction workers, Foreign Nationals with dark blue jumpsuits stained with gooney guano, and finally, Dietera, sitting at a table with a bunch of Olderhostile folks, which are in her group. So wait a minute, she's stuck sitting with them but Kilgro and Myhel can sit wherever the fuck they like, and hover over me to scavenge the skin off of my ribs? Dietera's group too is through the A.S.S. organization, so she is kind of obligated to sit with them. They seem to be having relatively normal conversations over there. If I moved over to their table, would Myhel and Kilgro follow? Would they take it as a rude hint? I can't be so brazen yet.

Free speech doesn't mean you should get what ya pay for. --- Drats

Back over here at our table, Kilgro and Myhel attempt to get more friendly toward me, while trying to cut Ben off, which is pretty easy to do since he's a soft-spoken, quiet kind of guy of few words and some social ineptitude, due to his historically hermitic behaviors.

Kilgro barges in again, "Do you like cetaceans?"

Myhel says like the Swiss Miss instant cocoa with tiny marshmallows lady, "Have ya eva bean up tah Michigan?"

I don't want to eat another bite of curry, but I must. I have to keep going. I can't bury my face under the bare table or into my assassinating curry. I have to keep spooning it in. What will the Foreign Nationals think of Mr. Kestrel? Already, I am noticing that they are noticing that the girls have taken keen notice and interest quickly in me. That can be a problem with so few women on the atoll, especially if the men act like 'guys'.

After dinner, we all walk out in a happy group laughing at silly jokes. As we pull our bikes from the rack, we proceed to parade down the main road four or five abreast. I notice ahead of us that some kids spastically shoot forward on their bikes, then stop and laugh, and then dart forward again. As we close on them I see they intentionally run over tiny little mice; which look to me like baby House Mice.

"Get those critters!" I hear one of the peanut gallery call.

These bouncy little pop-corn mice *are* House Mice, but they just happen to grow a lot smaller out here than in any place else in the World. This apparently happens on islands and atolls, like Komodo Dragons, Galapagos Tortoise, and Channel Island's Grey Fox; islands do weird things to animals' sizes, making them either uncharacteristically way bigger or smaller. Do you know what they call that? Why not? The doctor's kids run them over on their bikes as they shoot across the road in the darkness.

"You goin to The All Hands' Club?" Kilgro grunts hopefully.

"Nah, I got studying to do," I respond, hinting more at pride and better things to do than at courting sympathy. I've always hated that 'poor me' shit.

Anyway, even though they should be going in the opposite direction, I have a feeling that Kilgro doesn't want to leave me alone with Myhel and Myhel certainly doesn't want to leave me alone with Kilgro; so they escort me all the way to my bike rack at my barracks.

"It's New Year's Eve Eve," Myhel tries to convince me.

"You sure you won't come out? It will be fun," Kilgro insists with a final effort.

I try to soften the rejection, "No thanks. I want to hit the ground running at this job."

Though disappointed, I can tell Myhel respects my diligence. I'm already doing everything perfectly correctly to make her fall hard for me, and I don't even know it. I am just being me. They ride off.

I climb the 3 flights of stairs 2 or 3 at a time, throw all my clothes off, and lay down on my bed in my under-shorts to read. As with my previous studies, within a few moments, I am either totally sucked-in or asleep. Simultaneously somehow, WWII irresistibly intrigues me, but at the same time, infuriates me at the magnitude of fuckin stupid waste, and the environmental trashing and thrashing of our Planet. I don't think it has ever been acceptable to talk shit about WWII like we do about Korea and Nam, but, I will say it now. How can idiots attack each other like this and waste so many planes and ships and lives, and break up so many families, and destroy so many forests and jungles and trees, and dump so much oil and chemicals into the oceans? Why? For money? For power? Even though this was the Pacific, I guess we were stopping the Nazis from killing the Jews, ultimately. That oversimplification always seems to block any other credible suggestion, at least in every thing I am studying.

Only one page in, and there's a knock on my door. Oh no. Myhel, or even worse, Kilgro. I shutter for a second and flirt with the idea of playin' 'possum. However, it's not what you or I thought. The Sri Lankans want me to go to The All Hands' Club. Whew.

So I say to myself, 'Screw-it! Making friends with the atoll folks may prove as valuable as studying here right now.' I see that as logical, and not a rationalization or procrastination. So, I go with them. They are very happy. At the bar, I don't want to order real drinks that will take me too long to down, so I order a few shots of rum.

"I can't stay cause I have to study and work tomorrow," I tell my captors.

Overhearing, or more correctly ease dropping, the Navy chiefs give me dirty looks. I turn away and down my third shot, only to

53

have the OIC (Officer in Charge) put his hand on my shoulder as I choke on the harshness.

"So, welcome again to Halfway," he says sincerely. "We haven't formally met, but I am Lt. Flipflopbaker."

"Nice to meet you. How are you?" I say cordially, feeling some warmth in my cheeks.

"I'm fine thank you. You are gonna love it out here. It's a really great place," he continues with a warm smile.

One of the chiefs adds as a half-assed sophomoric challenge, "Yah but you better learn how to drink if ya gonna be out here."

"Don't listen to them," the Lieutenant says with a smile, "Drinkins probably the one thing everyone does *too* well out here."

I look to the seemingly perturbed Sri Lankans, after all, they invited me; came all the way to my room, and they have been shaking my hand and rubbing my shoulders all night, yet, I'm hangin with the Navy, whom, by the way, will be leaving the atoll entirely in just a few short months.

I respond, "Good point sir. I'm not much of a big drinker anyway", avoiding looking at the chiefs. "I'm heading back to get some studying in before I crash."

"Good, I'll head back with you. See you at O-seven-hundred," he says as he turns to the chiefs.

"Ay Ay Sir," the chiefs mumble and salute half-assed.

I wave to the Sri Lankans and say "Thanks you guys. See you tomorrow." They grin and wiggle the tops of their heads from side to side, as they do in their interesting culture. I can tell they are disappointed.

The OIC and I talk as we bike on the way home. He had gone to Annapolis, and seems like a really good guy. As he turns to go into his historic quarters (the OIC House, where Nixon signed documents to send an extra 50,000 American troops to Nam, while he simultaneously announced to the public that he was ending the war), he says, "Come by and visit anytime. I have some interesting memorabilia you may want to add to your tours."

"Thanks," I say with gratitude. "I will. Good night."

Wow, I'm glad to find that at least one of the Navy guys is cool. Maybe I can add a component to my tour where we go in and check-out the house? Back in my room, I read for about an hour, then start to fall off, dreaming again of goonies and war. I think about the Sri Lankans. Are they coming on to me? I think it is just a cultural thing, but they all seem gay and very touchy-feely. The way they smile, and rock their heads, holding my hand a little to long. Better be clear in this situation. Zzzzzzzzzzz.

On the next day of work, I wake up before my alarm and look around the room, wondering where the hell I am. I hear a Red-tailed Tropicbird scream as it hovers past my window, probably harassed by the squadron of Great Frigatebirds that guard the shores and the atoll's boundaries. Oh yeah, I'm on Halfway.

I throw on my uniform, excited about what new creatures I will encounter, and skip down the stairs with my backpack. Off I go to my first meeting of the day with the entire Navy staff. Waiting. Waiting for what should be a short meeting to end, as soon as possible.

As I exit into the hall to head straight into my second meeting, I bump into Dietera and Loon, with Kilgro badgering Dietera about what she thinks should be dolphin-monitoring procedure. Dietera does not seem invested in the conversation at all. She already stated what she knows to be correct protocol and does not bother to argue any further.

Maybe to escape the grating voice that is the insistent Kilgro, Dietera scans my face, then asks me, "Meeting with the Navy continues to be a painful experience?"

I say, "I have discovered immediately that they hate the APS and think we will fuck up Halfway like they did. Again, whenever the Lt. hovers about, everything stays cool, but like Jr. High kids, as soon as he turns his back, the hazing commences."

Then Kilgro bilges, "The Navy chiefs line-up to take their cheap shots whenever the coast is clear."

Loon adds somberly, "They already read me the riot act. They mention how APS wouldn't even be out here if it weren't for the Navy, and how the Navy built the infrastructure, and how it was the Navy that kept the Japs off of Halfway from the get go, and that how the APS bunny-huggers will do a great disservice to the military history, and on and on they mumble bitterly, as if the APS has come to Halfway at the expense of the Navy and were forcing them off and into other jobs in other parts of the World they don't want to do."

I pronounce, "Look, let me make this clear from the under-experienced viewpoint I hold in this moment. The base is being closed because, technologically speaking, it has been obsolete for decades."

Then Kilgro adds, parroted straight from the mouths of the disgruntled chiefs themselves, "The last time the Navy ever really needed Halfway was during Nam, and even then the top brass still considered it a little auxiliary."

Dietera then says in a matter-of-fact sort of way, "Actually, they 'needed' it late during The Cold War as well. When I was here studying birds in 1982 they had something called The Pony Express, when 100's of men came up. Flights came and left every hour because the Russians had signaled they'd be firing a test missile in the North Pacific. But it was all a cat-and-mouse game, where they would fake a signal so that we'd run Pony Express for weeks on end, all for nothing. Millions of taxpayer dollars a day. As an environmentalist the officers almost kicked me off because they'd be afraid I'd find this shit out and spill the beans, call Earth Island Institute or something. They barely let me stay, but wouldn't tell me what was going on. I had to get the story from some lubricated enlisted men at the bar, who probably were scared they'd spilled the beans once they sobered-up," Dietera adds credibly, "APS has no power, and will always take a back seat to the military."

"Yeh," I agree, "one Air Force C-17 cargo plane costs more than the APS' total annual budget to run over 511 wildlife sanctuaries covering 93 million acres. It's The Pentagon that decides to put Halfway into closure, and as an afterthought, someone determined it should be a sanctuary for the bird colonies and visitors."

Then Kilgro joins back in, enjoying empathy and camaraderie with the cool crowd for once, reiterating the point, "APS is being used as a scapegoat, cause the chiefs just don't like 'huggers'. They hate anything the environmental movement stands for cause they don't understand it and see it as a threat."

Hmm, pretty insightful coming from someone who shows such a lack of understanding of self-perception and self-projection. She comes off as so harsh. Maybe I should tell her.

56

Loon goes a little more radical, "Don't you think the last person a group of guys with guns, ships, missiles, and other weapons should be afraid of is a guy hugging a rabbit?"

We all laugh. "Isn't that funny?" Dietera says.

Loon goes on, "I don't have a gun. I walk around all day, everyday, without a gun, and nothing ever happens and I never need one. None of my friends carry guns either. That's the problem; if we are happy and safe without guns, then they fear we won't need them and they will be taken away."

"How will they feel safe if they can't hide behind their guns?" Kilgro agonizes.

I say, with a Darwin-esque surety, "What if they can't use their weak brains to defuse situations and must resort to fisticuffs?" Everyone laughs again.

Dietera interjects, "It's all about the money the gun industry makes, bottom line, every time."

I fill in the details from my adventure-riddled day so far, "Whew! Anyway, to get back on the topic, glad that's over, and optimistically I look forward to the next meeting, with the Navy contractors, who seem to be a bunch of dickey construction assholes." Everyone rolls their eyes. I explain, "Now don't get me wrong, I worked construction a little, and my brothers and Dad did it all their lives, so I love construction workers, but if you know what I'm talking about, these guys could give a fuck about anything. To them, I am just another obstacle to making an easier paycheck. I can tell right away they love to be in conflict with the APS."

Dietera says, "These guys have total contempt for nature."

Then Loon says angrily, "They boot goonies off the road and crush all manner of birds beneath the sand without a second notice."

Dietera says, "That's Zart's job to stop them from doing that and mitigate for bird losses, but he can't cover the whole atoll at the same time."

I take a deep gulp and head into the office. I keep that meeting to mostly 'yes' and 'no'.

"All of my guys have already been to the Orientation, and most of them ah short-timers and will be off island before ya can get to rememberin their names," one of the rusty lookin leathernecks says with grit permanently embedded under his nails.

57

Though hostile, nothing directly antagonistic comes out of this meeting. The chiefs seem to care, and are angry, but the construction guys just don't want to be bothered. They just want to get their paycheck and have a beer.

Finally, right before lunch, my last meeting of the day with the island managers, HIC, hangs over my head like The Sword of Damocles; for rumor has it, they are the devil's spawn.

As I head in to meet Dutrouex, Cherry Ballpig, and Deny, in the Hangar headquarters, I see Jewel carrying some mail out of the office.

Jewel says, "Hey sugar, heading my way?"

Oh man. She looks soft, and nice, and huggable. Why can't I just squeeze her right now?

I look at her with despair in my eyes and whisper, "How can it be this bad out here?"

Though kind of like a conservative Republican cheerleader, she cuts to the chase with laser precision, "Wild wild west and military mentality meet brainy biologists and emotional animal advocates? Oil and water sweetie."

Shit.

I step into the office and right away I know I am in for it, meeting them for the first time like a firing squad. Some stand, some sit on desks, some sit with their feet up; but they all put on their poses and try to look tough. There's the tall, skinny guy Dutruoex, with the big nose. There's the big guy with the huge keg hidden under his ukulele shirt and the giant, stinky stogie, and the quiet short guy who talks with marbles in his mouth. There are a couple of foreign nationals sniffing around, and a serious looking dude with a Marines flattop. Not a one of them looks happy. Not happy, like me. There are no introductions, so I just stand there looking them over.

"Falco, the group has a bit of a concern," Dutrouex their leader begins with a southern drawl, minus the Southern hospitality. "Ya want a beer?" he says as he corrects his manners, and he pops a Coors can open. Oh, there's the hospitality.

I shake my head no and give them the 'are we done here?' look.

"Aaahh, c'mon. Relax. We are all gonna be on the same island together for a long long time," he continues like John Wayne.

"Please don't tell me to relax," I say point blank but calmly. "I could go around telling all of you to relax and that would make me look like the cool one, right? What is this meeting about?"

Deny says, "Hey, ahh, you are not goin be telling the people that they really gotta stay a hundred feet from a friggin monk seal, and the best fishin beach in the island is gonna be closed, like just 'incase' of a seal?"

Ut oh. They already gotta know all the answers to these questions. They are just testing the water. Testing my metal. The attitude is so clear. These guys slept through 6th-grade biology, but are now going to tell scientists how to run the freaken atoll. Atoll. It's ATOLL you idiots!! Why do they keep calling it an island? Pick and choose my battles Kestrel. Remember, no one tells these kinds of guys what to do. They want to retain their 'real guy' status, and since I'm in no way interested in using manipulation as a tool, though I'm aware I could, I can see there's gonna be conflicts. Why should I waste my second day on the atoll butting heads with dipshits?

I stand to exit the meeting, "I'm going to follow the book, use appropriate discretion where necessary, try to be friends with everyone out here and have a great time, but most importantly without a doubt, protect the wildlife out here," I say with calm commitment.

A few of them laugh and smirk. I hear one in the back say something like "Oooooo, Capt. America." Another mumbles something sarcastic like "Greetings Earthling."

Dutroeux (don't worry, Drats never got the spelling of his name right so it will be spelled 4 different ways in this book. Same guy, and not important. Try to pronounce it like Due-Tro). Anyways, Dutreuox, the HIC manager, stands up. "Now now, as a major, I was a fighter-jet pilot for quite some time and I respect the fact that you are a proud American. Yah just gotta know where to put your pride in the smart place. Ya gutt me?" he finishes with his Georgian drawl impression of The Duke.

I still don't know what they are talking about, but I think they think I know. I leave puzzled and with my stomach echoing with hunger, over my footsteps, in the bleak hall.

I hop on my bike and zip over for lunch. I sit at the back of the Galley, alone intentionally, and shovel stuffing and gravy into my mouth because the only other item they offer looks like smoked shoulder or something, with a lot of grizzled fat on it. I sit there and I eat as I look across the room at all the people. I can see the Navy clique, sitting at their table all together, and the construction guys, and HIC, and the Sri Lankans, and the Filipinos, and the Thais, all at their own national tables. Oh look, there are the 7 APS folks and their volunteers all squeezing into one table. I start dreaming, reminded of my high school cafeteria. Clique shit. I turn my attention to the few women on the atoll, one by one.

Hmmm. There are 200 men and 11 women. Of those eleven, could I potentially date any of them, and would they be available to maybe become my one true love? Out here? If I pull a monk move the whole time out here, it's gonna be friggen lonely. Then again, I am always looking for 'the one.' I know to some guys that sounds chickish, but I have always been a romantic and believe that if I keep my aim true, I can find an awesome soul mate with whom I could share a great and passionate love with. But what are the chances that I can find one on this tiny atoll, out of these 11 women? I had a hard time finding the right girl in Boston, and even a harder time in LA. It's way to tight out here.

So first there's Jewel. We already know how hot she is. The problems: She works for HIC. Enough said. On top of that, just to allay doubters, she's only on atoll occasionally, Christian, and a little too cheerleader for me. She is a possibility, though, a long shot. She gets a lot of attention from all the guys on Sand Island, including the construction guys, the Navy chiefs, the foreign nationals, and the pilots and other HIC studs, with whom she does a great job of spreading the flirting around to. I think she already thinks I'm a nerd. I think she's the type that wants, ya know, a "real guy". Not like me. We would make an odd couple. She wants a guy who smells like a guy and talks like a guy and acts like a real man, a guy who knows his way around a frat, sees women as objects, possessions, not opposed to a good wife beating once in a blue moon; ya know, not like me. So I will play it safe and professional with her and see where it goes organically. I never like to push anything. I'm more of a suggester or a nudger than a pusher.

Okay, look at me being all judgmental and high and mighty. No, no, no. I know I am fucked up too, and well aware that she just might want absolutely nothing to do with me. I'm confident, not delusional. Sometimes a girl doesn't want me no matter what. Ya can't fight that. Nothing I can do about it.

As I sit at my table, looking around the off-white room with its screens and glass-slatted windows, and the neon bulbs, I see Ryle and a couple of the construction workers eyeing the girls. I can tell he makes vulgar comments about them, and some of his cadre egg him on. He's the disgusting one. Every word that spews from his mouth makes him look uglier and uglier. Ugliest, I could fairly say. At the end of their table sits Poor Construction Girl (PCG), an engineer and apparently the only female in their unit. Imagine that for a second if you've never been in that situation. I've never been in that situation, quite, but I can imagine how much it would suck. She looks like she has a hot little body, but she looks like a scary freak and seems to be attached to one of the other engineers. The scary freak face is probably a clever defense mechanism against preying intruders; the opposite of Kilgro's desperate attempts for attention. PCG would be hot if she simply tried an eighth as much as Myhel does, and that's why she won't.
Right away, I would say I see Dietera as much more like a sister or friend. Dietera came off to me as a serious scientist with basically no sensuality or sex appeal. We seem to vibe-off each other well as friends too. I'm not interest in falling in love with anyone much older than me, and I already heard through the course of my day that she's got a steady other back on the mainland somewhere with two kids from a previous marriage. Some people could find Dietera attractive, but her mind is on the birds, and that is it. I am a sensualist, and I also need good friends in my field too, so like Banette, I think it wiser to keep it a professional friendship with Dietera.
So, where does that leave me? If I am smart and patient, I will wait for quality, but I'm neither and I know I won't. Maybe they will come to me. That's a bad habit of mine; falling for girls who like

me. Like I said, I don't ever want to push anything. It's never as good.

'God, Myhel possibly,' I confer with myself, 'that's not much of an option. I left Messycka back in Boston. I feel love for her, even in this moment in the Galley, but I can also feel that I just don't care very much for her. I don't long for her like I would if I were really really in love, so that was never really real and deep with her. I know all girls are pretty psycho, but I can't date a *total* psycho I can't trust. Great sex can really confuse things, huh.' I let an audible laugh slip out. Drats told me when he decided to write this novel that, "The names would be changed, . . . to embarrass the guilty". Most of the time, I don't worry about trying to understand Drats.

As my second full day on the atoll draws to a close, and New Year's Eve draws nearer, I go to my room, lie-down to read for a moment, and fall asleep deeply for an hour. When I awaken, I look around in shock, then see that I wrinkled my uniform. I shake the pins and needles out of my hand and look at the manifest for the next flight, coming in New Year's Day.

With the sun setting, I decide to change out of my uniform and go to the All Hands' Club, where immediately, every foreign national grabs my hand and says heartily, "Merry New Year. Happy Christmas Mr. Kestrel." I laugh my ass off, inside. They hug me again and hold my hand. "Merry New Year. Merry merry New Year to you."

"So which one of you have wives back in your country?" I say in hope, not that there's anything wrong with gays; I just don't want to lead anyone down a dead end, pun intended.

They all wiggle their heads, saying "Yes yes I have a wife and he has a wife" and so on.

Why did I ask? I have a feeling everything like that is irrelevant out here, . . . like in prison. I guess they will figure out soon enough that even though I sing and write plays and dance and look and sound very gay, I'm straight. I calm down and have a nice time. It turns out at least Darom, for one, has two wives even! Later, he explains to me that as long as you treat them both evenly (which basically means give them equal money) then that's cool in Thailand. Women are more like possessions in Asia, like a dog or bunny; at least that was my experience living two years in Tokyo.

That second-class citizen shit really irked me and made me lose quite a bit of respect for conservative Japanese men. They are kind of like the Mormons of Japan. If you really have power, you don't have to control "your women" like friggin dogs. 'It's New Year's Eve, so stop thinking about that cultural stuff and just relax and have fun,' I convince myself internally. Though it doesn't feel right, and doesn't feel like any New Years Eve I have ever known, it's time to cut loose and party.

The music thumps away. I don't know who it is but I might guess Garth Brooks or something like that. I try to talk over it and ignore the annoyance. Then, the lights dim and the country/western abruptly stops. I wheel my head around to see Myhel right behind me at the bar.

"So whad are ya drinkin there partner?" She asks, trying to sound like a buckaroo.

"They told me this is an Alabama Shlammer. I never heard of it," I say politely.

"Oh, you better watch out for those," she warns with a Cheshire smile. "Those will sneak up on yah ya know? Those are definitely off the list. I puked my guts out on those one night, or, at a beach party."

Wow, blackout. She can't even remember? I better nurse this puppy. Wow. Myhel has make-up on again, like bluish eye-shadow, and a skirt, with heels. And no Kilgro. Decent. Actually decent. Funny how a friend can ruin a friend. I am not a big make-up or dress-up fan either, but when someone looks as bad as Myhel naturally, the make-up and primping can make a big superficial difference. Like when I've seen women with their hair messed up wearing sweats, and then you see them in a nice skirt and heels, with like that whole makeover craze thing that is happening. Big difference, but all superficial of course. I guess all it does is really just give you the idea. Like that Deadhead girl back in Boston. What was her name? I can't remember right now, but she was kind of peripheral, being my girlfriend's friend's friend. She always wore baggy, ripped jeans and tie-dyes, never any make-up, and sandals with dirty toes. So, I just knew her as the nice Deadhead girl who I said 'hello' to once in a while. One Halloween, I see this unbelievable goddess in a red dress with red pumps. I say 'Hi', then realize, it's the Deadhead girl!

63

"What are you suppose to be?" I ask in total shock. "I didn't even recognize you. You look incredible." My French girlfriend didn't like that comment at all.

"I'm your ultimate fantasy," she answered with provocation, and without the slightest hint of the repression she had always previously displayed, like she was pulling off this massive sociological experiment. Again, my girlfriend liked that comment even less. My knees grew weak. Oh my god. I had to make a point to NOT look at her for the rest of the evening, except when my girlfriend went to the bathroom, once.

"So, is there some kind of country/western theme to this celebration?" I ask Myhel with a sigh.

"Ha ha ha," she laughs boldly. "This is Halfway. It's a total mix and hodge-podge. But ya gotta realize that most of the guys out here are from Georgia, like all of HIC. Where as, the chiefs are mostly from Texas. They hate each other, but not as much as they hate people from the North, ya know," she illuminates to me.

"Wait a minute. They hate each other?" I respond confused.

"Ya well you know how these kind of guys are. I dated one! Ha ha. The Navy fights with the Marines and so on. Of course, when they have a common enemy, they fight together ya know, but they love to keep the little-boy competition going. I think it's something guys have to do," she says as she takes a big swig of her drink. "Hmmm, that's good."

A loud shriek of feedback rolls off the stage as some guys start tuning gear up. Smoke from all the cigarettes, and a cigar or two, singes my eyes.

"You think all guys are like that?" I say with an offensive wince. I have certainly evolved way beyond unproductive and petty fighting, in my mind.

"Noooo. Let me finish. Those are the guys that are now, off the list. The ASS and APS folks are always the opposite of that. We're scientists. That's why," she explains, slurring 'scientists'. "And the Olderhostile folks all seem to be pretty nice, no matter where they are from. They are definitely on the list."

I think quickly to myself. The Olderhostile people pay as 'citizen volunteers' to come to remote places like this to help nature. Of course they are nice. The challenge before me will be to get some of these chiefs and HIC staff to see how beautiful and important this place is.

"Do you like to dance?" she erupts, appearing loosened.

I can tell that she doesn't possess the depth of sensitivity to know what I am feeling, unless she is just a master of hiding it. She just wants to keep the conversation alive at any cost because she wants to sink her claws into me, mainly to show up Kilgro.

"Yeah. I love dancing. It's a lot of fun, but I have to warn you that I am a little bit picky," I say.

"Really. You're a picky guy huh?" she says with a smile.

"Well, no," not knowing what she's getting at. "I mean I have been singing in bands for a long time and studied arts in college, and it's kind of hard for me to just like anything like that Hootie shit. I have kind of narrow musical tastes."

"You sung in a band?" she says as she adjusts her dress like she has peed her panties a little bit.

Shit. I have a big mouth. Why did I give out so much information? At this point the crowd starts getting a little rowdy as the band prepares to play. Wow, a band on Halfway? As the stage lights (both of them) go up on the band, the driver of the Dolphin Van grabs the mic. and says, "Test. Okay. Test. You ready. Merry New Year! Merry New Year everybody," sounding a little like Dr. Nick from **The Simpsons**. He turns to the band and they tinker around with their equipment for another minute or so. Bad sign. I am already considering putting torn napkins into my ear canals after that feedback session. I should have taken Ben up on those earplugs.

I look around the room and see Kilgro leaning over a table of men in a low-cut top. It doesn't look like her 'engaging conversation' has their attention, but they are all looking her way, albeit, a little lower than her neckline. Myhel sees me looking, but I can't tell if she thinks I am gawking at Kilgro or looking at the scene in disgust.

I say, "I don't get that at all," shaking my head.

Myhel agrees eagerly, "So what, her tits are huge. So what. What is that a friggin fetish or something?"

I say in a whiny voice, "Do those guys want mommy?"

Myhel laughs hard and loud. The band on stage clunks their way through *Some Guys Have All The Luck*. The accent is classic. I hope they feel that I am laughing with them because I certainly don't want to hurt anyone's feelings, but no doubt I am laughing at them, and this whole scene. Ah, only on Halfway. At least it feels that way. This place is special. Maybe they say the same thing on Tristan da Cunha. 'Ah, only on Kerguelen.' Hm. Maybe we are never as special and unique as we believe we are. Maybe someone else, some other of the 6 billion of US, writes exactly what Drats writes right now, in their novel. Some guy in Hollywood, or up in the hills near the Kunlun Mountains.

I hear Kilgro over the music say, "When I was in Belize . . ."

Myhel grabs my arm, a little bit for balance, but mostly to squeeze my muscle and purr like a kitten.

"Nice bicep," she stammers with a smile.

I remove her arm from mine and head to the bathroom.

When I come out, Jewel stands directly in front of the door, leaning against the pool table. I look at her, square on. She slowly smiles. Oh man; I really should be finding a way to be talking with her, instead of getting tied-up with Myhel. Why can't I control my destiny? She is fine and a lot more my style than Myhel could ever be. As I open my mouth to say 'something', Myhel bursts over and says "Everything come out alright, ha?" with a vulgar laugh.

"Ya yah, fine," I say embarrassed, as she drags me off.

For the next hour, every time I try to see what's up with Jewel, she is looking at me. She always has cock-blocking HICs around her every few minutes, but she seems to get rid of each one pretty fast, only to be annoyed by the next one in line. But every time I look over at her she is looking right at me. I thought girls were supposed to be subtle.

Then later, near the witching hour, Jewel seems to be warming up to me, and has made her choice. Now when I look over at her, from the bar, from the dance floor, from the shuffleboard table, she is giving me a huge 'come on over' smile. It's just like gooney courtship, really. She must be a little lubricated by now too. You know that smile right? I'm not talking about that fake Vegas- give-me-money-shit smile. I'm talking about a person giving you that big, huge, YES smile. No, not 'yes you can do me'. I just mean YES: Yes to life, yes to love, yes to fun, yes to joy, yes to happiness, yes yes YES. Myhel tries to pull off that smile, but she feels too needy, too desperate, too yes for the wrong reasons.

Myhel is too insecure to let herself be free enough to understand YES. But Jewel is givin me a big fat YES.

My paranoid defenses go up. I think *they* are using *her* as leverage to try to work *me*.

"10, 9, 8, . . ." the countdown to New Year's suddenly begins. Everyone quickly spins around and grabs drinks, standing, some on the cushy booth seats, while others look to make eye contact with someone special. I look over at Jewel. She pushes one of the drunk HIC guys off of her chest, and struggles to give me a smile. Suddenly I feel a strong downward jerk on my neck and head and a feeble attempt to kiss my left lips. "7, 6, 5, ..." Oh god, it is Kilgro trying to get in on me before Myhel can seal it! Like sharks on a kill, they frenzy. Myhel pushes Kilgro off physically with both hands, incidentally slapping one of her breasts. How could she miss? Foreign Nationals squeeze us on all sides. It's mayhem.

"Whoah, that was a close one," Myhel yells with a drunken smile as she wraps her arms around my back and pushes her hips against mine.

"4, 3, 1 ..."

I look over at Jewel, surrounded by men hugging and kissing her. Tomorrow, she will fly off a thousand miles away, returning people to the real world, and later, collecting others to come and experience Halfway. I can barely see her for only a second, then again, the mass of heaving bodies absorbs her. Does she have somebody special somewhere else?

"Great way to start out your stay on Halfway, eh?" Myhel bursts. "Hey, that rhymes!" She says with a husky laugh, and on "Happy New Year", which still many of the FNs are calling 'Merry New Year', she puts a big, wet, tongue-filled kiss on me and wraps her right leg tightly around the back of my knee. And who says 'men don't know what women want'?

I pull my head up for air to see an orgy of faces around me all hugging and kissing and saying 'Merryd Nu Yea!' It is a loud blur. Finally, I am able to see Jewel, grabbed and escorted out by a couple of pilots and some other HIC staff, and as she goes through the swinging glass door and into the hallway, I see her glance back at me again. Our eyes meet. 'Seems like more interest than I thought,' I rationalize. 'It can't be an act. It's too good,' I say under my breath.

Myhel, Kilgro, and 3 of what appear to be Sri Lankans rush over and ask me to dance. It feels kind of like the band's last song, and it sucks, but I give into the thrust and break into a frenzied sweat. After a while, coming off the dance floor hot and sweaty, I look around and scan the scene before me. I quickly look around the club, and when I finish going through each girl, I settle on Myhel. I stop and think of my family again; like they are angels that can watch me from floaty angles. What would they think of her? Why do I care? Most of my family have barely ever met any of my girlfriends, and yet, it's important to me to know they approve. I'm glad I don't demand their disapproval, but why should I care what they think at all? Maybe it shouldn't be 'What do they think of her?' as much as it should be 'What do they think of me? The way I think? What I am thinking right now? The way I am thinking? What the hell is thinking?'

Again, why do I even care what they think? Why do I need to impress them? Is your family fucked-up? More fucked-up than mine? They have to be. Look at the history of TV. Dysfunctional families like **The Simpsons** are way funnier than The Beaver and Father Knows Least. Ibsen knew that mothers yelling at sons in kitchens would be show stopping. Great art always pisses people off. Lope de Vega's *El Cid* made people riot in the streets.

Myhel pops, "What's a ya New Year's resolution ya gut ah?"

My head searches left and right laterally, as I say, "I hope people march on the world capitols after reading my friend's book, demanding an end to Unholy Wars, eco-destruction, greed and the like. There is definitely no such thing as the oxymoronic 'Holy War'. I mean, c'mon, how can war, the most unholy act *Homos* can perpetrate, be holy? War is Hell, not holy. Of course there will be no wars, greed, or any other human evil if we trash The Planet, so without environmental protection, especially population control, everything else is a friggin waste."

Myhel looks up at me with her mouth open. She is very impressed, but I don't really notice. The conundrum bounces around my head. Does your family make you cry? Is there a point where you think about them and you just cry? That's a pretty bad point. I mean, I guess there are worse points, or there could be, if I use my vast imagination, but that's still pretty bad. Like take for example Sproc, who isn't as bad as my brothers Rosmarus or Manat. Sproc

68

USED TO BE Easy Rider. He emulated Peter Fonda and rode around on a chopped-out '49 Panhead and was tall, thin, and handsome, and he 'screwed society dude' and 'stuck it to the man', and he was a tax rebel, and rode around in the desert in the southwest and 'Inland Empire' and all that shit. Easy Rider was definitely a huge influence on him as a mean teen, and listening to the sound track on 8-track, I tried to understand: 'Why is this cool? Who says this is cool and which drugs are they on?' I look down to see Myhel slow dancing with me, on autopilot. Me too. She's kind of using me to hold her up, but sneaking sips here and there. She doesn't want to let go of me for a second. I walk over and sit down at a bench for a second, and she follows along tightly.

"But now; he's the red-necked conservative Christian guy who blows Hopper and Fonda away!" I say aloud with depression, waking from my deep daydream, with the music cranking and the mirror ball spinning.

"Isn't that funny how it turns out that way?" Dietera adds with her typical, mild tone of absolute correctness, as she slides into the bench in the booth next to me. "From my experience it seems like a lot of the most long-haired radical hippies were also the ones most susceptible to turn into rednecks like Dick Cheney-s", Dietera continues.

"And other dicks," I quickly interject for a laugh. Even Deny smiles a little from his table, 8-feet or so from me, but I can tell I might be walking down a dark political alley with him, not to mention the much more severe haters on the atoll.

I think to myself again quickly. Even the song *Wasn't Born to Follow* from The Easy Rider Soundtrack seems so hypocritical now. Sproc says Jesus was a rebel. Whether or not he was, Sproc is totally following now, like a freaken slave more than a sheep in the flock. When I suggested he should stop wasting his time with the bible and get involved in local politics to promote social, educational, and other progressive change for US all, he pulled his typical reactionary passive-aggressive move by running down to city hall the next day and telling them how much he was vehemently opposed to same-sex marriage because it is against god or some shit like that. He called me back right away, in Japan, and when he told me that, it reaffirmed to me what a lost cause he was. None of my brothers are good at communicating or being

69

loving or understanding at all, but they are great at fighting and kicking ass; kind of like the Marines; like Deny.

Like when my older brother Sproc partied at my house at UCLA in Santa Monica, off Wilshire, some 14 years ago. We were all in my room talking and laughing, and I was trying to shmooze a cute girl as usual. It was going well. She said she was a little paranoid about driving after the party cause she had some drinks, and I told her she could hang out here as long as she wanted with no strings attached. She smiled and looked like she would stay. That's when my brother Sproc came charging into my room with his then wife Poopsie in hot pursuit. Before she could 'stop' him, which is a total joke that she would even bother to try, he quickly snorted up a line of coke and threw the straw back down on the mirror and stated gruffly 'So There!' Some people will just never, ever, grow up; especially when it comes to drugs, hurting the one you love, or being violently reactionary. Poopsie whined 'Sprocy' with disappointment and disgust. The girl left my room and slipped out of the party before I could find her again. Sproc kept trying to get my friends and roommates to take a snort, but none of us were into that stupid shit at UCLA, at least in my band and my circle. Coke was big in the 80's, but we all knew better. That's probably why we were at UCLA and guys like Sproc weren't.

Sproc pushed a little, "C'mon," evoking a Jim Morrison pose.

I shot back, "I run track. I don't want to have a heart-attack before I graduate from UCLA!"

Sproc backed off. I don't know if he realized it at that moment, or ever, but he just wanted to party too hard. His chronic habits shot his tolerance levels through the friggin skylight. So instead of being Easy Rider, Sproc is now the guy with the shotgun that blows Fonda and Hopper away for no reason. No "reason" other than the fact that bikers and hippies were different from nice, abiding, peace-filled religious folk. He can't see that he's gone from being Easy Rider to killing Easy Rider, in about 13 years. I come back to consciousness again to realize that several people are now sitting around me and having their own discussions. I take a deep breath abruptly, to wake up, and relieve my internalized stress.

"See ya, thanks," I say to everyone as I hit the head again and then amble outside to get some fresh air. One of the foreign nationals asks me if I want a cigarette. It is almost 1 a.m. now, the party wanes, and it looks like I've dodged Myhel. Strange, maybe she left with some one. So, I think to myself 'ah what the hell. No APS staff are around anyway. I am burnt, tired, a little buzzed, and wow, I ended up dancing for like fifty minutes or something. I take a long first drag, and then start walking out into the moonlight to look at the crazy antics about: Albatross clacking their bills, petrels aaaanteeeent-ing (a nasal sound that you would think comes out of their noses), wedgies moaning, ya know, the normal Halfway stuff. The FN and one of his buddies follow along quietly, watching what I will do. The avifauna could care less about what US humans do to celebrate or inebriate. The birds, the beetles, the centipedes; they all party-on, relentlessly. I want to treat everyday like New Year's; like they do. I suddenly catch a major head rush as my brain capillaries constrict from the foreign toxin.

As we walk along, I remember what Ben had talked about in the first orientation; namely, the gooney chick mortality rate. As a matter of fact, I astutely notice that many of the carcasses I browse under the moon-glow are last year's birds, due to the desiccation of the feathers and other parts, and the thankful lack of pungent squid-hell smell. Basically, none of the goonies have chicks right now, but 99% of them incubate eggs.

This gooney chick swallowed so much regurgitated plastic that it died. This happens way to often and more frequently every year. Do we care?

I stop for a second and look down. Just like the hulking masses of chicks that simply resemble 'fish bags' I will see month after month on Eastern Island as well, and yes, even on Spit, I will find it —-- plastic mounds, surrounded by ex-gooney chick. Acute emaciation. That's right, you heard me. Quick starvation, mostly dehydration. Why? Humans throw and dump plastic everywhere and don't give a shit. The plastic floats on the surface indefinitely or washes up on a beach, like on Halfway. Oh god I hope Drats' publisher has the balls to publish the trash photos, including the infamous Japanese glass fishing balls (floats for nets), cherished by beach-comers as ornaments. The adult albatross search the oceans, and as they did for thousands of years, anything floating on the surface, especially bright and colorful, (like a comb, toothbrush or worst of all, the cigarette lighter), must be edible, like flying-fish eggs, squid, and other surface gleaning fair. That's just the way it has been for goonies for millions of years. So the adult swallows the crap, regurgitates it back to the chick, who, too young to vomit a bolus or pellet, can't eat any more because it's stomach is actually full of plastic, gets dehydrated, collapses, and dies with a bloated stomach full of our plastic. US. That's who is doing it to them. US. There is friggin plastic everywhere now and we are the only species that creates it. Sharks don't make plastic. Manta Rays do not pollute the oceans in any way. We do it to ourselves, and all of the other creatures combined, at the same time, and none of them, not even one of them, does it to US.

I notice that some of the carcasses have cigarette butts in them. I suddenly gag, and look at the cigarette I am smoking. It makes me sick, so I field dress it and dump the butt into one of the pockets in my shorts, disgusted with myself.

In the future, right near the end of Zart's term on Halfway, he and I will go scuba diving in Thailand. The boat crew will just let shit blow right off into the water: Water bottles, wrappers, even a Styrofoam cooler; right off the deck and into the ocean.

"Hey, you can't do that," I will protest.

"It not a problem," the Thai dive operators will respond. "The ocean is so very big. No problem."

Don't tell me the ocean is fuckin big. I know the ocean is big you stupid fuck. The point is, ah god forget it. Anyway, I will tell him, and later the owner on the phone, "I am not going to use, nor can I recommend you, to other divers, on the basis of pollution."

The owner will say with a jaded Kiwi twang, "All the companies do the same thing. It's the culture here. You can't tell people to change their culture overnight, mate." He will try to get me to reconsider and awaken me to his reality, "Who you gonna dive with mate? They all run the same way. Give it a fair go. I think you will be comin back to us," he will finish confidently. I will think about it for a minute. Forget it. I'm never diving there again. Fuck that. I don't want to be part of the problem.

Smelling the cigarette on my fingers, I shake myself out of my thoughts for a second, to see men staggering out of the club with their arms draped over each other's shoulders. The night is over. I hear what sounds like a military jet blast low overhead. That's weird. We aren't expecting any flights. Then it becomes silent again. It obviously did not land.

I go back to my room, and without even turning on a light, throw off my clothes and slip into bed in my underwear. I fall asleep before my head hits the pillow, and sleep off most of the morning. When I finally get up, the sun shines brightly overhead and glaring. Everything makes me wince. I stare at my watch waiting for my eyes to de-blur. 8:49am. Wow, I almost slept until 9? Unheard of! The Galley is closed. I grab an orange, and a Snickers bar, and then go over and sit on the toilet while I peel the orange. When I am done, I go back to sit on my bed and eat the orange, and then the Snickers. Sitting. Thinking alone. Thinking about last night. Thinking about the foreign nationals. Thinking about the dead gooney chicks. I look over at my schedule. There will be a plane coming in today, New Year's Day. That's something to look forward to. But what will I do with the day off until then? I have no plans. The lining of my mouth tastes like a sticky stinky ashtray. I think for a moment, and notice my mind drifts a lot more towards Jewel, and almost not at all towards Myhel, and then I slowly keel over and fall back asleep for another hour.

When I awaken, I finish what is left of the Snickers. I crumple-up the wrapper and hit the trash can with a bullet from across the room, cheer like a giant crowd in a stadium, throw on my workout gear and my sunglasses, and stuff my camera and bins into my beaten backpack. When I open my door from my glaring room to enter the dark hall, I almost fall over a mini fridge. So I throw my backpack back on the bed and bring the fridge in and place it next to the only outlet in the room, by the sink. I open it and examine it. No cockroaches. Doesn't smell bad or anything. No note. Hmmm. I plug it in and it gently begins to hum. I set it to the lowest setting, close it tightly, and grab my tattered backpack and head back out the door.

I bike up to the North Beach, near the old cable station buildings, and lay my bike on its side in the sand. Both Black-footed and Laysan Albatrosses present so many photos ops that it makes choosing shots impossible. They are attacking me too, and my bike. I look back to see a big nasty Black-foot tearing into a hole in my seat cushion, and ripping plastic off.

"Hey, beat it," I warn firmly.

I pick up my bike and roll it through the sand and over to an Ironwood Tree. I lean it there and start to head over the rise to the lagoon. When I look back at my bike, the albatross are attacking the tires and spokes, and a White Tern has landed on the seat. I continue walking in the grainy coral sand, which digs in under my toes in my Tevas, so I stop to take them off. The sand is hot, but not too hot to walk on. Just then, as I stand up straight, I see what looks like a driftwood log, but what could be something else. I pull my binoculars up to my eyes and focus to see my very first monk seal.

I had just read about this. When? Was that last night? No, couldn't have been. I passed out last night. Oh yeah, last night was the party. When did I read this? Man, I have been in such a time warp coming out here, I can't even remember. Anyway, it could have been on the plane.

The important facts: *Relict populations of an ancient line of seals that once filled the oceans, but probably will be gone within the next century, have but three know representatives to attest to their passage on Earth:*

Caribbean Monk Seals supposedly filled the islands when Columbus arrived, along with so many turtles popping their heads up for air that they looked like fields of Brussels sprouts. Now, the Caribbean Monk Seal is thought to be extinct, and Green Turtles, like all sea turtles, remain perilously endangered not only in the Caribbean, but throughout the globe.

The **Mediterranean Monk Seal** supposedly numbers in the 500s or so. It amazes me to think that a monk seal could still make it in the Mediterranean at all.

"How is the Hawaiian Monk Seal doing anyway?" I remember asking Myhel when she brought me a drink last night.

"The **Hawaiian Monk Seals** are said to be at about 1200 seals left. Yup. 1200!" she answered frankly, with earnest urgency.

Wow. I saw more people than that at a high school football game I went to before I left Boston for Hawaii. I saw twice as many Japanese humans as that at the Ala Moana Mall in Hono before I shipped out to Halfway. It makes you think: 1200 Hawaiian Monk Seals on The Planet! We have way, way too many humans.

"On the entire Earth!" she continued last night between gulps of her drink. "They are almost off the list, eh. Yet, we still think about US first. Me me me. US US US. There are 10 times as many people at a NASCAR event than there are monk seals left on Earth, and we don't even give a shit." I could hear her voice crack. At least she cares. That is key, and it also makes her a little more attractive to me. I don't think Jewel cares. I mean, Jewel cares about being a good flight attendant, and being a good Christian, and looking good; but you know what I mean, she doesn't really care about the Planet, which is practically the only thing that really matters at this point.

"What about the people out here?" I asked her over the sound of the party. "Do they care about the seals?"

"They are like 'Boo hoo hoo. So what. If they can't adapt or survive, then they ain't tough enough to make it with US'; like they are talking about Norway Rats and Rock Doves," Myhel explained with a hiccup. "Well, they do have a very low birthrate and high pup mortality. That means their numbers will stay low forever. But now, condos, hotels, and 4-wheelin has wiped-out their natal habitat ya know, with bright lights and noise scaring them away en a forcin them to abandon der pups, or to birth on less desirable beaches where Tiger Sharks do der huntin. I betcha, en I believe, no matter what we do on this Planet, that these animals have a right to live. They are part of this world, eh."

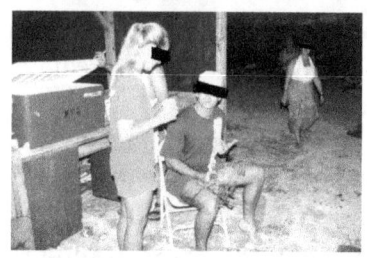

Myhel plies Kestrel with drink while Kilgro lurks drooling in the shadows like a famished ghost crab.

Fresh out of college, I synthesize and consolidate, "Overpopulation of humans is by far the biggest problem on Earth and would solve so many other issues. Water shortage, global warming due to excessive fossil fuel use, energy crisis, food shortage, species extinction; these all tend to lead toward a complete failure of society. All we really need is to have less kids, less often, and later in life. Humans belong too of course, but not at the alienation of other creatures. There are way too many humans and we're like rats in a cage," I said to Myhel at the club last night.

Now, my mind snaps back to the present, on the beach, looking at this incredible nature scene in front of me. I start to sing **Dorsal** alone, and I imagine that all is well in The World, and that everything is in balance and at peace. I imagine a group of us, and we all sit around relaxing up at the North Beach, discussing this very topic. It's like a wonderful daydream: My whole family sitting up on the beach and talking, civilly. Wow, the goonies blasting along just above the sand and waves, the sun setting over the turquoise lagoon, and the gentle, room-temperature breeze. If I could only get them up and into a football game, (my family, not the goonies) that would be fun. I belt out the second chorus, into the breeze and out over the tiny waves.

Wow, I feel exactly the same way about problems in the World as Dietera, Loon, and yes, dare I say it, even Myhel feels. There are a lot of US who want to save the Planet and stop people like Newt Gangrinch. I can't believe his name is even 'newt' and yet, he has no affinity to wildlife of any kind, including 'Herps', as we call them. What would you call what WE believe in? Animal Rights? Even maligned creatures like sharks deserve to live, period.

Drats wrote a song for the **Rudy The Red Bat** rock opera called *Winged-hand*, about bats, but originally, he wrote it on The Big Island of Hawaii about tigers and other monstrous and ancient sharks that still patrol our waters. I like the idea that the song is like a riddle. You never say the word 'shark' in the entire song. Sing it slow and smooth like a shark moving through the water.

Dorsal
by Drats

Slinking through the shadows, sliding through the dark.
Undulating motion, with a threatening arc
Rarely pierce the surface, diving down on a lark. Slipping through the porthole, of an old wrecked bark.
Detecting the smallest, slightest molecule of scent. Closing in on my prey, when hungry I'm hell-bent.
Whether night or day, I seek through the murk. Mechanistic functions, they're always at work
Past plant life formations, here perfect I lurk. Can't idle or stagnate, this is my one quirk.
Temperate or tropic, or Artic cold. Nothing can stop me, I'm millions of years old, I'm billions of years old.
I belong to the sea, I'm part of this world. I belong, only to me, I belong, I'm part of this world.
I belong, just like YOU! I'm part of this world.

I check to see that I am downwind. It blows firmly out of the west, right where the monk seal lies. I approach at a blind angle, and never see the seal move an inch. When I get to what I think looks like about 150 feet away, I lay down prone in the sand and turn my camera to the auto-depth mode. I zoom in tight on the seal's whiskers, until they come into sharp focus, then reel off one shot and wait for a reaction. Nothing. No way. I am so far away and down wind. No way. So, like a salamander, I slither on my belly forward another 40 feet or so. I sniff, to see if I can detect rotting flesh, since this could be a carcass. I can smell seal anus. Pretty heinous. I freeze for a moment, sensing nothing, then look around quickly to see if anyone is around or if another monk seal is coming up onto the beach.

Just under the small surf, in about three feet of water, I can see a large black shape. It then quickly separates into two smaller shapes, then merges again. I am dying to know what it is, but fear rising up on my knees will scare the seal. Monk seals scare easily. They don't live in big gregarious colonies like raucous sea lions. Breeding beaches are so critical to their survival. I haven't actually seen that for myself, but it's in the literature, and since it is a critically endangered species as well as a protected marine mammal, as well as being on a beach on a wildlife sanctuary, I'm gonna make certain that I, as the first ranger on Halfway, stick to the 100-foot policy.

I lay back down in the sand and the monk seal turns its head toward me and lets out a loud exhale, never opening its teary eyes. Good, it's alive all right. I take a shot, then another, then 5 more. Great shots! I then just lay there for a second thinking about this creature, and our World. How long has this species of monk seal been swimming around the Hawaiian Islands? How many cruised around here 500 years ago? Really, only 1200 left now? What would happen to US if the monk seal went extinct? Is this one male or female? Had it mated yet? Does that green algae growing on the face and snout bother the seal? I wonder if I went over there and just scratched it off, if the seal would like that. How can I convince it that I just want to pet it and hug and squeeze it tightly, to no harm?

How the hell are visitors and atoll residents going to know how to stay 100 feet from a monk seal? Do you know what 100 feet is? I played football for 7 years and know what 100 yards looks like, and I know 31 yards is about 100 feet. I ran the 110m high hurdles too, so that also gives me a cognitive measuring stick.

I know! I will cut out a life-sized cardboard monk seal as a demo at the orientation, so folks can eye it. I'll put it right outside the orientation area, one hundred feet away. Genius! That image jumps through my mind as I shoot my last shot. Now *I* want to make the cardboard cutout to satisfy my own need to know. Not curiosity, mind you, but need to know. I want to burn that image into my brain so I know exactly what 100 feet looks like, but at the same time, I wonder how they came up with 100 feet, as opposed to 85 feet, or 117 feet. ??

Suddenly, I hear a motor and look out across the lagoon, the bright coral sand sticking to my cheek and chin. It is a little red powerboat with 4 or 5 people on it. They are cruising, and laughing it up. Ut oh, this is gonna wake up the seal. I roll quietly away from the seal and up the beach; I'd say a good 63 rolls or so. Then I stop to check the seal; sound asleep; then train my binoculars on the boat to see what looks like Alain and Laura, the French chef couple, Myhel, and two other people I don't know yet. I stand up and brush the sand off, and then walk down to the shoreline. Those dark objects catch my eye again. They're Spotted Eagle Rays! They are beautiful and graceful and totally smooth as they glide effortlessly, but they have funky-looking Martian faces. I want to jump in with them right away, but I don't have a mask with me. At the same time, Myhel catches notice of me on the beach and directs Alain to steer the boat over. They cut the engine as the speedboat enters the shallows, and Myhel, intentionally sticking her breasts forward in her bikini says, "Ahoy there land lubber. Avast there matie."

"Hi, how's it goin," I respond in a happy voice.

"What are you doing out there?" she queries.

"Just taking some photos and checking stuff out," I say, without acknowledging the monk seal up the beach.

Myhel glances over at my footprint trail, "That's P134," referring to the monk seal. I look at her with surprise. She yells as she holds up her tank, "I already logged that one this morning. We are going scuba diving!".

"Wow, you are? Where?" I say.

"Anywhere the hell we want," she says, trying hard to sound non-nerdy. "Why don'tcha come with us, uh huh?"

"I don't have any gear," I respond.

"We have all the gear. Hop in," she says forcefully. The others smile with encouragement.

"Let me go back to my room and get my mask and fins and swimsuit," I say.

"Okay, we will meet you at the fishing dock in 15 minutes," she says with excitement. They start the engine and put the boat into reverse.

"Cool," I say as I turn and head directly back toward my bike. As I approach my bike, I look back at the seal in the distance. It has rolled over and now I can see the dyed markings left by Myhel and her seal monitor cohorts. I look with my bins to see if I can make out the "P134", but instead, I can easily read C18. Myhel wasn't even close. Hmm.

After rushing up the stairs and prepping everything in my room, I head back down to my bike. Though I hadn't really been there yet, I find my way to the fishing pier. Along the way, on the beach by the broken seaplane ramp, I shoot turtles sunning on the sand near the waters edge. This, along with the earlier monk seal shots, will also be used in my slide show later. 'Unbelievable World', I whisper to myself.

Green Turtles. If only Homos could learn to be this mellow.

I get on the boat. They fire it up and blast out into the lagoon.
"Do you guys dive too?" I say to Alain and Laura.
"Wei. We will try," Alain says, looking at Laura suspiciously.
"Cool. Hi, I'm Kestrel." I say to the two other guys onboard.
"This is Darom, and Dr. Chance," Myhel says politely.
"Nice to meet you," I say, shaking their hands as the speedboat bounces and slaps down against the little waves.
"Nice meet you Mr. Kestrel," Darom says. Yet another guy who knows me before I am introduced.
"How do you like the island so far?" Dr. Chance says in a deep, calm voice; like he's about to examine me.
I say with jubilation, "It's great! I love it out here. It is amazing. I saw a monk seal and sea turtles this morning."
"Yah, we see them every day," Myhel responds, deflating my over-enthusiasm.
"Too many turtles. Too many turtles," Darom adds.
I look at everyone else confused.

Myhel clarifies as Dr. Chance laughs, "He means we have a lot, not too many."

"The language barrier takes some getting use to around here," Dr. Chance adds.

I can't figure out where Darom hails from. At about 5 feet tall, maybe in his 40's or 50's, and standing right next to Alain at the wheel, he looks like he could be a jockey.

"Darom is going to be the captain while we dive," Myhel adds.

Once I hear his name again, I realize he is the Thai guy with two wives.

"He's the man of all trades, the jack of all seasons," Dr. Chance adds. "He's the boiler maker, the masseuse, the barber, and the boat captain. He's a Buddhist Monk."

I note that Dr. Chance looks like a normal white guy, probably in his 50s, and very calm and doctor like.

We pull in to a deep area of the lagoon. I look over the side and see the bottom, but it looks kind of blurry.

We all start slipping gear on. I don't have a wet suit, and I couldn't find my swimsuit in my room, so I wear a pair of my APS shorts and my t-shirt. I know, I am not supposed to use uniform components. I am to be in complete uniform or no uniform at all, but there is no way I am going to miss out on my first chance to dive on Halfway. I check my air level, take a quick draw off my regulator, and spit into my mask. Somehow, I am ready before everyone else, so I slide off the boat head first and commando straight down to the bottom, decompressing once by pinching my nose and adjusting my jaw. I ever-so-gently kneel on the moonscape bottom for a moment and look around. Nothing. I look up. No one has hit the water yet. I look at my gauges and equipment. Everything looks fine. I am in 22-feet of water, with what I guess could be about 50-foot visibility. I strain to look as far off as I can, for big sharks, and other mega-fauna. I hear three loud crashes above my head in quick succession and look up to see three divers enter the water. Myhel comes down and gives me the OK sign. I respond. She then signals for us to buddy up. Again I communicate concurrence. I look up and see that Alain and Laura are still by the boat, and I can barely make out Darom's head through my bubbles, looking over the side from above the surface. After a few minutes, Alain finally comes down to join us, but

Laura hands her fins back up to the boat. Alain signals for us to dive, and we start cruising around together.

It is kind of a boring dive compared to Hawaii, but we do see some Domino Dacsyllus in some solitary coral outcrops, a Spiny Lobster, some Yellow-lined Goatfish, and best of all, a shark. On basically my third day on the atoll, I photographed Monk Seals and Green Turtles, saw Spotted Eagle Rays, and now am diving with a Black-tipped Reef Shark, and then two. Awesome! They are swimming slowly back and forth. Almost pacing. They are mellow. Hanging around. Then they are gone for a few minutes, then back again for a while. It is wicked cool. If these two wanted to, they could do some damage, but at about 5 or 6 feet each, even if they ganged-up on me, I don't see them killing me. They maybe never saw a diver in their lives. They may be looking for a hand out or some other opportunity to score a tasty snack. Myhel is a little touchy-feely on the dive. I kind of thought she was grabbing my legs to stay in contact when the sharks approached, but I wouldn't let a guy touch me like that, so it feels a little more than platonic. As the dive goes on, my beliefs become verified. While I'm looking at the little coral heads and moonscape, Myhel is feeling my thighs and butt and surveying "my moonscape". She never once touches Alain, at all.

The staple; the keystone species of Halfway's beaches and dunes: Naupaka!

What's also really blowing my mind is the flora around this atoll, including underwater. The plants on the sand seem to be limited to bushy Naupaka, *Erogrostis* (a large beachy bunch grass), and some creepy stuff like Beach Morning Glory; at least from a native perspective. The alien shit on Halfway appears to be a totally

82

different story and runs the gamut from bouganvillia to ferocactus. But the natives are slim pickins indeed, and quickly being extirpated by *Verbasina*, Ironwoods, and other pesky invasives. Underwater too; oddly barren. No kelp or seaweed, and sparse coral. Nothing like the tropics or the main Hawaiian Islands. In the North Pacific, Halfway Atoll sits half-way between San Francisco and Tokyo, at least that's what we told the Japs. Actually, Halfway is about 800 miles closer to Tokyo, but who's counting? Of course they couldn't call it 'Slightly Closer to Japan Atoll' right? So, Halfway made perfectly justifiable American sense. Like getting Alaska for four-hundred and eighty-seven bucks or whatever it was, or getting Manhattan for some beads and forty-two bucks and shit. Is that what being American is all about? Making the killer deal? That one killer capitalistic deal? Speaking of killer; the corals here look practically dead, like they just barely hold on. Not vibrant, . . . surviving. I am still way glad to be on the dive, and for free, and with sharks, and tan Myhel looking actually doable in her bikini. Though she has a kind of dumpy body that could use some exercise and healthy diet, her personality does not seem as grating now as it was when she first stood next to Kilgro, and I was blasted by Kilgro's 'When I was in Belize. . .' horn.

As I pull myself up into the boat, Laura, Darom, and Dr. Chance all look at me with astonishment.

"Wow! You are quite an athlete. We need to get you on zee court," Laura says.

"What?" I respond, confused.

"You're the first guy I've seen pull himself up after a dive without needing help. They say Bent's like that," Dr. Chance adds. "A couple of the Navy chiefs can't even get back into the boat without help, when they are swimming!" he laughs, but I doubt he could either.

"Oh. I run, lift, hike, play Ultimate; so I like to keep in good shape. Who's Bent?" I ask.

Myhel and Alain bob at the surface now also.

"You don't know Bent? He's the new dive master," says Dr. Chance. "Good guy to know. Pillmold will be going back to Florida some day in the future."

Myhel adds, "Thank god." She's obviously not a fan of Pillmold, and I'm sure he is 'off the list' as Myhel always loves to put it.

I drop my mask carefully and start grabbing their gear and pulling it into the boat.

"That's Darom's job," says Dr. Chance.

"Oh, that's okay, I'm just helping out," I say.

"That's Darom's job," Dr. Chance says again. "They need jobs." Oh, I get it finally, through my thick skull. Wow, it is so easy to step on toes out here. I reach down and help pull Myhel into the boat, then Dr. Chance and Darom help Alain in. I can see that certain things are okay, and other things are for the Foreign Nationals to do.

I think for a moment, staring down into the shimmering blue. I gotta find the boundaries, but I gotta do what's right. All my life, when I look back at it, I say, 'How can I have done that better? How can I be good, positive, the best? I want to do what is the best for the best. I don't care if it's the best thing for me. If it's the best thing for the turtle, or the monk seal; then, that's also the best thing for me.' Am I whacked?

"What happened to you?" I say to Laura. She looks at me in anger and disappointment, but says nothing. Alain looks at her and tries to get her to smile. She gives back a half of a smirk.

"How was it?" Dr. Chance asks.

"It was awesome. We had two Black-tipped Reef Sharks," I respond enthusiastically.

"Those were Galapagos," Myhel corrects.

"Really?" I say with surprise, "I thought they were black-tips." I had never even heard of Galapagos Reef Sharks, but had dove a few times with black-tips on the main Hawaiian Islands and that's what they looked like.

"We don't get Black-tipped Reef Sharks out here. Just Galapagos," she says.

"Oh," I say, "What happened to you?" Changing the subject and directing my attention toward Dr. Chance.

"What dya mean?" he says.

"Why didn't you dive?" I ask.

"I don't dive. I just came along for the ride," he says nicely.

"Yup, good to have a doctor along for the ride, hut," says Myhel. Laura and Alain shake their heads in agreement. "And a great boat captain too," Myhel says as she pats Darom heavily on his little shoulders.

"Yah, but I'm off duty," Dr. Chance jokes.

"You're never off duty around here," Myhel responds.

Darom cranks up the outboard, and we all grab onto something as he throws it into gear.

"So that was your first dive eh?" Myhel shouts.

I answer, "Yeah! This is my first time in a boat out here too. I got certified in Hawaii, and I probably have 50 dives under me, but I don't know because I haven't been keeping a dive log."

Myhel asks, "Why not?"

I think for a second, "Why?"

"Darom, let's take him on a cruise. The long way home," Myhel commands, as she hands Darom some rolled up bills. She smiles at me. I think she feels like she's showing off.

We drive around the inner lagoon and cut through a surge-channel in the reef. As we head south along the western edge of the outside of the atoll, we see clear blue water. In some places, I see shiny spots of sand glimmering on the bottom, even though we are in at least 50 feet of water by my guess. It looks like it drops off precipitously in some spots.

"We should have dove out here. This looks incredible," I yell over all the noise and wind.

"We do sometimes, but Alain and Laura wanted to try inside the reef so it was off the list," Myhel explains.

As we turn the corner at the jutting Frigate Point, at the end of the runway, I can see a monk seal hauled-out near the south end of the West Beach, and at the same time, another monk seal lying on the South Beach. Everything is bright blue and beautiful, . . . spectacular. Though Halfway has been bombed, polluted, and abused for 50 years, it is so far away from massive human harm that it still possesses remarkable beauty; almost pristine in some ways. Not the land of course, but the vast ocean about, the shore, the dive spots, and the lagoon, still look amazing. Though known for its birds, Halfway Atoll Wildlife Sanctuary blows every other dive spot on Earth out of the water!

"Time to go fish now," Darom announces as he starts to throttle down.

"No, we are not going fishing today Darom," Myhel corrects like a dominatrix.

Alain and Darom exchange disappointed looks.

"So what part of France are you from?" I yell as Darom gently accelerates the boat back up to plane. Alain says something, but I can't catch it. So I just say "oh, mh," like I heard him.

Ahead in the distance, I see a large rusting hulk. "What is that?" I yell.

A rusty, surge-plagued dive with killer Amberjack and trevally aggregations.

"That's the cement barge," Myhel quickly answers before Dr. Chance can get his first word out again. She's such an eager beaver.

Oh yeah. I had read about that too. Halfway had a Navy water barge that would bring fresh water to the atoll when it was a Naval Air Station. Now it sits right next to the main channel, which we rapidly approach and turn up into. Right at the mouth of the channel, a group of Spinner Dolphins start greeting us with leaps and spins near Spit Island and the barge, as they try to bow-ride off our little wake.

Darom picks up the radio and says something in a foreign language.

"Hey ranger, aren't we breaking the rule?" Dr. Chance asks, being a wise guy.

"We didn't approach them. We are just going to the inner harbor," I clarify.

Dr. Chance laughs, "Those rules are pretty unclear don't you think?"

"Look, there is no ambiguity regarding the Marine Mammal Protection Act. . ." and before I can continue, . . .

"Yes, you can't approach them within a quarter of a mile, can't change their behavior, can't chase them. . ." Myhel adds. "That is certainly off the list."

"Ya but we just made them start jumping all over the place," Dr. Chance argues.

Spinners go nuts for boats, like dogs chasing cars. Healthy?

She responds, "But they were already here. We are just passing through. Believe me, I've already been through this with Tirgut and Kilgro a number of times. Plus, we even have a dolphin expert coming to the atoll to verify that our procedures are in line with the Federal Regulations."

"Yeh, but you still made them jump," Dr. Chance challenges.

I shoot in, "They could have started jumping right now even if we weren't here."

"What are you saying, that we shouldn't have boats?" Myhel retorts.

Darom just keeps driving. Laura and Alain look like they have heard these arguments before and wish the psycho bi-polar Americans would stop with their crazy hypocritical extremism.

I can see everybody's points. "Okay. Let me say something here." I start, "If we were to find that the recreational boat activity, including diving, was having a negative impact on the Spinner Dolphins, then we would have to modify boat use and traffic. The problem is, where is the burden of proof? I think we, as the Federal Government, need to find a way to prove that our boating is having no impact. That is hard to prove. So instead, we need to look for signs of disturbance."

"Like what?" Dr. Chance asks.

Myhel jumps in with, "High infant mortality."

"INFANT!" I respond harshly. Ooops, did I say that out loud. I better watch people's toes out here.

Myhel thinks, then offers, "Calf? Hep, up; 'infant' is definitely off the list."

I clarify, "I mean, a lot of this is hard to determine. If they left the atoll, that could be a sign that the engine noise or taste of fuel or oil in the water could be driving them off."

"Well it sounds like 6 of 1 to me," Dr. Chance says despondently; maybe unhappy to find that I'm 'one of them'.

I ask, "Dr. Chance, you're a doctor. Do you know everything about every patient you see? Now imagine that you couldn't even talk to them. How would you know what was wrong with them? Science is trial and error, right?"

"Yes, I can see that. I just don't want our boating ruined by a bunch of ASS or APS folks that don't know what they are doing. The Navy was here for years with no problem," Dr. Chance says ignorantly.

No problems!! Now I am getting pissed. Does he work for HIC? Was he in the Navy? The reason The FIVE System (Fluid Injection Vapor Extraction) pumps day and night out here is to get rid of the layer of oil on the water table all over Sand Island. AVGAS, diesel, you name it; spilled everywhere out here, extracted now at the rate of 500 gallons a day. What do you expect? It was a navy base, not a sanctuary. The water table is only 6 feet down in a lot of parts of Sand Island. These are all questions I want to pose, but instead, I start rambling at high speed to expel my frustration. I definitely do not want the only doctor on the atoll mad at me. It must be tough to be the only doctor out here. Look at The Cable Company graveyard: 4 out of 5 gravestones are doctors, one of which who supposedly tried to perform an emergency appendectomy on himself!

I try to appeal to Dr. Chance in a way he will appreciate, "I'm not the greatest biologist in the world. I'm a ranger. If the biologists tell me something is bad for the dolphins, I will believe them unless I see otherwise. Like a cop, I am suppose to use discretion in my judgments, but execute the law first."

Dr. Chance smiles. I think he likes my answer. Alain and Laura still stay out of it. I don't think Darom even knows what we are talking about. I think he is thinking about the one that got away. But Myhel, Myhel *really* loves my answer; I can see it. I can see in the flush in her cheeks, and in her body language, and her eyes. She is diggin what I am saying.

She has that same flush in her cheeks that Messycka used to get when she would enter my room, like every time, right away. She would ring my buzzer on Comm. Ave., then walk up the stairs of the old brownstone apartment building near The Green Line, where I would open the door and watch her enter my apartment (unflushed I might add). Then we would walk into my room and I would close the door behind me. Immediately, and it happened over and over again; her cheeks would get pinkish red, and her fingers and toes would tighten and squeeze-up. Then, neither of us would even have to say a word. I knew what she wanted. Could Myhel fill that niche for me? I've gone from finding her repugnant to considering dating her in less than a few days, but I know already in my heart of hearts, by a number of the things I've seen her do already, that she's not 'the one'. Therefore, I must be strong, and morally incorruptible.

We pull up to a ramp, where we take the boat out of the water. A FN waits there with a forklift, which he uses to tow the boat onto the trailer and pull it out of the circular inner harbor. We rinse everything with a hose, and head on our bikes back to 'town' as one big happy group. Why can't things stay this way in my life? Nope, not on Halfway. Not anywhere really. Konrad Lorenz says we need aggression. For an instant I flashback to one of his last chapters, *EccoHomo!* (This Man): *One is tempted to believe that every gift bestowed on man by his power of conceptual thought has to be paid for with a dangerous evil as the direct consequence of it.* He immediately refutes this notion, but I find it interesting that a lot of people think this now. Are they cynics, or realists?

I glide on my bike, looking up at the trees swaying against the blue sky, and all the bright white birds gliding along high above. As each party peels-off to their respective residences, we say bye and I am left alone, biking along with Myhel.

"You can shower at my place if you want. I put in a shower massage my Mom gave me last year for Christmas. Shower massages are definitely on the list."

"Wow. That sounds cool," I respond innocently. "How long have you been out here anyway?"

"I'm like one of the top 5 longest. Long story. Too long, hup. But I will never be able to beat a couple of the foreign nationals out here ya know," she says with disappointment, like she can't win this completely meaningless competition.

We go to her house and over to an in-law side entrance. She sputters on the hose-less spigot near her steps, and we help each other get the sand off of our feet and Tevas. Looking over at her, I can see she makes a real effort, and yet, she has an insecure twitch about her, and almost a kind of sorrow about her aura. We enter her room. That's what it is: One room, and a half closet, and a bathroom. We enter into the bathroom and she slips off her bikini with no hint of timidity. Not bad. Not good, but better than I thought.

"Should we shower together?" she pauses for a second, scanning my face, "to save water," she adds, detecting she's pushing too much and should retreat.

I laugh. Then she leans up to me and kisses me. Ut oh. What am I doing? Maybe I better wait on this. I don't even know if she's a psycho yet. I mean, c'mon, I know, all girls are psychos, American girls in particular, but *how* psycho? She kisses me again, and this time, grabs me and really starts making out with me, moving to grab my hard ass pretty darn quickly. We take a quick rinse, towel off, and lie on her bed. I'm too distracted to even notice that she doesn't even have a shower massage!

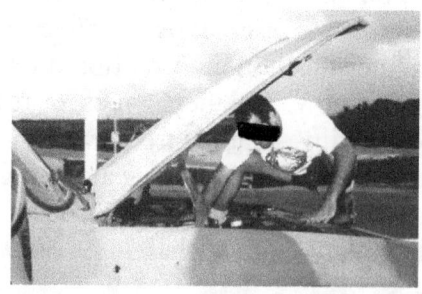

90

Like entering a Venus flytrap, trusting Kestrel troubleshoots an Army Surplus vehicle at Kamehame on the turtle project.

My mind races as usual. Am I blowing it with Jewel? This is wrong. Way too soon. I haven't had sex in over a month, and I haven't had good sex since I left Messycka in Boston eight months ago, before I went to Hawai'i to work on the Hawksbill Turtle Project. I wonder what most 'guys' would do. You know, the *'Movies for Guys Who Like Movies'* type guys. The guys with big pick-up trucks. The guys represented in beer commercials, who try to coerce you to be like them, and drink like them. Real men, like macho guys you see on TV like Howey Long, who go around acting like 'guys' basically cause they can punch-out pretty much any other 'guy' and definitely any other so called guy like me, who aren't really 'guys', according to them. What if I were 6'4" and 300-pounds? Would I go around all macho like that, or would I be a gentle giant? I mean, I'm way stronger and tougher then any of my girlfriends, and yet, I never felt a need or entitlement to violently dominate them, or beat them. I never punched any of them. I probably wouldn't go around punching guys out and acting like a macho jerk if I could, but you never know how you will act in a situation or in someone else's shoes, do you? I know Howey Long can punch me out, and I know he wouldn't consider me a 'real man' in his eyes, but that still wouldn't give him the right to do it. I've always hated bullies.

She reaches over and gently starts touching my hog. Wow, straight for the hog. Hmm. Not sure if I really like that. Maybe I should wait until the plane comes in tonight and do a little more research on her before I just let things happen. What is she looking for? Should I fuck things up by talking?

I stutter, "So, do you have a boyfriend?"

Fuck! What a stupid, irrelevant question. Even if she does have a boyfriend, she invited me over for a shower. She's touching my thing.

"No. I had a boyfriend I was supposed to marry, ya know, but I came back out here. Couldn't be away from the goonies," she states with zero credibility.

Woah, that sounds scary.

She blurts out randomly, "I'm afraid of the 'C' word now."

What the hell is that? My mind races. Chlamidia, Condaloma, Chastity, Cuticles. Don't mind the spelling. I'm a ranger, not a doctor. Neither is Drats. I can't imagine what the C word stands for, but to her it means she is getting ready to go down on me. "See word?" I stammer.

"The 'C' word," she repeats. Looking at my unregistering eyes, she explains, "Commitment."

"Oh. Commitment," I repeat aloud as I think for a second. "What's wrong with commitment?" I ask, afraid. After all, as I have stated, I want the real thing. I WANT COMMITMENT. I want to be in love again with a soul mate in a life-long committed relationship that is special, and has meaning. Nobody believes me. Nobody thinks I do, but I do. 'Commitment' is not a dirty word to me.

She goes on about how she just wants to relax and have fun on the atoll and how she just got out of a heavy relationship and likes sex and thinks I'm hot and blah blah blah, but I need to ask so many more questions; like how could she have been on the atoll for a long time and in a long-term relationship, and a bunch of other stuff that doesn't add up, so I say, "Ya know, I got a lot of stuff, the manifest, and everything to get ready tonight. Maybe we should pick a better time for this." Liar! Liar! Lair liar! Fuck, she can see it too, but what the hell am I suppose to say?

"We have plenty of time. I have a handsome gorgeous guy lying in my bed. Huh h, I'm not goin let that go to waste." She puts her lips over me just as her cell phone rings.

"Oh shit, it's Kilgro, he hh hah," she laughs with excitement towards me. "Hello," she says, abruptly changing to sounding perturbed. I guess she has to answer, and Kilgro is her boss. "No, I'm tied up with something right now," she grins. Between each sentence, she delights in taking a lick, as if to disrespect Kilgro on the other end of the line. 'Nah na na- na nah - nah. I have Kestrel Falco in my bed, and, Kilgro don't.' That seems to be how she thinks.

I crunch up to reach my shorts, in an attempt to start putting them on. Myhel signals for me to lay back, and pushes me down again. She continues suffering the Kilgro conversation. "No, I told you, I'll see you at the Galley at dinner and we can talk about it. No, it's New Year's Day. Okay, well you can talk to Tirgut about it. That's fine with me. See you at the Galley," and she hangs up.

"RRrrrrrrrr", she growls in feigned frustration.

I keep quiet.

"Okay now, where were we?" She says, as she goes back to business.

Good question. Where were we? Where were you? I'm not really here. I am someplace else. I have to stop this now. Wow, hard to say 'no' ya know, when she's sucking on it like that. She will say or do anything to get me to give it to her. Disease? Shit we haven't had *the talk*!

"Um. STDs?" I question softly.

"Nope, clean as a whistle. I just told you I was in a long term relationship," she says as she goes back to it, berating me for asking such stupid questions.

Stupid answer. How do I know the guy she was with wasn't screwing everyone he could? He was in the Navy for god sakes.

"Pregnant?" I say, trying to scare her out of it, since she *says* she derides commitment. Why the hell would she say that? Did she get that out of Cosmo or something? Seems a little quick to be the first thing to come out. I cover all the bases. She shows me the Norplant in her arm.

She giggles, "Let's see if we can raise ye 'ol mast on this sailor's ship."

I go to extreme full mast in an instant.

"Whooah. That was easy, huh," Myhel says with bubbling enthusiasm, and a sense of pride and accomplishment.

She slips up along my thighs hastily, straddles me, and gently slides down onto me. I reach up and squeeze her breasts gently while she ungulates like a slow-motion bull rider. She cums really fast, with a funny, orgasmic, repeated, repressed laugh that sounds like a cross between a cough and a choke, then falls over to one side with her head vanishing into the pile of soft pillows. She lets out a satisfying gasp.

"You okay?" I say in a deep, soft whisper.

"Hehheaaa. I'm great," she whispers back with a silly chuckle.

I pause for a second. What do I do now? I decide to forgo permission and rotate my body up and behind hers, like a wrestling reversal. I gently, slowly, one centimeter at a time, slip myself back into her. She gives out a little moan, then pushes her upper body up off of the bed and arches her back deeply. I start going faster and harder, then like jackhammer fast and hard until her boobs bounce so fast that they become a blur. I grab her left hip bone and pull her ass tightly up against my pelvis each time I thrust forward, while I hold her blonde ponytail in my right hand and pull her head back so I can see the pleasure drool from her mouth.

Okay, actually, it wasn't that great. I think Drats is exaggerating for a little erotic titillation. He's such a hopeless romantic, you know. It's not as good as it will be with Hamed More. It isn't as hot as it was with Messycka. Messycka was hot. It wasn't even close to how I would feel when I finally meet Chelonia, the love of my life, the passion of my soul. It is okay. I can't get into it that much when it isn't a girl I'm really really in love with.

Suddenly, it comes, and I quickly pull out and blast cum all over the bed and towels. Whoa, that was a big load. I have been saving it up, not being much of a masturbator.

Myhel laughs, "Why'd ya pull ouwt silly?"

I lay there silent for a moment. I don't know what to say, nor do I want to or feel like saying anything.

"Outt oh, cat got ya tongue?" She says, trying to add some levity.

"Come on did I scare ya already?" She says with a bit of fear in her voice.

I fumble, "No, no. Everything is okay. Everything is just great. Did you want me to cum inside?"

She says, "No. no. Not at all. No. Definitely not. I'm just sayin. . . I just told you 10 minutes ago I am on Norplant."

I think for a minute, but can't think of anything constructive to say and don't want to lie.

"What did you *not* understand about 'I'm on Norplant'?" she says with frustration.

"Look, I just don't cum in girls, ever." I say. "I either use a condom, or they drink it, or I blow it all over; but never ever inside."

"Ever? That's kind of dumb. What's the point of being on birth control if the guy won't even use it?" she states bitterly.

What an idiot. The point is, I don't want to be responsible for a life, a baby, period; and I definitely know tons of guys, especially in Japan, who said a woman tricked them into getting them

94

pregnant. I always have to laugh at those idiots. If you don't cum in them, they can't get pregnant!

I say, taking a more relaxed, scholarly tone, now that my sexual energy has been expended, "I think it's complicated, and mistakes can happen, so it is probably a good idea to be on birth control to avoid being impregnated."

"Yah, well you don't know shit mister. I have Norplant so I can control my own reproduction. It has nothing to do with you. You can cum anywhere you want and I won't get pregnant," she says defiantly, like she has just read *Women On Top* and has to prove how much she doesn't need a man. And yet, she's got Norplant, and she's been chasing my ass down all around the atoll for the last 3 friggin days. Hmmm?

"Why did you get Norplant in the first place?" I ask, puzzled.

She snaps back immaturely, "None of you bees' wax."

Oh, that *really* makes me want to trust her now, I think to myself sarcastically. Then I say, "So I could have cum in your mouth?" I ask.

"Yes you could have, and you could, but not on our first time together," she says with anger, setting some kind of artificial moral dating guidelines. "That would certainly be off the list don't cha know."

"Of course not, and I understand that," I smile.

"So why didn't you cum inside me?" she insists. Obviously, this is important to her.

"I barely know you or anything--anybody on this atoll. I don't know what's going on yet."

She sits thinking to herself. I look into her eyes but can't read her mind.

She says, "Well, why the hell did you sleep with me if you weren't ready or afraid or some shit like that, eh?"

What the hell is going on here? I don't understand at all what is happening.

I look at her for a long moment. She doesn't say anything more. She appears to be feeling that she has already said too much maybe, like she fears turning me off, which is true.

"I don't know you yet. I can't trust you. What if you are one of those women who is just dying to have a baby and will say anything? I'm sorry but how do I know? What if your Norplant stops working?" I am blunt, as usual. "I know lots of guys, in which case, the girl said she was safe, and months later the guy is stuck with a baby. No thank you."

"Look, we gotta stick together out here. This is a small place and people can go kookoo really fast, like overnight, ya know. I guess you want to keep this quiet huh?" she says softly, touching the hair on my chest with her pinky nail, changing the tone.

"What do you mean?" I really am unsure of what she is talking about.

"Well, we should keep our business private. This is a Payton Place. Why don't you walk over for now on, or hide yuh bike in the bushes at least so it's not obvious that you are oveh here. Having everyone on the atoll know my business is definitely off the list," she says like she has experience in these matters.

"Okay," I say reluctantly.

Myhel becomes very sweet again all of a sudden, and states, "And you can cum inside as much as you like. Don't worry. I do not want to be a mother. I am too young and have my biology career ahead of me."

She looks pretty earnest, and I feel I can trust her, for now. Is it the soft, warm kisses she gives me? Like one of those 'everything's gonna be alright' kind of comforting love kisses? That's nice. I know everyone's a good person inside. Maybe Myhel is too and she just needs a chance. Maybe I can get her to stay away from Kilgro, and get her to start eating healthy and working out. Bad sign. I want to change her already. As I reach to put my underwear back on, she grabs them and says, want to try again and see if you can get it inside this time.

"Okay," I say again, a little bit surprised, and surprising myself. I'm not even sure if I can get it up again right away, but after a few gentle mouth maneuvers and gently cupping my balls in her fingers, the mast stands erect again, and she mounts me again, and she rides on me in the exact same way until she cums again, this time taking 3 times as long. Still pretty quick though.

When she falls to the side of the bed, I get up and kneel down next to it. I slide her over into position, first starting slow, and gradually, getting deeper and faster. After about three minutes I am frothing at the mouth and drooling on her upper back and sandy hair. I slip my hypersensitive penis back out again, right before I ejaculate, and lay down on the bed next to her after having an even bigger orgasm. I am zonked. Little do I know that this will be the pattern for almost a year on Halfway. So mechanical, and daily. She would make naughty sexual innuendos, then she would go down on me just long enough to get me hard and wet; never a second longer; utilitarian to a fault. Then she would mount me and cum rather quickly. Then she would collapse and I could 'basically' do whatever I wanted, which would generally turn into me humping her from behind like a little rabbit, and her asking if I like it. That's one of the problems with biologists and why so many of them and I don't click. They lack creativity and imagination. Too many labs. If I compare her to the actresses, dancers, models, and other women I've been with, it's not even close. I know, we are not supposed to compare, but I certainly do. I know what totally awesome great sex is. This ain't it. She never brings up the topic of cumming inside again, even though I make a point of it to 'never plant a seed'.

Mind you, I'm not complaining. Of course it would have been great to be with the love of my life, or someone I really love and care about; someone who is more creative, imaginative, provocative. I think Jewel would have been more exciting for me. On the other hand, Myhel says she fears the 'C' word. She likes doing it with me everyday. What would you do? Who would you screw? Judge me. I'd like to see what you would have done on a tiny desert atoll in the middle of the Pacific.

I go back to my room and lie down for a minute. What have I done? Did I fuck-up already? God, I hope I can trust that girl. My spider senses tingle.

As night approaches, I learn the flight arrival protocols will be pretty much as monotonous a routine as doing Myhel. As the new flight comes in, I listen for a call, then I go whipping down the stairs, straddling entire flights, six stairs at a time, coming down with a shin-splint splat slap as I hit the concrete, hearing the hum of the engines, far off. It makes me think of what a scramble to battle stations would feel like, and if those engines were those of enemy craft.

On this night, New Year's Day, my cell rings. The plane will be landing in 10 minutes, or something like that. In the future, lots of times, I will be told as I arrive at the Hangar, huffing and puffing, that the plane won't land on schedule because they have to wait for dark until the albatross settle-down. So, if they get there a little bit early, to avoid bird strikes, they fly around the atoll. A plane flying around the atoll sounds really weird. Civilization! Rescue! Hope! Comfort! I don't know what I feel but I am excited to hear the first plane in days. Even though it's only been a few days, it's really weird. I mean, I'm compelled to watch it cruise around, especially since it's a propped plane. Ya, I know it's a turbo prop, but still, the hum of those engines flying around this place; very World War Two-ish and visceral.

On this incoming flight, I will meet the guests and others in uniform for the first time as Halfway's first ranger. On a completely different subject, I will also be meeting Zart. I'm anticipating something positive out of this, but should not get my hopes up too high. He might be a cool guy. That would be great. I will also get to peruse the manifest first to see how many possibly available chicks might be on this flight. Of course, if they have shared last names or belong with the Olderhostile group, I must consider them 'off the list', as Myhel always puts it. Everything exists as either 'on the list' or 'off the list' for her. For example: Spicy mustard, 'off the list'; hunky guys, 'on the list'. So which will be my focus? Hey, I am going to be a kick-ass ranger and that is that. That doesn't mean I don't want to at least fantasize about what options might be available, and of course, I get to say hi to Jewel again, who, as the plane pulls to a stop, and the stairs descend, just starts smoothly coming down the stairs, and gives me a quick little tease of a flashy smile. Hmm, did she hook-up on New Years? She looks great. What a pro. She partied late, flew to and from The Main Hawaiian Islands, and looks as fresh as a Beach Morning Glory in the dew. For some reason, I really doubt she hooked up. Simultaneously, squashing that beautiful instant right out from under me, Kilgro and Myhel pull up next to me in their ASS golf cart.

"Hey, you're not supposed to have that cart out here" snarls Deny.

"We have disabled people!" Kilgro fires back.

"They are physically challenged," Myhel corrects. Turning to Deny and projecting like a scratchy bullhorn, "Physically challenged. We are pickin em up, ya know."

At that moment one of the Olderhostile folks gets pissed. "Don't label us. That is very inappropriate." The "girls" blush with embarrassment for the first time, but definitely not the last time, in front of me. They look down and away from me in shame as they pull the cart out in reverse and load their first few scolding passengers. I keep looking for a 'knowing glance' from Myhel, but she never acknowledges our carnality. Hm. Interesting. She's an expert at this. Must have had practice.

After all of the tourists are off the plane, and I have 'meeted and greeted' them (as they grammatically incorrectly say in the biz), I see a big guy coming toward me. Looks like he might be a construction worker or with HIC, but within a second, I can see he's heading straight for me: The Uniform.

"How's it goin? Welcome to Halfway," I say heartily.

"Oh, I know Halfway," he says broadly, shaking my hand. "I should be welcoming you."

"I brought your bike," I say. "Nice one. It's not the typical beach cruiser out here."

"No. I put the handle bars and the breaks on myself, and some other junk," explains Zart.

"I rode it. It's nice," I respond.

He says, "Thanks. When I leave you can have it as my legacy. Ha ha. So how you liken it out here?"

"Wow, it's a trip," I respond, hipster-esquely. "Not really any hot chicks on the flight huh?"

Zart shakes his head in expectable disappointment. I know, bonding. We have to do it. It proves we are cool, tough, straight, smart; to the other guy. You have to prove that right away or you can't have respect and you can't be friends. That's men for ya; psychoer than women by far.

Zart and I bike back and as we pass the old abandoned Marine's barracks area, we hear a ghostly groan. We stop our bikes with rear skids.

"What the hell is that?" I question in a husky whisper.

"Those are moaning birds. This is your first time?" Zart whispers, as we hear another, and then another much closer and more insistent.

The Wedge-tailed Shearwaters (better known as wedgies), giving long squeaking baby-cry squeals, hold Zart and I frozen for a minute.

A nocturnal Wedge-tailed Shearwater glows in the flood light by the HAZMAT depot.

"I just read in the literature that the Marines, in their tents or barracks, were so disturbed, even haunted, by their mating calls that they would grab spades and smash them into the ground with the shovels. That's why there used to be many more shearwaters on the atoll. They were almost wiped-out. I haven't been to this area yet," I ramble quietly; friggin know-it-all.

"Yah, they are making a big comeback now that we started rat baiting. They like to burrow under the Naupaka," he says, "and they were known as the mutton birds".

Naupaka. I had just read about that too. Very interesting: A Hawaiian beach plant. Endemic? Primitive. I like it. Cool. Maybe I can learn something from this guy.

"After I dump off my stuff, let's hit the All Hands Club," Zart suggests.

Zart and I sit down for a quality one on one chat at a booth in the bar some 20 minutes later. Zart is a pretty big guy. Not huge, but more likely a lineman than a back.

"What's yer poisinn?" he asks with a Warshingdontonian accent.

I spiel, "I like to go hiking and be in nature, but it's not enough to be out hiking about, where you are walking around, viewing nature. I want to be *crawling* around in nature. I want to be on my hands and knees and crawling through the bushes and up trees and into caves, and like, see what it's like to be going on my hands and knees through the forest. I know it sounds a little dangerous, or crazy, but it feels so much more connected than like having hard rubber boots between me and the ground." My enthusiasm bubbles, not in a conniving manipulative way, but just because I really love and believe what I feel in my heart deeply; and it looks like Dietera, and now Zart, are allies in this same value: Love of Nature, first.

"NO, I meant to drink!" Zart finally explains when I catch my breath.

"Oh. Cider?" I answer.

"I don't think they have cider out here. Wow, you'd make a good politician," Zart responds.

I reveal, "That's funny cause I think of myself as a poet and my Mom wanted me to be a priest, so that covers everything on the Chinese restaurant placemat."

"Chinese placemat?" Zart wonders.

"Yeah. I'm the Year of the Dragon and it always says I'd be a good poet, politician, preacher, and sometimes it says teacher," I explain.

"Oh," Zart says, shortly. "We got a large Chinese population up in the Pacific Northwest, but I grew up kinda out in the boonies. Went to Evergreen State. So, which one of those would you want to be?" referring back to the placemat choices.

I think he thinks I know too much about too much.

"I've never seen myself as a priest, and I already am a poet, and a teacher. If I were a senator," I continue undaunted, "I would pass a bill that would say that when the US unemployment rate hits over 8% nationally, then all of the elected and appointed major federal officials, congressmen, cabinet members, justices, you name it, and all banking and stock exchange employees making over let's say eighty-thou a year, all have to take a 50% reduction in pay to help pay for unemployment and create more jobs. Until the rate goes back under 8% again."

"Wow, that's radical. I mean, it's a good idea, but it's radical," Zart explains as he draws another puff from his Cuban or whatever the hell that disgusting, vomit-making gagger is.

Did he mean 'radical' like 'cool rad'? I don't think so. I think his backwoods upbringing clashes with my prog-style. I'm not surprised; it seems my thinking appears to be too advanced for 92% of US around the World, but he is open-minded at least.

I say, "I think first of all, if the unemployment rate rises above 8%, then everybody hurts, except super-duper rich who never get hurt. We know the rich are directly responsible for unemployment, and by definition, they hoard, otherwise, they couldn't be rich. Congress shouldn't be paid the full rate. Let them feel the pinch too. That will light a fire under them, and make them less privileged. It would be an incentive," I explain. Zart almost looks like he wants to say something. I pause; he gets a puzzled look on his face, then laughs. Nothing.

I continue. "If the unemployment rate goes over 8%, then congress, etc., shouldn't be allowed to have any "disposable income", and then people would love and respect their politicians more for taking the hit with US, so it's a win-win situation. The only loser in this situation is that congress and all the aforementioned exec-types won't have quite as much play money when times are bad. Boo hoo hoo," I finish with a flash of a sick laugh. "I think if they let unemployment get over 10%, then none of them should be paid at all until they are able to get the rate back down. It's not my fault. I am ready and willing to work hard as long as there is a job. They should pay for screwing the economy up and fucking it up for the rest of US hard workers, by being greedy and pandering to special corporate interests."

"Did you ever hear that song 'Eat the Rich' 'Eat the Rich'?" Zart half sings.

Dietera cuts-in as she arrives with a round, "Yuh, that was Aerosmith right, or didn't AC/DC have a song like that too? I can never keep those suburb rock bands straight."

"Yuh, oh yuh." Zart answers vaguely, being a fan of 'suburb rock' but never having heard the term. He listens to Bon Jovi, Skynard, and other white-trash crap like Guns and Roses. Personally, I'd put Aerosmith way above those other bands. They Rock!

I can't tell what he's saying, but who cares. We are having fun. What a nightmare it would have been out here if I had to "talk" with the HIC or Navy chiefs all day and night.

I look at Dietera and Zart and say, "If all these people, these public servants, like US, and these big execs, the ones that were just smart or lucky enough to get filthy rich off of US, if they have to live on half their salaries for a while, they are gonna be fine. None of them are gonna die or anything", I say, repeating myself for Dietera's benefit, as I realize we are all starting to feel beyond buzzed. I take a break, a deep breath, and look around. The second hand smoke is killing me.

Zart asks, "Wow, you got a lot of energy. Ya better lay off the coffee."

I say, "I don't even drink coffee. It buzzies me out," as I spaz like a wounded wasp for a demo.

Then Dr. Chance comes over and slides into the booth with a drink in hand. He moves very smooth and slowly, like a doctor. I look over at him. I think I already asked too much. I slam the second half of my drink. Now I'm wasted. The Halfway doctor. Hmmm, Halfway doctor? It keeps popping into my head. Pooping, like little bunny turds in my brain. "Kind of an interesting post for a Navy flight surgeon who could be makin oodles of money elsewhere," I pry, but not vulgarly, by my impression.

"I'm not in it for the money," Dr. Chance tries to say in earnest, "…this place is the experience of a lifetime for me and my kids," he says.

Now don't get me wrong. He seems like a nice guy and luckily for me, I like him. It's been hard to find cool people to like on this Atoll, especially from HIC. He says he went to Tulane. He says he's a general surgeon, and had to be to get the job. I wonder though still, something smells rotten in Denmark. Malpractice suit? Shirking the IRS? Stalking ex?

He scans my face as I puzzle over him. "Anything wrong? I'm not gonna run you through the whole physical again," he says to my relief.

Don't get me wrong. I have no fear. Passing physicals is my specialty. I have always tried to at least maintain excellent physical shape. At least that is one thing in life we have complete control over. If you want to be buff, just workout and eat well, that's all that's to it. I never wanted to be in psycho-compulsive ripped shape, but less than 20% body fat, can run a mile in under 6 minutes, and can bench two-thirty kind of shape. I'm not a fanatic. I just want to be comfortable in my own skin and be able to hike, scuba, play Ultimate, and climb trees like a monkey.

"I don't know what this head tingling thing is," I tell Dr. Chance, as he really makes an effort toward good bedside manner, and I ask if there are a lot of others feeling the same way. "Sometimes I get it on the outside of my skull, under my skin and hair-line and I feel more like veins popping," I continue.

Zart returns to the table with drinks for all.

"Or like synapses snapping?" Dietera adds.

"I don't know what it is," I say, shaking my head.

"You know, the synapses are in the brain so it can't be that, but I don't know what it is, . . . popping flicks in the brain? Could be tension in your temporal veins," Dr. Chance thinks for a second.

"Outside the brain too. Hypertension?" I question with frustration.

"Hypertension is hypertension and that could just be what it is," he says affirmatively.

And that could be because I'm just such a stressed-out stress-case and I'm all fucked up. I have nothing to be stressed about out here really. If you think about it, it should be a pretty chillaxed place to have a good time, but I snap to judgments about people with arrogance. Why? Why do I obsess about my problematic family when I know I can't do anything to help them? Why do I let all these stressors drive me mad?

"Maybe that's why I run so much you know," I hypothesize.

"When I was in high school I would wake up at six-thirty in the morning, put on my shorts and my cutoff t-shirt, and, you know, I'd go for a run. I'd run the beach and come home. The following year I ran all the way down the length of the beach and then turned around and ran the length of the beach back on the wall, jumping the pedestrian gaps, and then I would run back the length of the beach one more time, running over the rocks, the sand, and climbing over the breakwater boulders and stuff like that. I would have that run out of my system and that's maybe why I was so hyper and maybe had so much energy for track, cause I just wanted to go go go, and it made me feel good. It fired those endorphins in my brain. They say you can't add brain cells, but I swear aerobics make me feel smarter. I mean, don't get me wrong, I still run, but in high school I would run every freakin day, and all day, all over, to school, in school, at school, in class, at practice, everywhere all the time. Now, if I'm lucky, I run 2 times a week. I try to lift once or twice a week, and I bicycle and hike and do all those things in combination." My rampage finally comes to a stop.

"Here on Halfway, another one of the peace dividends is that the Navy had their workout facility here." Dr. Chance adds, which as I explained before, the Navy guys didn't really bother to use. "Sometimes I see some of the other construction guys in there working out, which I think is kinda funny cause they spend all day sweatin and working physical construction, but then they have the energy to come in and lift," Dr. Chance observes.

"And then on top of that, I saw them taking Creatine and other powdery protein stuff to build up their muscles so they can be really huge," Zart gossips.

"Steroids?! I never do that," I respond stupidly. Of course I don't. Everyone can see that. I'm not built. I always lift to maintain strength, definition, and endurance. I try to double-up and get a cardio workout in every time I lift, by doing circuits. I don't put a lot of time between sets like a lot of weightlifters do. I work different parts of the body; like I will do chest, then calves, then shoulders, then abs, then start back with chest and do the whole circuit again. I spread it all around so that when one muscle group rests the other gets worked. This gets my heart, circulation, and even some fat burning going while I also work my muscles anaerobically. I stole that workout from Tim Daggett and the UCLA gymnastics team. I watched them workout a few times in the John Wooden Center, mostly staying focused on the girls. Oh my god, what perfect, perfect friggin bodies. Unbelievable. I wanted to date a UCLA gymnast so bad. Never happened. I'm not all-American enough for them.

Then Zart says, "Hey, Han and the Sri Lankans were invited to the Halfway House since the Navy will be leaving soon, and they invited us to come over."

"Great," says Dr. Chance as he stands up from the table and some Sri Lankans approach.

"No way," I say. "I think I'm going to sidestep the Navy until they take off for good."

Zart responds, "Hey, I've been out here for almost a year already and I've had plenty of conflict with many of them, but the lieutenant is an okay guy, and one of the older chiefs ain't so bad, and I'm bringing my conga for a jam."

"Jam?" I say. Zart has said the magic word.

So we all head over to the OIC House and meet the party crew out on the lanai. Lt. Flipflopbaker warmly greets us, only one of the chiefs is there (the older, nicer one), and a whole bunch of Sri

Lankans, Poor Construction Girl, the Navy secretary (who announces she will be leaving on the next plane), and a number of other folks.

The Sri Lankans cheer and toast our arrival. Then the jam begins. Several people, including Zart, rip into a great percussion jam. There are no other instruments, so I start wailing, and then, feel like I am hearing **The Police's** *King of Pain* in my head. I start singing, but change the lyrics to increase their relevance.

There's a seal pup starving on the beach today, It's the same pup starving that was yesterday,
There's a frigatebird caught in an ironwood top, There's an injured turtle and the sharks won't stop.

You get the idea. I am drunk, and improvising, but it fits, and everyone is just loving it. The longer the song goes, the more gusto and dynamics I pile on. Zart keeps a great beat, and a lot of the Sri Lankans have obviously been around a drum before. Finally, the ten-minute version of the song ends, and everyone yells and applauds, wipes off their sweat, and downs their drinks.

Han says, "Mr. Kestrel. You great singer. You not tell us. You singing ranger."

Everyone laughs hysterically. There is an incredible feeling of joy in the air. Zart also looks at me with some surprise.

I compliment Zart, "Way to crank the conga dude." Then I commend all the other players.

The Sri Lankans keep handing me drinks, and now I'm on autopilot. This, by the way, will end up being the first and last time I let that happen to 'my temple' on Halfway Atoll. Like I said, I like to party, but I also like to stay in shape, be a good worker, and set a positive example. It's so ironic that the bible-belt fanatics call the body 'a temple', yet they seem to be the most obese body-abusers out there at the all-u-can-eat buffet. In the future, every time the FNs invite me to a party, I write a note across my forehead with face paints, or with a sticky note – NO Alcohol Please! At first, the FNs have no idea how to deal with this. They think it's very rude that I won't imbibe with them. Yet, they eventually get use to it and still serve me soda or iced-tea, and they continue to love my singing and antics.

Okay. Good. So the initial shock is over. I know there is definitely some unforeseen hostility on the atoll, but at the same time, I have also found Dietera, possibly Loon, Dr. Chance, and now, Zart and the Sri Lankans to buddy up with. Plus, I've already gotten laid with pretty much the only eligible girl on the atoll (I don't count Kilgro as eligible), so I can handle the Cherry Ballpigs, Denys, and Kilgros out here.

I don't remember what happened after the next few songs. Someone comes over and starts talking. I take another sip and remember shaking hands with PCG. She seems to be pretty chummy with Zart. Another sip. Wait, didn't I just take a sip? Next thing I know, I'm looking at my ceiling again. Thank god it's not spinning. Thinking about everything that has transpired this day and evening, I can't go to sleep, especially since Ben said I don't have to work again tomorrow. I know I am in my bed, but I am having a hard time remembering getting here. So, after sobering up for almost 2 hours, and downing a 16 oz plastic cup of water, I quietly sneak out of my room, slip down the stairs like a ghost, and go over to Myhel's. It is dark. All dark. I look around. I anticipate the wooden boards to creek, which they do, but the albatross are pretty loud, so I step fully onto the porch. Then I tap on the door. A few seconds later I hear something swipe up against the inside of the door. I wait for another second or two, then tap again, looking around at the windows of the nearby buildings to see if anyone bears witness to this late-night booty call.

"Who is it?" Myhel whispers from just inside the door.

"It's me again. Is it too late?" I ask.

She opens the door slowly and quietly, then grabs my arm and pulls me in. I spin around and down onto the bed. I sit there. She takes off her long night-robe and throws it on the wicker chair by the door. She has on a teddy and panties.

"I was bettin you were comin back here," she says with a smile while she kisses me and climbs on top of me. We have sex again right away without another word, the exact same way as before, and both of us fall dead asleep, exhausted.

Holy crap.

As time goes by on Halfway, I feel completely comfortable and totally in the swing of things. Though still January, the winter weather starts to dry out. There are less puddles around the gooney chicks, and most of them are old enough and fat enough now to survive hypothermia, unless we get another cold, wet snap. I can feel each day getting a little bit lighter, a little bit warmer, and a little bit less breezy. None of the Naupaka, Beach Morning Glory, or *Tribulus* have flowers now, but they maintain their green foliage.

Though filled with dangerous entrapment and entanglement hazards and obstructions, albatross continue to live on; post the Homo sapiens destruction.

In my office, I look over the bookshelves and find a shark identification guidebook. I quickly flip to the page with Galapagos Reef Shark. Black-tipped Reef Shark sits right below it on the same page, as a comparison. They look almost identical, with the black-tipped slightly less pointed at the snout and with a slightly stouter body. Then I study everything about Galapagos Reef Sharks and see that their range definitely makes it to Halfway; but so does the black-tipped. As a matter of fact, it even says that black-tips live at Halfway! Hmmm, can I trust Myhel at her word, as a scientist, or as a person? I've learned in my life that you always end up paying one way or the other. This has all been way too free so far.

I walk into The Hangar one morning, a few weeks into the job now, to do what have already become, pretty routine orientations. I pass Myhel in the hall with a group of Olderhostile seniors in tow. Man, not a very diverse group are they? They all appear to be white, of money, and nice. Though I have been working on improving the orientation program by shooting slides and sending them off to be mounted at some mail-away company in NYC, I have already added interesting tidbits, and I have memorized my refurbished script, and it flows full of edutainment. As I head down the hall, I run into Deny, the procurement dude for HIC; not to be confused with Ben, the interim Sanctuary Manager. This guy Deny is ex Marine; 19 years in as an underling. Weird. Did he screw up and get booted? Why not stay in the extra year or so and get the retirement? Somehow, with his look, his actions, his persona, basically everything about him, he appears to be a fuck-up to me. He enlisted when he was 17, having his dad lie about his age for him, so he could go to Vietnam. By the time he got in, the war was over, so he hung around the Marines waiting for the next big chance at war. He carries his fitness better than the younger Navy chiefs, and looks to be in his mid fifties now.

He asks me how things are going. I tell him fine. A normal meaningless greeting, with nothing behind it. Then I say, "Hey Deny, you went to Nam?"

Deny responds gruffly, "Nah, I wanted to go somethin bad, but it was ovah before I could get in."

I say, "Really? What are you like 50?" calculating the years in my head and trying to be generous with my assessment.

"Nah," Deny replies, "46".

Wow. He didn't age very well. I'm 32 and I thought he looked old enough to be my father.

Then, he asks if I wish to order something to be delivered onto the atoll.

"Sure, I can get anything from Hono," he states with a can-do attitude.

"How come we don't have veggie burgers?" I gently inquire.

"What? I ain't orderin dhose," he responds.

"Why not?" I say.

"What's wrong with hamburgers? You got something against meat?" implying how un-American I am.

I think to myself for a millisecond. 'Oh no. If I have to explain this to him he will never understand. Since this is a long, complicated discussion, I fear it; but, as an interpretive ranger, I should try to be patient and explain it to him. Embrace it Kestrel Falco. Embrace the challenge.'

As I try to explain it to him, I can see in his moronic eyes, that he is thinking 'What a wuss. What a pussy. What a nerd. How can someone, especially an American, not eat meat? It's a gosh darn sin I tell ya.' I know the explanation goes nowhere, and that's when Loon walks up and says, "Kestrel, why would you rather eat veggie burgers; because of your health, because of animal welfare, or because of the environment?"

And I say, "Environment definitely!"

"That's unconscionable!" Loon replies quickly. "You government types call yourself wildlife supporters or whatever? What about the suffering of those animals? You still let people hunt and kill animals on your sanctuaries. What about what those animals feel, and the pain they feel and go through just to serve US, to feed US? Ya know, just cause we have the will and ability to do it doesn't mean we have the right, or are right. It doesn't mean that we should."

Wow, he kind of sounds like a radical, tactless version of me, and I say, "Yeah, I see your point and I feel for animal welfare, but still to me, the much bigger issue and picture is the environment." Man, I cannot get it out straight. It's hard when you're impassioned about something. "All I'm saying is, human personal health, and the suffering of farm animals, won't matter if The Planet is screwed. We have to think Planet first, then worry about animal and human welfare. It's not like we disagree. They all head up the same path of progress. They're interrelated."

Deny lets out an "Ohh geez. Yoo two should marry each other for krise sake."

"To me, the much bigger picture is the environment and how meat eating is destroying The Planet for non-livestock animals and plants," I continue to blather, un-phased by Deny's weak comment. "If the world went totally vegan, we could stop global warming and other environmental degradation like water pollution. We could save species. We could have enough food to feed everyone, and, as you stated, we could also live healthier, save medical expenses, and cut way back on animal suffering." Obviously, being fresh out of BU has me in mega ramble mode, debate hot.

"Oh god, come on," Deny groans. "You guys are whacked. It says right in the bible we are suppose to eat meat and enjoy it. God gave us meat to eat. You're spittin the meat back in god's face. It's a sin for krise sake."

"The bible is ridiculous," Loon fires back. "Don't use religious texts as defense in your arguments with me," he demands.

Deny looks pretty offended, like someone has just stepped on a flag or something.

I try to temper the debate to avoid violence. "Woah, dude! There have been some good instructions from the bible in the past so I think it may be a leap to call it 'ridiculous'. I know what ya sayin and parts of it are messed up, but all of the religious texts have some value, even as anthropological curiosities."

Loon says, "Oh yeh, name one great thing that ever came out of the Bible?"

I say, "Well, not only is the Bible one of the oldest great fantasy stories to be told, but it was also like one of the first major codes to tell people how to act in civilization and whatever. I mean, we gotta step back and look at the rationale behind having something like that."

Loon looks at me incredulously, "Oh, that's a good one? The epitome of simpletonism?"

Deny looks on in shock. He has never heard of such blasphemy before. He won't admit that he doesn't know anything about the Bible, but he knows it's American to take a strong Christian stance, just like most of the guys he knew in the Marines.

I defend, "Hey, you gotta keep it simple for the masses. As it is, I would argue that The Bible and other books are too technical and metaphorical for most modern people to even understand, with their lack of education."

We both look over at Deny.

Loon jumps in, "Thou shalt not kill. Thou shalt not kill. That's ridiculous. What the hell does that mean? Thou shalt not kill what?"

I say, "I know that's tough, and it's open to interpretation. There are a lot of bible-thumpers out there who say they take the Bible literally, yet, they kill all the time, everyday."

Deny says, "It is lidderall, and I don't kill no one everyday."

I say, "See?" looking at Loon. "How can that be? I think they think it means they shouldn't kill other people," trying to show that there is some good to be gleaned from the ancient past.

Loon states with anger and realization, "Well then that's saying that humans exist above all other creatures. That's what a lot of people say when they're reading the Bible."

I say, "In that case, it should read Thou Shalt Not Kill Man."

Then Loon adds, "But in that case is should be Thou Shalt Not Kill Man as long as you are not going to war, then you are fighting as a Christian Soldier or some shit like that."

This enflames Deny again, "Well, I'm not gettin any veggie burgers!" Deny puts his foot down, "Nobody but you two would eat em anyway."

We part ways.

Thank you Loon. Great diplomacy! I respect his view, intellect, and passion, but certainly not his alienating approach. The last thing I want to do now is get into it any deeper. Look, don't get me wrong, I see both of their sides but I definitely have to side with Loon on this one, except for his bible slamming. For now, he just needs to lay off the hardcore Earth First shit out here, especially considering the element we are dealing with on Halfway, if he doesn't want to instigate a civil war. I love that one "civil war". Ha ha ha, how can a war be civil?

I put my hand on Loon's shoulder and say, "Somebody said once, *An undefined problem has an infinite number of solutions.* In this case, the burden of proof falls on you. Every time I offer you a solution, it's wrong, because you change the definition. I'm taking unilateral control of this situation now because I know you are nothing but an obstinate obstacle. Look, I know there is a lot of bad stuff in religious books that have done way more harm than good, but we still have to look at the good. Ya can't just dismiss the whole thing as ridiculous. I mean, you could say that about everything: The works of Shakespeare, ya know, any movie you've ever seen, ah, pro football. You could make that argument about every human construct that exists and that some place value on."

"Good argument," Loon smiles as he walks down the hall, "but you still don't give a shit about the animals being raised in farms

112

for you to eat, and you work for HAWS. That's just wrong," he says as he turns and continues down the hall, getting in the last word.

He's right again. I am so close to vegan, and yet, I still make exceptions for myself all the time. I just had a Mahi-Mahi burger yesterday. Some of the FNs had caught some Mahi-Mahi, and an Ono, off the outer slope of the atoll mount to the south. They had a barbeque with singing and dancing, and lots of drinking again, outside their barracks. It was great.

I really love my job, even with the drawbacks; like some of the people out here. For example, a biologist came on the last flight. I hoped she'd be cool, like Dietera or Banette, and yet, she proved to be something completely else. Jellie, Mother Earth of The Turtle Project on The Big Island, apparently possessing even less of a bio background than I do, strode onto the tarmac. She doesn't need a silly bio degree. She does everything by feel. Intuition. Loving the Planet. She performs estrogen 'experiments' at the Hawksbill Turtle hatchlings' expense, preaches about the power of the syncratic menstruations on turtle patrol at Kamehame and Punalu'u, and she strongly states that men have screwed up the Planet. I agree with her: Men mainly have screwed everything up, and love will help the animals, but not blind, thoughtless, stupid love. Smart love. We have smart bombs. Why can't we have smart love? And men like Lorenz, E.O. Wilson, and Zinn, they haven't hurt; they have helped. I can see why she thinks men screw everything up. With a 23-year-old freak of a daughter, Jellie must have somehow got impregnated at around 17-years-old. So men have screwed her up, and literally.

For some reason, if you're smart, you can't also have love. Love is for the downtrodden, the sweaty immigrants in the barrios; not for US sensitive, intelligent, progressive to moderate, middle-class white folk. Nope, we can't find love, especially amongst each other. What if we spend billions of dollars on Smart Love instead of Smart Bombs? Where would The World be right now? I agree with her, don't get me wrong. Jellie and her dreads patrol of charismatically challenged hippy-wannabees love animals and would never do them *intentional* harm, so I see them as allies in the war to save the animals. It's the bad science that kills me. The lack of credible technique, the 'obvious insights' that turn into

113

anything but possibly correct, and a multitude of failings beyond that of even the most normal, basic, boring biologist, make her and her ilk a liability: A tricky, untrustworthy yet frequently helpful, if we can limit the damage they do, liability.

Pear-shaped Jellie isn't *that* whacked. I think her daddy is some kind of fancy shmancy scientist type at Wood's Hole. I tell Zart she looks like that weird "Hanka for a hunka cheese" guy, or like the Big Fig Newton. Zart laughs so hard, his eyes water and he can't catch his breath. She looks like she knows her way around a lab, and though not genius, at least she is not completely scary like Kilgro.

As I swim out here in the middle of the ocean, waiting, just waiting, my pinky throbs. It reminds me of how she fucked it up. I guess it doesn't matter, now that I'm about to be dead. Funny huh? The things we really give a shit about don't matter when we're dead. If I had lived, I'm sure over time the knuckle would have chronically kept popping out and causing me nuisance arthritic pain. Lucky I'm about to die, I guess. I remember back to that day, over a year ago, in February.

One day, Jellie asks Ben if she can have some help over on Eastern Island. She only has Myhel and Han to assist, and though Myhel may be a short, stout lass, and all 105-pounds of Han would give full effort, they simply are not strong enough alone to handle a pinniped. Jellie's job consists of radio-tagging monk seal pups for a number of studies, including mortality.

While Jellie attaches the transmitter, we will have to hold the freaked-out seal down. Though Jellie is of more ample size, not quite two Hans put together, she looks incredibly flabby and weak. "So that crew simply will not be strong enough," Ben explains to me.

I gladly volunteer, relishing another opportunity to directly impact wildlife in a big, positive way.

We tag one seal on Spit on the way over, then another little one right near the pier on Eastern. Not too small, because they have such high mortality rates that it's a waste of transmitters and too stressful for the pups; but not too big because then you've got a pissed juvie seal, that can kick your ass, on your hands. Speaking of hands, Seal Finger, the name given to the infection usually associated with the bacteria in a seal's mouth from a bite, ". . . is friggin gross and really nasty!" according to Jellie.

Jellie spies a seal with her bins. "Wait here while I check this one out," she orders, in charge.

I look down the beach with my hand blocking the high sun. "That one is way too big," I mumble to Myhel and Han under my breath. "What is she lookin at that one for?"

A few minutes later, Jellie waves us down to her part of the beach. "Let's do this one," she whispers enthusiastically. "Kestrel, you get the head. Everyone knows the procedure right?"

We all nod our heads and mumble as we grab what we need and get ready, like zombies, trusting that she knows what the hell she is doing.

Myhel whispers to Jellie, "I, I thought a seal this big would be, ya know, off the list, ya know?"

Jellie scolds, "Shut up." Her leathery skin crinkles between her eyes and temples, and between her eyebrows, and on the bridge of her nose.

We sneak up quietly on the seal and then quickly cut it off from the water. It bellows in protest, and by dancing around it in a circle, we get its head facing inland again.

"Now!" Jellie cries with a hysterical panic to her voice. I smoothly slip the hoop-net over the seal's head and lie on top of it in a way that pins it to the beach. Han jumps onto the tail while Myhel, having already had ample recent riding practice, straddles mid back. This is a big, powerful teenager. A third-year Monk Seal, or J3, can weigh three hundred pounds easily, and they feel like solid muscle; like a muscle sausage. Imagine how a big snake feels in your hands, but much stronger, faster, smarter, and slicker. One of the sleekest seals in the World, Hawaiian Monk Seals still have more strength than you or I can image.

I am looking straight into the seal's face, through the net. It has a strong, bull neck, and stinky breath, . . . worse than a dog.

"Keep an eye on his breathing!" Jellie yells. "Oh, ow, ah, watch the breathing!" she nags repeatedly.

Though I have the seal firmly, I can see it closing its eyes intentionally, as if saving its energy. Its nostrils open briefly to blast sand out. I am chocking it a little, but I feel if I let up any more, this guy will thrash me. It is practically twice my weight.

Jellie almost finishes with the tag. "His breathing?"

See? As a scientist she should know better than to go right away to 'He'? If it was a cute pup, I bet she would have said 'She'. Dietera or Banette would never let themselves be so anthropomorphic. "Done!" Jellie announces proudly. The seal tenses up. It can tell the alien abduction type probing part is over and braces for the next phase. This should be the simple part, especially on a big seal like this. Jellie, being the principle investigator and in charge of this project, should say "3, 2, 1, go!" At that point, all three of us should jump clear of the seal and roll away from its path to the ocean. Instead, Han has already been casually instructed to get off. Jellie, a little under her breath, distinctly says, though my ears can't believe it, "Okay Myhel."

The instant Myhel gets off, the seal strongly corkscrews around. Mouth wide agape, and only an inch from my face, my left pinky finger gets caught in either the net, or the folds of the neck skin. Either way, it happens so fast, all I hear is a quick, painful snap. I dive off of the seal and roll to my right. The seal quickly cranes around and starts to inchworm toward the pastel blue and white lagoon. Not having been cleared properly, the net becomes entangled in the transmitter near the seal's tail.

"Oh. Oh. Aw. Ah Oh ooh," Jellie continues, dancing in place like she has to 'go' really bad; like her feet burn, or like someone with a six-shooter makes her 'dance'. I imagine early *Homos* must have done this same dance at the sight of prey, or some other form of dinner, or at the sight of lions or bears.

The net hooks tightly onto the transmitter, and now the seal is dragging it into the water. This is wicked dangerous. The seal could drown, starve, or get munched by a tiger with that hooped net thing hanging off its tail.

"Oh. Oh no. Aoh!" Jellie frets.

I sprint to the plastic hoop, about the size of a thick hula-hoop, scoop it up, and then I run to the front of the seal and jam the hoop into its mouth. The seal growls, and bites down on it. Its wide eyes look frantic and freaked. I stand in the waves up to my ankles, with my uniform boots and brown socks soaked. Every time the seal tries to wiggle its head one way or the other to break for the lagoon, I cut it off. I break down like a defensive back, keeping my legs chugging as my boots sink into the soft, wet coral sand.

Myhel, Han, and then Jellie, all sprint to the tail and struggle to remove the net. Han pulls out a jackknife to cut it while Myhel tries to untangle it and Jellie continues to say, "Ooh. Oh a no, ah, Aoh, jeezzsh."

Somehow, someone gets the net off and I hear 'Clear!' I pull the hoop from its mouth and step aside. The seal looks around for the briefest second, knowing it is really free this time, and swims off, looking back once to see if we are following.

Jellie calms her hysteria, then looks around sharply and says, "Well, at least no one got hurt."

I instantly reflex my hand up to her face and say, "Really?!?"

My left pinky looks like one of the 'z's from the *ZZ Top* logo. Jellie covers her mouth and gags momentarily.

Han says, "Let's go Mr. Kestrel."

We head quickly for the boat.

"You didn't follow procedure mister!" Jellie says to me with a crooked eye, taking the first step to covering her ass.

"What?" I question in shock.

"You are not suppose to put the hoop in the seal's mouth. That could injure the mouth lining," she professes.

"You have got to be shitting me," I retort. "I saved that seal's life." I am pissed.

"Yah, see it your way," Jellie says with a blow off, realizing internally that she might lose this argument.

Han and Myhel both look at her with narrow eyes.

"How did you sex him so quickly?" I quiz Jellie on the boat as it bounces on the white caps, as we speed along the inner lagoon and across the channel to the inner harbor.

"Oh crap. In all the excitement, I forgot to sex him," she admits disappointedly.

"Him? There, you said it again!" I snap.

She explains half-heartedly, with a nervous laugh, "Oh you know, I just meant him. Doesn't mean it is really a 'him'."

I look around for an icepack, but I can't find one. "I know you think I'm taking it too seriously but I refer to living things as 'it' until I can secure a sex. You left us with the impression that you knew it was male," I say as my finger throbs.

"Oh, well I'm so sorry I left you with the impression that he was a male," she says extremely sarcastically, trying to marginalize me in front of Myhel and Han, like *I'm* the freak; and taking no blame for my injury.

"Hey, don't you take that tone with me. My finger is fucked up because of you. You were supposed to count to three!" I shout over the engine as we enter the inner harbor and pull straight up to a pier where the ambulance waits. Not waiting for long, but waiting. Waiting again on Halfway.

Yes, that's right, we have a real-life ambulance on Halfway; driven by the Filipino nurses usually, or occasionally, by Dr. Chance himself. Often, the ambulance would be parked by the runway with the fire trucks and other emergency equipment, waiting for the plane to land. It gives them all something to do.

Dr. Chance looks at us as we approach the driver's door window. "What happened?" he asks.

We all look at each other but no one says anything. Jellie looks away, upset.

"My finger is either broken or dislocated," I respond neutrally, giving the symptoms, without the causes: Something I almost never do.

"You in pain?" Dr. Chance asks as I climb into the front seat.

"Totally," I say, "severe, and throbbing."

"Well if it's hurtin, then at least it is still there," Dr. Chance says, putting a light spin on it.

Jellie becomes really pissed and indignant now, and won't talk anymore or answer anyone's questions.

Dr. Chance drives the ambulance back to the clinic while his little, cute 6 year-old son, one of 6 of the kids on the atoll now that more arrived on the last flight, hands me an icepack out of the doctor's tackle box. I smack it on my knee to get it frosty, then curve the icepack around my hand to get the ice pressed against both sides of my knuckle. Looking back, I can see the rest of them unloading the boat and preparing to pull the bright orange Boston Whaler out of the water.

"I bring you bike to you house Mr. Kestrel," Han yells in the distance. I gesture a thanks with my good hand.

At the clinic, Dr. Chance takes a quick X-ray and asks me details about the incident while he works the pinky, when suddenly and surprisingly to me, he pops it back in. I involuntarily jump out of my seat, my arms coming high off the table, as a reflex to the sharp pain that runs up the nerves in my arm. Dr. Chance hands me the X-ray. I hope Drats' publisher is not so lame as to omit such a picture; worth many more than the thousand words usually attributed to it; 5 or 7 times as many.

For the next week or so, Jellie just doesn't seem to be around. Though it's hard to avoid each other on this teensy atoll, she must be laying low. February arrives, with no sign of her. I haven't tried to dodge her or modify my routine.

My wondering ends with a stressed call on my cell phone.

"Kestrel, is Chipweldi there?" I hear Jellie ask directly, and sounding a little panicky again.

She is asking about my new supervisor, who just arrived on atoll on last Thursday's flight.

"Nope. No one is in the office. Everybody is off, or off atoll. I'm the only one on, but technically I'm off. I'm just working overtime finishing up some tourist maps. What's up?" I say, professionally, so she won't think I hold a childish grudge, but at the same time, not being a friendly friend.

A shiny metal brace and some white medical tape hold my finger now, with a little black padded cushion glued to the bend. I no longer keep the bandage around it to hold it in place, nor to relieve the shock of banging it or hurting it when I sleep. The finger definitely still hurts. I can play Ultimate, but I have to do all my catches as right-handed snags.

"Ohwhhh," Jellie moans.

"What's the matter?" I repeat.

"Things just aren't going my way," she says with a whine, seeking sympathy.

Oh no. Not again. First she trashes my finger, then she gets bit on the ankle by a little tiny friggin pup. Now what?

"I'm out in a golf cart with Kilgro and we ran out of power," she says.

"Did you call anyone over at ASS?" I ask, following standard protocol.

"No, we didn't call anyone or know who to call. Do we call like the motor pool? I think everyone is gone for the day and already eating in The Galley," she continues, with Kilgro egging her on, supporting her from the background.

119

I can see The Galley from my office window. "It looks like a lot of people are already done eating and they are wiping the tables," I report.

"Oh no! Can you come get us Kestrel? Please?" I can hear another 'yeah please, please please please' in the background. I haven't even really talked to Jellie much, since she has been on the atoll, but she works with Kilgro sometimes, and from my Big Island Turtle Project experience, I know they both already think shit about me. I don't think Jellie knows about Myhel yet, but I'm sure people are figuring it out slowly. I don't think anyone but Zart knows. Am I a fool to think that? That's what I think. Either way, whether they like me or not, I have to go help them. I'm the ranger. Technically, Chipweldi should be not only going to help them, but should also cite them for running out of power like irresponsible fools; not that it's dangerous really, but just a nuisance inconvenience. Chipweldi is so useless; I don't even bother to think of calling him on this one. I decide to just handle it myself like I have to with everything in my office.

I look around. Chipweldi took the keys for the pick up truck, against procedure again. What a fuck up.

"Chipweldi, it's the only vehicle we have and sometimes I need to use it. You know I used it all the time before you came on atoll," I told Chipweldi during his first two days on the job, a month after Zart returned.

"Hu he, I doesn't want the drunk guys driving around in the truck. I gotta be on call incase of emergency. Heh, hut," Chipweldi giggles. "If those guys screw-up big-time, it's a huge headache for me, and paperwork, hee hee hea, and then I gotta call em all in for a Come to Jesus session. Hee, I don't want to do that."

Stupid. Now I can't use the truck.

The only thing I can find keys for is the ATV. I bust down to the South side of the atoll near Bulky Dump, and see the two of them sitting in the golf cart. Such stark contrasts: A pear-shaped, high-maintenance headache of a dread-headed man-hater smell-hag, who claims she hails from the beaches of Hawaii, but really comes from ultra-conservative wealthy Euro-immigrant stock in Oklahoma. And her 'glimmer' twin Kilgro, who quite frankly could scare the spots off of a Magnificent Snake Eel. Jellie's dim green smile outshines her dark, black soul and tanned withered

120

completion. Her skin has a beaten leather quality to it, but a soft leather. Guys could fall for Jellie, even with her adult kid, as long as they got sucked into and went along with her whole game. Kilgro, on the other hand, never has a chance.

I crawl underneath, hooking the chain through the frame and axel of the golf cart.

"Don't touch the brake unless you absolutely have to. Just turn the wheel nice and smooth and straight and follow right along behind me," I order Jellie.

"When would I absolutely have to -- have to?" Jellie stutters with fear.

"Only if you are going to crash into something," I reply quickly.

"I'm not planning on that," Jellie says, looking over at Kilgro, who grins.

"Me neither. That's why I just gave you simple instructions to follow," I say.

"Oh. Like we need instructions from you. Thank you Mr. Super Ranger," Jellie sarcastically jabs, showing her insecurities again.

"How did you run out of power?" I ask slyly, looking over at Kilgro with a smile. She frowns.

"Oh, wha, oh, it's my fault now that I am stranded out here? Pooffff," Jellie rants with indignity.

"Well it certainly isn't mine, or your new helper's, or anyone who's off-atoll, or any of the guys finishing up in The Galley", as my voice ascends. Jellie stops and looks at Kilgro. That's right. Jellie got her into this mess.

I finish, "No one is to have carts out late if they have no one on duty to back them up."

"Oh, you are really great at blaming people aren't you? Just blame everything away. Nothing can ever be your fault," Jellie bitches.

Fuck. What an idiot loser. No wonder no one wants to go near her. Even desperate guys on Halfway who haven't seen a girl in a year still would way rather stay lonely than hook-up with Jellie and all her ample baggage.

I hop onto the ATV, kick start it, and begin driving back. Along the end of the runway, I suddenly feel the need to jump off of the ATV to dispatch a paralyzed gooney laying face down on the concrete.

"Kestrel, what are you doing? You are not going to do that right in front of me." Jellie stammers as I quickly approached the albatross with the loppers. "Oh no, oh god, gross." She looks away as I open the loppers around the bird's neck.

Kilgro yells as she gets out of her cart, "At least let me hold it and tell it goodbye so it knows we didn't do it out of evilness or anger!"

I yell without turning my head, "Too late." Snip! The albatross is dead. Just like that.

"Oh. You are sick. That is horrible." Jellie complains.

"What would you have me do?" I ask.

"You need to let her know she is loved," Kilgro says.

I yell, loosing my temper, "She! How do you know it was a female gooney?"

God; we will never see eye to eye on any of this stuff. I see what Jellie and Kilgro are saying, but the fastest thing to do, for the birds, not for me, is to put them down as quickly and painlessly as possible.

I stand next to the ATV and put the loppers away, "The animal doesn't understand me. It doesn't know if I am going to kiss it or kill it. All it knows is that I am coming near it and its stress level goes way up," I say.

Jellie chides, "They know. Animals can sense when I approach them that I do so with love."

"That's great. I do too," I say now frothing at the mouth and mad at the idea that I am going to totally miss dinner. "I love animals more than anyone I know, which is 100%, and you can't love them more than that. But huggin them, and saying goodbye, makes *you* feel good. It's for you. Stop being so fuckin homocentric! Tough love is the best love in this scenario and if you are incapable of giving it then you should get out of the field!"

I hop back on the ATV and crank it up. I think of them as bio-hacks, not as biologists like Banette and Dietera. I feel that if I go over and try to caress and speak nicely to that bird, all I'm going to do is add stress and pain to that bird's life. Am I wrong? I think people have auras and vibes, but I think their minds tell them things they feel for the animals and plants that those creatures simply don't feel back. Is Kilgro's intuition that much more powerful than mine? If Jellie is so much more sensitively intuitive than me, can she feel how stupid I think she is?

I look back as the towline becomes taut and I can see them both sitting back there with their arms folded, frowning. I feel like I should just cut the line and leave them. They can walk back. It's less than a mile. I can see Jellie pointing at the splint on my pinky and saying something about it to Kilgro; probably blaming me. When we get near the Seaplane Hangar, we ride over the large, concrete tie-down slabs, and I look back to see that the girls are having a grand old time yucking it up. The next second later, I discover that neither of my left tires are on the ground. My ATV pulls right, forcing me to jump and role off the ATV, which then flips and does a 363, eventually landing up on its wheels again. They laugh. Stupid. They had driven the golf cart way out to my right, forcing the weight of the cart to pull the ATV over sideways. Luckily, due to my tumbling abilities developed in football and in my UCLA theatre movement classes, I didn't get hurt, but this is incredibly aggravating to me. I look around. It looks like there is not a single human witness, just plenty of albatross laughing their vents off at me.

"What the fuck is wrong with you?" I flip out. They try to keep straight faces, but laugh at me. I am a gorilla to them: A simple Neanderthal. "Urgh, rughg," I cannot keep my cool.

I check the ATV, then tow their sorry asses back to the ASS office. I unhook the chain, and bail out of there without a word. They are going to blame me and say I am the hothead and all that kind of shit. In this case, it's *tow* against one, hee hee hee. I return the ATV, only to see Chipweldi slowly cruising along in the truck in the sunset. He has his headlights on, and as I pass him to pull into the office garage, he says, "Hay, you not suppose to be joyridin in the public equipment. He hi, I think I'm gonna tell Ben we need to have a Come to Jesus session onah you."

Rrrrrrrr! I am so pissed. Joy riding!? He is the one who is fuckin joy riding and almost got me seriously hurt cause he can't follow simple protocols. I shutdown the ATV, hang the keys, close the garage, lock the doors, turn off the lights, hit the alarm, grab my backpack, and sprint over to The Galley in my short shorts and boots. The door is closed. All the trays have been removed. Crap.

"Mr. Kestrel. Mr. Kestrel," some of the FNs wave me in. I slip past the door with the closed sign on it.

"You miss dine-her. We make a plate you. We make plate you. Wait. Please Wait." They look down at my legs and I turn my back to the counter.

I discreetly look down to see my knee is bleeding profusely. I didn't even notice I got scratched, but both knees are dirty and I am bleeding a lot. Luckily, Chipweldi didn't see that. He doesn't ever appear to notice anything. He would have had a field day on how I can't ride, or some dumb-ass shit like that to make him feel less inferior. I'm sorry I'm five-eleven and three-quarters, and he is like five-one or something. I know that must suck for people who really don't like being short. Luckily, I had a growth spurt at seventeen.

I grab some napkins while they are not looking, and wipe the sticky blood and dirt off of my hairy half-Italian legs. I quickly wipe off my hands, the scrapes on my arms and elbows, and dump the napkins in the trashcan. Mahalo!

The FN returns with a paper plate with rice, lentil curry, and a green salad with a mini French-bread roll.

"Thank you," I say gratefully.

"Anything for you Mr. Kestrel. You are great man Mr. Kestrel. Great man," they say as I walk out.

"Thank you. Thank you so very much," I gesture with a bow as I go back over to my office to get on my bike. I don't know if I am to bow or what, but I feel compelled to nod up and down to express gratitude. As I leave, I see Jellie and Kilgro finally ambling over to The Galley like they are out for an evening stroll. They look in the windows, but see no staff. They pull on the locked door, then turn away with frowns and walk off dejected. They should have hustled.

A few days later, after giving a tour, and posting flyers for an albatross documentary I have decided to show in The Station Theater, as an educational film series for all Halfwayians, I get a call regarding a gooney caught in an ironwood near the runway. I grab some new West Beach Trail signs I had just designed, printed, and laminated, and I hop on my bike with a pair of loppers in my basket.

Kestrel frees a misfortunate gooney from an alien ironwood.

What is an ironwood? I know, they use ironwood to describe 20 types of plants around The World. This just happens to be an Australian Pine. As you can imagine, the Navy planted them because they grow fast and dense, are easy to propagate with no effort, and are considered a trash tree and cost nothing. On the negative side, as you can also imagine, they are impossible to control and spread like wildfire. Speaking of wildfire, they also burn like Roman Candles, and cause a horrible strike hazard for our birds. After realizing what a problem they are, I have decided to start Ironwood Parties. This is how it works; we get a group of people in their workout gear to meet at a designated spot. We crank tunes on my boom box, I lead a group stretch, and then start going nuts on ironwoods; pulling most of them out by hand and tackling them. For the bigger, tougher young pines, we dig by hand or with shovels. After a meter or so, we try to pull them out by the roots. Within 30 minutes, everyone is huffing and puffing, soaked with sweat and covered in grainy atoll reef sand. Fun! We use almost no tools, and absolutely no power tools, so that we get a solid, hard, well-rounded aerobic workout, while we wipeout noxious alien trees, and leave no carbon footprint.

Now on my bike, whizzing by the Hangar, I see Mount Zart, one of our favorite ironwood party spots. Then suddenly, a gooney almost takes my head off.

"Oh yeah, I'm on a mission," I scream to the puffy white Pacific clouds, with gusto.

As I approach the runway, only a light breeze blows out of the west, and I am probably hitting around 31 mph. I am flying, and suddenly, there, halfway along the long row of trees along the string of landing lights, I look up and see an albatross, hanging by the neck with its wings dangling, about 11, maybe 13 meters up. I lay my bike over on its side and quickly make a three-fifty-eight scan. Nobody around. I quickly climb up the dead *Casuarina* and firmly grip the Laysan Albatross by the head, where I gently un-wedge it out of the crotch and with one graceful swoop, lower it to the ground and release it. It flops forward, and then falls onto its back, wriggling. One of its wings has twisted so far around that it has done a complete rotation and looks aligned again. How long had it been hanging here by its neck?

Kestrel tries hard, always giving 100%, and thinking creature first.

I quickly assess that the damage is fatal, grab the loppers, and decapitate the poor creature. Blood squirts out in laser streams, and the carcass shakes and shutters, shattered, for a moment or two. I move the carcass over toward the bushes and check the legs and wings for jewelry; you know, bands, tags, etc. I dump the gooney as far into the bushes as I can, and rub the bloody blades into the sand to dust bathe them. I hop on my bike and head toward the West Beach to post the new signs. Even though no one witnesses my act, I am so proud. That would end up being the funniest thing about my fieldwork. Day after day, week after year, no one ever really gets to see my work. You have to just be psyched and crank, even when no one is looking; just like when I run. No one follows me on my run. It's about my run.

I'm *not* proud about cutting the bird's head off. I'm proud that I am working for the U.S. Animal Protection Service, and that I give 100%, and that I am physically capable of helping animals in ways that many other weak, nerdy lab biologists never could. Who would I rather have doing this job? I would like to see Jellie or Kilgro climb up like a Spider Monkey and quickly end that creatures suffering. I understand that putting fatally wounded animals down, fast, efficiently, and safely, is like being an angel of mercy for these creatures. Jellie, for one, doesn't share my basic fundamental beliefs.

As I ride west, I think to myself. I hate killing birds. Hate hate hate it. The option has to be understood. Humans put trees on a barren sand atoll. Humans built hard asphalt runways, and cinderblock buildings, and tall metal towers with invisible wires. If an albatross hits one of these structures after spending years in a literally liquid, impermanent world, it will break a wing and slowly starve to death because it won't be able to forage for food over the wave tops. I'm not talking about a slow human starvation death, like 3 weeks. I'm talking about seabirds that can live for months without food, as they slowly wither away, or are eaten alive by rats.

Biking along now, the pinky nags at me and throbs. I'm dwelling on it. It is hard to forget when the pain keeps reminding you. Wow, a lot of shit can happen in an instant. One stupid thing and blam! The monk seal, the ATV; I could have gotten really hurt. Gotta stay sharp. Dr. Chance wanted to prescribe me painkillers for the finger. He is as prescription happy as they are in Tokyo. I said no way. That's the last thing I need, to be hopped-up on percocet or some synthesized prescription crap.

As I continue biking down the runway with these obstreperous ubiquitous thoughts railing throughout my cranium, I reach the west beach and turn north-northeast onto the soft sand. Just at that moment, I snap out of everything that had just been blasting through my head for like the last 7 minutes, and I focus on my first location and post my first sign. I head up trail, and I can hear an ATV humming over the distant reef surf. Who is it but, my current supervisor, Chipweldi. The ATV is running, but Chipweldi looks like he is picking his fingernails and his mind appears to be a million miles away. As I approach on my silent bike on the sandy trail, he looks up a little surprised from his seated position on the vehicle.

"Hey, what are you doin out here?" he says in a friendly tone.

"I'm mounting these new West Beach Trail signs," I respond cheerfully. This had been mentioned clearly in the morning staff meeting. Does he listen to anything? Is it 70's druggy memory loss? I think he just doesn't care.

"Hee, hee, I heard that ain't the only thing you bean mountin. Hee," Chipweldi chides through his lawn-gnome lips.

My head snaps towards him, my ears in disbelief. "What?" I question.

"Oh, ya know, that whole thing gives me a big headache," he whines.

"What are you talking about?" I ask, confused.

"Ya know, it's not gonna matter to the seals. They don't read the signs. Hee he ha," he says with his added nervous laugh.

5 different things shoot through my mind simultaneously, as usual. 'What?' I think to myself, 'This is my job and he is my current boss, and the biologists and seal monitors all agree that the seals are so shy (hence monk) that if they see hide or hair of a human, they won't haul out to rest and digest, and more importantly, they certainly won't feel it's safe enough for pupping. What is this guy doing out here? Why is he *working* for the APS? Does he really give a shit about anything?' Does he know already that I've been messing around with Myhel?

I stand there for a second, dumbfounded, and look down at the signs in my hand.

"Hey, how about we take shep by the hind legs? Hee hee ha," he says.

What the hell is that all about? Maybe this atoll really is gay and this is what happens to all the guys alone on the atoll, like prison.

"What'd mean, who's Shemp?" I am afraid to ask.

"What? You don't know what I'm talking about? Shep," he chirps back. As if I had just fallen off the turnip truck and knew nothing of being a Fed, he goes on. Keep in mind I have only become a ranger this year. "You know, he ha hee like screw the pooch. He hee ha," he giggles.

"I'm sorry, I'm not following you," I say, completely lost. Maybe I am dumb.

"C'mon. How old arh you? Don't ya know nothin? Let's goof off. How many times have you ever been told *that* by yuh boss?" he says with enticement.

Is this some kind of Frank Zappa-esque, late 60's stick-it-to-da-man shit or what? I come out on the West Beach Trail, posting signs and looking over some *Verbasina* that needs pulling, and imaging how I will bend the trail at cool angles, leaving open areas behind a hidden berm or log to use as natural blinds for monk seal viewing. The green beetles are plentiful, and I had not only just saved the hanging albatross from anguish and suffering, but I also took out a few centipedes with my Leatherman before I heard the ATV. I cut their heads off quickly and try to avoid touching any part of their segmented bodies as they wrap tightly around the metal and my fingers.

I have all this type of stuff going through my mind, and all the new military history I absorb and learn, running though my brain. I have all kinds of new and shocking stuff to do, to know, to learn about, and I run into the one thing I can't deal with. SLACKER! I was the smallest, weakest, least talented kid on my high school football team, and yet, I worked as hard as I could every single practice, knowing full well that my chances to get into a game were nil. Now my boss is telling me to fuck-off on the job. Is this a test? From him? No way. Now it *IS* a test: A test to see if I will be "cool like him", or if I will be a goody-two-shoes. I don't know what to say, but I can tell Chipweldi knows, by my reaction, that I will not join his cadre of time-wasters.

This guy is only one generation ahead of me, and yet, we are a million miles apart. I like to work. He doesn't. But you can't say that about a whole generation right. I'm so sick of that 'best generation of all time' crap. It's the individuals who make up that generation that matter. Every time I hear someone say, 'Kids these days', I have to laugh my ass off. Firstly because, some kids are good and some are bad; always. Some individuals are sometimes good, and some sometimes bad, but the parents raise the kids, as does society. How do the kids get fucked-up? Who makes the kids nasty? Human Nature? Violent cartoons? What would Lorenz argue? Hitler, Stalin, Mussolini; there are lots of examples of people from 'the greatest generation' who ya wouldn't want to have as an in-law.

I look at Chipweldi for a second, then look out over the gorgeous Pacific whitecaps and say, "I guess I'm gonna just finish posting these signs and get back to the office to finish the new visitor brochure."

I turn and walk over to my bike, pick it up, and start biking down the path, without looking back at Chipweldi to see his expression. I don't even want to know, either way. He's a waste. He turns the wheel backwards.

Luckily for me, less than a month after this interaction, Amb arrives on Halfway; the new Sanctuary Manager. He is to take over, and really take over. No interim command for him. He is one of the biggest big wigs of the entire Animal Protection Service. I am really looking forward to this. At one point, he was the manager of all APS Sanctuaries. He could be a huge boost to my career if I work hard and maintain my diligence.

Before I go to The Hangar to meet Amb, I swing by Myhel's room. After 'the second coming', I tell her I have to leave to meet the plane. She looks at me a little sad at first.

She says, resigned, "I know. Ya don't have to explain it to me. Guys just want to leave when it's ovah eh."

Hmmm, has this really been her experience, or did she pick that up off pop culture? If guys really do always bail on her after the deed, that don't say much for her. And now we've been doing it all these times, and I never pulled one of those rush off deals once. I like snuggling and squeezing her. Even if I am not in love with her, it feels nice, and though my heart is lonely, it makes me feel less so. I like the contact and emotional warmth: The distant, non-committal warmth, as she requested. I'm secure with my manhood, whatever the fuck that means, and I can hug a woman all I want and feel fine with it. I can hug a dog all night too, non-sexually of course. I love sleeping with a warm, heart-beating being. Bunnies, cats; you know what it's like sleeping with an animal. I've tried sleeping with snakes, but it's hard not to roll over on them, and sleeping with ducklings is great, especially if you can get them to figure out that we don't poop in the bed. Swirly, a rescued Mallard I once raised, learned to poop on the paper, and all together stopped pooping on the bed or on my shirt as he slept on my chest, occasionally waking to gently dabble my lower lip and the tip of my nose with his bill. The only thing I don't like sleeping with are men or boys. I'm not a homophobe, and I'm not a homosexual. If I can sleep with women and animals, why can't I sleep with men? I'm sure I could. I have no desire to. I wouldn't call that homophobic. I'd call that homo-disinterested. I think homophobia is a misnomer anyway. Homophobia should literally mean fear of *Homo sapiens*, or the genus *Homo*, like misanthropes. Homosexuals should really refer to it as homosexual-phobia. As a scientist, *"Homo"* does not mean gay to me. *"Homo"* means the genus of *Homo*, like *Homo erectus*, *Homo habilis*, and other Homos that went extinct at the hands of the big-brained *Homo sapiens*. Calling a gay guy the lazy slur "homo" is a totally misrepresenting label, to both the gay target, and to the entire genus *Homo*; of whom only 10-20% are actually homosexual.

As I realize my completely homocentric digression, the synapses firing at light-speed again, I say, lying next to her, gently, but sincerely, "Whoa whoa, wait a minute. I think I've already proven to you with the number of nights I've slept here that I'm not like that at all. Secondly, if you think for a second I would ever risk my job or performance for screwing around, you got another thing comin. I'm organized enough to have sex with you as much as either of us want and still do my job well."

I want her to understand that I don't want to play any power games. You know, like how the girl ignores you all day and tells you she doesn't want it, but as soon as a football game comes on or something else a guy might be really into, right away she is suddenly available and has lots of time and really has to have it RIGHT NOW, jumping up and down on the bed in her panties. It makes em feel more valued, especially if they have low self-esteem, which tends to be mostly tied to laziness in my experience. I get up and start pulling my white briefs and shorts on, unknowingly having said the exact right thing to get her to fall more in love with me. I have no idea how much she really feels for me.

She plays it very cool on the exterior. "I respect that," she says, "Oh wait a minute," she thinks aloud, "I have to go meet the plane too!" she says with a goofy 'U.P.' laugh.

We laugh, and with that I give her a hug and a kiss, trying to get her to just relax and avoid pushing things.

She starts looking around for her clothes strewn about, then adds with hope, "Can we ride together?"

"I gotta go get my uniform on and get Zart, but we can swing by if you want to ride over with us," I say quickly as I hop on my bike. Again, I can see a little disappointment in her eyes. Her fragility starts to show more and more each week. Maybe her idea about us having casual sex is not such a great idea for either of us after all. Like I said, it's been boring but okay for me, but it could be doing her some mental damage.

Back in my room, I bang on my buddy's door.

"Zart, you ready to roll?" I announce.

I hear the door open a moment later, but I am already all the way back in my room, buttoning my shirt by now.

"Yah, you nervous about the new chief," he says with a hearty laugh as he kills a Pete's Wicked Ale.

"We gotta swing by Myhel's on the way over there," I report.

"Hey, ya know, not that it's my business or anything, but you better watch out for her," he warns.

"What?" I say with surprise.

"She was married, or almost, then she came back here, and she has a reputation," he continues disjointedly.

Okay, wait a minute. I like Zart, but a barely know him. I know Myhel a little bit better, cause I've been sleeping with her. Why would he say this stuff to me? He's certainly isn't gettin any out here. Jealous? No. I don't see that in him really.

"Dude, can you be more blunt? I'm kinda more stupid then I look," I say.

Zart laughs, "You are a funny bastard. I'm just sayin, stay away from Myhel. I think you are gonna be sorry."

As we lock our doors and start down the hallway, our voices are amplified, so we lower them to a whisper.

"Can you give me a concrete example of what you are talking about?" I ask.

I can see Zart does not like the fact that I won't simply take his advice, and that he has to put himself through the effort of actually thinking and talking articulately.

"Does every friend of yours have to do so much work to hang around you?" Zart asks. "It's so much work to just talk with you. Can't you just sit and be quiet, and take a yes or no answer?"

Funny, I always thought one of my strengths was my energy and high level of hyper-activity, and my gregarious, fun-loving nature. But, NO! I have learned from my sucky bosses at BU, and from my family, and even from my friends like Dietera, and now Zart, and later from the love of my life Chelonia, that they hate me. They hate when I laugh and smile. They hate when I want to hear the true story and get the details. They hate when I question where they got their info, or worse, when I say things like "Who told you that?" or "What makes you think that is true?", or worst of all "Who told you to think that?" They really hate that one, but the point is, we all think things and got them from somewhere. If I ask that, it's like asking "Do you understand why you are asking me that?" Call it my Socratic method if you will, but that's the way I function, learn, have fun, enjoy life, and I hate the lazy cynics who can't humor me. Ty the Navajo Guy, another APS co-worker I had shared an office with, in the Mojave Desert as a bio tech, would ask me to step out of his office because my glowing aura shone so brightly that it blew him out of the office. Sorry? 'Why' is the most important question, always! Why? Why? Why? I hate when they give a news report and they don't tell you why. '15,000 people today were killed in a horrible genocide in Blewblondia, film at 11.' Why? Tell me why, right in that sentence, and I will be happy.

"All I can say is…" Zart whispers to me as he checks to see if the stairwell is clear, "she's a bad apple. Also, do you want the new manager to think you are with her? I would put some distance between you and her. She could drag ya down."

He still never gives me a good reason. "Dude, Myhel doesn't have a malicious bone in her body. She's a nice girl," I say. "If anything, Kilgro drags *her* down."

Zart looks at me as we grab our bikes.

"Okay then, I'll meet you down there," forcing an ultimatum.

"Dude, we are just riding bikes together. It won't give you leprosy," I joke.

"I don't know," Zart says with his arm twisting.

"Look man, I don't want you to do anything you don't want to, but I doubt there will be any guilt by association associated."

He chuckles, relents, and agrees to bike along with me; and . . . , he would turn out to be right, and I would turn out to be very, very wrong, about Myhel.

133

When we get over to Myhel's, she waits on the stoop, with Kilgro and Jellie already there also.

"What took you guys?" Myhel says as an inside joke, pointing out to me that it takes all of 4 minutes to go from her pad to mine, change into my uniform, and get Zart. So, like a bunch of old chums we ride along 5 abreast (especially Kilgro) down the middle of the street, all the way to the Hangar, only having to move out of the way once for a golf cart, once for the Dolphin van, and about 50 times for goonies warming on the asphalt in the sunset.

Kilgro blurts, "Wow, we've got the two hottest studs on the atoll with us. When I was in Belize, I always got to, ya know, hang with the best guys. I hope the new manager is hot."

Jellie laughs, rolling her eyes at Kilgro's non-feminism, "I think he's gonna be like 50-years-old."

"So," Kilgro rebuts, "I like maturer men. They appreciate you more."

The rest of us exchange glances, but fear broaching any related topic. It's better not to know.

The Hangar area looks like the Columbus Day parade in East Boston or something.

"I think everybody on the atoll is here," Zart yells to me.

I blankly stare off, thinking of what has been happening out here with Chipweldi, Deny, the Navy chiefs, and some of the other characters out here. How will Amb handle them?

At the Hangar, the mob scene and excitement continues. It is loud, like The All Hands Club. Everyone is definitely taking notice that Myhel is 'with me'. At one point she puts her hand on my arm. I pull it away softly and look at her with a little, subtle smile. She knows that's a boundary.

Bang! Suddenly, as the sun fades to darkness, we hear the first one. Bang! Then another. The Bonin Petrels, my favorite bird on the atoll, smash into the tall metal sides of The Hangar, disoriented by the lights. As each falls to the tarmac dead or stunned, a FN quickly, nonchalantly slips by like a ball boy at Wimbledon, and takes them away. Like a petrel boy, or carcass boy.

Amb comes off the turbo prop and shakes Ben's hand first, then meets Dale and Banette, Karolyn, Chipweldi, and then he tries to reach toward Zart and I, but has to push through a number of FNs who try to get in to shake Mr. Amb's hand. He reaches through the crowd to give me a handshake.

"Kestrel, been reading your ASS surveys. I'm impressed," he says. Myhel straightens up, and looks over at me with beaming pride.

"Thank you. I love my work," smoothly slides over my juicy lips. Myhel stands so erect now, she looks stiff.

Amb says, "Zart. Great to meet you. I heard from Ben that you *ARE THE* maintenance department out here."

Zart gulps and fumbles, "Awh yeah, I get plenty-a help from the Foreign Nationals," trying to walk the line between humility and still accepting credit, but shy as an Okie. He actually almost sounds like Barney from *The Simpsons* for a second there.

Amb swings back around through the crowd like a prophet and says to me, "I also see you logged a Slaty-backed Gull. Did you get a photo?"

I report, "No, but I did get some shots of the Intermediate Egret. That's a record for North America."

"Well I'd like to see those. How sure were you on the slaty-backed? That's pretty darn good for a guy who has barely been out here very long," he inquires.

"Well, I'm not a great birder. I'm a generalist, but I would say -- had to be 87% sure or so," I respond analytically.

Amb laughs, "Okay."

Myhel and some of the ASS folks also try to wedge their way in to greet him, but they give up. I can tell that Myhel wants me to introduce her to Amb. I don't.

Within Amb's first few weeks on the atoll, everything changes. Amb demands morning staff meetings *everyday* at 7am. I think this is a good idea. You have to establish discipline on one of the most remote places on Earth. The Navy knew that too of course. This idea grates upon Chipweldi instantly.

After Amb has a couple of days with Chipweldi, the questions start.

"How are things going with Chipweldi?" turns into "Do you know what Chipweldi is doing today?" and "Has Chipweldi passed on my instructions to you?"

It isn't good. You know how that is if you have been in that kind of tense office environment. Finally, one day, Amb calls me into his office.

"How is your relationship with Chipweldi?" Amb asks point blank. "Sir, I don't know what you want me to say. He is my supervisor. You are putting me into a difficult position," I answer honestly. That is all he needs to hear. He knows what is going on without another word from me.

"I will notify Chipweldi that from now on, you report directly to me. If he gives you any projects or orders, you need to okay them through me. Is that clear?" Amb says sternly.

"Yes sir, I think that's great and I look forward to working with you, but, ah, Chipweldi never gives me orders to do anything. I was already doing everything under Ben before Chipweldi got out here, so you don't have to worry about him directing me." I know that sounds like total kiss-ass, but I am so happy to have a hard, stern, strict boss, instead of a useless, giggling buffoon of a slacker.

Speaking of the devil, Chipweldi comes stumbling into the office, "Oh, hey, heh huh, don't mean to be barging-in on nothin." He looks over at me.

Amb interrogates, "Chipweldi, what was the last instruction you gave to Kestrel?"

Chipweldi quickly looks back at me again. He knows the last instruction he gave me was to 'take shep by the hind legs.' He must think I narc-ed him out.

"Uub, hee," Chipweldi struggles, "Stay the course. Yup, I'm sure it was stay the course. He's doing a fine job, fine."

Amb bursts out laughing. At least he can laugh at this situation. It has sucked for me. Amb sends out the memo and everybody knows that I work for Amb now, until Chipweldi can 'hit the ground running' and 'get up to speed' as Amb puts it. Next thing you know, Chipweldi has to go off atoll again! This time, I think it is for more LE (law enforcement) training. I can't believe how much this guy gets off atoll. I have been here for going on 8 months, with my birthday and The 4th of July right around the corner, and I don't see a way to get off any time soon. Not that I'm complaining. Generally, I think I am loving it out here.

That night, back at Myhel's, after having sex again in the exact same mechanical way Drats has described to you so many times before, I drift off into alpha state, and I mumble that Amb has become my super.

136

"Great, hu uh, he's a big wig eh, so that can really help our biology careers," she glows.

Hmmm. Help us? That's pretty presumptuous. First, that there's an 'us', which is starting to scare the hell out of me, and second, that he would help her or me. I know, networking and positive thinking, and all that stuff, but, she's okay, ya know, not as bad a Chipweldi or Kilgro. I think she's even better in the field than Jellie, but she can't hold a candle to Banette, Dietera, Zart, or me for that matter. She's just not the same caliber as even Loon. I don't know what to say, and at almost midnight, I start drifting off, when suddenly there is a tapping at the door. My eyes open wide as I look at Myhel in the dark room.

"Shhh," Myhel whispers in my ear. After a pause, then another tap, we wait again in silence. Then, a louder tap, and I hear, "Myhel, let me in," whispered from the other side of the door.

"Go away," Myhel says just loud enough for the perp to hear.

"Come on, let me in," I hear again.

"No, what do you *not* understand about 'go away'?" she says more firmly, but not firmly enough for my taste.

I slip out of bed and head for the door. Myhel tries to grab my arm to stop me but it's too late. I stand up against the door closely, trying to peak though any cracks of light to see who it is.

Suddenly, the door bursts open into me hairy chest, and instinctually, standing there completely naked, I reach out and put both hands around Ryle's neck. He freezes in shock.

"Don't talk no shit Ryle!" I belt out in a deep, testosterone-filled voice, the hackles standing straight up on my neck spine. Then, I push him out onto the porch by his neck.

"Oh, you're a naughty boy," he says with a smirk as he looks down at my thing while I close the door tightly and walk over to the bed.

"What the hell was that about?" I question Myhel.

She doesn't say anything for a minute. I head back to the door and can see Ryle standing on Myhel's porch, shaking his head, and then walking away, apparently buzzed.

"I am getting a lock put on that door. That's it!" Myhel says in anger.

Okay, I know I am dumb and naïve, but obviously he has the idea that it is okay to go barge into her room even after she said 'No'.

137

What the hell kind of relationship is that? I have to error on the side of caution, incase this is an abuse issue or something.

"Has he ever raped you? I will press rape charges and unlawful entry immediately" I say, shifting instantly back into professional ranger mode.

Myhel stays quiet again for another minute. Long story short, I never get a straight answer out of her, but it taints my feelings about the whole situation forever. Is she 'midnight booty call girl'? I thought that was Kilgro's job. Do they pay her? You know how active my imagination is.

I tell Zart about it the next morning as we prepare for work in our rooms. He says things like "See what I mean?"

After a day to ponder the event, I tell Zart I am taking a Myhel break until I get a handle on what's going on around here. Plus, like I said, I don't want to sound greedy, but I think even though she is the only really available girl on the atoll, I think I should seek amorous behavior elsewhere.

Timing couldn't be better. Only a week after the Ryle incident, a class of University of Hawaii students arrives from Hilo for a week of research, class projects, and volunteer work. I tell Myhel, with this group on atoll, that I have to take a hiatus from our 'relationship' so I can get everything in order and really do a great job and impress Amb. She understands, and says okay, but she adds this caveat; "I'm not seeing anyone but you."

Hmm. Why would she say that and why should I believe her? It's not that I was almost starting to fall for her, but I was starting to like her. Why didn't she communicate to Ryle that she didn't want to see him anymore. Did she? I thought she said she was afraid of the 'C' word. Doesn't that comment sound a little committal? If she just left a long-term relationship, where does Ryle fall into all of this? I'm not the first guy of her rebound?

On the University group's second day on the atoll, I get to work with and meet a number of them in person, including Danica, in the All Hands Club. With a group of students full of energy and laughs, and a lot of "how'z it bra" and "mahalo" and "aloha spirit", and all that other really cool Hawaiian culture lingo, there is a new spark of energy on the atoll. Not like the kind of hyper energy as if Boston or NYC students were here. Remember, these kids are ultra laidback. When I first worked in Hawaii, I saw 'mahalo' written on every trashcan, so I thought it meant 'trash', until the Kama'iana kept saying 'mahalo' to me. 'Are they calling me trash, like white trash?' I thought to myself. Later, I learned it means 'thank you'. D'oh!

Danica looks part Italian like me, a little big boned one could say, unlike me, but so sweet, nice, unselfish, soft, and so many other things compared to Myhel. At one mili-moment at the bar when no one else could hear, I say, "Danica, are you surviving your class out here okay?"

She is surprised that 'The Ranger' would take any interest in her little problems, and also the fact that with the other 8 cuter girls in the class, that I would speak with her and remember her name. Actually, the other girls in the class are exactly that, 'girls'. Danica might not be as good looking, but she still seems much more hot and juicy as far as I am concerned, because she is more mature. I can't handle little-girl immature sorority crap. The fishermen are all over that shit like pedophiles. No thank you. They feel like they are in Hooters or something. I like adult women who I can have actual conversations about things of consequence with. Hey, I just realized, that is another thing that is missing with Myhel. I feel no strong, real connection with her. We just have sex, and though a biologist, she's just not there for me on any level really. We just have sex: Mechanical, routine, predictable, albeit nicer than nothing, sex. That is all. I love and care about animals so much. She doesn't really seem to passionately care that much about other things. I think Myhel is narcissistic, in an attempt to overcompensate for *her feelings* about her appearance.

Danica answers with a smile, "My classes are fine, but I'm feeling a little tired and over-stressed. It isn't the class, it's the classmates."

"I hear ya," I empathize, as we hear a couple of her classmates explode into a cackling volcanic eruption. "You originally from Hawaii?" I keep the conversation going.

She says, "No. My family is actually from Italy and I was born in Santa Monica."

"Oh," I report, "I lived in Santa Monica, and Marina Del Rey and Venice, but mostly Santa Monica, when I was going to UCLA," with no hint of ego or pretension.

"Oh, a UCLA boy?" she smiles.

139

"Yah, I used to ride my motorcycle to school, or my bike, or the blue bus down Wilshire." I confirm for validity, since no one ever believes anything I friggin say, even when I'm totally sincere. I want her to know that I'm genuine, and not a bull shitter.
"You're not drinking?" she asks.
"Nah, I got so much work to do, and it's so overrated, ya know."
She smiles in agreement, "Ya, I been nursing this one."
Just then I get a glimpse of Myhel in the hallway on the other side of the glass door. She pushes through the door and enters the bar with Kilgro, Jellie, and Tirgut, the ASS Founder/President/Operator, who is also on atoll for a visit.
I make a hasty retreat.
"I gotta bail. Let me know if you need any help with anything while you're out here," I offer as I start to walk away.
"Wait. Actually, I am working on my reef ecology project right now and I have a few questions," Danica says.
"Oh, well, I would love to help you." I don't really know shit about reef ecology. Even though she is probably a 22-year-old undergrad, her sophisticated text and assignments would probably blow me away. "I have a full day of tours and programs tomorrow, so I don't know what time would work. . ."
"Well I need like 15 minutes. How about right now?" she says.
"Okay, let me go to my room and then I will meet you." I am attracted to her, but I think she legitimately wants to work on her schoolwork, and I am going to honor that.
"I'm in 221 Bravo barracks," she tells me discreetly.
"Alone?" I say.
Danica smiles, "Yes, silly, we all got our own rooms."
"Cool," I say quietly.
I slip out past the shuffleboard table. I think Myhel and none of her cadre see me.
20 minutes later, back in Danica's room, I am surprised to see that I can answer every reef question she poses. I don't know a lot of the Latin terms, but with a quick scan of the page, I can figure out which polyp goes with what.
I get a warm, gentle feeling from her, and I want to kiss her and hold her strongly in my arms, but I think better of it for right now. What if she complains? What if she says I hit on her and I lose my

ranger job or something? She is an adult, but she is also a student. I don't know where to draw the line here.

"Well, I better get going," I say at the close of our study session. It is quiet. I look up at Danica's hazel eyes.

"Really?" she says with a little hint of a smile. It is quiet again. Ah fuck it. I reach over and gently tickle the back of her hand with my fingertips. She rolls her hand over and lets me tickle her palm. Then she grabs one of my fingers like she is squeezing a hotdog. So, I just go for it. Staring deeply into each other's eyes, I reach over and give her a big, juicy, wet kiss; the kind of kiss I would like from Myhel, but never happens. As if I have been saving my real kisses, my spine comes alive. We hear white terns squawking on the air conditioner. She takes off my shirt and I take off hers. She slides my shorts down and I reach over her back to untie her bikini-top. We have sweet, nice, delicious lovin; once then, and then later again in the early morning before dawn.

Oh my god, it is so nice. Ya know what else? She isn't all worried about getting hers, like Myhel is. Myhel is all about making sure I get hard quick so she can ride me like a vibrating dildo machine and cum quickly. That's what it is all about for her, and I had forgotten what it had been like with Messycka, until being reminded now. With Myhel, it feels like it is always about her. With Danica, like with Messycka back in Boston, it is not about getting hers. She just feels happy, almost privileged, to give sweet love to a lonely remote atoll ranger, and she gets all hers in return, many fold. That's how I feel too. Love is about the spirit of giving. Giving giving giving. Not taking. I love givin it. I don't take it. I sleep with Danica for the next 4 nights in a row.

On the next morning, a C5 cargo plane lands at Halfway to take a huge amount of naval equipment, including vehicles, off the atoll for good. As they begin loading the stuff the Navy left behind, the guys seem pretty cool, and say we can tour the monstrosity. They have a big Patriots logo on the tail, and it turns out they are based out of Massachusetts. A whole bunch of us go on board. I am at once able to dodge Myhel and take photos for Danica at the same time. Strange, where would Myhel be during all of this commotion? Why hasn't she been questioning me about the nights I haven't been with her?

We tour the aircraft with Danica and the Hilo girls. Life is cool and fun again!

Inevitably, it happens. Just as I tell Danica I will see her later, I turn the corner and out of The Hangar, running straight into Myhel. She says, "Are you mad at me?"

"No. Why?" I ask.

"Well, ya know, the whole thing with the guy at the door. Gettin a lock put on that door is definitely on the list," she says sheepishly.

"Ryle!" I say. She flinches. She does not even want to hear his name, at least, in front of me. I reveal, "I think we need to have a talk about some stuff. I felt like an idiot, the way I reacted, but it was all reflex and shock. I want to think about the whole situation for a while. Can I get back to you after I sort a few things out in my head?" I say, reasonably.

"Okay. But this is a very small island," she warns.

"Atoll," I correct with frustration.

"No, island. I'm talking about Sand Island, where we live, not the atoll, where everything else lives. We are going to see each other all the time, every day."

"I know. I know that. I'm not saying anything about civility or professionalism; we know those are musts. I'm just saying I want some alone time so I can think about the entire situation."

She looks at me like she is going to cry, but also full of anger, . . . like rejection anger.

"What kinda situation here?" she asks impatiently, with a little panic in her voice. I can see her pupils getting really big, swelling.

142

I begin, "Remember the first time we were going to have sex, and I said to you that the last thing I want to do is to do it with someone who doesn't really really want to do it? You want to force me to hang out with you right now while I need time to think about you and how I feel?" I pause to let it sink in. Of course she does. I know the answer. She wants me in her bed every friggin night to make sure she maintains control of 'the resource', as a biologist might characterize my function in her bedroom habitat.

"I know. I know," she says. "If you love something you gotta let it free. I am a strong believer in that. Whad arh we talking bout here?" as she begins to well up.

"Whoa whoa, wait a minute. Just give me til the weekend," and I walk away. If I stay there, it is just going to go on and on until she convinces me I should stay with her or she is going to start crying and then there is no exit at that point.

That night, I go over to Zart's room and tell him everything that is going down.

"Wow, I thought you were doing Myhel, not that Danica chick. She's nice." Zart says, takin a swig off a Pilsner Urquell, "She's kind of the un-nicest looking one in the bunch though. Seems like you coulda picked better."

"Man, you get some fancy-ass beer don't ya? I actually like this one," I say, referring to the beer. Then referring back to Danica, "I wasn't going for looks. I like her personality and maturity. She's from Santa Monica. The other girls are kind of like a bunch of little cheerleaders. I can't get into that. What do you mean you thought I was doing Myhel?"

"Oh, come on man. I hear *everything*. I'm a very light sleeper. I can hear you sneakin over there even after you said you were gonna give it a break. Man, Myhel has screwed a lot of guys out here dude. You gotta watch ya back out here, and watch for diseases and shit," he says as he belts down the rest of the beer and immediately cracks another, letting a burp rip. "Women, ya know, they are a problem. They got problems. The ones out here got problems, ya know?" he professes. "I had Ashby (the Poor Construction Girl) naked and drunk at the west beach, skinny dippin, and she wanted to do it. I asked her if she had a condom, cause I didn't, and she splashed water in my face, punched me in the chest, and left."

"Dude! You didn't tag that while you could?" I say with excitement, like a locker room rat.

"No way," Zart answers with petulance. "I'm not gonna get AIDS."

I say calmly, "Duuuuuuuude, you may be right, but I don't believe that a girl would knowingly do that to a guy. Real guys might do that, and impregnate them to boot, but unless you think the girl is a total scum or a druggie, I would trust her. If she's a scum or druggie, I wouldn't do her period, and I suggest never cumming inside any girl, ever."

Zart disagrees, and stands by his actions with PCG. Hey, to each his own. I can't tell him what to do with his dick. He's right. I always say to men all the time, 'wrap it up' 'wrap up your junk' 'it's your fault if the girl gets pregnant'. A lot of guys won't buy that.

"So do you have a girl Zart?" I ask.

"I had a girlfriend up in Washington, but she moved to San Fran and the only chick I've hooked-up with out here was a Kiwi biologist who came to visit."

I ask, "How long was that for?"

"Like two weeks," Zart responds.

Then I look at him with realization, "Wow, and the rest of the time . . ."

". . .yep, total monk. There aren't any girls out here," Zart finishes with a dejected tone.

As darkness falls, I go back to my room and think to my selfish self for a while, lying on my bed. I should go over to Danica's right now, but I am feeling bad about the Myhel situation. Maybe I should go over and have sex with Myhel, then she will mellow out a little and not think I'm screwing around with Danica. That's deceptive. Why would I do that? What if one of the C5 crew guys is screwing Myhel right now, or if Ryle is over there again? Great; then she isn't fixated on me. What if one of the other guys is with Danica right now? If I don't go over there she is gonna think I'm not into her, or that I am with one of the other girls. Yuck! I am grossing myself out. This whole scene is making me sick.

Wow, the problems of a polygamist. This is how bull elk must feel keeping their harem together. I never wanted to be lucky enough to have these problems. Can't I just find *one* great soul mate who I can love forever? Myhel: Never in a million years. So that is where my problem lies. I should not be having sex with her, period. I am because I am lonely and alone and want it, but now that Danica's on the atoll, I feel like I should have never hooked-up with Myhel. That is fuckin wrong. Fuck. What do I do? I need to straighten out my act.

So, I decide to stay in my room. At 11 there's a knock. I lie there for a second, then realize I have to get it if I don't want to wake-up Zart or any other neighbors in my hall. I open the door a crack, fearing the worst, but instead, I am surprised to see Danica. I didn't even know she knew how to find my room. She quietly slips into my room, flips off her Hawaiian flip-flops, and crawls onto my bed. She looks so solid and delicious, and I think she just put some kind of nice silky cream all over her thighs and knees and feet. Oh man! She smells like a coconut-butter treat.

"Why didn't you come over?" she says in a soft whisper.

Now this is a girl that could be a potential soul mate. Even the way she securely handles this situation is much more mature and together than Myhel, who has easily got 10 years on Danica. But that also appears to be the problem for me. I am 11 years older than Danica. I think that is too much of a gap, even considering my non 'guy-like', immature character. I'm 32, or 33. She has to experience her 20s, or at least her early 20s, before she would be ripe for a real relationship with me.

I say, "I need a break," half-heartedly, even though I really want to kiss her right now.

"Well no sex is okay silly. You can still sleep with me," she grabs my hand and pulls me onto the bed to give me a nurturing hug. Ah, that's it. Love. Loving love. She knows what I want, what all real men really want; soothing, calming, settling love and comfort, and a soft voice to say, 'everything's gonna be alright'. Something Myhel can fake occasionally, but never supply. Myhel would be mad at me and think something was wrong if we didn't jump to coitus right away.

"Ya, but we can't stay here. It will be too noisy even if we don't make love," I tell her. What I really worry about is Myhel showing up here and making a big scene. This is the first time I use *The Zart Excuse.*

We slip quietly back to Danica's. When we enter the hallway to Danica's room, Myhel stands there, waiting. Waiting waiting waiting. How long has she been waiting, seething? Why? Is this a set-up? How did she know anything?

"What are you doing here?" she barks at me.

"What are *you* doing here?" I emphasize back.

"I am waiting to see what you are doing," she says with her arms crossed.

"Okay, well now you see," I say, and with that, we go into Danica's room.

Fuck that! I am not going to go around feeling like a cheater or something with a girl who has guys knocking on her door at midnight, won't give me a lot of straight answers on shit, and now is acting all bitchy like she owns me when she was the one who said she didn't like commitment to begin with.

"Does she think she's your girlfriend?" Danica asks, crinkling her nose in disgust, after we both sit in silence on her bed for a minute, listening to the door and looking at the light coming through the horizontal crack along the bottom.

"I guess I have to clear some things up with her bluntly. I have been having sex with her, but it has been kind of a mess and I guess it's good that it's over now. Making love with you snapped me to reality, and why am I wasting my time with her?" I ramble.

"Cause she was the only girl you could have sex with on the island. What are you going to do, wait to see if you can hook-up with the tourists?" she reasons. "Good luck with that," she says with a laugh.

"I know. You're right. I have to be strong enough to tell her no and stick to it," I say. "Fifty ways to leave your lover."

After another hour of snuggling and talking, we have great sex, twice. This turns out to be the first time Myhel gets really mad at me.

"I don't see you with her anyway," Danica says as I fall asleep. "Don't ever lower yourself to something like that. Look at me, I shot for the stars and I got you. I know I'm not the right soul mate for you either. I am too young for you and we have different lives, but that makes every moment I spend with you that much more precious. That's the way I like to look at things."

I drift off into a pleasant dream, happy in the thought that the Myhel drama is over.

On Saturday night, the flight arrives to take many of the visitors and students off the atoll. We all chat and drink in the All Hands Club until the plane lands, all of us that is, except for the stuck-up snobs who begin to start a class-warfare battle. They all head up to the North Beach, to the fancy little bar HIC built up there, against the will of the APS. The high-roller fishermen, and HIC cognoscenti, the what are quickly becoming NASCARians, and the animal-hater types; they wait for the plane, sipping mint juleps and margaritas. The Olderhostile people take a gander, but generally they, the ASS staff, the HAWS volunteers and workers, the FNs: Pretty much everybody but the really wealthy, continue to frequent the blue-collar All Hands Club, instead of going up to 'Boobies', as crass Pillmold would like to see the North Beach bar named.

A Red-footed Booby with spectacular breeding color on its bill; one of three booby species on Halfway Atoll.

Myhel and a group of others approach the Hilo students, and Zart and I, in the All Hands Club. She looks for trouble and makes some off-color remarks. We pretty much ignore her.

"Well now that all the students are leaving tonight, who are you going to hang around with now?" Kilgro says as a dig, as Myhel obviously turns back to see my reaction.

I am way out of their league. They have no idea how obvious they are. It is funny. I can tell she wants to hurt me and protect her friend Myhel, but at that same time, she does it in a nice enough way (to her, mind you) to leave the door open so that if somehow, someway, I get desperate enough, maybe I'll give Kilgro a late night visit.

The other thing that is funny about this is that somehow Myhel perceives a power shift in this relationship. As if now that "I'm caught", I will have to be her slave or some shit like that. I have to laugh at how puffed-up she is about this whole thing. It's all a front.

"Leaving?" Danica questions. "Actually, a number of us are staying on until the next flight." Danica smiles at me innocently. Myhel is livid, and walks off with her group. Zart pulls me aside. "This is looking dangerous dude," he warns.

"What do you mean? Be specific," I retort.

Danica smiles, Kilgro lingers, and the Hilo girls hang, after Myhel storms off. Note Kestrel's bandaged fingers from the Jellie monk seal incident.

Zart observes, "Well, you know. Myhel looks pissed. You better watch your nuts."

"Zart, this is what you did to me last time. What are you talking about? Does she have a gun? Does she have mafia connections? What?" I press.

"No no no, nothing like that," Zart says vaguely.

"What do you want me to do? I know it's over with Myhel. That's it. Aren't you happy about that?" I ask him directly.

"Yeah," Zart continues slowly, "I'm just tryin to watch out for ya buddy." Again, so ambiguous. I have no idea what he is trying to warn me about.

After the aircraft lands and I complete all of my duties, I swing by my room to change.

"Now where are you going?" Zart asks, as he peeks in from our bathroom.

148

"Down to Danica's," I say with a grin.

"All right," Zart warns in a drawn-out wavy rollercoaster tone.

I head down the stairs to Danica's, where Myhel and her friends sit in the lobby right near Danica's room, playing cards. They have drinks and look like they are camped-out for the night. What the fuck. I can't just walk past them and go into that room. I shouldn't care, but it's rude and wrong and I can't bring myself to do it. I head back up the stairs and around to the other side of the building. As I try to enter that way, I see, through the window in the door, that they would see me no matter which end of the building I enter into. I am cock-blocked.

I go out to Danica's ground-floor window, looking around to see if I will get busted as a peeping Tom. As I look into her totally dark room, I can barely make out her breathing body under the sheets.

"Danica. Danica," I whisper and tap on the glass. She gently jostles. I repeat. Her head raises-up off the pillow. Then she comes to the window.

"What are you doing?" she whispers with a soft, surprised smile.

I whisper back, "I want to come see you but friggin Myhel is blocking the door."

"You climb in the window," she suggests. It would be difficult for an average human being, but I'm a friggin Squirrel Monkey and could be in there lickety-split. I almost want to climb in just for the challenge.

"The only thing is. . ." she continues, "I think I drank a little too much and I just got my period so I am feeling like shit."

"Oh, I thought you went to bed a little early," understanding the explanation.

"Yeah, I almost feel like I want to ralph right now," she explains.

"You want me to get you a Pamprin or anything?" I ask considerately.

"No, I got one, but that's so sweet of you to ask. You are going to make a great woman really happy some day, but not Myhel," she says with a hushed laugh.

"I'm sorry. I feel like such an idiot. We are adults. This is such stupid high school stuff," I say, shaking my head.

"Goodnight fair love, I shall see thee tomorrow," Danica says as she slides her hand off mine, closes the window quietly, and floats back over to her bed.

"Parting is such sweet sorrow," I reply in my best Shakespearian accent. And with that, she reaches over and pulls the curtain drawstring as she reclines. I move away as stealthy as a Bobcat on a Brush Rabbit.

As I walk back toward my room, I decide to take the long way back to avoid Myhel. I hear some geckos barking, so I spend a few minutes catching and examining them. What fascinating creatures. Ya ever look at geckos close-up? Like really close-up? I peer into their psychedelic eyes, finger their trippy toes, and gaze at the semi-translucent bodies with their throbbing internal organs. Wow. House Gecko.

Suddenly I hear the roar of a gator coming over the little hill behind the married officer's quarters (MOQs). The headlights blast down onto my position, so I instinctively slink back behind the lip of the building. I am, after all, standing outside the girls' windows, alone, at 11pm. I can see two of the HIC workers, and Jewel, bouncing in the springy gator seats.

"Thank y'all for everythin agin. Y'all are sweet hearts," Jewel says as she tries to pry herself out of the gator. The drunkard in the back looks like he thinks he is helping her, but he just kind of reaches forward with his right arm and grabs her right arm. The driver also tries 'to assist' her, with his head intermittently bobbing.

"No no, I'm fine thank you. I got it," Jewel assures them. The guy in the back finally gets out and starts to follow Jewel.

"You want me should escort ya to room," he blathers like a gold miner in a Bogart movie.

Jewel quickens her pace. "Thank y'all. See ya bright and early," she says with confidence, though appearing a little tipsy herself. She out-paces him easily and he abandons the hunt.

"Ahh forgit it," he says as he staggers back to the gator, with its six bulbous tires. They speed off noisily flying down the road with goonies trying to jump out of the way. Note to self: We gotta take the keys away from these dickheads at night. No workers need to be driving at night. Those lazy bastards should walk or be on their bikes like the rest of us.

"Kestrel? What are you doin out her shugar?" Jewel says softly as she spots me angled in the corner against the barracks entrance. She runs her soft perfumed palm smoothly yet firmly down the side of my face, stopping on my neck. "You feelin sick?"

"No, I'm fine, although I am upset to see those guys driving around at night like that. That can make your stomach turn. That's why Zart and I find so many squished goonies all over the place," I say in quiet anger.

"Oowh, really honey? I didn't know that was a problem," she says compassionately. "Why you out here honey? Are you lonely?"

I giggle briefly at the thought, then answer, "No, I'm, I'm fine." I swallow, "I am just checking out these geckos. They are cool huh?" pointing up to the corner of the entrance ceiling, by the light.

Jewel vaguely looks up and squints, but doesn't even try. "Really, what you doin out here honey?"

I almost want to say praying, but that would be totally fucked up. I laugh to myself for a moment.

Jewel softly prods, "Is it a girl? It's a girl right?"

I look into her blurry eyes for a second. Mine betray me. She can read me like a book.

"You look like you need a drink," as she grabs my hand and pulls me toward the stairwell. "Why don't you come up for a drink? Just one drink," she stammers with a hiccup.

"Jewel, I would have loved for you to invite me up to your room many times before. Anytime before. But, this is a bad time," I explain as we hover outside the door of the building. Termites fly around the streetlights, and the petrels grunt and moan. Jewel frowns at me. She knows I'm not being straight with her. I admit begrudgingly, "If we go in that building, Myhel will see me with you. That will hurt her feelings even more."

Jewel makes a cute grunt herself and says, "Why do you care?" with a broad, sensual smile.

I say, "My Mom taught me to be nice." Jewel loves that answer. "Don't be silly, silly. I know, it's all about that Myhel thing. So what. Big deal," Jewel says with an air of class and maturity.

She knows about the Myhel thing too? How much? Wow, I'm the only one who doesn't know the secrets. What is there some kind of all-seeing secret society out here or something?

"She's in there right now," I say.

"She is?" Jewel says as she cutely peeks into the hall through the little window in the door.

Then, Jewel boldly swings open the door and stands in the hallway, announcing "Hi gals!" in a sustained legato.

They look up from their cards, say hi and wave, and go back to their game and conversation. Jewel looks back at me with a smile, and I slip behind her hot little juicy butt and up the stairs, three floors to her room.

We sit on her couch, talking about a bunch of things neither of us care about, with the TV numbly droning on in the background. I really don't feel like drinking, so I take little sips. Then, kinda out of the blue, I am sitting on the floor with my back against the couch, and she, sitting on the couch in a short comfortable skirt and a casual shirt, with her feet up on some pillows, looks very relaxed. After she finishes her drink, she looks like she wants to get up and get another, but feels that maybe she has had enough for the night. Instead, she reaches over and gives me a nice kiss. Nice. It is nice. I don't feel any fireworks but I go for it anyway. Without breaking lips, I twist up and onto the couch on top of her and start slowly undulating. We make out for about 15 minutes, as I feel her breasts and rub my hands all over her skin; but you know how you can tell right? It isn't happening. I can feel it. I stop and pull back, resting my head against the couch. We both stare at the TV in silence, entangled with our arms around each other.

"Maybe-" I start.

"Shh," she says. "Shh." She hands me another drink. We sit in silence. I don't take a sip. "I felt the fizzle. That's always what happens to me, even when I'm in love," she says with resignation. There is another long pause. I dare to speak, "Even when you are with someone who loves you?" I say sympathetically.

Jewel confesses, "I don't know if a man has ever loved me. I think they can't love me cause I'm just not passionate."

"No. You are. You are passionate. You are very passionate, and compassionate," I try.

"No. See. Compassionate yes. I can be the next Mother Theresa if I want to be. But I can't be the hot witch you want to get insider er pants," she says angrily.

"Whoa. Wait a minute. Come here. We can try again. After that language now, I am starting to get turned on," I say as a joke and try to make a move on her. We both laugh at how ridiculous I am.

"No," she says disappointedly. But she is right. Looks, personality, all that other shit don't matter. Either a girl is hot and juicy, or she's not. I thought Jewel, by her accent, and her nice body, and her conservative 'fooffiness'; but also by the way she flirts and teases; would be a hot, wild-child sleeper surprise package. Instead, --- major dud. At least she knows it, but it's sad that she knows it too. What to do? I was going to suggest that it's just because she is drunk, but obviously this has been an issue for her. "So then, a blow-job is out of the question?" I ask, adding some more levity to the maneuver. She laughs again and gives me a big teddy bear hug, squishing my ear into her chest. She doesn't want to fool around, and you know me, . . . I don't want to fool around with anyone who doesn't want to fool around.

Jewel confesses, "You know one thing, like love at first sight, I kinda thought for some reason, even though you and me be so different, that you might, just might be the one. Ya know, ya know what I mean by 'the one' don't cha? Like when we met on the plane. Like when we looked in each other's eyes at the New Year's party."

Oh my god. Oh my god. I can't believe she was thinking that. It's so weird how people get drawn to each other. I like a lot of things about her, a lot more things a lot more than I like about Myhel, that's for sure. But there is no spark. I see a little tear well up in her left eye, but she doesn't let herself cry. I don't know what to say. It's almost like I feel like she should try to be a nun or something. "I, I definitely think you are hot, and, and I'm surprised I'm not makin sweet love to you right now," I stutter. I am thinking maybe we should just force it and get her over this hump (no pun intended). Maybe it will suddenly get good then. I don't believe that though.

Jewel looks over at me with an understanding smirk, "I know you think you are trying to be all nice and all to me right now, but please don't talk to me like that."

'Yikes!' I think to myself. Should I say sorry? I just shut up. A few moments later, she changes the subject. I hang out with her for another half-hour or so, then fall asleep. When I awaken, she sleeps in her bed and I have a stiff neck, half on the floor and half on the couch. I can see it getting light, so I quietly put the blanket over her exposed shoulders, slip out of her room, and back to mine. At breakfast in The Galley, Zart is pissed. "What the fuck dude, this has got to end," Zart carps.

"What? What happened?" I respond.

Zart asserts firmly, "This Don Juan night raid shit has got to end dude. I need my sleep."

"What? What do you need sleep for?" I say.

Zart can't think of any possible reason, so he says, "Look, that's my business. Tell Myhel we are gonna ban her from the barracks for causing a nuisance," he says, stuffing greasy hash browns down his throat, as he dumps some more Tabasco on with a jerky, frustrated shake.

"What happened?" I worry.

"She came looking for you twice. Knocking on your door. 'I know you're in there'. Shit like that," he says perturbed.

Oh shit. I didn't see that coming. Of course, I bet you did, right? I'm sure the reader saw this coming a mile fucking away. You guys have great powers of perception, right? Too bad readers can't warn authors, or characters, in real time. How can you just go on sitting there, smugly reading, when you can see the horrible path I'm on? That's another reason Drats made **Rudy the Red Bat** a participatory musical in which the audience decides the ending.

At that moment, Myhel and her clique enter The Galley and stand in line with a group of Olderhostile folks. Although she tries to yuck it up, I can see, even all the way across the cafeteria, that she looks rough. She looks like she has been up all night, and maybe crying, and not happy. Certainly not happy looking, like when she was with me.

"Are you done eatin?" I ask Zart nervously.

"NO. Why, you want to run away?" he jabs like a cranky Frankie.

"Yes," I admit.

"Okay," he agrees, being the nice generous friend he is, and we dump our trays and get out of there. As we turn the corner to get our bikes, who do we run into, but the Hilo college girls.

"Here's the guy," one of the young, cute girls announces. They look me over for a second.

Danica steps toward me. "Hi Zart," she says right to Zart's face. He recoils back. "Oh, hi, hi, hi ya doin," he fumbles. Zart can't talk with girls. He can talk about them all he wants, but talking to them, that's a different story. Not as bad as Ben mind you, but not smooth for sure.

Danica gently peels my shades off and looks deeply into my eyes. "Last night that psycho knocked on my door, and then again this morning, looking for you. I almost tore her head off. I think we should go make-out on the table in there right in front of her and teach her once and for all that you are not her boy toy. Did you tell her you love her? Tell me the truth," Danica stays controlled, but very angry and sick of the bullshit. I think she is kind of in that position where she likes me, and likes to have sex with me, but feels empowered, with nothing to lose, and at the same time, cranky from sleep disruption, and her period. Mighty combo! I have to admit; I like her style and how she handles herself, just like I will in the future with Chelonia.

"No, I told you, I fucked up, I shouldn't have gotten involved with her until I knew more," I explain. "I am definitely not in love with her, and she's been wiggin me out. I certainly never, ever told her I love her. All true," I say with my hands waving.

Danica grabs my hands and pulls them together between us. "Well, seriously, I am out of here in a few days and I want to do my work. I want to relax and have a good time too. You are never gonna see me again after this and *you* have to live out here, so it's your call."

"Don't say that. I can come see you on the Big Island," I say encouragingly.

"You will?" she says with pleasant surprise. She is being insistent but doesn't want to turn me off, so she keeps a great balance of sweet and rational, as opposed to Myhel's bitter/sour, deceptive, and illogical behavior.

"Sure. I would like to," I say. Her girl friends all look over with surprise. Zart catches some of them checking out my ass and legs in my government shorts.

Danica smiles and comes in close, "Okay, well as far as Myhel goes, tell her to leave you alone and if she comes knockin again I will take care of her. I'm not afraid of her," she leans toward me then grabs my forearm firmly, "If I'm gonna be bothered by her knockin, I'd rather you be there to keep my attitude positive," she finishes, smiles, and then walks into The Galley with her classmates to get in line.

"See?" Zart says.

"See what?" I respond with a gulp.

"See, that's the kind of girl you should be with. She's way more together than Myhel," he says. "She's like one of the worst looking girls in the class, but she is smoking." Zart breaks a sweat, just from experiencing the proximity of the young, fit, college girls. "Yah, wow, she is something man; but she doesn't live on the atoll. I told you looks ain't everything," I say.

"Yah, well it doesn't hurt that she's got a nice, creamy body. Is that what it comes down to?" Zart asks. "You want one that lives out here? You'll never find a girl on Halfway."

I think about it for a minute in silence as we bike back to the barracks. What is he Mr. Picky? I don't want to go for months and months alone without sex, and I would never pay for it, so this is how it goes. I never say never, except regarding Kilgro, then it's never never never. I would also have to say at this point that Jellie is one-hundred percent 'off the list'.

"I'm deciding to cut Myhel off," I blurt out with conviction.

"When Danica leaves, you're just going to go back to Myhel," Zart responds.

I rebut, "No, off the list," I say with a Myhel accent.

Zart laughs, then says in a cranky tone, "What about, 'When I was in Belize . . .'"

We crack ourselves up.

My guilt racks me. Zart appears right again. Within a week of Danica's departure, I find myself again in Myhel's bed. My conscience bothers me daily about what I should do. Everything seems fine now, but I fear a little strain building. I can tell she wants more but fears rocking the boat. Sneaking over to have sex with her feels almost like conjugal visits. I've never felt this way in my life, with any girl, ever.

Zart knows what I'm doing too, and looks at me shamefully. That does it. I can't take it. I decide to spend some quality time alone. Instead of just studying, I decide it is time to flex my creative muscle. I have studied just about everything about Halfway by now, and I am considered *THE* military expert on atoll, even though wildlife remains my forte by far. I begin work on the Jorgenson play: **Adolph Jorgenson; Hero or Fruitcake?**; a whimsical comedy with musical components based on the true-life story of this colorful character. I string together the events of his pretty wild life; a story of shipwreck, international murder, and mad behavior, and the thing writes itself. I think my friend Drats, the author, would be proud of me.

We put on the show in The Station Theater to the entire atoll, minus the cast; which includes Zart as a cop, Dr. Chance as a ship's captain, and Myhel as his spent piece of tall ship trash, doing her best Kilgro accent the entire show. She actually tries hard and is a bit of a ham. I play Jorgensen, the lead. A token FN from each nationality performs as poachers, castaways, and as the smiling bartender. Hysterical.

Right before we start the show, I sing a surprise *a cappella* solo version of *Pure Imagination* from *Willy Wonka*, but instead of smiling, I think about all of the special creatures going extinct at our hands. I sing a long, slow, legato version with a lilting vibrato, and add my own Manilow-esque key-changes, diphthongs, and pain-riddled strain for mega-feel. Amb videotapes the entire performance. Too bad I didn't live to put it on YouTube. It's a great show. I had great source material, and expectations were so friggin low that anything I put on was gonna blow them the fuck away. We sing, we act and run around, and the crowd just loves it. One of our main props is a cardboard cutout boat from a refrigerator box. The FNs in the audience smile broad grins, gleaming reflections from the stage lights. The cast performs well, even with no acting experience.

Everybody, even evil people like Stark Kristian and Cherry Ballpig, laugh it up and have there photos taken with the pilots wearing grass skirts and coconut bras. Only on Halfway.

Evil? Wait. Wait one cotton-pickin minute. Can I call them evil, legitimately evil?

Right after the play goes up in the early fall, Myhel seems to well-up with much more emotion for me than she has before. "So, ah, I was thinking, you want to come back to my Mom's house for Christmas in the UP, eh?"

"What?" I say in shock. "That sounds kind of serious to me. Doesn't it?"

She looks at me with puppy-dog earnest.

I press, "I thought you said there was no commitment in this relationship?"

"Well, we've been seeing each other for almost a year now, and I thought we were boyfriend and girlfriend now."

"Why? First off, it's been like 8 months, and on and off. And we technically aren't even seeing each other right now. What gives you that idea?" I try to say kindly.

"I don't know," she says with a sob. "I already told my mom and my siss that you were coming hup up."

"What? I can't do that," I say with a sorry in my voice.

"Well, why not?" she demands.

"Because it's a false impression. We are not boyfriend and girlfriend. I don't know what gave you that idea. You never expressed anything like that to me. You never told me you liked me even. You said you were afraid of the 'C' word"

"I know," she admits. "I never told you how I feel."

I ask, "Why?"

"Because, if I told you I was in love with you, eh, I was afraid you would dah-ump me?" she says with a snivel. "Then I'd be off your list, completely."

"Well then what does that tell you?" I say directly. "We gotta listen to our heart's."

"I know. I know it is wrong. I was just hoping you would change and fall for me," she sobs.

"Oh shit. I'm sorry. You got the wrong guy. I am looking for a special girl in my life. I don't see that with us. You don't either. You want me, but you know it doesn't feel right." I get up and walk away.

"Wait, don't leave it like this," she begs.

"I have been through this before, and I think you have too. The best thing to do is just forget about me for a while and focus on you. Focus on yourself and your own life, and just relax and eat right and have a good time, and I will talk with you soon," I say.

"Ya know, what I think? If ya were walkin down the street in a big city somewhere, you wouldn't even look at me," she says with a hurtful sob. "Would you? Would you?" she says in the distance as I refuse to continue arguing or even looking back. "I wouldn't even be on the list. I wouldn't even be on the list."

Two weeks later, Myhel still lies in her room. Dr. Chance gives her drugs every couple of days. Fuck that. I am not going to get sucked into that shit. I didn't even do anything. If she likes me that much, she should have been honest in the first place.

So, I start really getting into the Ultimate team I started. Trying to get the FNs to play is a riot. They play cricket, soccer (what they call futbol), volleyball, and hoop. I can't laugh at their lack of Ultimate Frisbee skills cause they laugh every time I attempt to pitch the cricket ball. So many don't know how to swim. This gets me thinking about starting a swim program too. At first, I make some little modest plans about basic swim safety, appropriate rescue skills for someone falling off a pier and shit like that, but then, I realize with Myhel out of the picture, I have tons of disposable time on my hands. I go hog wild on a plan that includes snorkel trips out to the outer reef, diving boards and a slide in the inner harbor, and even a regular swim program up at the North Beach to teach the FNs how to actually swim. I know, all this creation of plays, and ultimate teams, and now the swim program, very homocentric of me, yes, I know. The Ironwood Parties are still happening, and I'm such a people person compared to so many others out here, that I, and Jewel concurs to an extent, need to be a positive face in the crowd out here. Jewel is trying to do the same thing. She and I are almost like liaisons bridging the gap between HIC and APS. I like Jewel so much more than I like Myhel.

Kestrel makes a surface dive in about 47 feet of water, outside the northwest reef.

I make the mistake of showing a second draft of the swim plan, complete with diagrams and timetables, to Chipweldi.
He looks at it for a second. "This thing gives me a huge headache. He he h," he says with a meaningless chuckle.
I don't know if somewhere out in Barstow or Boise or Independence Kansas, they get this guy, but no one, I mean no one,

on the atoll, gets, or understands, Chipweldi, ever, period. And you know what? I think he loves it that way. It's like trying to understand *Zippy the Pinhead*, or *Ubu Roi*, or jazz scatting. Yet, instead of modifying his behavior, he keeps plugging along the same old way. To me, he is the perfect example of when people complain about a waste of federal tax dollars. I certainly ain't a waste! Every American that meets me on Halfway, whether they agree with what some would consider my 'liberal' viewpoints or not, at least know they get way more than their tax dollar's-worth with me. I give people more information than they want to know, or can take. I use my boundless energy constructively and rip-out tons of alien plants with my bare hands. I am the anti-thesis of Chipweldi! Why does he 'work' for APS? How can we hire people this bad? How did he get to HAWS? I think he thinks he's a cool rebel or something. You know my philosophy about The World right: You either turn the wheel forward or you force it backward. You either help things out or fuck things up. Zinn said *You Can't Be Neutral on a Moving Train*. I am driving the wheel forward at an incredible rate with massive amounts of force. Chipweldi drags the wheel backward. He slows things down. He stops progress and projects. Why? Why why why?

I never show another piece of my work to Chipweldi. I give all of my necessary information out at the required morning meetings, and sometimes a little extra info, as you can imagine, knowing me, and then I do my best to avoid Chipweldi for the remainder of each day and evening. It's not hard. He goes off the atoll all the time, having all kinds of problems with Amb, the Sanctuary Manager, and apparently trying to avoid me just as well. He rarely contacts me, other than to ask if I could go meet the plane and do a snake search, usually for some cockamamie excuse, but probably tied to him wanting to watch a Cubs or Indians game. By the way, Amb thinks my swim plan is not only very ambitions, but he likes it a lot. I should go rub that in Chipweldi's face, but I won't and never do.

The next day, I stand on a high dune. Jellie walks up to me while I scan the goonies with my binoculars.

"Whatcha doin?" she asks like a child. I think she may be trying to make up.

I reply, "Bird survey. I told the biologists I'd help them out." (I'm referring to the real biologists, Banette and Dietera, not the bio hacks like her.)

"What are you looking for?" she asks.

"Golden Gooney," I answer as I scan.

"Have they *seen* one?" she says with general surprise.

"Yeah, that's why we are out here. Banette took the whaler and a vol and a FN over to Eastern and they will circumnavigate Spit to look for any over there. Dietera took other volunteers and are looking for them over here."

"You're pulling my leg right? Golden Gooney," she says in disbelief.

"Yes. It's the Short-tailed Albatross. It's from Tora Shima Island and it's the only other Northern Hemisphere species," I inform her. I could have told her way more, but instead I show some uncharacteristic restraint and maturity. Maybe being out on this atoll affects my personality.

"Oh" she says blankly.

"You never heard of them?" I say, looking over at her for the first time. She has a large bandage loosely wrapped around her ankle. I can see blood. "What happened?" I ask.

"Oh, stupid oaf me. I got myself bit by a monk seal," she admits embarrassed.

"Wow, how did that happen?" I ask, not to accuse her of any ineptitude or negligence, but to learn from her folly so I can avoid the same fate.

Defensively, she rambles, "Oh you know, I was just being dumb. Totally my bad."

I look at her for a moment. She is not going to give me any details and I decide I don't even want to friggin know. I go back to my spying. Later, I get from the horse's mouth, meaning Dr. Chance, that it was a little-teeny seal pup she shouldn't even have been near, and that she let herself get bit because she is a klutz. Great, just great. Dr. Chance was unfamiliar with Seal Finger, a horrible infection that can lead to amputeeism, transmitted by puncture wounds from pinnipeds. Nasty.

A week goes by without incident, and then we get word from Hono that a Coast Guard Cutter will be coming in. Everyone is excited to have 100 new people on Sand Island, though technically, they will

161

be living onboard their ship. This will be a good test. If Myhel breaks out of her morass and hooks up with one of the Coasties, then I will feel relieved that she is back to her normal routine, minus me. I needn't play matchmaker, or anything that contrived or manipulative. In this scenario, an extreme case like Myhel, I need to simply make sure she knows the Coasties are coming so she can ruminate on it, and then step out of the way.

So I say to Zart, "Any reports of any ASS participants arriving via the Coast Guard Cutter?"

Zart gives me a puzzled look, "I don't know," he says slowly, deducing where I am going.

"Better call in," I suggest.

Zart picks up his phone and calls Kilgro, something he is pretty sure he has never had to do. "Yah," he says, a little like a zombie. "Yah, you guys sure you don't have any ASS personnel coming in on the Coast Guard vessel?" Zart asks Kilgro over the large, clunky cell-phone.

I feed to Zart with a hiss, "Volunteer participants?"

"Yah, vols," Zart says, as I whisper to him and talk with my spinning hands. "Ya sure? The cutter coming in this week. How do you know?" Zart goes on.

I give Zart the thumbs-up as I quietly laugh my ass off. Kilgro's buzzing voice sounds really annoyed from even my distance, like a swarming hive of bees. Before Zart ends the call, it sounds like Kilgro turns and starts arguing with Tirgut about it. Zart hangs up. We wait.

About twenty-two minutes go by, as Zart downs 2 more brews. "What are the chances there will be some hot Coast Guard chicks on this vessel?" I quiz Zart.

"None. It's gonna be all guys dude. You can't be that lucky twice. You really lucked out with that Danica girl. She was perfect. No hassles man," he says as he takes a slug off a Benningan's or some other tripped out import I've never heard of. "See this?" Holding up a mustardy golden tall can. "This has it's own CO2 cartridge in the can," he proudly demonstrates.

I smile politely, but could care less, so I get back to what really matters. "Well, if there is a hot chick, I'll let you go after her first, that way I can watch how the 'father-hen' Coasties react and see if

you are gonna get your ass kicked," I laugh, though I think it's a
good idea.
"Why, can't *they* do her?" Zart asks, referring to the Coast Guard
crewmembers.
"No, no fraternization, that's why we have a chance with their
girls," I illuminate.
"If there are any girls," Zart fires back as he pops open a new can.
"Don't get your hopes up."
Hmm. He doesn't want me to get my hopes up. That's cause I have
my hopes up.
We wait.

The outer reef; close to where the tiger shark almost took Kestrel
out.

Finally, my phone rings. Somebody is upset because they just got a
call from so and so that Myhel said she heard that somebody
thought the Coast Guard blah blah blah, and the ASS folks blah
blah blah, and no paperwork and blah blah blah. That's all I need
to hear. I smile broadly at Zart, and eject my phone battery. It
works like a charm. Myhel knows the Coasties are on their way,
and will be thinking about it day and night until they arrive.
Zart says, "That was pretty smart dude."
I say, "I just learned that trick in a propaganda class I took at BU."
Zart worries, "Don't you think Myhel is gonna wanna get back at
you?"
I say, "Myhel went off on a tirade once, and told me 'Vengeance is
a dish best served cold.' That was back on the second time I broke
up with her. Now, she probably schemes about getting even with
me by flamboyantly and flagrantly flashing a new boy about me,
feeling it will cause me to long for her and beg her back. She will

feel better about herself and everything. If she hooks up with a Coastie, then I can feign anger, and tell her I never want to be with her again, and I will be justified. This will help her heal and get over me, ultimately."

Zart says, "You hope."

I reply, "It would be a huge weight off my shoulders if she would just obviously hook-up with a Coastie."

Well before it starts to get dark, I take off on my bike down to the inner harbor. I survey the inner harbor for more options for the swim program. The only problem is that the fisherman often clean their catch and dump the chum off the pier, with the major channel just outside the entrance to the inner harbor, right where Tiger Sharks would cruise by. The thin, pale blue clouds float past Spit Island and the rusty cement water barge. I can make out a couple of Brown Boobies sitting on top, silhouetted against pink and orange sunset swiffs and swaffs of streaky light waves and ocean shimmer.

"Hey, ya ever see any sharks in here right around the piers?" I make the mistake of asking Pillmold, the first 'dive master' on Halfway, supposedly a connoisseur and a wheeler-dealer business entrepreneur, but now, one of the fishing drones working for HIC. A bitter sexist, he's one of those guys who just ain't worth talkin with.

"Oh sharks, ya, sure, everyday! We got a thresher over here we named 'Big boy'. Ain't that right dick-brain?" he yells at one of his crew slaves.

Why did I bother? I already know better. I guess that's what happens when you're full of hope.

As I turn to leave, Pillmold bellows, "Hey, you make the maps right?"

I answer, "Yeh."

"Well you put a friggen shark right on the map," Pillmold complains.

"I know," I say, "it looks cool. We have a lot of sharks."

"Yah, but the tourists don't need to know that," I hear him yell as I quickly peddle away. Screw him.

Later that afternoon, I speak with Darom and a couple of the other Thai anglers. They have tons of info. Turns out that harmless White-tipped Reef Sharks have been seen early in the morning or in the evening in the inner harbor, and that is it. Those guys tend to be pretty nocturnal, no other sharks have been seen, and people should only be allowed to swim during midday hot hours and when someone is there. As I look at these rules, I realize it would be smarter for me to make it really hard for anyone to use these accoutrements alone. I design two diving boards from scrap materials at the Bulky Dump, that are so long and heavy to put into place, that it would take at least two strong adults to make it operable. With the slide, I add weight to the base and top, so again, leverage wise, there is no way to put it in sliding position without at least two very stout persons.

"At least two strong adults; that should save us from getting screwed or sued," I say to Amb proudly as I show him the plan the next day in the office.

"Great work? You put a lot of time and energy into the plan," Amb encourages. "You're the kind of Outdoor Recreational Planner we need out here."

What? That is Chipweldi's title! Wow! He's a GS-11. I'm only a GS-5 and I had to eek-it-out as a volunteer for months to even nail that.

"You sure you have no interest in going to FLETC?" Amb asks me again. This is probably the third time he has asked already.

"Yes. I'm sure, but thanks for asking," I politely decline.

The last thing I want to do is go to FLETC (the Federal Law Enforcement and Training Center, somewhere out in Georgia.). No thanks. I didn't get a Master's at BU and learn all about wildlife on my own to become a cop. I know I would make a great cop, way better than pretty much all of the ones I've ever met, but I want to encourage and enlighten people to love wildlife, not ticket them and bust them so they hate wildlife.

That evening, right before the sun goes down and the Coasties arrive, I decide to get some quick ultimate action in. "One last pass," I yell. I sprain my ankle in the soft sand. Oooooow, how that kills! I crawl around in the sand in pain. Severe pain. Zart runs (the best a heavy beer drinker can) to get the ATV. He and a volunteer help me get onto the back of the ATV. It is very bumpy and really hurts my ankle, but it is the quickest way to get me to the doctor.

That night I hobble into the All Hands Club on crutches. Hey, at least I don't have to worry about getting beat up. Even drunk

Coasties won't beat up a gimp. I stumble forward and up to the bar behind Kilgro, just in time to hear this gem uttered to three Coast Guard crewmen, eagerly watching with their mouths hanging open: "If you have needs, I can satisfy them."

"Well all right," the Coasties say enthusiastically.

I feel like I am going to be sick. No Myhel though. Hmmm. I tripod over to the music room and see Zart messing around with the drums. When he sees me walk into the room, he breaks into a steady four-four rock beat.

"Not bad," I say when he lets up. "Solid. You don't drop time," I encourage.

"Yeah, I was in a few bands. I wanted to be a rocker," he says, as he twirls one stick and swigs beer from the bottle of Heffenviesen on the stool behind him. A couple of the construction guys goof around with the guitars and bass on the other side of the rehearsal room.

"Hey, you ready to rock?" the guitarist yells at Zart.

"Yeah. What do you guys want to do?" Zart queries, tightening the top of one of the cymbals.

"Just play, 1, 2, 3, 4," the guitarist gruffly commands and counts in.

What a nightmare! *Knocking on Heaven's Door, Smoke on the Water, Whiter Shade of Pale, Cat Scratch Fever.* Somebody shoot me now. Grabbing the mic., I begrudgingly sing all of those songs, and order another drink, even though I am starting to feel pretty buzzed, and I belt into those numbers like I care. I implore them to pick something at least from the last two most recent decades.

The guitarist lectures, "Don't know anything new. Don't like the new hippy-hop stuff. Classic rock is the best. That's why it is classic. Classic rock is where it's at. The last great guitarist was Randy Rhodes man."

I definitely don't feel like singing anymore, but now an audience gathers with a bunch of people standing in the hallway, and squeezing into the doorframe. Many of them are Coast Guard men excited to see any action. Drunk Coast Guard men. I scan the crowd for a girl. I can make out one. One girl, that is it.

"C'mon. Sing a song. Play something!" We hear the crowd demanding.

The guitarist, of whom I still never got his name, rips into a very sloppy version of either *LA Woman* or *All Along the Watchtower*. Either way, the adrenalin rises-up into my head, and I look over at Zart with an extreme smile spreading across my face: Semi-insane, one might describe it as. Zart lays into his drum part as I scream *"There must be some kinda way outta here, said the juggler to the thief"* like a possessed banshee. I feel it more than I can see it. I sense it more than I can hear it, but the audience shrinks back in surprise at the sheer intensity and volume of the audible assault. This strength, and everything else combined, hardens and stabilizes my sprained ankle.

"There's too much con-fusionnnn. I can't get no release," I belt in twisted agony, and with an even more giant heave forward, a dozen gents explode into the room and crash into Ryle, Cherry Dewhurt, and JP, causing Pillmold to say drunkenly, "Hey! Watch-it!" He yells vulgarly into the face of a short, stout, fireplug of a Coastie. Pillmold clearly sees from his body posture that this Coastie ain't gonna take Pillmold's shit. Pillmold backs down a bit. The guitarist breaks a string. "Quick, fill-in", he commands as he struggles to change the string.

I look at Zart and the bass player. "Give me a slow, thick, jazz beat," I say.

Zart starts to play and the bass player follows along.

"Thank you for coming all the way out to Halfway this evening," I pronounce with lounge vigor.

The crowd perks up and wails.

"Do you feel like I do?" I scream like Frampton.

The crowd erupts into berserk chaos. "Yeh. Ya. Yeah."

"We got a broken string here so I'm gonna recite a little poem," I say smoothly.

"Booh. Boo. No way. Fuck that," the crowd violently protests, to my surprise.

What? Poetry haters? Next you're gonna tell me they want to punch mimes. I look around, and see my college notebook sticking out of my bag. I pick it up and open it to one of my communication assignments. My eyes fall onto a nice, fat, juicy quote. I can't remember which guy this is from or what the quote is about, but I figure I better start reading. I try to make it swing a little with the jazz, beatnik style, but most of it comes off stiff, like William S.

Burroughs meets Jim Carroll, avoiding as much pomposity as possible:

"Those who manipulate the unseen mechanism of society constitute an invisible government which is the true ruling power of our country. We are governed, our minds molded, our tastes formed, our ideas suggested largely by men we have never heard of. In almost every act of our lives, whether in the sphere of politics or business, in our social conduct or our ethical thinking, we are dominated by the relatively small number of persons who understand the mental processes and social patterns of the masses. It is they who pull the wires that control the public mind. --- Edward Bernays"

I look up at the crowd. They stare in a dazed shock.
I then say, with all seriousness, "I think he also invented Bernays' Sauce." I pause, then say, "Just kidding," with a chuckle.
"Amen!" One of the Coasties yells, only having have heard such language in church. A few join him in the laugh while everyone else stands in a kind of befuddled stupor. D'oh! I barely get that quote; I can't expect anyone else to get it right now, but, . . . the string is on the guitar.
Funny thing; right when I got to the end of that quote, Deny and my brother Manat shot through my mind. They are the masses they are talking about, just like these guitarists are, and the Coasties, and the guys who work for HIC like Cherry Ballpig. I'm aware that in a way, I am too. They don't ever really have an original thought in their heads. Why? Does it take to much work? Why do they just randomly parrot lines from tough-guy spoon-fed Hollywood crap? Do I do it that much less?
The musicians spazz about with excitement, like white men with no rhythm, and rip back into the exact same song. Convulsing my best Jimi Hendrix vocals, everybody looks at me. Kilgro and Jellie and the French chefs all stare at me with great surprise as they trickle into the room. No one knows I am the singing ranger, and I think they thought my solo number before the play was a fluke, or good theater acoustics. No one has ever heard of such a thing as a singing ranger. No one really notices Zart doing a good solid job

drumming, or that the bass and guitar players not only continuously fall out-of-time and out-of-tune, but they just basically totally suck! All anyone seems to be noticing is me. My dynamic movement, even on one ankle; my wide, powerful vocal range; and of course, my psycho-sick looking Ozzie eyes. Me me me. Craving attention. Is that what everything is all about? Let's face it. Be real. There is no such thing as curiosity. Everyone and thing has a reason for why. Not necessarily in a devious way, but they do. They want to know for a reason, even at the risk of death. Curiosity killed the cat. The cat wants to know cause the cat thinks this is something it could eat, or at least kill. Cats '*love* to kill', to make Konrad Lorenz role over in his grave. They *have* to kill. How do you like that Konrad, better? Saying a cat loves to kill is like saying an alcoholic loves to drink. Really? They *love* to drink? NO! They *have* to drink. Cats have to kill. It's like my obsessive compulsive brother Rosmarus. He doesn't like being a bully; he just can't help it. Rosmarus would rather cheat than lose. I would rather lose than cheat. These are not necessarily fundamental philosophical differences as much as philogenetic instincts coming to fruition in habituated adult behavior. I am a winner for not cheating, even though I lost. Rosmarus is a loser for cheating, even though he won, he lost. Rosmarus even said to me once, "Nice guys finish last, and you are a naïve sucker if you think otherwise." Too bad. Too bad he thinks that way, because if we have more people thinking like him and less people thinking like me, and if we have way more ultra-conservative war mongers than peace-loving environmental advocates, then we are really doomed. The cynical, greedy Republicans have taught us that, over and over again.

"Ya like *Cat Scratch Fever* man?" The drunken guitarist blathers at the Coasties.

I wave my hands and nod my head 'no' to try to encourage them and plead for another number.

"Yeah!" A group cheer roars. Everybody all of a sudden is having a great time and I *have to* sing Ted Noise, again. We rip through the song as everyone bangs their heads in unison.

"You are a great singer and a great front-man. You should be in a band," a few people say to me at the break.

"Wow man, you should have told me you are such a great singer," Zart says as he sucks back a Heiniken; kind of a low-brow brew for him actually.

I say to Zart, "Don't you remember you said that same thing to me after the Sri Lankan drum jam?"

Zart questions with confusion, "I did. I don't remember. I must have been hammered. That's a totally different kind of singing anyway. This is Rock n Roll!"

"What are *you* doing out here man?" another one of the Coasties yells at me.

I grab the mike and whisper to get the crowd to lower their level, "The ultimate irony of living at Halfway with 48 albatross nests on my front lawn is that when I worked at Hawaii Volcanoes National Park on the Hawksbill Turtle Program I was working down at Apua Point and I was by myself, and I had been snorkeling for a few hours and then I was laying under the army tarp, ya know, to stay out of the sun, and I was on the painful army cot, you know, the one with the bar in the middle of the back that fuckin kills?" I ramble at an unbelievable pace with long run-on sentences. The Coasties, FNs, and everyone else, nod their heads and laugh, hanging on every word.

I go on with, "I was just trying to cool down, and avoid the metal brace under my back, and trying to avoid inhaling too much of the hydrochloric acid in the air, floating around from Kilauea and more at the emergence point plume. All of a sudden, way off in the distance through the gaping triangle in the tent, I could see a huge white bird with straight wings over the ocean. Clear as day, though far away, I knew it wasn't a plane, so I grabbed my binoculars and sprinted across the lava muttering 'Oh my god'. Running across the black sharp lava as fast as I could, and getting out to the edge of the water, I struggled to set my binoculars (due to my heavy breathing), but finally, I did, and I got a look at it and it was a Laysan Albatross!! Sure enough. It was a Laysan Albatross, and I was saying to myself 'Oh my god. That was a Laysan. Oh my god. I saw an albatross. Wow! That's so cool.' Then the next day, I went around telling everyone I saw, 'Wow! I saw an albatross. That's so cool. That's so cool. I saw an albatross. Wow! That's so cool. It's amazing.'" I stop and take a breath before the next guy can interject. "Now I know you think I sound stupid and you are laughing at me, but on the Main Hawaiian Islands they are pretty rare, unless you are up near Kauai and Kilauea Point Lighthouse on the cliff, which also happens to be a Wildlife Sanctuary and a place where they used to nest and appear to be making a comeback. There are boobies there, and frigates, but albatross are still struggling to make it back there. Then I end up on Halfway, with so many albatross it makes you go insane," I finish with a big huff.

I get all puzzled looks again. No one knows how to respond or cope with my manic energy. I start singing *a cappella* and the rest of the 'band' jump for their instruments. I am on a roll. I feel empowered, and good, and free. Myhel still isn't here. That is liberating. I can have fun and not feel guilty. Why didn't I answer their question 'What are *you* doing here?' more directly? Like Billy Joel's Piano Man: *"Man what are you doin here?"* Do you know how many times people said that to me at UCLA and BU. "Man, what are *you* doin here?" Everybody who meets me and gets to know me assumes I can do much better. Me too. I assume I can do much better. Even when I took this job, Tirgut, the founder and owner of ASS, said, "It will be great to have a great ranger out on Halfway, at least for a little while."

"Little while? Do you think I'm a short-timer?" I asked puzzled.

"No, it's just that we never hold on to great people like you. They always move on to bigger and better things," she explained.

Back in the packed All Hands Club MWR music rehearsal room, I finish a song and the crowd goes nuts, but just at that point, one of the head Coasties announces, "Liberty is over. Everyone back to the ship. Head count in 30 minutes."

With that, the Coasties, many of them shaking my hand, shuffle out of the All Hands Club with disappointed groans. Han, the Sri Lankan, apparently a little drunk on Christian Bros., quietly says to me, "Mr. Kestrel, I sorry but we have close the club now."

The next thing I know, I'm back in my bed. Now, waiting to fall asleep, and fully exhausted, these thoughts run through my head, like they always do, at night, as I lie in my bed, alone. Alain and Laura, the French chef and his wife, really enjoyed the show. I think they like seeing Americans being good, instead of the lame hicks they have to deal with daily from HIC. I feel for them too. Alain and Laura shipped all the way out here, and the crazy idea of a French restaurant with fancy French cooks for no one. Asinine. There is no one here who could even appreciate Alain's wizardry and Laura's soft, ethereal presence? They are great chefs, great hosts, and do a really great job. 'Man, what are *they* doin here?' What's funny about them is the reputation of the French from my trip to Cannes and from everything I've heard. At The All Hands Club tonight, I heard Ryle say 'The French people are a bunch of assholes, right?' I heard him say it within earshot of Alain, to see if he could get a reaction. I could tell Alain heard it, but that was all. Alain appears to be too worldly to get embroiled with a dick like Ryle.

I think while I look up at the cobwebs strung across the ceiling of my room. Well, considering I am about to die and these are the last Frenchies I will ever meet, I have to say that Alain and Laura probably turn out to be the nicest people out here in the long run, as I stated earlier. He is not a particularly handsome guy and he is a little hefty (which you would expect of a good French chef), but only a little in the stomach area, with a scar on his face. Her? She has like a very unattractive boyish frame and face with a big nose and not really nice teeth. However, her gentle personality affects my attraction to her way more than her physical detractions, and the one time in my year on the atoll that I saw her at the beach in a little bikini; Wow!

I remember a week or so ago, and the reaction from a couple of the Navy chiefs and HIC workers the first time they were shocked to see her in a bikini after not even looking at her for months.

"She has a hot box from heaven, I mean like excellent body, nice legs, nice butt, but especially you know just her box is freakin fine," one of them said over a stiff drink at the bar that very evening. I could tell he was going to masturbate over her, if he hadn't yet.

The chief looks over at me, reading the disgust on my face, and says, "Whad arh ya got a problem with sumpthen?"

"Yah", I say, "I got a big problem with bigoted men that treat women like hunks of meat, or possessions, or objects."

"Oh yeah," the chief reeled like a gaseous intestine, "Like you treated Myhel any better. Get away from me you asshole James Bond. Ha ha ha. James Bond. James A. Bond, fah asshole, Ha ha ha," the chief rattles as the crowd laughs.

Though vulgar, he is right. The prevailing perception of my Myhel relationship makes me look like a hypocrite. On top of that, it makes my mouth water now to think of Laura on the beach as I lie here. I force myself to slide out of bed and lean down over the faucet for a gulp in the darkness. I lie down again and think of her. She oozes sexuality with zero effort, like the Brasilera girls do. Too bad I'll be dead. I can't enjoy a French or Brazilian or Italian girl again. Wait. Can you enjoy "it" in heaven? If we can't enjoy carnal or physical pleasures in heaven, then what is it more like an acid trip, where you just feel bliss in your mind but in reality your soul (or whatever else is left) just feels like it's in a state of utopian happiness? I mean, I love "it", so why not have "it" all the time up in heaven?

Thinking About It
by Drats

I can't stop thinking about it; TV, news and magazines,
Everywhere I look I see it, Imagined fantasy scenes
Am I a maniac, or are you too shrewd? Am I being open, or just
being rude?
About it every second I think; With every body I see, Reduced to a
peering dink, Is there something wrong with me?
Am I a dirty fiend, lascivious and lewd? I image it with you, is that
being crude?
I can't stop thinking about it, Young and old from every race,
Surrounded by a world of it, It's always shoved in my face, I love
it, Want it, think it's good, Maybe they want it too, To grab it if I
only could, Be honest about it with you
I'm constantly checking it out, It's the first thing I think of, It
brings bizarre feelings of doubt, It's got nothing to do with love, I
can't stop thinking about it, Please don't tell me you can, Is
everybody thinking about it? Am I a normal human?
Am I a maniac, or are you too shrewd? Am I being open, or just
being rude?

I stare at the ceiling, thinking about the night. I remember my own feelings of cognitive dissonance. I don't want to think about negatives, but I do. I always do. Take football and track as a perfect example. When I played football, I had a great coach, Defa, but I was generally a failure and my senior year was fraught with injury. We won the Div. 2 Super Bowl in '81, which was great, and I was always a team player and very proud that we won, but I didn't play even a second of that Super Bowl game.

In track, though my coach loved the kids, she proved to be pretty inferior, but under Ma Magee I was a great success who still holds records today. I helped my team win, was carried on my team's shoulders after beating Petras from Swampscott, and was elected team captain for the spring.

If you look at these two scenarios, you would think that I would forget about the football bummers and ruminate on the track hero shit. Instead, all I do is dwell on how I could have been better in football and how I wished I got to run a 'wing left, reverse right, on two, ready break!' The football players were dicks to me, whereas the track team loved and respected me. The football team stuffed me into lockers and abused me on the field with cheap-shots. On the track team, even my 'little' brother Manat admired me. Yet, I dwell on football. Why, why why? And it is the same thing now. Instead of thinking about all the nice compliments I got and how great I sang, and how entertained everyone was, I am thinking about negativity and assholes. Why? Is there a psychological term for that? Just like all my great singing gigs, and all the acting I have done, and the professional dance, which proved to be the most lucrative; I forget all of these things and only remember how people were mean to me and boo hoo hoo. Like when I was at UCLA, an oasis in a shit-hole of *Homo sapiens* pollution, called LA. I wanted to sing, dance, and act, probably in that order, but I hated Hollyweird. UCLA made me feel strong, great, optimistic, progressive, and I believed I could achieve great things. I felt like I belonged to a great school with a great class. Maybe I should have stayed and got a job there. What would have happened to me if I never left UCLA? Instead, I don't think about that. Instead, I dwell on how lame BU was, or how some lame ass psycho pussy like Tah ruined my band **InsectAffect**.

For example: Instead of thinking some nice, positive thoughts as I drift off to sleep tonight, I remember back to the disgusting gossip about Laura. At that point, Cherry Ballpig, the repulsive pig with a massive beer-belly of self neglect and with a rancid cigar stub dangling from the corner of his leper lips, had to say what maybe some of us were thinking but none of us needed to say.

"Ooaahwaah now I see why Alain is hooked-up with Laura. He must love doing that girl. Ha ha ha."

Gross. I always kinda think stuff like that to myself, like, 'Well, Alain's not the greatest prize and Laura's not the greatest prize, but I guess I can see how they got together, etc. But I don't jump to 'What are they like in bed?' Why do these guys have to take it down to such a graphic level? It's like the more graphic they are, the more cool and tough they think they are. I hope no one finds this novel too fuckin gratuitous. I feel that Drats only puts in swears and shit like that when necessary.

One of the fat chiefs says "Va va voom, je parle Francies" in a butchering French accent. "Then, it must have got pretty fuckin hot for Alain. Huh u huh. If ya can't stand the heat. . ." he says like a dope.

Obviously he's never really had a hot woman and doesn't know how to at least act like he's already been there. Again they detect my look of disgust. The objectification. My face betrays me so often. I can never lie cause I know that even when I tell the god's honest truth over and over again, people still think I'm lying. I'm not believable.

"What's a matter with you?" the bigger, meaner, uglier chief says. "I like Alain and Laura and I don't feel it's appropriate to say gross sexist things like that, that objectify women." It rolls off my tongue so fast that I can't stop my impulse before it spews out. All of the chiefs' eyes narrow.

One takes a big gulp of his beer, then belches, "We don't need no huggers telling us what to like or how to act, that's for sure," deflecting anything to do with my comment and taking the 'I'm more of a man than you are' personal attack stance and name-calling. The unintentional irony of his statement is that he is enlisted in the Navy, so he has commanders telling him exactly what to like and how to act, but *he thinks* he's a free and independent thinker, just like most programmed religious fanatics do. Ha.

"Well, if you continue to act in ways unbecoming of officers and gentlemen, you'll never be one," I retort.

"Ha! Officer? None of us will ever make officer," one of the chiefs snarls back.

"Not with that attitude you won't," I say with a laugh and walk off. Now my minds-eye remembers the rest of the events. As I leave the All Hands Club I see Myhel on her bike heading north. I can see her far ahead of me as we ride past the raucous goonies. Then, up ahead, I see she turns and stops in front of my barracks. My head bobs as my vision of the events gets blurry. I almost fall asleep with my perspiring scalp soiling my pillow case, but I maintain consciousness long enough to get back to the image of her ahead of me on her bike, in the dark. I think it best to avoid her. I already had enough confrontations tonight. I skulk around the long way to the far side of the BOQ, put my bike in the rack, and head up the stairs. As I get close to my floor, there she is, hiding in the hallway in ambush. I run up the stairs taking 3 at a time, but by the time I get to the third flight, I hear a voice.

"Kestrel," she says in a soft, controlled voice. I freeze and look down over the railing to see her looking up at me from the landing below.

"Ya, what's up?" I ask curtly.

"I want to talk with you," she says calmly.

"Myhel, it's only been a few days. We need some major separation time," I say, even though it has actually been at least over a month.

"Says you. I don't know what your problem is. Maybe you don't want to admit how you really feel about me or something and that's why you are running away?" she challenges. "I don't need any separation time. I am fine. How about you?"

I think for a second. "I thought you were falling in love with me and wanted to take me home to momma," I say quietly so the sound wouldn't ring through the stairwell. I look up and it appears to be clear.

"I know. I thought about it and that was my bad," she whispers as she starts to walk up the stairs a little and puts her hand on mine on the railing. "I am over all that. Let me just come talk to you," she says. She seems reasonable, so I say okay and she comes up into my room for the first time ever. We talk for a long time, then she starts gently rubbing her fingers across the zipper of my fly. I can feel half a loaf starting to rise. Shit! This is a fuckin mistake. I am better off alone. Then she kisses me on the mouth and starts squeezing my hog. We have sex twice in about an hour, then she sneaks back to her room in the blackness.

I bet you didn't see that part to the story coming. Neither did I. I bet you thought I'd never be stupid enough to go back with Myhel again. Why? Why do I do that? I can't control that? Now I lie here looking at the ceiling, remembering all that I can of what has just happened this night, but not knowing how or why. I have no control over myself. I sing, I drink, I have sex. I am like a base animal. I am not even above lizard-brain level. I'm like Ryle! I know, lots of guys would say 'Hey, you are horny, alone, might as well do it.' I think that's probably what the chiefs would say, and the construction dudes, and the HIC staff. I don't think the Sri Lankans would say that though, and I don't feel like that is me, but it is? I just did it! This is not 'her bad', this is 'my bad'.

I pass out.

The next day, I try to jog my hangover away. Bad idea. Never works. Then, even worse, I see Myhel coming toward me at the beach in biker shorts and a sports bra. She is looking more fit than she ever has, and much better than when I first met her.

"Howdy," she says with a jovial cat-that-ate-the-canary voice.

"Hi," I say, dryly, as we jog along the beach together. "Look! White-tailed tropicbird!" I say with shock and excitement.

"No, that's a red-tailed. We don't have white-tailed," she corrects me like a non-thinking robot.

I stop and wipe the stinging sweat from my eyes, remove my shades, then refocus with my hands tightly cupped across my forehead like a visor.

"Nope, that's a white-tailed, that's why I'm making a big deal out of it. I see red-taileds all the time, and I saw white-tailed in Halemaumau Crater," I retaliate. There is tension in the air.

"Oh, wow, you're right," she concurs, with her hand blocking the sun over her visor, kissing up to me, but not really caring about the bird. I could call it a roadrunner and she would agree with me, as long as everything is fine.

We stand there for a second watching the bright white bird soar in high circles, then glide toward the center of Sand Island with intermittent wing beats. Just then, we lose track of the tropicbird because a pair of white terns come down and start hovering above our heads. Their big, black eyes staring at me, I say, "I wonder if I could catch one of these guys?" and with that, I squat down a bit. As the tern comes lower to glance over my hair, I spring up and gently cradle it in my hands.

"Wow!" Myhel says, amazed at my physical prowess again, "I didn't think you could do that."

We both pet the tern for a second, examine the wings and the beak, and then I open my hands and it pauses for a second, realizing it is free again, and lifts-off gently, only to come back with it's mate and continue to hover just over our heads in complaint.

"Well I guess they don't learn their lesson, do they?" I say like Bugs Bunny. Myhel laughs hard and loud.

"You are so funny. How come I never meet guys like you?" as she gives me an awkward hug.

I push her back gently, hold her shoulders for a second, then let go. "Myhel, listen to me. Last night was a mistake. I am leading you down the wrong path. I don't see myself ever falling in love with you and you are in denial about how you feel for me."

She bursts into tears, "Fuck you. You are an asshole. All men are assholes." She starts to march off.

"See, this is exactly what I'm talking about. No one wants to be with a girl who is unstable," I say firmly.

"Unstable? I'm unstable?" she yells unstably. "Unstable I'm NOT. Being unstable is off the list!" she blubbers.

"Yes. This behavior right now is unstable, immature, and a bunch of other things, but instead of name-calling, I am just telling you that no guy wants to be with a girl like that, just like no girl wants to be with a guy like that. Even some of my theatre arts friends who love drama don't want this kind of reactionary explosive shit!" I say, losing my temper.

She keeps walking away, crying. I know she wants me to follow her and say, 'Oh, poor Myhel. Sorry you feel so bad. I was wrong. I love you and I will go to the UP to meet your mom.' That's what she wants me to say. No way. Sorry. You can't always get what you want.

Just like me. I want a girl I'm crazy about to say she will love me forever and soothe me and comfort me and be my trusted soul-mate and give me awesome head. Look, she wants what I want. I think we all want what we want. *All You Need Is Love* a very sensitive Brit once said. I believe that. I don't believe in letting something ride that isn't real and is waiting, just waiting, to explode in your face. I have to be strong enough to cut this off. Weeks go by and I focus on work and wildlife. A couple of times, alone in my room, the idea crosses my mind for a second, for a second. That is all. I think that maybe I should go see how she is doing. I think maybe I am stupid for letting this opportunity go to waste. Then I think about her personality, what Zart said, Ryle trying to bust into her room, and everything else, and I talk myself out of it again. Look, I am the ranger out here. I have to stand tall and strong, and dealing with her brings out all of my weaknesses. I have to have some balls sometimes, instead of just being all dick all of the time. Perception is a funny thing. I kind of thought Halfway was kind of a paradise when I first got here, like a heaven on Earth. Heaven appears to be turning into hell pretty darn quick, and how much of this fault is of my own doing. Most of the people out here all want to kill each other over programmed beliefs. At the worst possible time, just when tensions on the atoll seem to be simmering up to a boil, a new figure by the name of Misa Queen starts to rile up the rest of the stew, like Mother Nature whipping up little tempest tornados of testy turmoil.

With visitation way up and great accolades coming in about all of my fabulous programs, someone somewhere decides they have budget for a second ranger. Great! With two of us I should be able to get way more work done and finish a bunch of projects I'm excited about. But no, as I see her walk off the plane, my heart sinks more than it did when I saw Jellie. This turns out to be a completely useless idiot named Misa Queen. *'Don't tell Amb!'* would become her beg mantra to me for the oh-so-too-long a year she would be on atoll.

Zart says with a tone of disappointment, "There's your new ranger."

We all look at Misa Queen for a second. She looks dumpy and dumb, sloppy and fat, and frankly horrible. We see her hug Myhel and Kilgro at the Hangar, with her Polynesian poser beads, smelly dreads and stinky sarong flowing thing, and Hawaiian flip-flops, better known as slippahs. No other footwear could make that outfit complete. Jellie joins them, as they walk off to the golf cart.

"Shit. If ya can judge a book by it's cover, we are fucked," I say in disappointment.

"*You* are," Zart shoots back.

As I turn with Zart to exit, Jellie catches a glimpse of me and directs Kilgro to swing the cart around to make introductions. Jellie digs, "You've heard about our ranger out here."

Misa Queen looks at me with suspicion and says, "How'z it? You still getting in trouble with the girls?"

"Nope, everything's cool," I state dismissively, minus the wise-ass comeback.

"Well, now that I'm coming out here too, you will remember, there won't be any hanky-panky upfront," Misa Queen states like an over-protective, nervous freshman sorority virgin.

Zart almost spits trying to hold the laugh in. What a preposterous assumption. What on Earth has she heard about me? Banette and Dietera exchange looks of disbelief. Myhel keeps her arms folded tightly across her chest, and her lip tightly buttoned. She has put all of them up to this, but she puts on the hurt boo boo face to garner sympathy.

"I'm sorry. Why are we doing this to each other? Misa Queen just got here," I say placidly.

"You're right. I'd rather we not talk," Jellie snipes, taking my tranquil tone as a victory, as she splits with the ladies. I hear Myhel mumble with a growl, "Ooooh, he is off the list."

As some of the BRAC construction guys head for the plane for good, I notice I know none of them really. They are mostly the good guys who work hard and are pretty cool, including the guy who tried to play bass. The Lt. is also leaving for good. He waves me over to him to say goodbye to me alone, in the shade of the Hangar, humbly and cool.

He says, "The Navy will be completely gone from here in less than 3 months. I know you won't have any trouble with anyone with that short time left." He gives a knowing smile as he raises his eyebrows. "You give a great history tour, and I know you will keep the naval tradition alive."

Zart looks at me as we mount our bikes, "What was that all about?"

"I don't know and will probably never know," I reply.

As we ride back to the barracks, I see Myhel sitting on the stairs. Zart and I attempt to walk past her, but she stops me.

180

"Kestrel. Kestrel. Please Kestrel. Can we talk for a minute?"
Myhel pleads.
I should just blast past her, but I say, "Okay," politely.
"Remember I told you I come from 'The land of the ugly babies'?"
she asks.
"Yuh," I reply vaguely.
"What did you think of me the first time we were, together," she
stutters.
"From the first day I met you in your room and we took the
shower?" I question. She barely nods.
"The 'C' word, 'commitment'. The Navy guy back on Wouldbe
Island, who you moved back there to live with, only to move back
out here. The trophy wife things you said (which is wicked funny
that she could think of herself as such). I don't know," I stop with
confusion. She is right and I am wrong. I can tell that I would
never be serious with her and yet I am almost thinking I should do
her right now. I shouldn't even be talking to her right now.
"If you saw me walking down the street in a city, you wouldn't
even look at me!" Myhel says again as she starts to cry again.
Those words will ring in my head until my brain completely stops
cranking on the sandy bottom, outside the atoll waters. Her large
birth mark, sprawled across her brow and nose, which I barely ever
have even noticed and which Drats never even bothered to
mention, is way to superficial for me to even care about, especially
when she covers it with make-up. Yet, this remains a sticking point
and apparently not only blemishes her face, but her soul. I guess
since I don't have a wine stain or whatever they call it, I'm less
sympathetic, but seriously, it is so shallow to care about that little
birthmark. I'm sure she got shit about it as a kid, but we all caught
shit about something. What she should realize is that the little
birthmark on her face has nothing to do with anything else: Love,
Sex, Friendship, Success. Nothing! Yet she lets it. If I were her, I'd
be more concerned about my soul.
"I know I am crying right now and you think I'm a basket case, but
please come to bed with me. I will suck on you for 5 whole
minutes," she says in desperation.
I look down at her in pity for a moment. I can handle it. I think of
just saying goodbye and walking away.

Myhel says, "Look, I know you already told me you are never going to fall in love with me. I just want to have sex with you while we are out here on the island. All I really care about in life is a roof over my head, full stomach, nothing on me hearts." She makes a Freudian slip, meaning to say 'hurts' instead of 'hearts'. She goes on, "I am way low maintenance and all that stuff, compared to that Hilo girl." She tries to convince me as she reaches out and starts to tickle my knee.

"But when Christmas rolls around you won't want to take me to the UP to meet your mom?" I ask bluntly.

"Oh, well, hu, I thought we were boyfriend and girlfriend," she says apologetically, and yet with a glimmer of hope.

"Oht ooh. This is gonna be a huge problem. What gave you that impression?" I ask gently. "Ya know, we never even said that we love each other all this time. I thought you said you weren't into commitment?"

"I'm not. I wasn't. The C word is off the list. I didn't even like sex until I met you," the tears start rolling again.

"Whoa whoa whao! Where the fuck did this come from?" I state, but much nicer than that sounds. By now, you know how I am. I don't want to hurt her but I'm conflicted by all the mixed messages I'm getting. That should be enough to convince me.

And she says, "Ya well I thought things had changed and I was afraid to say 'I love you' cause I thought you would dump me." This sorrowful sight of broken tears pains me, for I can see that her fantastical mind cannot cope with reality.

"Well that is an important thing to think about right? If you are afraid to say I LOVE YOU to the guy cause he's gonna run away then you have to figure that you are in love or infatuated with him and he's not that way with you," I try to say this with understanding, not condescension.

I come to the realization that no matter what happens, it would be totally irresponsible of me to have sex with her ever again, unless my feelings for her really change dramatically. Danica and Jewel have already proven to me that I am not only not in love with Myhel, but there are already a bunch of things I don't even like about her.

This time, I am really through with her!

Chapter 5: Wicked Angry

The winter creeps back in, and the atoll starts taking on a darker and cooler feeling, leaving the hot summer days far behind. The noisy albatross will start returning any day now, after their short break from atoll life.

On our hands and knees, pulling *Verbesina*, we crawl along. I sing to break up the monotony and keep my spirits high, while working my vocal chords. Yup, always a multi-tasker.

Han looks over at me, knowing I've been through a lot. "Mizz Myhel still went her trip to the UP to see her Mum?"

I say, "Minus me."

"Oooooh," Banette caterwauls like a harpooned monk seal, "That must have been tough on Myhel, but she set herself up."

I keep pulling, furiously, as I say, "I have no idea how she told her family, or if she did. She lied about the shower massage. She was wrong about the Black-tipped Reef Sharks and the White-tailed Tropicbird, and I realize, she just wants to be like Queen of The Atoll. There is way more and way worse private stuff, but I still don't even know how you guys know anything to begin with."

Loon adds, "God, you haven't spoken to her in a month now, . . ."

And I say, ". . . and I am feeling strong and liberated."

I don't know if it's psychological or not, but it seems like my lifting workouts are more intense and I can run longer at Ultimate, which Myhel has still been attending and plays, at times. I just make sure I never cover her or go near her on the field. But seriously, the less Homo-centric I make my life, the more healthy, relaxed, and fun I seem to be.

We continue along, pulling out yellow weed after yellow flower. I look over and notice that Misa Queen has been watching everything vaguely without saying anything, hiding beneath a granny-esque Hawaiian sunhat and huge Jackie-O face coverers. She watches us pull, stopping to talk with each person who drifts by, taking consecutive long breaks, but I never see her pull a weed until the very end when we are all about to finish.

That same night, Hamed More and Riz Smaller arrive on the 19-seater. Funny: Smaller is dorky-giraffe tall, and More is wee-wee-little and seems to be less. When looking at the manifest, then seeing them step off of the plane, I immediately assume that the six-foot-tall one is More and the five-foot-tiny one is Smaller. Wouldn't that confuse you? As biologists, they are eager to meet me and the rest of the APS staff. They are both beautiful, intelligent grad students: Smart, nice, healthy, . . . great! Finally, like with the Hilo class, we have some semi-normal girls on atoll. Of course, this is going to cause problems on Halfway.

I can't even remember how it happened now, and I'm sure you're all sick of hearing of my 'Diddler on the Roof' sexcapades, but, within a week of her landing, I am in Hamed's room making sweet delicious love to her.

"Oh my god! What a radical difference from Myhel," I confess to Zart in confidence. "Hamed isn't as hot and wild as Messycka was; but nobody is."

Zart analyzes, "But Hamed, Hamed seems like a girl you could really fall for."

I say, "Girl next store, biologist, messed-up, but not half as messed-up as Myhel."

"I don't like the looks of this," Zart prophesizes.

And so, as you can imagine, things go down hill really really fast. Myhel remains really pissed off as I stay away from her. She tells everyone she can what a jerk I am, and then she tries to tell everybody that I dumped her for Hamed More when actually, I don't like the term 'dumped', because I didn't, I don't, and I never do.

"How can you dump a non-committal person?" Loon says, defending me.

"Isn't that antithetical?" Bent, the new dive master, agrees, as he volunteers to pull weeds with us; something Pillmold would have never offered to do.

I say, "Also, I stopped seeing Myhel way before Christmas, and started dating Hamed a week after she got to the atoll in mid January. That's over a month gap between officially ending it with Myhel and starting to date Hamed."

Han asks, "You date Hamed three weeks before Myhel come back to Halfway?" Now he is starting to believe me.

I say, "I didn't even know that Hamed existed when I told Myhel we needed a break."

Banette says, "Yet, a month or so on an atoll like this, where nothing ever changes and everything always looks and feels the same, and everyone appears to be waiting, just waiting, waiting, waiting, waiting. . . well then, it's easy for her to say you dumped her for Hamed, and it's an easy lie for everyone to believe, especially when they are dying to."

Banette is really smart. That is one of the things I really like about her, and Dietera and Loon. They are smart people. I think they might be smarter than me. I like that. Bent seems pretty smart too. Banette's apropos comments flash me back to that one funny night we ended up in Zart's room, several months ago, before the first major negative events began to occur with Myhel; right before Ryle knocked on her door and things seemed almost okay. I can't remember what happened that night or how we got there, but it was a sick crew: Kilgro, Jellie, Myhel, Jeff, Zart and I. 3 guys, 3 girls, 1 room, with a bathroom, lots of drinking, eleven o'clock on a Saturday night. Ya, you've been there.

Jeff was this short-term volunteer who got hitched out to Halfway for a 90-day stint since his dad had recently retired from the Animal Protection Service. He was a good kid, so you know you won't hear from him again in this book. I cast him in a bit part in the Jorgenson play, with like seven lines, as a judge presiding over the Adolph Jorgenson trails. At 19, he already enlisted in the Marines. There was no talking him out of it, Zart and I learned quickly, so fuck it. Anyway, he got so plastered that we laid him on his side on the cool tiles of the bathroom floor next to the toilet, just in case. After a drink or two, we would check him again to see if he was still breathing.

"I got to pee," Kilgro gruffly barks.

"You are not goin in there, ha h," Myhel shoots back, nervous at her moxie.

"Go ahead. I dare you to. You won't," Jellie goads with a husky laugh.

"Oh, you don't know me very well. I have stooped to much lower, lower things," Kilgro fumbles, trying to be cool, but sounding desperate as usual.

She goes into the bathroom and closes the door.

"I'm more worried about him than her," Zart laughs under his breath, but we both know we couldn't put molestation beyond her.

"Don't get any pee on him," I add from the peanut gallery.

We hear a grunty laugh echo in the shower.

It looks like we are pairing off, to me. Everyone can see easily that it looks like Myhel and I have it goin on, and don't forget, Zart already knew, so Kilgro probably already knew too. Jellie, I think, was the only conscious one there that was clueless.

I set Zart up with Jellie in his room. I thought I was doing him a favor. After we decided Jeff was passed out for the night and going nowhere, but he was sleeping like a baby and appeared to be fine, we finally got Kilgro to leave by repeatedly convincing her that she had to be out on the dolphin raft at sunrise for surveys. It was down to Myhel, Jellie, Zart and I. I cleverly lured Myhel to the bathroom, stepping over Jeff, and said 'Be right back' like a Cheshire Cat with a little Willy Wonka thrown in. Then I locked the door, so Zart could pull a move on Jellie.

We heard Jellie leave Zart's room about 20 minutes later, then Myhel and I did it in my bed, commando-quietly, then she slipped off to her room.

Zart was pissed the next day. He was not going that way.

I remember explaining to Zart, "I thought I was helping you out man."

As I look back at that event now, it seems like a lot more than seven months ago. I would never pull a stunt like that now, especially with Jellie. Everything on the atoll seemed new then, and open. Wow, how things change.

I think back again, "Ya, don't do me any favors," Zart said with aggravation.

Obviously, he wants nothing to do with Jellie. I don't get it; he's not that much of a prize, so why doesn't he just do her? Zart was mad about that night for a while, but he still keeps bringing up the fact that he wants a girl so bad. I know what he means; not just any girl. I shouldn't try to thrust Kilgro, Jellie, or Misa Queen onto him.

Today, I look over to see the sweat dribbling off of the tip of his large nose, and I ask him, "What are you looking for?"

He goes from one knee down to both knees and onto all fours to take a gulp of air. He only works half as furiously as me, but you can't expect anyone normal to be close to as hyper as me in my work. Zart says, "Oh, I want a girl, don't get me wrong, but she has to be the right girl."

Vague; a little non-descript as usual, but I guess true to my argument that basically we are all looking for the same thing ultimately.

I flash back to a huge party out on the beach to celebrate The 4th of July, traditionally, the biggest holiday celebrated on Halfway, with parades and beach parties. I dressed up like Captain Shnooks, the guy who supposedly discovered Halfway, even though there are records that show that Japanese sailors had hit the atoll a number of times but never established anything because, other than to collect albatross eggs and feathers, there was no reason to be here.

I arrived by sailboat, which one of the good construction workers sailed and beached in the soft coral sand. I stepped off the bow with a Capeetahn Krunch hat and recited a speech I wrote about the history of Halfway's discovery. If the publisher isn't lame, you can look at that photo now.

With a cardboard telescope and machete sword, The Capt. edutains visitors, HICs, and FNs alike.

Wow. What is fiction? I threw in a lot of pirate 'Argghh's for good measure.

As the party dragged on, I got some of the ultimate team together and tried to get a bunch of the basketball, volleyball, and bowlers involved for the first time. Note to self: Don't play ultimate with a bunch of drunk, testosterone-charged, Creatine-raged, dickheads. I had kind of forgotten about Ryle and didn't think he'd be looking for payback, but he was. On a play, as I bumped him a little to reach down and grab the disc off the shiny sand, he smears my face into the coarse coral, extremely hard and violently, with all the force he has. I can't see, but I come up swinging and miss. He and his friends laugh and walk away. Dietera skulks away; being the bio bird nerd that she has been her whole life, she probably thinks she's next in the persecution line. I stand there like a fool, looking around in a daze. What a fucking asshole. This guy Ryle needs to be put away. Have I mentioned how much I hate bullies already? The next day I went over to him in uniform while he was in the weight room. I had a bloody scratch on the bridge of my nose from the sand grinding he gave me. "Hey, howz it goin?" I say in a non-threatening manner.

"Good," he says, as he grabs a large white towel, throws it over his shoulder, and walks up to me all tough, inflating his chest, and with his buddy coming over behind him like he's gonna back him up or something. I'm thinking, 'What the fuck do these idiots think, like I'm gonna attack somebody or something. What stupid, stupid Coors-drinkin fucks.'

"Hey man, I just want to say that we are not in Jr. high school and that was just ridiculous yesterday." I try to open an intelligent dialogue.

He says, "I don't care about you. I don't give a fuck about you. Ppffff." He stands, as if bracing for a push or punch for a second, then turns and walks back to the equipment, with his back-up buddy.

I stand in complete shock. I barely know this guy. Why would he act so vile? Immediately! Immediately, this thing flings me, just flings me back to one of my first days in the schoolyard in first grade, when I attempt to reason with a bully in a rational way, then push back in anger, only to realize we are on totally different planes. This bully pushed me over a horizontal creosote log in the pot-holed parking lot. This was all the school had for a playground. I fell, and cried. He was obviously way bigger and stronger than me, and that would be the first in a long school history of having to knuckle under the bully, no matter what I thought. He went on to use that same strategy to make it to high school football captain. To the dominant aggressors, go the spoils?

Ryle, who stood in front of me in the weight room, was supposed to be like an adult. He was supposed to be a strong, smart, courageous adult American construction worker, and when I looked down at him, all I could see was a little-bitty 6 year-old going 'I don't care about you. Naah, na na, na na, naahhh.' He was frightened. His actions relay fear, not comfort and control like I convey, probably because I am too stupid or naïve to realize there is any present danger. I have to keep reminding myself, 'Yes Kestrel, *Homos* are that stupid. If I can't even reach out to my family who are supposed to love me, how is there any hope for humanity, and the other 2 million species on the Planet, to control their psychotic minds, let alone a rage-filled moron like this dude?' Sure, again I know I'm not perfect. I pulled pranks, throwing broken hockey sticks through spokes, using my knees in Buck-Buck, throwing rocks and stuff like that, but I was never ever a mean bully. That's what separates the old, archaic biblical man from the smart, new world man: sensitivity, intelligence, kindness; holding back when one could easily kill, rape, or steal. Lorenz proves that even animals, even going all the way back to fish, like ciclids, have internal behavioral mechanisms that prevent us from going hog wild. Impulse Control; something this guy Ryle obviously lacks, but why? Will 'Ancient Men', like Dick Cheney, continue to run, rule, and ruin the world over 'New World Men', like me, and for how much longer? I could have turned into Ancient Man. I was close as a kid at times. Some people reading Drats' book might be judging me and thinking I am still a barbaric Ancient Man in my actions, especially in relation to the Myhel situation and the fact that you may currently interpret my feminism as chauvinism, which is probably most closely humanism, or humaneness, which maybe we must now call creaturism or Earthism. I'm not perfect! Stop trying to make me perfect! Love me, love my flaws! I think *Homos* are all flawed from the get-go, no?

So I just look at Ryle in the weight room with a million neurons blasting through my brain. Just look at him and think to myself,

'Oh my god, Oh my god, what is going on here? What do we have here? How dangerous is this childish psycho? Oh my god, this is like my brother Manat, who seems all normal one moment and then snaps without warning.'

I wake from my revelation with two mitts full of flowers, and turn to Zart, now well behind me and still on his filthy knees, and say, "That guy Ryle has obviously had something against me from before."

Zart replies, "He doesn't like you because you hook up with girls and cock-block him from Myhel, or he doesn't like you because you won the eight-hundred bucks in Bingo and didn't waste it all on them by buying the bar rounds all night."

I think about what Zart hypothesizes and move on with my work until we have eradicated the area. Later that night, when I run into Ray, the bass playing Filipino FN; who stands with Jellie on one side, and Cherry Ballpig, master of sloth, on the other; I decide to broach the topic. They have scattered opinions, so I plead my case: "Okay, let me explain something quickly. See, as the first ranger on HAWS, my payroll wasn't established initially, so when I first got to the atoll I had to 'volunteer' for some months or so until the position came through."

Cherry Ballpig says in complete disbelief, "You didn't have any money?"

I reply, "No money, other than a $21 per week food stipend."

"So you were living off your savings?" Jellie questions.

"Yes," I reply, "from working at BU in the Student Union."

"I know you are a cheap guy, don't deny that," Cherry Ballpig accuses, as he wiggles the giant sausage of greasy cigar around his Sea Cucumber lips.

Ray leans there, very cool, dragging off of his own cigarette; a Filipino James Dean.

I announce, "I am proud of my thrifty ability to always live way above my means while always staying way below my means monetarily. My Mom taught me all about that."

Jellie acknowledges, "Our Mom's were born in The Depression. You can fault him if you want," Jellie directs toward Cherry Ballpig, "but there is no way I think Kestrel would ever have gotten sucked into playing a Bingo game to begin with."

"They begged him," Ray breaks his silence.

190

I mimic, "C-mon Kestrel. It's the last game put on by the Navy." I convince them, "Ben and the others told me."

Jellie sides with me for the moment, "There was no way he was going to hand over eight-hundred dollars to a bunch of drunks who apparently don't even like him and hold hidden childish grudges."

Ray looks at Cherry Ballpig, and says proudly, unafraid of repercussions, "On top of that, these guys are construction workers. They make killer bread man." He always tries his best to sound as cool as possible. He would have made a good beatnik.

I agree, "As a ranger, I'll never make as much money as a construction worker."

Cherry Ballpig laughs, like I'm full of shit. He's wrong again. I say, "Good construction workers in a union make almost double of what I make as a ranger."

Cherry Ballpig snidely offers, "Maybe nobody likes you because you think you're a stud getting a lot of attention being a big fish on a little atoll, doing tours and meeting guests, . . ." Cherry ends bitterly, revealing underlying tension.

Jellie snaps harshly, " . . . and lowly, bitter high school drop-outs like you and Ryle, who fucked off in school to be cool, instead of working hard like Kestrel did. Ryle hates his life; full of frustration, he lacks control."

"Like my brothers," I realize, "they need to have control over some part of their otherwise out-of-control lives." I begin to understand. "So I just bless and release. I just let em go."

Getting off the track, I realize it is not worth wasting the time to try to figure out what Ryle's problem is. About a month later, when that crew prepares to leave the atoll for good, at the end of the BRAC Projects, they take a photo in front of the plane and they all smile. I see that guy Ryle leaving and I think to myself, 'Haw hah ha haw, he's leaving.'

I stand by the planter boxes with a line of people as usual, with Chipweldi, Deny, Han, and Banette on both sides of me.

Zart says, "Well, I'm a leavin pretty soon, I guess."

"Oooowww!" Banette whines like Fran Dresher, "we are all gonna miss yooooou."

I think we all really feel that. He's a good guy. I bet Banette wouldn't whine over me like that. I can't see why anyone would have any sympathy for me. Everyone thinks I'm doing great, ah, too great for my own good, out here.

I ponder aloud, "Do heads of state or the president think stuff like 'Ha ha ha, that dictator I hate just left and I may not see him again'?"

Everyone looks back and forth at each other, then we look off in the distance to see that a number of jerks board the plane for the last time.

Then Banette says, "The funny thing about Halfway though; whenever a bad person leaves, we always feel way better than when compared to the magnitude of how bad we feel when a good person leaves."

Han says, "It way more important be good when you can, especially on a little toowelve-hunderadd-acre atoll island of sand."

Then Loon paraphrases, "But the relief of losing a loser makes us all feel like way better, whereas, the loss of a winner never makes us all feel horrible, but just a little sad, but we can deal."

Chipweldi and Deny look at each other and shake their heads. This is too much open expression and emotion for their comfort levels. They don't even feel comfortable with the mushy term 'comfort levels.'

Chipweldi giggles, "Are there exceptions to this rule?"

I offer openly, "Zart's term happens to be ending and he also prepares to leave Halfway for good. That's going to suck, and be very sad, but I feel really great about certain people who are leaving the atoll right now."

Han sympathizes, "Zart been Mr. Kestrel's best friend on atoll."

Banette says, "Dietera is cool too, but she is off-island all the time for other bird projects."

"I like Loon, . . ." I say.

". . . but he's too crazy," Deny yells past Chipweldi.

Loon takes offence.

Chipweldi says, "You kind of had no choice but to befriend Zart, . . ." disgruntled, like why hadn't I become his friend.

The tension is thick. While I've been dating Hamed, things have been touchy on The Myhel Front.

Han says innocently, ". . . he gave you no choice to be friend him Mr. Kestrel."

I start getting choked up and can't really look over at Zart. I admit, "We are definitely different people, and I worry about your drinking, having lost my Father to alcohol just a couple of years ago, but you're a great guy. Not 'guy', . . . dude," I clarify.

Deny rolls his eyes. He is disgusted by what looks like bromance to him. Deny walks away, but Chipweldi morbidly has to watch on, like he relishes my sorrow, and feeds off of it like a sucking leech.

Two weeks later, the time comes before I know it. Zart boards the plane to leave Halfway for the last time.

Banette puts a sensitive hand on my shoulder. They board the plane and it taxis away.

I say with a gulp, in a zombie-like monotone, "I feel very emotional as I watch the plane take off."

"Yeh, he, hee he ha," Chipweldi gloats, "With the Navy completely gone, Zart and you had just recently moved out of the barracks and into a chief's quarters, and now he has to leave. Tough luck. He, ha ha heh. I'm gonna have to book you another housemate or you will have to pay for the whole unit out of your pay," he says, throwing salt into my wound.

They know I'm too cheap for that and will gladly have another roommate. As we return to the chief's quarters, now my house, with Hamed, I become uncontrollably upset, and I start to cry. She doesn't understand it at all.

She is like "What? Big deal. It's just your friend Zart."

I look up and see her walking into my dim kitchen, with just the distorted glow of the streetlights illuminating the counter and sink in a slash of beige. Vague murmurs of seabirds mumble outside the glass lanai slats. A mousetrap snaps near the cabinets. I pick it up, throw the dead mouse as far from my building as possible, to be scavenged by birds or devoured and disintegrated by dermestid beetles. I throw the trap in the corner. She opens the fridge while tiptoeing naked across the kitchen tiles of cold, with her cute little pixieness. She has a hot little cute little body that is so hot that it drives me crazy, as the glow of the refrigerator light makes her plush skin contrast with purples and yellows. But, she is kind of disconnected mentally somehow. The cultural divide? She is a Canuck after all. But disconnected from everything else that is going on in The World? That's more than cultural. I have other friends who are Canucks, and they have feelings. This is one of the best examples: How can you not understand that someone's very close friend is leaving, basically your best friend, is leaving you on a little atoll with psycho Myhel and the other idiots to boot; . . . one of the best friends you ever had, and you are not going to feel emotional about that?

I relay, "Sure, Zart and I had some ups and downs, mainly all my fault, stuff you don't even know about yet, but we got along like pals really."

"Jeeeshh, what's the big deal?" Hamed says to me as she sips a cheap beer from a can and tip-toes back to my room.

These are the first red flags I start getting from Hamed's personality, but her flaws can't compare with Myhel's, whose flaws can't compare with Jellie's or Kilgro's, whose flaws absolutely can't compare with Misa Queen's.

I quickly learn in just the first few days of Misa Queen's habitation on the atoll, that this is going to be a rough ride. We've all got problems right? I'm the first one to admit that, but god, this dipshit Misa is most fucked. First off, Misa Queen can't do the tours. Any of them!

"Don't tell Amb," she spouts with shame, glimpsing around to see if anyone hears.

'Useless idiot!' is one of a number of derogatory comments I hear visitors and others say on the atoll after she has been 'working' here for less than a month.

'Worst ranger ever!' an Olderhostile couple scribbles onto their evaluation.

I look back over my records frantically at my desk late in the evening. I have not received a single complaint the entire time I have been doing tours, over a year now, except the fire hose comments, which I take a little more as back-handed compliments while still taking to heart the concept that a little less would be a little more in my case. As I look over the new evaluations returning from ASS, every evaluation regarding her is either harsh and horrible, or obviously from an old lady trying to be nice, out of pity. Like, "Nice try Sweetie." Or "Keep on learning. You'll be fine." None of them gush with the praise I have had draped upon me. I'm not bragging, though I am proud. I'm just stating exactly true facts. Like the one that said, "Ranger Misa Queen, it's not a competition. Not everyone can be a Kestrel Falco. Just relax and be yourself, and, oh yeah, probably a good idea to learn the facts." Ut oh. This is gonna be bad. How do ya solve a problem like Misa Queen. If I could get her to wear a little nametag or badge around her neck that identified her as, say, 'special', like as in Special Olympics, or something like that, maybe people would take pity on her, but that don't solve that fact that she stinks so bad that, I'd rather smell a Striped Skunk. She is beyond the suckiest ranger I have ever seen, and gives all rangers a bad name and a black eye. Is this the reason Chipweldi got here out here? Is this why everyone appreciates me so much? I don't believe in conspiracies. It can't be a typical Government maneuver to send APS rejects to remote places, like Halfway Atoll and Havasu, to sweep problems under the carpet. Ben is good, Banette and Amb are topnotch, as is Karolyn. In contrast, The San Francisco Zoo appears to be run by rejects from every other sector of the City departments. Even the misfits have to work in some sector. Why not cram them all into the zoo? Is Halfway like that? Is that what Tirgut meant about me not really belonging out here for APS?

Case in point: With so many visitors coming to Halfway Atoll Wildlife Sanctuary now, we decide that we should break the Historical Tour into two groups. Even though the visitors have been on the atoll for all of about 12 hours, and have only had my airport meet and greet and my 40 minute orientation, 100% of the folks slide over and squish into my tour group, leaving Misa Queen to stand there alone next to the monk seal cardboard cutout. It's funny too, because standing next to the cutout makes the seal look much slimmer and smaller than it should. Misa Queen looks around with a frown, embarrassed. She looks down at the seal, then up at the group, who snap pictures of her, then she looks down at her stomach self-consciously, as even more shutters go off, and crosses her arms in front of it in shame.

"Okay folks, half the group, starting with these people right here, need to go with Ranger Misa Queen please. Thank you," I say with authority.

"Yes, yes, step right this way," Misa Queen says with shrill desperate squeals, sounding perturbed at the crowd.

No one moves. As a matter of fact, some of them actually slink to the side away from Misa Queen, and an old frail woman in her early 80's grabs my right arm to assure I won't force her to go with repellant Ranger Misa Queen.

"I paid a lot of money to come out here, and I am very old and will not be back again," the frail women says as she clutches my arm with a grandmotherly grin.

Misa Queen's cheeks go beet red, as her other, much larger cheeks, dimple with cellulittic tension.

"Oh well," I smile and look back at Misa Queen with a subtle but sincere sorry in my eyes, and head off on a 69 person tour, solo. No problem for me, remember, I have stage experience and can project with the best of them. Instead of following along on the tour, as she should, Misa Queen slowly ambles back into our office.

With respect to telling Amb, I have to respect that. Never tell Amb. I figure, she is so bad, I don't have to do my duty and report how horrible she is. Amb will figure it out soon enough if he doesn't already know. It's not my job to supervise her and I've tried to help her so much from day one.

When I return from the tour, with accolades abounding, I see a pile of Misa Queen's paperwork on my desk. I ask her what it is, and she states "I don't do filing." What a weird thing to say. She seems like she doesn't really want to learn anything, especially about the World War II history.

I say, "These are your personal records and action forms. We all need to file these."

She refuses, so I put them in alphabetized order and file them neatly without another word. She looks over at me, as if she has won a battle and is turning me into her slave.

I think when Amb finds out how problematic she is, Chipweldi will be chastised for hiring her, and all hell will rain down upon them.

In the morning meeting the following day, Chipweldi says, "Kestrel, here is all of Misa's paperwork. Show her how to fill it out, fax it in, and file it."

I look at Misa Queen for a second. Her eyes shift back and forth in a frantic panic. She looks at me. I think she wants me to defend her.

"Ah, Misa doesn't do filing," I say quickly. Misa looks pissed. Oops. I guess I shouldn't volunteer info but I really thought that's what she wanted me to say.

"What?" Chimes Chipweldi, Karolyn, Banette, Amb and Ben, in laughter.

I would say Misa looks like a Mule Deer in the headlights at this point, but Drats has already filled you in on me pretty well by now, so you know I don't want to insult majestic deer. Maybe more like an evil troll, caught in the headlights. Sorry, I can't think of any suitable animal analogy. I love animals too much. I never thought I'd say this, but Misa Queen appears to be on the same level as Kilgro.

Misa looks around some more, her face fuchsia, her cheeks cherry.

"I - I don't do filing," Misa Queen barely stammers out.

A chorus of laughs break out, "Ha ha ha. Ha ha ha. That's a good one. Ha ha ha."

Amb's face turns straight, as he says, "You do now. Do you, or Chipweldi, need any clarification on this?" Amb switches to serious mode, and conducts the rest of the meeting professionally, but visibly annoyed.

Misa Queen's sour expression even makes gooney chicks look jovial.

Misa looks down at her tense, chubby hands like she's about to cry or pray. Everyone stops laughing and just nods their heads. I still don't get where she wants to go with this. Is that supposed to be

197

some ill thought-out feminist statement? Who's going to file, only men, from now on? Little fairies are going to run around doing all the filing? I don't care; I'll work over-time to do all the filing. More money for me. Weird. What is filing demeaning or something? I have never let myself feel demeaned by filing and I do it all the time. I don't let filing, or cleaning a friggin toilet, demean me. How insecure is that?

As the weeks go by, I can tell Amb loses his patience with her. Ben is forced to file a request with Amb, that Banette the biologist would prefer that Kestrel Falco help her in the field, since Misa Queen 'simply can't function'. This becomes impossible, because I am still doing every tour, solo.

"Kestrel, when is Misa going to be able to solo on the Historical Tour competently?" Amb demands in frustration.

"I don't know Amb. I don't know why it is taking so long. Do you want me to work with her personally again?" I ask, thinking to myself 'please say no, please say no'.

"NO. That's not your job. You trained her well and put in way more time already than you needed to, and *that* was supposed to be Chipweldi's job. She needs to study and get up to speed," Amb says, mad.

I would be mad too, but he is too mad about this. He is a leader and needs to stay cool. I'm sure there has got to be way more than Misa Queen on his nerves. I'm sure the constant battles with our 'cooperators' aren't making things any easier out here.

I finish grabbing my gear in the office, then head out to the field to work with the biologists again.

Loon, Dietera, Banette, and I scan ahead in the blinding coral sand, watching for petrel burrows on a survey.

"So word is you dumped Myhel hard for Hamed," Loon ejects.

"Okayyyyy, we should be working out here, not talking about gossip," Banette clarifies with a whine.

"We are not talking *about* gossip," Loon answers like a wise guy.

"Where did you get that?" I ask with sorrow in my voice.

Sorrow? Yes. I am sad that people are just that lame. Loon won't answer me and moves off with Banette.

Dietera slips up beside me. "I'm just telling you as your friend that there is a lot of scuttlebutt going about the atoll on you," Dietera whispers, but at the same time, not trying to make it into a big deal. "It's just small-time bullshit."

I softly say, "I wish someone would tell me what the hell is going on here." So clueless, like I said, clueless, clueless, clueless.

"I don't know how you haven't figured this out yet, but Misa Queen has it in for you," Dietera reports.

"The sick thing about all of this? I never said a bad thing about Misa Queen to a single soul. And I never got back at Ryle for ramming my face in the sand. And you know what? I never get anybody back. That's how I live my life."

"Me too," Dietera responds with earnest. "It's the only way to be."

"I would want to get some people back, but why? What's the point? If I can't bring happiness to people, and there are a lot of people who you just can't bring happiness to, then I'd rather bring them nothing. I know that sounds like a lot of holistic hippy stuff for a violent punk like me, but look, Misa Queen and Ryle already live in a hell they have created for themselves." Dietera nods in agreement as I blather on. "They already have more than enough rope to hang themselves. I just avoid people like that, instead of wasting good energy on vengeance or negative crap," I finish with resignation and disappointment.

Dietera senses this and says, "The next big shocker in all of this is that then, Misa Queen, who you went out of your way to help so many times, turns around and sidles up to support Myhel? Within a very short time, everyone on the atoll, especially the FNs, think you are a jerk and a womanizer because Misa Queen has been going around telling everyone that you broke Myhel's heart, who really loves you, to date Hamed, who is a cheap slut, according to Misa Queen," Dietera says.

I am shocked. I don't know anything about any of this but I can see why Misa Queen would hate a guy like me and immediately grasp onto siding with Myhel to hurt me. 'Siding'?! I even hate that idea. So childish, cliquey and juvenile, but that's where we are, and why? Because Myhel can't have what she thinks she wants, and she can't take it like a balanced adult. Worse than that though, I feel really bad for Hamed in all of this. Sure, her and I didn't hit it off like gangbusters exactly, but I don't want ridiculous shit to come down on her. She's basically innocent.

"With that said, I think you should be aware that she probably isn't the only one," Dietera continues to pour on the bad news.

This is very uncharacteristic of her, for I can tell she is such a mellow, Zen gal, but I can also see that she thinks the severity of this case merits intervention, and that I am worth saving.

"Remember, you are the good guy. There are always plenty of bad guys who want to take the good guy out. Believe me, I know. The politics even in the bird world are unbelievable. Obviously Chipweldi doesn't approve of your work style, or the fact that you actually work. Ha ha he," she says, mimicking Chipweldi's nervous giggle at the end. "There are others too, who feel insecure or threatened by you because they don't trust you and you're a hard worker and all that stuff. I think you can trust me, and maybe Loon."

"And Zart," I add.

"Yes, Kestrel, but Zart is gone," she states for reality check effect.

'Oh yah', I think to myself.

That night, Han addresses me in the Sri Lankan barracks. "Mr. Kestrel. You are a very bad man Mr. Kestrel. Very bad man. You hurt Miss Myhel. Miss Myhel, she is sweet lady. You don't like sweet lady?"

Oh my god, what a nightmare. How can I explain? "Look, you guys don't understand. It was wrong with Myhel, so I broke up with her. Then Hamed came on the atoll and I started dating her," I explain clearly.

The Sri Lankans look at me with distain. They don't buy it. I told you before, even when I am telling the perfect truth, nobody ever believes me.

"Look, what do you guys want me to do? How can I prove it to you? Why do you believe Misa Queen over me?" I prod.

"You must go back with Myhel," one of the other Sri Lankans says.

"What? Why? I'm not in love with her," I explain.

First, they look confused by the term 'love'. Many Sri Lankans still have marriages arranged by their parents. Second, a volley of comments erupt:

"Why did you sleep with her if you did not love her?"

"You must marry the woman you sleep with."

"You must produce baby with her," Etc. etc.

200

"Whoa whoa whoa! Hey you guys come from a different world than me," I reply.

"Yes, but you still must respect the woman," Han preaches, to me, the converted.

I say, like a professor, slowly and clearly, "Yes, I know, but we have different ideas of what that means. I don't think it is respectful to the woman or the man to force them to marry in an arrangement."

The Sri Lankans get a little angry, but as the conversation turns back and forth over this subject, I realize by the end that some of them begin to warm-up and realize I speak the truth, while others stand hardened against me from Misa Queen's vindictive lies.

Tex sees me working out by the office the next day. I have equipment lined up, and I'm taking a thorough inventory. I don't have to. Nobody told me to, certainly not Chipweldi, but I have time, so I decide to get it done and feel good about it.

Tex sees the consternation on my face. "Don't look like it's that hard to sort some shit," he mocks.

"Why? I really am so naïve aren't I?" I say to Tex.

He looks at me puzzled. It won't be until I am swimming miles off shore, about to be killed, that it will come to me. Misa Queen, and so many other spite-filled single women between the ages of let's say 32 to 63, HATE ME! They fuckin hate me!

"Why?" I question.

Tex looks at me again, vacant.

I offer, "Well, I represent white, hetero, men to them."

Rattas Dewhurt comes walking up behind me. She wants to know if she can borrow some flowerpots, from our government nursery, so she can plant alien flowers, which she brought onto the atoll intentionally, to give Amb and the rest of us fits. I don't even know she is there, but Tex does.

Tex says, "The good-looking guy they could never attain. The charismatic charmer with a joke and a laugh on his sleeve."

I agree, "When people are miserable, they hate people like me."

"Ha!" Rattas Dewhurt screams from a foot behind my head. "Who you talkin bout? You better not be talkin bout me," she growls with anger, actually, bitterly proving my point.

Tex laughs, inciting her more, but I look at her with surprise, and earnest disgust.

"What do you want Rattas?" I ask her point blank.

She begs for the pots, but I basically tell her to screw. She starts to walk off in anger, then adds, "You better not be talkin bout my new friend Misa Queen. She's from Texas, like Janus Joplin, and Dubbaya."

Tex says, "From a what I seen, Misa Queen is a boner fide embarrassment to our great Lone Star State."

Rattas Dewhurt doesn't like to hear that one bit, as she runs off to report it to Misa Queen and Myhel.

"We better not say shit like that," I caution Tex.

"Why the hell not?" Tex stands up for us. "She a insecure backstabber, that's why she says to you 'Don't tell Amb, Don't tell Amb.' She knows if the shoe was on the other hoof, she would run off to tell Amb in New York minute."

"You think so?" I ask Tex, but deep down, I know he is right about this one.

"Sure," he continues, "most happy, well adjusted middle-aged women like you and know you a stand-up guy, don't they?"

"Yeah," I admit hesitantly, thinking of Banette, Karolyn, Dietera, Tirgut, Jewel, and a number of other women I seem to get along with fine.

Tex says, "And not a dick, right?"

"Yeah," I humbly admit again.

"But," Tex continues, "if you gut a boss especially, and she is ugly and can't land a man for whatever reason, she a gonna take it out on you to make herself temporarily feel a little better bout her bitter loneliness. She hates you for what you are and what she thinks she can't gitt, but if you tell her yer queer, she'll turn around about-face and luv ya, so as not to be discriminatory."

"Hmmm" I say, as I wrestle with Tex's logic. How could a guy who has been so wrong about so much, start to mature and become a more whole person right in front of me, and be so right.

Tex says harshly, "It's so obvious, that's Misa Queen in a nutshell: Insecure, lonely, can't pull off a simple tour, totally blown-away by how great you are, non-attractive persona, and a vile, gossipin' liar."

I say, gaining confidence back, "Banette likes me, . . ."

"There ya go," Tex encourages.

I say, ". . .and, but she's a great, published biologist, okay looking, in good shape, and has a boyfriend." It comes to me clearly. "Karolyn likes me. She's a 50 something married secretary with adult kids."

"Darn tootin," Tex proclaims.

I say, "Maybe I should do a sociological study to prove this point? Either way, I'm not a threat to either of them, so they like me and appreciate my hard work. It's weird not being the underdog. I'm used to being the underdog. I was 94 pounds in 9th grade and they said 'You can't play varsity football unless you weigh 100 pounds.' I got chased around and beat up, by girls. By girls! Big, mean tough girls, but still, girls."

Tex asks, "You was the smallest person in ya class?

"Yes", I say, "always getting beat-up and picked-on, and it's still like that if I am in Boston walking around and stuff."

"Ya can't be ya self?" Tex asks with remorse.

I report, "I can't have any anonymity or autonomy. If I see people who know me, they're gonna put a chip on their shoulder right away. I have to respect that. I have to play that game. I can't disrupt the order. If I give an honest opinion, just like with my siblings, they would want to hurt me or attack me or my family. They wouldn't stand for the insolence. It would be like 'How dare you break the pecking order of the playground.' Yah know?"

Tex shakes his head, and listens to every word.

I say, "And ya know it's definitely not worth it. When you are dealing with townies in Boston, it's better to act polite or stupid, and walk away. As for that old saying 'If you get in a fight with a pig, you end up smelling like shit.' None of this is ever worth it."

Tex agrees, "It's not even worth dealing with such morons. Forgitt about em."

I continue, "It's better to just be like, 'Oh yeah, huh, oh? Um ah.' and just don't really even act like you have a brain and let it slide. Ya have to pick your battles in these things in life and the things you really want to make an impact on, change, and have an effect on. I don't see old style Revere and East Boston ever growing more loving, but maybe I'm wrong. By the time I was a junior, I was 155 pounds and had a 6-inch growth spurt. I never saw that coming," I tell Tex, as I finish stowing all of the gear neatly.

Late that night, I sit on my bed thinking: a little tired, a little drunk, and little depressed.

Hamed lies quietly under the covers. She touches my back in a rare show of compassion. "What. You still thinking of Zart?" she asks dryly.

"No." I'm thinking about everything else above, but I had already stopped thinking about Zart, and I have refocused on how to deal with the Myhel and Misa Queen situations. "There are things that are just kinda like hopeless cases where ya just say, 'Aaaahhh'. Ya know, it's not worth it. I think that's the way a lot of people feel about Cleveland, or ah, let's say, Detroit. 'Ya know what, they're screwed-up, there's nothin ya can do about it.' How many people have taken a stab at fixing Louisiana politics, ya know, you can use the best progressive methods, and still, their political system is a mess. So, yes, sometimes it's better to just nuke the area and start with a clean slate in 10,000 years or something," I say resigned, as I start to mumble and fall onto the pillow to sleep.

She has no idea what I'm talking about and she doesn't really care. This relationship is going nowhere. I should kick her out of my bed right now, but she's so cute and I want to do her again. Here we go again!

I see a video tape by the VCR, and I say, "One thing about Zart though, when he isn't actually drinking or smoking a cigar, or working, he has his video camera running. All the time, he goes around video taping everything. One night, he videotaped that "talent" "show" (I make heavy, separate air-quotes) we did at the All Hands Club as kind of a hokey throwback to the Navy morale-booster things. I thought it went great and everybody loved it, and blah blah blah, but firstly, video cameras should be banned from talent shows, seriously. Secondly, the next day when I saw the video tape, I was mortified."

Hamed More looks at me with mild surprise to my reaction to the tragedy unfolding on the television screen, as I play the tape and she sits up straight on the bed with her legs crossed Indian style. I have a hard time not looking at her, especially when she's naked. She has this soft, chunky endomorphicness, and plush skin-tone, that my wild impulses tell me to hug and squeeze. Do girls feel that way about men they are sexually crazy about? I've seen women act like that with babies, but not with guys.

Hamed More says, "What? This is a howl. You are embarrassed? C'mon. It' brilliant. The crowd loved it. Ffffff," she exclaims on a positive tone.

I say, "I-I guess I know I'm an over-the-top, hyper, ah, totally hyper-active person." There is a long pause. Then I explain calmly, "I have to make a note to myself: Less is More. Less IS More." Is it funny that I'm saying this to a tiny girl named "More"?

As we stare at the tape, we see Zart's tipsy camera work floating around the bar. Each person waves cheerily as the camera passes them. Then, the camera shot drifts off into a sea of dark hair and faces. The FNs mostly sit in a large group in the center, and obviously enjoy the show greatly. One can tell by the bright white smiles and bright white eyes glowing in the murky dimness. It's there! There, in that shot, in that frame, we both can make out Myhel sitting there, 'alone', in the group of FNs. Both of us swallow hard, and stare at Myhel's ghostly white skin and bright flowery dress, shining with her bright fake-blond hair, in the sea of Sri Lankans and Thais. I reach over and squeeze Hamed More's hand in half-hearted reassurance. She does not like any of this and appears to feel creeped-out.

I should just jump up and stop the video, but I fear that will make things look worse somehow, so I let the tape play and we stare at it transfixed. It's no blur anymore. We clearly see Myhel trying to hold up her fragile and frail image. She wears a lot of make up, and a long, bright blue attention-getting dress, and a large, colorful flower in her hair, which she picked from one of the gardens near the well-landscaped OIC house.

I erupt to Hamed More, lacking impulse control, "She intentionally sits in a position where no one can really access her or talk with her, but she feels like a princess on display with all of the nods and smile gestures shared generously with the servants."

Hamed More laughs, "Wow, you care. You care, don't you?" She accuses me of caring for or about Myhel. Now I'm getting pissed.

I say, "Look, I'm sympathetic to people who are insecure and everything, but I think with all this time on the atoll and all the drugs the doctor put her on, she has somehow become a little bit loopy."

205

Kestrel launches up from the bottom of a 20ft. deep surge channel near the outer reef.

I look back at the TV screen to see that Zart had finally wheeled the camera off of sad Myhel and has panned back up onto the stage, where we can hear Dietera and Zart cracking up off camera. One after the other, the performances go up. Zart never pans back to Myhel, luckily. Then, we come to the part where Hamed More and I enter the stage, with the assistance of Riz Smaller. We put on that old Vaudeville gag where we use a table to represent the floor, then I use my hands as my feet, slipping them into my hiking boots, while behind me and underneath my over garment, Riz Smaller uses her arms as mine. I can barely force myself to watch it. In this skit, Hamed More plays the sidekick. We perform volunteer work, eat meals and drink beer, go snorkeling, and of course, the hands and feet look completely uncoordinated and the crowd laughs hysterically. Hamed More is completely horrible, but she is just so cute, that I let it slide and avoid making even a hint of a criticism.

I say, "Wow, it would have been so much better if I didn't sing so much, if I didn't recite my poem for so long, if I didn't sing on the top of my lungs like David Lee Roth with the yelling."

Hamed More says, "Yeah like, yyyyeeeeeeaaaaaaahaaaawwwww," weakly imitating Roth's yell.

I say, shaking my head, "Just back it down. Just back it down."

Hamed More looks at me for a second. "What are you gonna do. Back down your whole life? Pffffffffffffffffffff." she moans.

I think to myself for a second. Her comments aren't usually so brilliant, for someone who uses that word 'brilliant' a lot. I should back down most aspects of my life, if not every. Yet, that's not obvious to her.

I shut off the tape and look at her for a second. She looks back at me blankly. Cute. Cute as a button, but blank. Blankety blank blank blank. Blank as a button. She reaches over and turns on the boom box. It's that song from The Verve, or The Verve Pipe, I think.

Hamed More reels, "Brilliant. Simply brilliant."

I get the idea that she thinks if she keeps saying that word then somehow people will think she is brilliant. At least she's not saying 'on the list and off the list', but I get the feeling that even if I really let myself fall in love with her, she will never really be 'on the list', and, *we* will never be brilliant.

Within another week or so, it is over. Flamed-out. I don't know what happened. I try to talk with her, but she isn't interested. I feel highly bummed. If she doesn't want to talk with me, I don't want to force her. I never like to push anything. I make it clear that I would enjoy having a talk with her as soon as she likes, by slipping a note under her door, and leaving a voice mail on her cell phone. I'm not too proud to beg, or anything like that, but I don't want her to complain that I am harassing her either, so I just back off and wait for her to contact me. She never does.

So this is the way life has become on Halfway. I'm not messing around with Myhel. Zart, the coolest buddy I had on the atoll, bailed. Hamed, and even Riz, who I am much more interested in than Myhel, appear to be beyond my reach. My 'co-workers', Chipweldi and Misa Queen, are friggin nightmares, and now Jellie is on island via the Big Island Turtle Program, Monk Seal Monitoring Program, and thousands of Reggae shows. Oh yeah, and though I've got the Navy chiefs, Ryle, and many of their ilk gone; I still have HIC staff, and most of the FNs, hating me. But, minus my difficulties and challenges, the atoll is spectacular: I just have to stop dealing with the humans and get into the diving and the birds, like I've told myself before.

One day as we head back from hucking at the beach, I say to Dietera, "Isn't it funny? The longer I spend out here, the more deeply I should be getting into the wildlife, but instead, the friggin humans keep getting in the way. I'm waiting, . . ."

Dietera says, " . . . just waiting, for one of these days, to be able to throw yourself fully into the wildlife experience without it being predicated on *Homos*."

Instead of logging another dive with Myhel, I break out on my own and go diving with, of all odd couples, Tex, and Loon! Y2K approaches quickly next year. Maybe we are all going to start getting along?

Tex says, "Bush ain't gonna be so bad. He'll be a hell of a lot better than that liberal Gore, 'Oooh, we have to save the planet.' Boo hoo hoo."

Loon responds, "Bush already says he wants to spend 87 billion to attack Iraq."

"87 billion? What's 87 billion?" Tex scoffs.

Loon goes off, "That same money could triple our own security without attacking innocent civilians."

"None of them are innocent," Tex strains over the engine noise.

Loon counters, "It could wipe out state debt nationally."

Tex shoots back, "That's the states' fault."

Loon tries to let Tex know that there are much better things Bush could do with the money when he gets into office than to spend money attacking a poor, weak, country like Iraq, but Tex doesn't care. Just like with my brothers Sproc, Rosmarus, and Manat, they don't want to come to an intelligent conclusion; they want to win the argument and maintain alpha status.

Loon tries again, "It's enough to give all the unemployed people in the U.S.A. jobs, jobs that we need like cleaning up environmental disasters and Super Fund sites."

Tex rifles back, "Why ain't they got a job? I got a job. Why can't they get a job?"

"Eighty-seven billion dollars would fund our ecology budget in the U.S. for like over 10 years! Are you fuckin stupid or what?" Loon looses it.

"You really are in idiot Tex. Every argument you make is a petty little cheap shot and totally unsubstantiated," I say in frustration. "Why don't you address the points being made?"

"Yeah, it pisses you huggers off. Ha ha." He laughs like a buffoon, then says, "You like to use facts and science, don't ya?"

I add homocentrically, to see if I can appeal to Tex on a *Homo* level, "I would spend eighty-seven billion dollars on healthy, organic, lunch programs for schools, or programs that keep kids in sports or arts and out of trouble."

"Ah, screw the kids. We didn't have any of that and we turned out fine," he dismisses.

"Really?" I laugh out loud. "You turned out fine?"

"Yeah," Tex defends as his rotund belly jiggles back at him in shame. His diabetes clock is ticking and he is not smart enough to even know it.

I say, "Dietera argues that most of the people who want to invade Iraq think they will somehow get some of that eighty-seven billion dollars."

Then Loon adds, "To support corrupt defense contractors and their lobbyists in Texas, much of it won't be accounted for after all is said and done, like what happened in Viet Nam."

Tex argues, "So it ends up lining pockets of people. That's still good."

"Yeah," Loon yells, "bad people. The wrong people."

Tex stares at Loon.

"This is why you can't even waste your time talking with people like this," Loon says, as he walks to the other end of the boat and starts getting his dive gear on.

I go over to Loon and say, "Oh well, I'm sure that ruined your day. I'm glad I've gotten to the point where I won't let it ruin mine."

Loon bitterly spits, "Guys like Tex are a waste of time."

The three of us buddy-up, and go over the side, leaving Darom alone in the small speedboat. As I get to the bottom, I gently kneel on the sandy coral to avoid stirring up turbidity as I adjust my gear. I look up and see that Darom already dropped a fishing line in the water and jiggles a lure. The Brown Chub inspect it. We have a typically spectacular dive on Halfway; cruising up chimneys, watching schools of bright Yellow Tang and a few random Masked Angelfish, and of course, lots of sharks; all Galapagos Reef Sharks. This is the first dive on Halfway in which someone, namely Myhel, is not grabbing my ass and thighs through my wetsuit, and it is great. On the way back, it is as if the tension drifted away in the currents. I think Loon and Tex are actually both good guys.

I say, "Hey Tex, we are going to be banding petrels at night coming up. Would you be into helping out?"

Tex seems shocked that I would invite him to such an event. "Sure, I'll do it."

When I return to my room, I keep my nose clean, getting into studying the reef fish carefully in a few books from the office, library, and an ID book from Bent, the dive operator.

One morning, on a return from an Eastern Island Tour, maybe a week after that dive, I happen to notice Dietera back at her clipboard, counting gooney nests.

"What's up?" I greet. "You're back on the island? I didn't see your name on last night's manifest."

"I was on there. I think HIC has stopped logging people working for ASS or APS on their manifests or something," she wonders. "I guess we don't count."

I think for a moment. That's weird. Are they trying to hide something or insult us or what? "Maybe they want to keep the count down. What are you doing?"

"Nothing much, just doing the plots while the Olderhostile folks return from enjoying your fabulous tour," she says without a hint of sarcasm. "What's been happening with you?"

"Why do you ask?" I query carelessly.

"Well, I just keep hearing things aren't going so well for you out here all of a sudden," Dietera states nicely.

Ut Oh, "What do you mean?"

"Look, Kestrel, I'm the last person to gossip and I stay out of all of that stuff, but a lot of people have it in for you out here," Dietera answers.

"I have actually learned that there are probably a number of people here now that hate me for one reason or the other," I say with regret.

Dietera keeps working as she speaks, "What did you do wrong?"

"I didn't do shit! That's what's pissing me off," I say loudly.

Dietera says, "Well, you were having sex with Myhel, and now you are with Hamed."

I enlighten her, "Ahh, you are a little behind the curve. I regret to report that Hamed already dumped me, and, I was but currently am not sleeping with Myhel anymore." Why do I have to explain myself? We're adults. I start to get really frustrated now. "So fucking what? She invited me over and we got together. This shouldn't be a big deal here, in Canada, or Europe or anywhere else."

"Well, I think when you are the ranger people want to look up to you," Dietera says realistically.

"But the thing is here, I broke up with Myhel before Hamed even came on atoll. Fuck! I know in a sense I am practically a role model and represent the APS, but I'm not a priest, or a monk, as Zart would put it. I never said I will take a government job on the condition that I have to be celibate or something."

Dietera looks at me for a second. She can tell I'm getting really worked up over all of this. "Look, none of this really means anything. Someday you will be out of here and you will never see any of these people again."

"Well I hope not," I reply. "I hope I get to see you and Zart and some other people again on the mainland."

"Yeah, well that goes without saying. The cool biologists and vols will stay in-touch. I guess I'm just saying don't let all this stuff get to you, ya know, . . ." Dietera says in her usual calm, intelligent voice; one of the few voices of reason on the atoll. " . . . but, at the same time. . ."

"I know, perception beats reality. I know, I sound wicked angry right? I sound wicked pissed-off. It's not very sane of me is it? I should be very connected and warm and calm and spiritually uncorrupt. But what is it in this world that makes US all uptight and wound and ready to fight all the time? Angry at everybody, snarling at people defensively? I once heard a comedian say, 'Ever notice that whenever you're in traffic on a freeway; everyone else is an asshole?' It's true. Is it just human nature to think that way? Or, is it culture? Is it nature or nurture?"

Dietera laughs at my enthusiasm and gesticulations, and adds, "Exactly, and out here it is the same thing. On the one hand, you are in the public eye and must act appropriately, but on the other hand, you gotta let the bullshit role off your back."

"Right! A lot of people have said, just like the late William S. Burroughs, 'You have to be in hell to see heaven.' We can't always be happy. We can't always be in a state of bliss. But, by having bliss once, or twice, for short moments; every day, every week, every month; just to remember that that can happen, that that

211

moment can exist; that makes the rest of our toil worthwhile," I assert firmly.

Dietera states like a guru, "Moderate your highs and lows, and don't get too bummed or pissed-off."

I say, "So yes. Of course I sound pissed-off. I'm pissed-off about so many things. That's one of the reasons my friend Drats says he has to write a novel about this. But, again, in the end, how mad am I, and by telling you how mad I am, does that make you more mad, or does that make you less mad? Do you feel more connected to the natural world, or less, and is that good or bad? Who's to say whether that's good or bad?"

Dietera laughs, "This is exactly what I am talking about. You are all worked up. Tranquilo."

"Look, when Hamed that Canadian midget showed up here, I felt like I was falling in love," I say to Dietera in earnest. I don't know how much to tell her but she is way behind on my latest exploits.

". . .but it was because of the island madness," Dietera finishes.

". . . and the shit I have already waded through with Myhel. Luckily, I am always very busy with work on Halfway and love my job. As a matter of fact, it's reef net removal time! Yeah! The Townsbend Krumsmell is here and we are removing nets with tow boards and little knives," I report to Dietera. She looks off in the distance to see if she can see the ship from our position. We can't. We turn as Dietera finishes writing her last notes and wraps-up her backpack.

"Where do you get all these ideas?" she asks with a chuckle.

"I don't know. Don't you think of radical stuff? Outside the box?"

"Sometimes. Most of the time I am focusing on how many feathers a species of bird replaces during a particular molt," Dietera answers.

I awake the following morning to the sea-sickeningly sweet smell of donuts and biscuits with gravy, onboard the SS Halfway, to fish the seamount. Stark Kristian ill-advisedly bought this jerky flat-bottomed river vessel for HIC as a supply boat to travel between Halfway Atoll Wildlife Sanctuary and the main Hawaiian Islands. We have come to the seamount to fish for bottom fish, mostly rockfish, to bring back to the Halfway Galley.

How did this trip even come to fruition? A few weeks ago Darom caught a Shortfin Mako Shark with some of the high-roller angler guests. They decided to serve it in the Galley. Blue state or red state origin quickly became evident. Jellie and the ASS staff, the Olderhostile folks, and none of the APS staff on HAWS, would touch the shark. I actually had a delicious piece of mako at a bistro in Copley Square on Boylston Street (back in '89, before I knew better) and I was guessing that even in the Galley that shark probably tasted pretty good, but, I could not bring myself to even look at it in line. So few sharks are left; so few makos, and all for shark fin soup, a horrible Chinese abomination. If we can't get Georgian's to stop eating woodpeckers and Floridian's to stop eating gators, how will we ever stop the Japanese from eating whales or the Chinese from eating shark fins? And that is exactly the case. The FNs and the HICs all line-up for heaps of mako, and they all think we're weird for refusing to consume.

With that, Stark Kristian asks the APS why he can't catch fish off atoll to use in the Galley? Seems logical, you know, buy local, fish local, grow-your-own, and all that junk.

"If we lose all the fishin around here cause we are eatin all of them, then the anglers won't come," Kristian argues erroneously. Eventually, especially after the mako incident and after some calls to the National Marine Fisheries Service, Amb said HIC could catch rockfish over the nearby seamount, only for on-atoll consumption, so as to save money, gas, and refrigeration of fish from Hawaii. It really will have no impact either way on the Halfway fishing program, especially considering the main species sport anglers like to go after out here are the Alua, or Giant Trevally, which don't make great eating anyhow.

"Kestrel, we need an observer on that vessel. Someone who actually cares," Amb stated frankly. "You will be leaving at 20:00 to be over the mount at sunrise."

Okay with me.

Now back out on the boat, I look around and rise up out of my bunk, to see the slightest glow of sunrise against the deep purple stars. I hear puking. Several of the crew yack over the side. Looks like a mix of Filipinos and a HIC.

"Don't let me tell you how to eat your biscuit," Deny says as he tears open one of my biscuits like an Oreo with his fat, greasy fingers. I know I sound stupid, but I really don't know how to peel open a biscuit and poor a fat blob of lard gravy on it. It's not in my vocabulary to eat shit like this. I have a fruit shake every morning for breakfast, with no milk or anything, just OJ, banana, and whatever I have ripe and ready. These guys are feeding me crap, and right when I wake up too. Like donuts, part of my childhood culture, but long since forgotten as a viable food option. 3 Boston Crèmes and 2 glasses of whole milk every fuckin Sunday morning. I got responsibility to bring the dozen plus donuts back from after mass at St. John's because my 'little' brother would fuck up the order or eat some on the way home, and my older siblings were already blowin off church or hung-over. Does anybody still eat that way today, and if so, why are they knowingly trying to kill themselves? What pain can be that great to make one want to eat to gluttony? What makes someone smoke or drink themselves to death?

I try to eat some of the biscuit, pushing the gravy off to the side. Pointless. I go into my trusty, beaten backpack and pull out a banana, and a bag of organic craisins I had begged my Mom to mail to me from the mainland. I know, from leading many a whale watch as a naturalist, that greasy, heavy, gross stuff, will certainly make you puke.

"So let me guess: You think we came from Gorillas?" Deny says with distain as he slides the back of the spoon across my plate and dumps the remains into the trash. He shakes his head as he looks at the waste of what he thinks of as 'perfectly good food.' If he cares that much, he should eat it instead of making a face.

"We didn't?" I quip back.

"I didn't!" he states assertively.

Ironically, he acts and looks way more like an ape than I do (no offence to the apes), especially considering his primitive views on evolution and diet.

With the unplanned vomit chum-line established, the fishing lines start going over the side. For hours, I mean hours, we catch nothing. They don't have a fish finder, but the depth finder shows we are right over a seamount, 122 feet down at the summit, and in anywhere from 367 to over 1,118 feet deep right around it. I don't know if we should be catching rockfish or not. I'm not an ichthyologist, but I thought rockfish liked cooler latitudes.

Waiting, waiting, waiting. Waiting to catch one fish. Waiting to break the monotonous jerky swaying of the vessel.

Finally, close to noon, Deny tells the Foreign Nationals to pull up their lines halfway. He starts the loud, stinky engine and begins to troll at about 3 or 4 knots. Within a few minutes the FNs start pulling in small tuna, including Skipjack and Yellowfin, and some Ono. They club the Ono, but stab the tuna in the heart to let the hot blood run out. Some of the tuna look too small to me, but the men are so psyched that they stab them before I can even suggest release.

After taking a few photos with the fish, we go barren again. Not a catch. So we make a beeline for Halfway Atoll in an attempt to return before dark.

"Hey Mr. Ranger," Deny says facetiously, "why don't you make yourself useful and coil this line."

Being one of the few who hadn't gotten seasick, I start coiling one line after another into five-gallon buckets. I never get seasick. I have been on the ocean a million times and know from whale watches that even when the clients yack, which tends to be what really makes me nauseous, that I never get sick. Looking down into a bucket while the boat rocks under low steam gets to me eventually. I stand, take a deep breath, swallow the diesel fumes hard, and walk out to the deck to get a blast of air. It passes, and though I may look green for a few minutes, I still don't get sick. I look over at Deny in the pilothouse, grinning down on me.

"Ya finish those ropes?" he asks like Quint to Hooper in Jaws. What an asshole. "Ya, oh yah, dos ropes arh all done," I respond with a mimicking accent.

People frickin hate it when you mimic them. I used to do that as a kid, but I'm too mature, savvy and cool for that now. 'The Halfway Regression?' I remember Dr. Chance small-talking me as he popped my finger back in, 'You seem like a really intelligent guy compared to a lot of the people who made it out here.'

215

'Thank you,' I replied, taking the compliment well considering my pain and circumstance.

'Watch out for 'The Halfway Regression'!' he warned with an ominous, doctorial tone.

He explained to me that people who live on the atoll, for a long time, atrophy, just like people who watch a lot of TV or play video games. Their brains turn to mush. Many become alcoholics, like Adolph Jorgenson (although I would bet you anything he was an alchy way before he got here), and that they tend to go crazy. Is that why I answered Deny like that? Are Myhel, Misa Queen, Ryle, and the rest of them wearing down my indomitable spirit and obstreperously positive attitude? Am I losing my smile? Fuck!

Was I a different guy in the first chapter, when I was first flying out on that twin turbo? I am so gung-ho; so positive. Nothing can stop me. No negativity, no jaded old men: None of them can tell me I can't change the World!

Deny makes his way down the ladder and looks at the tangled rope mess.

"You call that done!" Deny gets in my face.

"It doesn't matter if you can rip my ear off and make me bleed to death," I say frankly, devoid of emotion, like Spock, "get out of my face or I'll file a report."

Deny takes his glasses off and stands his ground, trying to stare me down. No idiot's going to win this battle, so I step back and turn aft.

"Pussy," Deny says under his breath as he climbs back to the bridge. I can see why he got discharged after 19 and a-half years in the Marines. I don't think he is really a bad guy; just stupid. . ., stupider than me. It's all relative: Maybe some of you Albert Einsteins out there reading this book right now think I'm an idiot. The motor chugs along and the FNs look bored. I want to get out of this stupid mind funk right away. I sneak up behind a couple of the FNs, start softly, then built to the chorus:

September seventh, '77, on the road to Mandalay.

It was, business a usual, in police room 619.

All the FNs chime-in right on cue.

Oh Biko, Biko, because Biko. Oh Biko, Biko, BEcause Biko.

Here am I Jah, here am I Jah, the man is dead, the man is dead.

Now Peter Gabriel is going to kill me, because *I know* those ain't the words, but I could never tell what he was saying and the FNs love it whether they know the exact words or not. Some more FNs come running down from the bow to join-in. Everyone on board now waits for me to finish my bogus verses so they can all sound off on the raucous chorus with gospel fortitude; except the three HIC staff onboard, who cast their eyes down upon US and shake their heads in ultraconservative denouncement. They don't like me singing with the FNs and treating non-white people like equals because it undermines their construct of authority. They don't like me singing an Anti-Apartheid song about a black dude being tortured by white dudes, especially when they are out-numbered by about 10 to 3 (11 to 3 if you count me on the FNs side, which you must, by the way) in a little bark out in the middle of the friggin ocean. They don't even like me singing a Gabriel tune. 'That ain't music,' I've heard them rail before with honky-tonk bravado. I wave for them to come down and join the fun, but they turn away and reject the invitation. We sing on for a good half hour, switching over to *Da Do Do Doo*, *Buffalo Soldier*, and other numbers with parts everyone who doesn't know English can scream over. It is great! The best part of the trip.

When we return in the dark, the lights are on at the pier and a few vehicles await us. The FNs start loading the catch into the icy coolers in the back of the pickup trucks. Amb approaches me after eyeing the catch.

"What the hell is this?!" Amb demands.

"What?" I say with utter confusion, exhausted.

Amb yells, "These aren't rockfish."

"They never caught any," I reply.

"It's okay, he said it was fine," Deny announces, trying to get me in trouble. Amb looks at me in anger. I laugh. Amb can't think that is true for two seconds, could he?

"You were supposed to monitor the fishing," Amb grumbles.

"I did. I have photos, data sheets and everything. You told me to observe. You didn't tell me they couldn't troll or anything," I state factually.

Amb is pissed, but it's his fault. He ordered me to observe.

"I don't see how I would have had the authority to tell them to stop anyway, unless you imbued me with such power," I say to try to soften the blow, but it enrages him more. "Amb, you gotta cut me a break here. I don't even understand what's going on here from a biological perspective. Shouldn't we let them go after highly fecund families like Ahi and Ono, and leave the slow, long-lived rockers alone on the bottom?"

Amb looks off in anger. I think he knows I am trying my best. For the first time, the days begin to plod-on on Halfway Atoll after this incident. We sit in a morning meeting, waiting for it to start, while Amb yells in the other room at Chipweldi and Misa Queen about something, and I am just glad to be in here, sitting around the table with our hands folded and our mouths zippered shut, trying really hard not to look at each other. We sit: Karolyn, Banette, Han, and Ben.

I whisper, "I think, even after doing stellar work, Amb feels like I let him down and seems to be acting passive-aggressively toward me, . . . which is too bad, cause he has enough to *really* worry about with HIC, Misa Queen, Chipweldi, and the other shit on atoll."

Everybody looks around cautiously. Amb still yells in Chipweldi's disheveled office.

Karolyn whispers back, "You can't let the bad guys force you to alienate your only good guys."

Banette and Ben don't dare to speak, but I think it's rude that we are waiting here, listening to the yelling. I consider instigating a group stretch. I think Han would go for it.

Then, I say, "I look at Ben, Banette, Karolyn, and even Han. You all seem to be dealing with Amb fine, from what I can tell."

Nobody wants to say anything. They seem very tight-lipped to me. "Not to complain," I say.

Ben says, "You love your job and still take pride in your work. I think all of us sitting here do."

I say, "No matter how messed-up the humans are, I'm not Homocentric. It's about the animals and plants for me."

Han says, "Especially the animals, even though you spend way most time the plants."

Banette says, "Since Zart left, you've been cranking in the Native Plant Nursery, mostly as a volunteer; and the Ironwood Parties are still going strong. Amb doesn't even know about that extra stuff you do."

"I will make a note to report that," Ben says with a smile to me.

"I already noted it," Karolyn says, on the ball.

So I see I am pretty sure that all of them, with maybe the slight exception of Ben, are truly my allies and supporters. It's just Chipweldi and Misa Queen I need to stay clear of. They are the APS concern.

I relax a little, and open up to them, "The work, the work is a slow, exhausting, but beautiful and fun work."

They all nod their heads in unison.

Ben says, "When NOAA returns again with their reef cleaning ship, immediately jump to tow-board duty again. That will get you off the atoll a little."

Sure enough, the day arrives before you know it. We get in the water and they tow us slowly behind a boat over the reef. With the tow-board, we hold on and look for debris, especially entanglement hazards, and use the board itself as a sort of rudder to allow us to take breaths and dive down in the deeper areas, curving and twisting from left to right, like you would on a sled. This method allows us to cover vast areas of the atoll quickly, efficiently, and when we find a ghost net, we give the captain a thumbs-up and drop off the board and down to the net, to cut it out. Most of the time, it's nice to find an empty net. Not so nice when there is a dead or struggling seal, dolphin, or turtle in it. We hook the nets to lines, and the crew pulls them up into a pile attached to a bright buoy. The larger boat collects them, to be hoisted on to the largest boat, the mother ship. The nets then go all the way back to landfills in Honolulu, after being weighed and documented, and if possible, identified. Responsibility is key in stopping flagrant polluters, but tough to discern. That's why after this experience, I learned it's way better to simply boycott fish that I'm unsure of, and stick with fish on the green list, like U.S. farmed Tilapia and wild caught Alaskan Salmon.

Over the last decade or so, I have felt so un-empowered about my decisions regarding fish consumption, that I pretty much stopped eating it all together until I moved to Hawaii. Red Snapper has become a euphemism for any species they can't name. If the restaurant does not blatantly advertise that they only serve local, sustainably-caught seafood, I switch to something vegetarian. White Fish, Pollock, Cod; those names are total bullshit most of the time. In the few years in Hawaii now, including Halfway of course, I have eaten more fish than I did in my first previous twenty-eight years of life: More fish than in my lifetime!

As we cruise along on the tow-board, we get the most incredible view of the reef, like a really fast drift dive. I feel like a jet airliner flying over the Rockies. Each topographic feature looks like mountains and ravines. We see all kinds of reef fish of course, but the turtles and eagle rays we come over are by far the coolest. At times, we see moonscape bottom, apparently lifeless. Then, suddenly, we come upon a lone pioneer: A coral head standing solo in a vast sandy plane. But it's not alone. In this coral head, *Dascyllus* poke in and out for cover, like the ones I saw on my very first dive. Wow, how did they cover all that open sand and make it to this coral head without getting nailed? These little black and white checkered fish would be easy prey, but maybe they are too small to be bothered with by most reef predators, and their eggs or other planktonic form may reach these areas via currents. I don't know.

Doesn't that just sound like the greatest job? It is. It beats shooting pigs. When I worked in the desert I had feral swine pulling up 20+ willow and cottonwood trees a night, faster than I could plant them. Shooting the pigs sucked. I even had to shoot my buddy.

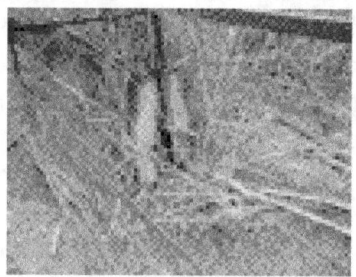

These two 46 and 44-pound shoats, caught in Kestrel's panel trap, surrounded by invasive alien salt cedar, became his only juvenile swine victims.

Buddy was a 250-pound boar who liked to put his snout up to the insignia on my government rig and take a sniff. Undoubtedly, he could smell my lunch and snacks. Bananas, wheat crackers; maybe he was even attracted to my gaseous farts? Either way, when I got the order to start shooting pigs, I shot 20, and he was number 4. I hated to see that smart, virile guy go; as much as I hated seeing the sows or the two shoats go. There is certainly no pleasure in it.

I can't believe as an APS ranger and biotech, that's Animal PROTECTION Service, that I would have my first and frequent duties include killing mongoose, feral cats, rats, and other stuff. I know; sometimes you have to take a step backward to move forward, and you gotta break a few eggs to make an omelet, but what I realized right from the first mongoose was that all of the things I had to kill were 'human fault'; "*Homo* fault?" No I can't call it that. Can't go back and kill the humans unfortunately, so starlings and *Verbesina* it is.

I think as long as I can mostly avoid Chipweldi, Misa Queen, and now even Amb, I can still enjoy myself out here by immersing myself into my work, and simply, just staying away from girls, and sucking-it-up.

The days become weeks, and months are going by now, but very, very, very slowly. In Boston, LA, Tokyo, and San Francisco, time seemed to fly by. I never had enough time to see my friends, make love to my girl, study, sing, and do everything else I do. On Hawaii's Big Island, and now here, time seems to reach out forever, like it did in the Mojave on those 110-plus degree days. Now I really feel the need to break the monotony.

One day, a slim guy comes up to me after orientation.

"Ben tells me you're a musician," he queries.

"No, I'm a singer," we laugh. "Why do you ask?"

"I heard you have a band out here," he reveals.

"Ya, actually there are a couple of bands. I've been playing with 3 Filipino dudes since Zart my drummer left," I explain.

"Well, I play guitar and would like to jam with you guys some time," he says.

"Sure, great!" I say with mild excitement, not knowing who he is, "We can jam tonight. What do you like to play?"

"You know, rock, pop," he responds vaguely.

"That's pretty vague. If a villain had a knife at your throat and told you to play a great song or you were dead, what would you play to blow him away?" I love asking questions like that.

"I don't know. I played with The Dead and Fairport Convention," he says nonchalantly.

"You know any King Crimson?" I ask with great hope.

"No, that stuff is too complicated. How about *All Along the Watchtower* or like *Layla*?"

Shit. That stuff is wicked old. I'd rather sing *Lola* than *Layla*. "Piece a cake," I smile with encouragement. "I'm sure we'll find tons to jam on. Right now the band practices for the big New Year's gig coming up. We know *Zombie, Boys Don't Cry, Drive, Losing My Religion*, and a couple of old Police songs."

"Well great then. Also, you are the diver right?" he says with enthusiasm.

"Yah, I have a lot of dives out here and since the dive masters have changed twice already, I'm probably the guy," I respond humbly, "though Bent is great. I wouldn't bother wasting any breath on Pillmold."

Myhel will have none of this. She lingers in the back of the room, pretending to listen to the rants of the Olderhostile folks, but she's not missing a single word from us. "Ah, excuse me, I've been here a hell of a lot longer and I took you on your first dive here," she growls like a wounded badger.

"Oh yes, that's right," I agree, totally professionally, and making her look petty and vindictive. "She had a good 20 or 30 dives under her belt out here before I arrived."

"Hah," she argues. "I had more like over one hundred dives before you got here." She bats her eyes at Troubadive, insinuating she's had more than one hundred *something elses* as well. The Olderhostile folks start to rustle in their chairs and look disappointed in Myhel's neglect of them. She's also lying, because she told me she had about 25 dives before I got there, and she also bubbled about the fact that her and I had surpassed the number of dives she had pre-me. I don't care. It's not worth it.

"Oh, was that with that Navy guy you married," I reply.

Myhel's face turns bright red. She is livid. Firstly, I'm pulling the same cock-block move she pulls on me with every girl who lands on the atoll. 'Don't go near Ranger Kestrel, he's a womanizer.' Secondly, bringing up the Navy guy not only makes her look attached, but also pours salt into the gaping wound she has created in herself, which she blames on me. I don't want to hurt her. I know how messed-up she is, but I'm not going to let her take advantage of me or walk all over me. My family already taught me that. If you don't fight back, people will walk all over you.

The Olderhostile folks frown and follow her out reluctantly. Then one of the ladies comes back. "When will we get your tour?" she asks with a smile.

"Ten A.M. in front of the office," I reply politely.

"See you then. Myhel encouraged us to skip your tour, but Tirgut and the reviews say you're a must," she says with a smile.

"Thank you," I reply politely.

That back-stabbin' Flying Gurnard. That doesn't hurt me at all. That hurts the tourists and the World. I look over at Troubadive trying to avoid portraying anything.

"Trouble in paradise, eh?" Troubadive says empathetically.

"You don't want to know dude," I say with a calm smile.

Troubadive pats me on the back. "No biggy," I say as we walk down the creepy hallway.

We jam that very same night with Troubadive in the All Hands Club.

Cherry Ballpig, now the self proclaimed Mayor of Halfway, comes up after and says to Troubadive, "Man, you were incredible. I know. I have partied with All-mond Bros. I have sold more pot than you've ever smoked," he brags drunkenly and proud.

Troubadive humbly accepts his praise. I laugh to myself because Cherry Ballpig claims to know The Allman Brothers but called them 'Almond Brothers,' and he's praising this guy Troubadive now. It's like me walking up to Fripp and saying 'Hey, you're pretty good', or going up to Adrian Belew and saying 'Hey, you ain't so bad.' Only on Halfway.

The next morning, I wake up early because Troubadive and some of the others want to dive, but the wind uncharacteristically howls. Darom stands in the Galley by the big glass slats. "Trees move too much. Move too much," Darom reports as he points to the swaying tops of the *Casuarina* trees.

We all stand there disappointed with the disgusting smell of the greasy Galley breakfast perverting our olfactory senses.

"Hey, how about we snorkel inside the reef?" I suggest.

A few interested takers say "Yah" right away, including Dr Oso's sons, a new volunteer, and Jellie, Kilgro, and even Myhel. It looks like the girls got word that Troubadive is rich and famous, so of course they have to throw themselves at him like whores. It's funny to see how Banette, Dietera, PCG, Jewel, Hamed More and Riz Smaller, and the other non-whores react to Troubadive like he is a normal guy. That's what he wants, but he does not want to snorkel.

"Nah, snorkeling, that's no fun unless we can ride some Pelagic Mantas or Whale Sharks," Troubadive says with deflation.

"Nah, we don't really have those around here, and the Spinner Dolphins bail every time we get close," I respond.

"Yes. We go inside reef. Inside reef," Darom states with his Thai accent.

"Alright then, let's go," Patch says with enthusiasm.

"Whoa whoa whoa. Who's going to monitor you?" I say, thinking safety. "I never want to be responsible for anyone's offspring. Even watching someone's pet can get sketchy."

"What's a monikahr?" Patch asks back.

"If you don't know what a 'moniker' is, then you can't go," Kilgro bilges unkindly, looking for laughs from the gang, but just appearing mean and petty.

"Whoa whoa whoa. Who said *you* are going?" I snap at Kilgro.

"You can't tell me I can't go," she snaps back.

"Yeah," Myhel, Jellie, and Patch agree.

"Okay, you guys go snorkel with Darom," I walk off with a smile. No skin off my back. Troubadive doesn't want to go anyway. Rushing up behind me, Jellie, Kilgro, and Patch push past the screen door and surround me by the bike rack. Myhel's plan is backfiring because she didn't count on me really not caring.

"What is with you?" Jellie asks.

"Yeah," says Patch.

"Nothing," I respond as I pull my bike out.

"You miss Myhel don't you?" Jellie attempts to ask compassionately. Oh my god, she is so friggin far off. In silence, I begin to ride away.

"Please come with us. It will be fun," Jellie implores.

"It's better if you guys go and have fun," I say. "I'm trying to stay out of trouble."

"What if Myhel doesn't go?" Kilgro groans.

"No, I don't want to screw things up. You guys go have fun," I repeat.

"She's not going," Jellie says.

"Yeah," says Patch. "She says you're a plyher," as we all burst into laughter.

"What?" I say in confusion.

Jellie explains, "Yup, now that Troubadive is not going she is going to stay on island so she can see if she can land him."

Though she tries to make everything sound like it is coming from an open, loving hippie; it looks pretty clear to me that she wants to make me feel jealous. She has no idea that I want Myhel occupied with another guy, so she will focus her obsessive possessive behavior on him.

"Good luck," I say with a relaxed bless and release type attitude.

"So will you come with us then? You know where to go, and what to look for," Jellie begs.

"Why? Darom knows the waters better than me," I say.

"C'mon," they beg again.

"Okay," I relent, "but Patch needs an official chaperon."

Jellie states, "I'll watch him."

I say, "I've changed my mind again."

Jellie looks at me with a quick scowl. I wiggle my destroyed pinky finger at her punctured Achilles. She realizes immediately she has no grounds to argue, as she looks at the road rash healing into nice scabs on my knees and arm from the ATV crash; all three injuries exclusively her fault by the way.

"Sorry Patch," Jellie apologizes, for getting his hopes up.

"Screw you!" Patch says as he pouts-off angrily.

Kilgro pours salt on the wound, "Uuhhhh! Where did you get a mouth like that, you little brat?"

The water inside the atoll surprises us as we blast along the surface. It's much smoother than we expected it to be. Darom, Jellie, Kilgro, and believe it or not, Hamed More, Riz Smaller, and even Myhel, all end up on the little red speedboat. Darom and I are the only guys, which really means it's me with a boat full of almost all of the eligible girls on atoll, and two of which I had previously hooked up with, and one, Riz Smaller, who I actually would like to hook up with. I take some pictures. I hope Drats' lame publisher has the balls to print these.

Myhel quickly tries to out-do Riz, who surprises me with her lanky looks.

I will never know, will I? I wish I got to see Drats' book finished. Bummer. Like that Japanese Yoshinoya commercial I was in. Everyone said it was great, but I never got to see it. I know what you are thinking: What was I doing in a beef bowl commercial? It doesn't matter. All I did was dance on a subway platform like some kind of Blues Brothers spy. I didn't have to eat anything.

I think Patch and the new Doctor's family took their own boat out because it looks like them far out across the 4.95-mile wide atoll, but I don't have my bins so I'm not sure. Someone should be out with them. They don't know shit and that is dangerous.

As we anchor the little red speedboat, Riz Smaller stretches out in her bikini on the bow. Wow, she has a way better body than I thought she did. Not to be outdone, Myhel quickly whips-off her robe to join her, climbing over the windshield with her bikini butt right in Darom's face. He smiles. She tries to compete. She could easily best Jellie and Kilgro in a beauty pageant, but Riz Smaller and Hamed More are real women. It's so stupid to even try to compete; just like meatheads trying to out muscle each other at the Loser's Lounge in Laughlin. It's what we animals do.

I decide to strike out on my own and I hit the water. Some small goatfish and other critters move around, but I find it difficult to get excited in 12 feet of water and a sandy bottom with intermittent coral heads. This all changes as I end up encountering an Alua while snorkeling quite a ways from the rest of the party and the speedboat, and my calf suddenly cramps up. My calf never cramps. This totally visceral reaction to the threat of this toothy Alua, or Giant Trevally, a massive jack that could break you in half, causes

226

my muscles to fail involuntarily. Like the pit bulls of the ocean, Alua drive sharks off kills. Like Wolverines, nobody wants to mess with an Alua, especially a big black 90-pound aggressive male like this one. He circles me in an elliptical pattern, coming very close at times, but not close enough to reach; not that I would risk getting fingers chopped off. I grab the tip of my fin and stretch my calf, keeping an eye on the big brute. He sees I'm in distress, but I try my best to play it cool. I look up above the surface quickly to see that I am a good 132 meters from the boat, and no one is even looking my way. Whoa, what if little Hamed ran into this guy, or Patch? They would be in deep shit. Eventually, the Alua moves off and I return to snorkeling, but much closer to the boat. I guess being a little more social with the humans I am trying to run away from is in my own best interest, on multiple levels.

Kestrel snorkels along the bottom right before encountering the male Alua! Kestrel gains 12 pounds in his first 6 weeks at Halfway. His stomach shows it.

When we all finally return onboard the boat and towel off, I tell my story of survival, to little interest, and I resolve to go after Deny to get more bananas shipped to the atoll to keep cramps away. I also decide I should stay within 50 meters of the boat from now on. What if that had been a big tiger, or a hammerhead, instead of an Alua? Interesting though, having that combination of characters in the boat, especially Myhel and Hamed, but also Kilgro and Jellie, and having nothing incendiary occur. I think something will blowup at any moment, but nothing does. Is Myhel out to prove she's not a freak?

A day or so later, the weather and timing make diving outside the reef a good option. I'm way ahead on all of my work, Amb is tied up with dealing with Chipweldi and Misa Queen, and Amb always says he's a strong believer in 'making hay when the sun is shining'. Nobody knows I asked Darom to take Troubadive and I out. This winter diving at Halfway rules, because there is like zero plankton bloom and the visibility on some of these colder dives can exceed, get this, 147 feet! Diving with the sharks is awesome. We hit a spot called Deep Pockets, with sharks swimming all around us and through the incredible topography. They dive down into holes and come back out the other side, as Troubadive and I do. Galapagos Reef Sharks, and a sleeping White-tipped Reef Shark in a cave, round out the species on this dive. The second dive had other sharks in the distance too, but too hard to make out. They could have been Dusky Sharks, but that's a guess.

Back on the boat, as we turn up the channel and back into the atoll after the dive, Troubadive says "Hey, how about a night dive tomorrow night?"

"I'm there," I respond.

Back at the dock, the anglers show off more tuna they caught today. Tuna caught offshore tastes better if it sits in the fridge for a night, but right off the fish at the dock is a bizarre novelty that's hard to pass up. Primal; a little bloody, but melts in your mouth. It's good, but just like anything else, I wouldn't miss it if I went totally vegan. I'm conflicted as I put this tuna into my mouth, but not conflicted enough to prevent myself from the act; just like hooking up with Myhel. If I were to make it back to the mainland, I would go back to eating fish very sparingly, like once a month, and only from the sustainable seafood lists, but since I die pretty soon coming up here, I never end up eating anymore fish, which is at least good for the environment. On the contrary, I actually end up directly feeding the fish, our ancestors, the ancestors of all land animals, so it all works out for The Planet in the end. I stand there thinking, as the tuna melts in my mouth, in a daze with a glaze over my eyes as I savor the tuna.

I mutter abruptly "We must learn to live together as brothers, or we will die together as fools." Unconsciously, impulsively, coming out of my daydream; staring out at the sunset over the water. A few of the FN fishing crew jostle for more fish. I can smell rust and diesel.

"What? Who said that?" Troubadive intrudes, as he rinses his mask and snorkel.

"Martin Luther King," I say as I shake my head hopelessly. Hopeless?

As the autumn wanes, off of the weekly flight comes the usual mix of Olderhostile ASS folks, some HIC workers who frequently fly free back to Hono (for god knows why), and other random tourists. One of the last people to come off is a short, older-aged woman with a scowl. As I try to greet her, as I do with every guest, she brushes past me like I am an insignificant nuisance; too important for me. That's fine. I don't care, but I notice. A moment later, I see her give a quick, emotionless hug to Amb and hear her emit "What a fuckin hellacious flight."

Wow, quite different from my flight experience in Chapter 1, eh? One man's meat is another man's poison. I'm guessing she's his older sister, or maybe an aunt or something, and it's good to remember that no one usually visits for more than a week, so I have no trouble imagining I can avoid her general unpleasantness. Unbeknownst to any of us, Amb is married, and actually has two college-aged sons. He is so business all the time that we didn't even know. And this, this mean thing, is his wife!

Not only Panburelie, but also an author arrives on this flight. After orientation the following morning, she asks me a number of questions. She's writing some book about the best places to kiss or some shit like that (totally Homocentric, with no mention of other species), and I find out that night she doesn't want to waste anytime finding out if Halfway is a good smooching destination. Several of my compadres notice her felicitations as she leaves the band jam room on the first night, suggesting that I stop by her room to tuck her in. She spurns advances from Cherry Ballpig and everyone else.

Troubadive says, "Looks like you got another live one there."

I snicker, "Ya right. I wish I could go for that, but I've already had enough 'lady-troubles' if ya know what I mean."

Troubadive says, "What? Oh c'mon. Don't let people manipulate you. That's sour grapes. They're just jealous and wish they had your charisma. If you want her and she wants you, don't listen to anybody or anything else on the atoll. You have free will."

With that one statement, he manipulates my attitude as much as Deny or anyone else has.

We end up doing it six times in four days, and now she happily prepares to leave on the next flight to write of her experiences. Just sex. The other guys on atoll would just die to hook up with her, and for me, I feel like it is boring and wrong. I don't really appreciate it that much after all. An avid tennis player, her body is pretty good for someone with maybe about 14 years on me, but it definitely isn't her body that turns me on, but the fact that she really wants it and exudes a lot of passion. I would call her vivacious.

As we stand at the planter boxes at the Hangar, I say to Loon, "I wanted her warmth, her sex, her contact, her 'love';"

Loon says, "but just to hold you over out here until you finally hit the real thing," like he has heard it a million times before from me.

"I rationalize to myself that if you can't be with the one you love, baby, love the one you're with, but that's only if you have not committed your heart to someone else already, of course," I say as I squint into the sunset.

Dietera laughs, making fun of my logic, "It's not like making love with her would preclude you from finding Mrs. Right. So you did, with no remorse or guilt, . . ."

And Troubadive piles it on, " . . . and you relaxed and enjoyed it, and it was great."

They all laugh at me, but I think Loon at least wished he had my problems.

This would have all worked out great, except for two things. First, even though I shaved, her chin had a horrible razor burn.

"I told her not to kiss me that hard, but she didn't want to hold herself back," I tell Dietera as Loon and Troubadive shake their heads in disbelief.

Loon whispers harshly, "The abrasion looks like a bright red eye, blinking when she moves her lips."

Troubadive sighs, "There is going to be a huge scab."

Dietera confirms quietly, "She couldn't even hide that with tons of make-up," not that she really knows anything of make-up herself.

Secondly, when she says goodbye at the Hangar, she rushes over and gives me a surprise hug and kiss right on the tarmac. It looks really really bad and I can see a number of people fuming as I turn my back to the plane and walk toward them sheepishly. It's like 'Come to Halfway Atoll! See the goonies! Become intimate with the studly ranger! See the World!' Like that friggin bad!

What gets to me, as I turn to see the writer climb the stairs to the plane, passing smiling Jewel, is that I knew she wasn't 'the one' before I slept with her. I still did it anyway. I don't think I'm out of control. I do have limits, like Kilgro for example.

Loon and Dietera approach me, with Troubadive, who still has a couple of more days on atoll.

"That was stupid dude," says Loon.

"You better get out of here," adds Dietera.

"What's the big deal? He had consensual sex with an adult woman," Troubadive states, confused. It's too late. Amb, Chipweldi, Dutruex, and Cherry Ballpig all head my way, with Deny in tow.

Cherry Ballpig yells across the hangar bay, fifty-percent mad, fifty-percent jealous, one-hundred percent stupid, "Do you have to have sex with every squid to come on the god-dam island?"

Amb wheels around, "I'll handle this, thank you. I'm in charge here."

"Well you better act like you're in charge out here," the tall, thin, Dutruex barks back, Marine style, "and take charge of your Halfway gigolo over there."

"He, he, ha. Oh yah, we got it," Chipweldi adds sarcastically, infuriating Amb even more and leaving everyone with a sense of absurd chaos.

"6:45, tomorrow, in my office, first thing," Amb says to me with anger in his eyes, pointing his finger. At least he didn't say 'or else!' at the end of his sentence. I keep my mouth shut and look at him with indignation. Fuck him. As everyone walks away in disgust, Deny leans over and says, "I could have had her you know. I could tell she liked me."

Everyone present knows there is no way that author ever would have hooked-up with Deny in a million years.

Wow. So I get on my bike and peddle off with the good guys.

"Wow. They are so pissed," Dietera says.

"She had a few years on ya, huh?" Troubadive says with a chuckle.
"Yes," I admit, "I've hooked-up with some older women, but never with anyone extremely younger than me. Isn't that weird? I think it is bad for me to take advantage of young girls, . . ."
Loon cuts me off ". . .but you don't have any problem with 'more mature' women taking advantage of you."
"No," I reply frankly, "The first girl I ever really fell in love with was 11-years older than me. I think a lot of people, like my brother Sproc and his ex Poopsie, think she was taking advantage of me. I didn't, and I didn't care."
"You didn't get hurt?" Dietera asks compassionately.
I answer, "I got hurt, but I knew I had to crash and burn to learn."
Troubadive says, "That's life."
"What's interesting right now in the media is this big like cougar push," Loon adds.
"I know," Dietera agrees vehemently, "It's like the big baby push. Is that a conspiracy or what? Who is trying to force US to have babies and why? Why is everything about celebrities having babies, and what's this whole 'baby bump' thing, like it's cute or sexy or something?"
I state, "Now first of all, I love Cougars, I mean the animal, the Puma, Mountain Lion, Catamount, ah, there are so many different names for the Florida Panther and its kin in the Americas, but it's this one cat, *Felis concolor*, thank you, ah the beauty of the Latin name, it will never change." Little did I know that the science brains were already planning on changing the genus from *Felis* to *Puma*, but that it wouldn't become official until after I'm dead.
"Hopefully," Dietera adds. She, as me, hates when they keep changing the names of animals around.
Troubadive agrees, "A Cougar is a big wild cat, not a woman."
I say, "Now, calling older, and in many cases wealthy, women who prey on young, poor, naïve boys cougars is, to me, demeaning to older women, demeaning to younger men who may be gullible or may just be stupid whores themselves, and most importantly, it is demeaning to Mountain Lions, which, by the way, have nothing to do with older women or younger men, generally."
Dietera and Troubadive agree respectively. "It's not good, because we are seeing these women as big, vicious cats," Dietera says.

"Man-eaters! I mean, I guess it makes sense and it's a good name for what some of these women may represent, it's just too bad that it demonizes Mountain Lions," Troubadive ends.

We dismount and park our bikes and head into The All Hands Club.

I veer, "I know we are spending an inordinate amount of time obsessing over a semantic term, and ultimately how important can that be? Lorenz said it best: Does our killer instinct threaten humanity with annihilation? I take it the next step. Will we annihilate life on Earth? For staunchly religious types, what happens in this life is transient and insignificant. It's only the afterlife that matters, so drive giant SUVs, eat gluttonous portions of meat, and just do the minimum to make it to nirvana or whatever you want to call it. That's where the damage is. Delorese Ambrose, whoever that was, once said, --- *Rugged individualism, a cherished value in American society, can cloud our vision, causing us to forget that leaders ultimately serve others.* --- I concur, and take it the next step further to state that we must work together, not apart. I fear that when Bush takes office, he will have enough power, consolidated through his dad and Cheney and stuff, that he will be able to overcome or ignore congress, and act unilaterally. Who are these 'others' they actually serve? The oil industry? The military industrial complex?"

Han joins us. Though Tamil, he has been considering Christianity, of all choices. He's interested, but confused with what we say.

"If we don't work together, we are doomed," Han says out of nowhere.

We all look at him for a moment. Keep in mind the Tamils have been at war in Sri Lanka for a long time.

I say ominously, "There's no way we can function as independent individuals, like Mad Max. We are only as strong as our weakest link. If we don't work together, then, The Planet, society, whatever you want to say or however you want to put it; LIFE!!, doomed!"

"Some argue that god wouldn't let US do that to ourselves, and yet, look at what we've done so far," Dietera states.

"Drats wrote a song all about this," I say.

"Let's hear it," Troubadive encourages. I mechanistically start to sing:

Mass Production of Destruction
by Drats

The more we learn the more disgusting we become, instead of putting our knowledge to benevolence
Not for our own good, but The Earth's whole sum, Horrific weapons and threats lead to violence
Mass Production of Destruction
Cities like cysts, drip with puss, Should more be born to a life like this?
Hordes of selfish people just like US, Power hungry idiots are Earth's death kiss
Mass Production of Destruction
To live for today means there's no future, To live for today means there's no future, for anyone.
Mass Production of Destruction

Troubadive looks at me in a little bit of shock, and it is quiet for a moment, then Loon and Dietera break into applause.
"Nice one," Dietera says. "That's why I really only look environment when I vote."
Loon adds, "Yeah man, that should have been a hit."
"I'd like to hear it with music. I'm having a hard time imaging it, but the sentiment is pretty intense. Do you really believe all that?" Troubadive says.
"*I* do," Loon jumps in.
I keep quiet. It's so hard to talk about lyrics. The lyrics speak for themselves and if I try to articulate my interpretation of them, it seems to cloud the meaning. No, I don't think all mass production is destructive, and I know Drats doesn't either, but he always puts his heart into his lyrics and he has repeated that theme in a number of tunes.
Myhel enters the club. She walks the long way around the bar so she has to walk by our table on the way to Jellie and Kilgro's booth. She looks back at me, and I instantly avert my eye. She sits with the girls and they whisper to each other and giggle rudely, looking over at our table. Kilgro and Jellie turn to us and try to start some trouble.

Kilgro snarls like a sick monk seal, "So we have a bunch of beer at the ASS house and were thinking of watching *Sex n' the City*. You guys want to come over?"

We all look at each other and smile. We must all be thinking the same thing. NO WAY!

"What? Are you guys afraid?" Jellie goads to no effect.

Ironically, she doesn't realize that we are not 'afraid': 'Horrified' fits much better. Can you image having a mistake and impregnating one of these horrific beasts? Yikes!!! Wrap up your junk dudes, WRAP UP YOUR JUNK. Women can't get pregnant alone.

I try, but I can't resist. "HBO! Puf. *Sex and the City* started out as a male masturbation fantasy and turned into an empowerment tool for insecure women. I only watch moments of the show here and there, but I hate everything it stands for and refuse to watch. However, *Inside the NFL* is pretty good. I never saw it before and like it. Good show."

"*You* like football?" Loon says in shock. "You don't seem like that kind of guy."

"I like football too," Dietera admits.

I state, "I played football for seven years and I love certain aspects of the strategy, but there are things I hate about it too."

Kilgro jumps back in like a game Labrador. "Hello. . . we weren't talking about football, thank you."

"I wish I was the commissioner cause I would make some major changes to the NFL," I state.

"Really? Like what?" Dietera asks.

"I have small changes in mind that will make football and baseball way better, and actually make soccer watchable in the U.S." I say, "Okay, the goal posts need to be 10 feet higher from the field and 10 feet narrower, so teams can't win by kicking 5 boring field goals from 40 yards out. You gotta get in the end zone. Secondly, the kneel-down rule is totally anti-climactic. What a friggin loophole. From now on, if you are in the lead under The 2-Minute Warning, the offense must throw a pass, inbounds."

"What? They can't do that," Dietera argues.

"Sure they can. They have way more complex rules than that," I respond.

"There's still a loophole. All they have to do is throw it to a dead zone in the field and let it fall incomplete," Dietera reasons.

"No. If you throw it away, it's an automatic change of possession. If you throw 3 incomplete passes and don't try to hit your receivers, then you will have to punt with a minute and a half still left on the clock. The losing team will still have a shot to score." Dietera thinks, "Hmmm. I guess it could work, but it sure leaves a lot in the ref's hands." She mulls it over.

Loon and Troubadive look bored, and the girls are completely aggravated at our lack of interest in them. Remember, there are only about 27 women living on the atoll now, almost triple the 11 when I first got here. Instead of about 200 men, we have about 147 now. Keep in mind that all 53 men who have left were all non-Foreign Nationals. They were Navy and construction workers. This leads to these three 'ladies' moving on to courting the FNs in the coming months, and throwing themselves even more at whomever comes on atoll.

I keep going, "Next, no more point after. You can only go for a 2-point conversion."

"Yes!" Troubadive adds. "The point after is so automatic. How many of those are missed a year?"

"In the pros, maybe 2%," Dietera estimates.

"Finally, here's the biggy. Each player must be signed for 5 years every time they are signed. I am sick of all this kookie trading. That's okay for baseball, but you need continuity and identity in football. Oh ya, and no more helmets," as I exhale and slouch back in the booth.

"No helmets!" Everyone breaks out laughing.

"Rugby doesn't use helmets. Aussie rules don't either. What are we wussier than them?" I challenge.

"Ya, but what about the concussions?" Troubadive wonders.

"Exactly. I guarantee you, without helmets, players won't lead with their heads and spear and there would be way less head and neck injuries, but maybe more broken noses like in the Knute Rockne days." I rest my case.

"You got some crazy ideas man," Loon says, of all people.

"Thank you," I say as I take the compliment well.

There's a quiet pause as we sit smugly, having solved The World's problems again with a chat in the booth. I look around the dingy club and notice the doctor is gone. Unfortunately, this evening's flight took one of our little talked about but very special and nicer residents away. Dr. Chance, and his wife and kids, left for good, after training and getting the new doctor, with his kids, settled in. Their house is right across from mine, so I go over to see how they are moving in on their first night on my way back from the club.

As I walk in, I see tons of stereo equipment and speaker wire; vintage 70s stuff, and records; lots of em. Skynard, The Outlaws, Tom Petty, some Bob Seger. There's a mounted alligator head leaning against the paneling, and a nice compound bow and quiver filled with heavy-duty arrows, a-la Ted Noise.

The first time I speak with his petite, endomorphic attractive wife Kracklin, she says, "Oh, Ranger Kestrel, you're the player right?" in a heavy Georgian accent. She smiles.

I have no idea what she means. She stands with her hands on her hips with a damp clothy rag bunched up in one of them. I told you I am thick. You gotta be blunt.

I start, "Ah. . ., yes, yes I am. I'm a big player. I started the team over 4 months after I got out here, but I've been playing since I was 17 or so."

Kracklin looks at me with astonishment for my honesty. "Well at least you ain't shy about it," she says sarcastically.

I say, "No, I'm very un-shy. I want everyone to play. Do you want to play?"

She looks at me with a shrewd, stern eye. Yet, I like her. She seems to be as cool as Dr. Chance's wife.

"Play what?" Dr. Oso answers as he enters the room. Like a bear himself in shape and stature, he's hairy too, and kind of groans and growls like one, but right away, I feel he's cool too.

"Ultimate," I explain.

"Ultimate?" The couple says in unison as their sons and daughter prick up their ears.

"Yes, Ultimate Frisbee. Did you guys ever play?"

"Never heard of it," says Dr. Oso.

"Me neither," chimes-in little Patch. "Our favorite sport is nashcah. Do you like nashcah?"

"Never heard of it, but Ultimate is a great game," I encourage.

"Can't be better than wrestlin bear or gator," Dr. Oso adds.

"Or ring toss," adds Patch.

"Or ring toss," Dr. Oso agrees.

"That's not what we been talkin' bout and I think you'd bestin apologize now," Kracklin states with an overbearing Judeo-Christian morality.

"Now? Apologize for what? I'm sorry, I don't know what nashcah is." I feel very embarrassed because I don't know what I did.

Kracklin looks over at Dr. Oso for a moment.

"Our son has a little speech impediment," he says in front of Patch. "He was saying NASCAR."

"Oh, NASCAR. Oh. Okay. I am so sorry. No, I don't like NASCAR or any motor sports. So do you want to play or not. I can teach you. I taught everyone. No one knew how to throw a Frisbee when I got here," I continue, gesturing with my wrist.

"You know that's not the kind of 'player' I ben talkin' bout," says Kracklin, ushering her kids from the room.

"Player!" Dr. Oso states with distain.

"Yes, he's a big player," Kracklin claims.

I think I'm missing something in the conversation here. I remember the Altman film, *The Player*, but I still don't have any idea about what's goin on.

"Cool. You're a player. Good for you. I was quite a player myself before the Mrs." Dr. Oso brags. Kracklin scowls and slaps his arm.

"Okay. What is a player?" I throw my hands up in frustration.

"You don't know what a player is?" Kracklin retorts in disbelief.

I question, "No, why? Does it have something to do with nashcah?" I say, mimicking Patch to perfection. Everyone laughs.

"A 'player' is like someone who likes to hook-up with women," Dr. Oso awkwardly dances around the explanation.

"Oh, you mean like every hetero guy and lesbian on Earth?" I state with a laugh.

"No, but a 'player' plays the field," Dr. Oso hints. "You know."

"Oooooooooooh. I get it, a womanizer." The light bulb finally blinks on in my head.

"Exshackatamundo!" Patch says, sticking his head back into the room. Kracklin herds him back out.

"Let me guess, did you talk with Myhel?" I ask suspiciously.

"Myhel and Misa Queen, as soon as we got off the plane," Kracklin says as she quickly reenters the room.

"Great. Look, you can do whatever you want and think what you want of course, but my bet is that once you get to know them, you will befriend me." I know that sounds like some mega ego there, but I do think that those two would turn anybody off, eventually. With that, I blast out the door and back to my lanai. I shouldn't be angry, but I am. I am really pissed at jilted Myhel, but even more pissed at Misa Queen, for being such a back-stabber after all the help and secrets I've given and kept for her.

"God be with you," Kracklin yells from the low, small porch, as I walk down the narrow cement walkway between the lawns.

"And also with you," I reply, on autopilot.

It's not just the Myhel and Misa Queen shit; that's just the icing on the cake. On top of all the other negativity coming my way; the fact that I am not sharing my life with a sweet love right now, and the fact that it actually looks like Gore lost to Bush and we are going to have another, even weaker, lamer, Bush in office; I get a psycho e-mail from my tripping brother.

You know how I've said never trust a fanatic, especially a religious one? Well, I am anti lying and manipulation. If the religion has to manipulate you to be in it, is it worth being in? Which religion does not use manipulation? The born agains use it. Here's the e-mail from one of my Jesus-freak brothers, for example:

Hi Kestrel;
Well after three very crazy, flat out years of effort, we actually did it period. We won the 1999 LAMEASS T2 class championship. With the win, we secured a factory backed sponsorship deal for 2001 season, which is really very good, like we still have jobs at least. With the economic woes the civilized world is facing, racing teams and even entire series around the world are closing. There's really a lot more to tell, but it's for another time, maybe a phone call. . .
Speaking of phone call, I called you some time ago. I was driving out of Socal aftr the Long Beach race and was remembering our visit from the previous year. . . so I called you. ... left a message. Wow I'm sitting here thinking as I write, it's really ben a long time bro. We've got tons of catching up to do.
So how are you doing? Last time I heard from you, you had just begun a ranger guide operation. How did that go? I've heard

you've been job hunting since you graduated, do you still do an
occasional tour? Are you still riding a motorcycle?
Man the last three years have been a total blurr. I think this is the
first time I've been home for more than 4 weeks since I got this
crazy job.
Well I've got too much to say for one who types as slow as I do,
it's too frustrating. I'll call you this weekend.
Peace, say hi to Stephanie.
Love,
Sproc
Rock on with the Rock

Fair enough. Seems sincere right? But no doubt, if I answer that
letter, and even keep it totally neutral, it's as if I'm looking for
trouble. Please let me explain the manipulative aspects of this
seemingly nice email. Fact A) I told our other brother Rosmarus I
didn't want to communicate with him anymore because of his
fundamentalism (emphasis on 'funded' and 'mentalism') which he
felt obligated to ram down my throat, and Sproc was pissed and
wanted to get back at me or try to hurt me, so he wrote me the first
e-mail he has sent me in at least 3 years, full of excuses. Fact B) I
haven't had a motorcycle for over 2 years, and how could I have
one on Halfway? Fact C) I hadn't been with Stephanie since '93,
etc, etc. Okay, so I cut the guy some slack, cause he's wet-brained
from years of drug and drunk abuse. I send back a nice letter
asking "Do you understand why you are contacting me now after
all this time?"
This flips him out and I get:

Yea, I do know why I'm contacting you. Because you are my
brother. The LORD will listen to your prayers and answer them.
You just have to let HIM in, fo HE can show you the only true light
of HIS divine glory.

He loves to use "the brother excuse", yet he does anything but treat
me like a brother. It's so hypocritical for him to call himself a
Christian when his actions resemble Satanism, or to call me his
brother after neglecting me for a quarter of a century. Don't *say*
you are my brother; BE my brother! He doesn't give a shit about

240

me. He just wants to add another selfish knot on his belt for heaven. Lorenz states that our fish mind, even more primitive than our reptilian mind, has no room for altruism. Mother courage has nothing to do with selflessness, but with duty. Mothers must save and defend their offspring or their genes will not live on. That's why Wall Street is so fucked up. These "humans" must get as much as they can for themselves with absolutely no concerns for any others or the whole. In this sense, becoming a born-again is the most selfish act someone can do, because it hurts their family, society, the environment, and everything else, only so that one person can claim they are on their way to a heaven, which might not exist.

I have to step outside myself for a minute here to just point out what an incredible waste of time this is. We spend all of this time on this Planet, fighting about god, thinking about god, dying about god, praying to god. I'm not non-spiritual. I just spend way more time on concrete things I feel like I can have an impact on, like pulling alien weeds.

See? Like me, Drats can think, act, write, publish, and have others read it and think about it too. It's all happening in the real world and there is evidence. If I spent that time praying, only a god would possibly hear my thoughts. But, back to the Sproc situation, we are different than animals too. I recognize that. We went to The Moon, we created modern dance, and we designed solar panels. We have an obligation to our Planet and ourselves because WE ARE SMART ENOUGH TO UNDERSTAND ALTRUISM AND WHY IT IS IMPERATIVE. Do you have born-agains in your family? How do you deal with that shit? As you can see, I need help. It's driving me crazy and I can't let what happened to them happen to me. Acceptance? Forgiveness? Help.

On the following day, I look out over the beach at sunset again. Sitting on the white sand in uniform, with my elbows resting on my tanned, hairy knees, I think and ponder the conundrums again. Why? Why does shit happen to me? Do I make shit happen to me? I hope not. I don't want to make shit happen to me. I should be loving paradise out here but instead, I'm uptight, and wicked angry, and ready to snap. I reflect on my childhood again.

Some brown noddies buzz by, low over the sand. They gronk. The sun drops behind the horizon again, and I witness another green flash. Zart isn't here to share the sunset with me or to try to get me to smoke one of his cigars. Han doesn't come out for the sunsets now that Zart is gone. Should I consider leaving Halfway already? Where should I go next? Alaska: The final frontier? I would like to live in Rio or Florence, with a hot Brazilian or Italian girl. Oh my god, that would be nice. My head wobbles back and I realize I'm falling asleep. The ocean surf lulls me with nodding rhythm. The sand; a soft, endless futon, molds to my every curve. The temperature is perfect. I feel almost as if I am in a well-regulated house.

The sea shine on the water diminishes.

How inappropriate to call this planet EARTH when it clearly is OCEAN. --- Arthur C. Clarke

With the rains here now, Halfway looks wet every day. We have sunshine sometimes, but everything still looks and feels wet. The albatross sit on new nests, or dance. I've heard rumors of some first eggs being laid by the black-foots. It has rained almost every day this week, and it's a little raw, maybe like even in the 40s on the coldest nights, with rain driven from northern squalls.

I twist. My backaches from the most recent Ironwood Party and all of the other manic activity I have going on-atoll. "Woo hoo!" involuntarily mutters across my lips, facetiously.

What the hell was I thinking with that author? Was it worth the risk? Was I doing it because I could? What was the point? I thought I could just have a great time with her like a normal guy and everything would be hunky dory, not funky dreary. But I have to kick myself again, because I totally knew from the get-go that she was never gonna be 'The One.'

Today, at 4:42am by the way, I can't sleep, but, I ain't seriously even thinking of going for that workout. I got way better things to do with my time. Really? Like what? Spend 3 hours flicken the channels when there's nothing on? I am so sick of people telling me that that's 'necessary downtime' and 'battery recharging' and that we must and we need to veg-out. I know we need to chill sometimes, but that's all relative right? Spend 2 hours on a run or 2 hours in front of the boob-tube. It's the same thing right? Except one is mind- numbing laziness and the other stimulates synapses. One makes you fat, undesirable, and turns your heart to Jell-O, while the other makes you thin, hot, and pulmonarily vital. We've got it made right? Will I be one of those 80-year-old guys in Santa Barbara who's tanned and looks like he still does triathlons? Do I want to be? Better than being sucked into virtual digital worlds like the next generation will be. Digital computer zombie social-notworking attacks. Why do I waste my time thinking about things like this? Is it the Halfway vibe? Always a weird atoll with a dark history, especially considering Japanese feather-collectors, castaways like Adolf Jorgenson, The Cable Co. days, The Battle of Halfway, and the Navy: Why should it be any different now? Is this neg-world just wearing me down and gaffing my shiny spots and pointy edges?

I sit up for a moment. I thought for a second that I had a sweet warm girl lying next to me, but I am alone. Totally alone, and sweating. Fuck, I gotta talk with Amb in like two hours. Ominous: Like Y2K approaching. It's the end of the century. People will be thinking progress, and progressively, not negatively, right? I'm psyched to see what the 2000s will bring. Clinton has gotten US a 14 Trillion-Dollar surplus. We should be able to save lots of species and wipe out lots of noxious aliens with that kind of cash in the coffers, as long as we can avoid war or other stupid wastes of money. I drift back to sleep for a moment and see myself diving for a disc. I flinch and jerk.

Motivations. What motivates US and why? It has to be a billion times more technical than Maslow's *Hierarchy of Needs*. We can talk about ID, EGO, and even Super EGO all we want, but it seems more like as we evolve, or de-evolve, depending on your position, we need a classification for what must be Super-Duper-Stupor EGO. What motivated me just a couple of years ago to workout like a madman, like I did since 6th grade football, yet, this morning I'm like 'What are you crazy? I'm not going to do that!'? What motivated me to almost kill myself to get to Ultimate games; blasting out on my Ninja like a bat out of hell? What motivates the guy to call me 'buddy' or the casino trash to call me 'honey'?

Kestrel deemed the Pacific Golden Plover Halfway's most beautiful bird.

A petrel crashes into one of the lights outside the building, bouncing on the ground. I sit up and look at it through my screen. It stays on the ground. I want to go back to sleep but I should go check on that little guy. NO, I should go back to sleep. What about my meeting? What should I do? As I sit up again, the petrel flies straight up off the ground like a puddle duck. I wipe my hands off on the sheets, after pressing them flat against the dusty dander screen, slouch back to my bed, looking at the ceiling, and wait. Waiting waiting waiting.

My mind races again, as I lay on top of the sheets. My brain darts around again, in and out of alpha.

Realizing I'm still in bed and conscious again, I decide to forget about homocentricity. I look at my watch. Finally, it's 6:17am. No more waiting. I whip-off the sheet and stand up strong. I take a deep stretch and a breath, throw off my sweaty briefs, and start with my normal uniform routine. I look into the mirror, then pound my chest hard with a fist. I bicycle into the office to find Amb sitting alone quietly at his desk, typing away. I'm glad he's so efficient.

"Kestrel, look, I know you are an adult and have rights, but you have got to think about perception on this atoll," Amb starts, trying to be reasonable.

"I know, and perception is more important than reality sometimes," I agree.

"Well the reality is that you appear to be one of the only guys on the entire atoll who is getting any female attention, ah, . . . company, ya know what I mean." Amb continues, "It can turn people against you, and against US and what we are trying to do out here."

"Amb, they are going to use any excuse to hate US no matter what. We already know that. So I can't hook up with a woman because they are going to criticize US? That doesn't make sense. It's not that I've been flaunting it or anything. I've been very discreet. I didn't expect her to pull that thoughtless, blatant move right in front of everyone," I defend rationally.

"I know, and I am the last one to tell anyone what they should do with their personal life, but we are living out here with a bunch of conservatives from the bible belt and you got to understand that HIC is putting me through the ringer out here."

245

I can hear the tension in his voice. I don't know what's going on, and I don't even pretend to know about what is going on with all these weird little secret un-marked jets that always seem to land around 3am for AVGAS. Why do they come in so late? Why are they dark gray and completely unmarked? Why do the CIA-types watch the aircraft carefully from only yards away, then jump back on and speed off? A lot, lot, more is going on out here than protecting monk seals, and I don't think I even want to know what it is; but it is definitely stressing Amb and the HIC folks out, big time.

"Just lay off the women for a while," Amb ends.

What? That makes me sound like a friggin addict or something. "Okay," I agree begrudgingly. Don't get me wrong, I know he has a point and I can always see where reasonable people are coming from, generally. The thing what bothers me is that I am not cheating on anyone, not lying, and not doing anything else sexual sinners usually do. Just an adult unmarried, looking for companionship, not punishment, for wanting to have consensual sex with adult women. Fuck! What the fuck! I'm not trying to screw dogs. I'm not trying to screw little kids, or drunk women. 'Don't have sex with women'? What am I supposed to have sex with?

As I go over to my desk, I immediately create a flyer advertising the next Ironwood Party at Mount Zart. The ironwoods sprout to chest height already; hundreds of them, like a little, soft, Christmas tree farm. This will get everything right back on track.

Just then, Misa Queen enters the office with a shit-eating grin on her blimpy, butterball, back-stabbing face.

"How'd your meetin go with Amb?" she says all Cheshire Cat-like.

"Fine," I say without a glance, sending my doc to the printer.

She hesitates. She wants to cause shit, but she sees no line of penetration. "You are doing the West Beach Trail Tour today right?" she queries.

No, I am not scheduled to do that tour, and I am supposed to be going over to Spit Island with Banette to see if we can find any Christmas Shearwaters. I think for a moment. Better to just keep my mouth shut until the morning briefing.

"Are you going to answer me?" she nags.

246

"We will go over everything in the meeting," I respond nicely, not letting on to knowing of her evil doings.

"Well I'm going to tell Amb that you are doing it," she states vehemently. "You don't have any one better to do, . . . I mean any *thing* better to do," she says sarcastically as she zips out of the room. What a baroness of wenches.

Turns out, she wants to go to Spit on the tern count because she has never been, and it is her turn to do the West Beach Trail Tour, which she just doesn't like because she didn't study her script (which I carefully wrote, printed, and even highlighted for her), and also because there is a lot of walking on the sand and she finds in 'tiring', because she's a human marshmallow.

Twelve minutes later, at the morning meeting, Misa Queen makes her announcement to a stunned crowd. Banette states with disappointment, "Oooh, I wanted Kestrel on the Spit count with me."

"Well, yah can't always get what ya want. Hee, ha, hee ha he." Chipweldi adds, defending his portly understudy.

It's so obvious now that a line has been drawn in the sand. Chipweldi wants to use Misa Queen as his little destructive tool, the monkey wrench wench to help HIC, and hurt Amb, Ben, Banette, and any of US who actually do want to move the wheel forward and do good. He drags on the wheel, grinding it down, slowly. He causes me to wait, and wait, and wait, and I don't like waiting.

"Misa Queen was scheduled for the West Beach, and she will be doing it, and I will be on it!" Amb says with anger and command. "If Banette says she wants Kestrel, she gets Kestrel. She is the biologist."

Chipweldi laughs nervously as Misa Queen shoots a hateful eye towards me. Me!? What the hell did I do?

I go back to my office and start stuffing the needed gear into my dilapidated green backpack.

Misa Queen quickly enters in a huff. "Someday you're not going to be Amb's little pet anymore, and he won't be around to give you everything you want when you kiss his ass," she whines like a Rush Limbaugh fan.

"Misa; do you think we need to have a meeting regarding your professional behavior?" I say, looking into her ignorant, petty, dead eyes, magnified by her Kilgro-esque glasses.

She swallows a bizarre kind of hiccup of surprise, then looks like she might cry, and stomps out of the room with a funny "F-f fine with me."

"What a waste of DNA," I sigh to myself silently with a sad chuckle.

I post my party invitations, then jump into the electric cart with Banette and Dietera in the garage, then head down to get the Boston whaler, and meet up with Jellie. We make the passage to Spit in no time. It's great to work with people who are actually efficient and know what they are doing, and are stable without huge amounts of drama taking place. I realize I know next to nothing about Banette and her personal life, and that is just fine. She is a pro, and a great biologist, and that is that.

It makes me stop and think for a second. My relationships with Dietera, Banette, Jewel, and even Dr. Oso's wife Kracklin, all seem to be fine. There is no sex involved in any of these situations. They all appear to be mature, stable, intelligent people, compared to Myhel, Kilgro, Jellie, and especially Misa Queen. I come to the conclusion that I know the difference between good people and bad people, regardless of sex, or their sex. Who do I dislike more, Misa Queen, or Ryle? It's equal. One's a gal and one's a guy. Who do I like more, Dietera or Zart? Same thing. Will Dietera and Banette rub off on Jellie. Will she notice how my work report with them is a million times better than with her?

Banette says, "How much gas in that spare tank?"

Jellie says, "How should I know?"

I reach over and pick it up. "Full, I yell to Banette."

Dietera says, "I think the best thing the next President could do in office would be to set the National gasoline rate at a constant $5 a gallon. We would always know how much gas is, we would buy more efficient vehicles, and we could use any surplus for environmental mitigation. Big Oil would never let that happen. Their accountants know exactly how far to push the consumer to screw them for the most profit." Distracted, I can't get back to my previous point before we land on the little sandbar of an island.

Spit Island shows us what the debris on Sand Island would look like if we didn't pay a couple of the FN's a buck twenty-seven an hour to pick it up five days a week.

As we step onto the beach on Spit, I am overwhelmed by the plastic pollution everywhere. Washed up on the shores, we see lighters and cigarette filters, tampon applicators and children's figurines. The coveted glass balls are evident. Banette and I kick them under the plant cover to discourage anyone (like Pillmold) from breaking the rules and disturbing the tern colony. As I turn a corner along the northwest edge, I can plainly see a beached whale of some sort. None of us can identify it, so I take some photos and decide to ID it in the office. A dark, slaty-gray, like most whales, with a really odd-shaped head, we examine it for a moment, and then we go on to count terns. I think we had 312 active Gray-backed Tern nests documented from last season.

Dietera, Jellie, and Banette on Spit right before we find the beaked whale. Dietera has her bins out as usual, having already scanned for Christmas Shearwater. Jellie displays the bandage from where the little pup bit her ankle. She still hasn't gotten the concept of

camouflage down yet. With such short legs, Banette's shorts get
wet even in two feet of water.

Looking through the field guide back in the office, I come across
Blainsville's Beaked Whale, a *Mesoplodon*. What a stupid name!
Not *Mesoplodon*, cause the Latin pretty literally means meso,
middle, and plodon, which is like tooth. I mean 'Blainsville'.
That's the name I don't like. Don't name animals after people.
God, our egos! I am outraged, but glad to know which species it is.
All of the *Mesoplodons* have beaks, and suck squid into their
funnel-shaped mouths.
The next day, at Mt. Zart, the FNs join in. Ironwood party! In a
slight rain, I lead a healthy stretch, then a toast to get the drinks
flowing. Running and diving into the saplings, we go nuts, pulling
and yanking like madmen. The trees pile up. When we get to 100,
we lift them above our heads like pairs figure-skaters and march
them over the large dunes to the shore, where we launch them into
the ocean so the seawater can kill the roots. They stay there,
jettisoned along the shore for weeks, then eventually dry in the sun
completely. Poor little trees. It's not their fault. They just have to
die.
It reminds me of all the trees I have planted in my lifetime. Where
are they now? Are any really tall and home to squirrels or birds?
I'll never know. I'll never see any of them again. You can never go
back. You gotta do a good job when you are there or you can never
make up for it and you can never go back. Ya gotta dig a one
hundred dollar hole for a ten-dollar tree. I know right now, as I sit
out here on Halfway, with Drats tick-a-type-a-tipen-a-way, that I
have to live this now. There ain't no coming back. If I ever were to
leave Halfway, I would never come back. Like when I bought a
Japanese Stewartia tree for $120 or $160 once. My brother
Rosmarus, who wouldn't think twice about dropping that much on
a big fattening prime rib dinner for his family, said, "Oh my god
Kestrel, I can't believe ya spent over a hundred bucks onah tree."
He blew six-grand on a Harley that frequently broke-down, caused
him loads of shit, and which he ended up disgruntled about selling.
I guess we all have our priorities. I want the other 2-million species
on the Planet to be healthy and happy.

I remember when I addressed him back then, for the first time in what could have been about a year or so. I called him and wanted to make small talk, "Rosmarus, how's the bike runnin?"
"We're not talking about that!" he quickly replied.
I never asked him again. I could have said the same thing to him about his bike, as he said about my tree. I didn't. Why do we do all the crazy shit we do? Why do we waste so much time doing wrong or bad things, then convert to a radical form of religion to satisfy our restless minds? If everyone did good, positive, productive things in our lives, wouldn't everything be better for everyone? That's the conundrum I always faced when I used to pray as a Roman Catholic child.

Dear god,
Please bless everyone, and make tomorrow a great day, for everyone.
Thank you,
Amen.

Then I would think about tomorrow while I stretched and snuggled in bed. That was one of my favorite prayers; short and to the point, and covered everyone and everything, not just ME. Then I would think, 'wait one cotton-picken second. I have a race tomorrow in the hurdles. I want to win. If I win, I will have a great day, but everyone else will lose and have a sucky day. If I lose, that will suck. Someone else will have a great day, but I won't cause I want to win.' It's the same with bomb makers. Every time they drop some bombs they are like 'Yeah, we dropped some bombs and they worked great! Now let's go to Congress to get more money to make more bombs. Yeah!' But, you know what I'm gonna say right? What about the people who got bombed? Blown to smithereens! I love that word, 'smithereens'. The bottom line is, I prayed for everyone to have a great day, EVERY ONE! It can't happen. And there can't be a heaven, cause how can everyone be happy at the same time? It goes against everything we know of balanced nature. Let's say for example, I am in love with Elizabeth Hurley, but so is Hugh. When we get to heaven, we are both thinking 'It's going to be great to do Hurley everyday when we get to heaven.' What do we get, a facsimile of Hurley, or the real thing? What if she wants Hugh instead (fat chance)? Then I'm stuck without what I want in heaven.

Kestrel leads a tour to Eastern on the landing barge, including Loon, Twistor, Bent, Hiromi, Olderhostile folks, and foreign nationals.

What if she wants neither of us, or . . . , both of us at once? Yuck! Whose heaven is whose heaven? Is each one different for each soul? Is heaven about what you want and deserve, or what you need? Shouldn't heaven be such bliss that you can get whatever you want, even at the expense of any other heaven inhabitants? Can I eat chocolate in heaven everyday all day without getting fat? It's impossible. That's one of the big problems I have with heaven and hell. They don't make any sense.
I'm not an Asimov fan at all, as far as his sci-fi shtick goes, but he had some good quotes:

The wish to believe, even against evidence, fuels all the pseudosciences from astrology to creationism. --- Isaac Asimov

Luckily, I wouldn't have to worry about any of these questions, because things were about to change on Halfway again for good ole ranger numero uno. A Japanese dive master landed on Halfway, with a tiny little petite bikini model, and a tall, incredibly darkly-tanned dive-master, named Hiromi. I had to say 'He-row-me' to myself over and over again to get the name. She told me she needed to learn about everything so she could take Japanese divers. My phone rings. I answer and it is Banette down at the harbor. "What's up?" I ask, always happy to hear from the good guys on the atoll.

"Amb says you are free, can you help me out?" she asks professionally.

I reply, "I'm working on some maps right now, why?"

Banette explains, "Amb wants us to go get a specimen of the whale from Spit."

"I am there!" I say.

In like two seconds, I am out the door and on my bike. I thought we were just going to grab a nice, quick, clean, biopsy. Much to my chagrin, we have to cut off the smelly head. Oh god, I want to yack. I reach into my trusty, beaten backpack. I grab some toothpaste, an old trick I discovered from excavating turtle nests, and I put a dab under each nostril. All I can smell now is wintergreen. I ask Banette and the volunteer if they want some. They look at me like I'm weird. I'm used to that look and could care less. Their loss. They continue to gag, like non-weirdos, while I happily butcher away as if I'm just routinely brushing my teeth. I put the head in a plastic bag, then gently lower it into a 5-gallon tub. Back on Sand Island, the FNs dig a shallow grave and we dump the head into the ground and shake a jar of dermestid beetles onto the exposed flesh. The FNs laugh at the white smudges beneath my nostrils. I wipe them clean with my sleeve, now that the smell is buried. In a month or so I am to remind Chipweldi to ship it to the Bishop Museum in Honolulu. Beaked whales tend to be so rare that every specimen is highly valued, especially the skull, for research and DNA coding.

Two days later, with Darom as captain, we go for a great, magical dive with Green Turtles, 6 foot long Amberjacks, and a couple of big black, mean Hawaiian Groupers on a sandy bottom in the middle of a trench at about 87 feet. Hiromi stubbornly stands on the sand, with her arms folded across her chest, trying to stare the grouper down. These guys are like 40% mouth, so I grab her by her skeletal arm and finally pry her away and convince her to give up the standoff. As we swim off, the grouper follows us with a threat, but then goes back to its territory.

As we ride back in the speedboat, Hiromi unzips her wetsuit, displaying some nice tanned cleavage. We stop in about 22 feet of water and Darom goes over the side for lobster. Hiromi and I talk some more, conversing in the best Japanese I can muster, and I can see I am getting the green light again with yet another new girl on atoll. Darom resurfaces a few times, frustrated, but then he comes up with a big, self-satisfied grin on his face as he dumps a really nice sized Spiny Lobster into the boat. We pull anchor and then repeat the routine at another spot of almost the same depth. A few snorkels later, Darom has a second lobster, bigger than the first. As he starts to pull himself into the speedboat, I take his mask for him. "Merci boo koo," says Darom, fit for his age, but a little out of breath; a proud man.

"De nada," I respond incorrectly. "Wait a minute, I think this guy might be too big." Darom lollygags in the water, waiting for the verdict. I slip my Leatherman off of my short's belt and start measuring off scute sections. "Yup, it's half an inch over maximum size," I report with a frown.

"Oh, Mr. Kestrel, -- only one inch, no?" Darom hopes.

"Look, I didn't see anything. I was just showing Hiromi the diving and didn't even pay attention to those lobsters. What lobsters? Lobsters?" I joke.

Darom laughs, relieved, "Tank you, Mr. Kestrel."

"But," I have to throw in a caveat for drama-sake, "you know why you should never eat the big ones right?" Darom and Hiromi puzzle for a minute. I look down at a few sharks that appear to be gathering around Darom's legs. Nothing to worry about, yet. "Hiromi?" I puzzle to her.

"Yes. I know why. Big ones da good ones. Best ones. Ichibon."

"Hai!" I answer, like a psycho general in an Akira Kurosawa film. "This is the baby machine right here man, right here in my hands, and you are going to eat it all for yourself?"

Darom looks at me like, for a moment, he would be disgracing all of Thailand, and as if it's his sworn duty to Asia, the world of seafood connoisseurs, and the animal kingdom, he snatches the lobster back from me and dives back down to the bottom, gently stuffing the lucky lobster back into it's liquid lair, safe from post-release mortality at the teeth of the Galapagos Reef Sharks. Darom returns to the surface with the shark escort and looks at me for a moment as he hands his fins up.

"Cup kun kah." I say quietly with approval. Hiromi gives me a nice smile too, for the first time.

As we power back in, I think back to when Zart was on atoll. Would he approve of Hiromi? Probably a lot more than he approved of Myhel, but maybe not as much as he approved of Hamed and about the same as he approved of Danica. I can remember Zart, on one of his last days, knocking on my bathroom door. I answered like Lurch "Yyyyyeeeeeaaaassssss?".

"Hey, you want a beer. I got some stout." Zart offered proudly.

I can't drink that shit. "Nawh, But thanks for askin," I replied. Why have him waste it on me?

Zart looked down at my stack of papers on my desk. He started to read the top page. "What's this?"

I looked to see as I grabbed my Tevas. "Oh, that's an article my friend Drats wrote when we were in Japan."

"He got articles and stuff in the paper?" Zart asked with complete surprise.

"Yeah. He has been published all over the place. This was for a Gai-jin paper. Go ahead and read it if you want," I said as I zipped around getting ready.

Zart takes a good 10 minutes to read it. Too bad, if I knew he was that interested, or amazed, I would have given him a much better one to read. This one was pretty standard.

Bike Beats Subway!
by Drats

Some gripe about crowding and expense, but compared to other cites, we love public transit in Tokyo!. What a shock when one first moves to Japan; on time and safe. Young drunks passed-out with total impunity? They would be easy crime targets in New York. If only trains ran a few hours later, so we could avoid either having to wait for that dreaded first morning train, or feel forced to leave just when the party starts, resembling what the cat dragged in. Solution? Go back to an old favorite, the most efficient form of transportation: The Bike!

Looking on line and in the Tokyo Notice Board for a lightweight, used racer, so that every part of Tokyo would be within striking distance, lead to sticker shock. Have you seen the prices here? One might as well buy a car! And used bikes? Many salesmen said, "Japanese people want new things." They said bikes have no resale value, so many discarded bikes end up on ships to other

countries. What a waste! So I settled on a new city hybrid.
Previously, a subway trip to Ebisu took about 50 minutes and costs
420 yen one way. On the bike, it takes 20 minutes and it's free. The
bike will pay for itself in 14 months, keeps me in good shape,
allows me to see the city, and gives me the freedom to leave a club
in Shibuya at any hour, and be home in 15 minutes, without a taxi.
Cyclists don't waste gas or pollute, take up parking space, congest
traffic, make noise, or anything! More bikes would make this an
even nicer city to live in and keep everyone's legs, hearts, and
glutes in good shape. A win-win situation. Some bikers go for
weeks without taking a train, and then when they do, say "Hey, I
haven't been down here in a long time".

Some drivers get mad because they think bikes get in their way.
Hysterically, they impatiently beep and buzz by, only to be stuck
behind a line of cars at the next light. The cyclist smiles and waves
politely as they slip by. Bike messengers wouldn't exist if they
didn't get around faster and cheaper than anyone else. Even with
years of experience, everyone needs to still wear a helmet and bike
gloves. But, if you know what you're doing, bikes beat the subway,
any day, in every way.

Zart raised his head up from the text, "Is that really true?"
"Yeh," I said dryly as I got ready to go.
"You can't really beat a train with a bike," Zart argued.
"Yes you can," I argued back.
"Well, I don't think so," Zart doubts. He looked down at a longer,
much more political article warning of the coming Bush
Administration.

The Founding Fathers wanted this democracy to last forever
because they understood that mere empires come and go. To that
end, they established an intricate system of historic checks and
balances to make sure the sort of tyranny they'd just fought to
defeat never rose up again. They gave us the Constitution and the
Bill of Rights to guarantee our freedoms. Americans would never
have a king, but instead a popularly elected President, and they'd
always be free to openly express their opinions, especially about
the government and its policies. The people would be the master of

their own rulers. It was a unique experiment in liberty, which evolved and endured for more than two centuries.

The Founding Fathers never figured on Imperial Presidency, or court-appointed self-righteous ruthless profiteering ideological extremists. Can you really imagine the American people are so stupid they'd buy all The Republicans offer without question? Voter apathy and ignorance have become increasingly critical to their neo-conservative election game plan. The Bush folks must figure that as national policy, stupidity works. They won't fund education or raise the minimum wage because they want to keep the masses down and keep military enlistment up. That includes the man currently about to be inaugurated as President.

Zart stopped for a minute and looked up at me. "Whoah, this is some pretty radical, Anti-American stuff," as he shwills his foamy stout.
"Drats didn't write that," I clarified. "I just read it and thought it had some good points, so I printed it. And it's not Anti-American."
"Yes it is. You're talking shit about our county way before this guy even gets in as President," Zart stated.
"Dude, I AM A PATRIOT!" I said clearly, directly, and strongly, towards Zart. "Patriotism is love of country, not love of crooked, messed-up, greedy, evil oil men who don't give a crap about the other 2-million species on the Planet. Pro war certainly isn't patriotic."
Zart thought for a minute as he suffered cognitive dissonance. He doesn't like what I'm saying, due to his geographic upbringing and family, but the 'species' thing resonates with him and he goes back to reading.

It's not just that the Emperor Bush has no clothes, he has no clue...

If we leave it to the enfeebled Democratic Party, Mr. Bush and his handlers will probably get away with all this, but thankfully there are good people in Washington ready to act. The Republican monolith, which had seemed invincible, is starting to show some cracks. The Cheney-Halliburton Administration is quietly running scared before their administration even gets started. This is due to a growing revolt in the single constituency that the Bush folks can't dominate: their own Republican Congress. The neo-cons apparently thought they'd bought it, but it appears now they only leased it.

If you seek political change in this country, here's the key. The REPUBLICANS are the only people who can effectively defeat George W. Bush. The Nixon years ended with a cover up, but the Bush years appear to be beginning with one, and it apparently continues to this day. When this is all sorted out, the original crimes will doubtless pale in comparison to the misdeeds of those trying now to rewrite reality into a winning patriotic saga. When it starts to go bad all the 'good' Republicans will book. The smart money never goes down with the ship. Never.

Let's face it. It's becoming very clear that Dick Cheney and his ilk are really running the show. To be charitable, Mr. Bush, were he the son of anyone other than 'George Herbert Walker Bush', of Midland, Texas, who got him a legacy admission to Yale, would be lucky to rise to middle management at Wal-Mart. If Bush Jr. starts another war, more of the blood of our brave, believing, faithful kids will irrigate the fields of Babylon. A lot of folks are starting to ask some very untidy questions already. We've sent our best young people to fight and die for oil in Iraq before.

We now have the best Government corporate money can buy, and that's the problem. The people behind Enron and WorldCom and Halliburton are encamped along the Potomac and fully in charge. It's good the folks who fought for and set up this country are all dead. An hour watching America Today as reported by Fox News would kill them anyhow.

Zart stopped reading and dropped the paper in disgust. "You don't really think the Bush Admin is gonna be that much worse than Clinton's do you?"
I just shook my head. I didn't really have anything I could really say to him if he didn't already see what was coming down the pike.

"This is going to be very, very bad for America, and the World. Mark my words."

I said, "Noam Chomsky said it best, 'If you want to stop terrorism, stop participating in it.' Notice that the terrorists didn't bomb Stockholm. They went for the jugular; the World Trade Center: The symbol of capitalism and everything wrong with it. Luckily, that bombing in the basement was just a warning, but it's only a matter of time until they figure out how to blow up a whole building or pollute the water supply. I think we should close the NY Stock Exchange. That way they will also have one less target, and we won't get jerked around by greedy traders anymore. It's just stupid, legalized gambling for the insider rich, and it always hurts the poor."

I looked at Zart for a minute. I could tell he felt confused and bad. I didn't want this to affect our relationship, so I said in earnest, "Look Zart, we had real environmental advocates in DC for the last 8 years. Bush will attack the environment ceaselessly. It's what Texas oilmen do. It's that simple. Do you understand? They want to have everything deregulated, for the benefit of their personal corporate profits, at the expense of wildlife. Bush thinks wildlife was put here on The Planet to be used and abused."

"I don't think that is absolutely true just cause he is from Texas," Zart kind-of defends.

I go on, but nicely "Bush already said in his campaign that he will roll back a bunch of Clinton stuff and supports the importation and sale of some of the most endangered species in the world. Bush already said he will threaten our historic Clean Water Act by telling the EPA and the Army Corps of Engineers staff to stop enforcing Clean Water Act protections for many of the nation's wetlands, ponds, and streams. He says he will drop Kyoto, and questions global warming, even after all the hard science data we have. We are in deep shit dude. I don't even want to know what it will be like in this world by 2004, but I bet we'll either be at war or have already had one."

Zart thought long and hard for a moment while I velcroed my shoes and grabbed my keys. He reached over and quickly scanned another one. This article was much worse!

Bush Plans to Go To War Within the First Year of His Presidency!

259

*Reports from multiple sources and entities state that the Bush
Administration will start an endless war that will spread from
country to country throughout that region, and do massive
constitutional damage.*

They want this to happen. **They** *being the neocon members and
associates of the PNAC, the Project for a New American Century,
an ultra-rightwing think tank and mouthpiece for Cheney,
Rumsfeld, Wolfowitz, and most of Bush's handlers, who state that
they will continue to use Christian Fundamentalism as a means for
control and manipulation. Cheney, Wolfowitz and their PNAC
fellows have been campaigning publicly for Mideast oil wars
leading up to Y2K and the next presidential election, but also say
publicly that Americans won't buy into these plans without a
catastrophe like a new Pearl Harbor. They want it to happen!*

Zart looked up at me for a moment. "I don't think you are
supposed to be reading this stuff," he said with confusion and
concern.

"What? As a ranger or a Fed, I'm *not* supposed to read political
matter?" I said incredulously.

"Not if it's against the country," Zart jabbed back.

I took a breath and tried again, "I just told you, it's not against the
country. It's for the country, and, . . ."

" . . . it's for the other 2 million species on the Planet," Zart
finished my mantra for me.

He had heard me say 'The other 2 million species on the Planet' at
least 3 times by then.

I went on with, "We are supposed to be engaged. We are supposed
to care. That is what true democracy is."

"But CFRs say you can't strike against the Gov or use your post to
advance politics, etc." Zart lectured.

"And I don't. I know my view and agenda permeates my
programs. No one would ever doubt my love for wildlife," I said
clearly. Zart nodded in approval. Then I said, "But I never dare to
try to tell people what to think or how to vote. I just state facts in a
way that is easy for them to understand, and hopefully I'm making
more of an impact than simply entertaining a crowd."

"Yeah, what was that word you used before?" Zart chuckled.

"*Edutainment*, but I didn't make that up." I explained.

"That is funny as hell. You are a funny guy." Zart glanced down on the paper again.

Who could possibly benefit from such a war?
Facts:
-- The president's poll numbers could double overnight.
-- The whole industrial complex, from weapons manufacturers, to firms like Cheney's Halliburton, and GOP funded Bechtel, will harvest hundreds of billions in no-bid contracts as we methodically blow up and renovate Afghanistan, Iran, Iraq, and anyone else we feel like. Most of the money will go "unaccounted for" as they say, and into the pockets of those in the know, and nobody will have the power to arrest or stop Bush.

Zart looked up in shock, "You don't think this is really going to happen, do you?"
"I think it is happening, and up to US to stop it," I said frankly.
Zart looked at me even more perplexed. "Stop Bush? But how?"
Zart looked down to read one more quote.

"It is our special task in wartime to protect innocent people. The Pentagon is responsible for every death caused by its bullets and bombs." ---- Unknown citation

"Wow, some people really think Bush is going to be that bad, huh? What's so bad about him?" Zart started to think.
"That's the problem. No one knows what the hell is wrong with him. That's the problem. I think he's psycho, but that's too subjective. You want to spout patriotism though? He got into Yale cause of his dad. He went AWOL from The National Guard, which he joined in the first place to stay out of Nam, and I just read that all of the records of his Governor of Texas gig are gone! You can't read them. Why? Dukakis never did that. That's sneaky ass bullshit." My blood started to boil. "I don't like his tax cuts for the wealthy. I know I always put environment and population control, with appropriate education, at the top of my list, but you can't give tax cuts to the wealthy, period. That is the biggest bullshit. Look at Stark Kristian. Does that motherfucker need a tax cut!?" I

261

exploded. "I think everyone's salary should be capped at two-hundred 'k' a year, max."

"What, even baseball players?" Zart questioned.

"Especially baseball players. Nobody needs more than that," I said.

"So what are you sayin, we need Communism?" Zart wondered. "First off, you gotta think past polarization and only black and white scenarios. Karl Marx said --- *Capitalism cannot help but prepare the stew in which it will roast.* Capitalism has been a good experiment, and we learned that people are fuckin greedy and sneaky, and now it's time for a mix of government, for and by the people, that doesn't let greed take advantage," I tried to relate. Zart couldn't respond, but he appeared to understand. "I'm just saying; John Muir said --- *When one tugs at a single thing in nature, he finds it attached to the rest of the world.* Thomas Jefferson said --- *Peace and friendship with all mankind is our wisest policy, and I wish we may be permitted to pursue it.* They all point to the same thing. We need to stop being like humans and start being more like unselfish ants that always put themselves after the colony. Humans need three hands. We can't do anything alone."

"But you think Bush is going to take US to war? He hasn't even been inaugurated yet," Zart doubted.

I tried not to get too animated, but my excitement surged, "I know. That's what freaks me out about this. He and Cheney are bent on war before they even take office. Bush can't make money off of education or the environment, so he's gotta use up Clinton's 14 trillion dollar Treasury surplus on something he can make a killin off of. They just need a good excuse they can use to scare the American public. The thing that gets me is that we know if you vote for a Republican, there is going to be a war, no matter what! You gotta know that. That just shows that a lot of stupid Americans want war and think that it helps more than simply the defense industry. Every major corporate leader knows it will hurt every other sector of our economy. Going to war is not about making our country rich; it is about making Cheney and a couple of the other most richest people richer."

Zart shook his head, "I can't take that. I feel like I'm talking with Dietera or Loon right now. That's too conspiratorial. Most Americans don't want war."

I shot back, "My brothers do. A couple of my brothers think war if friggin great and cool and all that shit."
"Can they draft? I'm still old enough to draft, right?" Zart worried.

He had an amazing little awakening right before my eyes. It was as if he blossomed, bloomed, whatever, for the first time. He looked around at all my stuff and said 'Oh my god.'
I said to Zart, "I worry about the schism in America and how radio shock-jocks and the like take advantage of the polarization. If there was another US Civil War right now, it wouldn't necessarily be the South against the North, but it would be the evil, psycho, neo-con, ultra Christian conservative right rich and extremely poor and ignorant center of the country, with all the weapons mind you; attacking and killing all of the poor, minority, vegan, liberal, positive, good, middle-class, artistic, and pacifistic educated people. It would be brothers against brothers again. How fuckin stupid is that? Our mothers and fathers struggled and fought for years to raise strong, healthy boys; so they can grow up to kill each other. Stupid."
"I thought working for the government was good and I am doing good, working for the federal government, not bad," Zart puzzled for a second.
"You are. I don't know how to impress this upon you. You are. So am I. I love being a Fed. I love doing environmental work related to wildlife and stuff like that. I'd rather have me doing it than some other guy who doesn't give a crap; but, that doesn't mean I like every single action that our congress people and our administration does and whatever. That's why we have to light a fire under those bastards," I stated with passion. "If we can't stop Bush from becoming President, we have to stop him from starting a war that will cause a huge economic downturn, for starters. Did you see Polanski's *The Pianist?*"
Zart shook his head 'no'.
"That war was so insidious. First they start closing Jewish businesses and organizations, then they start burning books and cutting off food supplies, then they start taking people away, and before you know it, they are throwing the old man across the street from his wheelchair and out of the second-story window. It can get out of control so fast. Look at Nam. That was supposed to be a

263

temporary police action and it dominated like '65 to '75 basically, in the American psyche. As a child, I grew up with Nam over my head every single day."

Zart thought for a second, "Yah, but a war with Iraq would be like the first one, right? Like a couple of months."

"Really?" I questioned, "I think the Rushkies thought they were gonna be in and out of Afghanistan like cruisen through an In and Out Burger."

"In and Out Burger?" Zart asked.

"You never heard of that? I guess they don't have those up in Washington. Guys used to cut the 'B' and 'r' out of 'Burger' on the bumper sticker so it would read 'In and Out urge,'" I said as I straightened my belt.

Zart bursts out laughing, spilling beer down his chin, then composed himself and took a swig again.

Now, back in the present, I take a moment as I reflect on Zart and look at the lyrics and papers piled on my desk in neat, alphabetical order. Most of the songs come from Drats, but some of them are mine. My living songs. I hope my talents prove true tonight.

That night, I find my instincts to be true again. Hiromi and I officially become girlfriend and boyfriend right away, to stave off any problems from the peanut gallery. To no avail, things get a hell of a lot worse. I start to think to myself, 'my god, am I wasting my time yet again?'

I ask Dietera the following day, "How do we know what's a waste of time? How do we know at the time that the thing we are doing is a waste of time?"

Dietera thinks about yet another one of my thumb-suckers. She's an expert at them by now, although, usually she expects a question more on the lines of 'How many times in the history of the coast do you think a massive Great White Shark took out a California Grizzly on its way to pillage a seal rookery on a rocky island?', or 'How come there's no green fur?'.

How do we know if, maybe right now, Drats wastes time writing this book, or if you waste your time reading it?

Dietera plays devil's advocate for a moment, baiting me a little, "Are we wasting time when we are having fun? What if we totally hate what we are doing? Does that mean we are wasting time or building character?"

"Ouch, I love that one," I say. "'It's not a futile exercise, it's a character builder.' 'Whatever doesn't kill ya makes ya stronger.' Ya right. Or makes you weaker, or screws you up later," I laugh. "Don't forget, they fed The First Emperor of China mercury balls, to prolong his life."

Sometimes, Drats sits there writing and I think it's this big waste of time? What if he gets published and this becomes a bestseller and Drats makes some money off of it? Then everyone, including even me, would say, 'Hey, good work, way to go, and, look forward to your next book'. It would be a success. A monetary success. What if Drats never got it published, never made any money off of it and no one even got to read it? Then, I would be like 'What the fuck; you spent all that time and energy writing that thing, and just like so many other major projects you've worked on in your life, this will be another one that will sit in the old steamer trunk with all of the other shelved ideas you would like to produce or create.' But, it serves a purpose, it makes him think, it helps Drats emote, even internally. Writing helps Drats release things caught in his tangled mind. It's probably worth it. All the people that Drats misses in his life, his friends and family who never bother to communicate with him; at least he is having an imaginary relationship with them, virtually, through his book. What motivates him to write this book? Nothing. Drats has no motivation. I don't care, nobody cares. If this book makes Drats rich, makes him famous, makes people hate him, it doesn't matter. It may be the stepping stone to producing **Rudy the Red Bat**, or something else great, but that doesn't really matter that much. I mean, he'll never be bigger than George Harrison, and George didn't matter that much. I ask Hiromi to name the Beatles. She can't come up with Ringo's last name, and she forgets George entirely. See?

Dietera asks, "How did your big threatening meeting go with Amb?"

I reply, "Basically, he told me to lay off the girls."

Dietera looks at me a little shocked, then chuckles, "But aren't you already involved with that Japanese diver who just got on the atoll?"

"I like Hiromi a lot, and think I could potentially fall in love with her, but there are definitely a number of barriers. Language is a big issue, but as you know, I'm a great communicator," I brag jokingly. Dietera thinks that's funny too. "However, I am also starting to detect a severe bitchiness about her, especially when we are alone, and of course, there are huge major cultural differences. For example, I made a comment about Bumper-riding and she looked at me like I was crazy," I say.

Dietera says, "Well, I guess that's a bad example, because some people would say Bumper-riding is crazy, unless you are from Boston."

I get overwhelming impulses, "Oh yeah, and speaking of Bumper-riding—it always seemed less dangerous than Buck-buck, which made the arm-jams and clotheslines we suffered in Red Rover look like playin house. I asked a teacher on the mainland if the kids he was supervising were going to play Red Rover, and he said "That's banned!" Banned? They banned Red Rover?! How the hell can they do that? That was a sick game, and if Red Rover is banned, then Buck-buck must surely be long gone. Bummer."

Dietera admits, "I never even heard of Buck-buck."

"I loved those games even though I was the smallest kid and always got hurt," I reminisce.

Buck-Buck basically entailed a team of kids jumping onto a bridge of other kids, until they could collapse it. To those of you who didn't have the pleasure and anguish of playing, I pity your upbringing. I could tell Dietera hadn't, so I dropped the subject. Jogging one twilight, I see a group of ladies sitting on a porch, playing cards and enjoying cool drinks. They wave me over, but with the sunglow in my eyes, I can't even make out who is there. I approach the railing and into the shade, where I can see all of them clearly. My cheapo little Casio watch starts beeping. I stop it. I wipe my face with my hands. "How'z it?" I look around to see Kracklin (Dr. Oso's wife from Georgia) and Rattas Dewhurt (Ernesto Dewhurt's wife, and I don't even know what she does) gossiping away and playing cards, while Panburelie (Amb's wife) appears to be throwing in little jabs when she can, while knitting.

"What was the beeping all about?" Panburelie groans dysfunctionally.

"Time's up!" I say with glee.

"No shit Sherlock." Panburelie shrills, "I think I figured that one out."

"Oh," I say, always trying to be nice, even in the face of evil, "it means my run is over and now I can just walk and cool down. I went for 48 minutes," I say.

"Oh great!" Panburelie says, "Give us your whole life story next time."

I'm perplexed. What the hell does she want? What did they call me over here for, to bitch me out?

Panburelie gets up to go in and use the bathroom.

Kracklin says, "Don't be mindin her. I catch ya drift."

"What?" Rattas Dewhurt complains, "This boy sounds like nothin more than an imbecile. Panburelie should let him have it. James Bond. Pffff."

Panburelie comes back out. I decide to bail. As I turn, I see Kilgro and Misa Queen right behind me. They climb onto the porch, which creeks with great strain, and sit around the table to be dealt in.

Kracklin says, "Kestrel, you think you ben havin a compulsion toward the women?"

Kilgro laughs out loud with a big, vulgar laugh only she could pull off. Rattas Dewhurt smiles and snickers, as she takes a sip of her drink with her spongy mouth and lips.

I dart back to my room and rinse off.

I sit there, in my room, alone. I don't understand why I am lonely, and I always feel alone. I know I need three hands, and I can't exist without the rest of my tribe, my colony. Yet, I feel so alone. I throw on some light clothes again and go outside for a gentle stroll, where I run into Han trying to show Jellie the trick to getting the golf cart plugged-in right.

"What is matter the Mr. Kestrel? I see you face," Han asks sympathetically.

I say, "Just been thinking about a lot, and reflecting."

"Oh, you should. You really should," Jellie heavily suggests, like I really need to get on the straight and narrow, like Point and his Arrow. God, do I come off that self-righteous, ever?

I say, "How much time in my life did I spend singing? Not in front of a band on stage, or even for anyone. How much time did I spend playing with myself, singing outside, or in the bathroom, or in my room? Why was I so excited about the idea of singing?"

I think for a second of the irony of these statements. I had just been thinking about how much time I spent chasing girls, and now I'm thinking about how much time I spent singing. None of these really are wastes, like I said. Learning to be a businessman who stabs people in the back for cash: That's a waste! Sitting in front of the boob-tube watching aimless sporting event after pointless drama after violent cop show: That would have been a waste! A waste of a life, yet, people continue to do it every single day.

As I turn and keep walking down the breezy road, an albatross loses control on a landing and crashes square into my back at about 39 mph. I yell, "Aahhh". Then I look back. The Laysan Albatross shakes it off, snaps its bill at me a couple of times, and slaps its big webbed feet on the coral sand. I rub my back, then, I run into Amb on his way to meet Panburelie.

Amb looks pretty stressed. He says, "Hey Kestrel, off the record, I just want ya to know, I understand why this all looks like a big mess out here. You seemed pretty taken aback by my comments at our meeting, and yet, you turn around and start blatantly dating the Japanese girl. I was never trying to imply you have a sex problem, or are deviant, but . . ."

Arriving with her knitting bag, Panburelie cuts him off, " . . . if this thing doesn't work out with her, it's gonna look bad."

I say, "I had a professor say once, be very careful using the word 'deviant' unless you don't mind being categorized in that category. He was referring to sex, which is probably the hottest topic for deviance you could shake a phallus at. If someone runs around flashing, then we call them deviant, yet, flashing is the number one sexual 'deviance' of reported sexual offences, we see in the USA. If it's number one, right before voyeurism, then is it deviant? Well, yes it is, because if less than the majority of the population is doing it, it's considered deviant behavior."

Amb says, "Anyway, stay focused and keep up the good work. I hope things finally smooth out around here, if you know what I mean, especially now that you have a legitimate girlfriend. This one is really legit this time, isn't she?"

"Yeah," I say vaguely unsure. "As far as I can tell right now."

"Well I don't mean to pry, but do you like her?" Amb wonders.

I stop and do my normal meditative reflection: Where am I now? Where am I going? How do I get there?

268

I reveal to Amb, "At this time on Halfway, things look 50/50. Zart's gone, but I am no longer involved with Myhel, and I'm staying pretty far from Misa Queen and Chipweldi."

Oops, should I say that? That sounds a little unprofessional, and maybe a little bit too honest. What else should I talk about? Dietera is still on atoll intermittently, and now I hook-up with this skinny tall, dark Japanese chick.

My phone rings, breaking my train of thought. "I gotta get this," I say dutifully, using the excuse to escape.

When I answer, it takes me a minute to realize it is Dietera, who informs me, from Maui, or Marin, wherever she is at this time, that I will be getting a new roommate. "Hey Kestrel, I just got word from Tirgut. Good news. They are sending Twistor out as your new roommate. You are gonna love this guy. Now, he's only seventeen. . ."

"Seventeen! Are you mad, sending a seventeen year-old out here to live with me?" I scream at Dietera as I walk back to my house, plopping down on my vinyl couch to gain my composure.

"No, he's really different. He's really mature for his age. He's like a teenage prodigy," Dietera defends.

"Prodigy?" I question.

"Yeah, total bird prodigy. He's been finding North American records for shearwaters off the San Mateo Coast since he was like 13."

"Wow," I respond. I guess I am kind of impressed, but I don't really know shit about this subject.

Twistor ends up being great, and one of my best friends, like Dietera and Zart. How lucky am I to go from Zart to Twistor? Loon got stuck with Misa Queen. Twistor is seventeen, and ultra quiet; a real mumbler. Virgin? No doubt. Nice guy? Yeah, but, he mumbles.

On the same day I decide it's best for me to leave the atoll for good, and that I should see if I can get my ranger friend Renn to come take my spot, Amb decides to send me to training off atoll. The first session will be on Hawaii, and then later, the second will be in West Virginia.

Ben will be taking over while I go back to civilization for training for the first time. Technically, they are supposed to give me 40 hours of official government training a year, and I have been on

Halfway Atoll Wildlife Sanctuary for 2 years today! They haven't sent me on any off-atoll training yet, though I did get boat and other trainings on HAWS. Amb wanted Chipweldi to do the orientations, but after learning what a completely nightmarish uphill battle that would be, Amb orders Ben to go back to doing the orientations while I am gone, because Misa Queen hadn't learned the historical tour yet, so as a punishment, Amb told her she could not do orientation until she can do that tour. From what I've seen so far, I doubt she could pull off an orientation.

Assorted shorebirds, like golden plover and turnstone, migrate through Halfway Atoll Wildlife Sanctuary, as they have for eons, oblivious to Misa Queen's homocentric drivel.

So, in retaliation, Misa Queen has pettily been avoiding learning the historical tour to teach Amb a lesson. Chipweldi never bothered to learn the orientation, even though as Outdoor Rec. Planner, it is supposed to be his job to train me on the orientation. I think that's what happens; when someone comes in and is really dominant and great, everyone else just kind of gives up. I saw that with my family a lot. They don't even know how to deal with me, so they give up. Amb would much rather do the orientation himself than have Chipweldi embarrass The Service. Again, don't get me wrong about Ben, he is a good guy and a hard worker; he's just not cut out to deal with humans, like most biologists generally, and APS personnel specifically. Again, that's what makes me stand out in this outfit. Even though I've been too dumb to recognize it, these guys see me as really special. Okay, they see Zart as special, and Han, and Ben and Banette and Karolyn, in their own ways as special, and I see Amb as special too. That's what sours the "non-specials". They know they're not. Kilgro, Chipweldi, Misa Queen, even Myhel; they don't feel special, and they don't like people who are; that's for sure.

So if Amb is going to finally put some investment in me as a career employee, and I am going to get a lot of paid time off atoll finally, then maybe I will stick it out a little longer, depending on how much worse things get.

As I go back to the Big Island for the first time in ages, and since I don't really think I see myself, or my relationship with Hiromi, getting going again on Halfway; I decide to put a call in to an old friend in Volcano. Renn had been the only one to befriend me in the lions' den of estrogen lunacy that was Jellie and the 14 girls of The Hawksbill Project. Renn reached out an olive branch, and I snatched it to pull myself out of there. She was the only girl out of 14, working and living in our housing area, who had a boyfriend, somehow legitimizing her friendship with me while also giving her more clout. I want to hang out with her for a day while I await my training program to start, and to see what she thinks of Hiromi too.

"Renn, what do you think about taking my job out on Halfway?" I ask frankly as we sip papaya nectar by the Hapuu Ferns.

"Why you leavin if it's so great?" Renn questions in a down-home kind of Midwestern way.

"I don't know. I've been there long enough. I want to give this thing with Hiromi a chance, but there are too many pressures and weirdness out there. I need freedom to pursue my goals," I say, a bit hectically confused.

Renn shoots straight, "Since when you got goals?"

I reveal, "I want to be in love and have a real love in my life and I can't do that on Halfway. I love helping animals, but I need to be deeply in love at the same time and I want it."

"Okay, I'll do it," Renn answers blankly. "I don't see much point in hanging around Volcanoes. They aren't gonna make me permanent or they woulda by now."

"Great. You can live in my house. We have a seventeen year-old biologist who just moved in with us. He's totally cool. You'll get along with him fine. Very mature." I add.

"Sounds good to me," Renn answers.

The following morning, Renn and I take The Master Interpreter class up at HAVO and polish our presentation skills. I'm kind of the hotshot in the class. Renn leads too, and she is really good, but not as good as me. Plus, when she introduces her little Dorian doll named Pig, she breaks into tears like a freak. Everyone looks at her weird, but I support her all the way, making them feel like the weirdos for lacking sensitivity. Then I fly to Hono to meet with the big brass at headquarters. That also goes off without a hitch. Wow, things just move right along off Halfway, don't they?

One point of physiological interest though: Vertigo! I have been on an atoll at sea-level for months on end. When I get on the huge escalator at the Ala Moana Mall, I suddenly feel dizzy and have to grab for the rail. It is also really weird to see people I don't know. I fly back just in time for New Year's, and to greet Renn and get her situated in our old chief's quarters.

With the sun hanging low in the sky, a perfect metaphor for my waning time on Halfway, Twistor and Dietera look at me, and around at the birds, as Renn arrives from our house on her first day here. She lays her beach cruiser, with its white-walls, on the old golf course's shortly cut, green Bermuda grass.

We look across toward the sunset and I see the silhouettes of 3 bikini goddesses near the edge of the waves, realizing that one of them is the girl I was with just last night. I had slipped out of her room and back to my house at 4am, only to be seen by a few of the graveyard-shift Foreign Nationals. Do they call it the 'walk of shame' in Sri Lanka too? It is Hiromi, PCG, and Kracklin. They are talking and laughing with Hiromi, and then when they pass by me, they laugh and Hiromi sits on the sand next to me. She frowns.

"Why you make girls so mad?" Hiromi asks frankly.

"What? What girls?" I state with confusion.

"Misa Queen say you bad man. You no nice to Myhel," she answers.

"Don't listen to them," I say with frustration.

Hiromi states perceptively, "I not care. I think Misa Queeen stupid lady."

"Honto ni? How do you know?" I ask.

"I talk with Kracklin and other lady. They say you okay. I look at Misa Queen face. She look stupid face," Hiromi says as she rubs my arm like she is rubbing salt into a fish. Maybe she likes the 'bad boys.' I hope she's not disappointed, because even with this heavy reputation, I'm anything but a bad boy.

The next day in my office, first thing in the morning, Misa Queen comes in all smiles.

"Here, I baked you a loaf of bread," she sneaks.

"Wow thank you. Why did you bake me some bread?" I ask. She probably spat in it.

"Well, cause you're my co-worker. Why wouldn't I make it for you? We help each other out," she states as factually sounding as she can.

"Oh, well I'm a little confused about why you would bake me bread one day and tell my girlfriend I'm no good behind my back the next day," I reveal, blowing her cover.

She goes beet red and starts to erupt like a constipated volcano, saying that "Ah girlfriend, right! Oh, like what are you doing? You are just gonna use that girl."

I say defensively, "Whada ya mean, she's my girlfriend."

And Misa Queen says "Like, Oh ya, sure, 'your girl-friend.' Right!" sarcastically.

I'm waiting for her to say more, but that's all she can say.

I sit at my desk for a second, looking at the loaf of bread. It makes me so mad that she has stabbed me in the back again, that I start to daydream of murdering her. I start to think it would be great to just go to the Big Island and strangle her to death and throw her into the Devil's Throat so they can never find her, and eliminate her from society, because she's such a waste product. Unfit to reproduce. Unfit to be a ranger. Unfit to waste resources. Unfit. Unfit. Slippery slope eh? Who gets to call who unfit? If they went by when we were in like 5th grade or younger, I might have made some decision-makers unfit list. Who's fit compared to a Tiger Shark or a Blainsville's Beaked Whale? That's why you can never kill anybody. Maybe even Misa Queen will turn around and do something good some day.

Focusing around my office concretely, I start working, so Misa Queen just turns and walks out. I turn to my computer and whip off a notice in a minute flat. I copy this shit off the Internet and post it in The Galley, much to Deny's and Duetroux's chagrin.

Dear Halfway People,

Deny says he needs reasons to order organic. Below, please see a list of reasons I snagged off the Internet. Please sign the adjacent

273

list if you agree that we should get organic food shipped here when possible.
Thank you,
Ranger Kestrel

Why Should We All Eat More Organic Food?

Organic Food is More Nutritious

Organic foods, especially raw or non-processed, contain higher levels of beta carotene, vitamins C, D and E, health-promoting polyphenols, cancer-fighting antioxidants, flavonoids that help ward off heart disease, essential fatty acids, and essential minerals. On the average, organic food is 25% more nutritious in terms of vitamins and minerals than products derived from industrial agriculture. Since on the average, organic food's shelf price is only 20% higher than chemical food, this makes it actually cheaper, gram for gram, than chemical food, even ignoring the astronomical hidden costs (damage to health, climate, environment, and government subsidies) of industrial food production. Levels of antioxidants in hazelnut, oat, and other milks from organic nut and plant materials are between 50% and 80% higher than normal milk. Organic wheat, tomatoes, potatoes, cabbage, onions and lettuce have between 20% and 40% more nutrients than non-organic foods. Organic food contains qualitatively higher levels of essential minerals (such as calcium, magnesium, iron and chromium) that are severely depleted in chemical foods grown on pesticide and nitrate fertilizer-abused soil. UK and US government statistics indicate that levels of trace minerals in (non-organic) fruit and vegetables fell by up to 76% between 1940 and 1991.

Organic Food is Pure Food, Free of Chemical Additives
Organic food doesn't contain food additives, flavor enhancers (like MSG), artificial sweeteners (like aspartame and high-fructose corn syrup), contaminants (like mercury) or preservatives (like sodium nitrate) that can cause health

problems. Eating organic has the potential to lower the incidence of autism, learning disorders, diabetes, cancer, coronary heart disease, allergies, osteoporosis, migraines, dementia, and hyperactivity.

Organic Food Is Safer

Organic food doesn't contain pesticides. More than 400 chemical pesticides are routinely used in conventional farming and residues remain on non-organic food even after washing. Children are especially vulnerable to pesticide exposure. One class of pesticides, endocrine disruptors, are likely responsible for early puberty and breast cancer. Pesticides are linked to asthma and cancer. Organic food isn't genetically modified. Under organic standards, genetically modified (GM) crops and ingredients are prohibited. Organic animals aren't given drugs. Organic farming standards prohibit the use of antibiotics, growth hormones and genetically modified vaccines in farm animals. Hormone-laced beef and dairy consumption is correlated with increased rates of breast, testis and prostate cancers.

Organic animals aren't fed animal remains or slaughterhouse waste, blood, or manure. Eating organic reduces the risks of CJD, the human version of mad cow disease, as well as Alzheimer's. Organic animals aren't fed arsenic. Organic animals aren't fed byproducts of corn ethanol production (which increases the rate of E. coli contamination). Organic crops aren't fertilized with toxic sewage sludge or coal waste, or irrigated with E. coli contaminated sewage water. Organic food isn't irradiated. Cats fed a diet of irradiated food got multiple sclerosis within 3-4 months. Organic food contains less illness-inducing bacteria. Organic chicken is free of salmonella and has a reduced incidence of campylobacter.

Of course, the other 2 million species on The Planet would also greatly benefit from more people going organic and vegan, but I intentionally fail to mention that evidence, to keep the focus on human health, hoping to hit the selfish gene. The petition list fills quickly. I should have anticipated the crowds and spread it out onto large text sheets. They lean against each other's shoulders to get a look, as one of the 90 year-old Olderhostile ladies gets a look at it and reads parts aloud.

Dr. Oso laughs at the petition in an inbred chuckle and says, "I ain't never eaten organics in my whole life, and me an my family doin just fine. I can take on a bear or a gator."
"You're a doctor?" a few of the incredulous Olderhostile folks mutter.
Dr. Oso laughs as he takes a bite out of a greasy cheeseburger. I think he thinks he's having the last laugh.
The entire 60-slot list is packed after just one dinner. Outside The Galley, a number of visitors and FNs say "Good Job Mr. Kestrel. You do good job."
Inspired, I really get back to atoll business. Some little things seem to swing my way, but not of much significance. Jellie, the ASS staff, and even the Olderhostile folks, all express interest in the veggie burgers and sign another petition I post on the Galley wall. On the next shipment on the SS Halfway, there are 10 cases of frozen beef hamburgers and 1 case of veggie burgers.
Deny is livid. "Where the hell did these come from?" he yells.
I don't know to this day how it happened, but someone circumvented his "authority", and much more to his chagrin, the veggie burgers, unavailable at The Galley like the hamburgers were daily, sell-out at the All Hands Club in under two weeks, and people complain, looking for more veggie burgers, while Deny looks at cases of un-eaten hamburgers getting freezer-burn and taking up precious freezer space. Ah, vindication.
"We got too many burgers now. Why can't you guys just switch over to meat? It isn't gonna kill ya," Deny growls.
"Yah but I'm not gonna eat those…" I try to reply.
"Just eat em. Why can't you eat em?" His growl turns into a whine.
"Well actually, it's gonna make my gut wrench cause I haven't eaten red meat since '87," I say.
"That's a bunch of baloney. What if you were starving, would you eat meat then?" he argues.

"Look, Deny, I'm sorry this is hard for you and you don't understand, but I don't tell you what to eat, so you can't tell people what to eat." I try to be understanding. The Marines probably told him he had to eat meat to be a strong killer and get protein. He's programmed, like my Mom, and like Sproc and Rosmarus and Manat.

"Why don't you just switch over to buying veggie burgers?" I plead.

Deny hates that idea. It's like admitting defeat. It's subverting his paradigm. It's making John Wayne sound like Marion Morrison. It's like making the U.S. military in WWII look like the U.S. military in Nam. It's an insult; a slap in his face, and to Americanism. I can see it. It's all over his face.

"Deny, I am a red-blooded American patriot. You can't make me eat meat. I don't understand how I'm wrong or anti-American by fighting for organic food," I state emphatically into his face.

"Oh, get away from me," Deny says, dejected as he shakes his head. His country is gone. His beliefs, no more. CB radios are obsolete. People know now that smoking is actually bad for you. Americans are choosing veggie burgers over bloody cow meat. It kills him. Will I feel like that when I see younger people doing things that "don't belong"? I doubt it. I can see why smart Americans make the switch. I'm sure, as long as I know why the change is being made, I would be pro-change for positive reasons. I think change is good, sometimes. Guys like Deny resist any change.

Renn however, begins to cause me some consternation. When she arrives, she decides to pounce on Twistor like a vulture on rotting fresh. Like a black widow on her misfortunate mate, she plunges her mandibles into that poor misguided little virgin. I am shocked and have no idea how to react. She's engaged, so in my mind, that means she would have no interest in Twistor. Wrong! I feel like I am losing my center. I try to determine what has happened. I like sex, so why shouldn't Renn like it too? Big deal. I can't judge her, yet, with Renn preying on this youngster, it looks more like rape and control than loving sex. At least no one can fault me now, right, I mean, once they get a load of this?

Oh crap.

Sub Chapter 6: Sex Bandulance?

Everything that lives, Lives not alone, nor for itself. –William Blake

Twistor sits on the beach, his eyes transfixed on the early morning horizon. Just as I walk towards him, an albatross hits him in the back of the head at like 32 mph. Twistor's sunglasses go flying about ten-feet forward. I run up to him to see if he is okay. He laughs.
Twistor says, "Did you see that?"
I reply, "Yeah. You are gonna have an egg on your head."
Twistor mumbles, "It wouldn't be the first. What are you doin out here?"
I think for a second, not really knowing what to say or if I should broach the Renn topic. I say, "No matter how much beauty there is on Halfway, or in The World, it seems like the ugliness keeps on winning somehow. It seems like for every Spotted Eagle Ray or White-tailed Tropicbird, there is a Cherry Ballpig or Myhel in The World to make things bad and screw shit up. That's a horrible thing to hear from someone like me who has always been so full of hope. No matter how much the humans bring me down, and no matter how gluttonous they act with their greed and their gods and their guns, I find a way to separate myself enough to still love the animals no matter what. None of any of this is their fault. It's US."
Winds whip around the atoll, foreshadowing the storms of philosophical and social conflict arising against the Animal Protection Service, not only her on Halfway Atoll, but throughout the network of lands and waters conserved and managed for the benefit of present and future generations. Even the APS mission statement homocentrically focuses on protecting animals and plants specifically for the benefit of humans again.
Twistor says, "Sometimes I logically deduce that the best good I can do for The Planet is to kill myself, but then I realize my potential to do great things."

Before I can answer, my phone rings. Amb calls me into his office. When I enter, puffing from my bike blast, he closes the door suspiciously, looking to see if anyone is listening, then says, "HIC wants to take complete control over the atoll, and one method they are using is to start nickel and dime-ing us on everything. Since the Navy has stopped their Airlift Military Command flights and we have no Navy presence left on atoll, HIC has taken advantage of this by starting to charge more for Galley meals, and food in the All Hands Club."

I have no idea what any of this is about or why he is telling me this. I start to think about the organic foodstuff and the veggie burger battle. Shouldn't HIC have to start charging more for food if the Navy flights have stopped? Are people like Loon, Jellie, and I causing friction?

Amb says, "By doing this, they also think they can encourage us to start going to dinner at The Chipper Haus restaurant, with the wealthy anglers and other noted guests of higher means."

The Chipper Haus is the fancy/shmancy French restaurant that HIC built and hired the French couple to come run. I'm sure the food is delicious in there. To save money, HIC's head honcho Stark Kristian decided to forego on the pressure-treated wood, and now the pillars holding the whole thing up have subterranean termite damage.

I laugh, "Of course, none of US government types, with maybe the exception of you, can afford French Cuisine. What a scummy trick to pull," I say in anger, empathizing.

Amb responds, "HIC says they are mad at us because we are inhibiting their ability to make money, when, in reality, if it wasn't for us, they wouldn't have been invited to be here and would not be able to make any money at all, . . ."

I interrupt, " . . . nor would they have an operational landing strip in the middle of the North Pacific for their sneaky spy jets."

Amb says, "I even got into a big fight with them over it this week, stating that in the contract, the cooperator is responsible for all food stuffs."

A day later, we get Dutreoux's reply, in a conference call with Stark Kristian in Georgia, and other APS big-wigs in Honolulu. Duetroux says, "Well you keep puttin ristricktions on where we can a fish and what we can a do and where we wanna build. You

279

affected our fishin industray and scared away da people who were a comin fishin here, and that's our bottom line."

I don't fall for this. I lean over and whisper to Amb, "These guys want to turn this place into Tijuana for partiers, not Costa Rica for animal enthusiasts; with big luxury hotels, swimming pools, and a spa. Pave paradise why don't you?!"

Amb pushes me away to focus on the chatter.

At first, the prices seem reasonable with $2 for breakfast, $3 for lunch, and $5 for dinner, the later of which I tend to skip anyways because I have enough provisions in my house to make tabouli and other things at home in my kitchen. My Mom and my friends Tina and Tim have sent me some care packages, and I order some heavier things to come out on the boat once in a while too, like Snapple, and Woodchuck. But now, HIC decides to flex their gouge muscles to see if we can do anything about it. They increase breakfast to $3, lunch to $5, and dinner to $8!

I whisper again to Amb, who doesn't appear to be trying to negotiate, "I can tell you right now, they never served a meal in that galley worth $8 dollars."

I shut up, at the risk of getting Amb perturbed. I'm perturbed. Remember, these are 1999 prices. Crappy, horrible-tasting, unhealthy, institutionalized cafeteria garbage, reminiscent of 60's prison food, that most of US can't even eat anymore and we constantly try to find ways around, and most of the time, consisting of a main meat course with practically no alternative. At first, The HIC and ASS staff still don't have to pay, and of course, the FNs can only be charged a dollar per meal, so it's up to the few of us, and the scant numbers of visitors on the atoll, to pay the food's way.

A gooney chick with its own delicacy; flying fish eggs, regurgitated straight from its parents.

About two weeks after the new food price conference call went down, another shift occurs. Mainly because of political battles, instigated by Jellie and condoned by Kilgro and the bunch, the All Sea Society has to start coughing up bread for their meals too. I get the impression that Deny and the rest think that this is a powerful hand they hold over us, and that this will discourage us enough to force us to leave the atoll and turn it over to them so Halfway Atoll Wildlife Sanctuary can finally become useful to them as the Spring Break capital of the world, or the next 'Atlantic Pity', 'Daytona Bleach', or 'Lake Winnipesucky', as Kilgro, Myhel, and Jellie refer to them now in jest.

Luckily, the APS finally stopped dragging their feet and I am on the official payroll. I'm being paid as a GS-5, but I'm doing the work of a GS-9 and everyone knows it and shares their frustrations with me.

Karolyn says, as I stand over her desk, piled with bureaucratic papers, in the admin. office, "Everyone knows you are doing a great job Kestrel. Just keep it up and you will be rewarded some day."

Ben states, as I help him untangle some fishing net debris in the garage, "You been a heck of a guy and I know you deserve more. I told Amb he should consider making your position a 5/7, but I wouldn't hold my breath if I were you. I appreciate your dedication."

Now that Zart's gone, I tell Twistor the whole story about Myhel and Hamed and now Hiromi, and about Misa Queen. He doesn't have much to say, as we ride along on our bikes in the moonlight. He agrees I should give the Hiromi thing a break, unless I feel like I am really in love with her. I will learn he will usually be this standard and accurate.

Cherry Ballpig pulls up in his pick-up as we insert our bikes into the rack in front of our house. Rattas Dewhurt is in the passenger seat. Weird. . . , what would Ernesto Dewhurt's wife be doing riding around with this asshole at night?

"Hey. Out causing trouble again?" Ballpig blabs.

"Nope, everything's fine, thank you." I say without looking at him, as I try to rush Twistor into our house.

Ballpig goads, "Okay, run away like a little chicken." Rattas Dewhurt laughs with a snort as some snot escapes from her white-trash nose.

"Ballpig, you want something from me or what?" I state directly. Big mistake. Remember, never get in a fight with a pig? Ballpig sees this as a mega challenge in front of Rattas, and he's the biggest pig on the atoll (sorry pigs).

"Ya. Oh ya. I got something for you," Ballpig whips open his door and marches across my lawn, kicking a gooney along the way. I stand still and he gets up into my face like a complete freakin moron. His huge beer-belly contacts my tight abs. He reeks of alcohol and cigar.

There is a pause.

"You better start realizing who is running this island, for your own good," Ballpig barfs. Rattas Dewhurt looks on from the plain white pick-up truck, idling with vibration, titillated.

"Atoll, it's an atoll," I say with a smirk.

Ballpig loses it. "I don't' care what you science geeks call it. Understand?" he issues.

"I'm filing a report on you tomorrow," I rebut.

"Pfff. Figures. Pussy," Ballpig says as he looks to brace for a strike.

I turn and walk quickly into my house. As I close the screen door, I can see he still stands, holding his ground like an embarrassing Sumo Baby Huey. After a few moments, I hear him scuffle back to the truck like a silverback and grunt as he strains to put his heavy thighs and ass back into the seat.

"I need to get outta here," I say out of nowhere to no one, as I note that Twistor has already been sucked into Renn's room.

On that evening, I look in my mailbox at work and see my new calendar. It has finally come: My last full day of duty on HAWS will be in exactly 90 days.

I sit at my desk for a second in the silence. I think about everything, again, like working out here, and the Hiromi situation. Will I finally reach top quality, for me at least, in any aspect of my life? I can't concentrate on anything right now. Am I burning out? I hop on my bike, taking the long way home, riding as fast as I can and past the giant silver fuel tanks. I come to an abrupt stop with a view. After dwelling a bit on this series of brief messes we call adult relationships, I almost become mesmerized by the look of the waves at sunset, and sing one of the saddest songs from the ***Rudy the Red Bat*** rock opera.

Sinking
by Drats

I sink slowly into despair, the longer we are apart.
I'm rotting inside.
Now I know what it is to be weak and too dependent upon someone else.
I've always been the logical one, rationalizing my emotions away.

I can't stand being away from you
I can't stand being locked up in here
I can't stand being away from you

I'm so hungry I can't sleep. Please be with me right away.
I'm just waiting for you
There's a giant vacuum of emptiness in my bottomless stomach.
I'm sick and I will only let you make me feel right again.

I can't stand being away from you
I can't stand being locked up in here
I can't stand being away from you

I'm sinking I'm sinking, the longer we are apart.
You dominate me.
I'm lucky to have someone to feel so strongly, this painfully about.
I sink slowly into painful despair.

I can't stand being away from you
I can't stand being locked up in here
I can't stand being away from you
I can't stand being away from you
I'm sinking I'm sinking

I know, this is hysterical coming from Drats, cause it is so sappy and junk, compared to his more predictably sinister, satirical break-up song below:

Let's Be Practical
by Drats

Hey can't you see? You're the cynic, You're the cynic
We're just objects and there's nothing wrong with that.
Hey you're not me, very different, very different,
and I object, nothing cynical about that.
There's nothing cynical about that.

I am practical you are eccentric, I am eccentric, you are practical
I am practical you are eccentric, I am eccentric, you are practical
Hey, it's not easy. It's kind of hard, it's kind of hard.
The sooner we realize the better off we'll be.
The better off we'll be.

I am practical you are eccentric, I am eccentric, you are practical
I am practical you are eccentric, I am eccentric, you are practical

Hey can't you see? You're the cynic, You're the cynic.

I guess everyone has their moods. At least these songs are coherent
enough to reach a mass, pop audience. Take Troubadive's guitar
work for example. He is a master technician, no doubt, and way
out, but accessibility is another matter. When his flight prepares to
depart, after extension after extension on his leave date, we hang
out with Troubadive as he whips out his guitar and plays on the
Hangar steps. He tells, not really sings, this whacked-out story
about The Flintstones, and how excited he was to rush home from
school to see it, only to become shocked at the fact that it was a
cartoon! I could relate entirely. My imagination always far-
outstripped anything but Dali or David Lynch. Troubadive is like
that too. Is it okay for him or me to be way out? We laugh, have a
good time, shake hands and hugs, and say goodbye again, to one of
the good guys on Halfway Atoll Wildlife Sanctuary.
You know by now it's not enough to have just one problem on
Halfway. As stated, even Hiromi has been a mega downer of late.
The first incident was when she was somehow hanging out with
the fishermen. I don't think she had a dive so I don't know what

she was doing down there, but she got so drunk that she kept falling over. Kracklin calls me on my cell phone to get me out of bed to 'get down there now!' as she states with her heavy drawl. When I arrive, the fishermen's smiles vanish.

"Hey, what's goin on?" One of them asks in a tough, deep voice.

The old Navy tug sits in the harbor; silent witness to our repeated follies.

I ignore him and go straight to Hiromi. "Hi honey." I give her a little peck on the cheek and a quick hug. "You ready to get goin?" I ask nicely as I look at the scrunched snarl coming from this girl I thought I had been falling for.

"Hey, mixed nuts?" Another one of the fisherman says, as the others laugh, like it's a poke at me or something. I don't get it and I don't care. I reach in and pick out a few cashews.

"Thanks", I respond, as I look around to see there has been a lot of drinking going on, but Hiromi is the only girl. Hmm, interesting, I thought Riz Smaller and Hamed More were dating the fishermen now, but they don't seem to be around, conveniently, and I thought that if none of the tourists were here, that at least Kilgro, and maybe even Jellie and Myhel, would be trawling down here, but no, -- only Hiromi. Why and how did this happen?

"Hey, you just picked out the cashews," he complains.

"Yeah?" I answer.

"Well why do you think they call it mixed nuts for? You shouldn't eat mixed nuts if you just want the ones," he says, as he tries to start something with me, over nuts, mind you.

"Whad ah ya doin? We're just havin some fun," one of the other fisherman spurts as the others join in with a chorus of 'yeah's and encroach upon me.

"I'm just making sure my girlfriend can make it to her bed safely," I say, as I scan their eyes.

"Girlfriend?" They burst into laughter.

I grab Hiromi by the arm and help her to her bike. I'm not a violent person, but as some of them close in on me and refuse to relent, I feel like I'm about to punch one of these mothers in the face. I am at the end of my rope out here on Halfway Atoll, and that can't be good for anyone, especially me.

"Why you glab me? I not your dog," she says, as I sense a puke coming on soon.

"I know, I am just helping you, okay?" I say gently, putting on my 'drunk talk' voice to try to communicate.

"I not need help. I adult. I not need you help. You not lubb me," she says with stubborn conviction. The fishermen look on.

"Okay, I'm not forcing you. You can do whatever you want," I relent.

She stops for a second, because now she has nothing to fight against. I look at her. She stands there straddling her bike. She looks back at the fishing shack for a moment. She can't stop. She wants another beer. Some of the fishermen are talking, while two of them still stand in the doorway, smoking, and looking at us. I get sick of them watching us so I start to stare back at them. It doesn't work. They don't care. They are pissed that they didn't get to pull a train on Hiromi. So close, they were just minutes away. See why I hate 'guys'? No matter what kind of womanizer I've been accused of being, I would never, ever, pull shit like that. This is somebody's daughter, sister, or whatever. No matter how wrong I was for sleeping with Myhel, I never treated her like a piece of meat. Even though, due to her dishonesty and maliciousness, she didn't deserve it, I gave her the full respect I give to every person, and every being for that matter, that I meet.

This also majorly pisses-me-off about Hiromi. Okay, people get drunk, I am the first one to acknowledge that; but me, breaking up this scene? What if Kracklin never called me? How many times before has Hiromi been drunk-fucked? She told me she used to date Navy guys in Okinawa. Does she pull this all the time? I don't! I don't want this in my life, period.

Finally, Hiromi says 'taboon', which means 'okay', and she starts to ride. She wobbles all over the place and goes off the road onto the grassy shadows, two times. Great. If Amb, Chipweldi, or anyone else sees this, this will be another black mark for me to deal with. I stow her bike in the bushes and double ride her, on my seat, home to help her into her bed, where I watch her for a while, to see if she is going to vomit. Then, I hear some fisherman rustling outside the door. I hear her doorknob clink and twist, but they relent when they find it locked, and stumble off to collapse in their own sweaty rooms.

She is trouble. I thought it was bad with Myhel. Shit, I don't want to put up with this crap. I put a glass of water on her nightstand, and leave, locking the door behind me. I should sleep there with her to protect her from rape gangs, but her acid breath smells so much of bile that she is making me sick to be in the same room with her. But you know what? I'm not going to give up on her just yet. She is a mess and she needs help, and maybe I'm the one who can do it. I should stop being so selfish and looking out for number one, and try to devote my life to helping others. I will help her.

The next day, on my way to morning meeting, I swing by her room. I listen at the door for a second, and sure enough, I can hear her puking. I decide it's better to be on time for the meeting, so I take off, knowing that she lives, at least.

That afternoon, when I get off work, I swing by her room again. She lets me in. I give her a soft hug and a peck on the cheek. "Look, I want to help you. Do you throw-up everyday?" I ask. She would hear none of it, but I know she has bulimia or some other problem, and she is a heavy, out-of-control drinker; something I definitely will not hang with.

Then, today was the clincher. Just one day after her massive hangover recovery and our discussion regarding bulimia, this afternoon, after work, I call Hiromi and ask how she is. She says fine. I ask her about the night at the fishing shack, and she acts like nothing happened, which is very Japanese Bunko, or culture. If you get drunk off your ass in Tokyo, and throw up on the Yamanote subway, that's okay, cause hey, you were drunk. Everything is conveniently forgotten by the next day in the office.

I say I need to workout and go for a swim. She says she will meet me up there.

On the North Beach, we approach each other. I give her a big hug, but don't really feel anything coming back. We drop our towels and hit the water. I scan the area for Tiger Sharks and monk seals before I swim 10 lengths up and down the shoreline. As I tire, I come back to Hiromi and stop, my chest heaving, and my arms pumped. I try to bring up the previous night.

"I not remember," she states.

"You blacked out? You can't remember anything?" I ask with great concern on my face.

"NO. I remember. I remember," she snaps back. I can tell she is copping attitude again.

"Okay, where is your bike?" I ask her with a gentle smile, trying to get her to drop her defenses a little.

"What? Wakerimasen," she says, which means she doesn't understand, but I can tell she is lying.

"Anata no jetensha wa doko desu ka?" I ask her in my bad Japanese.

She looks at me now, mad for a moment that I pulled Japanese out on here and she can't act like she doesn't understand. "My bike in the bike holder is," she says awkwardly.

"No it isn't. I can see your bike rack from here practically. It's not there. Where is it?" I ask again gently.

"I know where bike is," she defends again. I don't think I have the patience for this any longer, and I feel my heart sink. I can't let myself fall in love with this girl. I look out across this amazing paradise, scanning over the surface of the atoll waters all the way out to the reef, and then back to the sandy beach and all the birds zigging across the sky. This place is great. This water is awesome and I could stay in it all day. The sky and the color of the water is unbelievable. Yet, I am bummed and everything sucks because I keep chasing after 'the one'. The one, right, girl, I just can't find. I want to love Hiromi. I want to give her my all. Can I cope with her major issues? No.

She runs off and dives back in, beyond the surf. I approach her in the water and give her a hug again. Then I give her a kiss. It's as if she has no choice. She is a Japanese girl and if I want to hug her or kiss her, she just has to kind of take it. I hate that too. I feel no reciprocity.

I look into her eyes. She smiles, but she knows I have already been let down. I think it's better not to talk at all. Then, we see Kracklin and Jewel come down to the water in their bikinis with 4 of the tourist women who had come on with some hardcore underwater photographers. Hiromi becomes so uncontrollably dis-amused with my looking over at them entering the water at the foamy creamy edge, that she reaches under and claws my balls and sphincter underwater, with her long sharp dragon-lady nails, causing me to scream in pain. The ladies all freeze and look over at me. Hiromi just keeps smiling like nothing happened, with her bright white teeth and pink tongue beaming from her black tan. I found her sensuous and exciting only just a short time ago. I'm not fickle. This person has simply pulled a one-eighty on me. I can't hide my anger and painful expression. This is the moment that I realize this thing with Hiromi is over! Damn, I was hoping Hiromi would really be the love of my life, but I don't even feel like I love her anymore at all. I feel like I want to cry, and I feel a little pain in my chest. I was falling down that path, but not anymore. I dunk my head beneath the surface and hold my breath for a long as I can, avoiding conflict.

After thinking it over that last part of the swim, I decide to keep things cool with Hiromi for now, even though the scuttlebutt around Sand Island now is that she has hooked-up with someone else on the atoll. Talk is so cheap around here. She still seems to be into me, kind of. It just seems like she is falling into long-term married-couple bad habits and pitfalls already. Horrible communication, stupid temper, and irrationality, sex as a tool, weapon, or obligation, and worst of all, just generally carpy bitchiness; especially when no one is looking.

Over the next week or so, I catch her yacking a bunch of times, but she lies and says she isn't. "What, I not trow out," she defends.

At the All Hands Club, the night before the big New Year's Party, we celebrate my two-year anniversary on Halfway. Dietera, Twistor, Renn, and a couple of other people are actually still my friends, but I have been finding it more fun to just hang with the visitors, and stay away from any possible problem people on island.

289

"Where you been?" Dietera asks, trying to get caught up. "With all the negativity I've apparently brought on to myself, I decided to spend a few nights a week jamming with the Sri Lankans in their barracks, and at the All Hands Club with the Filipino rock band. After being off the atoll, I think this breather will be good for Hiromi and I, and show me her true colors," I explain.

I neglect to tell Dietera, or anyone else at the table, that I have also pulled some mega-hermit maneuvers when I could. If I happen to get two days off in a row, which is rare, I pack my backpack when no one is looking, and slink off on my bike out to the West Beach.

Kestrel prepares to vanish into the West Beach forest, for a few days, alone.

There is no camping on Halfway. Everyone needs to be housed in a barracks or some other old Navy dwelling. I never lit a fire. I would just spend a day, and a night, and part of another day or night, totally alone. It's weird being alone. Alone with my thoughts. Waiting for nothing. Walking out in the ironwood forest. Ducking if I heard a plane coming in, or people coming down the West Beach Trail I designed. Sleeping alone out there was weird and scary. Reading in the sun. Sprinting down the trail barefoot. Talking to the birds. Lots of tree climbing. Looking at the ocean and writing lyrics and singing song melodies. Doing vocal warm-ups, then singing in full voice at the ocean. Being alone on an atoll of less than 173 people, on a planet with over 6 billion people on it. 6 billion people! Not 3 billion, like what would be reasonable and intelligent. 6 billion foolish people trying to have babies. Alone is weird. Playing my flute. There is something wrong with alone, but I think these sneak little forays are very medicinal for me. Is this the first sign of island madness, or was that way back when I started hookin-up with Myhel? Where do the loners hide and hangout on this little sand speck? I think they curl up in some tiny cinderblock room with a ham radio.

Of course, much worse things can always happen. The nice looking young girls who are on atoll with the underwater photographers have just come strutting into the club wearing tight hot pants and bikini tops. Laughing loudly and pissing vinegar, they march straight up to our table as if they are in a chic nightclub in Miami. The Foreign Nationals get out of their way. They have no idea how to react to these types of women.

"Can we join you fellas, or this is reserved?" one of them brashly asks.

"No sure, have a seat," Dietera and I say. Twistor blushes a bit.

"Oh, don't worry. They're just girls. They ain't gonna bite ya," Renn says, semi-chastising poor, already hen-pecked, Twistor.

I gotta get this guy out of this, but one problem at a time. I love my friend Renn, don't get me wrong, but she is a psycho and I can't let her trash young innocent Twistor.

The girls had only been sitting with us for what could not have been more than 3 minutes, when Hiromi walks in, sees me, stalks over to the table, and belches out; "What you doinn with girls? You like girls. You dog face? You look dog face. I hate you now. You like these, huh, you like?"

Everyone looks at me for a reaction. Right now, I could care less. How dare she come at me all confrontational like that, and possessive, and fuckin freaky. I wasn't drunk at the fishing shack, she was!

"Hey," one of the hot girls pipes up, "you said you weren't taken. We didn't know we got a cheatin man here."

Laughter erupts from several people in the general vicinity of our booth.

"No no," I try to explain. "we are not married."

"Girlfriend, whatever, let's not split hairs," the other girl says.

"No, it's not like that, she's not my girlfriend," I blurt out.

Hiromi looks at me with fire in her eyes. "What? I not you girlflend? I not you girlflend?" she says with anger in her cracking voice. Then she reaches over to a table and grabs an ashtray. She first throws the ashes and butts on me, then the ashtray, which bounces off my shoulder. Then she grabs a bottle of champagne from Rattas Dewhurt and some other HIC's table and pours the last quarter of a bottle on me. I reach up and snatch the bottle from her, like taking candy from a baby, not that I care about the champagne, but more, because I fear what she might do with the bottle next. "Enough! Dame (pronounced dah-may). Zen zen dame!" I command. Telling her to stop in Japanese really pisses her off, and she stomps out infuriated.

"Well, you must be quite a lover to piss off a lady that much mister. I'm in," the finest of the girls puts her arm around me while she wipes me off with a napkin.

"Did you just blow-off Hiromi like that? What kind of relationship do you two have?" Renn puzzles.

"We don't," I respond. "That's what I was trying to tell you when we were on The Big Island."

"You were just sleeping with her last night," Renn counters, spilling the beans in front of everyone while drawing focus off of her own fornication-relations.

I lose my temper. "Okay, first of all, did you just see that display? That is unacceptable behavior and I don't treat people that way and I don't go out with shit like that." Everyone looks around, mildly impressed that I am standing firm ground. I don't bother to go into the personal facts that I didn't sleep with her last night and there has been mega storms in this relationship. "More importantly, I need to meet an angel that I can't get out of my head, so I know this thing with Hiromi is friggin dead. I wanted it to work. I wanted her to be my girlfriend, I really did. I am tired of all the bullshit out here. But you can't force it, and there are way too many red flags," I state.

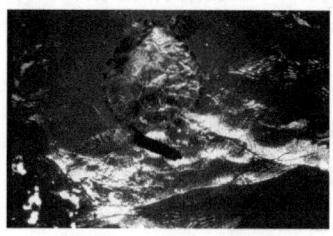

"Oh well then, our job is done here," the hottest fox says as she gives me a wet kiss on the lips and the three girls leave to have Pillmold and Deny buy them a round at the bar.

After that bizarre incident, which I have to imagine Myhel and Misa Queen must have had something to do with, we bike back to the quarters. Renn and Twistor now sit snuggly on the couch together, watching one of those lame, first-run Hollywood movies on HBO.

"Well, when it's your time to go, it's time to go," Renn says. "You have really made quite a name for yourself out here."

Renn goes on to explain that all of my enemies, like Myhel, Misa Queen, the HIC staff, and a number of other miscellaneous folks, have said that I'm a womanizer, liar, cheapskate, pretty boy, etc. You name it.

She appears to be trying to encourage me, but really aggrandizes herself to Twistor with a back-handed compliment, "It's just like when you were on the turtle project. Seems like you really know how to piss off the jerks, but you always end up making friends with the quality folks."

"I do?" I say with astonishment, then I sing like Adam Ant, "*I want all who get to know me, to be my admirers or my enemies,*" Twistor has no idea who Adam Ant could possibly be. I continue, "That's not true though. I would like to get along with everybody. I don't think I am as extreme as Loon or Ballpig. I think I'm in the middle more, or middle left," I reason.

"Yeah," both her and Twistor agree. "Banette, the French people, most of the ASS folks: They all think you do great," Renn states.

"Yea," Twistor adds. "The Olderhostile people freaken love you man. I can't believe the evaluations you get. Renn has been showing them to me."

"Really? I thought so. So what is the problem?" I ask.

"I don't know how you can't see it. A lot of people want to hurt the APS, and you are their All-American symbol. You haven't noticed? It's totally a dividing line. So far, the people that all hate you here are a bunch of assholes. What about Dietera, she likes you, right?" Renn confirms.

"Yes. She's great." I respond, thinking for a moment.

Renn interrogates, "You haven't hooked up with her too, have you?" They stare into my eyes.

"Nooooo," I say. "That's the thing that pisses me off. There are tons of people on the atoll, like you, who I never hooked up with, but if you ask anyone, the Foreign Nationals, whomever, they all think I've done everyone and their friggin grandmother!"

"I wouldn't worry about any of them," Twistor says in a consoling tone. "We know you are a good guy."

"Yeah, you just have to avoid stepping on your dick again," Renn says as a petty dig.

"I haven't done that once yet. I don't want to be with Myhel, Hiromi, or anyone else out here," I say. Then I think for a moment. I can't define any actual mistakes I have made with any of these girls. I haven't lied or been misleading. I haven't manipulated anyone, or gotten them drunk at the fishing shack. Hey! Who's watchin those guys? Why aren't their feet held to the fire?

"Well that's good, cause if you can avoid having sex with anymore chicks out here, it would probably do you a favor," Renn ends.

I think a lot as I lie in bed alone again. I think about everything that has happened, again. I have been trying to be a good person, but it has been blowing up in my face. Renn seems down to Earth, and her advice seems sound, and yet, I realize, that even though Renn has been on the atoll for a short time, I seem to be a third wheel every time her and Twistor are around. There is no way my engaged, 29-year-old friend, would be interested in this little, nerdy, quiet, 17-year-old, UNDERAGE, virgin, right?

Later that night, I hear a little funny noise coming from one of the other rooms. I gently move out of bed, so Zen that even the noisy, squeaky, old springs, don't squeak. As I get to my door, I get into push-up position and lower myself to the floor. Under the crack in the door, I can hear rustling, kissing, and other sloppy sex sounds. What the fuck? She doesn't take her own advice very well now does she? 'Don't pee where ya swim?' My ass.

The next morning, I act as if nothing happened and I know nothing. They appear chipper, but definitely feel a need to keep me out of the loop. Renn had been a good friend, and I could even consider her one of my best friends, but I have some issues with this. First, she is engaged. I wouldn't screw around with someone if they were engaged. Feels kind of home-wrecker-esque. What if I were engaged? Man, if I went so mental as to actually believe marriage to be a viable option, I definitely would not screw it up

294

by screwing around. I guess that's easy to say if I've never been there.

Secondly though, and much bigger in my mind, is what the hell is she doing? Does she have to feel complete control? I would never, ever, date a 17-year-old, period, ah, . . . except for when I was 17 and dating the girls in my high school plays and on the track team, like I was supposed to be doing. Renn is just so wrong on so many levels. I don't even know where to start. It violates my sensibilities.

Now, the atoll shit comes down on them. As APS staff start waking up to the fact of this little tryst, it becomes a good little diversion from me, and I enjoy being a little less scrutinized on the atoll for a short while. Somehow, I'm responsible and should do something about my friend Renn. I must deal with yet another political snafu, but my thoughts remain engrossed in my own little atoll problems. Many more people will focus their evil, pointy-fingered accusations, on them now.

I like Renn, I trust Renn, and I want her to be happy; but I can't help but feel pissed about the whole Twistor manipulation maneuver. Renn could be a total freak. Freak! Cool at times, so I accepted the ghost sightings, the old lady standing in the kitchen window, ya know, stuff like that; but now she appears to be going a little too psycho. I told you all girls are psycho, but there is TOO psycho. I mean, you don't want to be friends with a girl who is so psycho that she's practically at the level of "guy psycho".

"Hey, what are you doing with this Twistor kid?" I ask.

"Oh what, come on, like you wouldn't," Renn insults me.

I twist my head up into the air and take a calming breath, "Don't deflect onto me and start calling me a hypocrite. Are you into this kid or what?"

"Stop calling him a kid," Renn breaks in.

"What about your engagement?" I ask.

Renn curtly replies, "You don't know anything about that."

"I know. I guess I don't. I'm confused. I like Twistor," I say. "You are the one that told me you are engaged."

"Oh what, like I'm gonna break him, and fuck shit up or somethin?" Renn screeches.

"Look, are you going to avoid having a rational conversation with me at any cost?" I ask, looking for some empathy from the old Renn.

"There you go, trying to control and manipulate everything. You are the control freak. You want to control Twistor. What do you have like a Greek Acropolis man-love thing for him or something?" Renn blurts.

"Renn, where the hell is all of this coming from?" I ask sympathetically.

"Well it must all be coming from me because obviously you are sure that none of it could be coming from you; mister perfect ranger. All of your relationships have turned out just great out here, haven't they? You should be writing a fucking advice column for the hearts of Halfway, right?" She slices repeatedly with her sophomoric sarcasms, to no avail.

"Okay, I won't talk with you about it if you think everything is okay," I say as I stop and look at her resigned. "I don't enjoy this conflict oriented, confrontational sophomoric communication style."

"Oh, screw you mister high and mighty," Renn says as she pedals off on her bike and won't even look at me. "You're softmoronic!" I think to myself for a second, 'Fuckin psycho.' I stand there looking at her ride away. 'How could I have handled that better?' Suddenly, my phone rings. I pick it up and try to listen, but I can't hear anything, so I move my head and body around for a second, until I get a signal.

"Hey, it's Doctor Chance. Happy New Year. You remember our first New Year's out there together?"

"Yeah," I yell. "Where are you?"

"I'm working down at an Indian reservation in Arizona. You should come down some time for a round of golf," Dr. Chance yells back.

"Ha." I laugh because there is no way I would ever step foot on a friggin golf course unless I am mounting bird boxes or doing something else ecologically beneficial.

Dr. Chance continues, "I just had phone sex with my wife, since she's up in Oregon."

Thank you. Too much information! "Greeeeaaatttt," I say in a funny voice.

296

"Hey, before I forget, I think I left a credit card in the back of the ambulance," Dr. Chance says.

"The ambulance in parked right outside the All Hands Club right now," I reply.

Per his instructions, I hang up, bike over to the club, and I go into the back of the ambulance to get the credit card for him. I find the Coast Guard First Mate laying on the gurney in a seductive pose. She starts to unbutton her uniform shirt, leading her plump fingers down the front of her chunky body.

"Ooops. Sorry, just getting a credit card," I say quickly.

"This one?" she holds the credit card up in the air.

"Oh ya. That's it." As I reach for it she sticks it in her ample cleavage, grabs me and pulls me on top of her. She starts kissing me on the mouth.

What the fuck is going on here?

Dr. Chance was a funny guy and up to a lot of tricks, and he seemed to be a lot smarter than the new doctor, but, regarding this Coastie girl thing, I don't really see either of the doctors setting me up this way. I look out the windows of the ambulance, then look around for cameras or anything weird inside the vehicle.

She says, "What's the matter? What am I doing wrong?" as she peels-down her pants to reveal big, whitish, full-sized granny bottoms.

I think this is a trap, but for some reason, I go for it. After everything that I've been through and all the lessons I've learned, I still go for it, and I sense nothing.

It's not really good at all.

After I start pulling my shorts back up, she says, "Mmmm, that felt good," sounding like the ending to **Burning Circle**'s *Hate Race*.

I feel like I want to ask her what she is doing here, and how did she know I was coming, and all that stuff, but instead, again with all the shit that has gone down on Halfway so far, I just look at her for a second. Just then, Dr. Oso arrives and hops in the front seat of the ambulance. We both start to slide out toward the back doors of the ambulance, when Dr. Oso turns in surprise at the sound of jostling, and then says, "Hey, what, oh hey, what are you two up to?" he laughs.

I say, "See you later," then dart into the club. Dr. Oso keeps laughing as the Coastguard officer straightens herself in the shadow of the ambulance before he starts the engine and pulls off. He chuckles one more time. Most of my friends aren't in the club, so I consider biking home. Instead though, uncharacteristically, I hesitate. I'm not having an anxiety attack or anything that mental. I just feel paralyzed at the moment, like a Bonin Petrel chick in the grasps of a seven-point-two inch centipede. What happened? I gaze off at the skinny, dark men writhing to the drums and flute. It amazes me that humanity, no matter where you go and what culture you look at, they all want to express themselves in ways that could be perceived as potentially embarrassing to other cultures. Dancing around, putting on shows, playing music; there are always these nerdy, geeky cultural things we simply accept as normal. I thought some of these things were so cool and so great at times in my life. I look at some of these things now and I think about how silly it is to be dancing around in choreographed circles and crazy costumes. At the same time, that's what many would argue the spice of life is all about. Halfway, a microcosm for any conceivable universe, has Amb climbing up on stage to play the saw, wearing a Rasta dread wig and weird incognito glasses. The Filipino guys get up and play keyboard clumsily as they belt through a drawn-out version of *Whiter Shade of Pale*, singing with as much passion as possible. Now the Sri Lankans are up there, with a flute and a couple of drums, and they are kinda like 'Hey, we got a couple a drums and a flute. This is what we do.' It's a funny, trippy beat; almost like a choppy 6/8. When I jump in there, I show avant-garde performance art. We are all doing this stuff. Why? What makes US as humans do it? Why not avoid learning to play the guitar instead of spending hours, days, weeks of your life, studying? Why not do nothing? Is it because we would be bored otherwise, or that we fear we could not attract a significant mate? I don't know what would motivate somebody to jump on stage and play a drum for people, or a flute, or spin around and dance like a maniac. It is a need to express. It is not a want or desire, but a basic, actual need. I think each culture must have a deep need to express, not necessarily in competition, because I never believe art is a competition, but in a sense that each culture must somehow represent how they feel or believe, or view. Look at the machismo pride thing that goes into international beauty pageants, where one country really wants to show the rest of the world that they can produce the most beautiful female *Homo sapiens*. The most beautiful girl in the entire World, as compared to any other girl, of any other ego-centric culture, competing.

I can hear the bragging rights ringing in my ears, 'We have the most beautiful women.' 'No, our country has the most beautiful women, hands down.' 'No, I beg to differ. Our women are certainly the most beautiful.'

GOD! Gag me with a spoon, now! The funniest thing about this is when I was in Japan. On all these commercials, they always highlight Japanese beauty and Asian beauty, depicting the Asian woman as winning the contest, and showing all the Russian and Australian blonds as not only ugly, but sore losers to boot. They usually use just okay looking non-Asian models against the most beautiful Japanese model they can find. I also learned that Japanese people think that Japanese women are way better looking than Chinese women, which I also found hysterical, since most Americans I know have never traveled abroad and absolutely cannot tell the difference. I remember telling that fact to a number of Japanese people, and it really pissed them off. It's like telling them they came from the Mongol Steppes or the Korean Peninsula. Every culture has their biases and prejudices. 'No no, we are Japanese!' is always the vehement response.

I snap out of my post-coital narcosis to see that one by one the crowd drops like flies. I bike back to my room, still feeling a bit like a zombie. I want to call Dr. Chance back, but I can't legally do that with my Gov. cell phone. I have to e-mail him the credit card info, then cut up the card for him, so unless I mention the ambulance sex via e-mail, which I certainly don't want to do with Gov. email, I will never know how that whole thing got set up, or whatever the hell else happened. I should just shut the hell up and be happy that I had a fun time with a nice girl in the back of an ambulance on one of the most remote places on Earth.

The next day, New Year's Day, the divers are pissed because it is too rough to dive outside the reef. I tell Bent that I will take them diving under the cargo pier. He doesn't really approve and there isn't any money in it for him, but he can't really tell us not to and he can't take them outside the reef, so he just tells me to go ahead. Since a few of the guests are Japanese, Hiromi is scheduled to help with the dive. She shows up on time, but looks hung-over and a few years older. I say good morning and she quickly looks away and starts talking to the Japanese divers as if she didn't hear me. Good. That's fine with me. She knows it's over. She can act like a child all she wants. Each grimace simply proves to me that I've made the right choice.

As we dive under the pier, aggressive Amber Jacks attack us from the shadows, biting our fins and fingertips. At five-feet long and probably over sixty pounds each, it really hurts and some of the divers have broken skin. I suggest that we all stay under the pier, closely together, and to head for shore and out of their territory, but Hiromi grabs her Japanese divers, and instructs them to head out from under the pier and right out into the open water and sandy bottom, toward the fuel pier. Immediately, as soon as they enter the open, we see three different, large Amber Jacks and one large Alua, ram into the divers repeatedly and quickly. They're not biting. This is not about food. They are ramming! This is about turf!

Just beyond my visibility, I can also see a large shark coming in to check out the action. Shit, it's a tiger, and a good twelve-footer at least. I signal the other divers to stay under the pier and to head for shore fast, then, I dart over to the Japanese. I position myself between the group and the Tiger Shark, and head toward the shark slowly with my arms and my fins sticking out wide to the sides; kind of like a Spadefoot Toad splattered on a highway. The shark looks at me, then flinches, then turns and swims out of sight. I turn to see that Hiromi has the divers at the worst possible place now; the surface! Even worse, I can't signal them unless I too turn my back on the tiger and head up to the vulnerable surface. I look up and can see some puke on the surface. I look back and around in a three-sixty-eight, then hear a big splash and see two more divers enter the water from the end of the cargo pier. Though a good 62-feet from them, I hand signal them about the big shark and tell them to get out, but they want to know where it is. It's Bent and one of the visiting photographers from the BBC. They want to try to get some shots of the tiger. Good friggin luck. I use more hand signals and send them off in the right direction. A school of Sergeant Majors, along with some Yellow Tangs, quickly rush to the surface and around the divers to devour the vomit, as Hiromi and her group appear to be swimming toward the beach. Usually, we don't have much surf in this part of the atoll, but with the wind whipping, the exit is kind of rough for these now tenderized tourists.

Everyone sits or kneels on the cement of the fractured seaplane ramp and on the rocks, out of breath, with water dripping from our noses. An octopus clings to the rusted, corrugated steel along the seawall, and with a combination of color and texture, mimics the rust to perfection. I try to point it out to everybody, but nobody cares. They are too busy licking their wounds.

"Why? Why you not help? We need help. You not help me," Hiromi says with those hate-filled Godzilla-eyes again.

"Hey, what? Are you completely out of your mind? You should have stayed with me. I was trying to get you out of there," I say, exasperated.

"Why you bring us in deer?" she interrogates.

"Well, I didn't know the jacks would be flippin out and that there would be a tiger down there. What do you want from me, a crystal ball?" I shout.

"Shark? Shark?" they all mumble.

"I not see shark," she says.

I think for a second. Better to keep my freakin mouth shut if they didn't see the tiger.

"You see shark? I not see shark. You riar about shark too? Dog face!" Hiromi pesters.

I look out over the water to find the bubbles of the divers. I hope they know what they are doing. The trick with tigers; you gotta get close enough to see them, then you have to gently back away so they will come toward you and you can get a shot. It's a delicate game. If you come at them too fast, they will bail on you, and if you swim away from them too fast, they think you are prey and take a quick taste. These mothers can bite right through adult sea turtles; carapace to plastron!

As we pack the gear onto the cart, Amb comes riding up on his unicycle.

I say jovially, "Hey, good to see you back on that thing. I thought you gave that up."

"I did, because believe it or not, HIC wouldn't respect me cause I rode it. Then I realized, they are not going to respect me either way, so screw them," Amb says with a rare snicker.

I couldn't agree more. HIC is generally that shallow; and fuck people like that. Ernesto Dewhurt isn't. He seems to be one of the only HIC guys who isn't a major dick. That's why Drats never talks about him in this novel.

Amb continues, "A second SS Halfway trip went over the seamount again last night."

"What?" I say in complete shock. "No one told me about that."

"Yeah, that's what I thought. Nobody knew about it, but Dutrouex says you authorized it," Amb quizzes.

"What?" I laugh in disbelief, "No way. I don't have authority to authorize anything." I clarify my understanding of my position to him. He can't trust Chipweldi or Misa Queen, but he should still trust Banette, Karolyn, Ben, Han, and I.

"Yeah, well, if I find out differently, there's gonna be hell to pay," he says as he prepares to ride off, threatening me again.

"Wait a second. I take exception to that comment. I wouldn't do that and you should know me much better than that by now for sure."

"I don't know who to believe anymore around here. I thought Ben was your ally, but he says you can't be trusted anymore," Amb reports.

I carp, "What?" Why? Ben likes me and knows I'm a hard worker.

"Seems Myhel might have got to him. Do you know his relationship with her?" Amb seems to be digging.

"I think he's smitten and always wanted something he could never get," I answer frankly, because, disgusting as her and Kilgro are, it must still be obvious to Amb by now that Myhel sees herself as way out of Ben's league.

"That's exactly what I thought. I want you and Twistor down at that boat when it comes in, and we are going to go over that catch together," Amb orders.

"But, Amb, no offense, but shouldn't Chipweldi be doing this? It's his job. I have to meet the Coast Guard vessel for the debrief and practice with my ultimate guys after dinner. Chipweldi is the law enforcement guy. I'm just interp," I say without the slightest bit of whine.

"Chipweldi is gone! The only thing I can assume is that he went on the SS Halfway," Amb says sternly.

"Let's just call the harbor master and I'll check the manifest for you," I say efficiently, reaching for my phone.

"They didn't leave a manifest," Amb says with building anger.

"Shit!" spills from my lips, as my eyes widen.

This time Chipweldi went on the S.S. Halfway, and didn't bother to tell anyone. I'm not surprised that he didn't contact me. It's gotten to the point where I can go for days on Sand Island and don't even know if he's on or off atoll.

As the sun begins to set, Twistor and I ride our bikes down to the fishing dock, after squeezing in a little bit of ultimate Frisbee. We can see the SS Halfway limping its way in, and there appears to be some black smoke coming off the deck. As they pull in and start throwing lines to the awaiting FNs, I can see Chipweldi and the crew's stark faces. A golf cart, and a number of cargo items on deck, are blackened and melted.

"Don't even ask," Chipweldi barks from the deck, without one of his typically associated chuckles.

"I was sent down here explicitly to ask," I retort. Wow. I have really changed. I have lost me coolness, my sense of humor, and my happy spirit. I just can't tolerate moronic shit anymore. "Where is the catch?" I continue.

"Back off," Deny yells from the bridge. "You don't ask the questions around here."

"Yes he does!" Amb yells from the road as he steps out of Chipweldi's pick-up truck. "I manage this atoll and I told him to come down here. If I weren't here, he would be in charge. Is that clear?"

Deny looks down at Amb in anger. Chipweldi vanishes down below. The FNs continue with their work as usual, silent, but knowing the shit is hitting the fan.

Long story short? We discover in the next few hours that:

Number One: Deny and the HIC staff wanted to take a second shot at the seamount but knew Amb would deny them, so they conned Chipweldi into going, knowing that would also piss-off Amb.

Secondly, out over the seamount, or somewhere near there, a drunken fight broke out between the HIC staff, who were drunk, and Chipweldi, who was being his normally abnormal, annoying self. They actually tried to throw him overboard, and in the mêlée, a fire started and almost sank the ship.

Third: They determined it would be better to remove all evidence of the fire when they returned to safe harbor and try to pretend nothing ever happened. Unfortunately for them, we were all here at the pier to meet them.

Lastly, because of the fire and other stupid mishaps, they didn't even have any fish onboard! They wasted all that diesel to go all the way out over the seamount and back, without a fish to show for it.

I look over at Twistor and mumble, "What a waste."

The crippled S.S. Halfway, still smoking, leaks at the inner dock.

Twistor responds, upset as well, but a lot more controlled than my rage, "That really pisses me off."

I say back, "That pisses me off as much as those stupid boats that go up and down the Colorado River, back and forth past Needles, day after day, doing nothing, just driving up and down the river, wasting gas."

Twistor makes a rare judgmental and negative statement, saying, "Stupid." He is 295% right, but he still sounds more like Renn then himself. I don't like that.

I say, "Not fun. Stupid."

By 9:30pm, Chipweldi, Twistor, and the rest of us are getting on our bikes and heading our separate ways.

"Wow, I can't believe that," Twistor says with astonishment.

"Believe which part?" I ask.

"Ya know, the whole thing," he answers, as he shakes his head and we swerve to crush some mice under our tires.

"Only on Halfway," I chime.

Twistor thinks for a second, "What's going to happen?"

"What?" I ask, because I simply can't hear a word he says.

He repeats a decibel or so louder.

"Chipweldi will get written-up. It's probably a perverse badge of honor to him in his munchkin mind; and stripped, basically, of all his power; except the fact that he is the law enforcement officer, and the only one with a gun on the atoll."

Twistor looks at me for a second, realizing the situation, "So, in a sense, Amb is forced to keep him, for now."

I report, "I am going on another training, this time, in the new facility in West Virginia. Who knows what to expect when I get back here. Just take care of everything dude, you know." I want to warn Twistor, but at the same time I feel I have no right to give unsolicited advice, and I want to be friends with him, not like a father figure.

With that, the time comes, and I zip off to the East Coast for the first time in years. I have a lay-over on Hawaii for one night. I visit Danica in Hilo. She wants to make love to me, but in other respects, she seems very different from when she was on Halfway. A little detached, and I think she has another guy on her mind and thinks of me as more of just a booty call. I pass out on her bed, then wake up soaked from the humidity. She is no longer in the room, and I look up to see *Leaving Las Vegas* on the tv, and it just happens to be the horrible scene were Elizabeth Shue gets harshly raped in a hotel room or something. Yuck! Out of context, that scene turns the whole vibe kind of blah for me. I get up and go into the living room, where Danica studies from one of her books. We both say goodbye pleasantly to each other, and agree that it's probably best for the both of us to just move on with our lives. Yummy sex just isn't enough. There really are no hard feelings. Danica is a great girl. She's just not the one.

On the next day, the whole, long flight, my brain rattles like it always does. How easy would it be for me to just quit my job and stay on The East Coast? When things go bad, I either kick ass or run away. I have been sticking it out on Halfway, pun intended, but maybe I've worn out my welcome. Maybe I should quit and bail. I think about bosses. I think about girls. I think about coworkers, I think about Ultimate, I think about my family. Notice, I am trapped in that homocentric mind trip again! It's all about me. It's all about US. It has nothing to do with them, the other 2 million species on The Planet, but I can't stop thinking about all this crazy shit rattling in my head.

When I arrive at the training center, wow, what a nice facility. I would like to work at NCTC some day. Beautiful spot. Green, lush, humid, hot, full of wildlife, ya know, lots of American Robins and Eastern Cottontail Rabbits cruising all over the place, with a Blue Jay and a Northern Cardinal thrown in here or there with an Eastern Gray Squirrel darting up a Pin Oak.

We did not fall in love at first sight. I thought she appeared stuck-up in the first few classes. I learned a lot in that class, and I also learned that she would be the soul mate I had looked for all these years! With German, Brazilian, French, Italian, Thai, Japanese, and to a much lesser extent, American girls, I had not found my muse. Obviously, place of origin doesn't really appear to be an issue for me. This sweetest of girls, this Salvadoran flower, proved to be the most soothing girl in the World.

On the first day of class, I get placed next to a cute Taiwanese woman who looks kind of like Banette, but with a much more feminine figure. We become class partners, so she takes my focus. I don't notice Chelonia all week, until, as over-achievers, the teacher instructs us to sit across from each other for an exercise review on the last day. Since she and I had finished our assignments early, and no one else did, we get paired up.

Chelonia looks like one of those stuck-up foofy girls I want nothing to do with, but she throws me off with a disarming little, soft gentle smile. Wow! Mmm, mmmm, mmmmmm. Did you see how many 'm's that was? After the final exam, I approach the instructor to hand in my paper. She wants to make small-talk chit-chat with me, but I scan the room and see Chelonia finished before me and is already gone! I literally chase out after her. I run down one hall, then up a flight of stairs. I could be going in the wrong direction. Suddenly, there, 63 meters ahead, I can see her digging her keys out of her pocketbook as she walks through the parking lot.

I sprint over to her as quietly as I can. "Hi. Wow, you finished early," I commend, out of breath.

"Yeah. No point in hanging around," she answers shyly.

"I, I wanted to ask you, are you from the Near East or Central Europe or something?" I say to break the ice.

"Nooo," she says with pleasure, "Guess where," she gently commands.

I think for a second. I have no idea. Her long, straight, platinum blond hair, her fair soft skin with a hint of olive; I keep leaning towards Czechoslovakia. I stammer, perplexed. I told you I'm not much of a conventional beauty guy, but she is showing some tastefully done, professional looking "curvature"! Oh my god, she is so fine on every level. Zart would cream his pants over her. Oh, the irony of life: That I would actually get what Zart only dreams of, and yet, I could care less about those shallower physical endowments.

"I'm from El Salvador," she admits.

I try not to look surprised, but of course I do, and then I ask, without intrusion, "When are you leaving and where are you going?"

She replies, "I'm leaving on Monday, so I could have a weekend in the area, then I'm going back to San Francisco."

"Oh my god." I say, "I am staying until then too, cause I am going to go hiking in the Mahongaliodhella National Forest."

She laughs at my struggle and mispronunciation.

We speak for a while. It all becomes so clear to me now that I am off atoll. Then I ask if she wouldn't mind getting dinner with me tonight.

"That would be okay," she says with a soft smile.

I take her to dinner Friday night. At a Mexican restaurant, we enjoy a relaxing, delicious, mainland meal.

She says, eventually, after quite a bit of dodging, that she has never had a real boyfriend in her entire life, mainly due to her suffocating Dad. Humor is the way to the soul, so I lightly quip, "Is a good man hard to find, or is a hard man good to find?" I think I stole that from Mae West, but either way I am screwed, figuratively but not literally, because first off, she doesn't get it, and secondly, with her strict Salvadoran Catholic up-bringing, that kind of humor just doesn't fly. Her overprotective and watchful Dad made sure that no harm would come to her until she was well into adulthood. A gorgeous girl like that must be a nightmare for a dad to cope with when he knows that every guy in the hood wants to tag her. Good job dads! Keep them as virgins until they get to college!

She has plans for the weekend, and so do I, since I did plan to go solo hiking and camping, so instead of spending the whole weekend together, she agrees to meet again on Monday. She drives

307

me to the airport, since I turned in my rental-dental. I'm so excited that *I am even thinking* in run-on sentences.

It's quiet for a moment, because Chelonia doesn't talk much. She sees no reason to. She is the antithesis of my habitual rambling. I start to sing. She tolerates it, but I can't tell if she likes it. We listen to a report on NPR, and then I go out on a limb, "The problem is not propaganda, but the relentless control of the kind of things we think about. I don't know if that is an exact quote, or if I made it up, but either way, it's true. Sounds kind of like Marshall McLuhan or Malcolm McLaren to me." I laugh.

I think in the silence for a moment. As Drats writes this novel, he thinks about truth statements. Has everything he said in this novel been totally true? Well, first of all, this is a fictional work. There is no Halfway Atoll Wildlife Sanctuary. As a matter of fact, there is no Animal Protection Service either, nor is there even a Kestrel Falco. Names, faces, places, and occurrences have been modified, mangled, exaggerated, fabricated, and even squished into composite characters. This must be confusing for the reader. You know real monk seals still exist and that we have but only 1200 left in the Pacific. Love is real. The Earth is real. Our Planet is real. The World is real. Though the names and faces and times and places have been shifted around, this novel is truer than anything else I know in my life. The ideas and ideals are true. The minutia and details are for those who can't see the big, overall picture.

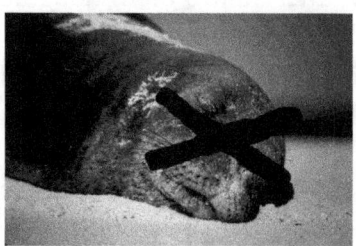

One of the few Hawaiian Monk Seals left alive at the turn of the millennium.

Look at how Chelonia has been programmed to think, for example. We all know that it's tough to fight with a normal girl, cause men tend to be rational and women irrational, right? So just to see if her and I even live in the same ballpark's zip-code, I ask her, "What do you want. . . if you could have anything?"

I know that is the stupidest question of all time. Women never know what they want. If I could have only had any girl in my life ever really tell me what she wants, it would have made my life so much easier. Myhel said she didn't want commitment. Hamed said she wanted me, then she didn't want me; maybe cause I cried over Zart. Hiromi said she didn't want me to help her get home when she was drunk and about to get raped by half-a-dozen fishing crew dudes. So what do girls want? What do they want? God Chelonia, just tell me what will make you happy and I will give it to you with all of my heart because I'm so smitten with love. It feels like a spell. This girl is precious man, a fucking California Condor, a Hawksbill Turtle man, and, she is nice. I am actually here talking with her and she is a real, nice person.

She hesitates as she thinks over my question. I don't like waiting, but I like the fact that she thinks before she blathers. I am floored. I thought I was falling in love with Hiromi not too long ago, even with all her problems; but now I realize, I feel guilted by Misa Queen and the rest of that shit out there, which forces me into a situation that is very very wrong for me. Chelonia is like a lightening bolt from the sky. Zing! This is the girl I have to be with!

"What do you want?" I say again, calmly, like a self-help guru. Chelonia thinks for a moment again, staring forward. She won't be rushed. Then, she says, "I would like to have a hetero male friend, who IS NOT interested in having sex with me in anyway or form" (including beating-off over her when he gets home, I imagine), "but IS interested in going shopping with me and helping me pick stuff out, and telling me how my clothes looks, and stuff like that."

I bust into a laugh, "Platonic! You're thinking like, that first of all, this type of person would exist and there would be a reason or a motivation for them to actually want to do this with you."

Chelonia looks at me in anger, "I'm frustrated cause my fantasy won't be complete until I can find someone like that, and I can't."

"No, the problem is that in your mind you are going to find somebody like that," I state directly. "How long have you been saying that?"

"I don't know, like at least seven or ten years, but I haven't been looking very much yet," Chelonia says sweetly and naively, like tomorrow she will start looking in earnest for the straight male shopper.

I laugh again, "How? Where? What? There's no such thing as curiosity and every thing and one has a motivation for their actions. So you gotta think about it. I am a hetero man." I persist, but gently, "Think about it my dear. Why? Why on Earth would I go shopping with a woman that I am not making love with nor have any chance to?" My over zealous affection begins to spill out. Chelonia puzzles for a second, "Friendship?" she answers.

"Sure, friendship, that's a great answer," I reply sincerely. "I play Frisbee with girls who are friends. I like to dance and will happily dance with a girl, even if it's just for the fun of dancing. But certain other things, I don't want to do with my friends. For example: I don't want to shoot heroin; I don't want to go hunting and kill animals; and I don't want to go shopping at a freakin mall. These are all things I don't want to do, even with a close best friend or a passionate lover. The only time I would go to a mall would be if I was forced to somehow. If I felt the relationship hinged on it, then I doubt I would be able to really fall in love with that type of personality anyway." I realize I'm supposed to be letting her talk, and learning about her.

"Okay, well I won't take you shopping with me," Chelonia says with resignation.

"Look, I'm not trying to bum you out. I just think you are being unrealistic." I try, "Honey, why would the hetero guy go shopping with you if there were no motivations? Ya know, financial, some other reason."

Chelonia says, "Just cause he likes shopping."

I guess there is no real way to explain some things like this; guys are hunters, women are gatherers. We developed this way evolutionarily for millions of years and can't be DEVO de-evolved in a mere few generations. I look at Chelonia and I can see her flaws. That's good. I know she is flawed, and so am I. I still feel like I am falling in love with her so much. So she wants me to go shopping with her. What is a guy to do, find a girl who doesn't like shopping and hasn't been programmed to find the killer deal? That's just as hard as finding a straight dude who likes shopping.

"You have to answer the most important question honey. Why? Why would a guy go shopping with you? To meet other chicks? Cause he has a clothing fetish? You better think about what kind of guy you are going to be shopping with," I say, without sounding too over-the-top ominous or threatening.

Chelonia thinks to herself, then she says, "Maybe a guy would go shopping with me just to make me happy; like you said, out of pure altruism. Maybe if he just really really loved me."

"Maybe," I respond. "I am a strong believer that if we were all altruists, the World could survive. I also agree that a devote guy who really loves you might go along for the shopping trip, but he is still gonna hate it no matter how much he loves you."

Chelonia counters, "Look at all the selfish people out there who are programmed into thinking that not only do they have to have a baby, but they can't even adopt the needy around the world, but have to have *their own* baby. How is altruism going to slow the overpopulation growth problem and baby ego?"

I say with gusto, "Exactly! Instead of egoism like Ayn Rand, I understand and appreciate that everyone needs to have a strong, confident, justifiable ego about themselves, and super-ego."

"I agree," Chelonia peppers-in.

"But," the caveat appears, "but not taken to the extent that negative egos go to."

"I agree," Chelonia peppers-in again.

I continue, "People who steal and trick, and put other people down to build themselves up. . ."

Chelonia cuts in again, ". . . Like a destructive ego."

I think, then say, "So there has to be a constructive ego that we call Altruistic Egoism. That's what it is."

Chelonia says, ". . . but, that's a contradiction. Ayn Rand said there is no altruism."

"That's wrong," I state firmly. "Altruism is me pulling invasive alien plants, for no pay, . . ."

Chelonia cuts in again, "I didn't say that. Think about yourself and then think about others. That is Ego Altruism. I need to find a word that works because I find 'altruism' to be too strong of a word or that it goes too far. I'm not saying not to think about other people. I'm just saying you have to put yourself first."

I counter, "First, I think you are going to have a lot of mothers and fathers, including your own, arguing against that statement. Secondly, I know you are not saying it is totally impossible to be an altruist, so let's avoid semantics. Okay? I'm pulling invasive plants out. Okay? I'm not getting paid to do it. Nobody is watching me. Nobody knows how hard I've worked or how many plants I've pulled out. Okay? I'm just pulling out these plants because I know in my mind, from my studies, that by pulling out these plants, it's gonna help native plants come in, help native fauna, native animals survive, . . . "

And before I can finish my point, she states firmly, "I understand that."

I stop for a minute. It is getting pretty heated.

"Chelonia", I say with a soft voice, "I'm glad we got back together here for a second time, and I'm so glad we are having this conversation, but, this is a real sticking point and I'm wondering if philosophically we are gonna be able to last, for, for a long time."

Chelonia says, "I already get your point. You really see yourself as a true selfless person, and I feel a little guilty about that because I think I should look out for number one, and, I want a guy who does the same so we will have money when we get older. I want to invest in a nice home."

I say, "Why would I want to do that? I never imagine myself as a homeowner. It's better to just rent and avoid having that cumbersome albatross around my neck."

Chelonia reveals, "I want my Mother to be taken care of when she is older. She has worked so hard on her hands and knees to raise me."

I ask, "What about your Dad?"

She says flatly, "He will be fine. He needs to take care of himself."

"Well" I admit, "I have toyed with the idea of taking a vow of poverty."

"What?" Chelonia says sternly.

"Yeh, I mean, money is fucking everything up," I say honestly.

"It's not the money that is bad, but the people and what they do with it and for it." Chelonia argues.

"Oh, come on," I say with alert, "That's the same stupid argument the NRA makes. 'Guns don't kill people. People kill people'," I snicker.

"Yeh, people kill people . . . with guns, HELLO!" Chelonia laughs back.

This interchange gives me real hope for the relationship. Maybe I should back off. There is give and take in a good relationship, and I can't always be right about everything, nor would I want to be in that situation with a girl. She argues with me passionately, but not stupidly or angrily. So, it's good. She seems to be equaling my rationality. It's a trap to ask people what they want, right? Americans never know what they want and feel entitled to get whatever they want, and though Salvadorena, she says that she sees herself as a San Franciscan American.

So Chelonia says, "I still think you are being selfish about pulling plants. You know you are helping the planet and the creatures on it, and you like them, so you are helping something you like, which is selfish, though not directly."

"But helping wildlife and plants helps everything. It helps stop pollution and wars and everything, not just me," I reiterate.

Then Chelonia thinks back to motivations. "What is your motivation then? Why do you pull invasive alien plants, while someone like Cherry Ballpig or Rattas Dewhurt never would?" Chelonia says, reflecting on my previous comments about the dynamics on Halfway Atoll and the kooky characters out there. "Whereas another person would not do that?" I think for a moment, "The reason I would do that is very simple: It's going to help the World. By definition, altruism is not selfish, and I receive no direct benefits from pulling the plants instead of weight-lifting or something. By your definition; every single thing on Earth is selfish if you put it that way."

"That's wrong. It can't be," Chelonia answers, thinking about her Mom again.

I ask with conviction, "Because I'm trying to help the other 2-million species on the Planet, . . . I'm selfish?"

Chelonia says, "Well you are not doing it to help humans, or just to help humans."

I respond, "No, I mean, I am doing it to help humans too, but humans, and myself, last, not first. Right? Or, humans equally with all creatures. How's that?"

Chelonia says, "Although ultimately, it will help humans, but you are not doing it only for humans. I see."

"Right," I say, "I'm doing it to help the other 2 million species on the Planet, including humans, and not to help me exclusively. So using transitive property, like a million steps away, it finally comes back to benefit me and is selfish. Is that what you are arguing? I'm selfish at the very very end, and I just took the long way around to being selfish?"

Chelonia laughs, "Okay, whether it's direct or indirect, which in this case is obviously very indirect, it still comes down to you helping the Planet and you being part of this World so you are still being selfish. You are doing something to help the species; to help the other 2 million species on the Planet, but then, eventually, that's going to help you live a better life."

"My motivation is not to help me. We have to look at intent. My intent is not to help me," I say.

"Right." Chelonia agrees, "You are not pulling up plants for me, like ME ME ME. That's why I said it was the lesser evil."

"What?" I state with surprise. "What does that mean, the lesser evil?"

Chelonia rebuts, "NO. I don't see it as a negative thing. It's not a negative thing."

"I don't understand," I have to admit, I am getting a little lost here. Chelonia says, "What don't you understand?"

"I don't understand what you are saying. Say it clearer," I prod gently.

"Ahhh," Chelonia stalls, "Being selfish is okay, to an extent. It depends on what level of shelfishness . . . "

I cut in, "Oh, like greed is good, greed is good, that kind of shit?"

"No. That's over the top," Chelonia corrects.

I understand, "I think you need a different word for 'selfishness'."

Chelonia says, "If people can help themselves, then they can put themselves in a position to be more altruistic to others. You are more likely to help other people if you have the means to. Okay? That's what I'm getting at."

I think for a moment. I can see what she is saying monetarily, in a kind of Donald Trump sort-of-way. Anyone with billions could become very philanthropic if they wanted too, but many of them don't, and many of them hurt a lot of people, and habitat, on the way to their millions. "I understand," I say, without elucidating my thoughts.

Chelonia smiles, "So selfishness and greed are two different things to me."

"Oh, I get it." I say, "We have greed, selfishness, and altruism, all of differing degrees."

Then Chelonia continues, "Yes. I don't hate the word altruism."

I respond, "Okay, I'm selfish because I want the Planet to be good. I want the Planet to be well, so I'm selfish."

"Yes," Chelonia says. "It's our Planet."

"It is a selfish act," I say with insistence.

Chelonia says, "Yes, less selfish, but still selfish."

"That is horrible," I say with regret.

"Why?" Chelonia puzzles, "Selfish doesn't mean negative or have a negative feeling associated with it."

"What?" I say in shock, "Yes it does. It's pejorative. It's like saying rape can be good. 'Did she have a good rape or a bad rape?' NO. Rape, by definition, is always bad, just like selfishness."

Chelonia argues, using one of my lines, "Who told you that?"

"It's derogatory," I say. " 'You are selfish!' 'Stop being so selfish!' " I say with the voice of an angry nun.

"I think about myself, okay? That's what I'm talking about," Chelonia admits.

"No, that's self, self aware, or taking self interest," I try.

Chelonia thinks again, then says, "Take care of number one."

"Self interested! That's what you want. Mean it in the most non-selfish way, and that's what you were looking for," I say with relief, buckling my pants and straightening my laces.

"Yes!" Chelonia agrees.

"So by your new definition, I am self interested and do it for self interest, but I'm not selfish about it," I say.

"Okay," Chelonia says, "but everything we do affects us. Subconsciously, you know you are helping yourself."

"No, like I said, it's not about logical outcomes; it is about intent. My intent is not to help myself. I'm not pulling because I think it is going to help me. As a matter of fact, I know I could be spending my time doing something totally selfish at that moment if I want; okay? Even if it's subconscious, I know it is not going to help me directly and I know I could be doing tv commercials or be a friggin lawyer and making way more money for me, and using my time in a much more "profitable" way (I use air quotes). It is for the

315

Planet, and it is not selfish, it's not self-interest. It is Planet interest. Earth interest. It's a recognition that we humans have done a lot of shit to this planet already. I don't have a big Catholic guilt thing about it because I know what has happened and that I am not responsible for it."

Chelonia agrees, "Right; you don't have that much to do with it really."

I say, "And now that I'm an adult and intelligent enough to know what's goin on, I'm gonna live my life in a way which is gonna have a really low impact, as much as I can, to help the Planet."

"Does that make you happy?" Chelonia asks.

"It's not about happiness. By your definition, the only unselfish way I could help The Planet is to kill myself. It's not about selfishness. It's not about helping me. Why does that disturb you so much?" I say with frustration as I feel the muscles under my scalp tense my veins.

Chelonia thinks for a second, as she pulls the car to a stop. "What is it then?"

I take a deep breath and a sigh, "All I know is it's about helping the other species on the Planet, so that there are people fighting for them instead of people fighting against them. Against nature."

Chelonia, still looking for an angle, asks, "Does that satisfy you? Is that satisfying for you?"

Okay, stay calm. She is testing me as much as I am testing her. "It's not about satisfying me, but if I could make a huge impact I'm sure that would be satisfying to know; but that is not my intention or motivation, because that could lead towards a huge let down, if I never reach a high level of satisfaction. If I could figure out a way to help limit human population growth to the point that we would eventually get back down to 2 or 3 billion people, that would be satisfying. Ya know, then I would say that would be extremely satisfying, but you are mixing apples and oranges here."

"Ha huh ha," Chelonia laughs as she hits the gas again. Funny, when she laughs, she sounds just like Milhouse Van Houton when he cries. It is very cute, and not an annoying, obnoxious, repressed Myhel or Misa Queen cackle. "That's a funny expression. In El Salvador, we say 'you can't mix oil and water' instead."

I respond, "Really. Ya, we got that one too. It's like comparing a great museum, like the Boston Museum of Science, with a sick institution, like the San Francisco Zoo. They are light-years apart. One should be a national treasure and the other should be shutdown."

"Okay," Chelonia says, as we pull into the terminal and I get ready to go.

Whew! I suddenly realize I just had the deepest, longest, hardest, conversation I've had with a potential girlfriend in ages. This event was deeper than Myhel, Hamed, and Hiromi combined, in one quality talk!

I say, "Come over here and give me a big kiss."

"No," she says vehemently.

I think she is only being playful, but she really doesn't want to give me a kiss. She is really virginal, and abominates any form for public display of affection, with the exception of some handholding, which I've noticed and relished. Finally, I semi-attack her and finally we share a long, sweet kiss. She looks like a beautiful love goddess. You know that feeling guys? When you look into the eyes of that unbelievable girl right in front of you, right in your arms, and you say, oh my god, she is so strikingly stunning and dazzlingly magnificent! That feeling like I don't want to go away from her, like, like I want to be with her all the time. Not ALL THE TIME time, but you know, all the time. "Get Married" would be the timeworn way of putting it.

After saying goodbye, I shuffle through the line, and at the last minute, I turn back toward the security gate. "I don't have to take this flight. I can miss it and say I was sick. I have like thousands of hours of sick time I never used."

This would be heart-healthy for me to stay a little longer with my precious, sweet, intelligently mellow Chelonia, but no, she will have none of that. We must show strength. She waves me on, like a brush dumping all of my feelings from the dustpan into the trash can. Mahalo! As I sit on the plane on the way back to Halfway, I feel tears rolling down my cheek. Don't get me wrong, I still love Halfway, but I so miss what I could be having on the mainland. It's a sacrifice to be out in the wild, but I know I love it.

Jewel sits down next to me, brushing the hair on my arm like she did on my first flight out to Halfway, so long ago. I look away.

317

Jewel says with a soft voice as she snuggles her head onto my shoulder like a teddy bear, "Eeeeevery flight, I gutt someone'z a cryin."

More tears burst out, but I keep my lip zipped, the whole flight. Back on Halfway, whenever I get a free moment, I decide I must call Chelonia, and I do. I call her, and email her, and email her, and even try live chatting, but that sucks, so we go back to calling and emailing and emailing. Even though Hiromi appears to still want to sleep with me, she has show herself to be quite the disconnected bulimic buzz-killer, and all I can do is think of Chelonia and the next time I will see this goddess. Hiromi doesn't understand what she did wrong, and after Myhel and all that shit, I really don't even want to deal with Hiromi on any level anymore, including explanations.

I start planning and thinking of ways to get Chelonia over here: As a volunteer, as an ASS participant, as an APS staff? Something.

I pace back and forth in my lanai, as I dwell on ideas to get Chelonia out her with me. I imagine animal help. What if I could get her to ride on a migrating whale, or if pterodactyl were still around and could be trained like horses to fly riders all over the place.

It makes me think of my childhood. My "little" brother Manat would look at me in amazement, never picking up a quarter of the dinos I knew. I just really, really loved dinosaurs. I didn't think it was a phase. I thought that's who I was and I would always love dinosaurs; always wanting to know more, always excited about new creatures and interested in being interested. I was so into it that I still don't consider it a phase now. In InsectAffect, when I was around 20, I told Drats about my love of dinosaurs, and my detailed recollection impressed him so much that he wrote a song. I sing it aloud:

My Dinosaurs
by Drats
Knee-high brown grass irritates my Mercurochrome covered scrapes
Grasshoppers pinned against the neighbor's fence as I foil their escapes
My prey ignores the raisins placed as food inside their jars

Even my prized mantis lost its appetite under the monkey bars
With imagined heroism I battle the creatures under my bed
Ma has to tie my shoes or I'll fall on my head
I recognize cheetahs as the fastest carnivores
And all I want to do is play with my dinosaurs, my dinosaurs
The sand box is a desert where camels, nomads and dune buggies
roam
My army men fear it cause it's a war zone
They've taken Speed Racer off I can't watch it anymore
My pinky still throbs from being pinched inside the door
With imagined heroism I battle the creatures under my bed
Ma has to tie my shoes or I'll fall on my head
I recognize cheetahs as the fastest carnivores
And all I want to do is play with my dinosaurs, my dinosaurs
I associate the street with evil, the old steamroller effect
Can't find that Sugar Daddy stuck on back of the couch, due to
neglect
Hot Wheels on the soft racetrack rug reach destructive ends
Brontosaurus, triceratops and the animals are my only friends my
only friends my only friends my only FRIENDS my ONLY
FRIENDS MY ONLY FRIENDS MY ONLY friends MY only friends
With imagined heroism I battle the creatures under my bed
Ma has to tie my shoes or I'll fall on my head
I recognize cheetahs as the fastest carnivores
And all I want to do is play with my dinosaurs, my dinosaurs

It's great to have had Drats as a friend, one of my best friends.
Friends are really really important. My quality of life is definitely
dictated by how many times I laugh my ass off with my friends. I
had a big family, but I still felt lonely and like I didn't really have
friends during a number of periods in my adolescence and adult
life. It makes you feel weird. It makes you feel like an outsider,
like you are on the outside of society, or humanity.
In my living room, with crappy shit blathering on HBO in the
background, as I finish singing My Dinosaurs, Twistor smiles. He
likes it, but is at a loss for words, as usual.
I say, "Can you relate?"
Twistor says, "Definitely."
"What?" I ask.

"Definitely," he repeats, an eighth of a decibel louder.

I think I heard what he said. "Like kids who get into birding, or piano, when they're 4 or 5 years-old, cause their parents were hardcore birders or musicians, and these kids become incredible prodigies cause they're so young and intensely absorbent. I believe that's what happened with Doger. Hanging around with dogs, you "innately learn" what it means when the ears go down; what it means when they show their teeth; what it means when they wag their tail; and the different feeling we get from the animal and its behaviors. Like Lorenz describes in his chapter on dogs, no one had to teach my oldest brother Doger about dog behavior, because he lived it."

As I finish my statement, I turn to see Jewel, Tex, and Pillmold, heading toward Twistor and I. Jewel and Tex look pretty content, but Pillmold has his scowl on again.

I continue my story, as I open the screen door and usher them in, "Now if anyone were to take the next step and say 'Look at the dog, how jealous it is. It must be feeling real consternation at this point and will probably have nightmares about other dogs getting more attention.' Of course that's an easy thing to think, and I would argue maybe a necessary way to think so humans could understand wild and domestic animals and survive."

Pillmold says, "Outh oh; egghead science talk again. You guys are just a bunch of one-trick-ponies aren't yah?"

If you could only see how funny this is coming from one-dimensional Pillmold. We ignore him.

Twistor asks me, "What do you mean, 'necessary for survival?'"

I reply, "That's why I love those sensationalistic show's *like When Stupid People Get Attacked By Animals*. Let's face it folks; WE HAVE THE BIG BRAINS, remember?"

Jewel smiles at me, because her and I have already kind of had this conversation, and she knows where I stand, but Tex and Pillmold exchange perturbed glances, not realizing what perfect Darwin Award candidates they are, . . . as none of them ever do, or they wouldn't be candidates.

"Whad arh ya sayin?" Pillmold pipes back defensively. "Like we gotta get out of the way of dem?"

I respond, "It is always our fault when we get munched or kicked."

Then Tex, Tex of all people, says, "We are supposed to be smart enough to avoid it," directed toward Pillmold.

Then Jewel, as if she has been really listening to my lectures over all her time here on and off Halfway, and in the media, and customer reviews, says, "We are so far removed from our connection to wildlife now, that we think we can walk up to a wild animal . . ."

I'm so happy to continue, ". . . Ya like to pet Bison, or feed wolf, or live with bears, or ride stingrays, or some other stupid shit like that."

Pillmold's eyes widen as he feels out-numbered.

I state, "Now let me add a disclaimer here. Obviously I am not one of those heartless bastards who thinks that animals don't feel or have emotions, or are beneath humans, or something like that; but on the other hand; I don't believe in anthropomorphism either, so were does one fall on that line?" Like Aristotle, I look into their eyes as they stand like statues on my black tile floor. Are they still receptive, connected? Yes. "Ya take somebody like my brother Doger. Some say they know their hunting dog had feelings and deep emotions. Ya know, when I was a kid, my brother Doger, 11-years older than me, had a huge German Shepard named Tiny, and that dog, man, he would say 'Tiny, go lay down under the kitchen table.' Ya know now, that's a pretty complex order, and what was the cue, what was the clue or word that signaled the dog? I don't know, but the dog would go and lay down under the kitchen table. Not anywhere else. And he would say to Sadie his Doberman, 'Sadie, go get in the car,' and she would run and go jump in the car. Now, he started playing with dogs as a kid, and this, I believe, is the key. My family almost never had a pet because our Mom is freaked by cats and anything that has fur. When Doger was a kid, as a matter of fact, when he hung around the neighborhood, instead of hanging around with a bunch of human kids, he hung around with a pack of dogs that roamed around. There weren't leash laws back then and some people let their dogs run around, and these dogs were just roaming the streets, some of them probably not being fed or protected very well, like you see in Thailand or El Salvador today, and he hung with this pack of dogs."

Pillmold looks confused and pissed. Twistor tries to clarify, "And this ties into the kids being sponges, or that you agree with anthropomorphism?"

Tex tries hard to follow along. Jewel seems to just like not being the center of attention for a minute, and looks like her calm, sensual self. I still like her, and still feel a little compelled to give her a nice hug. Of course I can't, so I don't.

Instead, I smile and say to Pillmold, "Now, you know when kids are little they are just sponges."

Tex nods.

I go on, "When I was little, I was really into dinosaurs. I had absorbed everything and all the adults couldn't believe how many dinosaur names I knew and how I could pronounce them correctly."

"Surprised?" Jewel blurts out with a laugh.

Pillmold says, "Peoples feel jealousy. Why wouldn't animals be able tah feel jealousy?"

I state clearly, "Lorenz claims it's response to stimuli. I wouldn't be so impassioned about wildlife, . . . and plants, don't forget plants, they are awesome too, . . . if I didn't feel within my deepest heart of hearts that they are precious creatures with intrinsic value and important to all of the World, because US, the "most powerful" species on Earth, have not only the ability, but the duty, to protect or at least leave these creatures alone to live their lives."

Pillmold retorts, "Nice brainwashin."

I look at this fool with a laugh inside. I'm the brainwashed one?? "I can't talk about this on tour or in any lecture out here without going into the whole 'sentient being' argument, where it gets really messed-up!"

"What's wrong with datt?" Pillmold concerns himself.

Twistor says, "I think what Kestrel is saying, first of all, is to say that an animal could be a sentient being is to first agree that *Homos* are sentient beings. To agree that *Homos* are sentient beings begs the whole philosophical argument of whether or not we have souls, spirits, an afterlife, eternal energy and where it goes, and all this other kinda shtuff. That's where we get into trouble first. That is, any people arguing whether or not animals should have rights and that animals need rights because they are sentient beings, must

322

argue that humans, US, we are all sentient. If US are sentient beings, and we too are animals, then animals are sentient beings."

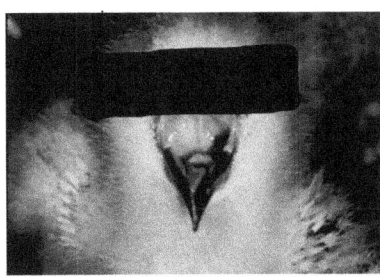

Humans bicker and scream. We're not animals.

Jewel plays devil's advocate for a while, because she claims to be a real Christian. "But, aren't humans sentient beings?" she slides with a smooth accent, turning "beings" into two distinct syllables with a big "yings" at the end.

I look at Jewel and Twistor, whom I think of as sentient, and then to Pillmold, who appears to lack sentience of any kind. "For all the evidence I see right now before me, there are a lot of *Homos* that appear to have no soul and no spirit; like our former Secretary of Defense Dick Cheney, who now, it appears, will be our new Vice President under Bush, for example."

"It's a good question," Twistor adds, "whether or not we are just sophisticated, some of US, intelligent animals, that have figured-out all of this stuff: How to make airplanes, computers, etc., but other than that we are no different than the other beings on The Planet."

Then Jewel, adding her patented compassionate side states, "Nobody wants to believe that when they read Romeo and Juliet, that we are just like the animals, right? That's a masterpiece and nobody can argue with Shakespeare, and that is very old, and though hundreds of years have gone by, no monkey has written a Shakespeare piece yet."

I say, "Yah but, an adult chimp can easily kill an adult human, but an adult human can't kill an adult chimp. They put their power into their physicality to survive, as we put our power into our brains, eyes, and fingers in particular. Writing a play is as human as biting a digit off is chimp, but I know what you're saying."

Then, out-of-the-blue, Tex comes out with "Okay, so let's argue that we do have a soul and a spirit and we are sentient beings; then why can't animals be?"

We all think for a moment.

Tex says, "There used to be arguments, 500 years-ago, that Africans were not sentient beings; that they were sub-human, soulless or something,. . ."

". . . like a different species, and which helped them justify slavery," I agree. "How could a good Christian in good conscience treat a fellow human that way?" I pose. "They have to lower them to the level of animals to justify enslaving, just like propaganda used against countries at war. Today, even if a friggin KKK leader said that blacks have no souls, he'd be laughed out of the rally. He would be seen as a complete fool no matter how stupid the congregation was."

This comment appears to anger Pillmold. "That's the way it was black then. Ah, I mean back then," Pillmold lets out a Freudian slip.

I say, "but, that was the paradigm of the time. Back then, we couldn't understand many African languages, so we thought they were stupid and soulless."

Then Twistor continues, "Today, we can't talk or understand animal (or plant) language yet, and we can't prove animals have souls, or can think on a deep level, or feel emotions, or anything on a level deeper than the most superficial anger or joy."

A chorus of 'whats' erupt, . . . not because they disagree with him, but because none of us can hear him.

"Well", Tex reasons, "until we can tap into animal brain waves somehow or teach them to communicate with US, like Koko the gorilla, we won't know that."

Wow! Keep in mind that the three of them all have very heavy drawling accents, yet, Jewel and Tex sound so much more sophisticated than they did when I met them for the first time on the plane. I am so proud that they actually have been listening and respect my passion, dedication, and enthusiasm enough to pick up on all this shit.

Twistor says, "That's what's so interesting about the studies with the great apes. When they taught Koko how to perform and understand sign language, and taught so many other animals so many things, they found that they were so, so close to US: 99.9% DNA compatible, so close to *Homos*, yet some of us still argue that those animals, that gorilla, are not sentient beings, but Manson is?" Pillmold thinks aloud, "A delicate, gentle ape vs. Charlie Manson?" He laughs to himself, because he certainly does not see a gorilla as gentle.

"Look into both of their eyes," Jewel challenges him. "Which has a soul? You tell me."

Then Tex says, "You tell US. Manson is a sentient being, but Koko the gorilla is not?"

Obviously, Tex had seen a show on Koko or something, on one of those hokey cable channels, and his animal empathy finally awakened. He cares! It looks like he cares! I feel my eyes getting wet.

Twistor, still in science mode, and oblivious to just how far Tex has come, says, "Secondly, the other arguments one could make is that there is no soul or spirit, and in that case none of US are sentient, which would also mean animals aren't."

"That would also mean we are all the same, as aminals" Pillmold scoffs.

Twistor laughs, "Either way; we are screwed."

Then Jewel says, "Either we all have souls or none of US have souls. That makes it kind of hard to eat a chicken."

"Hey," Tex chimes in, "If you 100% absolutely believe people have souls, then you too must believe animals do, and when you shoot, kill, or eat any livin thin', you are taking its life and killing a creature with a soul, just like a soldier or a bank robber."

Wait a minute! Is Tex just messin with us now?

"But ya have tah kill tah eat," Tex clarifies.

Nope. He's not messing with us.

Pillmold grinds his axe, "On top of all of this, Amb has been completely mishandling the whole Myhel deal."

We all raise our eyebrows in surprise. Whoah. Where the hell did that come from?

Then Pillmold spills the beans. "The first thing she did was report to Dutruex and HIC that you threatened her. That's why Amb is bringin ya into his office for an important meeten first thin in the mornin."

I say, "Okay, I don't need to know the second thing, thank you. Good night." I say as I usher everyone back out the door. Actually, I wish I could ask Jewel to hang, but instead, they leave, and I look at Twistor with more angst on my face.

With that, I put my hands on my hips. What the fuck? When will this ever end? Fuck. This sucks because I don't want to fight anymore, and now, I'm going to have my biggest fight yet. Pillmold is right. That really bothers me too. I have been hoping that he is simply always wrong about everything. I don't like when I guy as dumb and dangerous as him can be right. The next morning, Chipweldi is there, but Ben mysteriously isn't. It looks like Amb wants to keep Ben out of this.

As I walk into the office, I hear a voice. "Kestrel, we have to have a special meeting," Amb says dryly.

Don't you friggin hate that? I hate that tone, the bullshit. The whole threat thing, like he needs to be all serious to put the fear of god into me or something like that. Chipweldi sits there with his stupid grin.

"We had a complaint from HIC that you make threats to Myhel," he states.

"Whaaaaaaaahht?" I say incredulously. "No way."

Then it all comes rushing to me, as clear as the day it hit me in West Virginia when I first saw Chelonia, and as clear as that weekend hiking alone there, and on the third day, having reached mental solitude as well.

I state for the record, "I never threatened anybody."

I flashback to when Myhel showed-off a shirt that said *Absolute Bitch* proudly emblazoned across the chest in bright day-glo lettering. I never understood why she even owned such a shirt, but she did. She seemed to be a really nice, down-to Earth person on the surface.

I look at Amb, but never at Chipweldi. I've had it with going through the wringer out here, and Amb has had it with my relationship soap opera merry-go-round, so something's got to give.

I say out of context, "It's practically never ok to be a bitch. Ok?" Amb looks at me with surprise. "Now that, not only I had broken up with her, had dated and ended it with Hamed, had hooked-up with a couple of other girls here and there on the atoll, and now have totally fallen head-over-heels for the love of my life, Myhel proudly wears the bitch flag as a badge of honor."

Chipweldi laughs, "Hee hee hee, she wants to show everyone on the Atoll what a woman's scorn can be. He ha hee. You really did it. It's like messin with a Bobcat in a rail barrel. Hee ha ha."

What? Where does he come up with this shit? Amb tolerates Chipweldi, barely. He needs a witness, but I think he wants to send a stern message to Chipweldi at the same time. It's not working. Chipweldi is having too good of a time. Again, I never bother to even acknowledge him. Keep your eyes on the prize Kestrel.

I get technical on Amb, "When? Where was the threat? What kind of threat?" I say point blank, "What are the facts of her accusation?"

Amb answers as if he feels threatened, "I don't want to get into a non-juried 'He said--She said' shit thing in the office with you and Chipweldi. It is going to be too damn embarrassing."

Chipweldi laughs. He is loving this farce. For once, he is not the one who looks bad. He can barely contain himself. These are my bosses, so I remain respectful and contain my desire to break from protocol, but I definitely don't enjoy Chipweldi getting a rise out of all this shit at my expense. So, instead of being my own defense council, I keep my mouth shut for once.

I think about it for a long second. There was no way I was threatening in any way. So why would she do something like that? Why would she purge herself? Could she really be threatened some how?

Chipweldi breaks the silence with yet another one if his completely unoriginal sayings, "Cat gut yah tongue, or was it that author you hooked up with? Heheehe hee. For I guy who I thought was kinda smart, you seem to be several cans short of a six pack sometimes. Hi ha he."

I say to Amb, "Oh, wait a minute. I know. She's been talking this over with Misa Queen and this is the smartest way to get me off the atoll."

Amb folds his hands across his chest gently and leans back against the wall, also thinking. Then he says, "If she can get you booted off the atoll, then she will feel like a winner."

Amb looks at Chipweldi, who appears to go along with Amb, "Right now, she feels like a total loser. Hey ha," Chipweldi agrees like a drooling Long-tailed Weasel.

I look up at Amb with my eyes wide open, "By getting me off, she can be the Queen of Halfway again, picking whichever boy she wants, with no rejection associated."

Amb agrees, "Misa Queen would suddenly be the head ranger and appear to be knowledgeable for the first time."

Chipweldi looks up in surprise. He didn't know Amb had connected the dots between Myhel and Misa Queen, and Chipweldi certainly does not like me bringing up Misa Queen.

I say, enlightened, "I am blocking their ascension to their rightful places as queens of the atoll. Now I get it, and, now that I am leaving and it will be hard for her to serve her 'cold vengeful dish' as she puts it, why not try to get me kicked out of The Service, or put in jail, even better yet? At least we have a rock-solid motive: Ego."

Amb leans over to me, "How nuts is this girl over you?"

'You'd rather masturbate than be with me?' Her gushing words come flushing back to me as I sit at the table with both Amb and Chipweldi standing above me.

I say to Amb, "She would rather have me dead, in Fed prison, or whatever, than have me right in front of her reach but no longer an option in anyway."

Chipweldi blurts, "Wow! You should be flattered, hee he hu, but you know how compliments from freaks go. Was Jodie Foster flattered by Hinckley? Was Polanski flattered by Manson's attention? Hee, hee, hee."

I confess to Amb, ignoring Chipweldi's useless comments, "I remember I looked up at that big, crying mess, and said sensitively, 'No, don't look at it that way. Yes, I think it's best for both of us to have some time apart to gain some perspective on the situation here.' I went on, trying to be caring in a circumstance that can only be painful."

"Jeeshzzz." Amb gets a little more personal. He wants to see if he should waste his good name defending a lewd scoundrel like me.

"Were you truthful with her, basically?" Amb awaits my response.

I sit up straight. I am going to tell the truth. The straight up truth. What is it? Think it, speak it! "The truth, yeh, I would much rather be alone, masturbation or not, than be with a total lying, psycho like that. I never led her on or lied to her."

Amb assesses, "Well, I think you handled the whole situation really nicely but sometimes insecure losers take that as a sign of weakness and try to make themselves feel better somehow." Amb looks over at Chipweldi.

I know that, and I know he is trying to be nice right now. I have just fucked up over and over again, and like I said in the beginning, nothing comes for free. Just as I'm thinking this I see Dr. Oso drive by in the ambulance. A shiver jumps through my spine. Oh my god, I hope that ambulance experience doesn't suddenly come up some way, but from what I can see, they don't know anything about that and this is exclusively about Myhel again. Be careful with whom you hook up with Kestrel.

I throw myself on the mercy of the court, "What do you want me to do Amb?"

Amb says bitterly, "Vindictive, sick people, like Myhel and Misa Queen, just have to be avoided. I don't see any resolution to this."

Chipweldi complains, "There is no way around them. Hi he hee. In the work place, we are stuck with them."

I say, "I try to never be one of them, ever," as I look at Chipweldi, who winces a little behind his shades.

"How do you feel?" Amb asks me out of the blue.

"Now," I answer unprofessionally, and at the end of my rope, "on top of this crap, to add insult to injury, you call me into the office like I'm some kind of little fucking two-year-old, and sit me down with this shit. 'So you threatened Myhel?' Immediately assuming that I am at fault."

"Well, we are the government," Amb says, "we have to approach it that way."

I rebut, "First of all, no you don't, and secondly, you are the guy now I have been working on the atoll with for almost a year, and I've been on atoll for like two years. I've gotten all superior ratings, which are not easy to get in the Animal Protection Service, and I've been practically a perfect worker." I think about it for a second, then say carefully, "If I were a manager with a perfect employee who is doing a great job, and who had gone through jumping through all those hoops and volunteering for months with no pay, waiting for the job to come through, to be in the APS to

329

begin with; the last thing I would do as a good super would be to jump on someone before I even got any of the facts straight; especially if I thought there was an honest threat made, and if I knew there were extenuating relationship issues."

Amb and Chipweldi look at me, . . . considering my comments.

I say to Amb, "I understand, in this case, it would be my duty to assure in safety and rectify the situation so to avoid further escalation, if I were in your shoes."

Chipweldi looks at me. Do I know more than I let on, or am I just naïve and gung-ho? Chipweldi knows that's not what Amb is about at all. He wants to pound me down to assure I stay in line. That is all. He is in Daddy mode, like he wants to tell this little punk what to do or how to act, and I'm not going along with it well enough to scare the living shit out of Chipweldi.

So here I sit. He and Chipweldi trying to browbeat me, and me realizing I should just start acting like it works.

So standing above me, Amb continues, "So, what, why would you threaten Myhel?"

"I didn't threaten her or anyone. I just told her that if she doesn't want to talk or be civil and won't answer my calls and doesn't want to see me, that's fine, but it is going to be difficult to do on this little atoll. Then she started coming around me all the time and simultaneously saying negative, inappropriate, and unprofessional things about me to the FN and HIC staff, and to the ASS visitors. I told her that if she doesn't want to be near me then stay away from me. I told her at this point, since she's being so immature about everything, that that would be best. You see the game she's playing here Amb."

Amb looks at me. Shit, it's not going as he planned. He may have to defend me after all, instead of punishing me, which of course would be much easier and set an example to Chipweldi and Misa Queen.

Chipweldi sees an opening to make me look like a hypocrite, "Did you file and submit a report?"

Amb laughs at how ludicrous Chipweldi looks.

I smirk, then ply onward with the truth, "When I try to contact her and see how she is doing, showing the compassionate side, she locks herself in her room for 2 weeks and gets all kinds of drugs from Dr. Chance. When I stop trying to reach out to her, she comes around to start causing strife, making comments, being generally vindictive, etc." I make my case.

"Well, Kestrel, whenever you make a statement that can end with 'or else', that's a threat," Amb fires back irrationally, using zero discretion, as if he really needs me off the atoll.

"What? First of all, I never said anything like 'do this or else' or any ultimatum or anything like that. Secondly," I laugh, "you can add 'or else' to the end of practically any statement and someone can turn it into a threat. Would you like to come to lunch with me . . . or else? I mean, come on. A threat is a threat, not some kind of veiled thing that could be construed as a threat," I say. "Why would I threaten someone? What is the advantage for me to threaten Myhel? I wouldn't waste my time threatening somebody."

Chipweldi says, "Revenge?"

I say to Amb, "Revenge? Revenge who?"

Amb looks at Chipweldi puzzled.

Amb and Chipweldi look at each other like I'm full of shit. Now my temper flares, "Hey, I was a communications major and you guys know how direct and blunt I am. I wouldn't threaten anyone, and if I did, it wouldn't be that subtle and contrived, right?" I try to convince them but it appears to be working against me.

I should tell them to go fuck themselves. That's probably the only thing they would respect. I continue instead, "When my best friend Tim and I were at a party in Jamaica Plain back in around '93, we heard this drunk guy try to pick-up a girl in the kitchen. Just as the blaring song ended, we heard him say, 'How bout you make me breakfast?' The woman laughed and stumbled away. We said to him, 'You idiot! First of all, you should have told her you'd make her breakfast. At least she would get breakfast out of the deal. Secondly, the way you said it almost sounded like a threat. Tone is everything.' Then Tim and I started thinking of brilliant pick-up lines, and though we blew through 20 hysterical ones, one that Tim came up with stuck: 'If you wanna live, you gotta go out with me tomorrow night.'"

Amb and Chipweldi look at me, confused.

"It can sound threatening if taken the wrong way, or sweet and endearing if taken the right way. It's a matter of interpretation. Get it? It's funny." I throw on a swinger voice, "If you wanna live, you gotta go out with me tomorrow night." I pause for a laugh with

Groucho-esque timing and Chris Rock grit. I get nothing. I get all serious again and deliver, "I never came close to threatening anyone, including Myhel. She wants me off the atoll and is using you two as tools to get at me, and you are falling for it: hook, line, and sinker," I state definitively.

Where's Kestrel? Find him waving from the rushing surge channel.

Amb looks pissed to be assumed to be such a tool. "Are you stating that you made no threat?" he says, as if to hold some kind of ground, so he can be right or something, or maybe to get me to state something for the official record.

"You can put 'or else' after any fuckin sentence on Earth," I say, pissed back. "I don't hate Myhel, I just know she's messed-up. I don't hate anybody."

Chipweldi challenges, "Deny?"

I retort, "I don't hate Deny. I don't even really dislike Deny. I hate Cherry Ballpig, and Ryle, and I really don't like Kilgro and a lot of the HIC staff. I, I guess I could say that. I hate the fact that it looks like an even more horrible Bush is about to take office. But I don't really hate people, ya know."

Amb probes, "Misa Queen?"

I confess, "Oh god, alright, so I don't like Misa Queen at all, or Pillmold. What do you want from me?"

He looks at me angrily. Fuck this! I don't care what Myhel says or does, if my boss is too stupid to see this shit right before his eyes then he's really no better than Chipweldi, or Ben for that matter. If my own boss is going to fall for this shit, then she does win, and the Sanctuary and the wildlife does lose.

I compose myself, "I categorically deny any threat to any person or creature on this atoll!" I state in a loud, low voice, as I stand, "I assume you are through with me. Good day." I pause for a second. Neither of them seem to be interested in stopping me, so I slowly walk out in complete, controlled, disgust.

As I pace around the office, I decide that instead of calling Zart, I will call Chelonia, and I rant. It proves to be a good choice because she's simple, like Zart, but more insightful. I tell her, "I know Amb really isn't a bad guy, he just has all of these forces putting pressure on him. I felt like I was in a friggen military tribunal. I remember Lt. Flipflopbaker saying that 'The military takes care of its own. That's what they do best.' That's what they do best? Take care of themselves? I know what they are trying to say here but I fuckin hate hollow platitudes. He might as well have said nothing, or "Never Give Up", than hand out that tripe. Why do they exist; first and foremost to protect themselves?"

Chelonia reasons, "Well, if they didn't exist and threaten people and make other countries paranoid and edgy, then they wouldn't have to take care of themselves. I know their mission. It is supposed to be to take care of US, which actually translates to taking care of the moneyed, empowered interests in the USA. Of course one way to take care of yourself is job security, endless new equipment, and perpetual war. Without war, where would the military be?"

I say with enthusiasm, "Right, like it's like when Margaret Thatcher begged the Ruskies to keep The Wall up. Her and her constrained viewpoint ilk liked the status quo right where it was, thank you."

"Yeah", Chelonia says with regret, "We need war. Tons of businesses will go out of business if we don't have perpetual wars, and only progressives can see any differently. That's a huge dominant paradigm to subvert."

I yell, "WAR WAR WAR. Lee Ving from FEAR said it way better than I ever could. *Let's Have a War.*"

Chelonia states, "I don't know any punk."

I encourage, "Get the lyrics to that song. I know you don't like Punk and the sound of Punk, but seriously, great lyrics!"

Chelonia laughs, "Okay, I'll look them up. Don't worry about the Myhel threat thing. She is probably just trying to get a rise out of you, and if you get pissed, she will be all smiles. Just avoid her like the plague, like you said. She can't blame you for anything if you don't even go near her."

I question doubtfully, "Oh yah?!"

After about a week or so, I send Amb a resignation letter and tell him of my departure plans, in 60 days, instead of my original 90. He calls me on my cell phone before I can even make it back to my house; as soon as he gets the news.

He says surprised, "Ah, Kestrel, ah, I got your letter, ah, you, you leaving Halfway?"

I say, "Yah," curtly.

He says, "Well, ah, it wasn't ah because of anything I did, was it?"

I am so surprised, because I didn't think that he would react in such a way. I guess he didn't think I would react in the way I did either. Ya just gotta realize that some people just aren't gonna take your shit. My Dad was like that. Whether he was right or wrong, he was not going to take someone's shit.

I say, "No, ah, ya know, just time for me to get out of here. Writins on the wall. Ya know." That's all I say.

He says, "Well, ya know, we gotta talk about this. Ya know,"

"There's nothing left to talk about. I've made my decision. We've already talked a lot," I say, quickly ending his bid for control.

"Well if you leave the Animal Protection Service, it's really hard to get back in," he tries to convince me. I listen to him as he says, "Like, the APS doesn't look well on resignations. If you leave now, you will have a really tough time getting back in and getting a job," he warns.

I'm not worried about that," as I keep it very short and clean. "See you later," I say, when I hang up.

Bummer.

On a night dive, only my third or fourth in my life, and the first one on Halfway; we enter an unimaginable world. How can most humans spend their entire lives living in a normal, terrestrial, gravity-mode, without floating weightlessly in space, or diving into the inky depths? How come most adults I know have not ridden a bike, or climbed a tree, in more than a decade, unless we count those few who still murder turkey and deer from sniper limbs. Motives.

Sunset on a peaceful, deserted West Beach, as we prepare our gear for the night dive.

The splash of the anchor snaps me back to the moment. As the anchor sinks, the water appears flat calm. There is no wind, not even a hint of a zephyr. It seems more quiet than usual. With all of our gear ready, we hit the water together, because it's too easy to get separated in the dark. Bent, Troubadive, a couple of visiting divers, a couple of the photographers, and Darom as our trusty captain, round out the group.

It's funny to note the differences between the divers and the anglers. None of the divers drink Coors, watch NASCAR, or listen to country. The divers never seem to have as much money as the anglers, and are not pretentious, but they do appear to exist a notch or so above the sophistication of the anglers, who like to call themselves 'Sportsmen'. Weird euphemism.

As we get to the bottom, at about eighty-one feet, we shine our lights around to see total moonscape. Bad spot. I guess it's hard to see at night to determine location, and we don't have any GPS points logged.

Troubadive approaches me closely underwater, shining the light up so I can see his face clearly. He removes the regulator from his mouth and slowly starts blowing tiny pearl-like bubbles from his tightly pursed lips. I smile and give him the okay sign. He is demonstrating breath control. Every time we finish a dive I have less than 500 pounds in my tank, while he always stays down for an extra 20 minutes and still returns to the vessel with almost a thousand.

Bent told me, "That's because you are an ASP."

"What's that?" I responded in confusion.

Bent said, "An Air Suckin Pig," with a laugh.

Bent's right. I always seem to run out of air way before anyone and I need to breath more Zen.

I thank Troubadive, and we go off on a great dive that, for the first few minutes, appears to be disappointing, only to suddenly become very cool. First, we find an octopus, then a second. In the dark, they appear to cruise around on the bottom ubiquitously. We find some parrotfish encased in a bizarre phlegmy slime. They do this so they can sleep without White-tipped Reef Sharks and other predators turning them into a late-night snack treat. Then we see more octopi, and I stop bothering to count them anymore. As Darom would say in his heavy Bangkokian accent, 'Too many octopus, too many octopus'.

We return to the vessel and start removing our gear after the second dive.

Excited, I say, "Wow, that was rad! Weird though, no sharks."

A chorus of 'What's erupt. At the same time, I look astern with the lights glimmering and see four or five brown looking sharks. They could be Dusky Shark, or some other species I don't know.

Troubadive says, "You have got to be kidding. As soon as we hit the water, a couple of dozen sharks split into all different directions."

I look over the side in shock. Wow, I can't believe I didn't notice them or even see one on the dives. Sneaky.

Working hard at my desk the next day, crunching visitor data and tour participation for my quarterly report, (which I might add proudly, I initiated myself and instituted into the policy for all future Halfway Rangers,) I get startled by my phone. Oh my god, it's sweet Chelonia, calling me to say hello and tell me that she is thinking of me. What an angel.

She asks, "What's wrong honey? You sound depressed."

I don't want to dwell on the horrible Myhel story. "No. I am at work, and busy and focused, but I guess I'm bummed too, even though I had an incredible night-dive last night with Troubadive."

"Do you have time to tell me about it?" She asks.

I say, "Briefly. It was pitch-black down there."

Chelonia says, "No, about what you are bummin for?"

"Oh," I say, "I guess this all comes down to the fact that nobody cares. Did they ever? I don't know but it seems to me that even as shortly back as in the 80s, people cared and had hope that the World would get better."

Chelonia says, "Hippy hangover? Didn't the hippies in the 60s think it was going to get better, . . "

". . . and that they had 'Had Enough' as **The Who** put it?" I state. "The people in the 50s thought it was going to get better cause the economy was booming, and so were the babies. In the 40s we were optimistic cause we kicked ass in WWII, after believing in the roaring 20s, that the war to end all wars had already occurred, and it was time to Charleston our way into the future."

Chelonia thinks economically, "I guess the 30s put a damper on that one, but we definitely aren't in the 30s now; and yet, it seems like nobody cares about nada," she agrees.

I think about my Master's Degree thesis project. "When surveyed, Americans usually say they care about their family, health, and home, usually in roughly that order."

Chelonia thinks, "Do we? I mean, if we cared about our home, wouldn't we be smart enough to protect it? Take the Afghanistan situation right now, on the cusp of 2000, ---"

I agree. "Y2K. So ominous."

Then Chelonia says, "We all know that the Taliban are going cuckoo right now, yet, people in the US appear far more concerned with Clinton getting a hummer or the threat that maybe we might start getting taxed to use the internet. People in our country just seem to accept religious extremism, the most psycho extremism of all, like it's a right or something."

"It's not", I say.

337

Then Chelonia continues, "Just because we have religious freedom in this country doesn't give anyone the right to whack-out on society, or create new, even more bogus religions, like Moonies, Hare Krishnas, Mormons, and these neo-Christian born-agains. These people are as crazy as gun nuts, and in most cases, they seem to march along hand-in-hand."

Then I say, "How come no one but the smart guys, like Zinn and Chomsky, see this shit coming? If history teaches US anything, it's to keep our eyes open and look around, as Host Drats stated at the epilogue of each of his whacky *Bogus Weirdness* shows. Not out of paranoia, but out of the simple doctrine of eternal vigilance; the only way true democracy or socialism can efficiently function."

"I saw some *Bogus Weirdness* shows. Thanks for sending me the tape, but I am glad you put that artsy part of your life behind you now," Chelonia admits.

I am disappointed to hear her say that, but need to understand. "Really? Why?"

Chelonia reveals, "I just think you were good at that stuff, as Drats was, and very photogenic, but I think what you are doing now is much better. Is it because we live in a world of zombies? That's why nobody cares? You think the snappily-clad business executives who jumped from the 42nd floor during The Great Crash of '29 were in zombie mode in that moment?"

I say, "For their sake, I hope they were; but they probably were more alive in that last moment of death than any of US have been in the last decade."

When I do die on Halfway, coming up shortly, I won't really be in any kind of super-sensual world or anything. I think I will experience way more of an edge killing The Goons and saving Chelonia. I will be so tired and hurt by the time I die, I will simply feel like I am accepting it, kind of at peace in a way, being a meal as opposed to a waste.

Then Chelonia asks me, "So if we really care about our home, wouldn't we study history to discover the best way to protect it for future generations?"

"Aye, that's the rub. Maybe we don't care about future generations, hence the SUV (Saudi Undercover Vehicle) and mega Hummer craze. 'Tank you Ahhrnold'. We're all gonna die anyway in the coming god-induced Armageddon, cause we know god is just dying to punish all that he has created and reward those who faithfully accepted him into their hearts. So spend it while you got it and screw posterity," I explain with exasperated sarcasm.

Chelonia laughs at my presentation, and huffs, then says, "But, people still say they care about their home. They may be too lazy to study boring history, but they aren't too lazy to buy a gun and keep it loaded under the pillow for the day some stupid fucker makes the wrong move."

"Of course, those pillow guns won't have any effect on missiles smashing into towers or nuclear power plants," I state.

"I guess pillow gunners could shoot at the moon," Chelonia speculates with a yawn.

"It wouldn't solve the problem but there's nothing like feeling the power of shooting something. You gotta love a brand new gun," I say facetiously.

"Even if you can't control your offspring, your boss, your life, you can shoot shit and feel perfectly empowered for that mili-instant of existence," Chelonia says, just like I would.

"It reminds me of another song from the yet to be produced rock opera by Drats."

Chelonia perks-up a bit. "Sing it for me over the phone."

"Nah, it's gonna sound fucked-up," I say honestly.

"Please, I want you too," she begs without the slightest hint of a whine.

"All right." I begin to sing:

Nothing
by Drats

Captured in a world of nothing, Where everyone wants me to dance for them
Why do I feel this, obligation? Why do I continue with this procrastination?
Encircled by, invisible beams, Carrying me, to a far away land
Where nothing is left, and nothing makes me laugh, And nothing just might be my reward for . . . nothing
Climbing up from the valley, Of indecision and many rocks climbed

I find myself weeping at all who look at me, Please don't cry,
please don't cry
Jumping, for once I've reached the top, Jumping for joy, I'll never
stop
I've reached past my delusions, And my materialistic confusions,
At utopian peace with who and what I am.
Dying in a world of nothing, Where everyone wants immortality,
I think my children are my blood and my legacy, But my children
won't grow up the way I want them to be
Nothing is left. Nothing. Nothing.

I hold the last notes out long, smooth, and clear; very legato and
Sade-like.
"That's a very mesmerizing melody," Twistor says, as he enters
the office quietly. "We need to pedal along the runway. We have to
go on a mission to save a great frigate caught ninety-feet-up."
"Dya hear that honey bunny? I gotta go right now," I say
apologetically.
Chelonia warblers gently, "Okay my sweet love. Don't worry
about anything. Everything is going to be all right. Just relax and
have a good time. I love you honey bunny."
I say, "I love you too baby. We'll talk later. Bye."
I hang up, then instantly jump into action mode, and before you
know it, Twistor and I are flying across the runway on our beach
cruisers.
Twistor mumbles, "Sounds pretty serious."
I think he refers to the frigatebird. "What dya mean?" I ask.
"O, nothin." Twistor responds, embarrassed. I can barely hear him,
especially on the bikes.
"What?" I ask again. He looks embarrassed now, but I press him.
"Dude, what are you saying?"
"Just you and Chelonia. I thought you were really into Hiromi and
falling in love with her, and now you turn around and are like
heavily head-over-heels for this girl you barely know and you may
never see again."
"So," I reply with confusion.
"So," Twistor illuminates, "I don't see how you can swing over
that way so fast, especially considering you haven't even had sex
with Chelonia."

340

"Yet!" I clarify. "I know you don't understand me, and I know Renn may be saying some stuff to you, but you gotta understand one thing about me: Before I moved to Halfway, I had a girlfriend for six years I was really in love with. I don't want to play around. Since I was like seven or eight years old, my biggest fear was that I would never have a true love in my heart."

Twistor laughs with surprise, "Really? You?"

I relay, "Dude, I'm tellin ya. I was afraid that I wouldn't have a date for the senior prom, and that I would be standing outside the gymnasium, in the rain, looking in at all my classmates, having fun, and not caring about me at all."

"No way!" Twistor says in shock, "I can't picture you."

I say, "True. All true. I gotta show you some pictures. Anyway, I thought I could fall for Hiromi, but after meeting Chelonia, I know what I really want and need. Funny thing is, Chelonia doesn't. She is like my opposite. She does not need a man. Her and most of the women in her family basically stay away from men, and they appear to be happier for that. You are like that. You seem like you could be more than happy alone."

Twistor says, "Ya. I've been pretty alone most of my life, and I prefer it."

I reply, "I can't handle it. I have to be with a lot of people or I feel like I'm going to go nuts. I get so lonely. I don't know why."

As we bike along the rest of the way, quietly, I think about what Twistor said. I can see how everybody now sees me as a lascivious screwer: Basically, they think I'm a messed-up slutty guy who will have sex with anyone. That makes me really mad, but I can see how they can think that. It's obvious to me now that Myhel is the linchpin in all of this. If I had avoided sex with her as completely as I did with Jellie, the volunteers and interns, and especially with Kilgro, then probably, all of my other sexual activity would have gone unnoticed, or much less noticed.

My blood begins to simmer. I yell over to Twistor in the wind, "I am getting so totally sick of all this shit. I mean, whad am I some kind of sex-fiend or what? The fisherman guys are down there trying to screw whoever they can and no one is givin them a hard time."

341

Then Twistor parrots, "Like we said, it's because you are in a government uniform and a symbol of federal Halfway or somethin."

I puff with regret, "Like I have to stand to a higher, ah, calling, ah, or something like that. I mean, there is nothing really in my code of ethics that says I have to be celibate during this job."

Twistor says, "There isn't?"

I say, "What?"

Twistor says more forcefully, "Isn't there some kind of rule?"

I repeat, "No. No rule."

I think back to when I was in third grade. I had the hottest rookie teacher, and even at nine years old, I tried to accidentally bump into her boobs and cop feels off of her. She used to think 'Awh, you're so cute', and shit like that, and that I was all innocent, but hey, that wasn't as bad as when I was in first grade, when I used to throw pennies under the nuns' skirt so I could look up their dresses and see what was up there. What could possibly be up there, especially on a nun? How could I look up there? But, I had to know. I have to know about everything.

I think about how I am now. Oh, god, I must have been so incredibly obvious. And even in kindergarten, I would stick scrunched up tissues in the toes of the teacher's shoes, so I could watch her put them on at the end of the day and go 'Ow, ooh, something stopped my shoe from going on. Well how did these get in there?', and I would be like 'ha ha ha', with a villainous little laugh inside.

But, I mean, c'mon. Did I come up with that penny up the skirt idea? No way. I don't think I came up with that. That's too brilliant. So that means I'm not the only one thinking this stuff. I look over at Twistor. His face looks blank. Is he thinking what I am? Doubt it. How could he be? It's stupid of me to think that anyone could, but I do.

I asked Drats once if he thought his readers would learn anything from my libidinous folly. Drats replied, 'I have no idea who my readers will be or what they will think. I'm just telling the best story about you and that crazy atoll that I can. The book is obviously designed for humans to read, not animals and plants.'

I thought about that odd comment from Drats. You would think he is misanthropic with all his lyrics downing *Homos*. 'Are you misanthropic?' I remember asking him.

Drats countered with, 'Pfff, ya, right? What, me? I don't have a misanthropic bone in my body', he said sincerely.

I said, 'Yes you are. You are always talking about how bad we are and putting humans down and stuff.'

And Drats, in all his wisdom, retorted 'Yah, I'm talking about that. I care. That means I care. If I had total contempt for humanity I wouldn't even bother raising my voice and I'd join the other Coors drinkin, Limbaurff listenin, Christian cynics, and not give a fuck. I would simply look forward to heaven and screw this Earth.'

I don't remember if that was exactly what he said, but, wow! I see Drats' eyes burn with an internal desire. He is alive. Drats is intense. He is alive. I realized something in that moment about him. Drats doesn't write this book to be misanthropic. Why would he waste his time writing a book for humans to read if he thought humanity, or humsanity, was that hopeless, right? He still holds a glimmer of hope or he wouldn't have written it. Although, come to think of it, I think he thinks it's a very weak hope, hence the attempt at the book, a form of mass communication.

I hope that when Hollywood makes Drats' novel into a major motion picture, that they absolutely adhere to no computer generated crap special effects of any kind. NO. Drats would want the movie to be real. Make the movie real, . . . just like the other 2 million species on The Planet. Real, instead of being an avatar, a virtual fake thing, that we have everyday in our modern lives with its artificial constructs in our brains.

I yell to Twistor, "This construct of a world around us isn't actually real at all."

Twistor ekes out, "The house, the computer, the relationship; ya know, all of the stuff that we have in our life?"

I answer, "It's not really real. The only things that are really real are air, food, water; the basic things."

I think to myself again. That's the way a film should look. A film about Halfway. Halfway to Humanity. And the film should stick to conventions of reality. Even though there are the surreal components and bizarreness that happens, ya still gotta stick to things that people can actually do. I know so many people who

343

can't stand guys jumping off helicopters onto trains in tunnels at 99 mph and something no stunt guy could even pull off. Screw that. If nobody could ever pull it off, physiologically speaking, then why yuck-up the flick.

When Twistor and I get to the tree, panting, and dismount our bikes, a few tourists and FNs stand like statues, craning their necks up at the unfortunate creature.

"Wow. Ninety-feet," Twistor says. "That thing is up there," he mumbles.

I lay my bike over and stretch my legs in my service short-shorts. "A tree is a tree," I proclaim with gusto. "Just another day at the office."

Twistor looks around at the birds, watches me stretch, and does pretty much everything else he can to avoid actually talking with, or looking at, the people about.

I say, "I think there is hope for humanity just because of people like Lorenz, Zinn, and Chomsky, . . . , and me. I, I know I shouldn't put myself in their category, because of their genius and stature, whatever, but for every person who goes on Jerry Springher, or somethin, there's another person who is smart and isn't reproducing at a young age, and is not controlled by some kind of ridiculous imaginary spiritual entity from up above."

I hush my voice down for a second as the wind settles. I don't want to offend anybody now that they can hear me.

Twistor doubts, "Somehow, the intelligent, rational side is going to win-out over all other regular folk?"

I say, "Yes, and thereby, saving the other 2 million species on The Planet."

Twistor agrees, "Yah, we gotta be progressive and move forward. Let's stop fighting about Jerusalem like it's the big thing."

I start to climb up, as Dr. Oso arrives in his golf cart with his kids. "Hey, you're not goin up aftah that thing?"

I look over at him, but keep climbing hand over hand. I don't want to yell back and scare the bird even more.

"I ain't fixin ya up if'n ya break ya neck," Dr. Oso offers as support. "It's just a dumb bird, and ya don't wantah be paralyzin' yaself."

A Great Frigatebird perches with a grimace.

He is right. I would not instruct somebody else to do this maneuver, and if I saw someone doing it, it would be my responsibility to make them get down.

Rung by rung, limb by sticky limb, I ascend the tree quickly. Reaching the giant, black, Great Frigatebird, I note that the top of the dead snag feels brittle, like a huge section could crack and fall to the tarmac below. As I reach for the bird, talking in my typical high-falsetto, to calm the critter, it lunges its head forward, stretching its neck, and cuts the top of my left hand open, near the knuckles. While it bites my hand, I'm able to dislodge it from the Australian Pine. It only falls for a second, and then catches the breeze and flies off out of sight. I scoot back down the tree, after surveying the south beach, bulky dump, and the runway from this rare vantage point, and brush off my hands for another good job well done. Everyone looks at me with amazement. I'm sure some of them feel I am stupid.

I perform first aid on my hand. As we ride back, I ask Twistor, "Dude, are you into Renn?"

"Yah. You are not going to believe this, but I can't believe what an incredible pair we are," Twistor admits.

"Neither do I," I say, joking but serious. "It's none of my business, but Renn is one of my best friends, and I think you are a great guy, and there are some things that we just gotta talk about." I try to avoid sounding like anything but a cool friend.

Twistor looks over at me for a second. "Like the ghosts?" He looks to see my reaction.

"What?" I couldn't catch anything past 'Like'.

Twistor back-peddles figuratively, "Never mind. I didn't think so."

"No," I insist "what did you say?" leaning in to hear him.

345

"Everything is cool. Forget about it," Twistor tries.

I say cleverly, "Forget about what?"

Twistor shows the good judgment to trust me, "Has she told you about the ghosts?"

"Yeh," I say, "I don't think she is overly psycho, but she has some tripped-out stuff going on up there."

"That's what I thought," Twistor admits, "So do I," trying to make it work, but not even as close to as psycho, and malevolent, as Renn will end up being.

Then I say, "Hey, don't let it get you down. People all over Hawaii still believe in Night Marchers. I fell asleep on the beach and felt like I had a sea lion, of all things, on my chest. Of course, there are no sea lions in Hawaii. When I awoke alone on that cool night, it was almost starting to mist, and I couldn't rationally explain the feeling. Weird shit happens. That doesn't mean I jump to ghosts as the logical answer."

We ride silently for a moment, cutting past the wooden dolphin platform up in the trees. "I can't believe the spinners are back in such great numbers after all of the military destructions and disturbance out here," I ponder, changing the subject, as we pause to watch some Hawaiian Spinner Dolphins jumping and spinning, in the distance.

"So you never joined the military?" Twistor asks.

"No way. You still don't know me very well, do you? I can't even put my finger on a just war. There is no way I am going to put myself in a situation where I am an expendable asset just for the use of the interests in The U.S.," I proclaim. "There's a huge difference between patriotic and idiotic!"

He responds, "Yeah, well from what I've seen, you can get killed by friendly fire, or by your generals taking a gamble, or whatever. Why is that?"

I bring my binoculars down and look over at Twistor. "I don't know if anyone really really knows. The stupid wars generally keep happening because the Christians and Jews and Moslems have always been dying to kill each other, because they feel threatened that if there is a shift in the balance, one group may be able to actually take over and force the other groups to pray to their gods, eat their meats, wear their headdresses, and generally genuflect against their programmed will. Make them do their forbidden dances, as it were."

Twistor speaks wisely, well before his years, "The people that want to force you to join their sect of die, that, that is just crazy. You are going to get every single person on Earth to believe your belief, or you kill them. How mad is that? It's like cavemen, going out and killing other cavemen who are different, because they are different. Pure prejudice."

I relent as I see an odd couple walk toward us. It's Loon and Tex, with mist nets in their hands. "Wow, what are you guys doin?" I ask surprised.

Loon says, "Tex is helping me untangle and repair some Bonin nets. We figured we might as well do it out here instead of in the stuffy supply room."

"Tex. . . you, you are helping?" I say with a little surprise. Turns out, after all this time, that Tex really likes animals, likes helping with the mist netting and getting to hold the magnificent, albeit stinky, lumpy birds, and he was just putting up a kind of tough-guy front to be cool, in the beginning, as some kind of a personal defense shield. They sit down and get to work.

Twistor continues, "Anyways, I can imagine the U.S. having wars of ethnic cleansing, like Mormons killing Episcopalians, San Franciscans killing San Joseians, and the Christian soldiers laying waste to anyone who skips mass on Sunday."

I interject, ". . . and doesn't even make it to midnight mass on Christmas Eve, drunk. If you can't even do that, than obviously you don't even care and you are going straight to hell. Which is what this is all about: Nobody caring," bringing the main point full circle again.

"A little knowledge is dangerous," Loon adds as a wise guy.

The less you know, the smarter you feel. – Drats

Loon says, "It's the same story dude. Power controls everything."

Tex and Loon look at each other with anger.

Tex's jingoistic sensibilities smack into a wall of disturbing cognitive dissonance. "FDR knew, about Pearl Harbor? Before the attack? I won't believe that. Let me guess. We didn't land on The Moon neither?"

347

Everyone laughs. "I know we landed on The Moon, but you talk to a lot of Ruskies and Japs I know and they say it never happened," I explain.

I suddenly remember a test I just saw on this new thing called The Internet. I copied it and pasted it below my window in the bathroom so I can read it while I sit on the throne.

OK you history buffs ...

World History 101 - Mid-term Exam
(AKA "Those who ignore history ...")
This test consists of one (1) multiple-choice question.

Here's a list of the countries that the U.S. has bombed since the end of World War II, up until now, compiled by a historian, under the basic premise (in most cases) of turning them into democrazies:

China 1945-46
Korea 1950-53
China 1950-53
Guatemala 1954
Indonesia 1958
Cuba 1959-60
Guatemala 1960
Congo 1964
Peru 1965
Laos 1964-73
Vietnam 1961-73
Cambodia 1969-70
Guatemala 1967-69
Grenada 1983
Libya 1986
El Salvador 1980s
Nicaragua 1980s
Panama 1989
Iraq 1991-99
Sudan 1998
Afghanistan 1998

Yugoslavia 1999

Question:
*In how many of these instances did a democratic government,
respectful of human rights, occur as a direct result?
Choose one of the following:*

(a) 0
(b) zero
(c) none
(d) not a one
(e) a whole number less than one

It just blows me away. Y2K is coming. Is it over? Are we done
bombing or will we go back to WWII mentality? I think to myself
and create my own list: Iraq, Iran, Afghanistan, Chad, Somalia,
North Korea; and the list goes on of potential attack victims.
Loon says, "There are countries I can see Bush making excuses to
attack, not Gore. He would be too concerned about the massive
amount of environmental damage and resources go into wasteful
wars. As long as Bush can get enough stupid people to fear an
outside threat, he will have the consolidation he needs to impose
his will."
I think about Lorenz. He pointed out the same facts in *On
Aggression* in lower animals. As long as there is a perceived
outside threat, enemies will unite and aid each other to stop it.
Loon turns to Tex, snapping me from my deep thoughts, "First off,
historians argue that the U.S. knew the attack on Pearl Harbor was
coming, so it wasn't a total surprise, as many of our brave U.S.
citizens wanted to continue to believe for so long. FDR was
convinced by Churchie that we had to make this ultimate sacrifice
or wussy US would never enter to stop the Nazis. Even though
reports of the genocide were already pretty apparent, most of the
Americans didn't care cause we hated Jews anyways. Ah, racism.
Just like the cavemen. Just like the bulk of Americans today,"
Loon says with a funny voice. Wow, he is as rabidly anti-racist as I
am, and that's hard to find amongst 'guys'.

349

Japanese visitors walk through the Verbasina covered Sooty Tern colony on the Eastern Island runway, exactly where the Japanese had bombed some 56 odd years ago.

I jump into the ring again, "Secondly, even though General Yamamoto studied at Harvard and warned his pompous overlords of the futility of opening up this can of American whoop-ass, the arrogant and power hungry buffoons in command started their campaign of stupid-ass mistakes. Just like Bush undoubtedly plans to do if he really becomes president; go straight in with zero info, guns a blazing, Texass style. In WWI, navies targeted the battleships, which Yamamoto and most savvy strategists worldwide knew would have a *minor* impact in future wars compared to aircraft carriers. That's why they knew if they were to succeed in expanding their empire during WWII quickly, they needed to strike fast and sign a hasty armistice, making it impossible for the USA to even have time to repair it's aircraft carrier fleet before it was all over. The Japanese needed to wipeout the U.S. carriers, but you guys already know the whole story right, like none of our carriers or modern ships were in their usual slips. Later, from the decoding and the bogus decoy message about needing water at Halfway, the Americans knew the big sea battle would be out here."

"Yey, yah" they drone in chorus. They've all been on my tour and at my programs in The Station Theater. They don't need another recounting of the crusty Naval history.

Tex says defensively, "I'm aware of naval history. Why do you think I became a pilot instead of a captain? Planes rule."

I look over everyone and say, "The day of the carrier and the aircraft had arrived, and the U.S. had already told all their carriers to bail-out to sea before December 7th. So instead, the Zeros and other ample aircraft plowed 8 torpedoes into the USS Arizona and other WWI era obsolete slow pokes; total overkill; and missed the shipyards, fuel farms, and other important aspects of the Hawaiian bases. Stupid stupid stupid. Yamamoto could only shake his head and wish he wasn't a Jap. This Pyrrhic victory would haunt Japan for the next 4 years, directly, and still haunts them today on so many levels. I know, cause when I lived in Shinjuku for 2 years, folks there were always typically 'Japanese polite', but they definitely dug us Americans a lot less than say Kiwis, Ruskies, or, yes, dear I say it, even the French."

Twistor asks, "Wow, they still have residual feelings about the war 50 years later?"

I tell of an episode I encountered, "Dude, Confederates still hate me for being a Yank, a hundred and fifty years later."

"No way," both Tex and Loon say in a pinky wish.

"Yes!" I verify. "I was just back in West Virginia for training, and a woman from South Carolina, who works for the APS mind you, said she still hates Yankees. I laughed because I thought she joked. How am I, a Bostonian, supposed to hate people from a war centuries old? She said, "You don't understand what they done to us." Everyone looks at me in disbelief. Then I tell them about Japan. "I met an old, hunched-back rice farmer in Ino Shima one day. He approached me and said he was on a transport/cargo ship that got torpedoed by a U.S. sub in '44. He smiled with half his teeth missing and mangled, all jack-o-lantern style, and said 'We would have won, but you had science bomb.' Ah yes, the dreaded science bomb, dropped not once, but twice, just to make sure. Had nothing to do with the repeated fire bombings nightly of every major city in Japan, or the fact that 13-year-olds were flying kamikaze missions cause no pilots were left, or the myriad of other factors that proved that this whole thing really was about racism. *Tora Tora Tora*," I yell, pumping my fist, referring to the old propaganda film.

Everyone stops for a second and thinks. The breeze gently tickles my binocular strap and the moist salt air wets my nostrils. Maybe I sound like a know-it-all again, or too radical or something.

I offer, "So are we confusing caring with stubbornness? As I said, my premise here is that nobody cares. If nobody cares, why would the Japs and the U.S. be so obstinate? Oh, I know, it's about winning isn't it. We don't really care about our home, or we wouldn't let it fall apart and look like shit. As patriots, if we really cared about America, we wouldn't let all the redwoods get cut down and wouldn't strip mine and shit like that. We wouldn't let it be threatened by US."

Loon adds with fury, "We wouldn't let such a large percentage of US go hungry, be illiterate, or be imprisoned, if we cared. It's just like how we shit on our own brothers and sisters, our neighborhoods, our states, but then as soon as one outsider casts a disparaging eye, we are on their asses faster than H.W. Bush on a golf course after declaring war."

Everyone bursts into laughter, even Tex, but I think Tex laughs at how ridiculous he thinks that example is, while Twistor, Loon, and I laugh because we can actually picture former President Bush declaring war and then being seen on the golf course, like right away, even while troops were loading into C5s. So callus; so careless.

Twistor submits, "Okay, this has all got to be philogenetic, not civilized and cultural. Gorillas cover their turf."

I agree, "Even baboons; the most primitive, violent, hairiest, scariest primates of them all, have issues." I dig deeper, "Are you altruistic? Is there no such thing as a selfless act? When do we do something that is just plain nice, even though it doesn't necessarily help US? Example: Scientists believe that baboons split off from other primates about 15 million years ago. In studying baboons, they found that during the rainy season, when there is lots of grass and plenty of resources, the baboon clan will relax together, bunched-up in a large pile, and grooming each other. But, in the dry season when there are only patches of grass, the dominant males force all the other baboons off, to maintain control of the resource, even though there is plenty of room for the whole clan to still fit in a pile and relax together on the much smaller patches of grass that still exist. Most scientists argue that animals can't be altruistic, and these baboons certainly aren't. When we see animals do something that we perceive as altruistic, we are being anthropomorphic; projecting human emotions and actions onto animals, when really, we all may be simply doing what is best for ourselves. *We* don't even know what *we* think. Sure we are all tetra pods, with 2 eyes, 4 limbs, a brain in our head. . .,"

Loon interjects, ". . . Well, some of US."

I say, "Yet I don't even really know what I am thinking most of the time, let alone what my girlfriend thinks, my brother thinks, the guy down the street, the cat on the balcony, the Chestnut-backed Chickadee in the Wax Myrtle, etc."

Tex stares at me with complete dismay and disarray.

I clarify, "The grass is their turf. Our money is our power. When the shit hits the fan, do people grab their stuff and head for the hills, or work it out together?"

Tex puzzles for a second, "See, this is what I ain't getting from you bile-ologist types. You act like you are the biggest huggers in The World, but when ya git right down to it, it's all science, not love."

Twistor looks at Tex, then mumbles, "We love animals, that's why we are scientific about it."

Then Loon says, "I think you have to love the animals to be caring enough to go through all the science to help them. It's the same as loving flying, or anything else. You can't put all heart into it and no mind. That ends up being what you call a 'zoo', except their main focus tends to be bottom line over even love for the animals."

Twistor agrees. "Yeh, I don't think you can love animals and be pro-zoo at this point."

"Yeah", Loon adds. "They are more like animal prisons than anything else."

"I can see that," Tex says reasonably.

Wow! Tex can see that. That's pretty darn good. I wonder if Deny, or heaven's forbid, Cherry Ballpig, and other hardened HIC nature haters, will ever change their minds.

I finish by pointing out, "A major university did a study to see how closely we are related to baboons. They timed thousands of people using pay phones and found that the average length of a call was 3 minutes (when no one else was waiting to use the phone that is). But, when they timed calls while someone else was waiting to use the phone, the average call time increased to 5 minutes! The person on the phone wanted to control the resource!"

Loon realizes, "Wow! That's not altruistic, kind, or considerate at all."

I look at him and say, "Now, don't quote me on the times, it's that kind of minutia that is fucking shit up. It was something like that." "I don't see what your point is," Tex says as he strains to understand my subtext, fidgeting with the net.

"The point is: Are you a baboon? When someone else makes a mess, do you just clean it up even though you didn't do it? When people start the catty sorority dissing, do you join in so you can belong to the 'clan', or do you stay positive and constructive, even at the risk of weakening your own clan bond? Personally, I love baboons, but I try not to be one. Think about it, and always continue to try to do good things, even if you don't feel like it, or nobody is watching," I preach.

"What are you a goody two-shoes?" Tex asks with distain.

I look straight into Tex's sunglasses, through mine, "Yes I am. I wake up and think to myself about what I can do to make The World a better place today. If my existence is not making The Planet better, then why the hell am I here? I am not here to make things worse. I am here to turn the wheel forward."

"That's profound," Twistor mutters. "I don't consciously think that way, but I think I will." With that, Twistor gets a ring on his gigantic cell phone, which weighs about the same as a brick, and then he mysteriously mumbles, "Oh, ah, I gotta go. Catch you later," and he speeds off on his beach cruiser.

"Yeah, I like that philosophy. I know I get in a lot of fights, but I am doing it for the good," Loon adds.

We shake our heads in unison. Loon knows his methods sometimes serve his ego beyond The Planet.

I say, "This reminds me of another song."

Loon asks, "From that yet to be released rock opera extraordinaire entitled **Rudy the Red Bat** you are always talking about?"

Much to his surprise, I say "No, this was a **Burning Circle** song", then I burst into song:

Hate Race
by Drats

Whites hate blacks because they're dark, Cats hate dogs because they bark
If you examine it closely, The frat rats hate the sowhoritease.

354

Jews hate Moslems cause of gods, Christians call all others frauds
No one knows why the hate's there, Must be ignorance and fear.
Teachers hate the kids they grade, Men hate women that they've
"made"
Poor hate shtinkin wealthy greed, Irrational this hate we breed?
We bubble up all this green gunk, Protect our territorial junk
Base and banal this instinct, No wonder we're almost extinct.
Primal stupid hate-filled goons, Never evolve beyond baboons
Each other and ourselves we hate, Hate and Hate and Hate and
Hate.
We hate for superficial skin, Never knowing what's within
Enemy without a face, The race of hate, the Hate Race.
The race of hate, the Hate Race, Hate Race Hate Race.

I come out of this raging blast like Ozzie channeling Johnny
Rotten with a little Red-tailed Tropicbird thrown in for scream
sake. I take a deep breath and wipe my drool. Loon and Tex, the
two extremists, think *I'm* off the deep end.

Red-tailed Tropicbirds are pretty with their pinkish hue, . . . when
they're not screaming your face off!

I explain, "So by this, if we want to be anthropomorphic, it sounds
like the baboons care about their home, but actually, they may just
be trying to control the resource, to maintain power. Is that why we
list 'caring' about our home as one of our priorities? If our home is
big, and we can keep the feebs out, then we have the comfort, the
status, the power. Could be. But is that caring? I guess one could
argue it's caring about money and power." I receive a nod, and a
blank stare. "Okay, what about Lorenz and the studies of females
in aggressive male societies? Lorenz argues that a normal male of

355

a species would never attack a female. It's only the pathological male that would attack a female of the same species in the animal world. Humans are the exception in that case, which is so bizarre, and I think about how that relates to my brother Rosmarus. Like, in our entire lives he has always weighed at least twice as much as me, and often more, and he is so much huger than me, and he would say to me stuff like, 'not fo nuttin, but you'd make a good lookin girl.' He knows he could easily kill me, abuse me, hit me, beat me up and stuff like that, but he never really really killed me because it's kind of the same thing. Hitting me is like hitting a girl to him. But the thing is, we hear about it all the time, human males beating up girls; weak, pussy-ass bullies who think they are tough and need to show it by smacking around women."

Loon says, "Ah ha, why?"

I state, "Because they can physically dominate, . . . they do. Why do other animals not do that?" I trip over my own tongue because I'm speaking faster than I can think or faster than I can speak. "Why don't animals do that? Because they know better, and we know better. Going all the way back to Shakespeare and the Ancient Greeks and further back than that. We know we are the stronger sex and they are the fairer sex, and we are simply not supposed to beat on girls, period. Our job is to reproduce with them, and protect them."

Loon verifies, "And Lorenz found that to be true?"

I affirm, "Throughout the animal kingdom."

By the way, speaking of mental mind control. As all this occurs, I look across the beach in the distance to see two pale, anorexic looking figures walking, holding hands on the cargo pier. As I snag my bins for a peek, sure enough, it's Renn and Twistor. Walking with them, a few steps back, it's Myhel! Myhel of all people, with both of my roommates.

"Excuse me for a second." I call Renn's cell phone from a discreet distance. This is all I need on top of everything else.

"Hello," Twistor answers.

"Twistor, can you put Renn on?" I say.

"She's climbing on a ladder right now," Twistor answers.

I tense, "Look, what's going on? Are you dating Renn?"

"Yah, I guess you could call it that," Twistor answers, without a hint of understanding.

"I don't know if that's the best move dude," spills from my stupid mouth.

"Well, I don't know. Seems okay right now. I thought she was one of your best friends?" Twistor says slowly with confusion.

The girls yell from just above the water on the ladder. "Who is that? What do they want?"

I try to squeeze it in before it's too late, "And what are you doing with Myhel?"

Twistor answers, "Oh, she's fine. Renn says she's fine. Why have you been acting obsessed about her life?"

"Uuuuurrrrrhhh," I accidentally say loud enough for everyone on the beach to hear. "Dude, what the fuck. You are fuckin shit up."

Oh my god. For a second, I realize, I'm doing the same thing to neophyte Twistor that Zart did to neophyte me when I arrived. It's hard to understand the dynamics until you have been on the atoll for a while.

"Okay, well here's Renn," Twistor says stunned and perplexed, having already probably had too much cum sucked out of him to be able to actually think again like a sharp, focused virgin who doesn't even think about what or who he could be missing.

"No, I'll talk with you later. Don't say anything," I yell to Twistor.

"Say anything about what?" Renn says as she gets the phone.

I hang up quickly, then look at the pier with my binoculars again. Yup. Renn talks with Twistor, then I see her looking over toward the beach to see if she can find me against the ironwoods. I zip back to my room with every intention of getting my act together for tonight, but instead, I lie on my bed again, almost incapacitated by my engrossing thoughts.

Now, I really take a second to look at my whole situation. I have great health, due to my workout regiments, including the running, lifting, biking, swimming, snorkeling, diving, and of course; Ultimate and the Ironwood Parties. I'm getting enough fruit, and protein from veggie burgers and other bean sources we fought Deny for, and have avoided getting sick or picking up any serious diseases from Myhel. I'm doing a great job and really care about my work. I take a deep breath. I can handle everything.

The Ultimate league Kestrel instigated and coached on The North Beach on HAWS. Kestrel (second from right) sprints to the disc, with excellent form, dusting his defender.

Why did Drats call this chapter 'Nobody Cares'? Obviously, Myhel cares about something. I don't know what, but she certainly cares enough about something that she would go through the trouble of lying to try to hurt me.

Back on the phone with Myhel, I say, "I'm just not going to waste my time on a girl who sucks away my happiness, or for that matter, even a friend, a guy, a family member, who sucks, regardless of sex. I remove annoyances and aggravations from my life whenever I can. For them to not be able to see that, well I can see how they would misunderstand and could think I was being totally dramatic."

Chelonia asks me, "What is the worst thing Myhel has done, really?"

I recall, "'Oh he's not lookin fa Mrs. Right, . . . ' Myhel announced one night in a drunken huff at a group of tables pushed together in the middle of the All Hands Club, surrounded by Olderhostile folks and ASS staff. '. . . He's just lookin to get his dick wet,' she puked."

Chelonia says, "God; raunchy."

I say, "The rife hypocrisy in that statement sizzles my pubes. I can see and hear her saying it right now. She is doing it with some construction guy right now who only wants to get his dick wet. Myhel thinks all I want is sex in my life. If that were true, I'd still be doing her. What a fuckin idiot."

Chelonia piles on uncharacteristically, "What a simpleton. You have non-committal, mechanical sex for a while, then break up with her, and all you wanted was sex?"

I say, "No really, I haven't been in 'just-out-for-sex' mode ever. This is where we go all the way back about really understanding each other; really having a cognitive connection. Nobody can ever really study animals in the wild without the animals knowing they are being studied. No one can ever really know you, or me. As stated earlier, *New Reason* from one of the jail scenes in **Rudy the Red Bat**, explains these feelings most coherently. Yet, even when I sing a song or recite a poem, there are always differences in interpretation, depending on the audience, not on me."

I recite a quote to Chelonia over the phone, as I snuggle in bed, imagining her here:

The world is too dangerous to live in - not because of the people who do evil, but because of the people who sit and let it happen. --- *Albert Einstein*

"What the hell was Einstein talking about with 'people letting it happen' and 'can't simultaneously prevent and prepare for war' and all the other brilliant stuff so many of US just didn't get?" I ask.

Chelonia answers, "I think he's saying that ya can't just let heaven (on Earth) happen. There are too many fucked-up people that just have to bring their own hell into everyone else's heaven. Ya know?"

"Timothy McVeigh types," I go on, "Stupid idiots that think they are right and then go on to kill people to prove they are wrong."

Chelonia agrees, "I love rebels and people who stand up for what they believe in, like you do honey bunny, and like Zorro, but to blow up a bunch of kids to get back at the Fed for Waco?"

"How logical is that?" I ask. "And me, I love raving and jumping around and having a good time, but never at anyone else's expense. I don't go around killing animals for fun like some people do. I can't believe how fucked-up that is."

"It's not," Chelonia banters, "it's not logical, but you gotta understand honey, you are one of the logical ones."

"It's stupid. If he wanted to stop government control he should have blown up the friggin Stock Exchange. That's who controls US," I say.

Chelonia doesn't like that comment. I've gone too far cause it sounds like, for a second, I'm condoning bombing, and she is still pretty pro-Capitalist and doesn't see the Stock Exchange as the messed-up, evil, artificial construct that it is.

I recount to Chelonia, "I remember grad school at BU, and first hearing about Waco, then later the Oklahoma City Bombing. Instead of any of the work-study students I supervised thinking about and sympathizing with McVeigh, they all basically just laughed at him for being such a kooky tool as to think that blowing-up a bunch of little kids in Oke City would work somehow and serve his purposes. Twisted. Even gullible and impressionable college freshmen knew what a sick thing that was." Chelonia says, "Why wreck everyone else's heaven? Why wreck those kids' day, as they play in the daycare?" She sounds a little mad.

I agree, "Did McVeigh feel closer to heaven while bombing? Everyday of my life; every action I do; every time I have a relationship or even drive a motorcycle on the freeway, I promise to try my best to make this place on Earth my heaven. If you live that way (to steal a term from organized religion, 'blessed'), one quickly finds that the World is way more brighter and nicer than anyone ever gives it credit for."

Chelonia says negatively, "That's what's wrong with the World. We actually have to fight for heaven. We have to fight for our piece of heaven on Earth."

I concur, "We don't just get it given to us. But hey, if you want a mango, you gotta climb a tree. If you want cranberries, you gotta wade out into the bog. That's just how life goes. You can't have everything handed to you, like Raccoons in Back Bay garbage cans."

"In that way, it's not really heaven if you have to be fighting when you don't want to," Chelonia states.

Then I say, "It's the guys who were the jocks in high school, the big dickhead football players, the town bullies; they were the ones who wanted to stomp down on the brainiacs. They are the gun-toting Republican Christian bullies now."

Chelonia looks to clarify, "These are the violent ultra-religious folks who now make up the extremist right, and are a lot scarier than the extremists on the left."

"Nazis," I say. "Nazis and fascists are sick, scary bastards, and these fanatical born-agains can't see that they're Nazis."

"Well they're not Nazis. That's a little extreme," Chelonia tempers.

360

"What's the difference? Nazis wanted to kill Jews. Now 'Christians', and I use that term loosely, want to kill people who don't support the NRA, and Jews and Moslems and anyone else who won't knuckle-under for Jesus. I don't force my beliefs on people because it doesn't work and I don't have the right to, and most importantly, I think that would step on *their* heaven."

With that, Chelonia gives me a big warm hug and a fat kiss with her plump lips, over the phone. I can feel it. She says, "You are a little radical, but I'm glad we can share heaven together."

We hang up, and my mind races again. Nobody cares. Nobody cares anymore. Nobody cares in the whole World. Really? So far, the 90's have gone pretty well, seeming like more people care now than at any other time. I know it is scary that a scary baboon like George W. could win and take office soon, and it gives me shivers to think what he might do with the 14-Trillion-Dollar rainy-season surplus Clinton developed. I'm sure there's no way he could squander it in as little as four years. Why, that would be blowin like three or four trill a year. Even if he gave the ultra rich huge tax breaks, there's no way he could blow through that kind of dough, unaccounted for. I think the next century is going to be way better than the previous, and we are evolving, not de-evolving like DEVO says. I don't think we will ever really go back to war.

I realize I have been sprawled here for a while, so I jump up and head down to The Galley for dinner. I sit with Dietera and Loon, who are crunching bird data.

"It's New Year's," Dietera and Loon say cheerfully. "Your band ready for the big gig?"

"Yeah. We will be ready," I snort with gusto. Still thinking about the heavier matter, I ask them, "Do you know anything by the LA punk band **FEAR**?" They shake their heads 'no'.

"FEAR wrote, 'I don't care about you, fuck you.' In **InsectAffect**, we performed a period version with flutes in minstrel costumes, singing 'Fla la la la la, la la, la la, la. Thine existence concerneth me not.' The audience howled."

Loon questions, "You still asking if people care?"

I lean in and lower my voice to avoid barbs from the annoyingly insensitive peanut gallery at the adjacent tables. "I feel like I really care. I guess the first question is, 'Do I?', and the second is, 'If I do, how come so many others could give a shit? What are the

361

priorities?' When I read the *Utne Reader* or listen to NPR, it seems as though a lot of people really do care. When I listen to religious fundamentalists or watch Fox News, it seems like the World has turned ugly and nobody cares about anything, except maybe money, but is that caring too?"

Dietera and Loon have no way to respond. I attempt to relate it concretely. "This leads to caring on Halfway. I care so much; but it's the plants, animals and aquatic creatures; not the stupid humans. Am I a misanthrope? I want to love and want to be loved, but can't handle the idiocy, the zombies. I hate zombies," I say with frustration.

Dietera thinks for a second, then proclaims, "But you could look at it in the light of humans are animals, and we are all just the same." She continues, though a few of us look lost, "Do people go to war cause they care, or cause they don't care and they really just want to end it and try their luck at the next level? Is it true that most people are just assholes. How can that be when none or US think of ourselves as assholes?"

Loon jumps in excitedly, "Could be all black. Eternal sleep."

I say, putting on a tough guy voice, "That sounds better than working at a crappy job you hate, coming back to a gross lazy spouse who doesn't do shit, protecting your piece of the pie so no one can fuck with it."

Then Dietera adds, "Heaven, on the other hand, always sounds nice, but can it be? How can one place be so nice for everyone? Do we all suddenly become homogenized in our interests, likes, and pleasures?"

Then Loon says, "For example, what the hell are Romeos going to do in heaven? I guess there will be a bunch of Juliettes up there looking to get enraptured. See the conundrum."

Dietera tries to reiterate and focus. "How can heaven be heaven to everyone in heaven at the same time, every time, all of the time?"

Loon blasts, "I wouldn't want to have day after day of bliss and ecstasy. After about a week or two, I'm sure I'd be ready for some form of despair or agitation."

I agree, "Is it like the karaoke boxes in Harajuku, where each young couple or group of lonely 'nice' girls get their own little room, their own little piece of paradise? My brother Rosmarus is the epitome of not caring. You could say he doesn't even care about himself, if you saw his Saint Nick stomach, but he probably does care enough about himself to feel like he needs to be in control of some aspect of his life, and that he needs to win. This competitive spirit displays itself as not allowing others to talk, winning arguments by speaking louder than anyone else, and assassinating innocent waterfowl for pleasure. I know that sounds harsh, but it's true. It's the psychology of the hunt. When he was a kid learning guitar, his idealist views spewed forward (I sing with a Bob Dylan twang):

'Go to the river and watch the birds die. It'll give yah more than a punch in the eye. Hope someone knows. Hope someone knows. Hope someone knows.'

The song went along, thump, thump thump, thump. He sang it over and over again in a meditative, almost hippie-esque chant. How did so many of the hippies and the Deadheads grow up to be the exact opposite of what they had tried to be. I wonder what made Rosmarus snap? What was the one thing, the one straw that broke the camels back, that made him go from being what could have been a semi-loving hippie folk singer, like his hero Bob Dylan, into a vile, hate-filled ultraconservative? What made Sproc and Manat snap?"

I feel a sudden pain in my chest. I can't talk about my family with anyone. It lays buried so deeply inside me that if I even bring up one of my siblings' names, I could just burst into tears. Instead, I think about the hippies, while all the rest of my lightning-fast thoughts stay concealed within my mind.

"Hippies!" Dietera says between bites and adding-up bird info. "They kind of messed stuff up."

Funny that she says that, because I kind of see her as influenced by hippies and a little bit hippy (in a good way) herself.

I tell Dietera and Loon, "First, long ago, I was programmed to think hippies were bad. 'Where do you hide money from a hippy? Under a bar of soap.' Ha ha ha. That was my 1970 introduction to the hippy movement. They were dirty, lazy druggies, who needed to get a haircut and a job. I knew nothing of anything political about them, and the media certainly portrayed them as bad for American." I go on, "As I got to be a high school grad, I started learning all kinds of things about the hippy movement: How they protested a wicked stupid, fucked up war in Nam; how John

363

Lennon in '69, and myriad others said that the hippies will be the leaders some day and they can't make the same mistakes as the WWII-white male establishment; and how they subverted the dominant paradigm and tried to equalize society."

Loon and Dietera finish their logs and close up their science materials, then plow into their food. I'm done eating, so I keep talking while their mouths are full. I would probably keep talking, either way. "What the hell happened? Vietnamese people love basketball, English, and US now, but most Americans you talk to not only have neg shit against Vietnamese, but they hate hippies too."

Loon says, "But those are mainly wackos, right?"

Dietera and I both shake our heads in the negatory.

I say, "I'm not just talking about Arizona types who hate and are afraid of anyone or anything. You know these guys. They have guns and will shoot anything they 'think' is Un-American; which happens to be very Un-American in itself, by the way."

Dietera say, "But the hippies were American. It was one of the most originally American movements in history and impacted The World."

I say, "Exactly, so is it pro or anti American to be a hippy; to hate hippies?"

Loon chomps a mouthful of over-cooked, limp vegetables, and says, "Depends who you ask."

I respond, "I think I am way more patriotic than anyone I have met, but I would not join the military."

"Hmmm," Dietera hums with a mouth full of greasy spaghetti.

Loon spits, "Where does blind jingoism come into all of this?"

Dietera asks clinically, "Is there a definition?"

I go on with my story, "Funny thing, once I turned about 30, suddenly everyone started maligning, instead of respecting, hippies again, like the movement was bad."

Dietera answers with a laugh, "The early hippy movement, which was cool and revolutionary, died, as most movements do, only to be carried on by self-centered hangers-on who have lost the vision but just want to follow the crowd: Like Deadheads. Same thing happened with the punks a decade later. My main concern is that they can't raise kids - few of them turn out right. And this new breed sometimes smells so much like urine that they give the entire movement a bad image."

I get mad, "I smell sometimes. I try to take only 4 showers a week, unless I absolutely need more. I wash or condition my hair every other week, maybe that's why I'm not as bald as my brothers, though others would argue it's my lack of testosterone."

Loon wipes his mouth with a napkin, then says, "I know people who hate hippies for some of those superficial reasons, but really, the thing that kills thinkers, is your previous exasperation; 'What Happened?' Was everyone co-opted, manipulated, tricked by shiny material things? Shouldn't the hippies be in power right now straightening shit out? That's why hippies suck now. They were supposed to assure that 'War Is Over!' Personally, I would love to see relatively clean (but conscious about chemicals and bleach), hard-working hippies, take over and make the World a better place, using 60% of the military industrial complex to insulate homes, build wind and solar power stations, and high-speed hydrogen powered bullet trains; and keeping 40% of the military to defend."

I applaud, "That would be killer."

Then Dietera, also finishing her meal, if you could call it that, puzzles, "But since the hippies are apparently gone, then all I can be is mad at them. Have they just transformed? What's the excuse?"

I think for a second, of history, "The WWII guys are practically all dead, and everyone like Tom Hanks keeps spouting off about how great they were. The Korea guys are all retired, so they can't be pulling too many more strings. The Nam guys, like Senator 'McLaim', are in power now. That should mean that the hippies are ripe."

Dietera asks, "Why didn't George W. fight in Nam? He seems to be pretty pro fight, I guess as long as it's not him, the son of the first Bush, gettin killed."

We all sit for a second, sifting through and trying to find our answers.

I say with frustration and anger, "So where the hell are all the hippies and why aren't they driving public policy now? Did drugs fuck them all up, like Bob Dylan? 4 out of my 5 siblings got fucked-up on drugs. One is still a chronic Bud drinker and smoker. One probably did too much acid. One got into crack before they called it that. The other one said he was an alchy, but I don't know cause I don't think I ever saw him drink in my life. My younger sibling needs no drugs; he is already an emotional basket-case and hasn't drank for years, due to his lash outs and thrash outs."

Just as I finish, I look up to notice that Stark Kristian is back on atoll. He slowly passes our table, keeping a winced eye on me as Dutroeix says something in his ear, and Deny and Cherry Ballpig follow right behind, like fat evil alter boys. I look at Kristian and he smirks like a chimp and heads off to another table.

Dietera says, "I still don't get how some people end up completely screwed up on drugs while they have practically no impact on others. It must be a brain chemistry thing."

I say, "Okay now, hold on one second here. My Dad died from booze. My Mom is a religious fanatic."

Loon says, "So, you can't blame the kids, right?"

I snap back, "Bull fuckin shit. I didn't become an alchy, druggy, or worst of all, born-again shithead, so what the fuck is my excuse? And if I don't have an excuse, then, where the fuck are the fuckin hippies? Okay, I can't light a fire under my family; they hate me anyway. When, when are the hippies going to take over and straighten shit out?"

Dietera looks at us, depressed, and says, "Many will argue that they are in power now and they are not doing any better. You know, *Meet the new boss. Same as the old boss.*"

I say with doubt, bastardizing the names for a laugh, "Really? Bush, 'Cheatney', 'Rumpsfeld', 'Ashholecroft', all the guys that will be running Our country . . . former hippies?"

Loon adds, "With former FBI director daddy looking over his anemic son's withered shoulder?"

I almost yell, "How soon is now mother fuckers? Where is the separation of church and state and when are the poor Republicans going to learn that the rich Republicans need their votes, and that's how they became the guns and god party. Who are the easiest people to program?"

Dietera says, "Gun nuts and churchies."

I say in a southern accent, "Vote Republican or the Dems will take your guns away and take god out of our schools."

Dietera laughs, "Perfect. How can you lose? Any sucka would fall for that shit."

I say, "My mother, extremely Catholic, would vote for an adulterer over a black man. Hmmm, seventh commandment vs. a black dude. Hmmmm. If I try to ask her anything deep about the family, she'll give some platitudinal answer like, 'Well, that's what god wanted'."

Here's a new song Drats just wrote epitomizing that situation with my Mom:

Don't Go Looking for Trouble
by Drats

A crazy lady, once said I was crazy,
But she had turned into mega lazy
She wakes in front of the tube mass each day,
She'll make it if she continues to pray
She said, Don't go looking for trouble,
Don't go looking for trouble
But when I Don't go looking for trouble,
My troubles, they become Double
She said I was a stupid fool,
Because I spent my time in school
I shouldn't try to communicate,
Because our family is full of hate
She said, Don't go looking for trouble,
Don't go looking for trouble
But when I Don't go looking for trouble,
My troubles, they become Double
I tried to listen and ignore,
The things she said I would abhor
Don't ask questions, just pray;
And everything will be a-okay
She said, Don't go looking for trouble,
Don't go looking for trouble
But when I Don't go looking for trouble,
My troubles, they become Double
Has that method been working for you?
It's quite obvious that you are screwed
Your kids don't call you for a freakin year,
Yeah just keep praying, have no fear

Loon breaks me from my daydream, "I guess I can see why you care that no one cares, cause if they don't care, then life, and many species other than US, will suffer."

Dietera ponders, "Does anyone ever find true love and happiness?"

I remember, "Did you know a recent study shows that 80% of people who hit the lottery jackpot were less happy than they were when they were poor or normal, like US?"

Dietera responds, "What a fucked up thing money is."

I think again, "What about Robert Smith from **The Cure**? He was always singing *Just like Heaven* and *Love Song*, and other heavily romantic bits. Did he ever find peace and love, happiness? How do you cope with being a huge international sensation, only to find later you're not recognized on the street? Is it better to never have made it than suffer the precipice of stardom?"

Loon says, "Those are great songs, I'll give him that."

I say, "All I can come back to is me; to what I know. I know I want to be in love and find that highly romantic soul mate. It's got to be my Italiano half."

Dietera says, "It seems like you are mixing 'caring' into a lot of differing topics."

She's right. I realize, like the fire hose, I am overwhelming myself. "All I know is that I care. I said nobody cares. But I care. I care. I fucking care and I give 100%. I might have been the smallest, weakest kid on my high school football team, but I gave 100% every day I was out there. How can nobody care if I do? Somebody else must care."

Dietera looks at me for a second. "Kestrel, from what I've seen, you've always been a great guy, and guys who aren't great guys hate guys who are great guys. You are used to being at UCLA and BU. Now you have to deal with these 'real guys' in the 'real world' and it isn't easy."

I think about the battles with the HIC staff, and with my family. "Why do I feel compelled to standup for the underdogs? Why don't I just let them say all that god stuff to me? Why? Because it hurts me that's why. Because it disturbs me. They don't need that shit. But maybe I'm wrong. Maybe they do. I just care too much and love them too much to take it. Like I said, no one's gonna force their shit on me! I'm so conflicted."

368

They look at me with surprise for bursting onto the obsessively out-of-control sibling topic.

"I can give an example that people care," Loon illuminates. "The only way we can ever have fair elections is if we can eliminate money from them."

Dietera says, "It's impossible to eliminate money with the way the system is. It's designed this way on purpose so only rich people and people of that kind of upper-class wealth can be president and control power so they can protect business and money being made, and rich staying in control."

Loon says, "Yes, so what if we have the State Dept. distribute Presidential Exams, like Kestrel suggested before?"

"Yes." I get excited. "Anyone who passes this extremely difficult, on line exam on a secured site, gets background checked, then invited to Washington DC to compete against the other highest scorers. They are then vetted by the Supreme Court, Congress and the Executive Branch, and then go through a final battery of eliminating tests. Broken into 4 quarters, these final verbal, oral, written, and situational tests would deal with 25% Psychological Profile (assuring that the President will be psychologically stable), 25% Presidential Functions (assuring the President will be adept at handling all aspects of the presidency, including leadership qualities, grace under pressure, etc.), 25% Foreign and Domestic Policy (assuring that the President has deep policy knowledge and understanding), and finally, 25% Ethics (just incase he's another Hitler in Raygun's clothing.)" I spout.

Dietera says, "But no one is talking about anything like this right now."

"I know, but we can start a dialogue." I say optimistically.

Loon says, "Fill him in on the details."

I go on, "As previously stated, the beauty of these tests is that the President will be narrowed down to like the top *10* candidates. These 5 or 10 finalists will run for president, unaffiliated with any party, and will systematically be the best possible choices to lead the country."

Loon jumps in, "As a matter of fact, how about the President can't be a member of any recognized political power?"

"Yah!" I yell, though I hadn't thought deeply about that one yet. "Each of these 10 candidates get 1 hour on national television, 1

369

hour on public television and radio, 1 full page nationally syndicated newspaper ad, and 1 nationally televised debate; for free. That's it! No commercials allowed. Everyone is fair. Everyone gets equal time, equal press. There will also be an official government website with info on each candidate, paid for with tax dollars, with all statements verified."

"Nice dream. No negative campaign adds, and no manipulative and annoying commercials filled with lies," Dietera smiles. She likes the idea; she just thinks I'm crazier than Loon.

I continue undaunted, "On Election Day, we will have 10 capable candidates, and not a single bought-out politician to choose from, and the dispersion of votes will decentralize the parties and we will see a diversity of votes."

"The question is, can we keep the corruption out?" Loon asks.

I think again, "We all generally have a constructive side and a destructive side. It's the smart ones of US that control those sides."

"Maybe intelligence doesn't come into it," Dietera theorizes.

"Maybe they are just in control of their brain. The creative ones, as opposed to the destructive ones, who always stick to the destructive side of life, stay with tobacco smoking, gambling, and tend to have constrained viewpoints; they might be smart, but they just lack impulse control."

"As opposed to the creative, constructive, positive thinking unconstrained imaginative talents," I state. "I've been to Vegas. The losers just keep trying to get lucky while they kill themselves tryin." I state.

During this entire time, I have been noticing a run of mixed groups of folks, streaming in.

"Ya know, passive aggressive, obsessive compulsive, addictive and vengeful, etc. These are the same people that tend to believe in aliens, ghosts, Jesus, god or gods and guns, witches, ya know, supernatural stuff too," I answer frankly at rapid-fire pace.

Han, finding confidence in his voice, says, "They believe these things because this is what they minds teaches them."

"Some people need something to hold onto to keep their life together," I say uncharacteristically sympathetic.

"Or what?" Han challenges. "Or they will become completely out of control, Mr. Kestrel? I am Tamil, but I believe in Jesus Christ as

370

my lord and savior. But I will live survive with or not with my god either way. I will live."

Dietera says, "It is just like when the British were pushed out of India. It is like today, how the conservatives do not like vegans because it threatens the dominant paradigm in which they maintain their power via the existing structure."

I agree, "Like think of it this way. COW BOYS! Cowboys are defined by cows. Those boys are not war boys or business boys, they are cow boys; all about cows."

"Like this guy Tex the pilot," Loon says with a laugh directed toward Tex at the other table.

"Co-pilot!" Tex corrects, letting himself in on the joke and showing some sense of humor finally. Like Loon had stated at their first meeting, not all guys from Texas are bad.

"He thinks he's a cowboy. He has cowboy mentality. Yet, he grew up in an urban sprawl where he has never been on a ranch, nor does he know anything about cows," Loon says.

Dietera asks over to Tex, "You grew up in Houston or something like that right?"

Tex nods. He has nothing to feel ashamed of, but I can tell he would like it a lot better if it were 10 of him against the 3 of US.

I drive my main point home, "On top of that, these boys are defined by cows, an animal that most of US don't have much respect for. We think they are kind of stupid. They do not stand as proud symbols of the American West, like the bison do. If there weren't cowboys, and if there was no meat industry and no one ever ate beef, then there wouldn't have been cowboys. If there were no cowboys, then first, no one would have shot all the buffalo and cleared the land of natives to graze European cattle to put steak on someone's plate. There wouldn't have been cowboys and Indians; Cowboys expanding their gigantic ranching claims into redskin territory," I say with authority.

Obviously, Han had been studying so he could debate with Dietera and the other heavy philosophers on the atoll. He still fights his own internal battle about Christianity, and he is struggling with English at the same time. He's doing a great job.

"It wasn't that clear of a plan," Tex defends. "We are gonna wipeout the buffaloes, then drive out the Indians, then bring in the cows. And we are going to raise these animals and make them eat grass, then breed and slaughter them, so we can start the whole thing all over again? Ridiculous."

"I agree." I say, "I'm not saying that whole thing was contrived and planned from the beginning to be a big energy expensive thing in the end. If cattle had never happened, or let's say all humans were vegan, how would that have affected the taking of The Great Plains, Texas and Oklahoma?" Everyone looks at each other for a response to my question.

Loon says, "How would it have affected the way the settlers and Native Americans interacted, in the 17 and 1800s?"

Tex says, "Land owners have the biggest stake in everythin, cause they own the land. It's theirs."

"See, that privilege idea is exactly what I am talking about. Why do people own land?" I pose. "A lot of Native Americans believed owning the land was like owning the air and sky and sun."

"Why don't they own air, or water, or people? You can own a dog, but you can't own a person, . . ." Dietera considers.

". . . nor can you stake claim to the air. In our first stab at democracy, we said that only landowners could vote. Should that be the way it is now?" I say.

"You got a better idea?" Tex asks.

"What?" I exclaim. "First of all, I would change the whole voting system. I would make it so you can vote for three different candidates, or more, in preferential order."

Tex starts getting pissed, "What the hell are you talkin about? That sounds Commie."

Loon snaps, "That's the problem with you redneck guys. You are all talk talk talk, and shoot shoot and no listen, and the shit you say is stupid."

That comment totally cracks me up, because Tex has probably been the least verbose of all of us, or is in a tie with Dietera. Loon and I are the ones who spout off.

I take a breath, then softly, calmly add, "What I'm sayin is take this recent election. If my system were in place, I would vote for Nader first, then Gore. That way they know who I voted for in order, and they can count votes without having to pull off a corrupt run-off."

"Where will Bush fall on your list?" Tex drawls.

"See, that's the beauty of this system. I won't put Bush as third because he is a totally unacceptable candidate to me," I explain. "By voting Nader and Gore, I am showing that I want a Green or different party in office, and then I will accept Gore if we are going to be stuck with the Dems again, but Bush is absolutely not an option. If he was, I would vote for him in my third slot, but he is not."

As I hear myself speak, and everything else going on around me, I try to calm myself internally. My instincts tell me that Bush could never get in in a million years, and if he did, it would be very bad. Very, very bad. Maybe, worse than any president we have ever had. Yet, congress won't let him just run amok right? And the people, We The People; what about US? I think after Nam and Watergate and Iran/Contra, Americans are just too smart to let a guy like Bush get in and ruin our country by getting US into un-necessary wars for the good of his Texas cronies. I have to have faith that we are smart enough to avoid devastation, and that though he appears to be a puppet for the neo-cons, that there are too many checks and balances in the way to let just one person lead US down the path to war again.

"You sure got some weird ideas there," Tex announces.

"You can't see it? You can't see it working?" Loon begs.

Tex gives out a long "Nawh."

I say, "Well I may have weird ideas, but many people have no ideas. Some don't think for themselves. It's like their brains remain slaves to anything they're fed, unless of course, it's weird. Think for yourself! Don't let Fox News and Hollywood movies think for you. The PBS News Hour doesn't ever tell viewers how to think; they just give you the straight facts and people have to be smart enough to figure out what to think."

Dietera says, "Recent studies here and abroad determined that many Americans are too lazy to think that hard. We live soft lives; generally too well-off and therefore, too complacent."

Then Loon adds, "I think that if most people stop for a minute and think for themselves, they will realize we are all in this together and need to care and work as a team, or it's all over."

I say, "It reminds me of what Charles Sumner said:
- *No true and permanent Fame can be founded except in labors which promote the happiness of mankind.*

We do it for The World. We do it for the good of everything else *and mankind*, and despite mankind, not for ourselves. He didn't have the vocabulary really to be any less Homocentric, but if he did, he would have said '... *labors which promote the flourishing of nature*', or something like that."

Tex barks, "Who the hell was that?"

"I don't know," I admit, "but I think he was a governor or a mayor and they named a tunnel after him under Boston Harbor."

Everyone, especially Tex, sit at the table in a long silence; waiting, ruminating on the discussion, the heavy ideals, the mores and hopes expressed; profoundly moved. Tex wants to make a harsh comment about Massachusetts liberals again, but he abstains.

I come to a conclusion.

Each group of words erupts from my lips with a twist, then long pauses of contemplation,

"Good.

People care.

Good people care.

Good people, care."

As the winter weather wanes on the atoll, both albatross species have chicks on their nests. Discarded eggs sit about sparsely, building up fuming, putrid gasses in the heat of the baking sun, ready to blow. A year or so ago, I threw one of these gaseous time-bombs at Zart, ya know, as a joke, and he was never able to get the shtank out of his boot. Though Zart is a great guy, and generous to a fault, he never really forgave me for that transgression. I warn the tourists about the imminent threat, and tell them that even the slightest jostle with a toe can lead to a ruined pair of shoes. The pressure builds, not only in the eggs, but in my head.

Gandhi gave his grandson this list of …

The Seven Blunders of The World

Wealth without work
Pleasure without conscience
Knowledge without character
Commerce without morality
Science without humanity
Worship without sacrifice
Politics without principle

I struggle to think of a current politician in America who lives as a testament to, not a representative of, Gandhi's list. I live by all of these, with maybe the exception of *Worship without sacrifice*. I worship nature I guess, but it's not really worship. E.O. Wilson, in **The Ants**, basically states that it's the ants' cooperation that assures their survival. Ants have wars, really battles, but no nationalism. Are ants better than US? They never would have made it into space without US and the help of our super-duper space shuttles, but they have survived on Earth way longer than we will. They're still better. Certainly less selfish. Do ant colonies blunder? They certainly sacrifice, and are worth our appreciation and awe, if not our worship.

According to Lorenz, in reference to ducks, 'Heinroth found that the males could agree in a communal enclosure if all the females were removed.' No fuckin shit! I have been so blind the entire time I've lived out here. I thought people were like me, like US; ya know, good guys. I thought the pent-up, body-building construction workers, juiced-out on Creatine, steroids, and whatever, who weren't getting their dicks wet at all, and hated know-it-all ranger-types and college grads, and thin – good looking dudes who are smooth with the ladies; I thought they thought of me as just one of them, and that we all took each other at face value. NO. NO, NO, NO! I am wrong. Just like The Cable Company guys found out long ago.

Back at the turn of The Industrial Revolution century into the Technology century, around 1900 A.D., the first Trans-Pacific Communications Cable stretched across the bottom of the sea and through Halfway Atoll. The Cable Company built a compound near the North Beach, and the commandant brought his wife to Sand Island. According to the reports I crammed during my first days on the atoll, I clearly remember reading that the captain said, 'There was only room for one woman on Halfway, and that the addition of a second woman would soon lead to chaos.' The paradisiacal heaven of Halfway's bright coral sand beaches and blue lagoon quickly became atoll nightmare-from-hell when multiple women vying for attention abound.

Now, we are not ducks. C'mon, ducks are lame. I mean, look at them. They fly around with their fat little bodies, they got these doofy-lookin bills, the drakes put on these gaudy colors to show-off to hens, and no matter how you cook em they can't be any good to eat, right? Especially with lead in them.

I take all of that back about ducks. They are great, and WE can only wish to be half as marvelous as them in many respects. We are like them. They are tetra-pods, with modified arms that act as wings. They have warm, oxygen-rich blood flowing through their veins, up to their brains and into their large, complex pair of eyes, just like US. They risk their lives for their offspring, show magnificent colors and diversity, take-off in splendid migrations, and can be the most delicious of the goose, turkey, chicken, quail, grouse options; for fowlivores, especially for those who enjoy succulent fat.

Kestrel sneaks up and snags three weak pintails in a fishing net. The water catchment by the runway convinces lost ducks that Halfway is worth hanging around. It's not! They starve. Kestrel enlists Twistor to help him force-feed these birds in his kitchen to get them hearty enough to migrate back to a continent.

Not only was I the only drake getting laid on the atoll, but also, I was like completely controlling the resource and didn't even know that no other drakes had any shots at any other hens. I mean, anyone could have Kilgro any instant they wanted, and to a lesser extent, Jellie, but I get the feeling that the vast majority of the time, Kilgro couldn't even hook-up (unless it was with a FN, who would take any chance to experience any white woman they can because not only are there no white women where they come from, but caste, class, and the like make it literally a one-in-a-million shot for these guys. So they will take it, even with Kilgro, just so they can know that they did it, in their lifetime, if nothing else. Hey, look at me. I hooked-up with Myhel! There's no reason some of the FNs wouldn't hookup with Kilgro). Jellie just simply chooses not to hook-up. Though unattractive, she wants a guy and really liked Zart, but has enough pride and intelligence to assure she is not another Kilgro. I think in both of their cases, but much more so in Jellie's case, they are very sad, lonely people, who just wish they could have half of what Myhel and I had, and an eighth of what I had with Hamed or Hiromi. They want a man as bad as I want my ultimate girl. I understand. I think Jellie would definitely have gone out with Zart, but he had absolutely no interest in her in anyway. Once I got to know her, I understood completely.

All I've been tying up, figuratively, was Myhel, which, I guess in retrospect, was the only hen any other drake could really hook-up with. Not only did I occupy Myhel, but I also managed to have sex with most of the other available hens to come on atoll. So, in essence, I cock-blocked (dominated) the entire resource from the other fowl because I kind of screwed up Myhel for any other drake too, since she spent mainly most of her time with me, grieving over losing me, or planning revenge on me by having my wings clipped and my feathers oiled. I thought it was good to see that Myhel really was getting over me, until the whole bogus threat thing came up. Again, though I would rather focus on the other 2 million species on The Planet, like Dietera does, I am stuck in this homocentric conundrum of consternation.

I think back to yesterday, when one of Myhel's little tools, Misa Queen, waddled up to me outside the Bowling Alley. A totally useless piece of post-Jr. High racetrack trash, she clears her voice to get my attention or something stupid like that, and says, "Guess you're feelin bad now that Myhel has moved on and you blew it."

"What do you want?" I ask with a straight face.

"You know she has been having sex with. . ."

I cut her off before she can say the name. "You are a sick little person, aren't you? Please don't talk to me. That's not a threat in any way mind you. I'm just saying, don't talk to me." I try to cover my bases, but realize this statement too can also be twisted into a threat. Who cares? I am fuckin out-of-here anyways.

So that is the problem right? Men can get along fine, as long as there are no women around. We do crazy stuff when women are around. Crazy! We will kill for our women. The last thing I could give a fuck about right now is who vindictive Myhel sleeps with now. As long as she is off my back, I am happy as a clam.

Am I deluding myself about this whole Chelonia situation? I think about how I thought Myhel was; and now how I know Myhel is. Many women are programmed to be whores. Chelonia knows I have a Master's Degree and that I have the potential to make a little bit of money, but she would be stupid to be in it for that. And me? I want to have sex with her because she has a nice body and seems like a nice person, and I am pretty sure that will make me feel good. So her and I are the same in the sense that we both want to feel good. I know that, and yet, I am falling in Love with her so hard. Do I delude myself a lot? How does one know? Drats chose to write this novel from my perspective. What if he writes a series? How about **HN3H Part 2**, from Kilgro's point of view? That would be wild! How would Kilgro's versions of events go? Would I all-of-a-sudden be a bad guy?

I snap from my digression. Obviously, this 'female situation' for men is not only a *Homo* problem. One of the main problems with monk seal recovery is this mobbing behavior by aggressive males ganging-up on and sometimes killing the cow. These bulls don't do it on purpose; they just compete against each other to reproduce. Sound familiar? 'Yuh can't blame dose frat boys at Alphi Phi Oshmegma, or dose Marines in Okinawa, or doze football playahs at da cheerleadin pahty. Boyz will be boyz.' I shudder in my thoughts.

With only 1200 Hawaiian Monk Seals left on the entire globe, every pup counts. In the beginning, we caught a lot of flack from the Navy chiefs and the HIC staff for closing the south and west beaches, yet, our research conclusions show that over the last 25 years or so, we have had an average of 6 pups born on the atoll annually, with 7 being the record. However, though it has been impossible to tell, the pup mortality rate seems pretty high, based on the number of carcasses found, the number of total adults versus sub-adults in the area, and a myriad of other factors too complex to be entertained here. You should go on line and read the papers on Hawaiian Monk Seals if you want all the complex and most up-to-date info. Maybe you can donate some money to The Monk Seal Program as well. Anyway, I am proud to report that we had 7 pups last year, tying the record; and *14* pups this year, blowing the record away! Put that in your beef burger bun and scarf it, Deny! According to him, we didn't know what we were doing when we closed those beaches, and now we have doubled the pup pop. Instead of rubbing it in his face the way he deserves, I develop and host a special Hawaiian Monk Seal program at The Station Theater, and the entire atoll comes out for it with music, roti and lumpia, maps, posters, signs, stickers, and other fun materials, and of course, as always on Halfway, lots of drinking. You would think alcohol was free or something around here. I even had a game where contestants needed to guess where 100 feet was from the monk seal cutout. Most of the contestants, even the drunkest ones,

were all within 5 feet of 100 feet, but nobody was over. I was
amazed at how consistent they were even when I moved the cutout
a number of times to make for trickier angles. Above the stage, a
big number *14* hangs artfully on an old, ripped, sail, which I had
the kids paint. When Deny ever came in with Dutroeux and Cherry
Ballpig, and with Misa Queen and Chipweldi in tow, and craned
his head up to look at the number, I thought I was going to pee my
tight government issue short shorts.

"Congratulations!" I say with a loud, genuine voice full of pride.
After all, this is what I live for. This is not about me. This is not
about Deny having egg on his face. This is not about HAWS or the
APS in competition. This is about the seals. About the seals!
Because of US, they are doing great!

"What's the 14 foh?" Deny belches.

I spin around to the crowd after I finish firmly shaking Deny,
Dutruoex, and even Cherry Ballpig's filthy Cabbage-patch hands. I
shook them like a man. Like a man shakes hands. Like a real man.
A "guy". They didn't like that one bit! I could see emasculation on
their faces. Ballpig choked a little on his cigar. Misa Queen and
Chipweldi look at each other in astonishment.

"Ladies and Gentlemen, and anything else that happens to be
about," I bawl and yowl like a ringmaster.

"He, heeh, heh," Chipweldi let's out an uncontrollable chuckle.
Finally, some Agit Prop. Something right up his alley. Everybody
looks basically in shock at this moment.

"A toast ladies and gentlemen. A toast to ourselves and our good
work on this Earth!" I belt beyond human volume. "Fourteen monk
seal pups born this year! More than double any other year on
record, and that's with tourism, a fully operational airstrip,
restoration and research occurring; and not to mention, killer
recreation!"

I see Amb stand behind me near the steps to the stage. He bristles
with pride. Now he remembers what an asset, not ass, I am. I
cheer, "Halfway Rocks!"

"YEAHHHH!!!!!" The crowd responds and salutes.

I yell, "Halfway Rolls!"

"YEAHHHH!!!!!" The throng bounces forward as they pound their
drinks.

"Halfway RULES!" I scream with all of my power.

"**YYEEAAHHHHHH!!!!!!!**" The crowd goes completely nuts as the band breaks into *Boys Don't Cry* and I jump up onto the stage and throw on a wacky shirt made of grass and leaves and fronds. I jump around like Leona Helmsley with leeches in her leotard.

I look out to see the three HIC staff and two HAWS staff still standing in the doorway with their jaws dropped. The signs say 'Good Job HIC' and 'Way to protect the seals!', and the Olderhostile folks congratulate them and shake their hands. They fought me the whole way, tooth and nail, and now they are being honored for all the hard work done by me! What a fuckin great person I am. I did learn something in my propaganda class, didn't I? It's big, it's huge, but it's subtle still. So subtle. I'm singing a song, right in their faces, telling them not to cry, but the facts are the facts! The seals are doing great with the beaches closed, and all the naysayers can do is stand in the theater in utter shock. They try to play it off like they have had something to do with the success, and it seems to build their morale and spirit a little.

It's good to be good sometimes and feel good about being good. ---
Drats

Duetrouex approaches me during the guitar solo as I stand over to the side and wipe some sweat from my brow with a hanky. He can't let this indignation stand, but at the same time, he would lose mega-face if he shows any distain, so he says, "Ya know, this is all well and good, but I fought in Phantom Fighter Jets in Vietnam and our boys risked our lives over there, and that's serious, that's real."

I look at him and strain to get each word over the raucous celebration. He is calling this ridiculous construct of expensive fighter planes going up to shoot down other guys' multi-million-dollar fighter planes *real*, and Hawaiian Monk Seals, a species that has been on Earth for millions of years, and may be the oldest seal of all, stretching back even close to the age of the dinosaurs, *unreal*.

Duetreuox continues, "Ya come around here and protect all these animals and protect all these plants and be nice to all these animals, ya know, it's nice and everything, but, it ain't really doin shit sept a wastin taxpayers' money."

381

I look at him with a little surprise. Believe it or not, I'm actually surprised at this point, that he, the leader of HIC on Halfway, and our cooperator, could be so far from the same page as US. How can I get through to a guy like this when we don't share the simplest basic philosophy?

I say to him, but realize as soon as it comes out, that it sounds as preachy as the stuff I can't listen to from my brothers, "*In nature, is the preservation of The World.*"

He looks at me for a second, thinking, and then Dutreoux says, "That a Bible verse?"

I respond, "No, most of the time I avoid quoting hypocritical religious texts. It's from Henry David Thoreau."

Dutrouix scoffs, "Oohh, Henry David Thoreau," he repeats as if he were saying Benedict Arnold or some other traitor to America. He thinks Thoreau is some left wing, Ivy-league, ivory-tower bunny-hugger pacifist. He says quickly, "Ya know, that's a bunch of malarkey and I don't buy into that whole lovin of nature stuff."

I have to sing soon, so instead of formulating my usually well-thought-out rebuttal, I simply say, "What do you believe in?"

Dutriuox responds with, "I . . . I believe in America!"

I look at him and laugh, "So do I. It's the same thing. Every culture in the world, even ours, recognizes the importance of the natural environment. That's why we have refuges and parks. You don't like Thoreau, how about this one: *Keep a green tree in your heart and perhaps a song bird will come.*"

"D'oh!" Dutreuox quips, "Who the hell is that from, a Sixties hippy?"

I stutter back, "It's Chinese, it's an old Chinese thing like a thousand years old."

Dutreuix quickly dismisses, "Oh the Chinks."

And I yell, "See!? Anything! Anybody from anywhere, you hate. What's the point of even talking with you? What do you believe in, America, without Chinese Food?"

He yells back, "I believe in America, love it or leave it."

I say, "Okay then, there's where we disagree." Dutreuiox gives me the 'Whud djoo talkin' bout?' look, so I say, "I think that's a copout, I think that's bullshit, I think that's Nazi talk. To me, the saying goes 'America, love it, or make it better!' You don't leave it and run away. You make it a better place. And that's what I'm doing. I'm making it better. I'm making Halfway way better than from me not having been here," I finish awkwardly, flush with emotion.

Deny yells over, having picked up the last part of the conversation, "Ya, better for da girls, right?" mocking my sexual "success".

I grab the mic. to make sure it is off, then yell back, "Okay, conversation is over if you are going to start getting personal with me. It's unfortunate that you have such a narrow scope." I jump back into front man mode and sing the rest of the song with more fury and gusto.

After the song ends, I sit on the lip of the stage for a second to catch my breath and have a drink. A visitor approaches me and starts asking questions about the seals. A small group gathers and it turns into an informal interpretive moment; the best kind.

Impressed by my seemingly know-it-all answers, an old tourist throws me a curve ball by asking me what I think about the Israeli - Palestinian conflict.

I'm not in uniform, so I say, "Look, that thing has been goin on for friggin years, tit for tat, and it doesn't look like it's ever going to end and it's a very homocentric battle between two small groups of humans over very specific religious text disputes and has nothing to do with wildlife. I focus on animals, not cows and horses and your cats and dogs and pigs: OUR Animals! All of our animals, . . . is what I'm talking about. I say, 'When the African elephants go extinct, that's not some dude's elephant in Botswana. That's our freakin elephant. That's our elephant and it is gone and we let it go!'" I say with frothing fury as my eyes well up and I almost let a drop escape down the front of my emboldened cheek.

I know that this display of emotion might come to a shock to some of you by this late stage in the book. I hope Drats hasn't let my scientificness misrepresent my passion and love for this wild World.

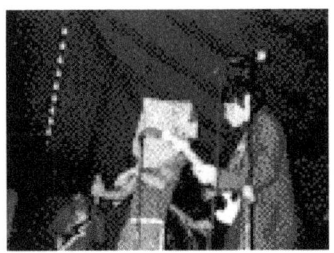

*As a singer, sometimes Kestrel let his head swell; like in this scene from **InsectAffect** in LA in the 80s.*

I say, "It's hard to articulately express exactly how I feel about our plants and animals, and yet, I have a Master's in it and that's my job. It must be so much harder for everyone else."

On my tours I have been using some anthropomorphism to assure that the laypersons on the trip at least understand what I am getting at. I learned from the HIC staff and the FNs that if I did not frame my statements into a context they could grasp, with big, broad, simple strokes, my presentations would blast right overhead. For example, when folks ask about the riotous gooney dances and can't comprehend the basic animal behavior involved, I would state something like, 'When the male arrives and struts his dance, it's like a person showing up to an expensive nightclub with gold chains and a Ferrari.'

"Ohhhhhhhh," all the tourists would laugh knowingly, as the kids would tug at their parents' shirts to extract an unwilling explanation. I describe the albatross chick mortality rate as the 'fly or die plan.' This makes it clear to the visitors. 'Nature is a struggle. You need to learn how to fly, or you will die. Period. Struggle is natural.' I then equate it too human struggles, so it relates.

During this session near the end of the seal party, Amb hears me say ' . . . we can't project complicated human emotions and super-ego driven behavior onto animals with only ids . . .'

Amb looks at me later, as I am organizing some maps in my office, and says, "Well, I would disagree with what you said about animal behavior. I had a black lab that knew what I was thinking and could really think,' he states firmly.

"Dogs don't really *FEEL* all the things we project onto them. Everybody who has a deep connection with their dog or cat or horse believes that and wants to believe that. It makes it easier for US to relate to, and understand, and love our animals. I understand that," I retort, scientifically paraphrasing Lorenz. "It makes complete sense that humans would understand animals as they understand themselves. Survival demands it. Instincts run deep."

Amb looks at me with a crooked eye through his glasses. Little did I know that being honest with his PhD ego about this subject would hurt me. He heard through Chipweldi, via Renn and Misa Queen I would guess, how I feel disappointed in Amb's hypocritical behavior towards me. Finally, even though Pillmold and the HIC staff may be the only ones actually verbalizing it, everyone on the atoll agrees that it was a very bad idea for Amb to bring Panburelie out here, and that she is a complete liability and that the island population as a whole, chafes under her. After only a few weeks on the atoll, she has alienated Amb and the rest of the APS from pretty much every group. She also causes divisions within the unit itself. Somehow, a nickname developed for her and spread around Halfway. *Badger*. I think it has to do with the tenacity, or personality of a badger, which again, I must take offense too, not on the part of Panburelie, but on the part of the magnificent and resilient American Badger. I have a lot of respect for badgers and I guess I find it hard to find any animal that I would think derogatorily enough of to compare it to someone this acerbic and plainly unlikable. Even when she dances to the Sri Lankans' music, she has a grind about her that resembles the grating of sharp nails down a chalkboard. People refer to her as Badger, but, only behind her back. They wouldn't dare confront the badger to its face. Funny, now that I think on this, swimming way out in the middle of the biggest ocean in The World: floating; just waiting; must waiting; I think about how the name really sounds like "bad – her". I think now, that is why this name resonated so well with the Sri Lankans and Thais.

All these events accumulate to lead to backstabbing, passive-aggressive behavior, taken out on me. Live and learn. Too bad I died before I could use my new skills.

I backslide to minimize conflict, "I agree that animals have more feelings than we used to give them credit for."

"Ah, so you think animals feel?" he says.

"Yes. Definitely. Lorenz lived with his geese for decades. He loved those birds and never once did he say they don't feel. I think that he loved and studied animals so much that even though he, and Faussy, and Goodall, are scientists, they love their subjects even though the subjects don't love them, and animals without a doubt feel pain and they might even be considered sentient beings," I respond quickly.

"Well then that conflicts with your tour statements," he says, as if to try to trick me but still never landing on a cogent point.

"Amb, you eat animals," Jellie says from the garage where she looks for some of our equipment to borrow.

"Yah," Amb looks up with a start. We did not know others were in earshot.

"So you eat animals with feelings," she continues, the staunch vegan. Amb doesn't answer. "And you too Kestrel? Sentient beings?" There is another pause. "Would you eat a person?" she says. Amb looks at her more crooked then he had looked at me. I feel him seething. "You love your dog and believe it has more feelings than Kestrel does, yet Kestrel won't eat red meat and you eat it everyday. Who is the contradiction?" Jellie insists.

Again the peacemaker, I try, to no avail, "Look I don't want to get into the metaphysical side of whether or not they have a spirit or soul cause we will never be able to prove it," I say. "It's like arguing about god. Esoteric. It's a huge waste of time."

I know this is way outside the scope of this book, but for Amb to say his dog is really connected to him and he ate a study subject shearwater and likes to hunt, sounds like weird contractions to me too, but I don't necessarily want Jellie on my side either. I put my trust, faith, and loyalty into this guy and now I begin to wonder if I should. I know, everyone is different and has different opinions, but there has to be logic in one's basic arguments and philosophies, no matter how articulate. I don't agree with Jellie on a number of levels, but she appears to practice what she preaches at least.

"You can't love mammals like they are part of your family, and eat them," Jellie challenges.

"A dog is very different than a cow. We weren't even talking about that," Amb deflects.

"Well you should be," Jellie scolds.

"Okay, so do plants have feelings?" Amb blurts out, at the end of his rope.

Jellie eats plants. How does she know whether a Bluefin Tuna feels more pain than a Beach Morning Glory or an *Erogrostis* bunch grass? She can try to use logic and reason it out, but she can't prove shit. None of US can.

Jellie looks back at Amb with an angry scowl, "I'm sure plants have much less feelings than a pig or a cow."

"You are? Are you sure? Fact: You can't prove that," Amb snipes back accurately, but pettily.

"I proved one thing. You're a jerk," Jellie states with a huff as she escapes like a coward.

Amb boils.

Speaking of plants, one of the things that makes alien plant removal so easy on Halfway Atoll Wildlife Sanctuary is that there are so few natives; so everyone can learn to identify them quickly. I put together a little identification book, with all the native plants, photos, and some info on each one, so the visitors and others can use it as a resource. I did the same thing with WWII era aircraft that were stationed here or attacked, but no one ever looked through the book, so I ended up creating a display in our office; putting the photos up on the wall. The vets really loved that one. Volunteers know they can pull any plants they don't recognize. I love growing and planting natives way more than eradicating noxious aliens. When I look at it though, I can clearly see I spend way more time, like triple the amount of time, pulling weeds and trees. As a matter of fact, I am so smooth as ranger, I can do all my work, tours, special shows and programs, meet and greets, orientations, research, and everything else, and still have time to join the bio crew on all kinds of projects, and pull trees and plants like crazy, maybe 5 days a week. It almost becomes a compulsion. I am working like a madman as fast as I can with a sense of urgency; like each day might be my last and how many great impacts can I have on this atoll before I leave? Every time I walk by a blooming *Verbesina*, I have to pull it, with its bright mustard flowers, and throw it somewhere to dry out. Every sapling Aussie pine gets the heave-ho into the ocean to let the salt attack and eliminate the chance of re-rooting or re-sprouting.

We also have a funky puncture vine out here. I think it is a *Tribulus* of some kind. Most of the native plants have one main similarity: They are all relatively soft. When albatross arrive after years at sea, they need a gentle and forgiving landing pad. The naupaka, morning glory, and the bunch grasses, with no need for sharp edges, hard trunks, or stabbing spines to ward off herbivores, offer soft landings. I would love to see Halfway 50 years from

387

now, with all the trees gone, and no goonies hanging, dangling, crucified alive.

While Amb watches Jellie make off with our gear, I use the diversion as an opportunity to slip out of the office and up to the beach. Amb shakes his head and looks off towards Jellie for a long time, then he turns to comment and realizes I am gone. As I speed off on my bike, I see a lone ironwood. As I bend to pull this one last small ironwood, in an area now completely cleared and replanted with natives, I look up at the dilapidated Cable buildings, and I remember when I dispatched a gooney in front of Zart, who said 'Oh Jesus, how can you ooh oh, god.' I miss Zart a lot. Even though we have stayed in touch a bit, it's hard with US being on distant and remote Sanctuaries. I feel melancholy for a moment, until I see Deny, then my testosterone snaps me back into agro boy.

Somebody once said, 'To have anything, you must give up everything.' It could have been Buddha. I don't know. Is Deny willing to give up his old-styled oppressive ways, or am I going to have a fight on my hands?

Deny asks with caution and distain, "Was there anything, anything other than veggie burgers that is, that we wanted to request from the shipment?"

Why does he bother asking? Why does he take a job where he has to rue his daily duties?

"Could you get some cartons of rice or soy milk?" I ask politely with a wince.

"You have got to be kiddin me. That's a joke, right? Now you gonna tell me there's somethin wrong with milk?" he says with his ire raised.

"Hey Deny, milk is milk right? I just want milk from something other than a big smelly cow," I say indignantly.

Deny looks at me with a repulsive eye, grinds his teeth a little, and turns to blow me off.

Oh no you don't. I go after him this time. This is his job, not his moral fucking duty or something, and I am out of here soon, so this is a battle I'm going to wage. "What I don't get about milk is why it is so fuckin revered. Like if I ever say anything against milk, some people look at me like it's a friggin heresy or sacrilege, like I'm attacking baseball or something, and isn't it like weird that this is just milk, and its just a drink, and its just milk, and what if someone was making fun of Coke, or something, but no, NO, milk is sacred," I say, without berating Deny.

Deny keeps walking. He looks like he wants to swing around and blind sucker me like a coward, so I stay the appropriate cushion back, kind of like a nagging housewife; just out of reach.

"On top of all the reasons cow's milk sucks," I continue, "like the lactose many of us can't tolerate; scientists today believe that in the next decade, that's like by 2010, biotech crops will cause huge jumps in pesticide use, which is not only very bad for the other 2 million species on the Planet, but will also show up with the hormones and everything else that has been turning up in milk. Should I bother to try to say any of this to you? Are you interested in any facts; documentation?"

"Oh sure," Deny answers sarcastically, "you'd just love to prove everything with your science and facts," he says in a way as if to embarrass me or something.

I say, "Of course I want to use facts."

Since when has the neo-con religious right decided that facts are evil or something? I know they are anti-science and Darwin and all that, but you can't be anti-science and have predator drones and depleted uranium shells. That's science too. I guess if it's military science, designed for killing, then it's not anti-Christian, like the other non-military sciences.

Then Deny says, "Yuh think cause you were right about da monk seals, you are right about everything?"

Ah ha! He admits that the scientists were right about the monk seal population and closing the West Beach. I decide to use my seamless logic in a way he can't help but relate too. "Deny, I am flying the Gulfstream back to Lihue on Saturday."

"What?" Deny asks, incredulously.

"Yah, I'm gonna fly it back. You got a problem with that?" I say dryly.

Deny thinks for a second, "Yah. You can't."

"Why not?" I ask.

"What? This is ridiculous," Deny states with confusion, jumping around, instead of thinking linearly.

I try again, "Please tell me why Deny. You have to give me a reason."

"Why? Why? Cause you ain't qualified," Deny says, like I am an idiot, missing the point completely.

"I can't fly the turbo-prop back because it's not my job and I don't have any training in it. I am not certified, and it would be foolish and dangerous, just like it would be if we let you manage the wildlife. Do you understand? You can't tell people what to do or think if you don't have any training or knowledge in the field. I trust you know a lot about being a Marine, and I would ask you questions about that if I needed info, and I would consider you an authority. But obviously, you don't know shit about wildlife, and you don't even know the basics about milk, and yet, you won't respect my well-supported viewpoint at all."

Deny says, "My daddy brought me up drinkin milk. And my grand pappaye drank milk, and . . ."

He really has no idea what a parody he's created of himself and his ilk. So embarrassing. I stand there unmoved.

Ignorant or over-protective guardians can do more harm than good. White Tern parents seem to know how to strike a balance.

Deny prattles on, ". . . and his grand pappaye drank milk, and his grand pappaye before, he drank milk, but he actually was a Flemish goat herder and drank goats' milk, which he didn't really like I heard. But seriously, he woulda wanted to drink cow milk if he could a got it, and now here, you can get it for free, and you are so spoiled and ungrateful to our flag that you would soil it with some slant-eyed gook milk?"

I don't take well to the racial slur, "That's enough Deny. I'll expect a case of non-cow milk on the next shipment, something in vanilla preferably, or expect a complaint filed. Thank you." I march away with a resolved smile.

I have finally learned how to handle that dick without letting him turn *me* into one. Too bad I learned so late. I legally do not have to stand there and take ethnic slurs or anything else from him; but you know how I am, and I politely do, to a point. It's all in learning how to act like a professional in the work world. He might be angry with me, but we already know he doesn't like me, and he does have to order that almond milk. He's not complaint-proof. Loon approaches me with a stack of clipboards and data sheets, and a plastic bag full of bird bands. Twistor comes out of the bathroom and enters the creepy hall, straightening his shirt. They had both heard the entire interchange in the echoic cinderblock cavern. We all look at each other for a second, as Misa Queen arrives at the top of the stairs, huffing and puffing because she has let herself become such a weak crème puff of a being. Her Motto? *No effort.* Never put out any effort. My Motto? *Always give 100%.* I relay in stunned disbelief, "Do people just snap one day? One day they have no major opinion, and then the next day, 'Anyone who doesn't eat meat is not only a wuss, but un-American?' Is that the stupidest shit you have ever heard in your life? Or how about, one day you are going along like a semi-normal human, and the next minute, Shazamm!, you're a religious fanatic?"

Twistor states, "This is why families are important. We have to have families, to teach US how to act. They teach US to be good people, . . ."

I add, " . . . and to be good to everyone else on The Planet."

Loon says, "Some people are trying to be good, so they can get into heaven or nirvana. Yet others feel, they don't really have to be good on Earth, cause this life is just a transitory journey to a better place, while still others feel no need for god whatsoever in their lives and still want to just be good all the time."

Misa Queen tries inarticulately to relate to the clan she has ostracized so thoroughly, "But don't ya think if there is an afterlife or not, that either way we should not kill people cause they don't believe what we do, or whatever?"

"That's the thing," Loon says, answering his misfortunate housemate, "It's like, one thing my family has taught me is that we have to be way more tolerant of fanatics and complete fuckin idiots cause it's not their fault that they got sucked into all this shit."

Twistor adds with understanding, "Yeah, too many drugs and dead brain cells, too much psychological disturbance, so ya know you can't blame them. We live in a society, a communal species, that somehow allows drunks and bums, and drug addicts, to not necessarily thrive, but survive in our society. It's weird how it happened with this generation though, where a whole group started out really hippy and progressive, and ended up psycho religious Republican ultraconservative scary. I think Vietnam and the assassinations, and the rock stars overdosing . . . "

I interrupt, testifying, "Before, when I would meet a fanatic, I would just laugh at them. My friends all agreed that we should be laughing at these people and hand out leaflets like *'Jesus love you. Everyone else thinks you're an asshole.'* But laughing at them doesn't work."

Loon states, "They can't be shamed because anyone who could be shamed would never let themselves get sucked into such a moronic cult to begin with."

Twistor theorizes, "The laughter appears to harden their resolve and make them feel all martyr-esque and shit."

Misa Queen still tries to contribute, "They are firmly entrenched in their beliefs or they wouldn't be fanatics. The only thing we can do with fanatics is try to be nice to them and recognize how messed-up their heads are."

Loon says, "That's why they are religious fanatics, that's why they have these psycho eyes and ridiculous beliefs. -- i.e. Abraham, or some guy in the bible, lived to be like 800, or a thousand, or something."

"Good example," I say to Loon, looking over at Twistor and avoiding Misa Queen as much as I can. "Why can't they be like me and say that there could be a god or some kind of spiritual power, and find love and oneness in nature and the universe? Why do they feel compelled to force their god down your throat?" I complain. "Because they are more psycho than me? I'm nobody's religious bitch, and nobody is going to force shit on me," I say with conviction.

Twistor tries to calm things down and bring everything back to reason. At seventeen, the inveterate mumbler seems more mature than me, which means way more mature than Loon and his regrettable roommate half-wit, Misa Queen. "So laughing at them, harshing on them, or 'reasoning' with them . . ."

Loon and I both can't control our laughs right now and let them roll, as Misa Queen watches on, perplexed as usual. "Ha ha ha h ha HAHAA! REASONING?" we gasp.

Twistor smiles, then gets back to his point, "It just adds fuel to the fire and causes more of those horrific "holy" wars, crusades, and most cowardly of all, bombings. So my strategy now is to just leave them alone and hope that they can sort out their issues and drop the god shit."

I say, "That's right, don't even talk about it and don't give them any energy toward it and maybe it will simply go away someday. My Japanese record producer in Tokyo not only brought Bob Marley to Nippon, but he also knew him personally. Shin was big on the scene in the Seventies, and he told me he met Bob Dylan, and that Dylan had converted to Christianity because of quote, 'too many drugs'. I know I can't do anything to help people like that, especially if they are convinced that they don't need help. If I keep trying, but they're not benefiting from it, and I'm not benefiting from it, then it's not working. The other thing is," as I reach around my backpack and whip-out a mangled paperback of *On Aggression*, I fumble through some worn pages and read, "Lorenz said, *I think it has been adequately shown that the aggression of so many animals toward members of their own species is in no way detrimental to the species but, on the contrary, is essential for its preservation. However, this must not raise false hope about the present situation of mankind. Innate behavior mechanisms can be thrown completely out of balance by small, apparently insignificant changes of environmental conditions. Inability to adapt quickly to such changes may bring about the destruction of a species, and the changes which man has wrought in his environment are by no means insignificant. An unprejudiced observer from another planet, looking upon man as he is today, in his hand the atom bomb, the product of his intelligence, in his heart the aggression drive inherited from his anthropoid ancestors which this same intelligence cannot control, would not prophesy long life for the species. Looking at the situation as a human being whom it personally concerns, it seems like a bad dream, and it is hard to believe that aggression is anything but the pathological product of our disjointed cultural and social life.* Wow, impressive right? I wish I had written that," I gasp as I relent.

Twistor says, "Those points eloquently speak for themselves. It's just like the tense situations of these disparate people all trapped on a tiny, remote atoll, like tropical cichlids in a tank too small for them, forcing them to rip each other apart."

I respond, "Like Lee Ving said, *We're like rats in a cage!* I say, there are too many humans. Way too many humans. *There's too many of US!*"

Misa Queen jumps in for one more try. Twistor, Loon, and I keep forgetting she's there and wish she would move along about her business, as she should but never does. She says, "I have a quote in my planner. *'Character is the governing element of life, and is above genius.' -- Frederick Saunders,"* she unquotes.

We can tell by the way she reads it, that she has no idea what it means. Is she admitting that she's not a genius and that it's her wonderful character we should embrace? I look at Misa Queen for a second. She takes a gulp. Loon has argued that her lack of character is 'even worse than her lack of a formed philosophy, lack of a developed intellect, and that she is actually worse on the inside than her more superficially, unpleasantly amorphous blobbular shape portrays.' Since he and her live in the old chief's quarters next to mine, he should know. Poor bastard.

She is looking at me, so I say, "I don't know who the hell that guy was, but I know that and feel I live by it."

Misa Queen apparently does have a motive in her lingering, as she tries to defend Myhel for a second, "She found 'Mr. Right', but you didn't reciprocate. Her hurt turned to anger . . ." Misa Queen whines.

" . . . and maliciousness, and even though she is really 'messed-up' as you put it, it ended up making atoll residents think that Kestrel is the asshole," Loon says, staring down at Misa Queen.

I take more blame to defuse the situation as much as possible, "I should have done damage control, but I never thought it would ever get this big and ridiculous."

Misa Queen points her finger like a nun, "Yuh have to have morals."

Loon erupts, "Oh god. Don't start with the moral shit. Does Myhel have morals when she is stabbing Kestrel in the back for revenge?"

Misa Queen looks shocked.

I jump down her throat, "Do you have morals when you bake me bread after telling my girlfriend what a scum I am?"

Misa Queen snipes irrationally, like a cornered Pygmy Shrew, "Didn't last, did it? That is another example of your immorality. My preacher man back home said that, not me."

Loon, dismissing her panicked response, asks, "Is religious fanaticism doing more harm than good?"

Twistor says, "Do religious fanatics help move the World forward or turn the wheel backward?" referring to one of the videos I played for him called *Turn The Wheel*.

"Are fanatics helping the World in some great way and we just can't see it because all we see is the negative murderous crap associated with fundamentalist literalists?" Loon adds.

I look at them, but not Misa Queen. I loosen my voice as I prepare to sing in the echo chamber. "We need to be moral and good, but we don't need organized religion to do it. Just like in **Truth?**," I say, then I sing:

Truth?
by Drats

Preaching as if they are gods, they try to make me nervous
Stepping on my head, as I struggle for the surface
And in the end, the tell me god is my friend
I pay the church and to my knees I bend.
I feel, that it's too unreal
They say that they know we must heel
Why do they insist they are right?
Don't they know the burden and constraint of human plight?
These words that are written of sin, are written by mortal men
By mortal men.
Pray for the ones who feel they have to pray
Cry for the ones who cry everyday
Resist the ones who confuse our youth
Pity the ones who claim to know the truth.
By mortal men, mortal men who make mistakes
Mortal men like you and I, who knows the truth?
How can they be sure? What do they know?

How do they know? They know? THEY KNOW?!

I stop and take a breath. Twistor and Loon applaud, quite accustomed to my antics by now, but Misa Queen looks at me like it is the first time she has really heard me sing, and the first time she has heard a song by Drats. She is surprised that she's impressed. According to Myhel, she thought I was a shallow womanizer. She knows I'm a great ranger, but she was convinced that I was a scum, until now.

I ask, "So Why? Why the freak out about burgers and meat and milk? That's why people can't get mad at their mothers and fathers. It's because my Mother and Father are not like me. That generation never learned how to emote. They don't know how to love, they have forgotten what it is like to be a kid, their heads are all back in WWII and John Wayne and all that other kind of stuff that we can't relate to at all."

Loon says, "I think *they* are afraid that *we* will take their guns away, and then their big monster trucks away, and their cigarette boats and snowmobiles and religious texts, oh my, and their steaks, and then, their bauh bauh," Loon pretends to start crying like a baby.

"Boo hoo hoo," Twistor joins in with a laugh.

I say, "It threatens Deny that I don't want to drink milk and he can't make me?"

"What the fuck are these control freaks on?" Loon blurts.

"Nothing! That's the fuckin problem," I answer as we all laugh. "I mean, even people from our generation, some of these people, are locked. It's like their emotions and feelings are locked somehow and can't be unlocked. I went to UCLA and had a Brazilian girlfriend and was lead singing in bands, and I kind of became kind of more like a hippy and became very open to new ideas and very loving and more expressive and able to say how I feel. The Catch 22 in this situation is that when my Mother passes away, my siblings are going to demand that I attend the service because that's some kind of unwritten rule that our family must abide by or something. Well my rule is that if I go back there, they have to console me and be compassionate and loving towards me, which I know they are incapable of doing." Everyone looks at me in shock for a moment, like I am the asshole. "I went back to my Father's funeral at Bichiano's, which was a huge mistake."

"Why?" Twistor asks.

"Now, every time I think of my Dad, I see that friggin coffin. I can't even remember him. And none of my family was there for me. I remember trying to talk with them. They all blew me off and wanted me away from them. I cried in the backyard alone, because I had no one to cry with. I just looked up into the night sky and cried at The Moon. That's what an only child must feel like. I am not going to suffer through that again. I can't ask them about my Dad, or talk about Dad with them."

I have bummed everyone out now. Me, Mr. Happy Funny-guy, has the group feeling pretty suicidal by now, especially Twistor, who is already starting to freak out about Renn.

"The casket situation was really sad and uncomfortable, and I don't want anymore of those with my family," I finish. "I don't ever want to see a casket again."

Loon adds, "Hey, that's what families are for."

"Oh yeh?" I snap back. "NO it isn't! Families are not supposed to pretend each other are dead. I feel that we are supposed to contact each other and everything like that. The basic problem is, if these emotions that my family have are locked as they are, then they will never ever be able to be open and loving, which means also, in a sense, they are probably never going to be happy. They are never going to be happy people, and that's why they turn to booze, religion, and other moronic antidotes. My family completely neglects me. I know neglect is not the same as hate, but it feels like hate."

"What is the answer then?" Twistor asks sympathetically.

"I think that each person in my family needs to take the time to find a really good, smart psychologist with whom they could talk with for a nice solid year. Maybe a shrink could teach them to unlock their happiness, and their emotions, and to throw away all the destructive crap they have accumulated," I respond.

Loon confirms rationally, "They are never going to be happy people."

Then Misa Queen adds, with her typical 'always fail' attitude, "What's the point of trying to dwell on helping these people if they can never be happy? Money could make them happy?"

397

"I think unhappy people tend to be unhappy whether they have shit-loads of money or not," I respond. "I believe in trying no matter what. I always try."

Everyone looks at each other in confounded conundrum. Misa Queen gives up, pretends to fumble through some papers, and drifts off down the hall, like a barge, cut lose, and zigzagging aimlessly down the Rio Grande. None of us care to notice. At the same moment, Dr. Oso appears with our APS FN from Sri Lanka, Han, who has his entire left arm wrapped in blood-saturated gauze. He suspends his arm up into the air with a sling. Dr. Oso holds it.

"What happened to you?" I say with surprise to Han.

Dr. Oso answers in annoyed frustration, "He got his arm stuck in a dumpster. Pretty mangled. The dumpster fell on his arm and broke im right away, and he had the where-with-all to direct the other Sri Lankans to gitt him out of there. First time we used the ambulance since you used it." He smiles, then fiddles with the arm.

Han smiles with a pained wince. Maybe Dr. Oso told him of my little gurney escapade.

"What are you guys doing, having meeting?" Han asks like a joke.

"No," I say. "We were having another heavy convo."

"About what this time? Sex in the back of the ambulance?" Dr. Oso teases with a wink. The other guys don't notice it or get it.

Twistor says, "So what is this? Is this the Nature/Nurture argument coming full circle?" picking up the topic.

I state, "I grew up in the same part of Boston as all of them. They aren't exactly still a bunch of Vinnie-buffs who wanna punch someone in the face up at Revere Beach, but. . . in other respects, we are just so different, and I'm not like them."

Loon says, "What's the difference?"

Dr. Oso interrupts, "Who are we talkin bout now?"

Twistor mumbles quickly, not to digress "His brothers."

I think for a second, as Han and Dr. Oso try to follow along as we walk down the long hall; never stopping his treatment of Han's bloody arm. "The difference is, I moved away, I went to LA, I had a New Jersey girlfriend who was eleven years older than me, then a Brazilian girlfriend who was in a cult. I had a French girlfriend. I traveled around the World, I met all these different people from all these different places and I got exposure and I was open to that." The fire hose nozzle blasts wide open. "I wanted to get out of that world I grew up in. I wasn't comfortable in that underworld and I don't want to 'be connected' and have people at Towne Hall doing 'favors' for me and all that shit. I just want to live an honest life and work hard, and not be anyone's slave."

Han takes great notice at this final comment. The Sri Lankans have kind of been slaves to India and the Brits, and even now, they are treated like slaves by the HIC staff and the fishing guys. Whether you can do anything about it or not at the moment, you still know the bully is wrong.

Misa Queen comes back down the hall to the stairs. She saunters at a government employee pace, well trained by Chipweldi, and following the exact polar opposite of the example I display. First she looks at Han with a bunch of false sympathy. "Oh, you poor thing. You okay? Owh." Then, now that she has had time to think about it, she tries to get a parting shot in, "Well, I guess if you are in a certain box of thinking you want to get out of that box," Misa Queen stumbles, realizing she sounds like an idiot. None of us can discern what she fails to say.

"Are you saying," Loon observes, "that if you grew up in a town where you were the biggest, toughest kid, and you had the cutest head-cheerleader girlfriend; you're gonna leave that?"

"You are the dominant," I say. "You are the alpha."

Dr. Oso says in agreement, "There's no reason to go on to Harvard or anything else. You are just content to stay there put, where you are."

"And never change anything?" Twistor mumbles. "Highly implausible."

Misa Queen looks about like a fool.

Dr. Oso says, "How did you get on this?"

"We were talking about cow's milk," Twistor remembers for us.

Loon ignites, "Yeah, really, how far back does the milk industry go, with these giant milk factories and a distribution system of millions of trucks hauling it to our doors? 60 years?"

"90 years?" Dr. Oso corrects, "I bet."

Loon goes on, "This is a joke and I can drink whatever the fuck kind of milk I want without getting harassed by cow sucking anti-freedom rednecks. This is America, remember?"

I jump in, "I'm an American, and I am FREE!" I yell like Kunta Kinte, as it reverberates down the halls.

Loon fires the next comment directly towards Misa Queen, paralyzed near the bottom of the stairs, "The thing is, we are so programmed and we can't even see it. Do you realize we get our milk from cows? We are sucking off cows."

Misa Queen argues, "We are not literally sucking off cows, . . ."

Dr. Oso feels this is a little too radical of a technique as well.

" . . . and if we did, to get milk, way less people would bother to drink cow's milk," Loon drives home.

Twistor thinks for a moment, "However, if we did not have a milk INDUSTRY, and we did not have it conveniently packaged and distributed across America, would people drive out to the country so they could suck off cows to get their precious protein and calcium?"

We laugh at the idea.

Misa Queen finally gets with the program and actually thinks in a scientific method. Stopping on the landing, before dropping out of sight, she says, "How did people figure it out in the first place?"

I start with my know-it-all response, "Okay, so as a scientist, and anthropologist, I can look at a cow and figure it out. They are not too big, like trying to milk an elephant or a giraffe, and they are not too mean, like milking a jaguar, and they are not too small, like milking a woodchuck, and they are not too fast, like milking a pronghorn, so I can see that. As a matter of fact, I would be pro milk if every dairy farm in American traded in their cows and switched over to milking native creatures all over their land."

Wow, Loon and Twistor totally prick-up to that idea, but Misa Queen can't even imagine what the hell the landscape would be like without millions of cows.

"What kind of milk da ya want me to get at the store honey?" I put on a funny Texan drawl and answer like a housewife. "Well, the moose milk was delicious, but let's go back to the half and half bison/big horn milk until the elk milk is back in season," I say, sounding like Granny from The Beverly Hillbillies.

Misa Queen looks highly offended now. She wants to, but feels like she can't leave as she shuffles her feet back and forth like someone with a motor-skills malfunction. She is obviously in Deny's camp and we are a bunch of eco-whackos to her. Keep in mind, she is supposed to be an enlightened Animal Protection Service ranger.

I go on, just to finish my point, "So cows make sense in a sense, but not undeniably. Lots of female animals produce lots of milk, and there have always been lots of options.

Twistor reasons, "Cows happen to be the most convenient for us, as goats are in so many other parts of the World."

Yes, I agree, "We humans, *Homos*, we drink cow's milk; a totally different species. We drink their milk." I reason, "Cows don't suck off moose. Moose don't suck off elk. Elk don't suck off bear and bear don't suck off walrus, right?"

Twistor adds, "Like an animal is suppose to drink milk when it's in its infancy because it can't ingest other food forms yet. Once one develops teeth and the other tools necessary to consume adult food, we are supposed to move away from mother's milk, so not to tax the mother, and to give her an opportunity to reproduce again."

Loon and I both nod in agreement.

Man, I am thinking to myself in this moment that this would be a great program to put on in The Station Theater, but I'm 100% sure Amb would nix it. This is more suitable for the avant-garde TV series *Bogus Weirdness*, by Drats. This would have been a great discussion for the live call-in segment.

Loon gets even more psychologically deep on the subject, "We don't move on to other items. We postpone our future by hanging back on milk."

Misa Queen still isn't getting it. "Why? Because it tastes good?"

Loon asks back, "Because it's subsidized and cheap and easy?"

Then Twistor asks, "Because it's healthy and all the other things The Milk Board and The Dairy Council would love for US to continue to think?"

Loon says, "None of those reasons are really good."

I start to head down the stairs as I look at my watch. "Like previously stated, my vanilla hazelnut milk tastes sooooo much better than milk, and though it costs more and should be subsidized like the dairy industry is, it is way healthier for US and worth the price. You know the list: No Lactose, No Cholesterol, No Chemicals, No Sodium, No Casein bonded to the protein, No Trans Fats, No lack of D or Calcium or Riboflavin."

Misa Queen looks on with surprise, as if she was hearing many of my words for the first time, like when Zart read the political materials on my desk in my room; a mini awakening maybe. Could there be hope for Misa Queen? I look her over. No. No hope. Too bad.

"We grew up on cow milk," Misa Queen defends like Deny did.

Twistor states, much nicer than Loon or I would, but still avoiding condescension, "We also grew up with DDT."

"Dairy farms will go out of business," Misa Queen worries.

"To be replaced by nut, soy, rice, and other milk farms," Twistor envisions.

"It's un-American!" Misa Queen imagines, thinking of what Texas would be without cows and cowboys.

"Don't worry," I say, "There will be soyboys and almond wranglers."

Now Misa Queen feels attacked and in a bind as we head toward the exit.

Loon lets loose, "Look at the dairy industry. Range-fed, happy cows up in Vermont are a far cry from these giant, waste-filled, polluted, disease-ridden, disgusting, abusive, factory milk 'farms' that simply have got to go, and anyone who drinks milk or gets other products from those places are culpable because, with or without guilt, you are taking from that source and perpetuating it."

Misa Queen, frustrated, loses the tiny veneer of composure she tenuously holds, "So what. One person doesn't matter right?" She sounds like a second-grader on the playground, but the nastiest one in the class: Veruca Salt, with some Kelly Ripa, Rosanne Barr, and Wicked Witch of the West sprinkled in for spoiled sassy ignorance effect.

Dr Oso still holds Han's arm up in the air. They listen intently.

As Loon begins to speak, we hear some feet shuffling up the steps, "Let me illustrate a shocking example: Have you noticed how many burger joints you can go to now and get a veggie burger? 20 years ago, good friggin luck. Why is this? Because consumers just like you and me demanded it, and now we have it. Same with coffee and decaf. Soon, non-cow's milk will be offered everywhere too. They already offer non-dairy creamer for people who are lactose intolerant. Isn't that even a funny term that The Milk Industry came up with? 'You are intolerant. You should learn to be more tolerant. You must tolerate milk like the rest of us Americans.' Dairy farmers, especially conscious and caring ones, need not be afraid. All they need to do to get ready is to start planting appropriate nut trees all over their massive ranch land." Then Twistor reasons, "Yah, and raising nuts and fruits is way easier than raising cattle."

Deny passes us on the stairs. He can easily hear that we still buzz about milk.

"Yah, that's what I said from the beginning. Milk is for babies. Milk is for fucking babies!" I say it loud enough for tough guy Marine Deny to hear.

We all split into different directions outside the Hangar, but Dr. Oso never lets Han's arm down.

That night, up at the beach, alone again, I look out. As I watch the albatross, with their long, pointed wings, flying around, I realize that they look lost. They look like they are just aimless. I watch this one bird carve giant circles back and forth, for four minutes. It's moving fast, and covering so much ground, with little, teeny, shallow wing-beats, and then long, effortless glides. 1, 2, gliiiide. 1, 2, gliiiide. Here and there. Other than that, their wings are almost straight out. At 49 mph, they zip around. What's all the flying behavior about? They are not foraging; they are not looking for mates. They are just flying around in weird circles, like most *Homos*, spinning their wheels.

I decide to go for a run. If you have shin splints like I do, and chronic ankle problems or stuff like that, then Halfway is a great place to run. Running on the beaches and the sand dunes up on the North Beach and through the Naupaka gives you the option of running through, around, or over the top of the mogul-like dunes. The soft sand and crushed coral, feels grainy, but good while even running barefoot. On the downside, in the summertime especially, the smell of the rotting squid-bags, festering in the sun, can be overwhelming. The dehydrated albatross chicks, dead or alive, attract large swarms of flies. One of the major jobs of the Foreign Nationals, going way back into the old Navy days, has been carcass patrol. Now they pick up tons of dead and dying gooney chicks. They bring them to the dump to be incinerated. Meanwhile, those rotting birds are supposed to be a major part of the ecosystem out here. Just as the redwoods depend on the dying salmon for survival in California, I bet these millions of carcasses have a huge environmental effect on the atoll. I mean, the Ghost Crabs not only feed on the carcasses, but I have gotten photos of them sitting on the carcasses, and being fast enough to catch the flies with their claws, and eat them! So we *Homos*, we go around and remove these food resources because we find them 'unsightly'. I understand about public perception, believe me, but I want to propose to the biologists that we remove the carcasses only from the North Beach where people tend to swim, and leave the rest of them on the other areas of the shoreline, like we do on Eastern Island, for the detritus to finally finely break down and nourish the reef. These animals didn't die for nothing. They are part of the environment too.

A week later when the HIC shipment arrives on the plane, with the tourists and Olderhostile folks, there are 8, count em, 8 crates of whole milk. I think there are four gallon-jugs per crate. That's cow's milk, from a cow. There is no non-cow's milk of any kind. Deny offers no explanation; just a 'fuck you' look. I have had it. I decide I will write an official complaint and put it on Amb's keyboard to sign before it goes off to HIC administration. I know Amb has much bigger fish to fry, but I have to put my foot down on this one. Deny should be working with us and supporting us, not fighting against us tooth and nail to push his defunct agenda upon us.

On the next flight to arrive, I do my usual meet and greet. I love seeing how excited people get when they first look beyond the tarmac to see millions of goonies.

It appears that everyone has gotten off of the plane, but when I look down at the manifest, I see that one soul, Eenis, hasn't come off yet. I look up again, and there, standing in the doorway at the top of the stairs, this haggard lady looks out in disgust. She holds on to the railing carefully, then makes her way down each step like an elderly woman might, being careful not to break an ankle, or a hip. At the bottom of the gangway, before she steps away from the plane, she dangerously lights up a cigarette. Like Madeline Kahn, right out of a Mel Brooks movie, she struts nervously in her heels over to The Hangar. Right when she gets under the awning, a petrel hits the flat metal wall and falls to the tarmac next to her. She gives off a whimper.

I approach her quickly, "Hello, welcome to Halfway. May I help you?"

She looks completely disoriented. She snaps her head around, looking.

"I'm the ranger," I advertise, "Do you need something Ms. . . .."

"Deny!" she yells like a rusty horn, "I'm looking for Deny."

At the Hangar, Deny never even acknowledges her. He just keeps on driving around and working, for once.

I look at her for a second. This must be Deny's mom, or a much older sister, or something. I see Deny driving around in one of the airport vehicles, and towing luggage.

Dietera observes, "Funny, in all the landings I've witnessed here, this is the first time Deny wasn't just standing around, with useless Cherry Ballpig and the like, doing nothing."

She is right again. Instead, he has a zip-around thing going.

I go around the atoll telling everybody that Deny's mom visits. Many of the Foreign Nationals greet her, holding her hand and calling her 'Mum'. I notice that they have the same last name from the manifest. A couple of days later, I find out that Eenis is actually his wife! This is hysterical to us, because Deny had been trying to pull himself off as a young tough Marine who also has been flirting with the young girls and trying to score, to no avail; the entire time he has been out here. He has been relentlessly after Jewel, and that has been one of the reasons why it has been hard just trying to stay friends with her. With him around, it deters my interest in someone I know I don't have that much in common with anyway.

I think about Deny with Eenis for a second, then shutter. If there is any logical argument for divorce, they make the perfect case study. Why stay in a loveless, dried-up, shriveled prune of an existence; for duty? Like with Amb's Panburelie, animals and human animals alike must recognize that our significant other reflects on us heavily. That's one of the minor reasons I knew from the start that Myhel wasn't the one for me, and yet, my association with her still drags me way down. That's why I could never look at Myhel seriously. That's why I can give 100% of my heart, my love, my spirit, to Chelonia with no reservations. Now Eenis comes out here, to our surprise, and completely changes the way we look at Deny forever. He tries to play the big winner, tough guy, but now it's clear to see what a total loser he is. Not simply because she looks very old, but because of her acerbic personality: The clothes, the cigarette, the whole package. Anyway, Eenis turns out to be just as miserable as the most miserable assholes on the atoll. She never smiles, always frowns or grimaces, chain smokes, and would much rather be pumping slots with quarters than spending any quality time with her husband, let alone communing with any other gooney. It's so funny to see the difference. The Olderhostile folks lay down on the grass in the guano, to talk to the birds, and take photos, and make friends with them. Eenis sees the birds as a complete nuisance, and the tourists as complete idiots for treating the animals with any form of kindness.

"God put the birds here for us to eat, not to pet," Eenis complains one day as she looks over the scant selection in the little store, sounding remarkably like Deny.

One of the Filipinos tries to explain it to her, "Madam, we cannot eat dey goonies. Dey taste bery bad."

I look over the desiccated raisin boxes, as Eenis hisses at me with disgust, "Well then, now I really have no use for them. I have no use for an animal if my husband can't shoot it for me to eat it."

After hearing that comment, Drats decided not to waste any more space in *HN3H* on her. I said 'she could be of interest', but Drats wouldn't budge.

I don't want to let her or Deny get to me either, so I decide to go for a bike workout. I peddle as fast as I can for an hour, going around the entirety of paved surfaces on Sand Island, and sweating profusely. As I go faster and faster, and drive harder and harder, I start to fantasize again. I have forgotten about everything else. I am hitting a cyclist's high and nothing can stop me. I am flying.

I see the white pick-up truck ahead of me at the end of the runway. Is Chipweldi on atoll? I haven't seen him in a while so I thought he was off. He must be keeping a limbo-low profile.

I look over and see a gooney chick, still sitting in the nest, but reaching for an old, defunct, bait station. Rats. I start to remember the rats on Mona Island, in my hammock.

Chipweldi states, "He he hey, whad arh you doin out in this neck of the woods? You preoccupied with philosophy again?"

"Nah," I reply, "I was preoccupied with the memory of another island I lived on and the rats climbing on me. I was dead exhausted from the 95 degree heat and 95% humidity, and just wanted to sleep in this unbelievable limestone cave at the edge of a cliff, some 90 feet above the water below. As I drifted into alpha state, I could see a cruise ship, way off in the distance, just before my eyes finally closed."

Chipweldi interjects, "This story goin somewhere."

I plow on, "I first felt vibrations, then, I could see the rat come down onto my feet. I kicked and growled like a startled sneak of Short-tailed Weasels awaking to the jolting sneeze of their kits. The rat ran back up the rope, and away. Later, as I fell asleep, the next one came down onto my head. I felt the vibrations but was too tired to open my eyes, until I felt it standing on my forehead and sniffing my face. I looked up and wanted to scat it away, but I was just too tired to lift a hand, and I fell asleep with the rat on my head, sniffing my face."

Chipweldi says, "So you can sleep with rats on ya."

I say, "My Godfather Danny told me about the rats in Nam and how they climbed all over him the first night. Around the mouth of his bag, he would try to breathe, but he could not sleep. He told me that on the second night he was that much more tired, and so exhausted, that he could cope with the rats."

Chipweldi asks, "After that, every night he slept with the rats crawling all over him?"

I reply, "Everything is relative. One night at my next research job, on the Hawksbill Turtle Project, we slept on the beach, but decided to forgo the tent, as we did on so many occasions wherever turtles nested on Hawaii. Even though cockroaches would land on you sometimes, it was great to sleep under the stars, by the surf. This time, it didn't pay off and we ended up getting caught in a heavy downpour around 11:30pm. We ran for cover in the military surplus Bronco, to fall asleep in the front seats. After we calmed down and fell back asleep, the rain stopped of course, and I felt a soft pressure on my lap, and peeked down to see if my co-worker had really just reached over from the driver's seat and put his hand on my crotch. Nope. Lucky for me, it was just a rat. Rat! Polynesian rat, an alien to Hawaii but introduced before the arrival of the white man. This little fella, smaller than most Norways, jumped off of my lap before I could flinch. I yelled, and it bounced off the dashboard and down the hole in the floorboards, from whence it came."

Chipweldi says, "Your co-worker?"

I say, "He awoke with a stir, vaguely asked what was up, and when I told him it was time for him to do his watch, he rolled over and back into a deep sleep. I got out and did his watch for him during the middle of the night, and later I had to cope with the chorus of early morning excuses like; 'Sorry, didn't mean to let you down man. Man, I don't know what happened. Dude, way to cover. That's teamwork. It won't happen again, you can trust me dude.'"

Chipweldi struggles to get it out, "Whad arh ya thinkin bout rats for?"

I recount, "Growing up in Boston, I got to see a lot of rat fights first hand. We had huge rats that all had weird, menacing connotations associated with them. Water rats, sewer rats, rink rats, city rats, subway rats; you name it. We had all kinds of rats. As I got older and felt compelled to learn about rats, I learned that in Boston we really only have Norway Rats; and the 'water rat' moniker above could be for the fact that like all rats, Norway's swim great. Muskrat live in the burbs and fens; totally different animals and not really like a rat at all, but like small, plant eating beavers, or large, aquatic *Aplodontia*. They certainly aren't like rats, you know, RATS.

Chipweldi yells, "Like *Willard*. I could see how someone seeing a muskrat or even a beaver at night could flip-out and think that they have just seen the mother of all rats."

I continue, "In the back streets; on Mass. Ave; in the alleys and the dumpsters behind the restaurants, and in the North End, everywhere, I saw rats in mega fights. My friends would keep walking, ignore it, and egg me on to get along. I had to stop and watch some of the action. The rats were so embroiled, they didn't even care that I stood in their midst; darting past my legs. The rats ran around, fighting with each other, and giving off piercing squeaks. It was amazing to watch."

Chipweldi says, "So . . . , this ties in with your beef with Deny about the shipment o'somethin."

Then I say, "So again, don't get me wrong. I understand how we got to cow's milk, based on our primitive evolution, availability and control transport of resource, etc. African tribesmen have mixed the cow blood with milk as a high protein drink for centuries: A controllable heard of beasts ready to be milked. Did cavemen watch ants milk aphids? I guess my big question remains:

I understand how we eventually got to milk, but why milk now and for how long will it be until we eventually get out of milk? Why cow now?

Chipweldi interjects, "Because there's too many gosh darn humans?"

I say, "We don't need the cow milk now. We need land with crops and forests, and tall grass prairies for the bison to roam about the prairie dog dens. That's what we need, not want, but need." Chipweldi looks at me like I'm a freak. I turn away from Chipweldi and bail. Later, I pull a crinkled piece of paper out of my pocket:

To be hopeful in bad times is not just foolishly romantic. It is based on the fact that human history is a history not only of cruelty, but also of compassion, sacrifice, courage, kindness. What we choose to emphasize in this complex history will determine our lives. If we see only the worst, it destroys our capacity to do something. If we remember those times and places (and there are so many) where people have behaved magnificently, this gives us the energy to act, and at least the possibility of sending this spinning top of a world in a different direction. And if we do act, in however small a way, we don't have to wait for some grand utopian future. The future is an infinite succession of presents, and to live now as we think human beings should live, in defiance of all that is bad around us, is itself a marvelous victory. ---Howard Zinn

I look at it. I stare at it. I think at this moment that I should decide to live my life that way. I read Zinn's words. I interviewed him at BU. What are the positives, and why do I dwell on so many negatives all the time? We live in a paradise. Nobody's going to just come and take that all away. Just as I have such strong, well-balanced affirming thoughts, my serenity explodes with Myhel screeching up to a stop on her beach cruiser with big white-walls, and sparkly tassels hanging from the holes in the ends of the hand grips. I can't remember anymore if we are in the phase of whether or not she is mad at me right now, and though I don't care, I can't help but be the bigger person.

I say, "Hi. Hello," In the most non-threatening way possible. Myhel stares at me through her shades for a moment, from under her visor. "Beautiful day isn't it?" she asks.

I fumble, "Oh ah a yeh, beee ayyy you tea ffffulll." It comes out like a new language. Like I'm speaking in tongues, whatever that stupid ass shit is.

Myhel says slyly, "Your performances with the band have been top notch eh. I'm glad we have more than one band on the atoll, so people have a choice, ya know," as if to say we are similar or on equal playing fields or something.

"Yah," I say, "your band is doing really well. I have noticed marked improvement." Whoops.

Myhel scans my face. She wants me to smile at her. She wants me to acknowledge her. She wants me to let her back in, or she wants to let me back in. Whatever. She tries to placate me, "Don't worry Ranger Kestrel Falco. Hassling you is OFF THE LIST. Okay partner?"

I don't know what to do. I don't want to respond. I say in desperation, "Hey, yeah. You guys picked up some new songs huh?"

Myhel smiles and leans forward to put her cleave right in my face, "Oh yeah, you know I like to have a wide repertoire."

Oh god. How the hell do I handle this? Maybe I can appeal to her intellect while making a helpful point.

I say, "Ya know what's funny about playin in a band. The fan reaction."

Myhel nods to be hip, like she has a clue what I'm talking about.

I continue, "It's like I remember that time when my 'little' brother Manat came up to me after a **Burning Circle** gig at The Middle East in Cambridge, Central Square."

Again, Myhel has know idea where or what I'm talking about. She is just so glad I am talking. I can't tell, but it looks like she keeps looking down at my thighs, right where they pop out from my shorts.

I say, "He came up to me after the gig, and he said, 'You know, I get what you are doin heyah. You arh gettin off. You're up deer gettin off.' I looked at him and said 'yeah yeah', just to kind of make him feel okay and agree with him, but in my mind I was thinking 'Oh my god. I mean, I thought he already had the Id part of this down. I guess not. He was really trying to grasp the Id part of it; the most basic part: The endorphins going off, the adrenaline rush, the power, energy, expression. Like, I could do all of that with a taiko drum and it would be the same thing. Redirected aggression, as Lorenz would put it."

Myhel questions, "It's not like being a singer?"

I look at her finally, "With a singer, then you get also into the Ego part, where you sing to try to emote or impress upon people why you are saying what you are trying to say."

Myhel probes, "And then of course there is the Super Ego, like yours. Where does that fit in?"

I reply, "It's all about the singer and how he smiles, giving the audience a little twitch. Fulfilling all these needs. But, my brother Manat, he just recognized the Id part of it. I was glad he did and agreed with him and said 'yeah'. I held myself back. I was going to say, 'That's all? You are just getting that Id part of it? Singing in a band is about a fun rush? That's it?"

Myhel looks bored. We haven't said anything about her or sex for a while. She begins to ride off, mumbling, "Talk with ya later."

As she rides away I think. It's so funny. This is how this whole communication thing is. I feel like I am a human, a *Homo sapiens*, while Myhel and Manat and Misa Queen and Rosmarus are *Neanderthalis*. I can't even talk with them. It is as if we are on different levels. I don't even know if they understand their own Id, let alone their Egos and Super Egos. Maybe they do, and I just don't see it.

I decide I need to get another great day of diving in. I am about to hit 70 dives at Halfway Atoll Wildlife Sanctuary, so I opt for a location sure to have plenty of sharks. On dive after dive, I have been seeing Galapagos Reef Sharks, which is fine, don't get me wrong, but I'd like to see some other species. The topography around Halfway is just amazing. I am so lucky to be able to dive like this all the time, and I wonder if I will ever be in such an opportune position as this again, ever.

Deep Pockets, The Cauldron, Chimney Tower: There have been so many names now, dubbed by Bent, that I can't even remember them all. A Hawaiian film crew comes looking for rare oddities like Masked Angelfish. They invite me to go along with them. We find angelfish, and Schlegel's Grouper at the corsair, at 120 feet.

On the way up I see a large shark by the anchor line. I look down to warn the others, but they're engrossed in a brilliant Dragon Moray Eel. I signal to Bent by first making a shark fin, then miming hammering my head. Hammerheads are friggin dangerous man. They don't give a shit about nothing and like to eat other sharks. We have Anvil and Scalloped Hammerhead Sharks to my knowledge around the atoll, and some have been recorded at about 20 friggin feet long; like a tiger, or a white shark! Bent looks up, then, signals to me that I am wrong. As we get closer to the surface, I see it is a 9-foot Galapagos Reef Shark with an escort of Remoras or Pilot Fish on each side of its head. Still, though I love sharks, I have to admit I am not excited about the fact that this reef shark is big and hanging around. We have to make a long safety stop at 15 feet and hang on that line, and that's exactly where the shark hangs; in anticipation?

We start getting the willies, and grab the rope with two hands, creating a shoulder-to-shoulder circle around the anchor line, with our tanks facing out. The cameraman sticks to his duty and shoots us from eleven feet away, as the shark circles slow and tight, sticking its head in for a poke here or there, and generally acting pretty aggressive. Not finding anything worth going for, eventually it backs off.

At the end of our safety stop, the cameraman heads up to the top first. Just then, the shark returns one last time and rubs its head against the right side of my face and mask. A little bit of water streams into my cheek and eyes, but I hold my ground firmly and stiffly, without removing my grasp from the rope. This shark is big enough to bite my head right off. The shark turns its body laterally now, and looks like it wants to bite me in the face. I reach up and push its snout away with my left hand while simultaneously, Bent pushes its tail off with his fins. The shark wriggles quickly for a second, then cruises off. Sorry Charlie. No food for you this time. Back on board the boat, dripping in the sun and rocking with the waves, the Hawaiian film crew asks, "Brah, are dahy sharks usually dhat hairy?"

I say, "Most of the dives are not uncomfortable in any way, and as I stated previously, having the sharks around is the best. I like the Amber Jack, Alua, Great Barracuda, Green Turtles, Spotted Eagle Rays, Mantas, and everything else out here too. I wish the Monk

Seals and Spinner Dolphins would come play with us, but they have no interest in humans, which I'm sure Lorenz would say is probably adaptively intelligent of them."

Seals and dolphins drink milk; . . . , when they are babies!

Chapter 9: Conundrum Smack!

The cold, wet, north central Pacific winter creeps back in for a second wallop, and on the atoll, we start to witness all of the albatross, returning like clockwork, to feed the surviving chicks. The albatross breed in the winter instead of the spring, so the younger chicks can benefit from the rainwater that drips down their bills and quenches their thirst. Though hypothermia is the number two killer of chicks, it is the much more dangerous dehydration, at the end of the breeding season, that wipes out much higher numbers of gooney chicks.

Good News! We have officially stopped all rat baiting, and the word is, they have been completely eradicated, . . . extirpated from the entire atoll. I haven't seen a rat since I first got her practically. However, much less lethal to birds, the mice seem to be having a population explosion, with no more mean rats to contend with. The anti-coagulant, which worked so well on the much heavier rats, works poorly or not at all on the miniature mice. We can't snap trap them outside of the buildings because of the birds, so all we can do is snap trap them inside buildings.

My eyes feel like they will explode with tears when, to my surprise, in the very end of December, the new tourists come off the latest plane. Here I am, standing in my uniform, in my sweaty little brown boots, and down the gangway come not just one or two, but my entire family, including a nephew. What a shock! I stand for a moment in disbelief, and then sprint to them, with the tears bouncing in my blurry eyes. I give each of them big, hard, long hugs. "Oh my god!" I exclaim.

I want to ask what they are doing here, and a million other questions, but I can't. I simply can't say anything. Me?! I can't say anything?!

After a good night's sleep, breakfast and orientation, my family comes on my Natural History tour.

Kestrel orients the Natural History tour group, projecting like Pavarotti.

Then at lunch, they say they are all going to hangout up the beach.
I tell them I will join them as soon as I can get out of work.
An hour after lunch, Chipweldi approaches me in our headquarters, "So it looks like the whole family made it out here to see ya. He, he ha, heh."
I respond politely and go about my business.
Then Chipweldi says, "Have you seen this newly approved vol app.?" he asks me.
"No." I look at the volunteer application for a second. It states that Chelonia has been approved, by Chipweldi, as a volunteer, and she can come to Halfway Atoll on the next flight, if she wants to.
I am so psyched, I could jump through the ceiling. But wait a minute, this is Chipweldi.
"What is this, and what's the catch?" I ask, so unlike the trusting soul that came here just two-short years ago.
Chipweldi snickers, "No catch. Look, I can see you kinda been dicked around by Myhel, and I know Misa Queen and I haven't been too good for ya. I got her on and Amb will sign off on it. You deserve it. He, hee hee, ha."
With that, I shake Chipweldi's hand for the first time since I've met him, "Thank you," I say sincerely, directly into his eyes.
Chipweldi looks away, "Oah, come on, hee ha he, you ain't gonna kiss me or nothin," he says, unable to cope with sincerity and appreciation.
I am walking on clouds, as I call Chelonia on the cell and tell her I booked the flight already. Though her energy is very low, and understated, as usual, I can tell by the way she says, 'That's great honey', that she is very excited.

415

Wow, this is the weirdest I have ever felt on Halfway. I'm as happy as I was when I first got out here. Halfway feels good again. With my family having landed, and now Chelonia on her way out, it feels like a whole new world. Once the initial shock of my family's arrival on Halfway ends, I have a moment to think, and I get worried as hell.

I remember back to our niece's wedding, when Rosmarus looked around for a second, pensively. In this quiet moment, we wait. Big deal right? Yes, yes it is. It is a very big deal. My family is a lot of things, but quiet ain't one of them. It feels weird and eerie when nothing's being said among us. It's a pregnant pause I fear.

'So, Kestrel, just answer one question: Do you believe in God?' Rosmarus asked with a capital 'G'.

'Do you believe in psychosis?' I asked back. Rosmarus's eyes showed disappointment. 'Obviously not,' I answered, 'Are you talking about god as you see it, like you spoke to god or hear god, or if I feel the presence of god welling-up inside me like you say you do?'

Rosmarus said, 'Like 'believe', meaning ya absolutely sure in ya heart that god exists? That kind of belief?'

I said, 'Then I have to say no. However, if you ask me a more intellectual question like, 'Do you think there could be a god?' or something like that, then we could have something to talk about. The question you pose to me now would be just like asking me something of the absolute opposite, like, 'Are you sure there is absolutely no god?' which is just as bad as 'do you believe in god?' Anyone who says they know there is absolutely a god or not a god seems just as arrogant in my book. The real question is: What the fuck is wrong with you that you feel compelled to ram god down my throat over and over again, year after year? When are you going to get out of this obsessive-compulsive phase, end this sorry situation, and when you do, will you go into an even more destructive phase, or will you finally be a happy, whole person? Why can't you just be happy and enjoy the great lives we have? Don't worry about god. Just be cool.' I have many memories like that to dwell on. I try to force them back out of my consciousness.

For the first few days on the atoll, my family stays relatively distant and neutral. I heard through the grapevine that they were impressed by my historical tour. They like anything with guns and bombs, planes and engines. On the third afternoon, they all kind of meet on the North Beach again. As I head up to look for my family, I shudder, and I bike so fast, and my mind races so quickly, that I don't even notice I am already there. I don't know what to think. I don't know what to do, or to say. I am so conflicted. I am so mad at them, that none of them call me or write me or anything, yet, they are here, and made this huge trip. Why? I am confused. Maybe they *do* love me and I am being paranoid. My nerves are on edge. I don't trust elements of my family. If they start their god shit, I'm gonna snap, I know it.

Sproc says, "So Kestrel, do you know how maddening it is? All ya have tah do is take god into your heart and you are in man. You are in like Flynn."

I stop and look around at everyone's frowns, then I laugh and say, "Wow! I know how this must look to many of you. Like I'm a dick for shitting on his beliefs or something, but you have no idea how maddeningly annoying this born-again brethren shit is. This is not the first time we've been over the same Jesus shit."

Rosmarus says sternly in a low voice, "Don't call it 'Jesus shit'."

I say, "As a matter of fact, I told Rosmarus a year ago to either treat me like a great guy or forget about me."

Rosmarus admits, "Yah, he said discussions about god or politics would be off the table."

I respond, "Yah, then a month or so later, you send me this e-mail that said: 'If you let HIM into your heart, HE will answer all your prayers with HIS divine good, blah blah blah.'"

Rosmarus says, "Yah, so then he don't wanna talk to me no more. He sent me a long letter."

I say, "Yes, I sent Rosmarus a long email." I pull the crumpled printed email from my pocket to explain myself:

Dear Rosmarus,

How's it going? I hope things are going great. Congratulations on the foreman position. Thanks for attempting to contact me recently and please don't feel obligated. I want you to be happy and have a happy life.

I don't want to add any sorrow or pain to anyone's life.

417

Even though we have some differences, I didn't think our family was that bad, and that we would stay in touch. Maybe I was being naïve again (as you have said). There are issues, obviously. Life is too short. Families should bring us happiness and peace, love and sorrow, hope and pain, joy and anguish, etc. The only time I hear from anyone (except Mom) is when someone dies or is in jail. That's Not Fair! I find that it's hard because I obsess and worry about you and wish I could make you happier, but I know you think I'm wrong and would never listen to me, and the feeling I get is that I bring sorrow to you. I find that for the short periods I'm able to forget about our family, I feel less stressed. I'm not sure why you are trying to contact me now after years of neglect. I am suddenly getting a flurry of contacts from Meg, Manat, and you. I hope it's regarding something positive. You said you "just want to shoot the breeze." Really? It's a little too little, a little too late, don't ya think? You have never called me to shoot the breeze in your life. I remember once you called me to tell me a Godzilla movie was on, but by then I was too old and you had no idea that I didn't even watch Godzilla anymore, and once you invited me to go biking with you, but your Harley broke down and you were pissed-off about the whole thing. Those were nice attempts though, and I appreciate those efforts, but that's about it.

What do you need from me? I think you would argue that you've never needed anything from me. I need and want a family who loves me, and doesn't project their own negativity and cynicism on me. Alternately, if I can just put you out of my mind, then my spirit and soul can forget and my anguish can diminish. When you start contacting me, all the pain and sorrow rushes back.

Think of it this way, what if I was dead and you were never going to see me again? Big relief? If that idea makes you happy I think you should embrace that, continue ignoring me, and go on with your life.

*When I called you 2 years ago to ask you if you had ever shot a pig, I was thinking you could give me some insight into how to make an efficient kill, and instead, I got a diatribe about the virtues of hunting. I don't even want to go there, because there is no point in you and I attempting to discuss hunting, **but the most important point is** either 1) your complete obliviousness to my feelings about shooting animals for pleasure, or, more realistically, 2) your* *complete lack of respect for my feelings, morals, beliefs, and what I have chosen to do with my career/life as a ranger. Either way, totally uncool! I can't say I'm surprised, because you have never had any respect for a pussy like me.*

The fact that JM (his wife) *had to twist our arms to get us together for that very brief meal at Fisherman's Wharf epitomizes your desire to avoid me. I was so glad that at least I got to see you briefly and show you the sea lions.*

Again, I know this sounds negative, but I don't want to hurt anyone. I don't want to bum anyone out. I don't feel like there is anything I can do about it. There is no way I'm gonna change and start hunting with you, eating steak and riding Harleys. I'm never gonna read the Bible or the Koran, or listen to Marshall Tucker Band, and you are never gonna eat healthy food and stop blasting away the lives of so many beautiful creatures. You have a lot of reasons to hate me, going all the way back to me getting all the attention at the picnic tables at the public yacht club. We can't accept those things so we have to let it go, or let it erode us internally. If we ever do talk again; sex, religion, and politics would definitely have to be off the table, but I can't see how we would be able to have an amiable conversation about anything. You might feel that I am being over-sensitive and you don't give a shit about any of this. I want to be a positive force, but I feel if I don't clearly express my feelings you will never understand. If people want to contact me in a friendly manner, that's fine with me. Otherwise, I'd rather spend my time in life doing things that matter to The Earth and having fun, instead of obsessing about negativity I can't help or change.

Kestrel

Our Mother, Saintia, looks around, and says, "Really? I had no idea any of you felt this ridiculous."

I say, ""Yup, that was an actual letter I sent. I can see some good points and some bad points now, and maybe some things I could phrase differently, and ways I could have made it way shorter, but again what's the point? I went off too much. I lost my cool. I went to far. This happens every time." I slide the paper back into my pocket and turn to Rosmarus, "Rosmarus, the thing that kills me about all of this is why? Why do you feel like you HAVE to talk about this stuff all the time?" I say.

"I don't have ta talk about it all da time," Rosmarus defends.

Too harsh right? Back off, be more tolerant right?

I thought, when Drats said he was writing this novel, that it was about *Homos* needing to work together and finding a way to share and live together on this planet cooperatively. I don't sound like I am being amiable and cooperative, do I? I have tried over and over again to tell the born-agains to stay off my ass. They won't. They can't. They are brainwashed and programmed just as much as the KKK, the Nazis, and Brittney Spears fans. Somehow, these brainwashed zombies think these things are good.

I say, "After I sent that to him, clearly explaining myself ad nauseum, he writes me a Thanksgiving email with a bunch of god references in it again. To defend myself, I could publish personal account after account. Here's another one I wrote about a year before I shipped out to Halfway."

Wow, that's a really interesting perspective of your life and Thanksgivings and I appreciate you sharing those thoughts honestly.

I am thankful that we can go hiking and see incredible wildlife still alive, though clinging to existence in a world of pressures from gluttonous, self-centered, ego-driven humans, oblivious to the fact that we have more than 2-million other species on The Planet, and Earth isn't all about US. As a kid, I thought I would never see Bald Eagles or Harbor Seals in Massachusetts. I saw them both on my last trips back. That is very heartening to me. We can make the world better if we want to; if we can put away our hate, prejudice, and spite.

I am thankful that we live in a world where no one can program anyone or force us to believe in their religion, mores, ethics, politics, or the like, and that I can think for myself and make intelligent decisions, at the same time taking full responsibility for my mistakes or achievements, and finding spirituality and love without restrictions or fear from rigid, archaic views.

I am thankful for having Dad, who taught me that labor unions were good, and hard work, and reading the newspaper, and being involved in the community, are all important.

I thank you for the prayers. I have plenty of grace and blessings, I know that. Mercy? Woooooh! I have to find a way to find mercy on myself and my sick mind and figure out how to cope with my heart and these emotional hurdles that keep me awake at night.
I wish our family LOVE, peace, and happiness and I wish we could find this joy without any form of "opiates" to keep us sane. I don't think I ever saw you drunk in my life, but I am glad you recognized any issues you had and obliterated them. I know you can. You have always been very strong.
Love and Peace, and thanks for being my brother,
Kestrel

I look around and defend, "See? I try. I tried really hard. Over and over again. It's impossible to get through to fanatics. I told him and Sproc multiple times, 'Don't talk to me about religion.' Their attitude is 'Fuck you little bro! I will even talk about it more.'"
Everyone looks around aghast now.
I say, "Even when I haven't heard a kind word in years, I get NRA propaganda from him."
Rosmarus says, "Ya say ya care about animals, and ya luv dis country, but ya don't care about protecting our gun rights."
I reply with a sigh of frustration, "I'm not going to get into an argument with you on that subject, and I don't know what gave you the idea I'm anti gun."
Rosmarus slithers suspiciously, "Oh, good. We need guns to protect ourselves."
I say, "From who."
Rosmarus rifles back, "From dangerous people with guns."
I say, "Wait a minute, so Rosmarus, you are saying that the regular dangerous gun nuts are needed to protect the rest of us from the insanely dangerous gun nuts?"
Rosmarus surmises, "Deer's a lot ah dangerous sick people out deer, . . . and ah I wouldn't call us 'gun nuts'."
I recover, "I know I wrote a lot of petty, angry things there. I am aggressively responding after trying so many non-antagonistic tones. What about how they respond? I am not forcing this situation; they are. Is that passive aggressive? I think you could call that active aggressive. So, that's it. I won't talk with them anymore. Is that what god wants? God wants believers to force

religion down other people's gullets? God wants US to kill people we don't like? God wants US to hate and annoy? This is Man, not god. This is Man writing this shit and manipulating this shit, for the benefit of the Greedy Greedies and the Richie Riches. It certainly ain't women writing about how they came from man and therefore were put on Earth to serve man and all that shit. The wives that fall for that deserve to be oppressed," I finish, avoiding my Mother's eyes.

Manat, the youngest, at almost 6'5" and at least 292 pounds, turns to me and startles me with a non-sequitur, "So what has it been like out here? You seen any sharks?"

"Yah" I answer off-the-cuff.

We all sit on folding chairs on the coral sand: My Family, Amb, and several other characters sit through a long, quiet pause. Pregnant. Waiting, waiting, waiting. If you were sitting in a movie theater watching a pause like this, you would start getting uncomfortable. Not a funny comedic pause, like on *Everybody Loves Raymond*, but more like a creepy, menacing exaggerated pause, like in surreal David Lynch films or in a Noh play. It's like a *Blue Velvet* kind of pause!

"What the hell Kestrel, you've changed," Nephew Chris pipes-in, "You use tah answer everyone's questions and be totally psyched and into it."

"He still is," Meg defends, always trying to say something nice. "Yeah, the tourists love him," Amb adds innocently, without understanding the tension and the subtext, and wishing he could do something to keep me on, but not daring to broach the subject and look needy. "Like a fire hose, right?" He laughs, shooting me a knowing glance.

Manat looks puzzled, and looks over at Rosmarus for a reaction. None.

"Look, Manat and everyone else, I know this might come off as petty or pig-headed, but I've spent a lot of time alone, day after day, night after night, thinking about our family. Anguishing over it. I think about you every day. I'm not gonna say shit to you. Manat says that I'm full of shit and that the rest of our family thinks I suck. I don't know what the issue is but I ain't sharing shit with you. I'm going to live a happy life with bright sunshine and light, and work where I'm appreciated, and spend time with people and creatures I love. If you guys don't want to stay in contact with me and want nothin to do with me, then there is nothin I can do about that," I say with sorrow.

"I didn't say that. . ." Manat tries to interrupt.

Rosmarus states firmly, "Hey, that don't mean anything. Manat doesn't speak for me, or anyone else."

"Rosmarus, I saw the hate in his eyes. I know I am not a genius in any way, but I know the difference between love and hate. He looks at me with hate in his eyes," I accuse.

Manat self-consciously tries to avert his glance, yet everywhere he looks, he cannot avoid the family glares, looking to see if his eyes betray him.

"I didn't speak for anyone else. I was talking about me," Manat defends.

"Really?" I reply, "So you hate me more than you hate Dad?"

"Kestrelllll", my Mom pipes-in with one of those 'Oh Mike' type tones from The Brady's.

"Ma, don't even try to cut it off. He needs therapy. This is it. Maybe he can get over this hump once and for all," I suggest against all odds.

"But Kestrel, we all came out here on a trip," she continues.

"I know. What better time and place?" I respond.

"I didn't come all the way out here for this crap," Manat says impetuously.

I ask, "Oh really? What did you come out here for?"

"Kestrel, that's enough!" our Mother raises her voice with a crack. This is way to painful for her to handle.

Interesting though, everyone else remains totally silent. I didn't expect Doger, or even Meg, to say anything, but I thought by now Sproc and Rosmarus would be ganging-up and running all over me with born-again religious shit. Instead, it is as if they feel this is necessary. It is like a process that needs to occur, like we had all been waiting for this to happen once, one day, waiting, waiting, waiting. Waiting for humans to find a way to communicate.

Waiting for humans to find a way to connect, to talk, just talk, and hear, and really listen. Waiting for a day when killing each other would not be seen as an option.

Like in Drats' feature length movie, entitled *Truth, Love, Extinction*, people, adult Americans, need to find a way to communicate. Pamela Smart, Matthew Stewart, William Kennedy Smith, and Mike Tyson: They all failed to communicate with the opposite sex in their lives, each leading to tragedy. Can't we talk and listen without killing?

Don't get me wrong. I am scared. You see, I know how I am deep down inside, and I know that if I can be that evil and violent, then other people can too, including my family, since we are so genetically identical. Yet, we are so very, very different. Manat could kill me in a fit of rage. He would not be smart or rational enough to realize he would be spending the rest of his life in jail, and never see his kids, and screw-up their lives. He might even kill me and then be tripped-out enough to kill himself, but probably not. He would just go on continuing to live in this self-created nightmare he continues to exist in.

In this moment, I remember Lorenz again. Oh Konrad, If you were only here to explain it to them.

It is quiet again. Waiting. Waiting on Halfway. Angers simmering. Finally, unfortunately, instead of making the breakthrough I so desire, Manat comes back with one of his typical cop-out Hollywood movie-tough-guy comments, "If I wanted to kill you, you would have been dead a long time ago."

"Oooh, let me guess, *Die Hard? Missing in Action 2? Top Gun? Force of None?*" I rifle back sarcastically. "I doubt that's even good enough for a Tarantino flick."

Everyone shakes their heads at me in anger and disappointment.

I calm myself, and say, "Look, I know I am fucking this up too, but how do I respond? Do you see what I'm dealing with here? He can't be open, loving, or honest. It seems to me that there is a streak of cowardice in our family, and it alternates kids. Doger, Sproc, and I seem to be relatively fearless, like our Dad was. Whereas, Meg, Rosmarus, and Manat, like our Mom, all also happen to have weight issues, and are chicken shit paranoid about something. Now wait a minute. What about Rosmarus? He is so big and tough. Is that what big and tough is? What about all those big gentle-giants among US? Was Andre the Giant a bully? I don't think so. I met him twice and he was a nice guy. I remember when I shook Andre the Giant's hand, and my hand completely vanished in his. It made me instantaneously sense-memory back to childhood and *My Dinosaurs*. But Rosmarus, no doubt, he was definitely a bully. He thought I was proud of him, but I must admit, though never to him, that I was so embarrassed when he was in high school, 5 years older than me, and he came to my junior high locker room to beat up a 9th grader. Granted, he was the biggest, toughest 9th grader in the school and could kick high school but, but still, 5 years is a big difference back then. Picture an eighteen-year-old dating a 13 year-old. Just ain't right, even in the Deep South. Anyone who needs to have that much control over something has issues, and that epitomizes the problem. I don't care if I'm in control or need to be. I never had control so I never need it. Rosmarus needs to have some modicum of control over his otherwise out-of-control, fear-filled life. That's one of the things he loves about hunting: That one instant when the shot hits the helpless little beautiful duck or rabbit. 'Yes! I am great. I am a hero. I "harvested" that animal! I am in control, right now, and for a moment, I am a man; a big, strong, independent man.' He doesn't like hanging around or talking with me because unlike Manat, I won't let him dominate. He has to dominate as the alpha, or he can't hang."

Before anyone can respond, I offer a graphic tidbit, using my "Italian Sign Language" to create boxes, columns, and rows in the air. I gesticulate wildly. I leave our Father out of the equation. We all knew he was into sailing, drinking wine, beer, and gin (not at the same time), and his omnipresent cigarettes. I have no idea what he feared, or if he did. He never showed me any fear. Do all kids see their dad's as fearless?

After I make the graph, I say, "I know that sounds like I'm harping on hunting again, but I try to be fair. Everyone, everyone in our family, has obsessive-compulsive issues:

Current Family Dynamic

Our Mom is obsessed with church, and her habit is house cleaning, (formally cooking). She fears furry creatures, especially when wet, and she loves babies, and tries to only say nice things. Doger obsessively drinks cheap beer and smoke cheap weed. His habit is isolationism from humans, and fears flying and socialization, unless it's with his dogs or chickens. Meg is hooked on cigarettes, prefers total non-confrontationalism, suffers from some nervous anxiety, and makes a mean apple pie.

This is where things turn sour. Sproc obsesses over Jesus, cars, and drugs. He is reactionary, passive-aggressive, and contrarian. I think he fears hell, God's wrath, or something like that but I don't know. He loves racecars and Harleys. Rosmarus also went through a 12-Step and obsesses over hunting and Jesus. Mainly, his habit is killing things, and justifying all the bad things he does with the bible. He may fear almighty retribution. I don't know if he loves anything other than killing.

Then there's me. I obsess about protecting wildlife, while I regularly worry about my family. Partying, singing and dancing; lots of sex, and hucking disc, make up my fun time. A bizarre psychosomaticism to needles (yet I'm fine with blood), still looms over me. And as you know, my loves: the natural world, music, dance, LOVE. Finally, there's Manat, who over eats to cope with emotions. Obsessed with enacting revenge on things to make up for his 'life being bad'. Holding some kind of generalized coward fear, but tough to pigeonhole. I'm pretty sure he loves his sons, and that it's not just obligatory."

Rosmarus says, "Kestrel, what the hell did we do?"

I can understand how he can feel that way, so I reason, "Okay, let me explain to you just for a second how I feel about this family right now with an analogy. After only meeting Chelonia in class, and then for dinner, and at the airport, and then talking almost daily on the phone, and sending letters and photos, and now even emails, I see Chelonia and I, with Gutszy Chilleramo of course (her little soft *Lepus*), sailing in a beautiful little turnabout. The dolphins leap in the sparkling sunset, right next to the boat; the bird life and all kinds of animals, marine life, terns and others, frolic. It's just gorgeous and we are so happy about the whole World, until we swing by the pier, to see the three of you standing there: Sproc, Rosmarus, and Manat, each holding four bags, one in each hand and one stuffed up under each armpit. These huge, heavy suitcases appear to be filled with lead. It's baggage; your baggage; all your old baggage, and you guys are like 'hey, c'mon, pick us up. Let us get in the boat.' I just look at you and I can't. I can't let you sink my boat with your stupid shit. Leave it behind. Leave it on the dock. Give it 'the deep six'. Send it to Davey Jones' locker. Take out ye olde baggage. No way! You are all way to stubborn to drop the bags. And what for? Why should you even

426

risk getting in a boat with someone like me who you don't like or trust? I sail away and try to avoid feeling guilty. There's no way I could let you in without sinking that boat."

Sproc quips sarcastically, "Oh boy, like we're the ones who all have problems", trying to get a rise out of me.

Manat snaps back, "Oh yah, we arh the only ones who have friggin baggage, pfff, right."

"I didn't say that," I defend, "but Hawksbill and Leatherback Turtles, and Monk Seals, and millions of other species are going extinct because of man and religion."

"Don't blame religion Kestrel" Mother berates, as if it is just simply improper and not done.

I reply clearly, "Well we need to lower human population growth to a sustainable level, but the churches want more and more flock, and work against the idea of dropping pop. They are not only against abortion, but contraception too! This population taboo thing has got to end. It's not about US. We have to think about the other species on The Planet. How many things do you do per day that is oriented toward them? Nothing! Extreme religious fanaticism on the one hand, and atheism on the other, has freaked-out a lot of religious types, but really has had no positive impact on global eco-issues. Religion is still about one little thing that's only been around for some 2000 years. I'm talking about humans going back millions of years and plants and animals going back way further than that. WE screw everything up right now and WE have to stop it."

Meg says, "Geez, Kestrel, what's all the tension about? None of us have seen you or talked to you in years."

I guess she is right and this will all seem kinda dumb when I am dead. I am upset, and disturbed. I say, "I should be in control of my own thought-process, use a constructive use of mental energy in a way to expel a lot of those feelings and redirect my aggression. Is that why I developed such a creative mind, and I am so different from everyone else?"

Sproc says, "Everyone feels like they are the different one from everybody else."

Then Meg rebuts, "Yeh, but all his life though, everywhere he went, people always said what a creative mind and active imagination he has, and how does he think of the crazy things he comes up with? That has always made you feel a little different." Amb chimes in, "He's the only person I know who ever wrote and starred in his own play out here."

I say, "Maybe that's the way Twyla Tharp felt, or Kate Bush." They don't know who I'm talking about. I rail bluntly, honestly, disclosing too much in unmanageable gulps, "What kills me about my family is not the hate, cause it really appears to be coming mainly from Manat; but it is this obligatory love."

Sproc says, "Unconditional love."

I say, "Being part Italian, we are suppose to hate each other and be men about it, but at that, blood is thicker than water and ya have ta luv ya botha. Really? NO. Hell no! I disagree. Look man, if people love you they love you and you can tell. I lay in bed at night and I think, 'Wow, my family friggin sucks.' I know, it's fucked of me to sell you down the river. I'm the jerk right? I made all the efforts to be nice to you, to never say anything negative, and to try to be positive and supportive. I don't get it and will probably drive myself crazy trying to understand why."

Our Mom says, "We are supposed to love our family no matter what."

I say, "Exactly. I'm supposed to be sweet and polite. I am supposed to assure that my Mom's feelings don't get hurt and there are no little wrinkles in the carpet."

Rosmarus looks at me, "But what? But what is dah problem?"

I explain, "Doger hasn't attempted to contact me in probably 30 years. I think it was cause he wanted me to help him move to New Hampshire the last time he initiated contact. Smell that fresh Derry air, and all that. He's an introvert. We all know that. Meg has tried calling me periodically like on my birthday, but I can't even pretend to start knowing what's going on with her and her life. I don't know if she is comfortable talkin with me or not. Sproc said I was right and we should stay in touch more, and then a week later, his cell went defunct, but when I sent him an e-mail asking him for the new number, no reply. He doesn't want me contacting him."

Sproc blurts, "The vibe ain't right."

Manat belches, "If I want to see a tantrum, I go mind my kids. Boo hoo hoo. We don't make an effort to contact you. Wah wah wah."

428

I say, "Look, I know what it sounds like. I'm trying to understand what is going on, and I'm trying to express myself, without yelling like a mongee."

Amb says, "Kestrel, if I may interject as an arbitrator, what are you trying to get at here?"

"I don't know what the issue is," I say with frustration. "Let's start with that. What is the issue? They say they care about me, but actions speak louder than words, and I know one thing, I would never treat someone I truly love the way they treat me. So instead of trying again to communicate with them, I just gotta let it go and try like hell not to feel guilty about it or obsess. I feel like I am the gregarious extrovert who could somehow intervene and pull all the shit together, but it's stupid to think I could actually succeed. After failed attempt after balls-out drama, it's just not worth it and I just don't care. Depressed? Maybe. I wonder what a shrink would tell me to do. Let it go? Fight for your family?"

Panburelie screeches, "Get hypnotized to forget them?"

Manat looks around, not expecting any of this, and feeling responsible, and says, "I don't know."

I say, "All I know now is that I don't feel any love for any of you."

Saintia, our Mom says, "I feel sad."

I say, "I feel disappointment, like when Dad died from alcohol, but I don't feel hate."

Sproc says, "You don't feel love, that's for sure, but you don't feel hate neither."

I say, "It just sucks, bums me out, and makes me say 'Screw Them!', like my friend Tina did to her family; like my best friend Tim did to some of his siblings (very diplomatically I might add, as usual, and much more so than I can ever be); like so many people who can't deal with such conflict."

Everyone looks around with dejection, but still, no one wants to say anything.

I tell them, "A comedian once said 'Have you ever noticed when you're in traffic, everyone else is an asshole?' Yeah, that's how it is."

Doger challenges, "You think our family, My family. . ., they are a bunch of fuck-ups and assholes, but not you. You're the good one."

Rosmarus says, "You're the cool one, the smart one, the nice one, the non-asshole."

I defend, "Sure, I'm not perfect."

Then Sproc says, "You have your flaws and weaknesses, but you're not lame like us," as if to humor my hubris.

I say, "I am out there in the traffic with everyone else. Can I be the only good one, the white sheep? Everyone else on the freeway isn't an asshole. As a matter of fact, probably 6% are assholes, and the rest of US are very conscientious about using our blinker, careful of other drivers, and respectful of old ladies crossing the street. When I drive, I pretend that everyone else in the other cars is Mom. How would you treat your mother in traffic? Extremely nicely."

Manat quips, "You, or a regular person?" trying to generate a laugh, to no effect.

I continue, "I may rush, and sometimes even quick beep, but I always try to be nice to everyone."

Sproc says, "So, no, you are driving and you are not an asshole."

I get to the point, "We have to stop this polarized thinking, and our family is not a bunch of fuck-ups nor assholes neither; we are just in traffic and fighting to get to our destinations."

Sproc preaches, "Well I hope that when you come to the end of your twisted journey my friend, you find that it ends with the lord Jesus Christ, and that's just the beginning."

Everyone gets uncomfortably quiet again.

I spout, "Yup, I'm done. Obviously. So how do I do it without creating more drama? I could do it the way all of you did it, just never call or e-mail, avoid any contact at all costs."

Manat says, "You do live 6000 miles away," as if to point out how far I have already gone.

Panburelie's voice scratches, "Halfway is a great place to go if you want to avoid people you know, with 28,374 albatross for every one of US."

Rosmarus says, "You've lived a great life with no regrets, and at this point you have no fear, nothing to live for, and that's why you need god now. That's bad. That's really really bad, but it's real."

Sproc says, "I'm feeling it. It's true."

Rosmarus says, "You ever feel that way? Like you ah missin somthin?"

Attempting to clamp down my feelings of pain for my family, eating away at me, I say, "Now, it is just enjoying being a ranger, and enjoying being open to really falling in love, that matter."

When they leave the atoll, maybe I will never see any of them again, and I guess that will be the only choice. I wish we could just relax and be friends, but we can't. Just like when Manat was trying to make *me* sound like the Baby Huey, I realize I give them little choice.

When my brother Sproc made the half-hearted attempt to say 'I love ya man', a few years ago, my response was 'Me too'.

Everyone knows that you can't say 'me too'. You have to say 'I love you' back, but when it's so insincere, and backed-up by years of neglect, it just brings me back to 'fuck you' instead of 'me too'. My Mom gives the dismissive 'God bless you and I love you' as fast as she can at the end of each call. I hate that one too, but I can't approach her on it cause she's way too frail and WWII old school, like this new character George W. appears to be. So again, I gotta let it go. Not easy, is it?

"Am I being a complete moron for giving you one last chance?" I say quietly and directly to Sproc. He looks at me a little flabbergasted, and is about to come out with a worthless quip, but can feel the gravity of my words.

"I'm serious. This is your last chance," I repeat.

"Oh, or what, like you ain't gonna be my brotha no moh?" he scoffs back.

I sing like Bob Dylan, nasal, *"When you ain't got nothing, you got, nothing to lose"*.

Sproc looks at me in earnest for a moment. He's thinking.

"What would be a Win-Win situation in our case?" I ask Sproc.

"What da ya mean Win-Win?" Sproc asks for clarification.

"Well Win-Win for you would be that I accept Jesus and am saved and we would all be going to heaven. Win-Win for me would be that I could have fun with my normal brothers again, and play football, and goof around, without having to deal with this mental anguish."

"We can have that. We can have them both," Sproc says with a preacher's fervor.

"No we can't." I stare at him during the long pause. Sproc looks sullen. "Believe me. It's like a curse I wear around my neck," I report.

"Well, I'm sorry you feel that way brotha." Sproc adds with dejection, but he really just doesn't have enough brain cells left to care.

"So there is no Win-Win situation, only Win-Lose. I have to bless and release, and just keep you out of my life. I lose a brother, but you are already so lost to me. I don't even know you. When I was a kid, and even when I was 18 and 19, I felt like I knew you, but it's not until now that I realize I haven't really known you for a long time and may never have known you. Which also means that maybe you never could have known me either. We are like a family of strangers who never talk. Now, I don't think I want to even know what you think or how you live," I admit in sorrow. "I think a Win-Win would be if you, Rosmarus, and Manat, all went into therapy for a year, worked out your issues, and then we were all happy brothers again."

"Kestrel, I can't believe you are saying that," Sproc says trying to guilt for finally expressing my true feelings honestly and articulately (a big NO-NO in Christian circles and Italian/Irish Catholic families.)

"Why? What can't you believe?" I quiz Sproc.

"We arh brothas. We are always gonna be brothas man," he lays it on.

"Brothers? Define that! I'm confused. Tell me what you think a brother is!" I demand.

Sproc struggles, "We'rh blood. We arh bi-o-logickale brothas. We grew up togetha. . . "

"Yah, and grew apart together to the point that you never contact me in any way," I rifle back. "Biological brothers don't mean shit. That's like saying we are the same as gators, with the same parents, but that's our only association with each other. Where have you been for the second half of your life?"

"I came out here," Sproc uses as proof.

"Ya, like some kinda friggin intervention," I retort. "Why neglect me all these years? Why come out here now? What is this?" I state bluntly, looking out of control to everyone.

Our Mother holds a crunched-up tissue in her hand as she wipes her nose and the tears she tries to hide. Everyone looks pretty mad now.

"I know, it makes it sound like I can never be happy. I am so glad all of you came out here, believe me, and I was in total shock. But I'm not happy that you are brainwashed into thinking like I am one of the unfortunate ones who will be 'left below' or burning in hell or something like that," I say to Sproc.

"But ya will, and it upsets me just as much tah know how easy it would be foh my brotha, my own little brotha, to be up deer in heaven with me, smiling down," Sproc says, starting to try to manipulate again.

I would like to say, just like Tweety Bird, 'Mmmm mmm good! That heaven sounds mighty tasty when he puht it dat way. Duh!' Instead, I laugh, "Smiling down!?! On what? The sinners in hell? Is that who we are going to be laughing at up in heaven?" I say incredulously.

"Hey, they made their own bed. God gives everyone the option for salvation. Ya just gotta be man enough to take it", he goads with a junior high challenge.

I state profoundly and soundly, "I would much much rather *NOT* be in heaven with a bunch of self-righteous, vengeful Lose-Lose situation losers. I hate what you guys have turned into on Earth; you think I'm gonna like your hypocritical shit any better for all of eternity up in heaven? With YOU? Why do you think I will never go back to Boston, though I love it so? I have created my own heaven on Earth, and it is great, and I love it, and I wish you and Rosmarus and Manat would stop bringing hell back into my life."

Sproc says, to try to sound hip, "I'm not bringing you hell man. You are just stubborn and resisting. I was just like you man. I thought my balls were bigger than Jesus dude," he says, like he is trying to convince me that 'Jesus freaks ain't square man; they're hip rebels who live by their own rules man'.

433

I spring back, "Okay, that comment right there proves I was *never* like you."

Meg and Doger burst into laughter. Sproc's face goes a little red. Doger says directly, "Sometimes dhat Fonzi ultra-cool act just don't hold up, yah know?"

"Kestrel, what do you want?" Sproc asks in frustration, "I'll never renege on Jesus."

"I told you. I want what I cannot have. I see no Win-Win situation here, so I have to choose a Win-Lose situation, in which I live my life in bliss without you. There's no way we are going to have a Kum-Bah-Yah moment and sit on the beach holding hands and singing *Imagine*. I don't want that either. That would be just too weird. But on the other hand, we can't have a brotherhood of man if we can't even get along as brothers. You won't let me have happiness, so I have to have happiness without you and hope in my absence you find happiness as well." I think the entire comment seems very reasonable to everyone.

Sproc struggles, "But you can have it all Kestrel. You can have happiness. You just need to accept Jesus, and you will be happy too."

"I am happy. I am happy without Jesus. It's your obsession with Jesus that's making me unhappy. Don't you understand that?" I explain.

"I don't have an obsession," Sproc argues back in the same defensive, reactionary way he always does.

I spout, "Look, I told you over and over again I don't want to talk with you about god, but you have to keep bringing it up. I can't trust you. You are out of control. That's obsessive."

"I'm in control," Sproc argues again.

"Okay, prove it by not mentioning god for the rest of the trip," I instigate.

Sproc argues back, "No, I can talk about god all I want, and that doesn't mean I'm out of control."

I look around to everyone else, "See where this is going. . . or not going? That's why I give up. Abandon all hope, thee who enters 'conversation' with born-agains". I say dismissively, "People are crazy. The trick is that everyone is simultaneously trying to make everyone else look more crazy then them. Let's face it, a lot of people, especially dishonest people, people who can't look

434

themselves in the mirror, religious hypocrites and the like; they will read a book like **Humans Need Three Hands**, by someone like Drats, and say he must be crazy because he is so radical or progressive. Really? You don't like what Drats wrote or what he is saying? You don't feel like Drats does? Really?"

"Okay!" Sproc yells loudly, "Let's say we don't talk about god at all. . ., then, can we talk about politics, like what a scumbag our last president was?"

Like a total sucker and just so happy to be off god, I take the bait like a fuckin fool, "I think, from even a cursory glance, it looks like George W. hates George H.W., and I'm not even a psychologist. There needs to be a Presidential Psychological Profile Test, seriously."

"What?" Sproc questions, "there better be ethics in there."

I rail on, "Then the top 10 finalists would run for President, WITH NO PARTY AFFILATIONS! The top 10 would each get a free one-hour TV slot to beg their case, a one-page article distributed by the AP or whatever, and an interactive website. There would be no campaign finance allowed at all, and no commercials. Money would have nothing to do with the election in any way. No one would be allowed to ask their religion."

Rosmarus lets out a giant, spitting, "Ppffffftttff!" in disgust.

I say, looking around at everyone, animated, "People who were smart enough to want to vote would have to take the time to research the candidates, and at the polls, the voters would have to take a test to see if they understand the candidates views and issues enough to be allowed to vote. If they did not understand the multiplicity of the election, then they would lose their voting privilege for that election."

Meg says, "Well, if that system were in place, it would have been impossible for Bush to get in."

Sproc and Rosmarus grumble.

Doger, the one who claims he has never even voted because it's 'just a big scam', struggles, "Yah can't do daht. Daht's whad a ya call, ah, . . ."

"Elitist", I say.

"Nayh, I don't know, is daht it?"

"Exactly," I say, "Instead, we would have a smart, policy-driven, psychologically stable Prez who knows what to do and how to get it done," I gulp for air. "We would have Gore or Nader. Certainly not Bush, if only smart people could vote. None of you would ever be allowed to vote, except for Meg."

Everyone looks at me with eyes a wide. Holy shimoli, how are they to respond to that? See? See? Overwhelming.

I look around. I haven't displayed this much frankness in front of Amb. "Am I crazy for suggesting this system?" I say, "Am I the crazy one? Please, I know I am freakin crazy, but, ya know, crazier than who? You?"

Then Rosmarus adds, "Geez, is this also what the atoll does to ya?" Sproc and Manat snicker.

Amb says, "Maybe so, but I'd like to see Kestrel take the same battery of tests as George W. Bush and see who comes out on top. You guys have a very smart brother you should be proud of." Saintia feels relieved that someone has said something complimentary.

I think to myself for a second. Lonely? Loony? Loonly? (combined, because I think when you get really lonely you get loony, so there should be the combined term 'loonly'.) What is loneliness and why do I feel it so often? Some people like being alone, like Ben and other Halfway hermits. Even Chelonia has told me already that she feels like she'd rather be alone than put in all the effort to have a love. I guess it all really makes me think one thing: I love my family and that's why I want them to be happy, but when I see they are not happy, it drives me nuts. They talk about heaven or being in paradise. Paradise? I'm already in paradise. I live in paradise. I have a beautiful love of my life who I trust and love with all my heart. I'm living in a place where I protect the animals and dive and swim with incredible creatures. I have enough food and clothes; what more do I need? I will never understand the empty, shallow weaklings that need more. . . more shit. I think if there is a heaven and I got there and god said, 'Hey man, good work, now how would you like heaven to be now that you're up here? You know, it can be anything you want?' I would say, 'Make it just like Earth please! I would like some Eastern forest, like Acadia, Maine, or the White Mountains, and some Redwood forest like Big Basin, and for good measure, a smattering of other habitats like coral atoll, ponds and marshes, you know, a nice diversity. Oh, and especially, don't forget Chelonia, to give me sweet love every day, and some Shnapple and some sushi would be killa. And of course, it goes without saying, tons of animals.'

See, I guess that's one of the problems the belief pushers have in getting un-programmed people, like Chelonia, Loon, Dietera, and I, to buy into the whole heaven thing. If you are poor, sad, desperate, have no hope, no faith or confidence in yourself, and are convinced this fucked-up life sucks and is full of suffering and pain, then heaven looks like a pretty good idea. But if you are intelligent and balanced, or if you are a rich, spoiled, greedy power broker who has more than everything you could possibly want and have complete disdain for all that is pure and natural and good, then screw heaven right? Who needs that shit? That's for the meek, who one day, oh yeah, one day, shall inherit the Earth. Right!

All the lonely people, where do they all come from? All the lonely people, where do they all belong? --- The Beatles

So, heaven can't wait. I don't want my family to be sad in this life, knowing and looking forward to the next eternal life of the soul, which will be so much better. I want them to get their shit together and be happy now! NOW! I found heaven on Earth. It was a long journey, and hard, but I made it, and if they want to, no matter how emotionally or psychologically troubled they are or have been, they can make it too.

I look across at Sproc and Rosmarus, then I softly say, "Where does my role come into all of this? I can't show you heaven. If I lead by example, you think I'm showing off to gratify my ego. If I tell you how to be happy, you think I am preaching to you. If I give up, as I have now, then I feel guilty because I should be straining to find a way to help you alleviate your sorrow. Like I said, the only obvious option is to let it go, like I had to with Dad at the height of his alcoholism. I can't make you happy. In fact, the feeling I get is that I make you sad."

Rosmarus growls, "You don't make me sad. You don't have any effect on my relationship with Him."

With my elbows on my knees I lean my head forward into my open palms, completely hiding my face, and massaging my stressed forehead with my tense fingers. I say, "If I am a cause of your sadness, no matter how wrong I think that is, I must do the unselfish thing and extricate myself from you. The hardest part is letting go. If I mean nothing to you, then, I, I guess I don't understand that."

My family all suffer from obsessive compulsiveness reactionary traits. Yet, I am just as bad if I can't stop obsessing about them and letting their sorrow become my sorrow. I can't let thinking about them ruin my life. I know how selfish that sounds but killing myself over them does not help them or me. I have to keep channeling the positive energy away from my destructive side.

My mouth gets dry. My tongue feels sticky. I flash back out of my thoughts and see everyone sitting in the chairs, staring forward like zombies. Doger takes another slug off his can of Bud; Meg, another drag from her cigarette as she adds some sun block to her lips. They can't hear what I've been thinking, but my paranoid mind believes that they can.

At this point, Amb peps up and tries to make a comment, but before he finishes his first syllable, his venomous beast of a wife blathers, "Are you enjoying the sunshine?" She cuts him off and strains to be nice: An obviously extremely difficult challenge for such a wench.

My family nods with grumbles. "ya, hmmm, ahh, oh, mmm.", too engrossed in the topic at hand to pretend to be any more cordial. "Only on Halfway!" Panburelie grinds out between her tight thin lips and gritting teeth, as she drags Amb off across the bright white coral sand to leave us to our deliberations.

Man. Amb, ya talk about some kind of dichotomous character right? I look at myself as a pretty dichotomous character. What an oxymoron. Everyone I meet in this field thinks I'm an eccentric freak, and there are the bio-nerds who are instantly afraid and repelled and call me 'strange' cause they've been stuck in their labs looking at the smegma at the bottom of their Florence flasks; and the hip bio-nerds that immediately gravitate toward me and want to be my friends, like Zart and Twistor. Amb though, he's s tougher nut to crack.

I watch them as they walk off, then, I see Ballpig by the deck of the North Beach bar, smokin a fat stogie. He spouts sarcastically, "Hey, you look like you havin a great time over there," belittling the tense family situation.

He knows there's a lot of tension, so he feeds off it. I oblige him and walk over to the small wooden structure with white paint and lots of windows.

I confront him, "Hey, you saying to people I threatened somebody?" referring to his claim to Amb that he witnessed me threaten Myhel. I climb up over the railing of the deck and stand where Amb, and everyone else can see clearly that I am making no threatening gestures of any kind, and just seeking truth and justice.

"Yah. I saw you threaten the girl," Cherry Ballpig announces loudly.

"You are a liar. Why are you lying?" I state.

"You calling me a liar?" he says with intimidating anger.

I'm not buying, "Yes. You are lying. I never threatened anybody. Why are you lying?" I repeat.

Ballpig' fat bald head beads with sweat. He's losing face. I just want him to admit he lied so everyone knows I am telling the truth. If I break off now he might never come clean, but he could snap too.

At that moment, he reaches up, and believe it or not, grabs my hair on the top of my head in a big handful, and growls, "If you were half the man that any of your brother's were, I'd take you apart right now. Wuss."

Now you know I abhor violence, and it just makes things worse, but something snapped in me like a fucking lightning bolt of testosterone rage. My shoulders and neck tensed into a cobra-like posture, and my pecks went rock hard. Ballpig lets go of my hair right when Manat, instinctively knowing my body language after so many years and so many battles, yells "NO! Look out!"

It's already too late. The right hook is on its way to deliver a devastating blow to Cherry's cheek. The bigger really do fall harder, because he hits that wooded deck with the slap of a 321-pound sack of lard. Bamm!! I stand over him. I could have easily killed him in that moment, but instead, I restrain again. "You want to take me apart? Stand up you fat fuck."

Ballpig, Chipweldi, Dewhurst; and Amb and Panburelie, off in the distance now; everyone there, with the exception of my family of course, stand there in complete shock.

"Holy David and Goliath Batman," I blurt aloud uncontrollably.

He has got to have at least 117-pounds on me. Ballpig wriggles like an Elephant Seal in his over-sized Hawaiian luau shirt, his stogie smoldering on the deck.

"See? See that? He's violent. He's violent," Cherry Ballpig says as he flounders and looks up at me.

I take command of the bully pulpit, "Okay. That's enough. Dutroeux; I am sick of this crap and before it gets out of hand, I want to announce the following: The Animal Protection Service is in charge here and runs Halfway Atoll Wildlife Sanctuary. If we don't cut the crap with this mini civil war we are having, something really bad, like more than hair pulling and a punch in the face, is gonna happen out here. We need to stop this madness now. Look at what happened with the fire on the SS Halfway. You are a Marine. What do you have to say to US, about Americans?"

I think for sure this could be a great opportunity for reconciliation. I see pride in Amb's face, and my whole family's faces. I've laid-out the common ground so easily for him. Leaders take the lead.

Dutrouex looks around for a moment, then mutters, "None of this will matter in a short time anyways."

I stop in my tracks. What the hell does that mean?

Dutrouex slowly saunters up behind Cherry Ballpig and helps him to his feet by his blubbery, smelly underarms. The HIC staff turns and walks away. The Olderhostile folks stand in stunned amazement. Amb stares over in my direction, but doesn't seem to be emoting. It looks like he is lost in thought; replaying the mistakes he has made that got us to this point.

"Kestrel, get over here," Amb says in a threatening gesture.

I look over at my family. Rosmarus and Manat love the fact that Mr. Pacifist has hypocritically used force; something they love and I loathe.

As I approach Amb, he leans into me and turns his back from the crowd to thwart lip readers, "Good job stickin up for yourself and the agency. You kinda had no choice there since he got physical first, but you should have refrained from hitting him. Now what do I got myself into here?"

I say, "I know how this whole thing works with the APS and even if I am the best guy you ever had working for you and whether or not you could see it, if you don't like my viewpoints, then that's going to effect the relationship. But we also know we can't find

440

people who think exactly like us, so we have to tolerate the differences and keep the eyes on the prize, namely, saving wildlife and habitats for the other 2 million species on The Planet."

Amb puzzles over everything I have said for a moment. My phone rings. It's Chelonia again. She must really love me, based on all of this calling. I whisper to her, "Ya know, I can't think about my family anymore. My brain is going to snap!"

Before I pirouette up and out of Amb's range, I say, "Bottom line is enough is enough. You need to put down you foot and be strong or these jerks will run us over. And we need Law Enforcement out here if they think they can get physical with us."

I walk a little ways down the beach for some privacy; my heart races.

I confess to Chelonia, "I am flipping-out. I need to be more Zen. The chaos starts to get to me and my life is going haywire all at once. I'm totally distracted and unfocussed."

As a calming drill, as we speak on the phone, I vividly imagine Chelonia walking beside me barefoot, along the West Beach at sunset. With her toenails painted a rich purple, her feet look so hot and sexy. This slows everything down in my brain. She wears a modest one-piece. What an angel. What a beautiful, soothing angel from space.

"Get your mind off it honey. Everything's gonna be alright. Tell me about that guy asking you if you were a native," Chelonia asks in a soft, sweet voice. I start off on a mega performance of my philosophical soul by stating, "I am Born in Calli, and Proud of it!" I listen for Chelonia to react with complete seriousness in my voice. She believes it. Why not?

"Native Californian," I say to her again.

"What?" Chelonia says with disbelief, having graduated from SF State with a MA in Education.

"First off," I laugh, "everyone knows that Californians don't read." Chelonia concurs in Valley Speak, "We're too busy driving around in our Hummers and waitin for the next perfect wave dude."

"Yah," I say, gagging on a spoon, "I'm so sick of this shit." I confess to Chelonia seriously now, "Can't people see, of anything you should be proud of in your life, just happening to be born somewhere isn't one of them?"

Chelonia says, understanding the basic logic, "We have no control over where our mother just happens to bear US."

I know I'm oversimplifying the social aspects, but I go on to drive home the point, "I'm not a Yankee. I had nothing to do with a war that happened a century and a half ago. I had a woman from South Carolina (of course) in one of my courses at the Federal Training Center in West Virginia, and she was a Fed mind you, and she, believe it or not, this was not a performance art piece or a Candid Camera deal or nothin, she pulled, 'You just don't understand what they (The Yanks) did to us (The Rebs)!' out on my ass!"

Chelonia gasps in complete shock. I'm not sure she totally understands, but I can tell she is way down on any kind of stupid-ass hate like that.

"What the fuck! You gotta be shitting me!" I blather. "Do the Jews, or is it the Christians, hate me cause The Romans (read Italianos) killed Jesus? Do I hate Polynesians cause their recent ancestors ate humans? This is the stupidest shit I have ever heard in my life. Don't judge people by where the fuck they are born; please!" I stop for air and a reaction.

"Don't you already judge Texans and hicks? You even say they are from Texass." Chelonia challenges.

"Yeh, I do. But I never judged anyone from Texas until I met them first-hand and they proved the stereotypes true, unfortunately. Hey, I went to France with an open mind too. That's not my fault. I'm sure, as I have said before, but maybe not to you, that I am sure there are cool people in Texas too, just like I know totally lame people in Boston too. We call them Massholes."

Chelonia chuckles, "So you are an equal opportunity hater?"

"First of all," I defend as I try to hold her hand through the phone, "I am doing it with love and jokes, not hate and killing and pain. I celebrate the differences. Secondly. I'm not misanthropic. I don't hate people; I just know we need about half as many of US on this Planet and we need way more 'me's and way less 'Cherry Ballpig's.'"

Chelonia seems mildly amused, slightly disinterested, and taking it all in stride, with an occasional nod over the phone. The Brown Noddies launch themselves from the stumpy nests cupping their feeble, frail, and fluffy chicks, and head straight for my sun hat. I duck and run forward a few steps.

A Brown Noddy stares down Kestrel from atop a Naupaka.

"Aeeeehhh, Aeeeeehhh," The noddy yells at me.

"Wow, they are mean," Chelonia adds with surprise, hearing them over the phone.

"Ya. At least they can't pull my hair with my hat on," I say. Then I continue, "Why do Californians take so much pride in being native, and I mean native in the most asinine sense, not Native American from a tribe? Why, the most important question of all time?"

Chelonia puzzles for a second, "Because they have absolutely nothing else to be proud of? Low self-esteem? They feel they lack intelligence?" She takes multiple stabs.

"They are born into a car culture, a void where they don't know their neighbors. Where they don't look at each other and say 'hi'. Where everyone and everything is so transient that all they can say is 'Hey, I'll give you a call, we can do brunch', and you know exactly what that means. If they have nothing to gain from you, you will never, ever, hear from them again. All the foreign students I tutored in SF all asked me why Californians act so closed and different from New Yorkers and other major cities in the U.S. they have visited."

"Es verdad," my little Salvadoran cupcake adds with her soft smile.

I didn't realize this until now, but she has gotten my mind completely off of all of the angst and mental turmoil of my brothers, not to mention the piddly-ass shit with Amb and Cherry Ballpig. It sounds so weird to hear her answer in Spanish too, since she never speaks Spanish to me.

"I lived in California for more than 11 years, and it's always the same. You go up to Portland, Seattle, Chicago, NYC, Albuquerque, and yes, Boston, and, Brazil, Italy, Japan, Thailand, Indonesia, . . ."

Chelonia cuts in, "Hawaii?"

"Yes, and yes of course, Halfway, and people will take you into their homes and give you the shirt off their backs. Why is California so fucked up, and why are "the natives" so proud to announce it everywhere they go?"

"It beats the fuck out of me," Chelonia answers, mocking my excited tone.

"Role out a futon, cook up some nabe. Crash my chair," I say with a Japanese accent.

Chelonia says with a laugh, "But why did you start out like you had been pretending to be from California? What was that part of the story?"

"I experimented with lying to a class I was teaching. They accepted me way more since they thought I was one of them. Suckers," I say with a laugh.

"You told them you were from California and they bought it?" Chelonia asks.

"Yea, why shouldn't they? But the point is, they treated me totally differently, just based on the perception of where they thought I was born. Total profiling. Probably like 83% subconsciously," I add.

"So can anyone answer this?" Chelonia asks with exasperation. "Why do Californians have an inferiority complex about the East Coast? There is no reason for it. It's kinda of the same way Canadians have been about the U.S. for a long time. It's a joke. I mean, Canada is great. It's very cold and snowy most of the year and that makes it tough, but other than that, it's a big sprawling country with beautiful wildlife and a generally good economy and good medical care. Most of the Canadians I have met have been really nice and yet, there's this kind of thing." (Like with Hamed, the o-so-cute Canuck I hooked-up with on Halfway, of whom Chelonia really doesn't need to know about.) "Once one bemoaned, 'America takes all our good hockey players.'"

"What?" Chelonia groans. "You gotta be kidden me. There are plenty more and better reasons for Canadians to be pissed at the U.S."

"I know," I respond, "This whole thing about Californians not liking people from the East Coast and calling them 'transplants' and always saying boring stuff about the Yankees and the Red Sox and this other type of stuff just cracks me up because I think they think there is this kind of rivalry or something."

"There's not?" Chelonia questions.

"I am here to tell anyone within distance that the people on the East Coast don't even give a fuck about Calli when it comes to petty bullshit. I have seen useless, ridiculous Sox fans say over and over again, 'Yankees suck!' That's what they care about. Period. Never in my life did I ever once hear anyone say anything negative about California."

"Never?" Chelonia asks as she paints her long pointy nails and adjusts a photo she has of me on her nightstand.

The air temperature is perfect. The sun almost touches the foam surf line, hitting the reef almost a mile out. Ah, beautiful, paradise, heaven. This is heaven. I sigh in relaxed relief.

We go off on a quick tangent to discuss details about her arrival, then somehow, I get sucked back onto the obsessive family track.

"One person, once, my Dad, when I told him I was moving to LA, said, 'What do yuh wanna go thehh foya? Ya know all the fruits and nuts roll to that end of the country. Ha ha ha.' Now he had never been there, and that was tongue-in-cheek. He meant nothing real or derogatory by it. He never tried to discourage me from going. But he had heard it was a bunch of weirdos, so he must have gotten it from somewhere. He had heard that on Johnny Carson or something anyway, so it wasn't coming from Bostonians, that's for sure."

Chelonia says, "We will tell you we have better wines, better sailing, better weather, better cities, better nightlife, better sports teams, and of course, better surfing and beaches."

Then I say, "Some of these might be true, but so what and who cares!??! Oregon has better berries and Idaho has better potatoes. Michigan has more rivers than Maine." I say, out of breath.

"Big fuckin deal!" Chelonia answers with a rare but welcome sign of spunk, again, practically making fun of my hyperness-mess.

445

"Out in Calli, we even have Northern Californians fighting with Southern Californians. Have you heard this NorCal SoCal rivalry shit?" I ask.

"I was in it. At Mission High School I kinda had no choice but to join a gang," Chelonia reveals for the first time.

That scares me a little, but better not dwell on that. Instead, I say, "Got it. Okay, pass legislation for zero development. Make it so that no one can get a building permit and no one can move into the state of California because there are just no houses. Utilities would not be allowed to increase capacity."

Chelonia says, "We have the power to do that if we want to. Instead of stopping the steady flow of transplants to California, Golden Staters would rather have these annoying transplants about to rent their condos to, and to sneer at and perpetuate negative vibes toward. I think that's a little extreme, personally," Chelonia states.

I respond, "What? Even Newton said:
I can calculate the motion of heavenly bodies, but not the madness of people. --- Isaac Newton
It's not *like that*?" I question rhetorically.

"It could be, but you don't know that it is," she says reasonably.

"Hey, I of all people know, that nothing that anyone says is necessarily true or right, but I strive to be right. It just comes down to percentages really."

"Go on then," Chelonia humors.

"Nawh. I love you honey. I have to get off now," I say.

"Okay, talk for another time. Sweet dreams. I'll be in your arms again soon," she says in such a soothing voice.

When I return to the beach from my call with Chelonia, my family still sits there, now in the waning twilight. It is spooky.

I take a deep breath, and I try to lighten things up a bit, saying, "Rosmarus, Sproc, I have an idea. I am going to start a religion out here, kind of how Joseph Smith did. I will state that god spoke to me and sent messages in bottles for me to transcribe into what I will call *Halfwayism*. Then, miraculously, cause ya gotta have some miracles thrown in, the bottles and notes and any other evidence will ascend into the heavens. Is that cool? Will you join it?"

"No," Sproc chimes. "There is only one true god and one true religion, and what you arh talkin bout is blasphemy."

"Oh really?" I fight back. "And which one would that be again?"

"Our lord god," Sproc answers.

"No, which religion?" I pose.

"It don't matter. As long as you know Jesus," he answers firmly.

"Which happens to be your religion. So the Jews and the African tribesmen are going to hell," I quip.

"NO, see that's what's great about god. He is forgiving and will forgive deer sins if dey accept him," he recites like a robot.

Oh no. Here we go again. My fault. I started it. How do you reason with something that completely outrageous?

I froth with my frustration obviously peaking. "What about Catholics? They believe in Jesus," I query.

Sproc looks at me with anger because Mom is sitting right there. She has already said 'stop it' twice, but we keep talking right over her.

"They are wrong," Sproc answers.

"So they are going to hell?" I proceed. Sproc won't answer.

"What about Methodists? Hell? So tell me exactly who is going to heaven, exactly, since you know," I order.

"I told you, you have tuh accept Jesus into your heart," he answers ambiguously.

"So the Boston Church of Christ accepts Jesus. Are they okay?" I ask.

"Are they Baptists?" Sproc asks, not sure.

"First of all, they are a friggin cult, but basically you just answered my question. Your religion tells you that you have to be a Baptist or you won't get it. Right?"

"NO! No. You got it all wrong. God isn't like that," like he knows what god is like.

"Oh, so I can be Pagan and still get in?" I ask.

"No. Look Kestrel, you have to come to church with me and read the bible to really understand," Sproc says with a glimmer of hope.

"Yah, how about I jump off a cliff to see what the fall is like? Which versions of Baptists are going to heaven? Do you even know? What if you are in the wrong Baptist group? How do you know?"

"I know. God told me," Sproc says.

See? See what the hell I'm talking about? It reminds me of the song Drats wrote for his alternative band **Burning Circle,** which is not in the rock musical *Rudy the Red Bat*:

Precipice of Faith
by Drats

Oh great god, on high above
Take me to a place of perpetual love
Oh good god, maybe if you're out there, please come talk to me
I'm having major problems I've got personally, yah

Well, we all try to be so happy, hope our little prayers are heard
Just asking for some favors, nothing too absurd
Please god, help me, can't you hear my plea?
Please, are you listening to me, listening to me?

Chorus
I'm calling you, dear god I'm calling you
You're calling me, dear god you're calling me
I'm calling you, can't you hear me calling you
You're calling me, dear god I'm calling you

On top of the mountain, looking over the edge
500 feet or more, solid granite ledge
Look down get ready, suck in my gut hard
I'm flying off this precipice now, for you god.

Repeat Chorus

This is what kills me. How are we to survive on this Planet, and make amends, and get along, and be tolerant? We can't. If I can't even talk with my own brother, my own flesh and blood, without him going off on aliens over the rink and ghosts in Connecticut, then how on Earth is the president to have a productive discourse with fanatics just as programmed as my own family? No wonder brothers fought against brothers in the Civil War and this scares the shit out of me that it could get to that point again, with fascist red Sparta-states attacking pacifistic blue Athena-states. Maybe Bush is just as programmed? My siblings; we are from the same state, in the same town, from the same house and same parents, and we can't even talk. ***Humans Need Three Hands!*** Two hands just aren't enough. Alone, we are isolated, nothing is said, things go without saying. We fail.

Speaking of 'what kills me'. This is another fear I have. I don't ever worry that someone I don't know is going to walk up and shoot me. It's my family. I am much more likely to be shot by Sproc or Rosmarus in the 'name of god' (how's that for irony or hypocrisy) like so many of these gun wielding murders that happen across our land. Manat on the other hand, he would just shoot me out of spite, cause he always pettily professes to be 'a vengeful son of a bitch'. Guess I'm lucky I died out here for a good cause instead of being wasted by psycho fratricidal brothers for nothing. You ever see those stories on the news? Every time they show a photo of the gun nut who snapped, they always look like one of my brothers, especially Manat. Whenever I hear something like 'Massachusetts man kills four of his family members at hockey rink, then gets killed by police,' I always think right away, 'Please don't be Rosmarus. Please don't be Manat.' So far so good.

"Kestrel, I been thinking 'bout getting a bike goin again." Sproc reveals, interrupting my deep thoughts

"I'm never going to talk with you ever again. When you leave Halfway, I will never see you again. Just leave me alone and let me live my life," I say with a tone of failure.

"But . . ." Sproc stops himself for a long second, then decides not to speak.

I say, "I hope you do make it to heaven and you are happy, but I think if it is a just god, you will probably be going to hell for ostracizing your brother so vilely. I don't mean that to sound manipulative. I'm just saying if you believe in god then you should fuckin act like it."

"I am acting like it. I'm spreading god's message," Sproc answers with a grin.

I snap, "Okay asshole, let me put it this way: Have you ever been fucked in the ass?"

"Kestrel!!!" Our mother yells out loud with tears rolling down her cheeks. Sproc bristles like he wants to fight.

"Have you, or not?" I demand. Sproc looks at me with a violent stare; gritting his teeth, replete with un-Jesus-likeness.

"Every time you bring up god and try to force that shit on me, it's like you are raping me. Do you like that? You like fuckin your brother in the ass. Fuck you! Nowhere, nowhere in the bible does it say you have to be an asshole to your brother to get into heaven. As a matter of fact, I think it probably says don't fuck with your brother if you want in. You are goin straight to hell for being a fuckin dick to me."

Sproc jumps from his seat and races toward me, totally 'un-Christian-like', and lunges for me with both hands. I fall backward out of my seat into the sand before he can reach me and I pull my chair up between us. Chaos!

Everyone yells "Stop -- Stop it!"

Doger and Rosmarus grab Sproc and pull him back, but Manat takes the opportunity to blind sucker me again, punching me in the face while I am holding the chair with both hands and looking at Sproc. I never see it coming.

"What? What are you going to do? Beat me up to convert me? Is that how it works? Oh yeah, you're getting into heaven. Right!" I say as I back-pedal and throw the chair down in the sand at Manat's feet.

"Kestrel stop. Stop it," both Meg and Saintia continue to yell.

"Thanks for coming out to Halfway, dicks!" I say to Sproc and Manat as I stomp away.

"Manat, what the fuck did you hit Kestrel for?" Doger asks.

"I'll get any shot in I can on him. I owe him big time," Manat says maliciously. "I'm totally gettin into his head."

"You're an idiot," Sproc says to Manat. Manat looks at him surprised, thinking he was on Sproc's team or something.

"Oh, mother of god. Jesus, Mary, and Joseph. Kestrel is right. Our family is very very sick," Saintia says, crying heavily in her hands. Meg grabs her around the shoulder and hugs her; a rare display of physical affection in this family.

"What is wrong with you guys? He's your own brother," Meg says, also starting to cry. "How can you do that to each other? What's wrong with you?"

Doger sits down on his chair as Rosmarus and Sproc stand in shock watching me walk off past the BOQ in the distance.

450

"I didn't do anything wrong!" Manat says. His face is all red and tears begin to well up in his eyes. He turns in the opposite direction and stomps off down the beach alone like the son of Godzilla. What a mess. What a fucking mess.

At that point, Banette and Chipweldi pull up in a golf cart. Amb ordered Chipweldi to help Banette do some bird banding, and to find some suitable locations for the petrel scope program Hamed More will be doing. In this program, visitors get to look at a monitor attached to a long tube down a petrel burrow. I made flyers for it and dubbed it *Down Petrelscope!* I thought it would be a fun play-on-words with a nod to the naval history, and give Hamed More a chance to see that I want to be helpful and nice to her even if she has completely blown me off without so much as a word. Banette pulls the cart up on the sand right behind where Amb's chair still sits.

Ben walks up, sees the large group of us, minus me, almost says hello, but then appears to be overcome by shyness, and turns and walks away quickly with his head down, without a word.

"Ben is such an introvert that he doesn't even socialize with the people on island," Chipweldi says, trying to start a conversation. "Anyone!" Two of them mumble randomly.

Chipweldi continues, "He drinks Diet Pepsi, and saves the cans in a closet in his house. Hundreds of rinsed cans, that some day will be taken away on a magical recycling barge. Hi he hey. Will it come? Will he get any money for them? Ha hii. I don't think so. That's not why he's doing it anyway. He's not in it for the money," he states frankly.

"It's principle," Manat adds perceptively.

"He wants to show everybody his dedication, but he's too humble to actually show it. So, they sit hidden in his closet. I don't even know about them. He comes to lunch in the Galley, which to me looks like the highlight of his day," Chipweldi continues.

Banette observes, "He always sits near Myhel, and she really enjoys the attention." Everyone looks at her. "Anyway, has Kestrel always been such an optimist?" Banette asks with a soft, pleasant accent, completely unaware of all that just transpired.

People nod. Banette says, "Remember, this is almost 2000. Life is good. The economy is fine. Clinton is waging a war all right; on

451

tobacco! On illiteracy! That's my brand of war. Bruce Babbitt is pro wildlife sanctuary. We are expanding."

Sproc snarls, "He's a scumbag."

"Who?" Chipweldi inquires.

"Clinton," Sproc snips. "Bush's son as president will be way better. He's a Christian," Sproc says. With that brilliant statement, everyone quietly stares at the water in disbelief.

Hours later, when I return to get my bike to start a video program in the theater, I can see they are all still sitting there, in silence. I can't leave it like that. I'd like to come over singing and dancing, but I can't think of an appropriate number. Singing *Dear God* by XTC or *New Reason* by Drats will simply cause more commotion. Rosmarus sees me lurching toward them in the *Casuarina* shadows, and wants to re-break the ice.

"So Kestrel, you look really filled-out. You been working out?" Rosmarus asks.

Now usually I would not consider this a loaded question, but in this scenario, it is heavily loaded. I am the only skinny one in the family. Doger is big and strong, and not what one would call skinny. Sproc actually is pretty skinny, especially in the arms, and needs to work on his stomach and chest. Meg battled with weight issues most of her life, but once she became a mail carrier, that solved that. Hey, I have an idea; let's force all morbidly obese Americans to take jobs as postmen, etc.

I say, "Yeah, I lift twice a week, just to maintain, but I bike, run, and play Ultimate, not to mention lead walking tours, about everyday. That's one of the great things about being on Halfway. The Navy had a mega infrastructure here, cause at the height of operations, they had 3000 guys out here."

"Didn't the Navy take a lot of stuff with them when they left?" Manat queries, trying to also act like everything is as normal as possible.

"They took a lot, that's for sure. I think it was 2 C5s and then a number of other trips on the C130s, not to mention a transport ship," I reply.

I don't dumb-down the codes for Manat since he had been in the Air Force.

"As I mentioned in orientation and on tour, we do have HBO," I continue. "Too bad you missed the Navy," I say with a roll of the eyes. "Actually, Lt. Flipflopbaker was a little bit older, and much more mature nice guy. He really didn't fit in with the whole Navy thing. He was kind of a tall, skinny, weak, runty officer, but the other, younger chiefs on the atoll where all slobs. As a matter of fact one was threatened about being kicked out of the Navy cause he couldn't run 2 miles without stopping. What kills me is that we are on this beautiful atoll where we can run, bike, swim, snorkel, lift weights, play hoop, volleyball, racket ball, bowl, and most importantly, play Ultimate! How can you let yourself get fat out here?"

Now Rosmarus and Manat look at each other. Obviously, they think I have an axe to grind and a point to make about their obesity; but I don't. I swear to god I don't. I am just telling them facts, without any weight or bias. They will never trust me to be simply honest, because they never can be, so they think I'm manipulating when I'm not.

I continue unabated, "It was funny cause he was here for years, but he waited until his last two weeks on the atoll to start running. Why would you even join an outfit like that if you can't even run?" I say.

An albatross blasts by our heads with out-stretched legs, like mini brake-flaps. We pause for the whipping sound of the wind across its wings.

I report about the Navy chief, "It was funny because he said in the Galley that he had to go on a crash diet, and at one point I saw him doing double-sessions."

"Why was he doing all this?" Meg asks.

"Cause when he got back to the mainland he was going to have to take physical tests and run two miles," I reply.

"But why didn't he just workout the entire time he was out here?" She wonders.

"He is what we call a procrastinator," our Mom answers with disdain.

"All he had to do was run two miles basically," I say with a 'poooff'. "He was having a lot of trouble doing that. It was hard to have a good diet when the Navy was here too. I gained 14-pounds in 6 weeks when I first arrived. Even though the stuff the FNs cooked was somewhat healthier, when the Navy still ran the kitchen, they covered everything with greasy, institutionalized gravies, and fattening buttery gunk. Lard should not be considered an ingredient."

"Not fo nuttin, but didn't you say you stopped eatin red meat back in 1987, fo eva?" Rosmarus asks with an accent straight out of Revere.

"Yeah, I didn't eat any meat again until I started backsliding in my Master's program by eating fowl once in a while after 1993, when I lived near that wing place on Comm. Ave., but out here and on The Big Island I started eating fish at least a couple of times a month. I still haven't had red meat since '87."

Why do I have to keep reminding him about this? I think he feels he needs to eat twice as much meat to make up for me being a veggie pussy.

"Fowl?" Meg asks in a slow, puzzled way.

"Yeah, mostly turkey when I can, occasionally duck. I would eat even less chicken if other stuff was more available," I state.

"But how much are you eatin meat?" Rosmarus worries.

"I don't know cause I don't keep track of it, but I would bet I average at least one serving of fish or fowl per week maybe."

"Per week?" Rosmarus says. He looks me over and thinks I'm lying. In his mind, how could I be so fit and strong without eating meat. "Wheya getting ya protein from? People goin way back were huntahs ya know. It's natural. You love nature, right?"

I say to Rosmarus, "I don't even want to go down the hunting/anti-hunting path." I look over at everyone else, "I don't even want to go down that subject with him. It's just so far removed," I explain to the others.

Then Jellie appears, dragging a kayak by, with Pillmold sniffing her tail, "Well, I saw you killin birds. You lop off the head of an albatross and you don't even care."

I get really mad, "No, we are talking about intent. I wouldn't think of Konrad Lorenz as a radical by any means but even he said, quote:

To any man who finds it equally easy to chop up a live dog and a live lettuce should seek suicide at his earliest convenience!" ---
Konrad Lorenz

It's all about intent. I never once killed an animal that I was happy to kill or felt good about killing, or a sense of accomplishment. Hunters go out there to kill them for fun, that is the deed, that is the intent. It is like totally opposite. I kill them to put them out of their misery and sport hunters thrust them into misery."

Pillmold argues, "You don't kill just to put it out of its misery. You kill a lot of stuff that isn't even dying at all."

I rebut, "Okay, or because they are an invasive alien that's going to wipe out a species."

"And he tries to do it as quickly as possible," Banette defends scientifically, yet sympathetically.

I state, "There is nothing fun about it and that's why we can't, we won't even be able to have the most base philosophical conversation. Hunters kill for pleasure and I never will or have."

Rosmarus says, "But, yah playin god. Who made you god?"

I fume, "What?! You are playing god way more than I am. You. You," I stammer at the shear hypocrisy. I flip back to a slightly less charged topic. "Protein! I think you are thinking about that myth? What are you talking about?" I say, though I really don't want to.

"Ya gotta have meat to get ya protein, and you need protein for muscles," he announces erroneously.

"I don't know where that comes from; the American Meat Council or The Dairy Council or I don't know where the hell that comes from, but there are plenty of cultures all over the world that survive well with less than 10% of the protein Americans eat, and on less than 1% of the meat that you put away. We can get protein from a lot of other sources like from certain leafy greens and vegetables, beans and tofu and lentils and almonds, humus and all kinds of stuff. Plus, what about all the artificial meats out there? If you like cheese, there is vegan cheese out there."

Meg laughs, "It tastes like crap, but it's there."

I say, "You like steak, try wheat meat or seitan."

Sproc jumps on that, "Did you just say satan?"

I ignore his ignorance, "There are so many options. Any meat you like to eat, there is a meat free substitute with protein even easier to absorb than from red meat. They have vegan turkey."

The explanation appears to be going nowhere, as usual. If they taste any of these meat substitutes and they don't taste exactly like the real thing, which they won't, cause they can't, then they are gonna say, 'Nope, see, tastes like shit.'

My question is: Why do they bother asking? If they really don't want to know that answer but just want to hear themselves ask the question, why bother? At this point, it starts to feel like a lecture more than a legitimate answer, so I zip it.

"Kestrel, you don't drink milk either huh?" Nephew Chris adds. Here we go again, back off the milk wagon. "Okay, great example. Everybody thinks you have to drink milk for strong bones and protein. This is cows' milk, not human milk. The whole concept behind being a mammal is that we feed off *our* mother's milk until we are weaned. We are just the only species that was 'smart enough' to figure out how to keep drinking milk after we are weaned. Can you imagine if we demanded that our mothers' continue to breast feed us into adulthood? Women wouldn't stand for that in a million years, so we steal milk from cows and goats. That's gross. I just went over all of this stuff with our supplies guy Deny. When we were growing up Mom fed us vitamin D enriched whole milk. When we reached high school and she got hip to *Weight Watchers* and health, she switched US to 2%, then 1%, then skim."

"I remember that!" Manat pipes-in with a rare smile, "That was the 'blue' milk that was all gross and watered down."

"It took us a little while, but we got used to it. I am used to all of these delicious almond, oat, rice, and soymilks now. I can't even drink cow milk anymore," I finish.

"So we are not supposed to be drinking milk?" Sproc asks, with major doubts.

"Well, ya, sort of." I say cautiously, "I mean, people aren't suppose to fly or go into space, and we are doing those. Chelonia and I both SCUBA dive, that's pretty unnatural for a human, but think about it; no other mammal keeps drinking milk. Milk is for babies. And there is no animal in the wild that goes up and drinks milk from another species, and certainly not for its whole life."

"When was the last time you had whole milk?" Sproc queries, in an attempt to prove me as hypocritical as him.

"I actually tried some in The Galley my first week here. It's funny, but it practically tasted like heavy cream or almost like eggnog to me. It was so think, and heavy, and rich," I say.

"So, that makes you feel good that you don't eat meat or drink milk or nothin?" Sproc continues, looking for a lethal ego opening.

456

I am not going to give him an easy one, "I don't know exactly what you mean by that, but the main reason I stopped eating animals was to protect and save the other 2 million species of animals and plants on the Planet." Sproc looks at me, as if to say 'ah-ha', but doesn't really have it formulated, and finally, we all pick up our chairs and stow them under the porch of the North Beach bar.

Later that evening, I go into the computer in my office and print the most recent report showing how devastating a meat diet is. I copy and print it without permission, as Drats has done in many cases in this book:

The debate over climate change has reached a rarefied level of policy abstraction, but at base, these policies aim to do a simple thing, in a simple way: persuade us to undertake fewer activities that are bad for the atmosphere by making those activities more expensive. Driving an SUV would become pricier. So would heating a giant house with coal and buying electricity from an inefficient power plant. But there's one activity that's not on the list and should be: eating a hamburger.

It's not simply that meat is a contributor to global warming; it's that it is a huge contributor. Larger, by a significant margin, than the global transportation sector. According to the latest U.N. report, livestock accounts for 18 percent of worldwide greenhouse gas emissions.

Some of meat's contribution to climate change is intuitive. It's more energy efficient to grow grain and feed it to people than it is to grow grain and turn it into feed that we give to calves until they become adults that we then slaughter to feed to people.

Some of the contribution is gross. "Manure lagoons," for instance, is the oddly evocative name for the acres of animal excrement that sit in the sun steaming nitrous oxide into the atmosphere.

Two researchers at the University of Chicago estimated that switching to a vegan diet would have a bigger impact than trading in your gas-guzzler for a Prius. A study out of Carnegie Mellon University found that the average American would do less for the Planet by switching to a totally local diet than by going vegetarian one day a week. That prompted Rajendra Pachauri, the head of the United Nations Intergovernmental Panel on Climate Change, to recommend that people give up meat one day a week to take pressure off the atmosphere. The response was quick and vicious. "How convenient for him," was the inexplicable reply from a columnist at the Pittsburgh Tribune Review. "He's a vegetarian." The visceral reaction against anyone questioning our God-given right to bathe in bacon has been enough to scare many in the environmental movement away from this issue. The National Resources Defense Council has a long page of suggestions for how you, too, can "fight global warming." As you'd expect, "Drive Less" is in bold letters. There's also an endorsement for "high-mileage cars such as hybrids and plug-in hybrids." They advise that you weatherize your home, upgrade to more efficient appliances and even buy carbon offsets. The word "meat" is nowhere to be found.

That's not an oversight. Telling people to give up burgers doesn't poll well. . . and environmental groups shy away when asked for their policy on meat consumption. "The Sierra Club isn't opposed to eating meat," was the clipped reply from a Sierra Club spokesman. "So that's sort of the long and short of it." And without pressure to address the costs of meat, politicians predictably are whiffing on the issue, creating no bills to address the emissions from livestock.

Well, stick that in your meat pipe and shmoke it until it's jerky! When I hand this print out to my brothers in The Galley that night, they won't even look at it for more than a second.

"Hey," Rosmarus yells across the table, "if I handed you something from the Bible, would you read it?"

Good point. No, I probably wouldn't, unless it was really, really short, and interesting, then, maybe. Like Thou Shalt Not Kill. That's a good one. I like to ponder that one.

I try to reason again with the Christian who kills ducks and a number of other animals for fun, "But these are facts from a reputable source based on scientific findings."

Rosmarus responds, "Yeah, but the Bible is the word of god, not the word of man."

Oh boy. Forget it.

"What's the madda? Cat's got ya tongue?" Sproc goads with his elementary school psychology, feeling victorious.

On the following morning at breakfast, I give a copy to my family to share. They all look at it more this time. Did any of them read it and comprehend it? I don't think so. It's probably like when my Mom sends me a religious card. I read it, try to digest it, and in most cases, fully understand it. In some cases I agree with and subscribe to their viewpoint. Catholicism isn't all bad, but sometimes they are way off and there is no question that the church and Vatican need a major update on issues like contraception if they think they are going to flourish or even survive. I am more contentious than my family when in comes to logical discourse, and try harder, so I would have read it more than they did. I can't dump my lofty expectations onto them.

When I ask them what they think about the report, it reaffirms my belief that none of them can read very well. They look very vague. Ya know, you can take a horse to water right?

So Rosmarus turns to me out of the blue and says, "So Kestrel, wheya goin aftah this?"

"Oh, ah, what are you talking about? I was thinking about taking Chelonia to Bali," I respond with confusion.

"You know, ya think ya goin uptah heaven or what?" he asks quietly.

"What kind of a malicious bastard of a god would create a petty heaven and hell and be so insecure that it needs *me* to pray to it. That's totally insane!" I say with dragon's breath.

"One-point-five billion Christians around the world can't be wrong," Sproc adds factually, in an attempt to show he is not always completely irrational and can use statistics too.

I try to make a joke. "Hmmm, interesting logic. Most Americans are obese; therefore, I should be obese?"

Doger shakes his head in disappointment over Sproc and Rosmarus and utters, "That's a copout."

And there's where it stands: A bunch of adult Americans; a nuclear family, and yet, NOPE; we can't talk. We can't even talk. It's quiet for about a minute. We wait.

Doger, the least likely to break the silence, says, "Hey ya know, Kestrel, that picture you took of that like little baby fox, that one that I gut up in my house, that's my favorite picture. I love that picture."

I stammer, not knowing how to deal with a nice normal comment and some kindness, "Thanks, I'm glad you liked that. I, that, that was a hard shot, I, I think I had to go back there at like 4:30 on the next morning and hang out in front of the den in the dark and the cold, and then wait for it to come out into the rays of the Acadia sunrise to get the shot. Then I tried to sneak away so the pups and the vixen wouldn't know I was ever around."

Meg says, also trying to stay positive, "Oh that puppy was so cute. That was like one of the most cutest puppies ever."

I say to the crowd of dog lovers, "Yah, I know you've bred a lot of dogs and stuff, and I've said it before. Think of the cutest puppy you have ever seen, of any breed, and the fox kit is cuter. Think of the toughest, strongest dog you can imagine, and pretty much, any adult wolf could kill it. And, think of the smartest, most intelligent dog you have ever known, like Tiny or Sadie, and a Coyote can out-smart it ten out of ten times. I mean, these wild dogs, with their wildness still in them, it's just amazing how magnified or accentuated their respective attributes, strengths and talents are. That's why wildlife blows me away, because they are wild! This is like a wild animal, a totally free creature, looking at me, and deciding what it should do." I stop myself, and realize it's me who looks like the psycho preacher again, so, I try to sound chipper so everyone isn't brought down completely, "I gotta go get some work done. I'll see you guys later." I head out of The Galley and over to my office.

Back in The Galley, they all sit, playing with their food. Most of the people have already left, except for a few straggling Olderhostile folks with Kilgro and Jellie.

Suddenly, Manat says, "He's full of shit anyway!" with a blow-off. Rosmarus looks at Manat with a discerning eye. "Manat, you know I've talked with him. In one of his e-mails he said 'Either treat me like a great guy, or forget about me.'"

Manat looks at Rosmarus, semi-embarrassed, but remains silent.

A solitary Gray-backed Tern stands on Spit, mocking Homos with silent study.

"So you are the one who is trying to drive him away from the family. Why?" Nephew Chris interrogates.

"Rosmarus, Chris; you know what I say, 'Don't go lookin for trouble," Saintia says.

Now that's pretty good for her. She got both names right. Usually, when she's excited and yelling at one of the kids, especially me, she says, "Doger, Meg, Rosmarus, Manat . . KESTREL!" It takes her a good 3 or 4 names to get to the right one. The perfect argument for birth control: Don't have so many kids that you can't get their names straight.

Manat puts his hand up to hush our Mom, "No no, I can take this." Turning to Rosmarus, "You drove him away from the family way more than I did, . . . I mean with the whole religious thing and animal brutality and everything like daht. He said dhat the things ya do ahr sadistic or something like that. So don't blame me. And also, yah, I do want him away from me and my family. Not, not away from the whole family but at least away from mine. Whenever he's around, everything's fucked-up. An' I don't wan him pushin his non-war or anti-war views on my kids. If my kids want to grow up and be in the military, den dhat's fine with me."

Meg leans into Manat and says in a calm, quiet voice, "Manat, you don't like him around because he makes you feel bad. Why does he make you feel bad?"

"He doesn't make me feel bad. He doesn't make me feel shit. He don't mean shit to me. Shit!" Manat gets angrier and feels more out-numbered as he obviously makes the very clear point that he really *does* care.

461

Everybody stops and looks at Manat like he's the baby; the same look he's gotten all his life. Everybody knows. Everybody knows but Manat. He breaks down, and starts crying. Again; not a surprise. We have a very emotional family, though we have no mastery of expressing these emotions. It reminds me of the time I was working at BU. I hated my bosses. They were disgusting losers. At one point, the big boss gave me a glowing review after I had just been promoted. She asked me, "Are there any things you would like to make comments on, etc.?"

I said, "Well, let me think about it, and I'll get back to you."

"Okay. Fine," the ogre replied with a drag off her cancer stick. That should have been that, but I went ahead and actually thought about it and responded honestly to her nothing-but-polite formality of a question. A day or so later, I wrote a letter telling her how hard this job was for me and that I could not stand the stupid ignorance and the horrible working conditions here, and that the students hate the bosses. When she called me into her office, right in front of me, I saw a mega meltdown, not externally, but internally. My boss, with the ashes falling off the end of her cigarette as it waved about her head, had a meltdown. She knew! She knew what a miserable, horrific, scum she was. She just didn't want me bringing it to her attention. So she went off like she was strong, in control, and in charge, telling me all my flaws and problems and deflecting everything on to me. I felt involuntary tears start to roll down my face. What a sick lady. What a sick, sick, sad person. Anyway, the point being, I was like 31 or something, and there I am, crying in my boss's office. We are crunchy and hard on the outside, but sensitive and disturbed on the inside.

So back to Manat out on Halfway; his face red, getting all emotional, he bubbles, "Whenever he's around it makes me look stupid. It makes me look like I'm fat. It makes me look like I'm a weak doofus. Every time he's around."

"Manat, nobody thinks that way," Mom says, "You think that way. You think everybody thinks that way. Everybody knows that you and Kestrel arh very different, since you weh babies wrestling in your underweah. You've always been different. Completely different! That doesn't mean he's bettah than you or worse than you. In some things he's betta than you and in some things you arh

462

betta than him." She goes on as if talking to a retarded child, and Manat gets more frustrated and flustered instead of consoled or reaching any semblance of mature understanding. "We in the family all know that," Mom finishes.

And Doger, who almost never says anything, looks again, and says, "Manat, you gotta be fuckin shittin me. D'yo think any of us really think that way? We know that Kestrel is the way he is, and he's hyper and he's active and he's crazy, and psycho. You, you ahh the way you arh. And ya know, that's the way things arh. What the fuck?! So you not even gonna try to hurt Kestrel and put all this hate on Kestrel for nothin? What the fuck?!"

That was the moment. That was what Dad would have said, minus some of the swears, and we needed 'the Dad', in that moment. He said it. They all stop and look for a moment, some of them shaking their heads.

What the fuck?! What the fuck is right.

As I place my bike in the lanai of my Chief's Quarters, I look across the grass lawns, and there, I see Pillmold a grinnin. "You goin out to meet the plane?" he inquires with a wave of his arm. "Yeah, I just heard it's coming in and I just got a call from Amb," I respond officially.

"Oh, Der Commandant?" he says with a broad smirk. I look at him kind of funny and he laughs with a Chipweldi-esque 'Hee hee hee.' He walks away, but in that moment I realize how petty the HIC staff have become and how they continually try to portray Duetraux as 'in charge' of Halfway; not the Federal Government mind you, but the private concessionaire. I think about Cherry Ballpig, and Deny and Stark Kristian. Holy shit! Halfway is a Wildlife Sanctuary and a Federal Property for the benefit of its wildlife and all people. The private operator was lucky to be invited onto Halfway to try to make some money, like people from Marriot or some other company surely would have, but these people at HIC don't even know what a Marriot is. They think they run the atoll, and they think that maybe the APS will leave and they will have the Atoll to themselves, where they can rid it of pesky monk seals and albatross. It's a joke! This is an American Atoll, an American property owned by the taxpayers and run by the Dept. of the Interior. No matter what they do and how they do it, or try to screw shit up and make it unpleasant for us, it won't matter cause the Animal Protection Service will be on the atoll way longer than HIC will be around, for sure.

After my aircraft duties, I head to the All Hands Club for a veggie burger. I'm happy to have a non-meat protein option. It almost feels like a therapeutic release, like reading the *Utne Reader*. I see Renn walk in with Twistor, with Myhel, Kilgro, Jellie, and Misa Queen in tow. She is holding him by the elbow, like she is escorting and directing him in. I realize that Renn is taking total advantage of Twistor, and Myhel is taking total advantage of both of them to try to get at me before New Years, or before I fly off for good. I think the best way they can get at me is to hurt those I care about. Should I even have a great girl like Chelonia come out here? This is going to cause a mega strain and I am going to tell Renn to stay away from Myhel until I am off-atoll for good. I don't know how I will deal with the Twistor situation.

The friendly Sri Lankan bartender with the huge smile asks them, "What you ben having?"

Renn says, "We will all have Alabama Shlammers. Except him." Twistor looks over at her with surprise.

"No drinky drinky for your dinky dinky," Renn says in a nauseating display of public abduction, as she subtly slides her pencil-like fingers over his fly, hitting each bump on his zipper. "Remember, you can't do it as well after a couple of drinks," she murmurs with underlying beratement.

What a fuckin control freak Renn is! She is not trying to protect him from drinking because he is only seventeen. She wants to assure her play toy stays ready for action!

So I think about mental mind control. I think I am relatively smart, and yet, I can't control my mind. As I look at Misa Queen and Kilgro especially, I think to myself stuff like: 'I would like that person off the Planet, yet how would I do it quickly and painlessly, and how could I get away with it, and what if I were to do it in this way that nobody were to find out?' But then, after purging the tension, my mind starts saying, 'Nah, you don't want to do that. Killing yourself or anyone else is not gonna solve anything or make anyone feel better, and I'm gonna feel all guilty about it,' and shit like 'Did I do the right thing?', and 'That there is no going back and that it's permanent.' So I talk myself out of my totalitarian daydream and know that I must do good and right on this Planet, not bad. But then the conundrum arises again. What about Hitler? If I saw Hitler standing in front of me in 1938, would killing him be the best thing I could do? Yes, millions of people would agree with me. There would be no reasoning with that dictator/hater, and if I expressed my feelings I would jeopardize my own life without hurting him and stopping his blitzkrieg. I know I've picked the most extreme case, and I've argued many times myself that the means doesn't justify the ends and vice-versa, but in this case, most people would tell me to 'Take Hitler out!'

Renn and Twistor look at me for a long moment, "How'z it having your family out here?" Renn asks without the slightest hint of what it has really been like for me.

It's been so heavily emotional, but I can't dump all of this shit on them, so I say, "Like I said, it's hopeless." I gasp. It's so sad to hear the eternal optimist say that.

"Why Kestrel? What is hopeless?" Sproc presses, as he enters the bar and approaches from behind me.

I stammer. Should I even tell him this?

"Yes," Renn supports, "Tell them how you feel."

I start again with an analogy he can relate too, "I see The Last Supper. Instead of the apostles, it's our family. Mom sits in the middle, and the brothers and Meg are on both sides of her, with a lot of the nieces and nephews kind of floating around like cherubs. Everyone is there, except for Dad. It is so dark and gloomy. It looks like everyone is sad and crying, with their heads bowed beneath the crosses. It's horrible and bleak, but just outside, in the sunshine, Chelonia and I, with Gutszy Chilleramo the bunny, skip and dance with the birds and animals running around in paradise. My World is sunshine, bright sunlight, and green, and happiness. Blue skies, Pronghorn, Cougar, Golden Eagle, tall grass. You live in a dark, cloudy, negative cave. We create our own hell. We can have heaven on Earth even if the preachers scare you into thinking you can't." It feels like a huge weight sloughs off my shoulders, but will it have an effect. Can I 'Break On Through to the other side', as Sproc had sung so many times, pre-Christian daze?

"Well I'm sorry ya feel dhat way brotha, but I am livin in the sunshine too," Sproc says, trying to sound cool.

I try again, "It's like this: There is a good list of people and a bad list of people. I think MLK, Jesus, Gandhi, Chelonia, JFK, me, Mother Theresa; we are generally on the good side. Then there is Bush, Cheney, Satan, Rumsfeld, Hitler, Rosmarus, Manat, Manson, Ashcroft, and you, on the bad side."

"What?" Sproc protests.

"What, you think you are more like Jesus than Satan in the way you act? You gotta be shittin me," I say incredulously. "If I like somebody, or love somebody, I call them, write them letters, send them photos, email them, ya know, generally communicate."

"God, how much attention do you need from your family?" Sproc fires back defensively, glancing over at Rosmarus, who looks perturbed.

"It's not about attention. I'm just saying when I don't like someone; I don't communicate with them, like ever. That's what you do to me so that's how I feel you think," I respond soundly.

"Don't tell me what I think. I know what I think. It's unconditional love bro. Unconditional," Sproc states with anger in his eyes, like that is that.

"Oh, so how am I to know whether you hate me or have unconditional love for me?" I ask as if I'm supposed to be psychic. Sproc gives me that all-knowing biblical bullshit look, "It's all in the bible my friend. If ya spoke to god ya wouldn't have any o' these questions."

"So the bible tells you I love you," I confirm.

"Well not exactly. Ya gotta be more open," Sproc reels in.

"You mean I'm oversimplifying again, or open to brainwashing, or what?" My frustration in this idiocy builds.

"What answer ahr ya lookin foh?" Sproc says like a fortune-telling zombie.

"How do I know you have unconditional love for me if you don't communicate with me? Period!" I query.

"You know because I told you man, and you know that I'm yar brotha and will always love you and pray fo ya," as he slides back into semi-hippy mode.

I question, "So if I were gay you'd love me unconditionally still?" Sproc recites from his sick preacher, "Homosexuality is an abomination against The Lord."

"Don't let me put words in your mouth Sproc. Basically, what you are saying, . . . is that you have a relationship with god. You talk to god, pray to god, and by doing that, I know somehow that you love me even though you never communicate with me on any level??"
"Yeah," he answers curtly.
"So, how do you show you care for me and love me? You don't show it. I am just supposed to know that you do?" I interrogate, way beyond where I should go for his psychological sake.
Sproc thinks for a second. He doesn't like the direction of this conversation since he's not completely controlling it, and we are still not on the topic of the bible. "I have a good relationship with my preacher, and some other people in my church."
"Sproc, you don't have a good relationship with a single person on Earth. You don't communicate with your brothers; hell, you won't even contact Mom. I'm sure that relationship with your preacher is wicked deep," I state sarcastically. "Are you the only sheep in his flock, or does he have to divide up his time?" I pause for a moment to look at myself with disgust, and I change my tack, "I'm just saying everything is in your head. Your brain is your relationship with god. It's fine to have faith and everything, but you live in the god world in your head and you are missing out on the real world you are in right now, which may end up being the only World we have, and is certainly the only world we know we have."
"Hey" Sproc says yelling, "I ain't missing out on nothin. Nevah have. None of that shit mattahs cause I have a great relationship with the only person it really mattahs with."
"Aha! Exactly my point. The only deep relationship you have, On Earth, is with god, who you are now calling a person, and who isn't on Earth. Your only deep conversations happen in your head with an imaginary being: Not a real person right in front of you like I am right now. That is too many drugs," blurts from my mouth. Oht oh, I went to far.
"HE is real!" Sproc responds violently, "Kestrel, I just don't get what your problem is, ya know."
"It's irrelevant whether you believe god is real or not. The point is, your last 25 years of life, the last quarter of a century, the last half of your life, you have been spending all of your time, energy, and 'love' in your head, or soul or whatever you want to call it, and not in the real World with real plants and animals. I don't want to get

in a ridiculous argument with you about the existence of god, something nobody can ever prove," I state with exasperation.

It's true. Just like Drats with this stupid novel. He spends hours in a trance, in an imaginary world, working on the computer, writing this book, sometimes at 2 am, sometimes at noon. Sproc lives in his imaginary god world in his head, and Drats lives in this imaginary novel world. The difference? Drats writes his down. Drats publishes in hopes of sharing his world with others. Why? Is your world just like mine or totally different? Good to know, don't cha think? My imaginary world is constructive, communicative, and sharing, like Drats' world is. Sproc's imaginary world is totally dark and private, full of hate for gay couples and abortion doctors.

"Who says its gonna be ridiculous, ya dramah queen?" Rosmarus pipes in before Sproc can say it.

"Okay, it's ridiculous right from the start. This whole premise is ridiculous. First of all, you are agro." They look at me with confusion. I say, "Aggressive. You are staring at me like you want to kill me or beat me up. I'm not even gonna start a conversation with you about god, something you are psychotically passionate and incredibly confused about, until you learn how to calm yourself and learn to find inner peace through Jesus or whatever the hell you believe in", I reason with hope.

Sproc tries to put on his calm voice, "That doesn't' mattah. God put everything we need here to serve us."

"Bbbbbrrrrrrrrrrrrrrrrrrrr!" I am going friggin crazy! My hands morph into tense talons. Whenever I get into this crazy conundrum I always ask myself 'How on Earth do you tell a crazy person to go get help?' I mean, just like an alcoholic, denial is the first thing. If they are denying alcoholism, forget it, right? And, it's the same issue with psychosis. I always think to myself that if I just had the money or medical coverage, I'd like to take the time to find a really intelligent, cool psychologist who could help me get over all of the stuff that I'm mentally freaked out about, and retain my cool and mellow. If I could present it that way to Sproc and Rosmarus, and to Manat to a lesser extent, and who knows, maybe even Doger and Meg, though with our distant ages and disparate lives, I don't know if it would even be warranted with them, I could maybe help my family. One would think, if I presented it in that kind of way, reasonable people would think it was reasonable. Right? But what would really happen if I pressed the suggestion that they see a psychologist? They would say, 'YOU see a psychologist!' The last thing they would do is go see one. 'Psychologists are a bunch of quacks. A bunch of college guys who don't know shit,' according to them.

Ya know, the people who need it the most won't get it, because psychologically, they rebel against the idea, even the notion. If I could tell my family to go talk to psychologists for a year, and I will pay for it, and then see how they feel about all the stuff that they have inside, maybe they could find a way to be happy in life. Right now, they listen to ultra-conservative radio programs and make jokes about liberals, and they harbor psychological anger issues deep down inside, and that just the idea of even suggesting them to shrinks could put them over the edge.

Saintia says, "Kestrel, can't you see you are just as wrong as them by telling them not to believe in God?"

I reply, "What? I never ever once told them not to believe. All I've ever said is don't push it on me. That is a huge misconception."

Turning back to Sproc and Rosmarus, "You are mad because you want me to be like you, or believe like you do, but whatever I believe in, that's me, not you."

Sproc says, "Bullshit. When I told ya I believed in God n some otheh stuff, you were all harsh about it."

I reply, "I was in shock."

Rosmarus says, "In shock dhat we would do somethin dhat stupid as to accept a higheh powah?"

I bite my tongue. Fuck. It's true. I think they are stupid and they know it. That's why I get no respect. I don't deserve it.

I try again, "That's your giant ego that set you up for that 12 Step crap. Higher Power? I've believed in higher powers my whole life. That's what happens when you are a runt who gets beat on all the time. I don't need any program to convince me that there are higher powers, and bullies out there. You are spending all your time in your head, instead of with real people in the real world. That's my point."

Saved by the bell. Suddenly, my phone rings and I step out into the hall to hear it. I hang up quickly and walk back to my family group, shaking my head.

"Things still ain't going good for you anywhere, huh?" Manat carps.

I ignore him again. I figure, I will just keep ignoring him until he says something either nice or intelligent. I sit, aggravated with my own situation, running the reel through my brain.

Sproc shatters my daydream, "You said you wanted me to be happy. I am happy praying. Whadya mean all agro. I am excited about my beliefs. Just because I'm excited or angry doesn't mean we can't talk or whadeva," Sproc argues.

"You know I think it's great to be passionate, but . . . cause you're emotional, you're not rational," I reply.

"What's wrong with dhat?" Sproc pleads.

"If we both start out emotional, all it's gonna do is escalate, ya know, and I don't want to escalate anything anymore. It's not worth it. It's not gonna go anywhere. It's not gonna benefit anybody," I say with utter despair.

"Well, okay, I don't understand. Why are you feeling so hopeless?" Sproc asks.

Wow! Now some would argue that he shows some caring and compassion and can't be the ogre I make him out to be. You don't know him as well as I do. If he knows *why* I feel hopeless, then he can give me bible suggestions to help me find hope, and ultimately, Jesus.

I tack and jibe, not to win an argument, but to make headway, "Are you? Are you happy? Or are you scared and freaked out?" I ask directly.

"Now who is using sixth grade psychiatry?" Sproc finally has a chance to use 'my line' back on me.

"It's 'psychology', and no, I'm not, I'm just saying what I've said to you before and why I am saying it again. I am not interested in manipulation, or controlling what people think, or making judgments, especially those based on feeling only. We have to use facts in this World. Facts." I switch to an analogy he can relate to. "If you don't gas-up, it will run out of gas. You can pray all you want, but you still have to put gas in your car."

"So, I know that," Sproc answers obliviously.

"It's the same with everything else in life. You can pray to god all you want but that doesn't fill me up. I don't know what you are saying in your prayers, or how much you pray, or if you are praying for me or somebody else. I can't hear you praying." I try to get him to understand, "I need you to call me and talk like a normal guy and joke around and have some fun and avoid talking about or obsessing over god. If you were happy, you would not need god so much. Did you ever notice that? Happy, successful, normal people don't really need to make a big deal about god. Mom is very devoted, but she hasn't tried to push god on me since I was in high school."

"But you know that I am ya brotha. You know that I am. I got you covered." He feels empowered, since he has covered me with prayer power.

"Okay Sproc, I am your brother and I will play the brother game. As my brother, I need to get over a hump and I want you to help me with this. If we can't get over this hump, then there is no point in talking. I am not making an ultimatum; I am just talking again about what is realistic. If we can't talk, then it's useless to try to do so."

"Whad, whad hump!?" Sproc asks as Rosmarus pricks up his ears.

"Da bible," Rosmarus utters.

I quickly cut in, "No, nah, no, okay. The basic fact is, you did tons of drugs, you killed tons of brain cells, and it made you crazy, and you became a Jesus freak. Now, do you agree with that or not?"

"No, I don't agree with that!" Sproc answers with complete indignation. How dare I suggest such a thing.

"Okay, then that is that," I say, as I sit back in my chair, resigned.

"What?" Sproc asks.

"Okay, we can't talk," I say.

"What. What makes you right? How da yuh know you-ah right?" Sproc says in anger.

"Okay, this is my last attempt. You know I am persistent, but not to a fault. I don't just make stuff up. Everything I state is based on all the stuff that's gone on all our lives forever, ya know? So what do you want me to say? Okay, classic example: All right, the spaceship over Larsen Rink. Here's the thing, I don't know if you are psychologically capable of discussing that. Okay, if you think for two-friggin-milliseconds that you saw a spaceship when you were a teenager, over Larsen Rink, in the Centre of towne, a town of 23,000 people, next to East Boston and Revere with hundreds of thousands of people, next to Logan Airport with their radar

471

systems, and Hanscom Air Force Base, and Pease or whatever the friggin military places we have all around that area; and nobody and nothing detected these Martians except you? You? The Museum of Science and the Planetarium? M.I.T. and Harvard? And no one detected them? You got to see the spaceship? You were completely clean of any drugs of any kind? I mean, if you hold to that, and that is your Truth, then we can't talk about anything. Now what did you really see? Use your mind's eye to go back to that day, that time, and picture that time and place, and see the spaceship."

Remarkably, Sproc closes his eyes into a squint and humors me. Maybe miracles can come true.

"Can you see it? What do you see?" I gently prod.

"There is definitely a spaceship there," Sproc responds quickly.

"A UFO, or a spaceship?" I query.

"Spaceship or UFO," Sproc fires back.

I continue, "Tell me what you see. See the spaceship. What do you see?"

Sproc opens his eyes and laughs, "I see a fuckin spaceship man."

I stay the course, "What year was it? What grade were you in? Who were you with? Why were you there? What were you wearing? Okay, think to that day. You didn't do a drug? You didn't even get stoned? Was that the one day of your teenage youth that you weren't stoned? You didn't trip on any purple microdots in homeroom?"

"Nope, nothing," Sproc answers assuredly.

I'm shocked, "What? How can that be? You smoked weed everyday of your life like a chronic stoner from what, age 14?"

Sproc glances over at Saintia, our mother, then admits unenthusiastically, "Yeah, something like that," then he looks around at the rest of us with a macho sense of pride. "But weed was way weaker back dehn. It was a different time."

I go on with routine precision, "Well then you had to be wasted when you saw it. Was this post your first acid trip?"

"No. I think this happened way before I dropped A," Sproc says.

"When was the first time you dropped acid?" I ask, cause I thought he told me he was like 15 or something; the same age I got my first grey hair.

Sproc says blankly, tired of the interrogation, "I can't remember."

"You can't remember your very first experience with acid? It wasn't special or memorable?" I ask in disbelief.

"I can't remember a lot of stuff from back then. I don't want to neither," Sproc says like a tough guy.

"But you can remember the friggin spaceship!?" Rosmarus says with anger as he looks at Sproc incredulously.

Sproc defends louder, "I wasn't wasted and I know what I saw!"

I let up a little more gently, trying to get him to break through, "Can you give me a time, date, year, type thing? If it was pre-acid then you were just a little kid," I damn compellingly.

All eyes turn to Sproc now. He can't explain the spaceship so this puts a huge hole in anything he has to say about god.

"Why, what's dah point of dis investigation?" Sproc deflects.

"To make ya look like an idiot," Manat says with a snarking bite of bile breath.

I ignore Manat and ask Sproc, "Do you know?"

"No," Sproc says with resignation.

"Do you know the year you first took hallucinogens?" I press.

"I wasn't wasted. I saw a spaceship!" Sproc says for the final time, wet brained.

"Okay, well you believe you saw something that is impossible, and therefore, using transitive property, I think the stuff *you* think, is fake or wrong, and it makes me sad, and I don't want to talk with you until you have had at least a year of good, helpful psychological treatment," I suggest with loving care and compassion.

"Fuck you! You callin me psycho?" Sproc tenses.

Speaking like Sade in a gentle whisper, I say, "Yes, you are acting psycho right now." I sing, *"Just cause you feel it, doesn't mean it's there. Just cause you think it, doesn't mean it's real."* Then I say, "Just because you're paranoid, doesn't mean that they ain't out to get you."

Sproc deflects yet again, "What about you? You are a fuckin psycho."

I smile calmly, "Yes, I know, I embrace my psycho, I don't deny it. You are in denial, just like Dad was." Ut oh, don't drop the 'D-bomb'. "You and everyone else in our family lets the destructive side win. I embraced my psychoness and turned it into songs and

473

award winning videos, and my story out here is being transferred into this novel Drats is writing right now."

Everyone looks pretty angry right now, at each other, but mostly at me for stirring this shit up instead of letting everyone's mind and soul fester in a quagmire of unrelenting hypocritical nonsense and foolishness.

"If we can't talk about anything rationally, then we are going to have an irrational conversation," I try to appeal to their reason.

"SO WHAT? Let's have an irrational conversation. Why does everything have to be so friggin rational with you. I thought you were an ahhtist?" Sproc yells, mainly to be contrarian; not against the dominant paradigm, or anything philosophically thought-out like that; just to be contrarian against me.

"You are really interested in having an irrational conversation?" I blather. I'm losing it but can't let it show. I take a deep breath to try to bring my heart rate back down.

Sproc responds, "Now you know how I've felt my whole life. How do ya think I feel thinking my little brotha was gonna turn out gay, or be in a satanic band? How do you think your brothas Rosmarus and I feel when we know it would be so easy foh ya to go to heaven if you just accept Jesus into yah heart and stop being so goddamn stubborn. I don't want to see ya in hell. It would kill me."

Oh my god! The nightmare of hearing this? What the fuck! I can feel tiny capillaries against the outside of my skull wiggling like caffeinated nematodes!

I grab my head with both hands, then say, "Look, I am an eternal optimist, but I've gotten to a point where I realize that there really is no hope sometimes and you have to be able to recognize that. You live in a world of crosses and consternation about the afterlife, and guilt and shit, and fear and pain and suffering, and this Earth is just some crappy Purgatory world for you to use and abuse. But I'm treating this life like there is no world beyond. I could love this World and be happy, if it weren't for all the religious types fucking it up for US. You think this is some kind of shitty world you just have to get through until you get to heaven, or nirvana or whatever. That's what you wanna believe, but why not make THIS heaven or nirvana right now?" I sweep my hand out in front of me like Charlie Heston parting The Red Sea. "Why not make THIS Planet that we live on Great? Be loving, and peaceful. I know, it's the battle of nature, the law of survival, the struggle of the fittest, but we are way too smart for that with our big human brains. We are humans. We are brilliant. With our big brains controlling our egos, we can very simply have a good World. But the problem is, it doesn't matter how much I try to do good; it isn't me that's screwing-up the World. It's not my people who are screwing up the World. It's not the people on my side. Believe it or not, you would think it would be the Jews and the Moslems and the Christians, and all the religious people who would be shedding the most 'light' on the World and who would be working so hard to help and save the World, and doing the most good, but actually, they are the ones causing all of the pain and suffering in the World for everybody else." Whew, I squeeze-off the valve on the fire hose.

Sproc sits slouched and frozen like a granite gargoyle. Rosmarus raises his eyebrows, "Get rid of religion?" he says, again like, 'over my dead body'.

I don't think I said that! "Religion needs to function mainly as a good part of society, or it needs to be modified to do so, or eliminated if it continually hurts society. No religion can be perfect, but they are all so far from perfect right now, and so stuck in archaic ways, ya know, ya take the Catholic priest issues, . . ." Our Mother cuts me off, "No, Kestrel, don't even talk about them."

On the landing craft ride over to the Eastern Island tour, the Hawaiian Spinner Dolphins greet Chelonia and Kestrel's family by Spit, with hyper-energetic displays.

I ricochet, "See? She won't even let anyone talk about it. That's the problem, isn't it? Brush it under the rug. Our family is great at that."

475

Then I turn to my Mom kindly, "I know, I know that, and I respect your beliefs and everything, but I just gotta point out that you got to realize that you can't force celibacy onto men, normal men, ya know, issues are gonna arise. It's unnatural, it's going against nature, it's like saying 'you can't have any water for your entire life. Don't drink water!' You can't. It's going against our physiological nature to not drink water. It's basically the same thing. So you take the Catholic Church with the priests; if that hadn't happened, and if fanatical Moslems weren't blowing themselves up with suicide bombs, and if the Jews and Palestinians would stop bombing each other back and forth, I mean, if all of these things, religious type violence and hatred were ended, the World would have other conflicts we would have to cope with, but it would still be a much better place. You don't have to necessarily eliminate the religions; you just have to eliminate the violent fundamentalism associated with the religions. Can that happen?"

"I'm not worried about it. I have my peace with HIM," Sproc answers like a programmed zombie with vacant eyes.

I slap my hand against my forehead as the unbearable conundrum drones on. I say, "Okay. I get it," just to end the conversation and to try to bring my blood pressure down. "I know, this is my fault. I'm the one letting myself get all worked-up. Again, if I didn't care, it would be so easy to blow-off this whole situation, just smile and say things like 'OK' and 'Yup' and 'Fine'. I could save time and psychic energy, and get on with my life. That's the problem with caring, and maybe why so many people simply don't."

Sproc says in the all-knowing voice again, "No you don't. You will never 'get it' until you get HIM." He points straight up with a narrow grin beneath his long, chopper pork chop fu.

I'll never be smart enough to let the comment finally ride. "What do I want out of all of this? Peace. Peace and love. I have to find a way to not hate Myhel and Misa Queen, for their transgressions against me or their problems. I have to find a way to befriend guys like Ryle, but that's impossible. I have to abandon my family, or live with them on my terms, which will undoubtedly lead to strife. *Don't Go Looking For Trouble.*"

Everyone looks at me with confusion. "Why does Sproc believe? It makes him feel good to believe and bad to not believe. I don't want to convince him not to believe. I don't want him to try to convince me to believe. I want him to be happy, but there are conditions. If he was a friggin heroin addict and he was very very 'happy', there's no way I would say 'Hey dude, as long as you're happy.' No. No way. You may think it a stretch, but it's the same thing. You, and Rosmarus, are out of control Jesus junkies. You can say you are happy all you want, but you are addicts."

Rosmarus turns it on me, "Forget about what would make us happy. What would make you happy?" as if to suggest I'd never be satisfied in any case.

I say again, "I would like you, my 3 problem brothers let's call you, to be genuinely happy. Laugh, sing, have a good time, work hard, enjoy life, and all that stuff; and dump the hate, prejudice, religious hypocrisy, animal torture and murdering, gluttony, spite, vengeance, cynicism, and all the other crap. I've seen other families where things seem to be okay. Is it such a tall order?"

Rosmarus shakes his head, "Your expectations ahr way too high?" With that clean rejection, I go back to my room to be alone for a while. What!? Me? Wanting to be alone? But my whole family is out here and Chelonia is landing on the next plane to touch down! Maybe some of Chelonia's only-child independence has begun to rub off on me already. After calmly meditating for about twenty-four minutes, and calmly relaxing my breathing and getting centered, I decide to call Chelonia.

"Hello Honey Bunny," Chelonia answers cheerfully, "I'll be seeing you in less than twelve hours."

"I know," I say with excitement, "way less than that, like just over six."

"I can't wait honey," Chelonia warbles.

I say involuntarily, "I can't wait to hold your soft body in my arms."

"Whoawh!" Chelonia utters, a little too much for her meek modesty.

I save myself, "I'm laying in bed on New Year's Eve, before the gig, and as usual, my mind races again."

Chelonia says with excitement, "This will be a special New Year's on Halfway, . . . 1999 will roll over to 2000, the new millennium! We will share that together."

I say, "I have total hope that things will be way better this century than last. No more stupid wars; people are too smart for that now. No more religious fanaticism. We have already figured out that is causing a lot more harm than good. No more evil, sick leaders; we've already had enough Hitlers, Nixons, Thatchers, and Rayguns to ever be stupid enough as to let a psycho lead."

Chelonia says, "Ooh, it is like a new world flying out from SF."

I say, "I am enthralled that we met at the training class and that the APS has really paid off for me in one way I never expected."

Chelonia says, "What are you thinking about really?"

I say sincerely, "I was just thinking, ya know, all the gigs I played with their ephemeral applause and back-slapping. 'Man, you were great out there tonight. You rocked!' they would say with exuberance, but those moments don't last even in my memories. Without photos or tapes or videos of those shows, I wouldn't be able to remember even a thing about them. 'Man, you should be signed. You got it all.' Even certain photos that I haven't looked at for a long time; they are completely forgotten." I reach over the side of my squeaky bed and open my old band photo album. "Here's a photo from a *Death and Taxes* gig back in '88 at The Whisky A-GO-GO. We might have opened for *Jane's Addiction* that night. I can't remember, see?"

Chelonia says with sympathy and understanding, "So you are reflecting a lot right now? That's good sometimes, as long as you don't dwell. What are you trying to figure out exactly?"

I say with confusion, "What was I? Who was I? What the hell was I doing? I never questioned any of it. It felt right and I loved it and did it. Why the fuchsia taffeta prom dress? I don't know; it just seemed to fit on every level."

Chelonia analyzes, "You weren't making a statement about drag or anything; it just worked? Maybe like Steven Tyler in eyeliner. Maybe like Suzanne Vega like a whisper of a waif. If you come across a photo now, you try to look at it and remember?"

"Yes", I say, "I try hard to remember. It hurts my brain."

Then Chelonia says, "I know what the druggies would be thinking, . . .", having had experiences at Mission High, City College, and SF State.

I jump in, ". . . and I'm telling you right now, I didn't do *that* many drugs. Hardly any, compared to many people I know, including the druggies and ignos from my town, to the burnouts in my bands. Everyone always laughed at me and called me a 'lightweight'."

Chelonia pops, "Like me!"

I think again, "I should be able to remember. What did I do? What the hell was I doing?"

Chelonia questions mysteriously with a breathy, "Why?"

I think aloud, "Why again." I pause, then confess to Chelonia, "It's like all those girls I had sex with, where I was really turned on, and really into them, and really wanted them really bad, and really felt this like love thing, or falling in love thing, and there was a really deep spiritual connection, and at the time, it was all incredibly important to me. Gone. I can't even remember what the sex was like."

Chelonia can hear my voice tiring, and says, "What it was like to hold them tightly after?"

I admit, "Some of them, I struggle to remember something about them."

Chelonia asks, "Their names?" There is a silence. She answers herself, "Their names."

I relay, "Some of them, after being so deep and intimate and revealing, I can't even remember their names! I have to call that one 'the older punker up the beach' and this one 'the Japanese virgin who always suspiciously kept her wrists covered, . . .'"

Chelonia asks over the long-distance buzz of a line, " . . . even when she was naked?"

I rectify, "There are definitely others who I will absolutely never forget their names, faces, the way we made love and what it was like. The promises we made or some other special, shocking, or unforgettable moment. Do those same women remember me the same way?"

Chelonia says with great doubt, "All of them, the same way you do?"

I answer quickly, "Impossible."

Chelonia says, "Memory is so selective."

I say, "Yuhh. You can remember a store where you tried on a pink hat. 'Remember? Let's go back there. What street was that on?'" I say in a cutesy girl voice, "You can't remember? I don't believe you," mimicking her exasperation.

Then Chelonia fires back, surprising me yet again, "Yet, you can tell me where we saw the Merlin chasing Short-billed Dowitchers, and I'll say 'Really, I don't ever remember seeing a Merlin. What's a Merlin again?' God that pisses you off."

I try to get Chelonia to understand and appreciate the difference, "You know how many Merlins I've seen in my life? Maybe 4."

Chelonia parrots, "Maybe."

"Let's see," I start the list in my databanks, "there was the one on top of the dead snag in the Blue Hills Reservation with all the fall colors vibrating in yellow, orange and red behind it. There was the one that blasted past my head in Belle Isle Marsh, flying as straight as an arrow, I would even say straighter, literally (and don't worry, I know what 'literally' means) at what had to be 71 mph."

Then Chelonia says, "There was the aforementioned one dive-bombing the dowitchers at Elkhorn Slough, which we saw from our kayak . . . remember honey!!!" she says with a grin coming all the way over the phone.

"Forget it." I say with dejection, "You don't remember, but you can't get pissed at me about the stupid pink hat thing either. And, and . . . damn, where else? The Farallones? No, was it Cadillac Mountain? It definitely wasn't Hokkaido. That was dominated by White-tailed and Steller's Sea Eagles, and those Japanese Cranes and Tundra Swans. Hmmm. Anyway, I can't remember, but it must have been 4 at least. So see, *I* can't even remember that."

"I see what you are saying," she says sweetly.

I say, "Chelonia; what a girl. What a great, great, girl. I just want to give you all my love honey."

Chelonia answers quick and serious, "Not too much."

My mind quickly flashes to Hiromi. What a stark contrast to Hiromi with her histrionic 'You not lubb me! I go back to my loom!' Chelonia would never waste my time (or hers more importantly) on stupid shit like that.

"Thank you honey. I will be there to see you soon and make everything alright." Chelonia enchants like a siren, "What do you need to just get off your chest honey?"

I say, "So now, instead of my human-centric rock performances; like the one I am about to put on at midnight on New Year's Eve, in only hours from now; and my ego empowering performance art to trip people out; I'm all alone, day after day, working as hard as I can in the sweltering sun to build a native forest (known as a habitat creation site, not a restoration site), eradicate alien plants, take out centipedes and mice, etc."

Chelonia says, "So, as far as the Earth is concerned, what you are doing now, bit by bit, day after day, is so much more important and effective than a million gigs."

I agree, "Or **Bogus Weirdness** shows."

Chelonia asks, "I thought you were enlightening and influencing people with your art?"

I say, "Yeah, but years later *I* can't even remember it."

Chelonia reasons, "Can they be expected to?"

I answer, "People still sing along with *Sweet Home Alabama* even though it is a totally racist song. I even saw a black guy singing it."

Chelonia laughs, "The words mean nothing."

I go on, "On this theme of 'What Happened?' I'm going to try to remember a poem called *What Happened* that I wrote on my 20th birthday on the graveyard shift at the Sunset Marquis Hotel in West Hollyweird. It was the dead of night. My phone hadn't rung for over an hour and twenty minutes. Sweet Steffy at the front desk knew it was my birthday somehow (it wasn't until way later that my lame blunt guyness fingured out that she had liked me all this time and we hooked-up in what turned out to be a poorly-timed bloody menstrual jam.)"

Chelonia says, "Oooooioooooo!"

Yikes! Too explicit. I gotta remember my audience.

I tell her, "She snuck me a coffee cup of schnapps so I could 'celebrate' at my station that night of my birthday. Talk about alone, dejected! I was in Hollywood California man!"

Chelonia says, "You should have been partying it up."

I say, "I should have already been a star by then."

Chelonia asks, "Why do we remember those things? Something like that?"

I say, "If I pushed a little girl out from under a speeding train, I'd be hero for a day."

Chelonia asks, "How much mileage would you get out of something like that? A week?"

I answer, "A year?"

Chelonia rebuts, "No way."

I say, "Not even close to a year. Everyone in Winthrop still knows that Mike Eruzione was captain of The Lake Placid Gold Medal Hockey Team. My "little" brother Manat is a firefighter. Has he ever saved anyone's life? He had to have by now, but when I ask him, he always says "Naaaah", but then goes on to tell me about back in his drunk-abuse days, and how he punched-out 3 guys at once in a bathroom; so he certainly doesn't suffer from false modesty, right?"

Chelonia tires of my belabored brother battles, and gets us back on track, "So *What Happened?* Here ya go. You're going to really try to remember this poem from more than a decade ago."

I start to recite it with my eyes closed, from memory:

What Happened?
I can't feel.
I can't feel even mixed emotions as the lights of a plane streak and strobe past the dark violet violent sky at night.
Speckled and freckled with marshmallow clouds resembling flack fired from ejaculating anti-anti pistols.
Palms sway, and traffic tastes like strawberry schnapps sliding down a Styrofoam gauntlet of blue, Chrysler 5th Avenue, parking deception.
Mother cries on the line, as coke kills athletes, and an acquaintance books reservations for a 3000 mile separation. A separation not unlike that, of the receiver and Father!
Nooooooooooooooooooooooooooooooooooooooooooooooooooo!
Fans. Fans simply circulate hot molecules stretched across a forehead, connected to my, a, the mind.
Entries in a bank magazine equal neg returns, and infinite debt is as imminent as life/cockroaches. Don't accept gifts from an Italian airlines. Instead, look them straight in the eye with your distorted answering mechanism, that twists drums and anvils and stirrups and hammers to accelerated hang-ups, and dead lobsters that leer at you, and induce unconscious yearnings for yet another year to be pulled from your fleeting moments, that end in ash, and begin. It's funny. It's funny to wipe the moisture off of the bulging, protruding, translucent red lips of the answering zombie, controlled by his conscienceless phallic peninsula of pulsating

vibration. Ironically answering all questions, but the trivial ones
related to oneself.
You numbly ask: 'What Happened? Why am I here? Where am I
now? Where am I going? Am I going, or should I be coming
instead, and what's the point if I can't feel anyway?'
Goodnight yesterday. Douse it in 151, or a blueberry tart.
I can't feel.
I can't feel.
What Happened?

"That's it," I say.
Chelonia says, "You have to stop? Not bad for a poem you wrote decades ago, but there's a lot more left."
I say, "I remember segments. I think that's the whole thing, but it might be out of order."
Chelonia states, "You just can't remember what order they go in."
My mind drifts, then I suddenly start remembering all the make-up I used to wear, to be artsy, not fashionable. Like during the Tree People benefit, I had a tree on may face. Shit like that. Not cute. Definitely not sexy; just cool and artsy.
Chelonia wonders, "What kind of bands were you mostly in?"
I rifle back, "Artsy progressive rock bands, theatrical stuff."
"What with make-up and get-ups?" Chelonia wonders.
I say, "Nothing like KISS make-up. Ha haa ha."
Chelonia laughs with me, "That shit cracks me up. I love when Terry Gross and others stick it to dickhead posers like KISS."
I say, "What the hell was with that band and why, when I was in Jr. High, did a bunch of my friends think they were cool? Pick the best KISS song ever, seriously, if you can think of one, think of the best one you know and how 'great' it is and how it affects you. Now think of any run-of-the-mill song by any other band: *You Gotta Another Thing Comin* by Judas Priest, *No More Mr. Nice Guy* by Alice Cooper, *Under My Thumb* by the Stones."
Chelonia agrees, "Pick whichever one you want, and they are all way way better than anything KISS ever put out. I can't even think of the name of a KISS song right now. I always thought that band was a joke, and the funniest part of that is they didn't realize that they were a freakin joke. Oh man, on MTV, when they took their

make-up off!! Then when Simmons tried to play the bad guy in that shitty Tom Selleck robot movie. God, he sucked."

I laugh and say to Chelonia, "The only thing that semi-saved that flick was the fact that I was so in love with Cynthia Rhodes back in the *Rosanna* days. Oh yeah."

"Oh yeah. I can see her dancing and smiling right now," Chelonia also visualizes. "You liked her?"

I say, "Wait, her face is changing. Oh my god, it's Chelonia, but you look just like Cynthia Rhodes in the *Rosanna* video. Oh my god, you are so fine. I love you so much."

Chelonia says, "Wait."

I say, "Wait. She's changing again. Now she is swinging her hips like a samba girl. Doink. Doink. Oh, I get it: She turned into Sade and is singing *Love is Stronger Than Pride*. But it's still your face."

Chelonia laughs, like Milhouse Van Houten crying, and says, "I love your dreams, when I'm lucky enough to hear of any of them."

I'm suddenly reminded, "Oh yeah, and I was talkin bout love, or forgetting. Anyway, personally, this poem was big for me. It's a living poem in the sense that I still have a copy of it in my binder. I have, I don't know, maybe 31, or 65 poems and lyrics that one-day or another, I just threw away. If I threw them away they couldn't have been good, cause some of the stuff I still have sucks, but I just can't dump em cause they mean something to me. *What Happened* was kind of like that annoying song they always played every time Bob Hope entered the stage. *What Happened* maybe didn't make sense to anyone else, at least on a concrete level."

Chelonia asks, staying engaged, "You couldn't explain it yourself to anyone?"

I say, "No, but I felt it, understood it, and believed it. When **InsectAffect** would improvise, I would speak, sing, and yell this poem incredulously at the audience in an Artaud-esque assault of the senses kind of way, right in their faces, like they were idiots for not getting what I was saying. It seemed to me like they liked it. After a gig with **Burning Circle**, 8 or 9 years after *What Happened* debuted, an acquaintance approached my 'wee little' brother Manat and said, 'What did you think of the show?' Manat responded, candid as always, 'That's my brother foh yah; he's never happy unless he's right in yah face.' Manat wasn't shittin. I have photos proving I spent almost the whole gig out in the audience. I was so psyched when Sansome came out with a wireless headset mic., a la Kate Bush. I could hang upside down with gravity boots like a bat from the light rigging at Madame Wongs West, sing from the top of a mountain in the Mojave, climb around on the machinery in a sheet-metal factory—you name it." Chelonia says with relief, "I am so glad you are not *that* hyper anymore. Your poor Mother must have went through hell with you." Then Chelonia murmurs, "You feel better?"

I say with a groan, "It bothers me that I can't remember the rest of *What Happened* in order, but I guess I can't be expected to remember the names of those girls, the names of my band mates, the names of the kids I went to high school with; if I can't remember quite possibly the most monumental poem of my life!" Chelonia accuses, "You can remember Cynthia Rhodes' name no problem!" Then, changing the subject, "How much time will we have before your band goes on tonight?"

I say, almost drooling, "Your flight will land right after sunset, and we don't go on until the stroke of midnight, so about 6 hours or so, but you will have to meet everybody and everything, but no matter what, I want to spend at least a half an hour alone with you just reconnecting."

Chelonia says, "Can't wait."

I say, "It's New Year's Eve after all. I don't want to pull a total Halfway and show up at 9, to be hammered by show time and pitiful. Amb wants me to help him be on security duty, due to the Coasties being back on atoll, until my band goes on at midnight. He told me we need to really watch out for smokers in a government building, especially since the seniors have been complaining a lot of late to ASS, thanks to Jellie's coaxing."

Chelonia asks, "Originally, weren't you to be going on a pelagic bird survey at 4:30am?"

I respond, "I'm too tired to do the math, but I'm glad I cancelled on going on the trip. It would have been too exhausting. Would I have passed that up when I first got to Halfway? No way, but with you coming here now, it's a different world. I can miss a Christmas Count."

485

A White Tern chick hangs on for dear life, as it watches Kestrel blast by on his way to greet Chelonia.

I can't wait any longer. Next thing I know, I'm already dressed and at the airport hugging Chelonia, then setting her up in my house, then laying on the bed and squeezing her for another twenty seven minutes, then I'm in the All Hands Club. Blurrrrrrr.

I can hear Loon in a loud voice, expressing his opinion over the roars of drunkin laughter, "King George, the tyrant, taxed without representation. King George W, the idiot, will consolidate more presidential power than any president or king has before. This is not constitutional. This is anti constitutional, and anti U.S."

Pillmold and a couple of HIC staff from Georgia just laugh, "You so funny. It ain't anti me," they heckle back.

Loon tries to reason with fools, "We are supposed to have checks and balances between the Supreme Court, Congress, and the Exec Branch. Yet, as Homer Simpson recently quipped, 'I'm going to act the best way America knows how; unilaterally!' This may be what will happen next century. As the solo super power, we will do whatever we want."

"Good. We should." The drunks chorus back, "Who would you rather have running the world, the French?"

Loon states, "That means the mega corporations can dictate everything. Where is Constitutional equilibrium? Look at Charles Savage's work *Take Over*. How can a guy like Dick Cheney, who defends both the Iran/Contra Scandal and the Gulf War, and supports action against Iraq again, still be in power? I can't even believe that's what ultra ultra conservatives want."

It's a sign of genius—answering thine own questions. That's what it would take.

Pillmold parrots, "What dah ya want a utopia?"

I put my arm on Loon's shoulder and I smile, "When we get to the point where every state of the U.S. drops in percentage of obesity; when no one has enough money left to buy an SUV, let alone fill it with gas; when everyone of US is so sick of a Prez who, with the stroke of a pen pulls out of a missile treaty or blows-off Kyoto; then, maybe then?"

Loon says in full realization, "Nah. We don't have any balls. We don't have any balls at all. We deserve to get bombed and terrorized and taken over."

I mimic a rural accent and say, "Ooops; sorry. Can't keep reading this book. Gotta sit in front of the boob-tube for a few hours now to watch the game, or Wife Swap, or Survivor, or golf, or some other mindless shit like that, P-Diong!" as I make a ping like I just spit into a spittoon.

Loon is 'Loon' for a reason, but he stands up to multiple drunks. Maybe that's stupid. I admire his moxie.

I relate, "It's just like the funny thing I found with my family; I'm dammed if I do and I'm dammed if I don't. I told my mother on Mother's Day that I want to have a closer relationship with my family; something deep and real. I told her that if I try to be nice, polite, and conversational (as she is), then I feel fake or they think I'm fake, but they definitely don't like when I tell them my opinions, and they can't handle the truth. She replied, 'I know, isn't it horrible, we just have horrible communication in this family. Every year I send Sproc's daughter a birthday card and all I get is a receipt from the bank that the check's cashed. Never, ever a thank you card.'"

"Yah," Loon listens.

"It sounded to me like she was agreeing with me. Then I stated, 'Yes, just Friday I finally got to talk with Rosmarus (after years), and he said there was no problem between him and I and that everything was cool, but, though I think he believes this, deep down inside, I feel that there is hate or dislike or something.' I told her I said, 'I want a family that loves me or let's me go.'"

The bar gets a little quiet for a moment, so I lower my voice and lean forward. I knock over my bike helmet and my gloves spill out onto the stained floor. I pick up my gloves and get a whiff of Bonin Petrel musk, from when we were banding like a month ago. Wow, that permeating smell really lingers.

Loon asks, "Then what?"

I explain, "I told her he responded with, 'My Lord commands me to love my brother as I love the Lord.'"

"Oh god!" Loon puffs.

"Exactly!" I reply. "I said to my Mom with a chuckle in pain, 'Oh boy, so he is *commanded* to "love" me. Boy that makes me feel great, not!!' My Mom got angry. I said to her, 'I know, it sounds like I am not being very tolerant, but what can I say?'"

Loon thinks for a second, and for once, has no reply. He can't solve my problems either.

Before I even got to the All Hands Club, when I was helping Chelonia organize all of her stuff in my room, she sensed this tension, and asked how I was handling the brother situation.

I looked at her and said with sorrow, "Look, my brothers can say anything they want, and call me naïve, and all that crap, but something happened to them over time."

Chelonia puzzled, "You don't think they just snapped in one day?"

I said, "No, I don't know, but something happened, and they snapped. They became what they are; bitter haters, born-agains, whatever!"

Chelonia wondered, "That's not going to happen to you?"

I reported, "Just like I said when I looked at my Dad in the casket; I said to myself, 'that's not going to happen to me'."

Chelonia touched my cheek tenderly, and said, "No, that you won't die?"

I said clearly, "If I know one thing, I'm going to die."

Chelonia answered, "That is something we really know."

I concurred, "I'm talking about the facts that he killed himself, which I won't do, and with a drug (booze), which I won't do, and in an open casket for people to look at, which I won't do, and at a funeral home, which I most certainly won't do!"

Chelonia then revealed why we have become such fast soul mates without having carnal knowledge of each other, when she spieled, "The bottom line is, all of the answers are there, and we know it. If we were to take the 30 billion dollar bonuses the bank execs get, we could stop all foreclosures across the U.S. and eliminate hunger. Maybe like 1% of Americans would somehow still go hungry, maybe. If we cut our military budget in half and used the savings and technological savvy of the industrial complex to insulate every structure and home from Bangor to Blythe, the energy saved would eliminate the need for foreign oil, and thus, foreign wars. These aren't new ideas. Carter was talking about this in the 70's. I think things are going to get worse in the next decade, not better, and we will look back on the 90's as a good time. If we got alternative energy sources up and running like the Japs and Krauts did, they wouldn't be better than US now and we would be the ones with surplus energy, without any new drilling or eco-destruction. Of course, this is not where Halliburton and all of these types of companies make all of their money. They need war, destruction, devastation, so they can 'make a killing'. Making bombs, using them, then going in and cleaning up afterward (maybe); what a great way to keep yourself in business; as long as we continually have someone to bomb: Economy of scale and demand. It's just a question of will and bottom-line (money). I'm not deluded or naïve about that, but it doesn't make it an excuse either. If we were to convert every piece of arable farmland in the United States into organic farmland, and organic rangeland and pastures filled with fruiting trees and solar panels and wind turbines, we could easily mitigate everything we do to exacerbate global warming."

I then said to Chelonia, as I kissed her and got out of bed to get dressed, "I told Rosmarus once that if we eliminated the meat industry altogether in the U.S., we could save the Planet. The inveterate carnivore glared at me as if to say, 'You can have my prime chuck when you pry it from my cold, dead hands.' Does eating meat make meat eaters psychos?"

Chelonia, still a meat eater, not only at the delicious home-cooked hand of her Mother, but even at fast-food places, said, "What percentage of NRA members are vegetarian? Why is there such an association with meat-eaters and guns, obesity, ignorance, and fanatical Christianity?"

I trumped her with this, "Okay, how about if we just converted from cows to deer, elk, turkey, duck, goose, rabbit, Pronghorn and bison and let them range wild, or tried to make our country just a little more naturalistic? For some reason, Rosmarus, and people like him, who claim to be red-blooded patriots, just think that we have to have factory farms, milk from cows only, and that's just the way it is. Constrained."

489

Chelonia then asked, "And how does your Mother react to all this behavior?"

I told Chelonia, "She says, 'Don't go lookin for trouble!' in a cowardly reply. I reported my dismay regarding Rosmarus's actions and lack of lifestyle. I was flabbergasted by her response.

Sooty Terns glide over the atoll at night, giving every conversation a sooty ambient soundtrack.

Chelonia asked, "Did you communicate that with her?"

I told Chelonia, "Yes, I said, 'What, but you said . . . I thought you think that we should be closer? . . . and communicate better, and clear the air, and brpppppppffff!', and my lips splattered out of control with a confused gasp of frustration. That has been her mentality the whole way."

Chelonia still followed the discussion logically, "Has that strategy been working for her?"

I answered regrettably, "Apparently not; yet she's not smart enough to learn from her mistakes, and move on. She's a microcosm for the Palestinian/Israeli conflict, or the Capulets and Montagues, or lions and hyenas."

Chelonia said softly, as she fell off for a nap, "Well you may be becoming a little extreme, but maybe now you know it's really hopeless and you will never contact them again nor return to Boston."

I said, "Yah, it's sad, it's hopeless, and I've got to be smart enough to let it all go or let it destroy me from within."

Now back at the All Hands Club, practically all hands are here. There's no organized bingo game or talent show this time, just tons of people (for Halfway that is) converging on one bar for one thing: To Drink. Stark Kristian stands around with a group of big-eyed game fisherman, all looking to impress each other with their manliness.

Right in the middle of the cacophony, the overly loud, distorted speakers blare the most horrible band featuring Myhel, singing the most wretched song 'Margarita Fucking Ville'. God, how I have always hated that song and everything it was trying to 'not stand for', but stood for in the eyes of millions of drunkin alcoholic losers who need a song to enable them. Right in the middle of all of this, Kilgro, with her Olderhostile group, appears perturbed.

Some of them fiddle with their hearing aids. Not a good sign. One of Kristian's buddies grins at his friends and then goes frat boy by dumping his drink on a blue-haired's bonnet for a yuck.

"Oh, sorry lady, ha ha ha," he laughs and makes a sick face at the rotund angler to his right, with a huge, stinky cigar that smells like he rolled-it with the toilet paper he had just used.

Kilgro stands up and hands a napkin to the lady, puts her hands on her ample hips, and stares at Kristian, who notices her but could care less and ignores her. One of the elderly gents, a skinny feeble guy, makes a vain attempt to stand up and defend what, for all we know, could be his wife, but the music is so damn loud and the big lugs don't even know he's barely alive. I think, 'god, if one of those beefsters even fell over backward accidentally, they would kill half of that table'.

I have to go say something to Kristian, so I make my way down to the bar but am blocked by Rattas Dewhurt, who turns to me with a huge grin on her face and says "What you drinken? Or, you workin?" looking down at my legs in my uniform shorts.

I say, "Why are you asking? Are you buying?"

She switches to a quick frown, "Where I come from, women don't buy drinks."

I say, "Oh, okay, then why were you asking?"

She replies, "Why were I asking?"

"What?" I struggle. At that moment the song ends and there is a brief silence. I take advantage of it.

"Could I please slip by you? Thanks." As I try to move past her she sticks her boobs and hip out against my front. "Your husband is looking right at us," I state.

She backs off a little, trying to look around, but probably unable to see anything past the booze goggles. It's funny that she is looking around for Ernesto, her husband. He's on stage, playing with the band, but she seems to have forgotten.

She slurs, "That was a great number to end with, wasn't it?"

I say, "You kidding? That song sucks."

Rattas starts to take in a deep breath, then spews, "Fuck you. Margaritville does not suck. I love Jimmy Buffett. I was there. *I lived* at Margareeda-ville. Fuck you."

Holy shit! That's not very loving and peaceful, and all that cheeseburger in paradise shit, is it? This must be why I avoid Parrothead Conventions. I slip away without a word. Oh well, I already knew she was the enemy. She already hangs out a lot more with Cherry Ballpig than she does with her own husband Ernesto. Keep in mind there is no cop on Halfway. Remember Chipweldi? No cop. If you get in the thick of it you gotta get out of it. I would have loved to grab her by the hair with my left and punch her in the face with my right. Just once. One, solid bunch in the face for that useless white-trash grump. But, as usual, I didn't. I take it and walk off like a real, emotionally stable, intelligent person. Like I always do. Some people would call me a wimp. I think I'm smart. I get over to Kristian just in time for his demented diatribe, "The rich people, w'all know we voten Republican; it's gettin enough votes to beat da Dems dat gets in da way. Dat's why we need the guns and god party. Who are the most programmed and program-mable people on da planet?" Stark adds with a slur. "Churchies and gun nutzss. All ya have ta do is convince them that their guns are gonna be taken away, and that abortion and gay shit is against god (and the Democrats), and you got yourself enough votes to compete. They have all these new test weapons they want to buy and sell, and they want to kill a buncha rag heads and get Soddam once and for all, in the kyster, if you know what I mean," he winks, anything but subtly. "I ain't no fudge-packer meself but I'd love to stick it to that fat-ass grease Heeb." Everybody on the periphery of the group has been trying so hard to ignore everything he spouts; but that comment ain't gonna fly.

Kilgro stands up and says, "Excuse Me Mr. Kristian, I don't care how drunk you are and how much money you have, I won't have you mixing Moslems and Jews in the same breath" she states defiantly with an authoritarian, Dr. Ruth kind of brow-beating nag, yet, insecure about her intellectual capabilities and tone.

"Sand gnats," Stark Kristian bellows, "They are all from the same place and they are all the same."

"Oh, and where are you from Mr. Kristian?" Kilgro's voice cracks with an angry cry.

"Wha . .? Pffff. I'm white!" he says with a snort as he holds his arms out to balance himself and as he looks around in a spacey way. He bursts out in a huge laugh and his yes-men buddies slap him on the shoulder and punch him in the arm.

"Yep, He's right", the boys chime in.

"Hey, what you gawkin at boy?" Kristian says with a laugh, to his reassuring cronies as he finally puts my face into focus.

"I'm not gawking, I'm trying to get your attention, and obviously, I can't, because you guys need to move it into the pool room or outside," I say calmly but firmly.

"Okay, no problem." Kristian starts walking out with his drink, and the others heel along all the way out to the patio.

As they get outside and all start lighting up, I look at the lot and realize the futility of the situation; "We are having a nice fun party tonight on our little island in paradise. You good-ol-boys wouldn't be planning to ruin any of this now, would you?" I say in a voice that is obviously well short of patience.

"Don't worry," Stark Kristian replies with his typically evil sounding voice, "We just good ol boyz havin a little fun. Ain't meanin no real harm."

"Let's keep it 'a little'." I say, pinching my fingers to a quarter-of-an-inch apart, as I turn and walk back into the bar. "If you come back in smoking, I will be forced to file a report."

They all look at me like they want to beat the shit out of me. I know they do. Kristian has to display his dominance and remind his underlings who's in charge, belching, "What? You gonna right me a ticket. I can buy and sell you. You don't even have nothin. You don't own nothin." Kristian gawks at me with the lifeless eyes of a Cuttlefish. Dr. Oso enters the patio with his wife Kracklin, and he lights up a cigar and listens in as well. I can see Jewel through the door, surrounded by a cadre of suitors as usual. I can see her glancing over at me in sorrow, knowing how hard it is to deal with these vile greed ogres. Kristian goes on, "Possession my boy. It's about the guy with the most toys." His cronies laugh and practically chuckle 'here here'. "I own a stock car, and a whole

493

race team, and jet aero planes. You have no idea 'bout ownership and responsibility. That's why we cant' have people like you runnin the goddamn works."

Dutrouex jumps in, "That's why we need people like Deny to be in The Marines. Can you image you or Loon in The Marines for crise sake?" All the men scoff.

I think for an instant. First off, I would have been a kick ass Marine, and probably an officer, especially if Dutroeux got to be a major. I would never join. That's a choice. They can't understand that. Then I say, "Ralph Waldo Emerson said *The landscape belongs to the person who looks at it*."

My statement goes right over their heads.

Kristian groans, "That's why you can't be leaders, see? Why not just give everything away to the commies? Ya evah look at my aircraft? You can look all ya want, but they still ain't yours! Ha ha ha."

He's right. His planes will never be mine, nor would I ever want them.

Back in the paneled bar, the music blares. It is finally New Year's Eve, again. One of my first nights had been a New Year's Eve, and now one of my last nights out here was to be one too. I couldn't have known this would be my last New Year's Eve *ever*.

I look around the bar for a second. What a sight. Only on Halfway. First, I hone in on Loon talking about this new term they picked up from Clinton's vice-president Gore, I think: 'Global Warming'. Loon is in full professor mode again; almost standing at the edge of the red vinyl booth were he sits, very erect.

"As carbon dioxide increases, our average temperature could rise from 1 to 5°C, in this century! It could already be too late, yet, we want to party to celebrate the New Year!"

Several on-lookers bust-out laughing. He is totally right, but it comes off like a George Carlin-esque comedy act.

"Won't it be nicer in Canada if the globe warms?" Jellie asks like a totally naïve idiot. Her lack of science credentials in some areas beams like the TACAN System out on the runway.

Loon fires daggers at her from his eyes, "It's all tied in. Every 1°C degree rise in temperature means 10 percent less staple crops, everywhere they are currently grown. That will shock the markets. Glaciers will disappear, along with the water they supply to

494

billions of people. Ocean rise will cause storms to wipe out coasts. Halfway will be 10 feet under water. Where will the goonies breed?"

"So we can just convert crops into bio fuels," Kilgro adds over the din of the horrible band on stage.

"That's not efficient. The corn used to fill an American car once could feed a person for a year! It's gonna drive food prices up," Loon defends.

"So human food supply worries you the most? I thought you were kind of anti-human?" Jellie says, in a way to try to pick and gnaw at him, yet still seeming like a totally mellow, chill hippie on the outside, to those weak-minded volunteers and such who idealize her.

"Food shortages wiped-out previous civilizations. If we get wiped-out, we will take a lot of animal species down with US, just like the bush meat industry does in Africa," Loon adds.

He cares. See, he cares. Nobody cares my ass. People care. My mind drifts off to Chelonia. Where is she? She said she would be here by now. Oh my god. After all those years of searching, to finally be waking up here on Halfway with Chelonia next to me. Yeah yeah, I had other girls, right? On Halfway. Girls that I woke up sleeping next to and I'd be happy and say 'Oh good, I'm glad I have a girl.' I felt that way with Danica, and sometimes even with Myhel, but this is different. This is unbelievable. This is like unbelievable. I can't believe that when I wake up in the morning this angel is here, with her soft body, and her soft, soft voice. Her soothing hand, and her calm, calm demeanor. Ya know, totally unflappable. The antithesis of my volcanic energy spurts. It's the hand, the soothing hand; I'm talking about just a soft, flat hand with long fingers and long nails, that she doesn't need to put on any erogenous zone that you would think of, but just on your stomach. She just rests a soft warm hand on your stomach. It almost has like a gentle heating-pad effect. That epitomizes what it's like. Ya wake up, roll over, and there she is. There's no regrets, no remorse. There's no thinking like 'Gee I wish I had a hotter chick with me' or any of that kinda shit. All it is is, 'Oh this is awesome! Here she is. My girl. The love of my life'. A once in a century kind of true love. Did anyone ever have a love that was this, . . . this much? I mean even goin back to high romantic crap,

Romeo and Juliet, Tristan and Isolde, ya know, the love suicides in Japan. Um, no, I don't think so.

No, I don't think so.

Everyday, leading up to the arrival of my family, leading up to the arrival of Chelonia, and leading up to the final gig on New Year's, sees the winter creep in again, and the atoll gets dimer and cooler feeling, with stronger winds and more frequent squalls. The albatross dance on tippy-toes, dig their long nails into the sand, and scream and clack. A lot of sex is going on everywhere, with goonies mounting goonies, then mounting other goonies, then two goonies trying to mount a gooney, then goonies getting in bloody fights, bill to bill.

On our hands and knees, pulling the little sprouting *Verbesina* yet again, we have been crawling along, in the same area we did last year at this time. I sing to break up the monotony and keep my spirits high, while working my vocal chords. Yup, always a multi-tasker. But this time it only takes the group about an hour to cover the same area that took us three hours before. Each time we go back, there are way less aliens to pull, and the natives I planted when I first got out here now look well established and appear to be spreading on their own, out-competing aliens.

At The All Hands Club, as I leave the patio and start to direct my attention on focusing on Chelonia, Pillmold slides over to me with a gaunt look on his face, and says, "So what'z the word on da weeeeeed around here?"

I look over at Pillmold, and he is looking straight at me. Then I look around at everyone else in complete shock. This is the first I have heard anything about pot on Halfway. I say, "What weed?"

Pillmold retorts, "Awh, c'mon. *I've sold* more weed than *you've smoked*. I know there's weed out here. You must be tied into it. You're a singah."

I look over at him again. "I have no idea what you are talking about. I haven't seen it, smelled it, or anything out here."

Pillmold turns his nose up at me and squints his eyes as if to try to detect if I'm lying. Recently we learned that Pillmold not only camped on the beach, which is illegal, but he picked a closed beach, the southern edge of Frigate Point, where we had the best pupping success, and on top of that, he built a fire, which he illegally used to cook the fish he illegally caught and ate, off the reef. He groaned for the next three weeks in the clinic with *Ciguatera* fish poisoning. He's lucky he didn't die, I think. I did not enter the clinic once to check in on Pillmold. I am staying out of it. Let Chipweldi, the "Law Enforcement Officer", and Amb, handle that mess. I always teach every new atoll visitor about everything, including the dangers of those little dinoflagellates that can wreak havoc upon the bioaccumulated gastrointestinal system. Pillmold slept through my orientation. Also, Patch and Kracklin have been keeping me posted, and said that Pillmold confessed that he thought the Animal Protection Service was lying about the *Ciguatera*, so that we could 'keep all the fish for ourselves'. Pillmold defended to Dr. Oso, "Hey, we know that Stark Kristian, the CIA, and The Military, . . . they all lie all the time about everythin they be doin. Why wouldn't the huggers be no differnt?" Why do doctors even bother saving guys like this? Hippocratic oath?

Drifting back to the present and New Year's Eve at The All Hands Club, I look around in anticipation of my band going on soon. Chelonia enters the bar and walks toward me. I told her not to dress up, but being Salvadoran, and on top of that, narcissistic, she is dressed way too hot for Halfway, in a skirt and heels with her sexy toenails painted in shiny Concord grape, reflecting like the back of a Metallic Skink. The screech of the band Myhel "plays" in almost forces us to withdraw sonically, especially as she hits some clams on the keyboard due to the distraction and attention Chelonia garners from all. Immediately, the guys descend upon her as they always have on Jewel. Chelonia shows strength, sauntering past them and straight up to me with a soft smile.

Unbeknownst to me, Myhel has twisted her band's arms into playing *Wicked Game* by Chris Isaak. She somehow imagines that when I hear her anguish over me, that I'll go running back to her and all of her transgressions against me will be forgotten.

I say to Chelonia, "Let's go for a quick walk," oblivious to Myhel and her pleas. I'm not even there to hear it, and my mind is a million miles away up in heaven with Chelonia. Myhel's hell, the 'C' word, and the threat accusations, all seem like a distant nightmare now.

As we step out into the moonlit breeze, with the pines rustling, Chelonia says, "That's very uncharacteristic of you, the extrovert always wanting to be in the crowd."

I look over at her and give her a big hug. I don't know what it is, but I just can't stop hugging this sweet angel. I'm in danger of smothering her, yet I can't help myself. I am so in love with this girl.

I admit, "Now that I have you, it's as if the rest of the world doesn't exist."

I grab her in a wrestler's grip and squeeze her tightly, lifting her off the sand and then dropping her into a deep dip. We kiss passionately.

Walking along the beach, Chelonia and I grapple with developing adult philosophies, and feeling-out any possible chinks in the armor of our love.

"I like to hear your thoughts. They are scary, and strange at times, but interesting," Chelonia says, as we deeply, passionately kiss again and search the darkening fuchsia and chartreuse sky for sounds, like an incoming aircraft. I look off to see another one of those funky 'spy' planes coming in, but this one is not at 3 am, and it rockets in very fast and low. I look down at my phone to see that it is on and working, and to confirm that I have received no calls.

"Hmmm. That's very weird," I ponder.

Chelonia asks. "Do you have to go on duty?"

"Usually I should. I don't know what's going on. They should have called me," I think again.

"Well, if they need you, they will call you. Finish your diatribe," she demands.

We laugh, then we see the plane land with no running lights. Suddenly, out of nowhere, we hear a sonic boom and see a second jet, maybe at like 22,000 feet, sweeping up out of a dive and away from the atoll, and climbing fast. My cell phone flickers and crackles oddly. We quietly watch the plane go out of sight, as the night converts to its deep black coat. Chelonia had seen her first green flash today as the Sun went down, and now she is getting the opportunity to see some of Halfway's unnatural phenomena.

I finally get back on my California native spiel, per her request, "The big hypocrisy on top of all of that is that none of these losers are fuckin natives. Ya know, it's like very rare that any of them ever have any Native American blood and are usually Jewish or Mexican, or Italian or Russian; even loads of Asians proudly call themselves natives," I say with annoyance.

Chelonia says, "Well, when they say 'native' they obviously do not think they are talking about Native American. They mean native to California, like born and raised. I think of myself as a San Franciscan, not a Salvadoran, or a Californian, but I can't say I am a Californian native. I guess there is 'Native' with a capital 'N' and 'native' with a lower case 'n'."

I say, "I meet guys who almost right away tell me that they are native when there is a good chance that they probably aren't even native. Their names are Garcia or Jorgenson, and none ever dare go as far as to actually equate calling themselves natives to *Native*; they just mean that their mommy squirted em out within the state boundary," I rail, trying to make my big, concluding point.

"That's it," Chelonia says in agreement.

"That's all it means. The Natives made it to Calli some 14,000 years ago or something, maybe even way before that, then the Spaniard missionaries, Russian fur trappers and others came, then people from all over the world moved there, so who are the natives? I would like that one cleared up before some insecure prick tries to start using it to leverage their alpha dominance over me," I say as I shake my fist like Lee Ving. Chelonia laughs harder than I've seen her. "Seriously, the natives were here in California for ten-thousand years; the Spaniards and the whites were in California for 150 years each. That's it!" I strut around like a cock, pushing my lips out like Mick Jagger. "When I meet somebody from California who is all proud about being NorCal or some stupid shit like that, I say to them, 'Which tribe man? Which tribe?'"

500

Chelonia asks, "Then they start back-peddling right away?"

I put on a voice that sounds all stoned out, "'What you talkin bout man? I ain't talkin literally.' Chelonia says, "Wow, you are pretty sensitive to this stuff, but I do see your point. I don't think I have anything like that that really irks me. I guess teenagers having babies really pisses me off. So what, you were born here and you have no tribal affiliation of any kind with the Ohlone, or Chumash, or Miwok or any other tribe around the Bay Area. Right?"

"Exactly. That's what I say to them." I say.

We hear the engines shut off near the Hangar.

I say, "So now that you came out to Halfway, I don't have to lay in bed and think to myself like that every night."

Chelonia asks, "Think things like what?"

I say, "What was it all about? All the times my heart was broken. All the rehearsals and gigs. All that time on stage, staring out at the glowing faces in the Fresnel lights?' It's nothing now," I say, retrospectively.

"Nothing," Chelonia says without the hint of a question.

"In the 80s, at UCLA, I had such eternal hope and optimism. I thought, I believed, life—the World, would get better. The future wasn't going to be like *The Road Warrior* or *Blade Runner*. It was not going to be like the Nam era with drafts and assassinations of the few of US who were actually good, who actually cared. It was going to be a World of people, NOT like US. Totally NOT like US. We were gonna get our shit together in a post-religious, yet spiritual, Green, happy World. What happened?"

"We have no one to blame but ourselves," Chelonia admits with guilt.

"US!?, and yet, I can't blame me." I remember back to when I came to that same revelation, staring at shattered pale lead paint, chipping off the ceiling; with White Terns making their rackety little mating dance just outside my window, stomping up and down on the AC unit with their webbed feet.

Just because I don't know it, doesn't mean it isn't the answer! ---
Drats

We walk past an air conditioner with a tern nest on it. "Why do you even have an AC unit?" Chelonia murmurs.

I continue; "This is exactly what I am talking about. Who? Who, with the exception of blivit Cherry Ballpig, would need a friggin AC unit on Halfway?" I rave.

Chelonia joins the fray; "Are we that fuckin WEAK?!" she laughs, mimicking my over enthusiastic psychoses.

"This ain't the Mojave. In my 2-plus years on Halfway, I don't think it ever got over 95, and even that was for a short hour at midday, and by 7pm, the Pacific breezes had already brought it down to 82. I hate AC. Suck it up," I say in full spew.

Chelonia looks at me for a second, straight in the eyes. She's doing her best to read me. "Why do you obsess honey?"

It comes to me like a lighting bolt, and just as quickly off my tongue; "I never fit-in with the drama crowd cause they were always so friggin dramatic. Now here I am being accused of being a drama queen. Big deal. Suck it up. Look, all I ever wanted was love. All I ever wanted was a sweet, sweet love who loved me with all her heart and whom I could love with all my heart, and trust."

"Why was it so important to be loved? Did you somehow feel unloved?" Chelonia heads down the wrong path.

"I don't think so." I think for a second, aware of the possible existence of denial, yet detect none. "I know," I admit with regret, "you know that story. I used to think life was so long and important. I use to think that what I did really mattered. I used to think that each individual counts, and makes an impact, and that people care. I wish someone would tell me they care."

Chelonia looks at me in dejected silence. She doesn't think they care. She doesn't have faith in humans. She's a little Newtonian, like me, but not existentialist. She doesn't go to church, but like almost all Central Americans, she definitely believes in god.

I blow on, "So US won over Them, and Me won over US. I'm waiting for the 95% of US world wide to stand up and take most of what the top 5% of Them has. I'm spearheading a coordinating effort, in which our resources are spread evenly and everyone has a little, but enough—plenty," I say, realizing that it sounds like Communism and is much more oversimplified than I had hoped it to sound. "As I've said, I have no regrets. I've lived a great life. I don't know what I would have changed in this journey. Maybe I would have been a little carefuller about who I dated."

Chelonia scans my face to see if I implicate her.

"My life definitely would have been better if I met you like about two years ago. That Myhel shit was totally moronic," I blurt quickly to allay her concern. "Maybe I wouldn't have wasted time thinking about how to enact revenge on all of the people who have hurt me. Maybe I would have handled my band relationships with a kid-glove instead of an iron fist. I don't know. I don't know. All I know is here I am again dwelling on these conundrums and wondering what happened?" I tell her, as we both vividly imagine the scenes, looking up at the stars, this time not alone, on Halfway. This time, for the first time, with someone I really love, who apparently loves me.

I trip over my tongue, pointing up sharply, "Hey hey; I forgot to tell you that Hale-Bopp would be visible. Look, there is it."

Chelonia says, "Did you hear about the idiot religious fanatics who said it was a space ship to take them to another world? I think some of them killed themselves to prepare themselves for the journey."

I reply, "I hope none of them had a chance to reproduce before they left."

We both chuckle, then stare at the sky, sharing a special moment. We can see two distinct tails. Wow, what an incredible world we live in, and what an incredible amount of human morons inhabit it with us.

"What went wrong?" Chelonia surges forward.

"I don't know. It's just like the mystery of my family. Like I said, they're not *that* fucked up. Yet, they are certainly fucked up enough. Ironically, Doger is the least articulate of all, yet he cuts right through, pure to the core. When I think of my sad born-again Christian brothers, I get all confused and conflicted. A million ideas about denying responsibility for US and our actions, blast through my brain in a millisecond. Doger sums it up with 'it's a cop-out'. That's it." I say with a gulp of regret.

"He's right. You couldn't say it better than that. Neither could I," Chelonia sympathizes, having some annoying born-agains in her own family to cope with, and being a secret-kind-of girl who conserves dialogue too.

"I can't take it. It's like way to painful. Aren't families supposed to bring US happiness and pain, laughter and sorrow? It's like the song *Listen?* Drats wrote with **Death and Taxes** when both Drats and I lived in L.A. during the UCLA years. Frustrated with a Beatles wanna-be guy we worked with at a day job in the Rhino Records shipping warehouse in Santa Monica, Drats wrote this song, which I feel applies to my life experience in general. It goes like this:

Listen?
by Drats

It's hopeless to try and write lyrics for you,
I try almost everyday
You're to complicated I can't get through,
I make no headway
It doesn't matter how long we work on this,
Together we'll never gel
I know I'm trying to bridge an abyss,
But maybe, you are as well
I don't understand why people are like that,
I don't understand why people are like that
I don't understand why people are like that,
Neither do I
You frustrate me, an easy job hard,
You inspire me to continue
Simmer my anger, a retard,
It's something in me in you
Ignorance is worse than the greatest evil,
Collaboration at every level
To fear the unknown, a remnant medieval,
Your idleness is the devil.

Chelonia genuinely loves when I sing to her, though I don't think she's as enamored with the dancing around as much; too fairy-esque for her taste maybe. She expects men to be semi-macho. I look at her to see if she understands. I don't want to pervert it with an explanation, but I feel it's important, so I clarify the theme; "We have to take responsibility for ourselves and for US."
"Even in our bleakest moments, it's always worst for someone else," Chelonia chimes in right on time.

I know she means 'worse', but I'm trying to pick and choose my corrections now, since my constant pointing-out of her English-as-a-second-language flaws could wear on her, and could be the type of nagging thing to just nitpick our relationship to death.

"I cried because I had no shoes, until I saw the man who had no feet," I concur, with a old quote from somewhere ricocheting in my brain.

"My friends argue—'Maybe they feel that they **need** this born again crap? Maybe they have to have it to stay alive?'" Chelonia postulates.

"I'd rather be dead than walk, stalk the Earth with the rest of the dead, unthinking, unfeeling, irresponsible, praying Zombies: Sucked- in and programmed by all the bullshit. I don't believe I have any right to tell people what to like or what to believe in, but when they ultimately damage The Planet and try to force their shit on me and others, then forget it."

I hold my hands out like Frankenstein's robot and stiffly stalk Chelonia's neck. She ducks and runs around behind me. Both feeling sleeping now, we decide to head back to the club via a quiet walk on the beach. We see a seal hauled out in the naupaka bushes. They usually hunt at night to nail octopus and avoid tigers, but this one must be full. It lifts its head and looks concerned. We back off and go back around to the road in the dim light.

"Maybe everything I do on Earth for US, and the Earth, especially the Earth, adds up and really matters and I just can't see it," I think again.

Pause. Waiting. Waiting again on Halfway. Chelonia has absolutely no problem with waiting. She is an expert waiter. She practically waited until she was 27 to have a real boyfriend, . . . me.

"Look at this Lincoln quote, for a second," I encourage, as I notice a wrinkled piece of paper in my pocket:

Abraham Lincoln warns: 'What constitutes the bulwark of our own liberty and independence? It is not our crowning battlements, our bristling seacoasts, our army and our navy. These are not our reliance against tyranny. All of these may be turned against us without making us weaker for the struggle. Our reliance is in the spirit which prized liberty as the heritage of all men, in all lands everywhere. Destroy this spirit and you have planted the seeds of despotism at your own doors. Familiarize yourselves with the chains of bondage and you prepare your own limbs to wear them. Accustom to trample on the rights of others and you have lost the genius of your own independence and become the fit subjects of the first cunning tyrant who rises among you.'

"Wow!" Chelonia responds, "That's pretty heavy."

"Yeyh," I acknowledge, "In my closing days as a ranger, and with the end or the Millennium, I have become so concerned with everything that's coming down the pike for wildlife and the environment in general."

Chelonia says over the noise as we reenter the club, "Clinton put a bunch of environmental policies in place, which they say Bush will reverse immediately, as like his first actions in office."

I scan the scene. I don't know if Jellie had a falling out with Kilgro, Myhel, Misa Queen and their ilk, or if she just finally realized how evil they are, but she has been hanging out with US now in the bar and at The Galley over the last month or so. She stands by our table, since she can't squeeze in. I'm very weary of being wary, because I have been screwed over by so many people so many times now, and with my family and Chelonia on atoll, I am guarded for the worst. I keep an eye on her.

Renn, Twistor, Dietera, Bent, and Ray (the Filipino bass player in my band, though it's more like I'm in his band) converse in a large booth with Chelonia and I.

Dietera states, picking up where Chelonia left off, "I just read a report in the *Utne Reader* that says that one of Bush's first actions will be to take punitive measures against Gov agencies that want to stop oil drilling. So he is cutting the APS by 9%, the National Park Service by 10%, and the USGS by 23%! Oil comes first, and don't you forget it!" she squeals the last line like an ornery prospector.

"Crap!" I exclaim.

"Well," Twistor says, always looking on the bright side, "At least you met Chelonia. That's a good thing to happen right before you leave."

"Yahh." I think for a moment. "Some girls are so pure. Like Chelonia; the antithesis of Myhel. She is so pure. She is so pure that she is primitive. She is like a baboon that has to be false

506

mounted 20 or 30 times a day until she finally gets the idea that 'Oh yah, we should be doin it. Okay, I'm ready.' And then we will finally get it on someday."

Everyone, including Jellie, burst out into booming laughter.

Totally embarrassed and private, Chelonia blushes.

Jewel comes walking over, "What'ya'all laughing at over here?" as she slides into the booth with us. Jellie, too self-conscious, wouldn't dare do that.

Renn says sarcastically, "Kestrel is telling tales about how he has been infected by the love bug, and this time it's for real." She rolls her eyes.

Renn and Jellie laugh, almost scoff, and Jewel chuckles, but Dietera, Chelonia, and none of the boys even smile at their jaded stupidity. I can see in Jewel's eyes that she is happy for me and a little jealous.

Chelonia and I zip up to the bar, where I lean over to hug and kiss her involuntarily, but her look stops me immediately; and I remember her big peeve about public displays of affection. No PDA!

I'm fine with the no PDA thing. I don't have to display my love to prove it or anything like that. I am very affectionate and love to be, but I don't want to make anyone else feel uncomfortable.

"What are all these Foreign Nationals doing out here?" she strains over the noise.

"Foreign Nationals, what the hell is an FN? FN. Does it make any sense? When I got to Halfway there were FNs from Thailand, Sri Lanka, and The Philippines. Of course, nobody from other first world countries; they pick the poorest of the poor from developing countries, pay low wages, and these guys were contracted under the Navy going back years and years, getting like $1.25 a day. These guys work on Halfway, glad to be out here, away from their families, sending money back, away from their loved ones." I explain to Chelonia, who listens and looks around as we bring our drinks back to the booth.

Dietera adds, "When APS took over from the Navy, they said 'Okay let's pay these guys at least minimum wage', but then they realized in a sense they couldn't because they'd be makin so much money that it would create such a disruptive imbalance that back home people would try to kill each other to get out to Halfway, or take family members hostage for ransom." She stops to take a look around. The Navy chiefs are gone. Cherry Ballpig or Duetreux are not within earshot. There is no one to berate US.

Chelonia says in her sweet voice, "Balance and moderation. Everything's a cycle. Balance, like my sign."

"You're a Libra?" I question.

"Yes. Did you already forget when my birthday is?" she asks, peeved, and crinkling her forehead just between her eyes.

"No. I know when your birthday is. I just don't know the horoscope. Do you believe in astrology and that stuff?" I say with trepidation.

"A little bit," she half-admits. I look into those soft brown eyes. What an angel on Earth. Okay. I don't care. I can live with that. She already seems somewhat irrational in some other ways anyway. What am I going to do, break up with a girl for being irrational? I'd end up totally celibate if I only dated rational girls. I continue, "So, even to have a job, in The Philippines with a 25% unemployment rate, that any job is golden, Halfway was so obscenely lucrative, even at a buck twenty-five an hour," I conclude.

Chelonia grabs my arm, "What a huge symbol of discrepancy between our worlds."

I agree, "Plus, the FNs get treated like 2nd class citizens. It's too bad too, because the foreign nationals totally add color and spice to the bland, pallid monochrome culture out here."

"When are people going to grow up?" Chelonia responds with a shake of the head. "How completely racist that is to treat them, order them around, and tell them what to do," she finishes with distain, looking around at the drunkin HIC staff with new found, justifiable disgust.

Twistor chuckles, "Hey, what about the centipede trick? Did you tell Chelonia?"

I turn to Chelonia to explain, "FNs love the centipede stunt. You haven't seen one out here yet, but they are friggen huge and are evolving into the top terrestrial predator. Zart kicked one in our dark hallway when we first moved into the chief's house, and he screamed like a little girl, but luckily, he escaped getting bitten."

"Yikes!" Chelonia exclaims. "I'm fascinated by insects, and I love to look at them, but I'm not into anything that scary or painful. How bad is it?"

I state, "I heard an archeologist, who got bitten up at the North Beach at night, describe it like a Bugs Bunny character coming down on your foot with a ball-peen hammer in an old Warner Bros. cartoon. Youwch!"

Chelonia imagines the over-sized, red throbbing foot, with steam whistles blasting perpendicularly out of the scientist's ears and all, . . . and grins.

I say, "Centipedes aren't insects by the way. Anyway, the foreign nationals catch one carefully and chill it in the fridge, then delicately extract the mandibles, removing any ability to inflict pain. The legs actually still hurt as they dig in and grab you, but they can't inject venom. Invasive aliens, and known to kill young burrowing chicks like Wedge-tailed Shearwater, Bonin Petrel, and ground surface dwellers like Christmas Shearwater, these large, orange monsters are not protected, but I still think it cruel to mess with them like that. I'm sure Jellie, Loon, and everyone to my left don't appreciate it either." Everyone looks in silence.

"Way to nuke the party, dude," Bent says.

"I gotta go get something in my office." I make a quick exit, as the group keeps talking with Chelonia. I quickly get on my bike and zip over to the office in a minute flat.

Amb steps into my office just as I reach my mailbox on my desk. "Kestrel, I wish you would change your mind, but if you are really bent on leaving, then we will be throwing a good-bye party for you at my house."

Crap. The last thing I want is a goodbye party. I hate those. I'm not very smooth at those.

"I'll be there. Dyo want me to bring anything?" I reply politely.

"No, of course not, just you and Chelonia. I'm glad to see you are really happy," he says, maybe finally realizing that *I* wasn't a messed-up freak, and that the Myhel situation just got out of hand cause *she* is a messed-up freak.

"Thanks," I reply.

Everything is very cordial. I wonder what Amb thinks of all this. He has to know by now that the whole Myhel thing and the threat complaint were bogus. He knows now that I am in love with

Chelonia and showing my true colors as a good, trustworthy guy. Does he feel like he fucked up, or does he even care? Does he think he will find another ranger like me, dime-a-dozen, or does he fear he will be stuck with another Misa Queen?

I grab the latest manifest and rip back on the bike to the club where everyone remains in basically the same position. "He is throwing a party for me," I tell everyone. They immediately know I must have bumped into Amb. "I wouldn't throw a party for an evil threatener. That's just the kind of guy I am," I say.

They all roll their eyes at my overreaction and hypersensitivity. "Maybe he wouldn't either?" Twistor says, wise beyond his years. Renn adds, trying to draw attention back on herself, "Yah, maybe he is ok with you now. I think I'm the one on his shit list now."

I think to myself for a minute, about all the angry visitors scowling at the end of Misa Queen's program. 'I don't know. What? I'm not sure about that one.' Those comments still make up the main bulk of the statements coming from Misa Queen on tour. Occasionally, she throws in a 'Don't tell Amb!' to me, even now, just incase I forget that I am not supposed to narc her out.

Just then, Panburelie flutters up to us like a Pallid Bat on shrooms, "What kind of music would you like at the party. I have some weird *Dead Can Dance* stuff that I think is right up your alley and you would like to dance around to. The kids want to listen to *The Spice Girls* and do a little dance for you," she snarls as she struggles to tug open a smile, and more jovial than I've ever seen her in the little over a year I've known her.

I respond, almost holding back tears, "Sure. That sounds great. Make sure they do *Say You Will Be There*," I say facetiously.

"You actually know their songs?" Panburelie says with surprise.

"Actually, I might have butchered that title and I don't know any others, but that song is good," I relay.

"What do you really like? I mean, you were a singer so you must have certain tastes. Didn't you audition for Blue Man Group too?" Panburelie inquires.

"In every decade I had like one musical artist who shaped my world. Why music and not other art genres? Why did Rock n Roll seem to be the only music that existed?"

Dietera exclaims, "Because it wasn't like art."

I nod, then say, "So in the 1960s it was like Motown and Hendrix, and the Jackson 5 and Ricky Nelson and they were all in a conglomeration of music when I was growing up. But I have to say that when I was growing up Jimi Hendrix blew me away. I mean, when I heard his guitar I thought it was charging maniacal elephants trumpeting. Elephants screaming and scramming, like they had elephants on stage, but it was just feedback through the amps; but those elephants gave me an earful."

"Were you scared?" asks Panburelie, with Amb now entering and listening intently with a smile.

"No, I loved it, but I didn't understand it. I didn't understand what I was listening to or how the sounds were made. I just knew I liked it a lot," I explain.

"Then, it was disco!" proclaims Meg, who now has also entered with the final family crewmembers. Meg remembers what a femmy little disco dancer I was in 1977, wearing my bright yellow jacket with the collar up like Fonzi.

"The seventies had to be Mick Jagger and The Rolling Stones. The whole seventies for me was just like one after another Rolling Stones album coming out. Mick Jagger was great, the greatest singer in rock and roll, and I knew even by the time of the end of the seventies that technically he wasn't as good as say Mike Reno from Lover Boy, but Mick just had that great voice," I say as I lean over to Chelonia with my hand over my mouth discreetly, "that voice that sounds like he's cumming the whole time he's singing, right?" Chelonia blushes and slaps my arm.

"No secrets you two," Saintia says in a vain attempt to maintain some motherly clout, but playfully.

"Then in the eighties, that's a tough one. There was a lot of different stuff, but mainly, Kate Bush influenced me after I got out of punk and new wave. A lot of people might laugh at that cause they think she's not that great or she's kind of weird, and this and that. I could relate to everything she did. Everything she's saying, everything she was doing, everything she was doing theatrically, and theoretically, was weird and different and I felt that was me, and I wanted to be weird and different because I always loved trippy, artsy shit, and also to be very sensitive, caring and emotionally expressive, and sing about wildlife.

"Now Kate doesn't sing about wildlife!" Rosmarus says to my surprise.

"You know her?" I say in shock.

"Sure, she did that Gone With da Wind Song. Ah, Proud Heathcliff, or sumten," Rosmarus fumbles, trying to sound hip.

I want to be supportive, "Yah, she's more into interpersonal relationships. There were so many things in her music that really resonated with me, I mean take the lyrics for *Love and Anger*. This hits on the head one of the ways I feel about our family."

"Don't know it. Please don't sing it," the peanut gallery mumbles. Manat lays-out a snare on a muddy trail, "Yah. Tell us what would you do as President? Would you use your power for your own pleasure?"

I say rapid-fire, "If I were Pres, I would turn it into a reality show, where everyday, all day, cameras would roll, and anytime anyone ever wanted to know what the president was doing, all they had to do was click on their TV. No sneaky antics. No under the table shenanigans. Even the Ruskies, Iranians, whomever the threat of the month may be, would know what I am doing everyday. What I'm doing and what I'm working on. I certainly wouldn't golf, that's for damn sure. I think I'd pass a law that a Prez can't play golf, especially when US soldiers are dying, which, of course, if I were prez, wouldn't be happening because no soldiers would ever be dying," I clarify with a gasp.

Then my brother Sproc looks over at me through his black-rimmed glasses and says "Kestrel, I already prayed for you. You are taken care of."

"That's mental," I reply.

Sproc snaps again, "What?"

"You think you can say a prayer and that gives you all this power and shit. That's mental. I'm glad you are not running the country thinking shit like that," I say, straight, "I've heard rumors that our new president thinks dinosaurs were here like 4,000 years ago or something. God help US is right. Talk about mental."

Sproc replies like a child, "Oh, what are you an expert on 'mental'?"

"Yes, as a matter of fact, I am. Do you know a better candidate for head of 'mental'?" I oscillate.

"Yeah, I think I've been just as much 'mental' as you," Sproc competes.

"Ah, so you admit that you are fuckin mental," I say.

Sproc, pissed, looks at me for a long moment.

"Now you look pissed. That isn't very Christian of you." I love saying that to him and Rosmarus. I shouldn't love that. I state honestly, "I am so bitter and wrong. The conflict rages within and without me. Can't I control my mind and get over this shit? Like Kate. Sweet Kate. Of course she has the answer."

"So singing that song is like a religious experience for you?" Renn assumes. Is she stoking the fire?

"No. I definitely wouldn't put it that way," I stifle quickly, "but I have headed out to the beach on my bike and up to the rickety wooden seal-observation platform at the end of the abandoned runway. On top, facing the wind with the sun dropping to my left above the foamy line of ocean hitting the reef in the distance, I have belted it out with all the love and passion in my life and heart. How do people who can't sing like me purge their pain? I think Clinton did with his sax. Not George Clinton, Bill."

Dorsal fins of spinner dolphins from the deck of Kilgro's powered pontoon raft, near the North Beach observation tower; and the water-pressure tank, with its rotating airstrip light.

Jewel rings like a southern belle, "You just stand there and give a performance quality delivery to the goonies and white terns hovering by?"

"Yah," I reply with a smile.

"Just sing it!" Jellie commands, "Screw ya brothers. We want to hear it."

I sing it with a welling richness, building with feeling as I strain to understand each word before it travels from my brain to my lips.

Love and Anger
by Kate Bush

It lay buried here. It lay deep inside me.
It's so deep I don't think that I can speak about it.
It could take me all of my life, but it would only take a moment to
Tell you what I'm feeling, but I don't know if I'm ready yet.
You come walking into this room, like you're walking into my
arms.
What would I do without you?

Take away the love and the anger,
And a little piece of hope holding us together.
Looking for a moment that'll never happen,
Living in the gap between past and future.
Take away the stone and the timber,
And a little piece of rope won't hold it together.

If you can't tell your sister, if you can't tell a priest,
'Cause it's so deep you don't think that you can speak about it, to
anyone,
Can you tell it to your heart? Can you find it in your heart
To let go of these feelings, like a bell to a Southerly wind?
We could be like two strings beating, speaking in sympathy...
What would we do without you?
Two strings speak in sympathy.

Take away the love and the anger,
And a little piece of hope holding us together.
Looking for a moment that'll never happen,
Living in the gap between past and future.
Take away the stone and the timber,
And a little piece of rope won't hold it together.
We're building a house of the future together.
(What would we do without you?)

Well, if it's so deep you don't think that you can speak about it,
Just remember to reach out and touch the past and the future.
Well, if it's so deep you don't think you can speak about it,
Don't ever think that you can't change the past and the future.
You might not, not think so now, but just you wait and see
--someone will come to help you. Yes !

I finish with a huge lump in my throat. I look at everyone with tears in my eyes. Chelonia rubs the back of my neck and my shoulder. "Everything is gonna be alright honey. You are so great," she whispers almost like a kiss.
I say, "Well? Can you feel it too? What?! You don't know this friggin song? Am I the only one? Kate must have felt it. Fights with Paddy and the others? I can't assume anything cause I really don't know shit about her nor would I gossip if I did. I'm just saying it sounds like she has had my problems. We resonate --- kindred spirits. That might be a huge insult to her but I felt that the first time I heard her music and saw her."
"So you're saying you went from Mick Jagger to Kate Bush?" Manat asks with surprise.
"Not directly," I explain, cause he has got a good point. "Kate Bush **was** the 80's for me. I listened to *The Dreaming* repeatedly as I went to sleep. Then in the nineties, Radiohead."
"I knew he was gonna name something weird like that, that nobody's heard ov," blasts Manat.
Going back to negativity, he reinforces what I've learned from millions of interactions with him; it's better to just ignore every single thing he says. I go on unabated, "It had to be **Radiohead,** I mean, I didn't like their punkier stuff in the beginning. I didn't think *Creep* was that great even though I loved singing it and it was perfectly in my range. You know, when *Ok Computer* came out, oh my god, what a tour-de-force! That was definitely the best album of the nineties, and it's going to be very hard to find an album that is gonna be better." I think to myself for a moment. "I like Fiona Apple right now too," trying to sound a little more mainstream.
Kracklin says, "Yu let me borrow that Radiohead, me n Oso. I just don't get it."

515

Kracklin not getting Radiohead totally verifies why I like it. If NASCAR country/western-types got that shit, then I probably wouldn't. Why does anyone ever think any of this matters? I wanted Kracklin to like Radiohead. It doesn't matter that she doesn't.

No one else has anything to say, as Loon and Tex approach the table. Even though we are brothers, I have no idea how any of them feel about anything that has transpired, or if they understand it. It is funny to see Loon and Tex, as polar-opposite as my very own brothers, still hanging amongst each other and in a non-malicious way, feeding off each other.

Tex says, "Whad arh ya been havin a say-onz overrr here?"

Jewel says, "No, yawh missed everything shugar."

Then Bent says, "There have been a lot of big heavy philosophical discussions. I should have got in on more of these way earlier. Though I have to admit, everything seems extremely disjointed and unresolved."

Then Twistor mumbles to Loon, "and some singing."

Then Ray reiterates, "and some singing."

Tex looks exasperated, "Oh great. Can we never just have a good time talkin bout nothin?"

Loon says, "Yeh, you love talking about stuff you are expert on."

Tex looks at Loon, a little pissed. The rest of us snicker.

Suddenly, someone, I don't know, a Filipino foreign national, disoriented, on the stage behind me, picks up the microphone, and announces with a heavy accent, "Merry New Year everyboady. Now the next band will be start now."

Chapter 11: Last Chapter

Inside the warm, stuffy All Hands Club, the revelers ring in the new millennium. Out on the outer reef, White-tipped Reef Sharks search for a fish to gang up on, in the coral 'pukas', as the Hawaiians call the little holes. On the surface, all matter of seabirds, truly pelagic in that many of them never even see a continent in their long lifetimes, glean what they can from the infinite wave tops, as they have for millennia, with no recognition of the turn of the century whatsoever.

Like any other day on Halfway. Like any other day.

On Eastern Island and Spit, it is always pitch dark. The birds sleep in silence on their nests, no longer harassed and destroyed by rats. Boobies, frigates, tropicbirds, terns and noddies, all sit out the night with bills tucked-in. They sit through the wind. They sit through the rain. They don't celebrate the New Year at all.
New Year's Eve at the All Hands Club on the Millennium baby, 1999 to 2000! Think of that. Think of what has happened over the last thousand years. Over the last 2000 years! Going all the way back to year zero. We have basically gone from The Dark Ages to The Computer Technology Age. Go back two thousand years. Oh my god. I think this is significant, and more than just a date; a place, marking time.
At about two hours til the stroke of midnight, my other band mates start arriving with red faces, obviously, and I would dare to say appropriately, shit-faced looking. They are about to play their first gig with a real American singer to a packed-drunken-mixed crowd

who just sat through three, or was it four, horrible bands. This is a rock and roll band, in the tradition of The Sex Pistols, etc. I am ready to go hog wild. I love singing with a band so much. I am going to explode all over them! My band is proud and eager. Filipinos have strong musical traditions, and everyone seems to play something and love to sing. In karaoke, the Filipinos are the only ones likely to sing English love ballads and pop songs, while the Sri Lankans and Thais sing in their tripped-out languages and tonal scales. The band also knows my reputation, false as it may be, and think it's cool that they are backing the "James Bond" of the atoll. I wear "the suave uniform" well, and when clean shaven on rare occasions, could pass for a model, but the rumors aren't true and I haven't hooked-up with even half the women the scuttlebutt suggests. Either way, their perceived reality seems to have brought their blood pressure up and there is a buzz in the air. I see Amb looking pensive. I have no feeling at all that anything will get out of control here. Does he know something I don't, like when he assembled that friggin bang-stick right next to me while we were diving?

"Kestrel! Get ready. You ready. Hey," Ray, the leader of the band yells to me. The room gets a little quiet for a moment while they announce another raffle or some shit.

The gang moves in around me now that they know they can actually hear for a second.

"Kestrel, finish what you were saying," Dietera says.

"Yeah," adds Loon with a smirk, "you were saying something deep."

"Who was that on the phone?" Chelonia asks. "Is the plane coming in?"

The plane! The fuckin plane! I didn't even think about the fuckin plane with all the shit going on.

"No. I haven't had a call on the plane. I got to make a call," I say in a rush loudly.

"NO! Finish what the hell you were saying," they yell, almost in unison.

Chelonia cracks one of those soft, rare, sweet, smiles she never likes to whip out.

I take a deep breath, then open the hydrant, "So scientists have been wasting all this time on cloning lately. Are they mad? We

518

already know we have way too many people to sustain an American Dream life-style on this Planet, and it don't look like we will be moving to the Moon or Mars anytime soon. Two SUVs, an RV, a jet ski, two or three pets, a huge house, kids, a mega home entertainment center. Can you image if each person in Bombay and Beijing felt entitled to consume like US? Instead, as we all have illustrated a number of times before, why not switch over to figuring how to develop a third hand. There is so much we could do with a third hand. See, I just had to stop gesticulating to take a shwig of my drink," I state with conviction.

"That totally broke your train of thought," Dietera adds, though I can't tell if she is humoring me.

"Drummers could play more polyrhythmic poly-rhythms," says Troubadive, who is back on the atoll for a second time, to show off the diving to some of his buddies.

"Running backs could straight-arm tacklers with one hand while holding the ball with two, cutting way back on the number of fumbles," adds Doger in a rare contribution.

"Or," I offer, "they could straight-arm two tacklers while holding the ball with one arm." We both laugh. Doger is a good guy.

"What on Earth are you talking about?" says Jellie with Kilgro eaves dropping-in over the table like two iron dirigibles.

"I'll tell them what I'm talking about." I start in a loud, deep voice, a la Lou Rawls, "We need three hands!" I exclaim like a madman.

"Ha ha ha ha ha." I look around quickly. Amb did not hear me, but instead of repulsing them, Kilgro and company appear almost more titillated. Yikes. Backfire.

If I had only had three hands, I wouldn't have gotten killed right when we were so close to expelling our raiders and securing victory.

I go on, "Oh yeah, and driving: What about driving? Drive-thrus are designed for US to pick up a crispy chicken sandwich, then we're suppose to peel off the wrapper, eat it without dropping special sauce on our fly, adjust the radio, hit the turn signal, answer the cell phone, and fiddle with the climate controls and power windows without running down a zombie pedestrian." Everyone's laughing pretty hard right now, but I am serious. Serious and furious. "How can dim-witted humans be expected to manage all this with only two hands? What on Earth was god thinking? How come elephants were the only ones, the only ones on the whole Earth to get a third hand? Couldn't Snow Leopards and Wildebeest have used a trunk?"

Troubadive says, "What about squid and octopi?"

I respond, "Okay, that's overkill. I'm not saying we need eight limbs. Let's not get out-of-control here. They are *Cephalopods* anyway. "

"God gave us two hands Kestrel," Rosmarus says from his bible knowledge. He holds them together in the prayer symbol.

"Yah, don't be sick," Manat adds with a sarcastic roll to the eyes, trying for a bit of a laugh.

"I'm just talking about one more hand. That's all we need. One more hand," I say almost like a chant. "There are so many functions I do on a day to day basis where I have two hands full and need to grab something with my mouth or pin it between my knees or under my armpit."

Sproc adds, "That's the way god made us and science shouldn't be messing with it."

I turn to Sproc to see if he recognizes the inherent contradiction in his statement. "The Germans had an old saying; '*When the rooster crows upon the dung heap, it means the weather's going to change, or not.*' It's the same thing I said to you guys before."

They look at me puzzled. I continue, "If you are golfing out in the rain and you don't get struck by lightning, you could argue that you were not struck by lightening because god loves you. Specious reasoning doesn't mean that it's true. You love racecars. God didn't make racecars, man did. If you are anti-science and technology, then you should be anti-race car. Anyway, unlike the literalness you ascribe to the bible, I am not being literal. Humans don't need a literal third hand; they need a hand from all of the other people in society who are fighting against them. We need to work together."

Rosmarus, Sproc, and Manat all 'pffff' at me. They know they are real men and they don't need no help from no one!

"Yah know what else?" I add factually to get their philosophical juices flowing, "If there weren't anymore fat people, there wouldn't be anymore fat jerks."

My brothers stop to puzzle over that one. I know they think I am referring to Rush L. or them personally, but actually, I am just making a simple point of perception.

"Some New World monkeys use their feet, and their tail," Dietera fuels my flame as she tries to get us off of the personal family stuff and back onto the topic of three hands.

"I always loved that; 'New World' hee hee hee." I laugh, and everyone busts a gut and spits their drinks.

"That confused me so much as a child," Jellie states.

"When watching Wolfgang Baer's *Wild World of Animals,* the narrator would frequently say, with a stuffy academic Brit accent, 'This Old World species could never have survived the ice-age crossing of the Bering Strait. . . blah blah blah.' 'Old World', 'New World'?? What the hell are they talking about? Brazil split off from Nigeria at the same time. The plates were all here when Gwonbongaland broke into continents. Oh, I get it; 'Old World' refers to what Brits want to again point out; that they are the hub of civilized Greenwich Mean Time world, and the rest of US delinquent criminals down in kiwi world need to shut-up and follow along," I rant. "New England! The New England! My ass. The patriots showed them what they could do with their new England. It's Massachusetts man. That's a native name by the way."

"There is no 'New World'", agrees Loon.

Dietera adds, "There is just the part of the World that none of US ignoramuses knew about until Columbus fumbled upon it to call it India, thousands of miles from the real India."

"Isn't 'Wolf' 'Gang' 'Bear' a great name for a wildlife film-maker?" Troubadive notices.

I agree with gusto, "It's like football players named 'Young Blood' or swimmers named 'Spits'. I loved when I found out that 'Engelbert' 'Hump' 'Her' 'Dink' was a stage name." We all laugh.

"Dude, come on!" Manat says in disbelief.

"It is." I confirm, "That is wicked funny, and even funnier cause it's unintentional right? I mean, he wasn't fronting **The Circle Jerks** right? Punkers weren't supposed to be slamming while he sung *After the Lovin,* right? Still maybe the cheesiest of cheesy songs ever written, including anything by Neil Diamond." I suddenly blurt, "Did you ever see *Neil Diamond Parking Lot*?

Drop whatever you are thinking about right now and add it to your mental rental list. No wait; add *Heavy Metal Parking Lot* and *Neil Diamond Parking Lot*, and watch them in that order. You will not be sorry."

It's a bizarre time on Halfway as I look around the familiar All Hands Club for the last time. I don't know it is my last time. My family, who never travels anywhere, decided (and to say that they 'decided' has to be taken with great weight), to visit the remote atoll. My family never decides to do anything. It's not a totally dysfunctional family. They still talk with each other, kind of, visit on major holidays, and even occasionally do favors for each other. They exchange pleasantries, try to avoid controversial arguments and be civil, and fire political and philosophical comments sideways. So when I got an e-mail from my 'little' brother Manat saying the entire nuclear family planned a trip half way around the World, I said, 'You're shittin me!' I did not expect they would ever come, nor did they give me a date. Here they are now, part of this incredible scene. The Sri Lankans are dancing and hugging everyone. Darom sits high on a stool, so he doesn't look so small, with a huge grin on his face. Funny how every culture likes to smile, and dance and sing. We really are all *Homos*, aren't we. All one species no matter how different we want to act or claim to be. Darom chirps, "Too many drinking, too many drinking." He means 'everyone's drunk'.

A couple of the young interns on atoll grab Cherry Ballpig of all people, and drag him up to the dance floor for a stab at Billy Idol's *White Wedding*. Unbeknownst to Cherry Ballpig, this just happens to be the extended remix version. Cherry Ballpig is already in trouble before the second chorus. He has already thrown his cigar down, after trying to hold on to it while he awkwardly gyrates, and now he sweats profusely, and I can see the two young, healthy, college-aged 120-pounders laughing at him. They are laughing right at him but his ego tells him he may have a chance with these girls, so his id forces him to push it to heart-attack. He should pace himself. He started out way to fast and gung-ho, and now, he feels compelled to keep up this mad pace.

As the song plods on, I actually start to worry. Everyone at our table is laughing at him, but Rosmarus and Manat look away sympathetically. Now the FNs are watching and laughing too. The song goes on and on and the girls won't relent, thinking this is the funniest thing ever. Eventually, the song finally ends and Cherry Ballpig moves to make the socially-inept action of attempting to hug the girls at the end, both of whom skitter back like Ghost Crabs with an 'oooooooeeeeewwww' slipping from their tight lips and nostrils. He sits back with Rattas Dewhurt and the rest of the HIC table, soaked in sweat. That is definitely the hardest I've seen him "work" in the 2 years I've been out here.

What is all this **Bogus Weirdness**? Where does it come from and why should anyone care?

Bogus Weirdness was Drats' ranting outlet for views he couldn't express to the rest of the world, his family, and friends, directly. It was an art show mainly, but also featured live call-in segments with special guests, from radical mouthpieces to conventional academics. Drats always hoped it would be influential enough to change the World, just like the song *New Reason*, also a number from **Rudy the Red Bat**.

New Reason
by Drats

What is friendship? What is love?
Who dares to claim to know?
Even family trust in the lord up above,
Would the almighty place us in a grave so shallow?
Feed won't satisfy the hunger still we spree,
External substance burns the internal cavity
It is impossible to really hold some one else,
It is impractical to hold on to oneself
Fruitless desires become life-long dreams crushed,
It's harder now that we know we have no choice
Look at the pain-stricken faces hushed and rushed,
Screaming you can't even hear your own voice
Alone in a world of ambition never reached,
Loveless loneliness, deepest faith breached
Cold darkness spirals to infinity,
Once you realize you're alone there's no place else to be.

I can't really express those feelings any better than singing a Drats song. My family makes it extremely difficult to converse intelligently. Rosmarus and Sproc want to talk about god, therefore, I automatically end up on the evil "no god" side. It's stupid. If there is a god, it sent Chelonia down to me as an angel just when I had given up on the idea that I could find a pure, sweet, true love. She is really an angel. Sometimes she totally pisses me off, but don't ya think an angel would have to piss ya off once in a while? When she heard my family was comin, she took the plunge and said she would also make the long trip on that little twin-engine turbo-prop from Lihue. She knows how I suffer over my family obsessively, and she wanted to be here to help me keep my head on straight. What a girl.

MMMMMmmmmmMMMMMMMMMMM. Are you counting the 'm's? Chipweldi simply sealed the deal by signing her on to volunteer. I hope she likes pulling *Verbesina* weeds.

So they've come to the atoll, experienced the wildlife, and avoided the feared sabotage by Myhel, thwarted mainly by my resignation from the atoll. Misa Queen has been demonized throughout the atoll now, by all her vile actions and her unabating defense of Myhel, even in her most evil hours. What cracks me up about Misa Queen and her whole situation is that still, to this day, after everything she has proven: Chipweldi still defends her to Amb until the bitter end. He keeps stating things like, 'Hey, she's a reef ecologist. Even though Kestrel might be a great ranger and knows all about the natural history and the naval battles and all, he doesn't know anything about reefs. That's why we got her. He knows the military history and the bird biology . . .'

Amb cut Chipweldi off at that point, 'He knows about the aquatic fauna too. He is a diver.'

Chipweldi stands corrected but just goes on defending her. I agreed, and was very excited to find that she is a reef ecologist and can teach me a lot about stuff I know nothing about, like reefs. I have never been living out on a coral reef before, so I thought it would be great. But, every time I ask her anything, any question about coral reefs, no matter how base or elementary, she immediately expects that I am trying to ding her, or she tries to be unhelpful and guard her "knowledge".

Misa Queen has whined more than once, "Why are you trying to ding me? Amb always dings me."

First off, I have to get her to explain what that is. Secondly, she wouldn't be getting dinged if she was good. Banette and Dietera never get dinged. They are great biologists who work hard. What is this 'dinged' shit? No one ever dings me, I mean, professionally. I guess you could say Ryle physically dinged me, and Myhel told Dutrouex I threatened her, which I guess caused Amb to ding me in front of Chipweldi. But if she wants to be a great ranger, she needs to stand up for herself and avoid obsessing about being dinged. I've learned as time goes by that this is her defense mechanism, which she uses to get out of work, or to manipulate people. If I ask her what the date is, she has no idea. If I ask her which way is West, she wants to know why anyone would need to know such a thing. She is a fuckin lame poser who can't remember a friggen thing I tell her, and she just graduated from UH Hono. How did she do that? Anything I ask her about coral, she either tries to withhold from me insecurely, or, she really just doesn't know about, which makes me start to think that maybe she lied to Chipweldi about her coral reef knowledge. I look at her now and think she is just one, big, liability.

I love Dietera and Twistor, and miss Zart every day. These are my true friends, as Renn had been, but it's funny now after seeing how Renn treats Twistor, that I have no interest in ever being her friend again. Strange? If it were a 29 year-old guy with a 17 year-old girl living in my house, I would put a stop to it. What's with this double standard?

I hear a voice break over the din.

"Hey Uncle Kestrel. Not for nothin, but this party is 'okay'. We should throw a really big raging beach pahty tomorrow with all the left ovahs, like an all day pahty," says my nephew Chris, who loves to party and wants to throw a mega blast before they leave the atoll. "Aahhr you guys doin any U2 or Bon Jovi tonight?" he hopes.

I go deeply back into my head. Sense memory is such a funny thing. There are some little musical gems that I like that maybe nobody else really likes or remembers or thought about, and which weren't a hit and you think you would never hear again, and it's practically been removed from the public-consciousness. Then when you hear it, it totally transports you to another place, and time, and space. I think of The Cocteau Twins: When I hear *Heaven or Las Vegas* or *Sugar Hiccup*, or songs like that which I haven't heard for ten or twenty years, I think to myself 'oh yeah, that's when I was running the hurdles and graduating from high school. That's when I was at UCLA and the World was bright and optimistic. That was when Bush senior was gone, and things looked better under Clinton. That was when the World was going to be changed and turned around, and the old fuddy-duddies from the WWII Bush mentality of war, and the old religiously oriented fanatics, screwing everything up with war and prejudice, were finally going to pass the torch beyond Korea and Nam and the wasteful "Cold" War, and into a time of peace, fairness, and prosperity.' It all looked great, even up to Y2K and beyond. But no. Now that I have come to Halfway Atoll, my dreams and hopes have been shattered. We are not going to live in a World of peace and love as long as we have Cherry Ballpig, Dick Cheney, and people like Chipweldi, Misa Queen, Sproc, Rosmarus, and Manat, fuckin shit up. Never never never.

Now, when I hear those songs, I get so sad and melancholy. I was so into the idea of living in a post-war society. I was just so much younger then, and I thought people were like me and altruistic. I think I was happy then, because I was busy, and young, and hopeful. I was full of hope, and the idea that people like me would make this a better Planet. I was just happy. Happy to be alive. Happy to be searching for the perfect girl. Are the people in the World happy now? Back then, I was having a lot of fun. Nothing was a 'biggie'. That's not true. I would make things into 'biggies' that didn't have to be, and things that I certainly wouldn't make into biggies now. Did our whole World change recently, or just my perception of our World?

My phone rings again, startling me from my philosophical daydream. This time, it is word from the Hangar. Not only is our regular flight landing at 11:30pm, but another flight just showed up on radar and will be arriving at the same time, and I have to check it for snakes. This is going to be tight. My band goes on at midnight, but duty calls.

I head out of the club and greet and meet the first plane. Standard routine.

Before I can even reach the second plane on the tarmac, which appears to be a private jet full of rich ravers, they start to pour off it and create chaos. Some appear to be snorting coke as they come down the gangway. They wear brightly colored, high-end disco clothes with sequins and sparkles, and crazy hats and crowns.

"Yo, hey, hold on there partners," I say with a jovial cry, "What's going on here?"

"We are going to be the last people to count down the New Year of the Millennium on the Planet, and we were the first ones to count down too; earlier today, almost exactly twenty-three hours ago," a snooty brat says as another women vomits under the gangway.

"Hey, this ain't spring break in friggin hell-hole Havasu," I say with an alert in my voice.

Some HIC staff appear with Deny and Cherry Ballpig, and golf carts and the Dolphin Van. They start yelling at me like dismissing a pariah dog. "These are special guests. They are fine." "We'll take care of them." "Go back to the club," Deny and Cherry Ballpig yell over each other.

I stand perplexed. What the hell is going on around here? I look around to see I am the only APS staff here. I call Amb on his cell, but no answer. He probably can't hear it in the noisy club. I call Ben. I get his voice-mail. Knowing him, he is in bed already, alone. In bed, alone, at 11:40pm, on the New Year's of the Millennium. I shudder as I try calling Chipweldi, whom I haven't actually called on his phone in ages; like maybe a year. No answer. He's the cop on the atoll and is supposed to answer 24-7! That useless fuck.

I look around now in the heat of frustration. HIC has already carted these invaders off. I have no paper work or manifest. I don't know who they are or where they came from, and I don't even have an orientation planned for them. I don't even know how many there are, but being a bird surveyor, my mental image tells me 27. Well, the worst thing I could do now would be to let a snake get on the island, so I quickly do a cursory check of this remarkably nice and expensive Lear Jet. I don't technically know if it is a Lear Jet, but it looks like one so that's what I'm calling it. Top shelf and ultra modern.

I shine my light in compartment after compartment, then turn to rush back to my bike and the club. I notice one swing-arm to the landing gear door has a deep compartment in it. 'No, I already checked, everything is fine. Don't bother. I've checked a million planes and never a snake.' I rationalize, but something makes me go back and check, almost as if I could smell it, like when stalking pigs. You know how I am. I have to cover every base. I am the polar opposite of Chipweldi and Misa Queen.

As I shine the light into the compartment, I realize it is pretty deep. Nothing near the outer lip, but as I shine the light deeper, I see the eye-shine. Chills shoot from my quads up my spine and into the back of my neck and head. I involuntarily jump and hit my head on the bottom of the fuselage.

"Ffffffox poop!" I yell, avoiding swearing, only to realize this is one of the few times no one is around to hear it. I hear a roaring swell of voices echoing from The All Hands Club, like Coyotes, wailing at the moon.

I rub my head hard and look around as I squat beneath the hot engines of the aircraft. If Chipweldi were around I could have him have Spot help me. Spot came on atoll a week or so ago as a German Shepard multi-purpose snake-sniffer, drug-mugger, and police dog. He's not actually trained to kill snakes, but he could help me kill the snake in tandem. I picture the Shepard and I going at it with the snake. Hmm, I feel the dog would inadvertently bite me in the excitement.

There is no one around, I have no time, and I have no choice; so I reach in as fast as I can and snatch the snake and drag it onto the runway, dropping it hard on the asphalt. It hisses and takes a lame strike at me. It looks stiff from the journey, and a little kinked. Damn, my worst fear! It's a Brown Tree Snake, maybe from Papua New Guinea, or from Guam now that we accidentally introduced them there and fucked-up that island. They are venomous, tough bastards. I circle the five-and-a-half-foot snake like Riki Tiki Tavi, hissing back and making my circle faster and tighter. The snake tires of holding its head high, and striking, and it can't protect its tail. Finally, it tries to make a slither for it around one of the wheels. I grab its tail and fling it 30-feet in the air. When it comes down with a splat on the asphalt, I take to the air like Bruce Lee, coming down on its head and neck with my government boots. I keep my left foot on its neck while I stomp its head repeatedly with my right, feeling pain resonate up my bad ankles and shin splints.

The poor creature's long languid body twists and writhes on the tarmac and wraps around my leg. It's horrible. I love snakes so much. It stops moving and I jump clear of it. I look at if for 10 seconds. It's dead. I take out my Leatherman and cut off the mangled head carefully. I already destroyed it as a specimen anyways, and this is one species we want to make sure never makes it to Halfway Atoll Wildlife Sanctuary. Cutting it off to assure it's dead, I do so carefully, because I have read plenty of stories of people getting bit by dead snakes and sharks, stung by dead jellyfish, and the like.

I look at my watch. Shit, 11:51pm. I look at the snake, then look at the plane. I am not suppose to board any planes, but hey, they are suppose to have a manifest, a flight plan, and there is no cocaine or other controlled substances allowed on Fed land, not to mention, they brought a friggin snake! I run up the stairs of the aircraft after wrestling with my rationalizations, and into the cabin. No pilots. The plane is a mess with coke and ecstasy capsules all over the place. There's some kind of trancy house music playing, like Sasha and Digweed or Tim Robert. It's actually progressive house, but I don't know better. You know, raving DJ shit. Then, way in the aft of the jet, I see that there is someone here. I didn't see him because he blended in so well and did not move at all. You see, the color of the interior of the plane is white, and this 'guy' let's call him, is completely covered in white. It looks like white powder; like baby powder sticks to and covers every bit of his massive body. He wears powder-white shorts that almost look like a loincloth, or diapers. He looks like he may be 300 to 350 pounds, with each of his pecs bigger than my head, yet, he probably has less than 15% body-fat. He has intravenous tubes and wires coming out of him. As I walk toward him quietly, I am careful to avoid stepping on any of the debris on the floor.

Slowly, like Kung Fu on the rice paper, I approach him. Why? Why am I going near him? I don't know. I am drawn to this freak and I am on a mega adrenalin rush with my family, and Chelonia, and the band show, and just killing the snake, and no phone contact, and now this!?

At about 8-feet away I stop. I can see he is barely breathing. What a magnificent specimen. He looks perfect. He looks like a big, huge, perfect man. No one is monitoring this guy. What are these strange liquids going into this guy? Shit, it's 11:54pm now. My band goes on at the stroke of midnight. I have to kiss Chelonia. It's our first New Year's. It's the Millennium. What if she kisses someone else? There are a lot of desperate guys all over that bar and she looks like a friggin goddess tonight. Fuck! I don't know what else to do at this point, so I grab some pills and dump them in my government shorty shorts as evidence, and I blast down the stairs. I grab the dead snake and sprint back to my bike. I leave the snake at The Hanger, in plain sight, over the garden boxes; and bike my ass off back to the club.

When I get there, it is packed. Olderhostile folks, HIC, ASS, and APS staff, every FN on the atoll, and about 119 Coasties, jam The All Hands Club. As I run in, I can see the deer-in-the-headlights faces of Ray and my Filipino band mates. 'Where the hell have you been?' their eyes betray as they follow me toward the stage. Chelonia throws me my backpack and I take a quick duck behind the amps. As I start to whip off my uniform shirt, Amb approaches me.

Peering around the big black stack, "Cuttin it kinda close, aren't chya?" Amb asks.

"Amb, there was a plane, and a snake, and other weird shit," I explain to him as fast as I can.

Ray and the band get on stage and start tuning up. The dj plays Madonna off her Inimmaculate Contraception Collection of "greatest" hits. How can you refer to anything associated with her as greatest, other than greatest self-promotion genius? The snare hits and feedback blasts from the PA as the band fumbles about. Amb responds, "What are you talking about."

I respond, "I tried to call you from the airport. There are some weird party people who just landed on the atoll. They have drugs on them. Here." I hand Amb *one* of the ecstasy tablets. He looks at it.

"There was a Brown Tree Snake too!" I say.

"Whaaaaatttt?" he yells in shock.

"I killed it. Where's Chipweldi? Where's Ben?!" I ask frantically, as I get my shiny disco shirt straight, and Ray and the band shoot daggers at me with their eyes. The countdown starts.

"Great work Kestrel. None of this is your fault," Amb says as Panburelie pushes him aside.

Of course it's not. Why would it be my fault?

"Have a great show. Knock em dead!" Panburelie growls as she grabs Amb by the arm to pull him away.

Amb cuts back in, "You are officially off duty. I will take care of everything. Make sure your family enjoys this special holiday with you." He turns, as Panburelie yells single digits into his face.

I jump on stage, spot my goddess, then jump back off to push through the crowd.

"7 . . . 6 . . . 5 . . ."

Three guys vie to kiss Chelonia at the end of the countdown, and Myhel, Kilgro, Jewel, and a number of other women all seem to be blocking me, but she reaches and stretches through the squished bodies, and I grab her wrist and pull her towards me. We have a long, deep, passionate, loving kiss, as the band kicks into *Zombie* by **The Cranberries**.

"3 . . .2 . . . Merry New Year Evybody!"

"I love you so much honey," I say as she falls back into the crowd.

"Kick ass!" Chelonia screams back to me, still maintaining her own sweet way.

I climb back on stage and hit the first notes of the verse in the bottom of my range, a snarling Iggy Pop sound, leaving room to build to my Freddie Mercury falsetto. As I sing and look at Amb's reactions, I realize something. Wait a minute. Where the hell is Stark Kristian, Cherry Ballpig, Deny, and all the Richie Riches that came off that plane? None of them, or a number of other characters, are here.

When I hit the chorus, I really open up into full voice, screaming and wailing. Some of the Olderhostile people get up and cover their ears. They walk out of the club, shaking their heads in discomfort. They don't like when a nice, professional ranger they know, gets up on stage and screams 'Zombie' over and over again at them. I told you we are a rock band. I didn't say The Everly Brothers.

We play song after song while the crowd dances in front of us. The band does a good job. No major flubs or breakdowns.

When the songs end, the Coasties scream for more and chant, but we don't know any more songs, so we stop. Some Coasties get on stage and anticlimactically fumble through a Blues Traveler's number, but mostly people leave. Others stay around to party.

Panburelie slow dances near the edge of the stage with Amb, and the bartenders still pour drinks.

Everyone feels totally spent.

When we finally ever step out of the club after an excellent concert and a great party, with hardly any hassles from the usual downer atoll residents, our eyes explode open to see a friggin war zone. The Coast Guard had been in the club with us the entire time. When they step out, they look as shocked the rest of us. The Richie Riches have been romping around, trashing Halfway, setting fires, killing maybe as many as 100 birds; some of which they appear to be throwing around, like uncontrolled ravers on a roid-rage. It's like a sick nightmare. I stand frozen, my eyes as wide as the flying saucer my brother Sproc believes he saw over the rink.

"You gotta try what we are on," the head rave bitch yells with a primal scream as one of her friends whips it out and starts shooting his pee right in her face. She laughs and sticks her evil tongue out, long and pointed, as the urine drips down it. I'm surprised it's not forked!

"Yeah, check this out." Half a dozen of the Richie Rich ravers lift and press a golf cart above their heads and throw it onto the lawn, crushing albatross nests and burrows. These guys have like super-human strength! I look around at the destruction.

They don't care!

The primal revelation hits me like a heart punch. The essence of man isn't remembering and reminiscing about all the great victories in life, but instead, to dwell on all of the chances that could have been but got away. That's what drives us forward, phylogenetically. We are supposed to be smart enough to control that drive. We are supposed to care enough about others to control that drive. Either way, this homocentric party kills innocent albatross right in front of us, and these are the people who brought the friggin snake, so my discretionary tolerance feels lower than a Chuckwalla pressed against a hot bolder.

I see a couple of ravers running by and say, "Hey, I can't believe I even have to say this, but you gotta stop."

They laugh and run past. I could catch them with my lightning fast 400-meter hurdle speed, but then what would I do with them?

The head Richie Rich girl appears again from behind the Station Theater, in her plastic and Botox splendor, she reels, "You can't tell us to stop!" She says it as if she is about to fall flat on her face. "We can do whatever the fuck we want, and nobody can stop us."

"Wrong. This needs to stop right now and these birds are oblivious to how much money you have," I state with reason.

"These, these birds right here?" She looks with distain. She doesn't care about them. She doesn't care about me. She doesn't care about US. She doesn't care about shit.

There seems to be a general panic going on. One of the ravers pulls out a magnum and shoots it in the air with a 'Yahoo!' Attacking these motherfuckers physically disappears from my mental options, but I gotta do something. I fly back into the club, but Amb is already gone.

The Coasties, many of them stumbling drunk, parade off to their cutter. I grab the highest rank I can find and relay the situation. Finally, after a few hours more of complete chaos, they get the situation under control, and have the Richie Riches all back at the jet.

What if the Coasties hadn't been on atoll at the time? What was the contingency plan for a ship or plane to land here and create complete chaos? We always feel so safe in America; never vulnerable to attack. But we are out here. So remote. So exposed.

I see the head Richie Rich bitch struggling with a couple of Coast Guard police with batons and riot helmets. Finally, she's not smiling anymore.

"Let go of me. Don't touch me. Dyou know who I am, you ignorant oafs?! I'm the princess. I'm the head cheerleader. I'm the girl you could never have, losers!" she yells with shrillness.

As three of her steroid-monster buddies rush to her rescue, as well as anyone on coke and ecstasy can, some Coasties rush over as well. In the melee, drunks versus druggies, I see the head rich bitch get jostled, and her diamond tiara drop off the back of her head. In what looks like slow-mo to me, it bounces off of the wooden Halfway Atoll Map, which shows the nautical miles to a number of points beyond like Easter Island, The Marquesas, Genoa, and stuff like that, and the studded tiara lands in a bucket of viscous tar being used for runway patching.

I move over quickly and see that the fight is under control, so I reach down and pull out the tar-covered tiara.

The head Richie Rich bitch turns around to look at me, and when she ever sees her diamond-studded tiara encrusted in thick, heavy, petroleum tar, she has a massive flip-out fit.

"WWWhhhhaaaaaatttttt! Oh MY GOD! You have got to be kidding me! This is a joke! You did that on purpose. AAAAAAAAAAAAAAAAAAAAAHHHH! You did that on purpose. You will pay! That is worth well over a million!" she fumes like Kilauea.

I don't know what to do. I am exhausted and infuriated, especially about all the dead birds, but I could give a fuck about her tiara.

She looks at me with pure evil in her eyes, and spits, "Don't just stand there like an idiot, you fuckin idiot. You idiot. You dumb ass idiot."

I say, "Okay", then nonchalantly throw the tar tiara over to her, thinking she will be able to catch it with both hands. I realize instantly that this was one of those bad choices I try not to make but that my brothers, especially Rosmarus, always seem to. I meant no malice, but it turns out that one of her big blingy rings is caught in her lacy party dress and instead of reaching up, she bends forward to try to loosen it and the tiara horseshoes right around and onto her head. Hole in one! Tar and all. It happens so fast, yet all in slow-mo.

Queen bitch screams, "You fucker. You fucker. Get the goon. Get the gooooonnnnnn!" she yells, as the Coasties drag her toward the aircraft. She reaches up, wanting to get the tar tiara off of her head, but she restrains herself from touching it and ruining her nails on top of her hair and tiara. Her wasted and hung-over cronies rush to her aid, as the head Coastie and Amb talk things over. Amb looks beside himself.

After a cool down, time out, and some emergency hair care, the head Ritchie Rich bitch approaches me on the tarmac at the foot of their gangway.

In a brief moment of sincerity, she says, "Look, I know what you think of me and you're totally right. I can't change who or what I am anymore than you can stop wishing to be filthy rich like me, or Paris Hilton. It's what we are. I feel trapped," she continues under her breath, "but if I show one ounce of sensitivity toward you, they will ostracize me, and believe it or not, even with all my fortune, they're all I have. I know you can't understand."

With that, tears well up in her eyes and she almost, almost cracks a smile, and then turns and heads for their psychedelic luxury jet, glowing and fluorescing in the dewy first rays of sunrise. I stare at her. Her body looks perfect, like a doll, but still, I would never ever go near anything like that. That proves right there that looks can mean absolutely nothing when you're dealing with someone like this. All I have been concerned with are the other 2 million species on The Planet, yet, she thinks my biggest concern is her, or should be. As she climbs up the stairs, twisting like an eel on a hook, with her conniving little beefy pet bozo standing there three steps up, wearing a George W. kinda shmirk on his face, she turns to US like a queen on a diplomatic visit, and says in a shrill and disgusting voice, reminiscent of Cruella Deville, "Ya know, maybe a visit from The Goon Squad would set these peasants straight." "No!" chimes-in the muscle-head bozo, like the obsequious little horrible thing he is.

"No, these plebes *need* The Goon Squad. The Goon Squad! Yes!" she agrees with herself as she throws her perfectly ugly Botox-filled mannequin head back. "The Goon Squad would be perfect for this gooney island," as she looks at me with a punishing glare. "It's an Atoll you asshole. ATOLL!" I reply with fury.

After hours of citations, explanations, pay-offs, and what could have even been blow jobs and drug exchanges for all I know, the Coast Guard finally lets the plane go. Don't get me wrong, I'm not harshing on the Coasties. They saved our asses. But, I can't say I know what the hell is going on. I would have cuffed them, and sent them to jail in Hono.

As I walk back toward The Hangar, I feel tired. Really really tired. My eyes ache with the increasing brightness. I think I'm getting too old for this. I once pulled all-nighters semi-regularly. The birds scream all around the airport as the breeze begins to pick-up and the albatross get airborne, running along the runway with slapping webbed feet. Shlap shlap shlap shlap shlap.

When Chelonia and I get back to my room, we throw off our clothes and get onto the bed, sticky and dirty feeling, like I had been in Vegas. Yuck! Chelonia modestly keeps her bra on, and pulls on a pair of short, tight pajama shorts. I keep my briefs on. It's probably around I don't know, 5am, . . . 8am now. My eyes remind me of their sore tiredness, my brain hurts, and soothing Chelonia puts her soft hand on my lower stomach.

"Are you okay honey?" she says in a soft, loving voice; a voice so completely opposite from the Richie Rich bitch, or Kilgro, or Myhel for that matter. A soft, loving voice, and a soft, loving hand.

"I'm okay," I can barely muster, pained by the death of so many innocent creatures in the name of a friggin party.

Chelonia picks up an article from my nightstand. "What's this one?" Trying to get my mind off of it.

I can't even see if it's lyrics or what. I just stay resting with my eyes closed, relaxing. It is another article Drats wrote for a Japanese paper while we lived in Tokyo. She starts to read it aloud as I close my burning eyes:

Save Old Japan
by Drats

Living in Tokyo, it is very sad to see some of the old Japan slipping away. My friends, Japanese and non-Japanese alike, complain about the rigidity of old Japanese culture, the way that women are often treated like second class citizens compared to many Westernized countries, and that cell phones, scooters, and karaoke are still "Japanese", but they are just modern forms. But, if we truly lose old Japan, what will be left? Japan already adopts many of the worst aspects of Western culture, while the West only adopts the best from Asia. McDonalds, hip hop fashion and music, Denny's, oversized SUV's, intentionally earsplitting Harley's, business suits and ties, overpriced boutiques, cheesy young girls singing inane pop hits, Bay Watch and Starbucks! Much of what the Japanese adopt as their own is the rue of most cool hipster Americans. I admit, I had a tofu burger at McDonald's a few months ago, (had to try it, it sucked!) but that was the first time I stepped into a McDonald's since the early 80's.

From Japan however, Americans make-out like culture bandits with a hefty trade surplus on the goods. Americans take affordable, reliable, fuel-efficient cars, trucks and motorcycles from Japanese makers. We import great electronic equipment, sushi bars and chefs, tofu, taiko drumming, judo, karaoke, and karate, spectacular ancient art forms like Kabuki and Bunraku, and of course, beautiful women who marry American men. Japan gives America its best, and America gives Japan its worst, and the Japanese eat it up. Even if I do complain about the inconvenience or illogicalness of "the Japanese way" and things I do not like about this culture, it is not my culture. It is unique, and I would hate to see the old Japan die or be co-opted like so many native cultures in Africa, South America, and on remote islands, turned into tourist havens. If Japan can adapt to modern society and business, and survive as an Asian leader, but at the same time, maintain the best parts of its heritage and expel the worst aspects of American consumerism and MTV, then there may be hope for old Japan. If we kill the goose that laid the golden egg and made Japan the gem it is, if all of Tokyo starts to look like Roppongi at midnight, if all the cute young girls in Japan work as hostesses or in soaplands, then what will be left, and why would anyone with any heart or soul ever want to come here?

Gai-jins must be sensitive to these issues, and understand that we can be part of the solution, or continue to be part of the problem. Imagine if Martians came down to Earth and their culture was totally different than ours. If we did not respect it, if we did not understand it and trampled all over it, who would be wrong? When Homer visited Japan on **The Simpsons***, he walked through the paper doors, much to the ire or his wife Marge. "Why bother?" he said. He did not want to even take the effort to slide the door open. Are we crashing through the doors in Japan right now? With the economic bubble burst for so long, is there a glut of gai-jins, less interest in learning English, a frustration and breaking point that the Japanese are finally reaching? And, if so, will this ultimately save old Japan?*

"Wow, he wrote a great article honey," Chelonia says with a soft kiss from her plump, juicy lips.
"I feel the same way baby," I think I say.
I fall asleep, dead to the world. As I reach REM, I suddenly wake from a blast of a dream.
I mumble to Chelonia, "Why are humans violent? Why do we act like baboons?"

Chelonia thinks for a second, and then tries to answer the way I would if she had asked the question, "Modern scientists argue that a gene on the Y-chromosome, which we inherited from lower mammals, causes males to protect and bond with clan members, kill, rape, and steal from opposing clans or rival tribes, and this increases survival and reproductive success (like how early *Homos* out-competed Neanderthals, or how Euros wiped-out Natives everywhere they colonized, ya know with the guns, germs, and steel thing or whatever)."

I concur, "Like US, like them; we live in a colony."

Chelonia continues, "Females must have been attracted to big, healthy, prosperous colonies, just like they are today. They must have been attracted to big, strong guys who were strong enough to protect them and their offspring, but not so big and strong as to completely hurt and dominate them. That's what women want right, a strong good man, not a strong bad man. Maybe a Jack LaLanne, versus a Mike Tyson, let's say."

The image pops back into my head, "What about that huge guy in the back of the plane?"

We both think for a moment as the mayhem from the previous night rocks through our heads. The carnage! Those poor, innocent birds sitting on their eggs.

I say, "According to Yerkes, 'One chimpanzee is no chimpanzee'. I would take that the next step and say 'One human is no human'. I know that morons will argue that we are not chimps and we didn't come from chimpanzees, and all that other crap, but the bottom line is that one human is no human, period. I know this goes against everything that is our western culture, cowboy, gun-slinging Clint Eastwood American ideology *High Plains Drifter* crap, but we gotta realize that we (i.e. you) are alone. You are nothing! There is no such thing as a rugged loner. If you are riding around on a Harley out in the desert, you are not really alone and independent. Somebody had to go make that bike."

Chelonia looks at me for a second. I'm not sure if she's following, then she says, "Someone had to mine the ore, and vulcanize the rubber, and continuously (daily!!) drill for oil, and refine it, and get it to the gas station so you can fill your hog."

I say, "You think you are alone, a rebel?"

Chelonia answers, "That's cause you can't think for 2 minutes. Your mother fed you and gave you clothes."

I say, "Your father gave you shelter and taught you how to ride a bike so you could balance on your Harley later. You can 'think' you are alone, and 'think' you are a MAN all by yourself and independent and doing everything by yourself and for yourself, but you are not."

Chelonia states obviously, "You are part of a colony that grows food and mines resources."

I say, "The more that people fight against each other's minute differences and try to kill each other, and the more that we try to rebel against our own colony, the worse it will make it, and the more doomed *Homos* and many other animals will be."

Then Chelonia ratchets it up, "The more selfish, greedy, and individualistic we get, the more we destroy everything! One human is NO human! Period! Selfish religious fanatics, though many ironically denouncing evolution, apparently seem to hold more of the baboon gene than the rest of US."

I show Chelonia some quotes I've jotted down in my little arts log, where I put poems, lyrics, and concepts for tripped-out performance pieces:

For the animal shall not be measured by the man. In a world older and more complete than ours they move finished and more complete, gifted with extensions of the senses we have lost or never attained, living by voices we shall never hear." --- Henry Beston
Every animal knows more than you do. --- Native American Proverb (Nez Perce)

"Okay, and I got one more for ya; 'Everything in nature is wild and freeeeeee, like meeeeeee.' Okay, that's my bastardization. *All good things are wild and free* was Henry David Thoreau, but," I clarify, "I always adapt pertinent quotes to me, cause I want to be wild and free and I like to be wild and free, but ya know what I am really realizing? We can't be completely really wild and free. There is no wild and free."

Chelonia agrees, "If we are completely wild and free then we are not responsible to anyone else. We have to be responsible to everyone else cause WE have responsibility for the third hand."

I can't believe that we seem to be reading each other's minds. I say, "If we want someone's third hand to help US in our time of need, then WE need to be ready to do the same for others. Like how Boston helped Halifax after the big explosion. WE didn't have to go help them. WE didn't have to do shit. But WE, the Bostonians, blasted up to Halifax like it was our own backyard. I am so proud of Boston for doing that. I mean, you could stick with the stubborn primitive two-hands method, which I might add, has done great disservices to *Homos* thus far in our meager two-point-whatever million years we've been around, and be like a Ted Kaczynski Uni-bummer type guy, doing everything totally by yourself in some shack up in the mountains of your own private Idaho, and all that crap. We can all pull Rambos and yell, 'I don't need anybody else. I'm an island. I stand alone.' We want to be wild and free, but not at the expense of everything else that's wild and free. I can't just run amok, wild and free, without considering everything else. So that's why I don't know, as Henry David Thoreau states, if 'All good things are wild and free'. Consider an ant colony. It is free, not enslaved, but only free to go unhindered by humans or other creatures consciously, or unconsciously. Yet, each member of the ant colony displays undying loyalty and gratitude with their own lives for the protection, survival, and even basic day-to-day function of food production, etc. An ant will die for the colony in two seconds, and it will die without it. So this sense of wild 'freeness' is also tied to its commitment to its world, meaning, its species."

Chelonia states, "All individuals ultimately strive for their species to thrive, and in turn, this success drives other species to thrive on Earth."

I say, "As I stated, E.O. Wilson says basically if the ants were to die by some ant fungus or other catastrophe, that the entire Earth would come to a standstill. Lorenz says that it's not the family that makes up the basic social unit, but the anonymous flock, group, school, or herd that makes up the most basic and fundamental societies on the Planet. The problem with humans now, especially in certain places like the USA, is that we think our family, health, and house comes first. Screw the community. Screw the neighbor down the street, and the politicians, and the tax collectors. This is why *Homo sapiens* society will fail; not because of a lack of family values, but simply for a lack of shared community among our fellow peoples. We all know, . . . it's hard to nuke Moscow when you have a Russian exchange student sharing the breakfast table. We need to see the whole World in this way or it is over! Keep in mind that *Homo sapiens* is supposed to mean 'wise man' or 'knowing man'."

Chelonia argues, "This is the way we have to look at it as intelligent humans now. It's not just about protecting our own species. Now, we are smart enough to know that we need these other creatures, even from the ones that may annoy some of us, up to the ones that would eat us. WE need all our ants, and all of our other species. This is not only our mission: It is our duty and responsibility."

Getting antsy, and afraid to look at my watch, I say, "It's gotta be like 7:47am by now." I rattle away, "I can't lay here anymore."

"Slow down," Chelonia says. "You need rest too. You could be way off. It's so hard to judge with the endless din of gooney partying spilling all over your closely shorn front lawn. Maybe it's only 7:21am?" Chelonia suggests with a seductive laugh.

The irresistible force drives forward against the immovable object; "Note that I don't think about whether it's 7:30 or 8, like normal lazy rounders. I never think in those terms. What's the chance that one of US will look at our watches at exactly 3am?" I ask rhetorically.

"1 in 60 per hour, times 24 hours, if you mean on the hour, if my probability studies serve me," Chelonia says like a little know-it-all, mocking me and mimicking my voice to a 't'.

"That's why it cracks me up when we set our alarms for times like 6:30 or 7am, exactly," I reason.

"Did we fall asleep at an exact time?" Chelonia says, humoring me again perfectly.

"I certainly don't, obviously. So then, why wake up at an exact, rounded-off time? My alarm right now is set for 6:32am, or 6:34. I can't remember but that's the point: It don't mean shit anyway." Chelonia continues my thought: "Especially considering it's probably around 7am right then when you are lying in bed, and you have a meeting in about 2 hours with Amb."

"Yah, we gotta figure out what the hell happened last night," I say with great consternation.

I rest for a few seconds, then hear Chelonia fall back to sleep, and exhausted, I start to drift off too.

Obviously, we are both way off and disoriented after that hellish night. We didn't go to bed until around five, and now it's about 8:42am.

I kiss her again and know better than to keep talking. We twist together on top of the sheets and really kiss and hug. Really, really, make-out, but I can tell, since she squeezed on her skin-tight shorts, that she's not ready for the act of love. Not like with Danica or Hamed More. Not like with Hiromi. Not even like with Messycka, who I told you was the hottest ever. The difference is I can really trust and love Chelonia in a way Messycka would never allow me to, and I don't feel any need to force the issue of sex until it comes organically. This love is so good and real. Not like anyone I've loved in my entire life; and certainly nothing like the mechanical routine Myhel performed on me repetitively.

We hug quietly, and I fall back into a deep sleep, then I awaken to the obstreperous sound, in my head, of air hissing out of my regulator, as I look at some Morwong fish at 97-feet. I reach up and feel the sweat beads on my forehead, convincing me for a second that I am down near three atmospheres.

Chelonia says, "Rise and shine the World is mine. Are you awake honey bunny?"

"Yeh. Wow, what a night. I think I gave myself a headache just from the shear power of my voice," I say with grogginess.

"Yay, you can really belt it," Chelonia says as she squeezes me.

An albatross field in panic and chaos after the Richie Riches'
raiding romp. How many burrows collapsed?

I finally fully awaken from all these thoughts and dreams, the image of the Richie Riches, the tree snake, and the pale monster in the tail section; and the ringing in my ears from being on stage. After some heavy spooning, I throw on my uniform, change the battery in my cell phone, and prepare to zip down to the Galley to eat, before my last tour on Halfway. I walk out my front door, past the 48 active gooney nests, and the white terns on the AC unit, and the black noddies preening on the roof. What a cool bird. Nice cap. A Bonin Petrel sits in the grass; an uncommon sight in the daylight.

I see quite a bit of destruction from the night's revelry. Wow. What happened? The FNs are running around trying to clean up all the blood and carcasses.

I go to my office, put everything in order, and look to see if I have any notes or anything. Swinging by Amb's office, I see he has the phone pinned into his neck while he types at 52 wpm. I give him a little wave and he signals me to stop. Amb says quickly, with his hand over the mouth of the phone, "We can't have the meeting right now. Do your tour and any obligations you need to deal with. We will debrief after your tour," Amb orders, serious and stressed. Then, I get ready for my tour, and when I walk out to see if anyone has gathered, I see a huge group of about 54 folks, ready to go.

When I come to the finish of my last Historical Tour, I feel it welling up in me as I walk toward the monument. The end is still ten minutes away from me, but I can see the polished stone shimmer past the ironwoods, down the broken asphalt road, and in the open parade field filled with goonies. Maybe 300,000 goonies, counting chicks.

When I finish describing the battle, standing by the monument and using the engraved map as an educational tool, I get choked up. This is my last tour as first ranger. It was a master tour. Amb had come on it, knowing it was my last one. Why? I had been on the atoll for 2 years and 4 months.

I say the final words: "So, with that, The Americans won The Battle of Halfway, turning the course of the War in the Pacific, and forcing the Japanese into a defensive posture for the rest of World .. mmh, eh, . ."

It happens, tears well up in my eyes behind my dark polarized cop shades and under my broad-brimmed *Rat Patrol* Aussie desert hat.

544

At that very same moment I look up as I try to catch myself, to a cast of sullen faces looking at me like they had just listened to *Love Ridden* by Fiona Apple. They all look so moved, so close to tears, and yet, Renn has to blow it.

"Oh, boo hoo hoo," she mutters.

Amb looks over at her in anger as several veterans and Olderhostile folks gasp at her rudeness and sense of impropriety. I know I certainly have not been one for propriety, but this even offends someone like me!

She is jealous that even though she is a way way better ranger than Misa Queen could ever be, she could never pull off a tour like I just did. That was a classic. People were proud of US and felt great about the Animal Protection Service as well as American pride. They stood there, enthused and heartened, inspired and enlightened, edutained and viscerally impacted; and yet, Renn has to make a belittling joke of it.

Amb looks up to see my reaction. The consummate professional, I say, "Thank you. That's the end of our tour for today, and I will give you a moment of silence to view the monument, and I will stand over here on the road to field any questions or comments you may have; especially any of you who are vets, or have been to Halfway in the past. I would love to listen to you. Please beware of petrel burrows under the lawn."

I walk over to the road and stand there alone for a minute, wiping the tears from my eyes so no one will see them. Chelonia knows I'm crying, but she hangs back with my family, who are not only visibly moved, but shocked that a 'liberal bunny-hugger' like me would spend so much time, energy, and enthusiasm, on a war that happened 56 friggen years ago. Renn heads toward the office with Twistor while Amb stands talking to one of the guests in the back of the crowd. Twistor looks over at me sheepishly. He didn't like Renn's behavior anymore than Amb did, but he doesn't feel like he has any power to say anything to her.

An Equal Opportunity presenter, Kestrel gives his final, tear-jerking Historical Tour, to Primates and Procellariiformes alike. Gooney chicks seem to relate to the flight stories especially.

First one, then three, then five people; stand around me, asking me questions:
"Why couldn't the Brewster Buffaloes shoot down the Zeros?"
"That sounds like pure luck. Are you sure that's how the Americans found the Japanese carriers?"
"I heard that some of the sailors were eaten by sharks and strafed in the water. Is that true?"
I would get everything. Some true, some false, some from cheesy Hollyweird war flicks, some from misinformation or propaganda, some from out-dated textbooks, and some from that sensationalized, profit-driven *Discovery* or *History Channel* crap. Weird how the folks who always source shows on **PBS** like *Battlefield, War Plane, The American Experience, Nova, Nature,* or *Frontline*, always seem to have the straight scoop and the most intelligent questions, and many of them tend to be British or at least have Brit accents? It is also funny how misinformed the military guys themselves are, even about their own branch of the service and the true role it played in WWII and on Halfway.
Amb comes over. As some folks break off and shake my hand, he can hear them say, *"Great job. Really powerful." "Best tour I've ever been on. Thank you. Really."*
A couple of people try to hand me rolled up bills or slip them in my hand when they shake it. I never let the money touch my

fingers. Some of the old ladies even move behind me to try to stick some fives in my tight government shorts, like I'm a stripper with a bulbous bike butt.

"No, thank you so much I really appreciate it, but I can't. Thank you though," I say with sincere yet duty driven regret.

As soon as the visitors step out of earshot, Amb leans in softly, "Where did Renn go?"

"I saw her heading into the office," I reply.

"She should be out here listening to you field questions. Does she give a damn about the military history out here or what?" Amb asks.

Now I don't rat on people. I didn't rat on Misa Queen, the fattest rat on the atoll, but, I already told Renn, when training her, that she needs to listen to me field questions. I can't make her do what I say. I'm not her super, just her trainer.

"Also Kestrel, I saw that and I know you would never take money," he says with confidence, looking straight in my face. "I know you also told Misa Queen that," Amb says, looking at me even more intently.

I look at him. There is a quiet moment.

"I was right there when you told Misa she couldn't take money, right?" Amb gently presses.

Now he is forcing me to rat her out or appear an accomplice to her illicit ways. Though I know he trusts me now, I could jeopardize that by appearing to be aiding Misa Queen somehow, which is the last thing I would do anyway.

"I made it clear to her multiple times, verbally, and in writing," I say to Amb professionally.

"In writing?" Amb says with surprise, like he now has much more evidence than he thought he had.

Actually, I don't know what he is talking about, but I get the strong impression that either Misa Queen has been taking money, or she has been saying that I have been.

"Yes sir. I know you've been slammed and haven't had a chance to read it yet, but as stated in my monthly report, I created a training manual for rangers. It covers every single thing the next ranger on Halfway needs to know, and includes all my mistakes. It states it in there and I even added the CFR (Code of Fed. Regs.) number to it," I say.

"Oh. Good work. Did you have her sign a statement that she had read it? Did you show it to Chipweldi?" Amb goes on.

There is another pause. How do I answer this one?

"Ah, sir." I wait for him to save me. It takes him another second. "You didn't get her to sign anything, and you asked him to look at it and he didn't bother," Amb answers his own question, knowing the routine all to well around here.

"Misa Queen said she doesn't have to sign anything, and Chipweldi totally blew it off sir," I say quickly and quietly as more visitors approach. They are an old couple from the North East, I think New Hampshire, and they offer more accolades and condolences. "Best tour we've ever been on, and that includes Pearl Harbor and The Alamo." "You are really gonna miss that guy out here."

We smile and say 'thank you' as they turn and stroll away.

"Well, you are better than the Park Service," Amb chuckles. "Good job." Then when the coast is clear, he gets back to business. "Next time you see Misa, tell her if she takes money again, it will be her job. Tell her not to accuse you again either. Tell Renn to see me in my office," he says sternly. He is gonna nail her ass. "I'm not going to have a meeting about last night until tomorrow. I have too many fires to put out right now." Then Amb walks back toward the office.

"A ranger's work is never done eh?" exclaims one of the bubbly tourists. "That sounds serious," another one adds as Amb walks beyond earshot. I know he is using me because I am leaving. I think he is smart for handling it that way, especially since he can't get any help from Chipweldi.

After the tour, I stand there for a second alone. Everyone's gone now, off to the Galley or to take pictures of goonies. What a World. What a wonderful wonderful World we live in. Why do we have to have the Cherry Ballpig and the Dick Cheney types? Why the Richie Riches? Why the Misa Queens? Even Renn has turned on me because I don't approve of her Twistor manipulation. Again I realize: It's humans that are the freakin problem. Humans. We are like rats in a cage. There are too many humans. Do I ever have a problem in my life that is non-human?

We clean up and get back to work. What a party! Things seem to be settled-down on Halfway; like a huge ball of contentious gas had been released, or like a calm before a storm. Even my family, who still have a few days left on the atoll, seem to have mellowed to the Halfway vibe. The sunshine, the place, the bikes on the street, you know. Hey! Maybe that's what it has been this whole time. Maybe, maybe living in Boston made them psycho nuts, like Sox fans? Maybe if they lived on Halfway we would all reach equilibrium. I think of Goering:

We got around to the subject of war again and I said that, contrary to his attitude, I did not think that the common people are very thankful for leaders who bring them war and destruction.

" . . . But, after all, it is the leaders of the country who determine the policy and it is always a simple matter to drag the people along, whether it is a democracy or a fascist dictatorship or a Parliament or a Communist dictatorship," Goering said.

"There is one difference," I (Gilbert) pointed out. "In a democracy, the people have some say in the matter through their elected representatives, and in the United States only Congress can declare wars."

"Oh, that is all well and good, but, voice or no voice, the people can always be brought to the bidding of the leaders. That is easy. All you have to do is tell them they are being attacked and denounce the pacifists for lack of patriotism and exposing the country to danger. It works the same way in any country."

From The Nuremberg Diaries, written by G.M. Gilbert, in which the author interviews Hermann Goering, Adolf Hitler's Deputy Chief and Luftwaffe Commander.

I laugh to myself. That is ancient history. There is no way, even under an apparent idiot like Bush, that intelligent, well-educated Americans would ever fall for that shit again, especially with the new millennium now upon us. But wait a second; he did get into office somehow. I puzzle for a minute, then take a deep breath and look out over the vast parade grounds. Good-bye Halfway. I can't stop the tears from rolling down my face. The goonies look up at me like I'm a psycho.

I go about the rest of my day uneventfully. When I return home on my bike, I see a swarm of activity. Amb got Panburelie and some FN's to get the Halfway House ready for my going away party, while my nephew Chris continues with the preparations for the beach component.

"Okay Chris, tonight we can have the mega party. It coincides with Amb's big goodbye party for me anyways, so lets combine them," I say enthusiastically.

"Woohoo!" Chris yells with gutsy enthusiasm. He climbs up the stairs to the second story porch of the OIC House and shouts to the heavens, "Hey, who's ready to pahty tonight? C'mon, we want to have a real pahty so BYOB and let's get this thing stahted."

I can hear Chris' full announcement clearly over the din of goonies way down by the chief's quarters. As I step off my bike and leave it at the edge of the sand and lawn, I see a large number of revelers magically arriving from disparate buildings, carrying trays of lumpia and curry, and lots of cases of beer, coolers, and the Halfway regular hard shtuff: Christian Bros., a big fave of the Sri Lankans. I don't even know what it is, but I think it's either bourbon or some other whisky-type thing. I'm glad I don't. I'll happily let some drunk correct me on what Christian Bros. is. That won't bruise my manhood.

Jinx! Kestrel unknowingly foreshadows his demise,
just moments before the Goons arrive. Photo by Chelonia.

Dr. Oso gets his 100-watt stereo blaring Fleetwood Mac's *Say That You Love Me.* The vibe feels pretty good and the sun shines. Everyone seems to want to relax after the catastrophic attack of the Richie Riches. I take a deep breath and just relax. I also notice

550

some very odd characters approaching the OIC house too. I reach up to block the sun from my eyes. An FN distracts me for a second as he hands me a beer, while another gives me a clove. I don't really want the can of yucky beer, but I pop it to toast them. I hate smoking, and it screws me up of running, diving, and Ultimate, but it's a good way to get a head rush to get the party started. As I light the clove, one of these huge characters approaches me, singling me out intentionally, and says, "Hey, got a light?"

He takes my cigarette from my mouth before I can even offer, then he uses the simmering end to light his, then he throws my clove away on the grass. The sun in blasting right in my eyes, but he looks just like the huge guy I saw in the aft of the psychedelic plane.

"Hey," I say in protest, then look over at my brother Rosmarus. I see something I have never seen before. There is fear in his eyes. A chilling, wide-eyed fear that gives me shivers. The kind of fear I've seen in Manat's eyes regularly, but that Doger, Rosmarus, Sproc or our Father would never show.

Funny thing about bullies: When they meet someone who is actually a match for them, or heaven forbid, superior, they buckle. Everyone was always superior to me, so I always had to buckle to survive, or fight and lose, but at least fight. Running was always the better option.

This guy, and his three other cohorts, are painted from head to toe in some kind of bright white clay-powder, including their faces; even their eye-lids. They look like headhunters or something, from some bizarre South Pacific island, (save for the hi-tech sneakers and workout shorts), as if they had just finished a ritual. But as soon as they open their mouths we know they certainly aren't Polynesian. These are American guys all right, and they are huge, I mean WWF huge! Not World Wildlife Fund; World Wrestling Federation. I think all four of them are over six-seven, cause Manat is six-five and they got inches on him, and they have to weigh over 303 pounds each, with maybe 13 to 16% body fat! They look like they have been taking steroids and pumping iron for the last 20 years.

The one that threw my cigarette away is bald, and apparently the leader. We'll call him Lead Goon for lack of a better name. And there is Goon 2, Goon 3, and Goon 4. So this is the dreaded Goon

Squad, and somehow, within only a very short time after the Richie Riches left, they miraculously appear on Halfway, and look to Fuck Shit Up!

At this moment, Chipweldi arrives in his 'police' pick-up, with Spot sitting behind the seats in the back of the cab. Goon 2 walks over to the passenger window to distract him and Chipweldi says, "Hey, where the hell did you guys come from, heh heh, heh, ha?" Lead Goon then approaches from the driver's side, reaches in with both hands, and snaps Chipweldi's neck and jaw like King Kong did to that Allosaurus in the original classic. Then the Goons join the Lead Goon and they flip the truck onto its roof. The windows smash and the sirens go off for a moment, and then Spot comes blasting out of the broken window and straight for Goon 3.

"Here little doggie. Come play with The Goon Squad," Goon 3 bellows.

Spot lunges and starts shredding his left forearm, which the Goon gladly presents to the growling German Shepard.

Goon 3 laughs, "Oh, nice little doggie. Gee, they makin shep-hards awful weak these days." And with that, Goon 4 grabs the shepherd by his hind legs, Goon 3 grabs Spot by the scruff of his neck with his free right hand, and the other Goons each take a forelimb as they make a horrible wish. Multiple bones crack as Spot lets out a sickening yelp and a whimper, releasing Goon 3 and collapsing onto the asphalt like a jellyfish. Everyone, who has been in such a happy and up mood, suddenly stands stupefied in complete shock and horror. Spot continues to whine in pain, obviously paralyzed. Dr. Oso, in shock at Chipweldi's brutal murder, and now Spot's demise, steps backwards into his antique stereophonic system; nudging it with his chunky thigh. The song jumps as the needle skips over to *Sara*, a beautiful and lovely song, in stark contrast to the currently horrific scene.

Unfortunately, Chelonia just happens to be standing right by the foot of the stairs. Lead Goon wheels around and grabs her with both hands around the neck, and lifts her off the ground by her head. He could squish her like a grape. One of her wedged high heels slips off her delicate, supple little foot, and she goes limp. "C'mon. Let's kick this party off with a good ol' fashion rapin." As he turns and starts carrying her up the stairs by the neck, like a chicken to the cutting block, her eyes fix on mine and I see tears quickly run down her precious chubby checks.

Lead Goon pauses five steps up to display her to the stunned crowd. "Aawwwh, look, tears of an angel. I love when they cry. A rape without a tear is like a piss without a fart. Har ha ha har." He turns and proceeds up the stairs with the other three Goons in tow.

I turn to Rosmarus and say, "It's on."

"No," Rosmarus replies half-heartedly, but he knows it's on too. There's no way any of us could stand by and let this happen, even if our fates were to be that of Chipweldi's or Spot's, we have no choice.

I say to my family with the shake of my head, "I'll see you in hell", more as a provocation to action than any statement about, or admission that, a place like that would actually exist. In this moment, hell seems more like a possibility than usual.

Then quietly, quickly, I nonchalantly slip into the kitchen on the ground floor, and then up into the Halfway Room, where the cool Navy memorabilia still sits on display in pristine condition. The 50-caliber machinegun is a huge rusting hulk, so I can't see using that for anything accept comic relief. I slip a large Ginsu-type bayonet knife, the kind you could use for chopping coconuts open, and a small serrated close-contact murder knife, like a switchblade, down the back of my shorts in the small of my back, and head for the stairs after the Goons. Under my breath, I say to my nephew Chris, who stands stiffly by the stairs like a beanpole, "Get the guns out of Chipweldi's truck, and make sure they're loaded." Then I start marching up the stairs.

Plan? What is the plan? I have no plan, but I know whatever I do, I can't fail. I move on pure instinct now.

Lead Goon and Goon 2 enter the house and go into the master bedroom. Goons 3 and 4 stand outside with their huge arms crossed, like threatening gargoyles carved as temple guards to ward off demons. These guys would even scare off demons.

Goon 3 says, "Where do you think you're goin little man?" They stare at me with threatening menace.

"I've always wanted to give it to that uptight bitch in the ass. Can't I watch?" I say with a sardonic grin, trying to sound as base and ignorant as them.

Goon 3 says approvingly, "Oooo, a sadist."

Then Goon 4 follows with, "Hey, maybe we should let him go in. They can have a tandem butt fuckin. He's small enough to do for a girl," referring to my 177-pound lack of stature.

Goon 3 tilts his head back with a hearty laugh as he pictures me being raped, and with one surreal, seamless move, the big chopping knife comes out of my shorts and into his Adam's apple, the point stopping against his third vertebra. In the next millisecond I am sliding down the stairs on my belly head first, kind of like flying, like Superman flies, but maybe more like Tobogganman. Goon 4 lunges to grab me, but I am already in full slide, banging my forearms, chest, abs, and quads the whole way, but I can't feel any of it. I just killed a man! Sure, he's a fuckin freak, but I still killed someone. My eyes are pinned wide. My muscles convulsing, tight and bristling. The bruises would have been bad for the next few days, if I had lived long enough to let them flush with blood.

Goon 3 slumps to his knees, as the blood trickles down his white chest. He half-heartedly tries to reach up for the knife, but he can't and blacks out. Goon 4 rambles down the stairs after me. At the bottom, I roll and the smaller steak knife (still in my shorts) carves into my right buttocks.

Inside, Lead Goon drops Chelonia onto the bed like a sack of potatoes, ripping her pants down and her Victoria Secret panties straight up and off like wet tissue paper, abrading her soft, baby-like skin.

The Lead Goon barks, "Okay little piggy, let me in."

Goon 2 laughs, then says, "Hey, let me do her first."

The Lead Goon responds, "What? Get the fuck out of here. I'm not takin sloppy seconds after you, you fuckin herp victim."

Goon 2 barks back in his face, "Why? Why do you always get to go first you fuckin asshole?"

Lead Goon says, "Cause I'm the biggest, baddest motherfucker there is why and no one can stop me. Cause I'm in charge! Don't you forget it."

Goon 2 snorts, "You still think I can't take you, you fuckin pussy?" The veins bulge in his arm. Chelonia lays there, watching all of this, and hoping it will come to blows. She tries to think of what she can do, but she is coming up with nothing and her mind involuntarily starts thinking about her Mother and how much she loves her.

Kestrel and Chelonia, in a happy moment together, visiting The Fells in downtown Boston, enjoying the waterfowl. Why can't we have happy weeks, happy years? Why just happy moments, moments of bliss? Why do goons force their hell onto US? Photo by Nephew Charlie

The Lead Goon shoves beta-male Goon 2 hard over the left peck. "Shut the fuck up." Almost a punch, Goon 2 stumbles back and hits the dresser, smashing the mirror. "Fuck! I'm losen my hard on," The Lead Goon says.
Goon 2 teases, "Can't get it up huh? I'm already ready."
The Lead Goon says, "You ain't ready for shit. Now shut the fuck up."
Boy, these Goons don't have much of a vocabulary, do they?
While they bicker, unbeknownst events continue to occur outside. There are disadvantages to being too big, as the expression goes, and these guys are way to 'big' for their own good.
Goon 4 still has 6 steps to go as he lumbers down the stairs after me, and that's where my nephew Chris, in a ballsy move, reaches through the stairs and railings, catching the Goon's right ankle and left toes, and causing him to do a mega face plant, smashing onto the concrete landing. This seems to be nothing to him; as if he can't be hurt, or can't feel pain. His hulking mass doesn't smack. It more like bounces, kind of like a racquetball slapping the court. But as he starts to rise up onto all fours to resume chasing me, Rosmarus brings his 330+ wait down on him hard, knees first, on the middle of his spine, and the Goon goes prone again.
Almost simultaneously, Manat comes with his 280+ pounds onto his head and neck, getting him into an illegal chokehold. Goon 4 tries to swing his left arm around to deliver one or two poorly

555

angled punches to Manat's kidneys, but Rosmarus, already doing what he can to twist the Goon's massive right arm behind his back, grabs the left arm too, and twists them into a pretzel-like Nelson. Rosmarus uses all his strength just to control the Goons arms! Goon 4, in desperation, grabs for what he can, grasping part of Rosmarus's ample stomach and beginning to squeeze and twist, Abominable style. Rosmarus winces, but won't break his hold, knowing that Manat is dead if he does.

I quickly pull out the steak knife and, like a sowing machine, stab the Goon in multiple places in his lower back, but it is like sticking a thumbtack into a futon. He barely even bleeds; just little pin-whole punctures of blood. Realizing my futility, I head back up the stairs, taking three at a time quickly and quietly, with Meg, Doger, and Sproc right behind me. Like Army Ants on a Stag Beetle, a group of FNs swarm onto Goon 4 with Rosmarus and Manat, landing on any exposed extremity available. I assume he's out of the equation now, and I don't have time to worry about how.

All different kinds of strengths. Arm wresting: That's the basic kind of strength. My brother Rosmarus could probably break my arm if we arm-wrestled. But then, what about chin ups? That's a totally different kind of strength. I can do way more chin ups than anyone else in my family, and that's a useful strength too. Rosmarus and Manat couldn't do that. What about running the mile? One could argue that that's endurance, but that's still definitely a kind of strength, combining strength of heart, lungs, legs, and will. Ahhh and here's where we start to blur away from physical strength, . . . Surviving a shipwreck at sea; that's a totally different kind of strength that takes a fat-layer, ability to float and tread water, and other physiological characteristics into consideration; but we are still talking about all physical strengths. But then, will comes into play. Some shipwrecked survivors floating out on the ocean, the big ocean, just give up. They don't want or care to live anymore. They get tired of waiting. Waiting. What about mental, metaphysical, intellectual, spiritual, and soul type strengths? Do they all count as forms of strength?

Look at how quickly and easily these Goons go down. It's child's play. To take them on head-on would have meant completely suicidal annihilation, but with a simple slight of hand, they fall even easier than Jenga. I'm actually kind of insulted come to think of it. Did they think they were going to be able to walk onto our atoll, MY HOME, and have their way with US, take my clove, drink my Zima, take Chelonia, that easily? Talk about lack of a plan. That's what adaptation is all about: Survival of the fittest, not the strongest, and certainly not the physically strongest, but the fittest.

Inside, back upstairs; Lead Goon is almost ready to penetrate. "C'mon man," Goon 2 harangues the Lead Goon in the bedroom. Chelonia, now feeling so close to the inevitable, finally finds her voice. She is such a pure, quiet, sweet girl. She has most certainly never considered attempting, or even imagined, initiating sex. She never wanted to and has never felt a need to do so, and she has never been comfortable with talking about sex, especially anything dirty. Sometimes she looks deeply into my eyes right before we kiss, and brings herself all the way up to say, 'Chico, Chiiiiiiico'. She likes to subtly blow in my ear. She actually prefers to speak English in bed instead of her mother tongue, and that's probably just it. She always speaks to her mother and father in Spanish, and can't bring herself to sully the mouth she uses to speak with her Mom, a saint, with dirty Spanish. But, if she were to pick a time to start talking, this would be it.

She turns up off her belly and grabs his John Holmes-style monstrosity, and says in the softest angelic voice; in almost a mumble that you are not sure if you actually hear, yet you know exactly what she says, "Here, let me help you with that." She gently begins to lick it, trying to pretend she had done it many times before, though she lacks experience. Damn. Why couldn't the Goon have grabbed Myhel or Kilgro, or someone else with lots of experience? As she closes her eyes, she pretends it is me so she won't gag, and she does it well enough to stop the Lead Goon in his tracks.

Chelonia thinks to herself, 'The longer it's in my hand and mouth, the shorter it will be anywhere else.'

Lead Goon makes her pause for a second, "You better not be thinkin of biten that you little shit, or I swear I will punish you."

"No, I like it," Chelonia murmurs in a lie. "I always wanted my boyfriend to let me suck on him and ride on top, and he would never let me because he wasn't big enough or hard enough cause he was too small and weak and never could."

557

Goon 2, standing by, smirks like a cross between George W. Bush and Danforth Quayle. "Hhee hee," slips out of his mouth as he starts stroking himself in his shorts.

Lead Goon looks over at Goon 2 in disgust, then back down to my little angel trying to save her ass. "I'm glad you think you're gonna like it, cause I am gonna fuck the fuckin shit out of you bitch," he yells.

When I get to the top of the stairs, I do my best Goon impression, pounding on the door with a big heavy fist three times. I hear Rosmarus at the bottom of the stairs commanding Manat, "Make sure he's dead." Goon 4 has finally gone limp but Rosmarus wants to be sure, so Manat maintains the chokehold until he feels the muscles relax.

"10 fingers," I whisper to Doger, then Sproc and Doger silently boost me up onto the roof.

Meanwhile, nephew Chris and a number of others continue to have big problems with the guns. First, he tries to get Chipweldi's pistol from his holster, but he is jammed in the truck upside down and his dead weight makes it impossible to get to. I had always complained that Chipweldi was dead weight figuratively, but I didn't think that even in death he would continue to hinder us. So Chris, now with Dietera, Banette and Twistor's help, move on to the shotgun, which of course, is still tightly snug and locked in its rack, and with the roof crushed and shattered glass everywhere, it seems just impossible to get to.

"Help us!" they say.

Many of the FNs who had been standing in shock, suddenly jump to action and finally produce the guns. They check the pistol quickly, to see it only has one bullet in it. They find no ammo for the shotgun. Some of the FNs and Banette blast back to the office with Chipweldi's keys, asking Karolyn if she knows where the ammo is. Of course she does, and she acts incredibly efficient as usual. That's why you never hear about Karolyn.

Back inside the bedroom in the OIC house, the Lead Goon barks, "Now what?" responding to my loud knocks. "Find out what the fuck those fuckin idiots want."

Goon 2, interrupted and perturbed, gets his hands out of his pants and heads for the door.

Chelonia starts talking between licks, "I love WWE Smackdown. Those guys are so buff. Have you ever been on wrestling? I bet you would have kicked ass."

The Lead Goon complains like a pedophile, "Can't you get your mouth over it a little more? Damn you've got a small mouth. That won't stop me."

Spot continues to whine in pain, splayed out on the hot tar. Jellie, Mother Earth that she thinks she is, pets the poor dog on the skull. She probably thinks this is the best use of her time in this instance, but she offers no pain relief or end to Spot's suffering. She offers the dog what she believes is comfort and love. With a last expending of power, Spot reaches over quickly and bites Jellie hard on the hand.

Rosmarus and Manat, finally satisfied that Goon 4 is dead, go over to the cop truck to take the weapons from Chris. Their emotions go from the climax of feeling the guns in their hands and the adrenaline from killing the Goon, to the catastrophic realization that the others are off finding ammo, and that they are basically back to being weaponless.

Back in his house, rummaging through his sloppy closet, Dr. Oso searches in panic, "Damn kids. I told you not to buy them so many damn toys."

"What are you lookin for?" his wife Kracklin replies with her heavy Georgian accent.

"I'm lookin fa my bow," Dr. Oso yells in frustration and panic.

Kracklin yells back, "Are you nuts? What on God's green Earth du ya think ya gonna do with a bow?"

Dr. Oso stops and looks her square in the eye, "I'm gonna protect my family damn it."

"Don't be stupid," grabbing his arm as he continues to look. "They'll keell you. Didn't you see what they did to Chipweldi?" Kracklin begs.

"O-course I did woman. But you see what they doin to Chelonia right now?" implying that she is next.

Kracklin stops for a second, then yells, "Kids, you get the hell in here right now. Where the hell is your daddy's bow?"

The kids come marching in, "Don't he keepin it unda the sofa?"

Dr. Oso quickly falls to his knees with a heavy thud and pulls out a pig-hunting bow and a quiver of large-tipped arrows.

"Careful," Kracklin nags.

"It worked for the Dukes a Hazard. It's good enough for Ted Nugent. It's good enuff fa me. Hee hee hee."

Back at the door to the bedroom in the OIC House, Goon 2 finally gets around to seeing what all the banging is about, and swinging the door wide open, finds Meg standing there. She stands right in front of Goon 3, so Goon 2 doesn't even notice him slumped there with the big knife in his throat.

"Hey little lady, I didn't know there was a line formin'. You next?" Purrs Goon 2, with still a half-o-loaf and ready to go.

Saintia yells up from the street below like a Catholic church bell, "What in god's name would your mother think of you?"

The goon chuckles a bit, then pauses for a second to think about his mom; something he hasn't stopped to think about in a long time. Saintia is yelling at him just as his own mother had.

With that, he comes out of his brief daze and starts to notice Goon 3. He looks around for Goon 4. As smoothly as I had been with the chopping knife, Meg shows single-minded focus, slipping out and inserted two steel U.S. Postal Service pens directly into his irises before he can bring his gigantic hands up off his hips. With the slight of hand of a magician, she bulls-eyes his pupils. Before he can even yell, Sproc kicks him from behind with his steal-toed cowboy boots, right in the 'guliones' (as we say in the North End), and Doger, with his construction boots, kicks sideways, kind of Kung Fu and mule style combined, blowing the Goon's left knee out as he crumbles, screaming "My eyes, you fuckin bitch you blinded me. My Fuck Ffuuuuuuckk!!"

Back on the bed, Lead Goon growls, "What the fuck now?" He gives Chelonia a head slap, which knocks her hard back onto the bed. He pulls up his pants, and heads for the door with a huge hard-on. Chelonia lays motionless, flat out on the bed, unconscious with a concussion and a sprained neck; . . . ALIVE?

After a few quick kicks to the ribs from Sproc and Meg, and punches to the head and face by Doger, but being very careful to avoid the beast's grasp, Meg closes the door and they quickly descend the stairs.

From the roof, I wave at everyone to disperse. Then the door flies open. The Lead Goon looks down to see Goon 2 trying to decide if he should pull the pens out or leave them in his eyes, crippled. He looks to his right to see Goon 3 still slumped on his knees with the dagger in his throat, then looks to the bottom of the stairs to see Goon 4, face down and motionless. Like Lou Ferrigno, in what almost appears to be slow motion, he raises his arms in a flex and gives out a mighty roar. Those who had been scattering suddenly kick into gears we didn't know they had, and Lead Goon starts stomping down the stairs like Godzilla.

Once he gets about half way down, I slip quietly off the roof and into the bedroom, swinging through the doorway like a Spider Monkey on a sturdy vine. I have no idea what I will find but I try to convince myself to be optimistic while bracing myself for the worst. God, the worst. What could the worst be? Bloody carnage? Entrails scattered? Would they have eaten her? Why couldn't he have picked Rattas Dewhurt, or Misa Queen?

As I enter the room I see her lying on the bed. The mirror broken, I think to myself, 'That dude has already suffered his bad luck: Two pens in his eyes. There is blood on the dresser, but that could have been from the dog bites. No blood on Chelonia though. I kneel quietly next to sleeping beauty. A pulse, she's breathing. She's alive! Gently touching her check, I whisper, "You're okay baby. Everything's gonna be alright. Just like you always said to me. I love you honey bunny." I throw a sheet over the lower half of her soft, exposed body, and off I go.

Just as I reach the door to check the status, the Lead Goon gives up on chasing everyone who have now scattered out of sight. He pounds a beer that he picks-up off of the railing. Rosmarus and Manat have the pistol now, but they are not sure about what to do. They know one bullet from that peashooter might just piss the oaf off, and we don't have the element of surprise anymore.

"You gotta get close enough tah shoot 'im in dah face or this nine millimeter will only enrage 'em," Rosmarus theorizes. "I shot a pig once with a 9-mill and it took 21 shots."

Manat responds, "We better wait for the shotgun, but if he gets Kestrel, we'll have to bull-rush the fucker."

Manat bristles with aggression. He's in his element now, and loving this insane action. Interesting as well, are the revealing methods of dispatching. Rosmarus and Manat used brute crushing force, while the rest of US picked and chose our clever strategic openings; basically, chinks in the armor. Brute strength can work sometimes, but it can only get you so far, as the Goons have displayed up to this point.

Licking his wounds in pure fury, having lost his three mates, Lead Goon decides to head back up to the room. At least he knows he has a victim there. His eyes open widely when he locks on to me standing in the doorway.

"You!? You are dead!" Lead Goon yells.

He crushes the can and throws it down as he charges up the stairs. I slam the door, locking the knob and deadbolt, and quickly jam a chair under the knob, and then I hurdle through the window to the left, smashing the screen and glass louver slats. Landing on the second story veranda outside the window, I turn to find Lead Goon standing at the door, but turned toward me. I figure by now he is no longer interested in raping. He has to have vengeful murder on his mind by now. But I want to make sure so I stand there in defiance, baiting him. He charges toward me and at the last second, I flip over the railing and plummet two stories down to the lawn, where I execute a paratrooper's roll and sprint for my bike.

Spot whines and whimpers again, Chelonia groans as she begins to come to, Chipweldi is still dead, upside-down; and the Lead Goon starts huffing and puffing back down the stairs. Obviously, endurance is not one of his strengths.

Hiding behind houses and bushes, Loon, Renn and Twistor, and Troubadive, try to figure out what is going on. All of this discussion has been occurring while the Goons have been being dispatched. Instead of focusing on how to stop the Lead Goon, the scientists had already relinquished that task to my violent family, and they already busily try to figure out the most important question of all: Why?

Dietera already develops her newest conspiracy theory. "Let's see," she thinks out loud, "The Richie Riches were ultra elite, and the ultra elite have bought out Washington, and the incoming Bush Administration will be itching to get into another war so they can take the country's hard-earned surplus away from schools and the environment and give it to Texas defense contractors, but they can't get any more recruits who are sucker enough to go get blown up, and with Republicans in control there will never be a draft, heaven forbid their kids and those of their corporate buddies have to sign up (or be ridiculed later for not)."

Renn questions, "These guys are from our government?"

Dietera says, "I don't know. I think something like the Pentagon may be designing the ultimate soldiers, these giant lunk-headed Ahhrnold wannabees who they can send off to fight in foreign wars," Dietera ends.

Kate Bush had a song called *Army Dreamers*, 'Ooh what a waste.' There is a pause. No one knows what to say.

Dietera goes on, "By using prisoners, like lifers, who are already off the radar and have no one who would even know or care if they are still incarcerated, and picking the most violent ones, who all lift and workout anyways, you would have these stupid, violent goons, who have nothing to live for, would be easy to program, and would go on to fight forever rather than march willingly into the execution chamber."

Troubadive responds to Dietera with skepticism, "The flaw with this reasoning in my estimation is that if you were always fighting an enemy hand to hand, WWF style, or like gladiators, this strategy kind of works. But today, soldiers really need to be smart, computer savvy, sneaky ninja-like, and know how to avoid getting blown up. Not storm-trooping monsters."

Dietera says, "I agree, but they haven't evolved to think that way yet. These appear to be more like terror weapons, not strategic weapons. I know you are anti-conspiracy theory and all that, but look at what Stark Kristian revealed in a drunken stupor after the Jorgenson play. We know he has secret deals with the CIA, who he works for, and other entities that want to control the World and steal elections, to make a huge amount of war loot. Heart's and minds! No one wants to be raped and killed by these monsters."

Twistor adds with a fast, muted mumble, "Wow, that sounds so radical to everyone here, but. . . . Dietera, do you remember the Richie Rich bitch? She said on the tarmac that they would send a Richie Rich Goon Squad to fuck Halfway up, after the beefs with APS on New Year's, and especially after the tar tiara incident. But you are taking it the next step and saying Bush-types and the CIA develop the giant Goon Squad in response to low military enlistment and strong opposition to the draft?"

Dietera answers like a true scientist "Could be. Ultimate soldiers who are strong, violent, and take orders without thinking."

Goon 2 finally tries to pull the pens out of his eyes, but goes into shock and keels over unconscious.

"Maybe some roid-ragers got so out of control that even the military couldn't contain them and they went on AWOL rampages," Troubadive speculates.

"Yes," Dietera agrees, "and the Richie Riches got their hands on them and could control them like Rottweilers."

"That's why they were juicing up that goon in the plane," Amb recalls from my report, as he crawls down close to the group and looks over the scene.

They all watch as they see people scurrying around and trying to stay out of sight of the Lead Goon.

Loon says, "We The People, US, have lost the right to make a stand cause we're too busy sitting down, sitting in the pews of our mind-numbing bible studies, sitting on our comfy couches watching our mega giant home entertainment theaters so we don't have to get up to change the channel, get out to interact with people with differing viewpoints, or get up to fill our gas-guzzling SUVs with gas at 5 dollars a gallon, 5 dollars a gallon, 5 dollars a gallon. That's my mantra," he says, just like I would.

I sprint away from the building with blinding speed, to show him it would be futile to try to chase me on foot.

Out of frustration, the Lead Goon field goal kicks a parent albatross off of a nest, right near where Chelonia had been taken near the foot of the stairs. It flies in a flurry of feathers, and slides across the asphalt with its side caved-in, like a listless mass. Then he inadvertently steps on an abandoned egg and screams "Fuuuucckk!" again, in full roid rage. The sulfur and acids ruin his high-priced Hip Hop designer sneaker.

I don't know if he doesn't know about the petrel burrows, but I assume he doesn't, so I turn and blast right past him, cutting at the last second, and through a dense burrow area, tiptoeing through the sand dunes as lightly as possible, as I had done a million times before running the ropes in football practice, trying to guess, predict, where the burrows will be. At about seven-eighths of my flight, I sink a little into one cave-in, but smoothly recover. The Goon isn't close to as lucky. A quarter of the way in, he hits a different hole with each leg and snaps forward to a hyper-extended stop and groan. "Aaaaauuuurrrrgggggggghhh!" He was already pissed. How much more pissed can he get?

Lead Goon has no way to chase me on the bike, and I'm thinking, 'Hangar all the way. If I can call for help we can get the Coasties back out here to arrest, or preferably, shoot this fuck.' So I run back onto the road, snag my bike, and blast for the Hangar. The Coast Guard ship that was here last night may only be 6 hours away, and we know we can get a C-130 here in less than 4 hours. The Lead Goon watched my retreat, then scans the quiet hood. He pulls his legs out of the holes, one by one, then walks over with a limp and pokes his head into the Dolphin Van, finding an empty ignition. Then, he hobbles over to Cherry Ballpig's white pick-up. I hope Cherry wouldn't be so lazy as to leave his keys in his truck, like the lazy sidewalk super he is. That's what my Dad used to call all the rubber-neckers who would hang around the construction sites and do nothing while the laborers and bricklayers busted their asses: Sidewalk Superintendents. Yup. And that's all Cherry Ballpig was ever good for; if you can call that 'good'. I even have a photo of him sitting on his fat ass in the truck while the Foreign Nationals run around to off-load a cargo ship at the fuel pier. With a quick turn of my head, I see him reaching for the door handle to the truck, now about 71 yards down the road. Fuck. Though Spot continues to whimper and the corpses lay strewn about the building front, save for the goonies, Halfway looks dead; completely dead; like Omega Man dead before dusk, and I hope some zombies will poke their heads out and pick this mother fucker off before he gets in the truck. What happened to the guns? Where are all the ex-military Halfway Icarus Corporation types who always brag about how fuckin tough they were back in Tallahassee and Cartersville? All that chest beating I had to put up with these last 2 years and 4 months. Where are they now, the All Hands' Club, drinking 5 cent skunked beer leftover from the Navy? Suspicious.

Just as I'm thinking all of this, Dr. Oso slips open his screen door a crack and levels his bow.

"He's goin away. Let him go," Kracklin pleads. "You know you can't hit the side door of a barn with that thing."

"Well, he's about the size of a barn door, so shut up woman, yuh messin up my aim," and with that, he lets the arrow fly and quickly ducks back inside, locking the door. Now these arrows are designed for killin pigs: 'Big fat pigs with thick fur and 4 inches a hahd blubba', as Dr. Oso had told me days earlier. As the Lead Goon opens the door to the truck, the arrow whistles in and hits the thug right in the side between the second and third rib.

"Aaaaarrrrgggggh!" The Lead Goon bellows.

"Hee hee hee" Dr. Oso laughs, "I got him. Can't hit a barn ehh? Patch Nebbers, did you see that shot?"

"Way to go," he answers in an almost inarticulate drawl.

Lead Goon looks around quickly, scanning all the buildings, but sees nothing; so he reaches around with both hands and breaks the arrow off at the nock, leaving the rest of the arrow in to block the bleeding, and quickly jumps into the truck and takes off down the road before another arrow can fly.

"You just made him madder," Kracklyn protests. "All ya did was make him madda."

Dr. Oso snickers with pride, "Hee hee hee. Yeah. Hee hee hee."

Now I see the truck bearing down on me fast. There is no way I can get to the Hangar before he gets to me. Again, instinct quickly takes over, and instead of making a right towards the Hangar, I slow so he can get right on my tail, then I feign a right and make a quick left around the fire hydrant, our only hydrant on Halfway, and around the concrete posts the Navy put around it so drunk sailors wouldn't drive into it on their way back from the All Hands Club. Lead Goon, anticipating a quick right, swerves and goes flying off of the road into the sand, where the truck gets stuck. He flings the truck back and forth from forward to reverse a few times, then, he flings it into neutral, goes out to the hood, and lifts and pushes the truck out of the soft coral sand and back onto the road. Blood drips from the broken arrow in his side.

I just about make it to the column of ironwoods, when I look back over my shoulder. I can see, the chase is off. He gets back in the truck and heads for the Hangar. Damn, that was a bad move on my part. He's going to go to the Hangar to destroy our communications capabilities, so he can, one-by-one, kill everyone on the atoll! I led him there. I coast for a moment. Now what am I doing? I know! I'll take a boat. If I'm out on a boat and I set off an Epirb, eventually, help will be on the way, and there will be no way for the Goon to get to me.

566

Back at the OIC house, the Foreign Nationals, including one of the Filipino nurses, reach Chelonia in the upstairs bedroom.

"Okay Mum. They can't take nothing away from you. Mr. Kestrel is killing them all. Don't worry mum," they say to Chelonia as she lies on the bed in pain and with an incredible headache.

Saintia and Meg enter and my Mother puts her hand on Chelonia's forehead, "Are you okay?"

Chelonia barely says, "Yes. What about Kestrel?"

My Mother and Meg look at each other with concern.

"We are doing everything we can. We already killed three of the Goons. Our family is wicked tough. I'm sure we are gonna kick ass," Meg says with enough confidence to allay Chelonia's fears for the moment.

"We have to get up and save him," Chelonia says as she struggles to sit up.

"No, you need to rest," my Mother says.

"No, I need to help Kestrel," she says, and with that, Chelonia finds the internal strength to get up.

The rest of my family hides in a shed by the OIC house with the guns. Amb enters quickly, after seeing the Lead Goon drive off after me.

"What happened?" Amb asks quickly.

"These guns are messed up," Manat yells.

Rosmarus adds, "The shot gun has a triggah lock on it, and the pistol has no ammo in it and looks like it would backfire if ya shot it."

"Fuckin Chipweldi!" Panburelie blurts in frustration, coming in from behind Amb, "God rest his soul."

"Where's the ammo for the shotgun?" Sproc urgently asks in a panic, "Kestrel is out there right now."

The group of them, about a dozen or so, run down to the APS office where Ben, Karolyn, and Banette had pulled out some old ammunition from all of Chipweldi's cabinets and supplies. Chris, frustrated from having been looking for a while, says, "What about other weapons? Anything? A speayah gun? Geez!"

Chipweldi's office is a complete mess with boxes piled and papers and pamphlets strewed about. Finally, they find everything, including a second 12-gauge shotgun in an unopened box that Chipweldi just never got around to getting to. With boxes of old ammo, a new and a dirty shotgun, and a service revolver, which might not even work, they pile into two golf carts and one ATV. Sproc and Doger commandeer a third cart from ASS next door, and they all spin off toward the Hanger, thinking that's where the Lead Goon and I are duking-it-out.

Life is such a funny thing. There are so many things in life that are mysteries to US; things that we never solve; resolutions to our 'movies' that never come. These things that we never understand force us to learn to live with and tolerate ambiguity in our lives, or drive ourselves nuts over it.

Rushing to the dock, Kestrel passes an unfortunate albatross hanging helplessly by its neck in an alien ironwood; looking as limp as Chelonia did in the mitts of the Lead Goon. Again, selfish Homocentric needs surpass alleviating the suffering of a random individual of another species. Kestrel glimpses the bird for a second, then searches back behind him, and peddles on.

When I get down to the dock to take a boat, I run into some obstacles. Unfortunately, there is no way for me to take a boat. I can't put a boat in the water by myself. I can't find any keys, and I don't know how much time I have. Over by the dock, I see a really nice speedboat. Where the hell did that come from? I know, the Goons! That must be their boat. Who else's could it be?

As I approach the boat, I see it is decked-out with everything: Supplies, drinks, food, and all the hi-tech gear needed, but no keys again. I never learned how to hot wire anything, but Sproc would probably know how to do it. Where the fuck are my siblings? I scan the Seaplane Hangar carefully, but see no one approaching. Back at the main Hangar, the Lead Goon walks into the radio room to find Ernesto Dewhurt and one of the Sri Lankan FNs.

568

"Hey, you can't come in here," Ernesto says, as he steps forward with an Army maneuver. The Lead Goon gives Ernesto Dewhurt a straight punch to the chest. Ernesto Dewhurt flies back against the cinderblock wall with the ugly blue paint, and falls to the floor in agonizing pain, holding his cracked ribs. All 130-pounds of Sri Lankan FN sits there quivering.

The Lead Goon picks up the radio to make a call. He can't reach whatever party he was trying to reach, and slams down the radio in frustration. Then he picks up a chair and smashes the electronic equipment thoroughly. He then lumbers back down the stairs and into the pick-up, where he speeds off toward the dock, to get to his boat, . . . the boat I'm on right now!

As he heads down the road and passes on the southern side of The Galley, my brothers and others pass on the north side of the buildings, arriving in their slow, overloaded golf carts, without even knowing that the Lead Goon is gone. They start running up the stairs.

"Where is he? Show us where he is," my brothers demand.

Everyone points, searches, yells, and looks totally out of breath. When they get onto the second floor, they see the Sri Lankan shaking in the hallway.

"Help. Help." he begs.

They run to him, thinking this may have something to do with me, but instead they find Ernesto Dewhurt on the floor and the radio destroyed.

"Where did he go?" "Where is Kestrel?" They ask frantically. No one knows.

Ernesto Dewhurt can barely let out tiny, constricted groans.

"Let's try the dock," Amb surmises and suggests.

So they all head back down the stairs. Amb tries to call me on my cell, but unfortunately, in all the commotion, sliding down the stairs, jumping through windows, etc, it is long gone and I have no idea where it is. The phone sits on a manicured lawn somewhere, ringing.

Back at the dock, I fumble around on his boat, looking for something I can use. An idea. A clue. What can I do? Ut oh! Too late! I hear a truck and look up to see Cherry Ballpig's pick-up doin about 86 mph past the Seaplane Hangar. Fuck! I am fucked,

569

and trapped. There is nowhere to go but ocean. I wonder if this big lug can swim.

I reach down and grab any wire or hose I can with my tightest Ninja-action grip possible, and I start ripping like a madman. Fuel spills, wires spark, and then, I slip over the side into the harbor water with the Epirb I had grabbed off of one of our MWR boats (Morale, Wellness and Recreation, I think), and I start swimming for the other side. As Lead Goon makes it to his boat, he sees me. He stops for a second, then bangs a u-turn and speeds around to the other side of the Harbor to greet me. Seeing the interception, I start to swim back out to the middle again, so he drives back around to his boat, boards, then pulls out a machine gun from one of the storage compartments. Fuck! Why didn't I find that gun? He aims at me and I surface dive as he pulls the trigger and sprays bullets over the top of the water. I hold my breath as long as I can while I travel a good 27 meters underwater before my next quick breath. He shoots again when I pop up but now I'm a good 111 meters from him and he just wastes ammo. So, he pulls a key from his pocket and tries to start the boat in vain. He realizes the damage and starts to repair the lines and wires the best he can, for someone with such a small brain.

The inner harbor entrance and dredged channel, spilling into the big ocean.

I don't have any great ideas right now, so I start to swim for the harbor entrance, and get swept out into the channel with the outgoing tide. If I come anywhere close to land, he will shoot me. As he continues with boat repairs, keeping an eye on my position, I see the cavalry start to approach the dock. When the golf carts and

ATV get to about 44 yards away, the Lead Goon stops what he is working on and reaches down for the machine gun.

Ain't it funny that it's all men? There is not a single women involved in any of this right now, and why would there be? Why would smart, intelligent, non-violent women, get involved in this stupid man battle? Men are way more psycho than women.

Ben leads the group now, because he got on the ATV and it's way faster than the golf carts.

"He's got a gun!" Ben yells back to the others, running well ahead of them, but he reacts too late.

Lead Goon opens fire. At first he misses and Ben tries to navigate off-road and into the woods, but eventually, the big target and the ATV get hit, and both go down. Sproc, Manat, and the others, slam on the breaks. The Lead Goon starts shooting at them, but after only a few bullets are spit out, the cartridge is empty. My brothers and the others whip their golf carts into reverse and get the hell out of range while The Goon reloads and takes aim. He realizes they are out of range, so he saves the ammo and goes back to work on the boat. He has only one more line to connect, and bang, the engine turns-over, sputters, then purrs.

"He's gonna get away," Manat yells.

"Good. Let him go," Rosmarus answers.

"But where the hell is Kestrel?" Doger asks.

"Look!" Amb screams. Standing on the back of the golf cart, Amb can barely make me out beyond the waves. "He's out in the channel. He's way out in the channel."

"We gotta save him," Sproc yells.

"We need boats!" Manat yells.

So with that, they all turn back to the boathouse as Amb starts calling Foreign Nationals on the cell. While keys are being found, the forklift is started, and FNs descend on the docks in large numbers, Manat and Rosmarus decide to drive around to the Harbor entrance to see if they can help me. As they get to the water's edge I can barely see them. The tide is going out and the channel is sucking me out to sea at a good 3 knots. It looks like they are trying to call me and wave. Just then, I see the Lead Goon's powerboat burst from the Harbor and out into the channel. I see Rosmarus brace his shotgun against the golf cart and take a shot at the Goon. The Goon slows and turns toward the shore. He pulls up his machine gun and sprays bullets over the golf cart. Manat and Rosmarus duck. Manat takes a shot in the right triceps and Rosmarus takes two to the left side of his ample abdomen. The Goon turns back to look for me again. As he does, I duck below the surface again, making it impossible for him to get a fix on my position. Rosmarus, in excruciating, burning pain, fires another round. A few of the pellets in the shot pepper the speedboat. The Lead Goon tries to speed up a little because of the rocking of the rocky surf, and returns fire again, but Rosmarus and Manat are too well hidden now and the bullets only hit the golf cart.

"I'm hit," Manat says in pain.

"You okay?" Rosmarus groans.

Manat realizes then that Rosmarus got hit much worse and has serious, as opposed to, flesh- wounds, like Manat's. Don't get me wrong; I'm sure a shot in the arm doesn't tickle. Performance Artist Chris Burden proved that when I saw him get shot by a rifle to 'see what it feels like to be shot'.

As two little MWR motorboats hit the water almost simultaneously, everyone climbs on board. Everyone that is, except anyone from the HIC staff again. Where the hell are all the x-military guys and Dutruoex and Cherry Ballpig? They always brag about how they run the "island" and that they are in-charge and that they have all this combat history. Where are they now? Where are the fishing guys and why aren't they scrambling all over their boats to help?

As everyone climbs into the MWR boats, Doger slips on some slime on the deck and does a split. Luckily, he is in good enough shape and he bounces back up from it like James Brown. They can hear the gunfire in the distance. Some of the FNs struggle to get another boat going, but it has a large, rusting, metal FAD hooked to it with large chains. A FAD (Fish Aggregation Device) is basically a big hunk a'somthin you moor in the water and wait for algae, seaweed, barnacles, kelp, and a whole bunch of other shit to grow it into a tiny, then a bigger, then a tuna nursery. They start their engines and are off. As they turn the corner to enter the channel, the Lead Goon guns the engine and pulls a bat turn to head right for them. The boats split and try to out run the Goon, but his boat is way faster. As he closes in on the little speed boat Sproc drives, he pulls up his machinegun to spray some fire, but the boats are bouncing so much that the bullets are just flying everywhere. Doger takes his time and waits for the right moment, then blows a hole through the side of the Lead Goon's transom, knocking out an electrical wire. The engine stalls, so the Lead Goon unloads his entire magazine, hits nothing, then reloads and starts repairing the wire.

Sproc and Doger try to drive past the Goon's boat so they can get to me, but each time they try to pass, they get within range of the Goon's machine gun and the hail of bullets forces them back toward the atoll.

Amb swings the other speedboat by Rosmarus and Manat, who slide down the rocky riprap bank, injured, across the gnarled concrete, and into the speedboat.

"We better get you guys some medical help," Amb announces as he heads back for the harbor.

"Fuck that! We gotta save Kestrel," Rosmarus barks.

"Yah, these are flesh wounds. I've had worse," exclaims Manat in a Monty Python's *Holy Grail* rip-off.

Ironically, full of bravado, my brothers are probably much happier in this moment than at any other time in our lives. This is fun. We are bonding by killing a Goon! Amb knows he has no choice but to turn back into battle. Rosmarus reloads the shotgun while Manat feeds him shells.

Kestrel gets a close look at the rusting water barge as he's swept out into the big ocean.

A long stalemate ensues. My family can't get past the Lead Goon to save me without getting killed cause he's blocking the channel. Amb considers taking the boat all the way around Spit Island, but that might take too long and if the Lead Goon gets his boat running, then they wouldn't be there in time to protect me. The Goon can't get his boat started. The Epirb has been signaling now for a good while, and the tidal currents pull me way out to sea. Sooty and Grey-backed Terns fly over me, but only the White Terns come down to within a few feet off the surface, to egg me on with their persistent little mitt mitt mitt mitt mitt mitt mitt.

As I swim way, way, way out here in the ocean, I say to myself, 'I might die. This might be the end of the book right here. If I do, I will die not understanding what that Goon Squad was doing out here and why. I can die in peace, cause I saved Chelonia. Oh Chelonia, my sweet Chelonia. Love of my life. But what the hell was the fuckin Goon Squad doin on Halfway? And why? Why would they be this kind of like, genetically modified soldiers and who would make something like that? Are there laws, like right now, in the U.S. that would prevent the Pentagon or some other entity from making something like that? Are we already creating something like that? Too bad, I have plenty of time to think about this right now, but that process won't help me.

Chelonia drifts through Kestrel's mind like the dew evaporating from a Beach Morning Glory.

With nothing to do but wait, my mind starts to race as usual. Waiting on Halfway again. Waiting for something to happen, and having no control over my own situation. I'm treading water with the Epirb blinking away. The Coasties should at least have a C-130 in the air that will locate me, drop a raft, and call a ship to swing by and pick me up. Time drifts by. I decide to untie my boots and

let them drop, but I keep my socks and everything else on for
warmth, and I keep my belt on in case I might need my
Leatherman. I feel a chill starting to permeate my core. The last
time I looked back, the atoll seemed very far away. It must be way
further away now. The machine gun has a much longer range than
the shotguns, so there mustn't be anyway for them to kill the Goon
unless they can trick him into running out of ammo. I strain to look
back, but the wave heights make it impossible for me to see what is
going on way off in the distance.

The problem is that I have been doing the elementary backstroke
now for what I'm guessing has to be a good long time. I haven't
wanted to look at my watch, but I feel I have to. I start to sing
songs, in my head, to pass the time, and I sing, **Blue October's**
Into The Ocean, which has a nice catchy chorus and feels pretty
appropriate. Finally, I take a peek at my watch.

Three quarters of an hour! Fuck! You gotta be shittin me! I have
been treading water for 3 fucking quarters!

Dolphins breach the surface, startling the shit out of Kestrel. The
whole pod vanishes less than a minute after appearing, offering a
momentary false hope of comfort.

I don't feel like a current is taking me anywhere anymore, but I can
still see the damn atoll, and that ain't good. If I can see them then
the Goon can see the plane, and the ultra-bright international
orange raft. He will surely get to me before the Coasties do, and
then what? I highly doubt he'll murder me right away. He will want
to torture me for a while. Shit, what's worse? Fuck, I guess an
option is not being captured. Maybe he's not even after me
anymore. Maybe I should swim back to the atoll. NO! Don't start

575

thinking that way. If the Lead Goon were dead, there would be boats out here looking for me right now. I do have a way to puncture the raft. When the Coasties drop it, if there would be some way for me to let the air out of it, I could sink it and get away from it as fast as I can. Am I thinking straight! What are some drawbacks?

A) If I trash the raft, I won't have anything to float on and I may drowned from pure exhaustion or hypothermia before the Coasties get to me, and the Coastie rescuers will be looking for a raft, not a guy in the water, and I won't have any protection from sharks,
B) If I swim away quickly I might burn up my energy (see A above) and also, that's why I've been doing the elementary backstroke so smoothly and rhythmically all this time. We have tons of big tigers around Halfway, not to mention Oceanic White-tip Sharks, Short-fin Mako Sharks, etc. Now I don't mean to sound like a pussy about sharks. Let's face it; I'm bleeding, I'm moving ever so smoothly but on the surface, and the odds are with me that a shark is either not around right now, or would not recognize me as food. So this leads to some leaps in logic my mind takes at this point.

Tigers are the most indiscriminate feeders of the shark world. I know, cliché, but true. They eat tires and junk like that. They are very well fed around Halfway, with all the turtles and monk seal pups around, but one still may want to take a taste; hence the smooth, rhythmic, silent, elementary backstroke, which also allows me to breathe uninterrupted, keeping my breaths shallow, weak, undetectable, and non-existent. I wonder if my socks give off an odor to the sharks? Sharks want you to struggle. They want to hear or sense, or feel you, gasping in panic. They want you to be in distress. But look at me; I am so smooth. They better watch out for me. I probably taste bad, like puked-up clam chowder up the wall on New Year's at Kelly's on Revere Beach at 2am. Or, I am poisonous, or have a hidden stinger that will nail them right in the gills. Oh yeah, better watch out for me sharky. I'm too good to be true. Such an easy meal? Better watch out.

This theory doesn't work for tigers. They just don't give a rat's ass. Like a toddler, they will stick anything in their mouths. Any-eee-thang! That's right. Even Mr. Smooth Stroke up here, miles off Halfway. Damn, what is their Latin name again? I can't remember right now, but I know it has something to do with evil, mean, fat, glutton. Damn Latin. I wasn't allowed to take Latin in Jr. High with the smart kids. The teachers right away put me in all the lower level classes where Doger, Meg, and Rosmarus had been. Funny though, in my lifetime I've probably ended up needing Spanish way more than Latin. Were the teachers right?

Suddenly, I realize, I am wicked thirsty.

I hear a voice in my head say, 'Don't forget: You are unique, just like everyone else.'

Why am I thinking about this in the middle of the biggest, deepest ocean in the world? Oh, I know why, so I won't continue to think about these:

Oceanic White-tip Sharks, (not to be confused with the inshore little White-tip Reef Shark which we like to play with while they sleep on the bottom in caves, waiting for night to fall so they can prey on little crabs and octopi) are what the Aussies call 'bronze whalers', and the sharks most suspected of nailing shipwrecked sailors in WWII, the last great war. I love that: "Great War". Who comes up with this shit? Isn't "great" suppose to mean "great"? I was taught in parochial school that 'god is good, god is great. . .' Great meaning great enough to cast me into hell forever? I always thought great was a positive superlative. The Great War, the Great Chelsea Fire, the Great Blizzard of '78! These all seem like oxymorons to me. Shouldn't we call it The Horrible Molasses Fire, The Devastating Quake of 1906, etc.? Why the hell do we call them great? The Great Barrier Reef, now that's great. And that's where a lot of white sharks, popularly know as the Great White Shark, appropriately using the term 'great' in this case, and the bronze whaler, more scientifically known as the Oceanic White-tip Shark, like to hang out. Unlike white sharks, Oceanic White-tips tend to stay pretty pelagic. I'm 4 or 5 miles off the coast of one of the most remote atolls in the world in about, well let's say, 2731 feet of water. Bob Ballard found the USS Yorktown about 170 miles NW of Halfway in something like 27,000 feet of water, and it drops off like crazy outside these atolls. As I said before, the ocean is big; but the ocean is also deep. Very very deep. Way deeper than my feelings for my honey who I may never see again. Maybe even deeper than Kubrick and Lynch put together. Oceanic white-tips love deep ocean, and they're not called bronze whalers for nothing. They can be big, and they are always strong and mean. I begin to monitor the delirium as it pecks at my brain cells like a Pileated Woodpecker. Multiple cells pop and burst simultaneously. C) I don't have a way to kill myself if the Goon does come after me. Weird thing to think right? I would never usually consider killing myself, and instead, simply fight to the death or flee, but with all that's transpired, I have to put in to the table. Do you think I could bite my own wrist hard enough to cut the artery and either bleed out or attract a shark to do me in? Should I use my Leatherman to cut myself open? I'm sure that would be better than being tortured, but I can't even bring myself to give blood. Damn, I should have stuck a mirror in my shorts. I could have used that to signal the Coasties and to slit my wrists if needed. Who am I kidding? The idea of this makes me want to faint or puke. There is no way I can self-inflict myself. I'm not only too positive and confident for that, but a little too psychosomatic too. We all have our strengths. At this point, I'm going to fight until the end.

I remember a dream I had once: A drowning dream. I remember going up to the beach just outside Boston, and calmly walking into the water on a gray day. I began to slowly, methodically swim, further and further out, past the breakers and light houses, and looking back to see the land miles away, as it is now. I remember kicking into high gear in my dream and swimming as far and as fast as I could for as long as I could until I was completely exhausted. I imagine I must have been flailing in my bed in this dream. Then, when I felt I couldn't go another stroke and I had passed way beyond Nahant, Hull, and Great Brewster Island, out beyond where The Boston Lightship was, I took a deep surface dive, and went down into the blackness as far as I could. My eardrums bulging, I look up at the surface light, dim, maybe 40-feet up, and I let all of my air out in one cathartic push. I never make it back to the surface, but the dream ends right there with me awaking, gasping for air. Even if my subconscious was trying to drown me, my awake-state was all survival.

A little seawater trickles into my mouth as I am almost falling asleep, causing me to startle.

Oh yeah, now Short-fin Mako Sharks; there's a remarkable piece of evolutionary work. Makos are the fastest sharks ever. Why? Ah, I love that question. Makos are designed to eat tuna. Tuna are designed to swim wicked fast over vast amounts of ocean. Like Pronghorn in Wyoming, tuna have an unstoppable combination of speed and endurance. Though all fish are cold-blooded, tuna are pretty warm blooded as far as cold-blooded fish go. This enables them to swim at high speeds forever. Dolphins have a hard time keeping up with them. Why? Why why why? Like the oceanic white-tips, tuna live a pelagic existence. Their prey; like sardine, anchovy, and other small baitfish; can be spread out all over the ocean, and the ocean is big. If they're gonna feed themselves, they gotta hustle.

Makos love to eat tuna more than sake-filled salary men in Osaka. Take my word for it, that's a lot. While there's no way makos will ever be able to match tuna's long-term endurance and catch them out in the open ocean, the sharks employ best options like a combination of infinite patience and blinding speed. Makos find tuna hanging out around bait-balls. Don't you love that? Anything that has to do with humans has to be named homocentrically. Since we like to use anchovy as bait, and we men always like sports or like to talk about our balls and how big they are, then we call them "bait-balls". There's no ball, and anchovy have a pretty complex social order and place in the ecological web to be denigrated to only bait. Even among US, canned sardines are relished with gusto in certain circles. My Dad and Uncles always had canned anchovy onboard our boat in the confined galley with the swinging stove. Sardines do make awesome bait if you want to catch mongoose, cats, rats; anything that could prey on turtle hatchlings and needs to be eliminated, or, it's always fun to spread some sardines around your friends' tent while they sleep, to get the skunks and coons to come around and freak them out. However, I would never try that in bear country.

Makos can burst to 60mph. How do you clock that? Scientists say they "know" how fast they go, but there is no way to do it.

Maybe I should swim back to shore. I can't take it anymore. My face is sunburned. I'm dying of thirst. It's so salty. So salty. The last things I have had in my mouth were the sip of Zima and the drag from the clove. Yuck.

I look up and back. I can't see the atoll anymore. I must be way the hell out. I see some frigate birds soaring way up in the sky. I wonder if they can see me. They must be able to. I wonder if one of them is the one I saved way up in that ironwood.

I think about Chelonia again. She said, "I don't agree with the whole Darwin thing. I mean the strongest aren't surviving in humans."

I looked at her with surprise, then said, "Humans are Darwin in reverse. When we were part of the food chain, the fat, weak, stupid, lazy *Homos* and primates got eaten pretty freakin fast, and way too fast to reproduce. Now, I blame modern technology, especially medicine, for weakening the gene pool."

Chelonia said, "Now, weak stupid humans breed, while the intelligent ones know better."

And I said, "Darwin in reverse, like I said. Nothing eats us. We eat everything! The strongest and fittest get assassinated, leaving a child or two behind. The weak and lazy get welfare to help manage their seven kids from five fathers. In nature, in balance, it wouldn't work that way at all. We contrived it to be so."

I look up again to see a large dorsal fin right by me. I look under water and see a huge Tiger Shark floating along right next to me, looking over at me. I know I flinched, and it must have detected that, but I keep treading water ever so delicately. Even if I swim toward this monster, I doubt I could intimidate it. I'm guessing 18-footer. Easily 17-footer and well over 2091 pounds. Why not just finish me off? I take a breath and clench my fingers into fists. Then I relax again and get right into 'the zone' like I did with the snake and the goons. If it wants to kill me, I'm dead. If it doesn't, I'm not. That is my mindset. I'm not going to be a pussy about it. I am defenseless. Give it up.

One rule that apparently epitomizes nature, or natural behavior, basically follows the simple premise that if you leave critters the fuck alone, they will leave you alone. A rattlesnake will not bite you unless you do something really wrong. Most animals wouldn't even 'bother' us or see us as prey, if we just left them alone. *Homos* basically have learned to adapt to eat anything on the landscape. We will eat anything we can collect, catch, and kill, basically. Nothing matches the tenacity of early humans. Grizzly Bears come close, but have never caused the wholesale destruction of entire species. We can't blame the California Grizzly for that one. To my surprise, I see that the animals are so forgiving. Deer that would bolt within a mile of you in the 1960's now let you get within 22 feet of them with almost no reaction. There is that fine line of being too close to nature, and having it become so tame that people get injured; now a huge problem. I'm thinking maybe I should take the initiative and attack the shark, possibly scaring the shit out of it with surprise, or, confirming to it just how weak and helpless I am.

Suddenly, I feel vibrations and hear engines. Speedboats! I look up and the first thing I see is the Lead Goon gunning right toward me. I wait until he gets close, and then I surface dive and head behind and under his boat. As I come up for air almost beneath the boat, he guns it and the propeller sucks my arm in and slices me.

I lose my left hand just above my wrist.

Funny, I don't really feel it. The Lead Goon spins the boat around. I look at my stump in shock, then surface dive again right before the hull hits me. I come up for air again in a swirl and a tumble, but I can barely see in the waves and commotion. I push the stub against my chest to try to stop the bleeding, when I see the Goon coming back for me again.

I then see the Lead Goon make a sharp turn and head off again. His boat is way faster and more powerful than our little Boston whalers on Halfway, so it takes them a while to catch up, but they have finally made it to me. Darom would have been proud of how Manat and Sproc captained the boats in the rough ocean, under gunfire. Amb holds on to the bouncing craft as he keeps attempting to make phone calls for help. He directs the FNs on shore, has spoken with the Coast Guard, and has tried to contact HIC staff a number of times. Somehow the FNs have been able to get some sort of rudimentary communications system functioning. My brothers fly close by the Goon on both sides. They are kind of in a Catch 22 conundrum. They can't just come and pick me up or the Lead Goon will just bear-down on them and blow them away. Instead, the two boats emulate 'mobbing behavior', staying close enough together to act as wingmen. Whenever the Lead Goon gets close enough to start firing at one boat, he immediately comes under fire from the other. It's like a pair of ravens on a Red-tailed Hawk, or the way the White Terns harangue the Black Kite.

As he pulls up the machine gun to shoot at one boat, they peel-off, while the other boat takes a shot at his back. A third boat has joined the allies finally, but they seem to be hanging back. It looks like I can see Chelonia on board! Oh my god. It's Chelonia. It's Chelonia. She is fine. I start to take stronger gulps of air. I almost had felt like crying, and giving up, but now, I'm heartened again. I'm going to make it!

This cat and mouse battle rages on with neither side ever making a lethal hit. Like Gray Wolves on a Moose, every time the Lead Goon tries to close in on me, or either boat, the other boat pesters him and he has to break off or come under lethal fire. With his machine gun though, Doger and Rosmarus never get their respective boats within range for a nice clean shot. Sproc and Doger's boat stalls in a steep turn and floods. When he sees their dilemma, The Lead Goon runs his massive cigarette boat right over the top of them, forcing them to jump overboard and then pull themselves back into the damaged boat. The shotgun is soaked. Doger tries to fire it. It won't work. Everything is soaked now in the boat. There is no way to clean the gun.

In the process, the Lead Goon damages his own boat too, and turns and fires his full clip at Doger and Sproc as they dive back into the water. As the Lead Goon's boat stalls, he looks around for another machine gun clip. Manat quickly pulls his speedboat up next to him as Rosmarus says, "Hello", like Curly on The Three Stooges. The Lead Goon looks up and loads the clip. Snap Crack! Rosmarus squeezes the trigger and hits the Lead Goon square in the chest. He takes it, standing there like a stiff statue until Rosmarus can pump the shotgun and fire a second shot into his upper chest. Manat pulls out Chipweldi's revolver while Amb lunges to take the wheel and stabilize the bouncing craft. Manat fires; five out of the six 9mm rounds actually fire, and two of them hit the Lead Goon in the neck and head. He stumbles and slips backwards, and then clumsily falls overboard.

The old blue, little, beat-up speedboat we hardly ever use, and one of the fishing boats, now join in the search from me, and are underway and heading in my general direction, like a mini armada. As the little speedboat pulls up, I see Chelonia's face beaming with sunshine. She is so happy to see me.

I bellow with the bravado of a drunken sailor, "Chelonia, Love of my life. I will always love you with all my heart. Forever. Forever."

As I try to pull myself toward the boat with awkward, exhausted, one-hand strokes, the tiger returns. With one hand cut off by the propeller, I use my second to stave off the shark. Without any threatening Hollywood score or building suspense, the tiger quickly takes off my right arm at the shoulder.

Chelonia screams, alerting everyone within earshot.

Unable to get either of the stalled boats restarted, Manat and Rosmarus, both injured, strain to yank the Lead Goon's body back into the boat. He is too heavy. They can't. Now distracted by the scream, they give up, and let the hulking body slump back into the water, their wounds smarting.

If I only had a third hand, I could have made it back to the boat. Stupid tetrapod. Instead, with these last words, the 18-foot remedial-school-bus of a bastard does what they do best. The shark surfaces with a quick, powerful serge, to latch down hard on my head and shoulders, and quickly pulls me under and far below to relish its meal, unharassed by my brethren.

If I were able to get last words to Chelonia, she knows they would have been 'Don't hurt the tiger. It's not the tiger's fault. It's the Goon Squad's fault.' She would agree with me. It's always people's fault. Even in my last thoughts, my attention span spills off randomly to homocentrism.

The shark munches me down near the bottom; some thousands of feet down or so. It shakes and twists my torso back and forth, as alua and other fish come blasting in to get their fill. These may actually be individual fish that I dove with before. The Epirb ruptures then explodes under the intense pressure. I'm already dead, so I don't feel the shark eat me. Everything is completely black and I am completely unconscious. There is no light or sound, or anything, just blankness, like being in a deep, numb, dreamless sleep, but with even less consciousness. For the first time in my life, my mind is finally blank. How do you like that? It took total death to finally quiet my cuckoo mind. No more waiting.

As the boats limp in toward the atoll, Chelonia states, "Kestrel is probably glad that the shark got to eat him. He has no regrets. He had an awesome life."

Everyone stares off over the water in silence. Saintia says *The Our Father* and other prayers under her breath.

"It doesn't matter," Chelonia mutters. "Who cares? It happened and Kestrel is dead for it. Big deal. Kestrel would say 'Stop being a pussy about staying alive!'" She stares off toward the atoll, stoic and numb.

As the functional boats tow the damaged ones up to the docks, everyone on atoll gathers, still in shock.

Nobody dares say a word, until finally, Tex blurts, "No one will ever know who the roid-raging mutant freaks were or why they showed-up on the second most remote place on Earth," quoting the phrase I had used so many times during so many programs to accentuate our geographically significant locale.

There is a long, quiet pause. Everyone is looking around. There is always something tragic about rangers and other service employees being lost in the line of duty. Maybe cause they make such low money and take such high risks. Everyone still looks around for someone. They are looking around for me! At first, many feel happy and relieved to see the Lead Goon gone, but then, . . . as the realization hits them, the absence of my energy is felt, and the sullen faces betray the tragic outcome. Their hands spring up to their mouths reflexively, as they burst into uncontrollable tears; including Tex.

Suddenly, the roar of engines in heard, and everyone looks up to see the Coast Guard C130 fly low over the atoll and out to where the Epirb signal had been coming from.

The usually incredibly quiet Chelonia, climbs up to the highest part of one of the old Navy tugboats, moving like a streamlined sloth and fighting through both the physical and psychological pain.

Saintia yells, "You don't have to say anything if you don't feel like it honey," choking back tears.

"No!" Chelonia counters. "I want to. I have to."

She pauses for a moment and a silenced hush falls over the somber atoll in the glowing, golden light. Even the relentless birds go quiet.

"Ultimately, in this last instant of life, it becomes so much more clear to me than it ever did. I am not clairvoyant, but: **Humans Need Three Hands!** With two hands, we were able to build magnificent towers and missiles that shoot to the Moon. But, this whole rugged individualism, like you are either with me or against me shit, and other macho crap, needs to end. With two hands we've been able to create all these incredible things. But also, with these same two hands, we've been able to destroy, and have these towers smashed, and have these missiles mounted with nuclear warheads, and that's where the third hand comes in. Humans, naturally, don't act like rugged individuals. We are social animals. Humans have to be with other humans. Look at how nuts every loner you ever met was. They are loners because they can't cope with humans, which causes socialized humans to avoid the loners even more, leading to a vicious cycle. Humans have to be with other humans, no matter how much psycho strife ensues. Humans need love from other humans. It's been shown over and over again going back to B.F. Skinner. Any kid that's isolated and left alone turns into a total social deviant freak. Look at Kestrel's case: Very gregarious, out-going, extroverted, non-confrontational; yet his isolation from family and loved ones over the years tore away at him and ate up his insides. It's easy to believe that being away from people and running away from society will make things better, but it only turns you into a mental munchkin."

Many members of the crowd straighten, and stiffen their lips.

Rosmarus says with realization, "Dah third hand (or fourth hand if ya have to stay symmetrical) is dah othah person. Kestrel was not being literal."

Then Meg says, "The other human who helps you."

Then Manat says, getting it, with a groan, "The third hand is dah person dhat makes you complete: Da person who *needs you.* Dah third hand not only helps ya build dhat towa or missile, but dey also help yah maintain it, and keep it safe."

Then Doger says quietly and deeply, "When ya have a third hand it means dhat its not just YOU, it is US."

Saintia says, "It is another person you have to think about too."

Chelonia quotes me quoting others, "*No man is an island unto himself.* Somebody said that once."

Sproc agrees, "Dhat's true."

Then Dietera says, "If we go back phylogenetically, the fossil record shows that humans just split off from baboons 15 million years ago. This compared to the four hundred and twenty-seven million years Tiger Sharks have been here. Now you look at how quickly we learned, from just the 1960s and Jane Goodall's work, how similar we are to chimps. How quickly those battlefronts change within the blink of a historical eye. Many many people in the scientific world applauded her, and many people in the religious world blasted her for the blasphemy of even suggesting we were even remotely related to apes."

Jellie chimes in, "Compare the pre-1960's world to now when, yes indeed, we technically should have what is supposed to be a post-religious society. Flare-ups by the psycho fundamentalist religious idiots still seem to predominate, as they did before Jesus, and during the Roman Empire, and in the Dark Ages."

Rosmarus and Sproc would usually bristle at such heresy, but they can't feel a thing.

Banette, more tempered, reasons, "Still, there is a science world out there, still investing in the science world, with computers, with the network of what exists today and with communications worldwide, with everything moving at an exponential rate. We are learning so much from DNA and everything else that we will be proving incredible things about our own ancestry in the next 5, 10, or 20 years."

Loon agrees, "We are going to have so much more information and a lot of it will be really illuminating. Of course there will be those that want to maintain age-old power structures and will fight and regress and repress and rebel against social progress, no matter what the facts are."

Kilgro grunts, "The facts are the facts and the science is the science."

Everyone stops to think of what she just said. Everyone is in general agreement with her statement, and people are ambivalent about approving of her or arguing such a point.

Chelonia, still up on her pedestal, rings out "The concept, the idea, that we, US, are supposed to be individuals, alone on this Planet, is what kills people, or makes people commit suicide. The lack of hugging, the lack of love from family and friends, the lack of caring from others, these things that turn us into sick twisted freaks, proves to us again and again that we are communal beings. That's why. That's why humans need three hands. Kestrel convinced me that all the problems that we have on this Planet are just constructs humans have created. If we wanted to, there is enough food, enough water, enough appropriate educational distribution systems, that everyone on this Planet could be comfortable, let's say, surviving healthily."

My materialistic nephew Chris peppers, "We have decided to reject diss choice and instead, collectively agree, dhat some people should have moah than everybody else."

Ut oh. Pure capitalism brainwash. A number of our other family members look him over like scowling Great-horned Owls. His neck shrinks back in between his shoulders like a Western Pond Turtle.

Chelonia's voice cracks, "If US, in one of the most sophisticated, developed countries in the history of The Planet, cannot find a way to control first, our minds, including our egos; then how are we to control our greed or our need to compete destructively?"

Loon says, "Good, positive, healthy, constructive competition, especially when it's fair, rarely pervades."

Chelonia, like my apostle, states, "We all have a positive, constructive, enlightened side of the mind, and the dark, destructive, negative, under-enlightened mind. We question which one we should control and which one we wake up with in the morning. When we wake up, do we wake up with the negative destructive mind or the positive constructive mind?"

Han questions, "What we could control our owned minds?"

Dietera theorizes, "Obviously, the Goon Squad was completely out of control of their minds, and therefore their conscious-less bodies took over."

"Which lead to their horrible destructions; but look at Chipweldi, and Myhel," Renn spits like a bitter backstabber, "and so many other cases I can make examples of, of people who can't control their minds, and can't control their emotions, and humanity suffers the consequences, and it harms The Earth in the process."

Twistor looks up at her in surprise, through a think glaze of tears that thickly hang on his lower lids like super glue. Twistor says, strongly inspired, "Each individual must show respect and take responsibility, for the whole, not for oneself. Reading positive things and avoiding getting sucked into negative thought processes that waste one's time, energy, and life, along the way, aren't worth it." He looks at Renn sternly, implicating her in his general statements. "In my life, I worked so hard to fight for the other 2

587

million species on the Planet; to protect the underdog, to defend those who couldn't defend themselves; like Kestrel did every day!" Twistor feels the pain much deeper than Renn does, even though he knew me for less than one tenth the time. He feels the little love he clings to with Renn disintegrate and evaporate like a Kelp Fly in a Ruddy Turnstone's intestine.

Chelonia pleads, "If Kestrel's poems and lyrics die with his name, it doesn't matter. He could have turned the wheel backwards. We get frustrated cause we need a third hand. Until those stupid scientists figure that one out, we will have to continue to struggle, to try to take on more than we can handle, everyday."

Troubadive somberly says, "A surging ebb and flow."

Chelonia, looking down at him replies, "A balance."

Sproc says with illumination, "We choose, US, how we want to fight, and how much, and how much we sell-out, give up, or acquiesce. Kestrel neveh stopped fightin. I'm happy he gave a tiger a meal instead of rottin in a cansah warhd with chemicals pumped into his embalmed body."

"Embombed", Loon laughs, exactly as I would, "Think of that word for a minute."

Dietera nods, "Toxifying the Earth."

Chelonia cries out, unable to stay stoic any longer, "I'm racked with guilt. He died trying to save me."

Dietera counters, "Chelonia, you saved Kestrel."

Everyone breaks into simultaneous applause and cheers. Chelonia stands in shock.

Dietera explains, "You saved him from a loveless world."

Dr. Oso says, biblically speaking, "She saved his soul from rot."

Kracklin, usually more of the biblical fanatic, corrects him, "Well, we don't have to be that extreme. She saved him from thinking that every girl was like Myhel, and Misa Queen. They are not."

I'm dead right now? Big Deal! What would I do if I could live longer? Continue to give Chelonia all the love I can everyday, holding her tightly in my arms as we fall asleep, over and over again? Fight goons and morons who want to hurt wildlife, want to hurt The World? It has to end. It has to end. What would I do? What could I do? Love? Live? You're still alive. How will you live your life?

. . . one can only hate where one has truly loved and, even if one denies it, still does. --- Konrad Lorenz

The sun sets in the western sky, shimmering on the turbulent Pacific. The crowd disperses back towards the living quarters.

What a beautiful World, full of our own heaven, if we want it.

Fin

Praise for Drats and his paradigm shifting work: "… high energy, enthusiasm and good humor. He is a hard worker and dedicated environmentalist." -- Michael C., Executive Director of Lectern
"Not an introverted birder or scientist, but a good communicator who reaches out to lay-persons in terms they can relate to without alienating them. I am glad he skips the pomposity. Humble, inclusive, yet funny, and at the same time, knowledgeable as a general naturalist, making the perfect philosophical guide for beginners and experts, adapting to audience without condescension" -- Peter P., PhD, Ornithologist/Author
"I hate Drats. He makes me want to kill myself all over again." -- ghost of Adolph H., Nasty Leader/Dictator
" . . . a fine job." "well organized" "educational" "illustrated" "easygoing but highly informative …" -- Ruth L., Park Ranger, Natural Palk Zervice
" . . . evoking images of schizophrenic sea monkeys on acid." -- Libby M., Critic, Music Connection Magazine

Must we use violence, when absolutely pushed beyond choice, to save our World from a horrible fate? With the consolidated effort of his united family, will Kestrel snap into action, forcing the ultimate duel?
If we can't even save tiny little Halfway from buffoons and goons, how on Earth are we to save our Planet, ourselves? If we can't even make peace with our own siblings, then are we on our way to another Civil War?
Are we already at war against Nature, against US?
Howard Zinn said, "You can't be neutral on a moving train."
The world keeps turning. Do you grease the wheel?
The less you know, the smarter you feel.

Exaggerist Edutainment
JayaDrats@Hotmail.com

Thank you for reading this and other books, and for thinking of the other 20 million species on The Planet. Please leave a comment at our email address.

Other works by Drats include:
Rudy the Red Bat *(a children's book)*
Rudy the Red Bat *(the live participatory musical)*
Kapu Problem *(a novel)*
Animal Olympians *(a novel)*
Stoned Man *(a screenplay)*
Truth Love Extinction *(a screenplay and film)*

About the Author and Editors

Born low-class but hyper as hell, never given a chance but surpassing all expectations, Drats created and fronted the Los Angeles avant-garde band **InsectAffect** and sung and wrote lyrics for the industrial progressive bands **Death and Taxes** and **Burning Circle**. While working full-time (usually graveyard shift), he put himself through college and grad school while performing in rock operas, avant-garde theatre, and video production. He became an award-winning video producer, and then worked as a federal ranger and biologist, and as a naturalist and writer, for over a decade. He holds an MS from one of the top 10 communication schools in the country. Two well-known scientists/author/blogger, with experience living on Pacific atolls, edited an early draft.

Kestrel at home with the other goonies, during a rare peaceful moment on Halfway.

Majestic albatross glide over infinite whitecaps. Day after night after night after day, relentlessly; the natural world pounds out its rhythmic beat as wide-eyed optimist Kestrel Falco flies out to the remote center of The Pacific Ocean. As the first ranger stationed on Halfway Atoll Wildlife Sanctuary, he restlessly jostles excitedly in his chair. With shorts and a t-shirt, he looks more like a teen than a man in his early thirties. Son of a lower middle-class bricklayer, psyched and amazed, he bristles with enthusiastic awe as he gazes out the window of a small plane, high over the massive seascape. Has Kestrel gotten far enough away? What does he run from?
What are the roadblocks to understanding, and peace?
What was your altruistic act today?
Join Kestrel on his chaotic, quasi-metaphysical journey through our sometimes-surreal world, navigating through family, friends, co-workers, enemies, nature, and sea and Earth; dodging dangerous sharks and deadlier goons, and most importantly; his search for real true love. Can he survive Halfway, the second most remote spot on Earth? If he can't, can we? All he needs is a hand; a third hand . . .

www.ingramcontent.com/pod-product-compliance
Lightning Source LLC
Chambersburg PA
CBHW052345020726
47503CB00001B/108